PRAISE FOR *OUTFOX* AND #1 *NEW YORK TIMES* BESTSELLING AUTHOR SANDRA BROWN

"Sandra Brown is a master when it comes to rogue characters, increasing the level of tension to cause the pace of the narrative to move faster and faster... This time she not only nails a story that has several surprises, but also maintains the quality that everyone expects in her novels."

—Associated Press

"Sandra Brown is a publishing icon, and OUTFOX may be her best book ever... [a] fast-moving story that will please her millions of fans."

—*New York Journal of Books*

"An engrossing thriller... Well-defined characters complement the twisty plot, which ends with a gratifying final revelation. Brown once again shows why she remains at the top of the suspense field."

—*Publishers Weekly*

"Sandra Brown continues her string of remarkable hardcore thrillers with the canny and clever OUTFOX... Sultry, scintillating storytelling of the highest order that never lets up or lets us down."

—BookTrib.com

"OUTFOX is packed with suspense and love. It is an extraordinarily satisfying and entertaining novel."

— *Washington Book Review*

OUTFOX

SANDRA BROWN

GRAND CENTRAL
PUBLISHING

NEW YORK   BOSTON

Grand Central Publishing
Hachette Book Group
1290 Avenue of the Americas, New York, NY 10104
grandcentralpublishing.com
twitter.com/grandcentralpub

Originally published in hardcover and ebook by Grand Central Publishing in August
2019.

First trade paperback edition: February 2020

Grand Central Publishing is a division of Hachette Book Group, Inc. The Grand
Central Publishing name and logo is a trademark of Hachette Book Group, Inc.

The publisher is not responsible for websites (or their content) that are not owned by
the publisher.

The Hachette Speakers Bureau provides a wide range of authors for speaking events.
To find out more, go to www.hachettespeakersbureau.com or call (866) 376-6591.

LCCN: 2019944317
ISBN: 978-1-4789-1687-1

Printed in the United States of America

LSC-H

10 9 8 7 6 5 4 3 2 1

Prologue

───※◎※───

A cheerless drizzle blurred any view of the body on the beach.

Mist formed halos around the lampposts along the pier, but didn't diffuse the glaring portable lights that had been put in place by first responders. In a grotesque parody of catching someone in the spotlight on center stage, they shone a harsh light on the covered form.

A police helicopter swept in low. Its searchlight was unforgivingly bright as it tracked the length of the pier. Its beam skittered over the marina where boats rocked in a lulling current that was out of keeping with the surrounding chaos.

Before shifting out onto the surf, the searchlight cut a swath across the corpse. The chopper's downwash flipped back a corner of the garish yellow plastic sheet to expose a hand, inert and bone-white on the packed sand.

Since the discovery of the body, officers representing several law enforcement agencies had converged on the scene. The colored lights of a search-and-rescue helicopter blinked against the underbelly of low clouds hugging the harbor. Beyond Fort Sumter, a US

Coast Guard cruiser plowed through the waters of the Atlantic, its searchlight sweeping across the swells.

TV satellite vans had arrived, disgorging eager reporters and camera crews.

On the pier, the inevitable onlookers had congregated. They vied for the best vantage points from which to gawk at the body, monitor the police and media activity, and take selfies with the draped corpse in the background. They swapped information and speculation.

It was said that the deceased had washed ashore with the evening tide and had been discovered by a man and his young son while they were exercising their chocolate Lab on this stretch of beach.

It was said that drowning was the obvious cause of death.

It was said that it was the result of a boating mishap.

None of these conjectures was correct.

The unleashed Labrador had run ahead of his owner, and it was the dog, splashing in the surf, that had made the gruesome discovery.

One of the spectators on the pier, overhearing the exchanges of facts, fictions, and laments, smiled in self-satisfied silence.

Chapter 1

Three weeks earlier

The automatic doors whooshed open. In one surveying glance, Drex Easton took in the hotel lobby. It was empty except for the pretty young woman behind the reception desk. She had a porcelain-doll complexion, a glossy black ponytail, and an uncertain smile as she greeted him.

"Good morning, sir. Can I help you?"

Drex set his briefcase at his feet. "I don't have a reservation, but I need a room."

"Check-in isn't until two o'clock."

"Hmm."

"Because... because for the convenience of our guests, checkout isn't until noon."

"Hmm."

"Housekeeping needs time to—"

"I realize all that, Ms. Li." He'd read the name badge pinned to her maroon blazer. He smiled. "I was hoping you could make an exception for me."

He reached behind his back to remove a wallet from his pants pocket and, in doing so, spread open his suit jacket wide enough to reveal the shoulder holster beneath his left arm. Upon seeing it, the young woman blinked several times before rapidly shifting her gaze back up to his, which he held steady on her.

"No cause for alarm," he said quietly. He flipped open the wallet that contained a badge and photo ID that classified him as a special agent of the Federal Bureau of Investigation.

He didn't like to overplay this card, doing so only when he needed a shortcut through rules and red tape. It worked on Ms. Li, who was automatically willing to please.

"Let me see what I can do."

"I would consider it a big favor."

Graceful fingers pecked across her keyboard. "Single or double?"

"I'm not picky."

Her eyes scanned the computer monitor. She scrolled down, then back up. "I can have housekeeping service a nice double room for you right away, but the turnaround could take up to half an hour. Or, there's a less nice single available now."

"I'll take the less nice single available now." He slid a credit card across the granite counter.

"How long will you be staying with us, Mr. Easton?"

She was no slouch. She'd noted his name. "I'm not sure. Two other…Two associates of mine will be arriving shortly. I won't know how long I'll be staying until after our meeting. I'll have to let you know then."

"No problem. You may keep the room until you notify me of your departure."

"Great. Thanks."

She ran his credit card and proceeded to check him in. She had him initial the room rate on the form and sign his name at the bottom; then she returned his credit card along with the room key card. "That key also unlocks the door to the fitness center on the second floor."

"Thanks, but I won't be using it."

"The restaurant is just down the corridor behind you. Breakfast is served—"

"No breakfast, either." He bent down and picked up his briefcase.

Taking the subtle hint, she pointed him toward the elevators. "As you step off onto your floor, your room will be to your left."

"Thank you, Ms. Li. You've been a huge help."

"When your associates arrive, am I at liberty to give them your room number?"

"No need, I'll text it to them. They can come straight up."

"I hope your meeting goes well."

He gave her a wry grin. "So do I." Then he leaned forward and said in an undertone, "Relax, Ms. Li. You're doing a fine job."

She looked chagrined. "This is only my second day. Were my nerves that obvious?"

"Probably not to anyone else, but sizing people up quickly is a large part of what I do. And if this is only your second day, I'm even more impressed with how you handled a troublesome guest."

"Not that troublesome at all."

He gave her a lazy smile. "You caught me on a good day."

———✦———

The less nice single wasn't a room the hotel chain would feature in an ad, but it would do. Drex opened his briefcase on the desk and booted up his laptop. He texted Mike the room number, then went over to the window. It afforded a fourth floor view of a freeway interchange and not much else.

He returned to the desk and checked his email in box. Nothing of importance. He went into the compact bathroom and used the toilet. As he came out, the hotel telephone was ringing. He picked up the extension on the desk. "Yes?"

"Mr. Easton?"

"Ms. Li."

"Your associates are here."

"Good." Sooner than he'd expected.

"Would you like for me to send something from the kitchen up to your room? Perhaps a fruit platter? A selection of pastries?"

"Thank you, but no."

"If you change your mind, don't hesitate to call down."

"I'll do that, Ms. Li. Thanks again for accommodating me."

"You're welcome."

Although the open drapes let in plenty of daylight, he switched on the desk lamp. He adjusted the thermostat down a few degrees. He glanced at his reflection in the mirror above the dresser and thought he looked presentable, but hardly spiffy. He'd showered and dressed in a rush.

At the soft knock, he went to the door and looked through the peephole before opening it. He stood aside and motioned the two men to come in.

As they filed past him, Gifford Lewis said, "The girl at the desk stopped us to ask if we were Mr. Easton's associates. She's moony for you."

"Anything Mr. Easton wants," Mike Mallory grumbled. "As long as she was offering, I could have done with the fruit platter and pastry selection. You could still call down."

Out of habit, Drex checked the hallway—which was empty—then shut the door and flipped the bolt. "You wake me up at dawn, say, 'Find a place where the walls don't have ears.' And don't waste any time doing it, you said. I don't waste any time, I find a place, and here we are. Never mind the fruit platter and pastries. What's up?"

The other two looked at each other, but neither replied.

With impatience, Drex asked, "What's so top secret we couldn't communicate through ordinary channels?"

Gif stationed himself against the wall, a shoulder propping him there. Mike rolled the chair from beneath the desk and wedged his three hundred forty pounds between the protesting armrests.

Drex placed his hands on his hips, his expression demanding. "For crissake, will one of you speak?"

Mike glanced over at Gif, who made a gesture that yielded the floor to Mike. He looked up at Drex and said, "I've found him."

Mike's tone conveyed all the gaiety of a death knell. The *him* didn't need specification.

For years Drex had been waiting to hear those words. He'd imagined this moment ten thousand times. He'd envisioned himself experiencing one or more physical reactions. His ears would ring, his mouth go dry, his knees buckle, his breath catch, his heart burst.

Instead, after his hands dropped from his hips, he went numb to a supernatural extent.

Gif and Mike must have expected an eruption of some sort, too, because they looked mystified over his sudden and absolute immobility and silence, which were downright eerie, even to himself.

A full minute later, when the paralyzing shock began to wear off, he walked over to the window again. Since last he'd looked out, nothing cataclysmic had occurred. Traffic hadn't stilled on the crisscrossing freeways. No jagged cracks had opened up in the earth's surface. The sky hadn't fallen. The sun hadn't burned out.

He pressed his forehead against the window and was surprised by how cold the glass felt. "You're sure?"

"Sure? As in positive? No," Mike replied. "But this guy looks real good on paper."

"Age?"

"Sixty-two. So says his current driver's license."

Drex turned his head and raised his eyebrows in a silent question.

"South Carolina," Mike said. "Mount Pleasant. Suburb of—"

"Charleston. I know. What name is he going by?"

"Un-huh."

That brought Drex all the way around. "Excuse me? What does that mean?"

Gif said, "Means that you're not getting a name until we know what you plan to do with the information."

"What the hell do you think I plan to do with it? First thing is to haul ass to Charleston."

Gif exchanged a look with Mike, then pushed himself away from the wall and squared off against Drex. He didn't take a combative stance, which would have been laughable because Drex was physically imposing and Gif was nowhere near. But he set his feet apart and braced himself as though Drex's self-restraint was iffy and reasonableness was way too much to hope for.

He said, "Hear me out, Drex. Mike and I talked about it on our way over here. We think you should consider…That is, it would be advisable to…The smart course of action would be to—"

"*What?*"

"Notify Rudkowski."

"Not a fucking chance in hell."

"Drex—"

Louder and with more emphasis, Drex repeated his statement.

Mike shot Gif a droll glance. "Told ya."

Drex's ears had begun to clamor after all. Now that the reality was setting in, his blood pressure had spiked. The window glass had felt cold against his forehead because his face was feverish. The blood vessels in his temples were throbbing. His scalp was sweaty beneath his hair. His torso had gone clammy.

He pulled off his suit jacket and tossed it onto the bed, wrestled off the shoulder holster and dropped it on top of his jacket, loosened the knot of his necktie, and unbuttoned his collar, all as though he were preparing for a sparring match, which, if necessary, this argument might result in.

Willing himself to at least *sound* composed, he asked again, "What name is he using?"

"Assuming it's him," Mike said.

"You assume it's him, or you wouldn't have suggested this secret meeting. Tell me what you have on him, starting with his name."

"No name."

Mike Mallory was an all-star when it came to excavating information from a computer, but a people person he wasn't. He harbored a general contempt for his fellow man, considering most to be complete morons, Drex and Gif being the only possible exceptions.

He was so good at what he did that Drex put up with his truculent attitude and lack of social graces, but right now he muttered an epithet that encompassed both Mike and Gif, who, on this point, had taken Mike's side.

"Fine," Mike said, "call us nasty names. We're thinking in your best interest."

"I'll think for myself, thank you."

"After you hear everything, you may decide against taking matters into your own hands."

"I won't."

Mike shrugged. "Then it'll be your funeral. But I'm not digging your grave, and I'm sure as hell not climbing in with you. Fair warning."

"Fair enough. I'll find out his frigging name myself. Just put me on the right track."

Mike nodded. "That I'll do. Because I don't want him to get away, either. If it's him."

Drex backed down a bit and rolled his shoulders, forcing them to relax. "Does the mystery man hold a job?"

"Nothing I could find," Mike said, "but he lives well."

"I'll bet," Drex said under his breath. "How long has he been in Mount Pleasant?"

"I don't have that yet. He's lived at his current residence for ten months."

"What kind of residence?"

"House."

"Leased?"

"Purchased."

"Mortgaged?"

"If so, I couldn't find it."

"Cash purchase, then."

Mike raised his beefy shoulders in an unspoken *I guess.*

Gif speculated that maybe the property had been inherited, but none of them really thought that, so no one pursued it.

Drex asked, "What's the place like?"

"Based on the real estate listing, it was pre-owned, not new," Mike said. "But an established neighborhood. Upscale."

"Price?"

"Million and a half and change. Looks spacious and well kept on Google Earth. It's all on here." Mike groped beneath his overlap for his pants pocket and produced a thumb drive.

Drex took it from him.

"Won't do you any good without the password, and you're not getting it till we've talked this out."

Drex scoffed. "I can get the password cracked. When applied to you, the word *geek* sounds ludicrous, but you're not the only computer geek around, you know."

Mike raised his hands. "Be my guest. Get a geek to go digging. But if you're found out, how are you going to explain your interest in this seemingly law-abiding citizen?"

"A bribed hacker won't care what my interest is."

"A bribed hacker won't blink over taking your money, then—"

"Stabbing you in the back with it," Gif chimed in.

"Your hacker would get the man in South Carolina on the phone and tell him there's a guy in far-off Lexington, Kentucky, who's spying on him."

Gif picked up. "For more coin than you're paying him, the hacker would sell you out."

"Then it would be *you*, Special Agent Easton," Mike continued, jabbing a stubby index finger at him, "who would be spied on, caught committing God knows how many violations and crimes, civil and criminal, and that would squash this and any future chance you might have to finally nail this son of a bitch, which has been your main mission in life." He wheezed a deep breath. "Tell us we're wrong."

Drex sat down on the end of the bed, propped his forearms on his thighs, and dropped his head forward. After a moment, he looked up. "Okay. No hacker. I'll moderate my approach. Satisfied?"

The other two exchanged a look. Gif said, "Exercise a little caution, some discretion."

"Don't go off half-cocked," Mike said.

Gif added, "That's all we're saying."

Drex placed his hand over his heart. "I'll be cautious, discreet, and fully cocked. Okay?"

Neither approved of that last bit, and they didn't look wholly convinced of his sincerity, but Mike said, "Okay. Next question?"

"Do you have a picture of him?"

"Only the one on his driver's license."

"And?"

"Looks nothing like he did the last time he surfaced."

"Key West," Gif reminded them, although they didn't need reminding.

"You'd never know it's the same man," Mike said. "Which means I could be dead wrong about this fella."

"If he is," Gif said, "but you rush in hell-bent and create havoc in this guy's life, you'll land yourself in a world of hurt. Especially if Rudkowski were to get wind of it."

"Rudkowski can go fuck himself."

"Rumor is, he's tried, but can't quite figure out how to go about it."

Gif's quip got a rare snort of humor out of Mike and a reluctant grin from Drex. Gif was good at defusing a tense situation. Of average height and weight, with thinning brown hair, and not a single feature that was distinguishing, Gif's averageness was his camouflage. He could observe others unnoticed and unremembered, which made him a valuable asset to the team. He was also a reliable predictor of human behavior, as he'd just demonstrated.

Drex's impulse had been to rush in hell-bent and create havoc.

Needing a moment to collect his thoughts, he motioned toward the minibar. "Help yourselves." He stood up and began pacing in the limited space between the bed and the window.

Mike and Gif made their selections and popped the tops off soda cans. Mike complained that he needed a crowbar to get the lid off the jar of mixed nuts. Gif offered to give it a try. Mike scoffed at that and called him a weakling.

Drex tuned out their bickering and focused his thoughts on his quarry, a man he first knew as Weston Graham, although that could be just another of his many aliases. Having eluded the authorities for decades, he could have turned up enjoying a Frosty at the Wendy's across the freeway or burning incense in a monastery in the Himalayas, and neither would have surprised Drex.

He was a chameleon, exceptionally good at altering his appearance and adapting to his environment. Among the ones in which he'd lived comfortably and without arousing suspicion were a penthouse on Chicago's Gold Coast, a horse ranch outside of Santa Barbara, and a yacht moored in Key West. Other locales that he had oozed his way through—those that Drex knew of—weren't that ritzy. They hadn't had to be. All had been extremely profitable for him.

When his cohorts had resettled, Drex asked, "What put you onto the guy in South Carolina?"

"I run my trot lines continually, but what finally tipped me?" Mike said around a burp. "An online dating service. Figuring he vets his victims somehow, I troll those services periodically just to see if something clicks. Day before yesterday, I came across a profile that did. The wording of it jostled my memory. Felt like I'd read it before.

"Took me a while to find it, but there it was. Except for the physical description of himself, it was word for word, comma for comma, identical to this most recent one. Likes, dislikes, five-year goals, philosophy of life and love. All that bullcrap. But the kicker? It was posted six months before Pixie went missing."

Patricia Montgomery, known as Pixie to her friends, had vanished from her Tulsa mansion, never to be seen again.

"Coincidence, Mike," Drex said. "Acquaintances of Pixie's who were interviewed swore that she never would have used a dating service to meet men."

"The acquaintances of all the missing ladies have sworn that. They've also sworn their friend was too savvy to be taken in by a con man. But Pixie disappeared within days of selling her stocks and emptying her bank accounts of her oil fortune."

Gif said, "The only thing missing from her home was her PC. Her seducer left behind tens of thousands of dollars in jewelry and furs but took an outdated computer."

"So there wouldn't be evidence of an online flirtation," Mike said. The leather seat beneath him groaned as he leaned forward to take the near-empty jar of nuts from Gif. "You're frowning," he said to Drex.

"I want to be excited, but this is awfully thin."

"You're right. Thin as onionskin. So I went back to his victim after Pixie. At least the one we *suspect* to have been his victim."

"Marian Harris. Key West."

"Eight months before her disappearance, the same damn profile was posted. Different dating service, but one that also caters to 'mature' clients with 'discriminating tastes.'"

"Word for word?" Drex asked.

"Like a fingerprint."

"Bad joke," Gif said.

The man they sought had never left a fingerprint. Or if he had, no one had found it. Freakin' Ted Bundy.

Mike shook the last of the nuts straight from the jar into his mouth. "Pittsburgh didn't take him as long," he said as he noshed. "He solicited 'companionship' with 'a refined lady' only three months before Loretta Doan's disappearance, more than six years ago."

"Are all the services you scanned nationwide?"

"Yes. Relocation isn't a deterrent to him. I think the asshole likes the changes of scenery."

"When was this most recent profile put out there?"

"Couple of months back."

Drex grimaced. "He's looking for his next lady."

"That's what I deduced. So I gave it a test run. I replied, using buzzwords I figured would make me sound like a prime target. I described myself as a childless, fifty-something widow who's financially secure and independent. I enjoy fine cuisine, good wine, and foreign films. Most men find me attractive."

"Not me," Gif said.

"Me neither," Drex said.

Mike gave them the finger. "He must not have, either. He hasn't taken the bait."

Gif thoughtfully scratched his forehead. "Maybe you oversold yourself. You sounded too self-assured, sophisticated, and smart. He looks for women with a dash of naïveté. Vulnerability. You scared him off."

"Or," Drex said, "he picked up on the buzzwords, smelled a rat, figured that this dream lady was actually a fed on a fishing expedition."

"Maybe," Mike said. "But another, more likely possibility—the one I fear—is that he jumped the gun. Solicited too soon. He hasn't responded because he hasn't ditched his current victim yet."

It was a reasonable theory to which Drex gave credence because it caused his gut to clench. "Meaning that she's in mortal danger as we speak."

"Worse than that."

"What's worse than mortal danger?"

Mike hesitated.

"Give," Drex said.

The heavy man sighed. "I repeat, Drex, I may be wrong."

"But you don't think so."

He raised his catcher's mitt–sized hands at his sides.

"Why do you think it's him?" Drex asked.

"Just promise me—"

"No promises. What makes you think this guy is our guy? *My* guy?"

"Drex, you can't go—"

Gif said, "Rudkowski will—"

"Tell me, goddamn it!" Drex said, shouting above their warnings.

After another pause, Mike mumbled, "He's married."

Drex hadn't seen that coming. "*Married?*"

"Married. Do you take? With this ring. I now pronounce you."

Gif confirmed it with a solemn nod.

Drex divided a perplexed look between them, then shook his head and huffed a laugh of bitter disappointment. "Well, that shoots everything to hell, and you've wasted my morning. If we hurry down, the restaurant will still be serving breakfast." He pushed his fingers through his hair.

"*Shit!* Here I was getting all excited, when what it looks like is that our lonely heart has struck out again and is still seeking his soul mate. But he's not our man. Because a wife doesn't jibe."

"It did once," Gif reminded him.

"Once. Not since. Matrimony, do you take, with this ring, hasn't fit his profile or MO in years. Not in any way, shape, or form."

"Actually, Drex, it does," Mike said solemnly.

"How so?"

Gif cleared his throat. "The wife is loaded."

Drex looked at each of them independently. The two men couldn't be more dissimilar, but they wore identical expressions of fear and dread.

He turned away from them, and where his gaze happened to land was on his reflection in the dresser mirror. Even he recognized that, since he'd last looked, his countenance had altered, hardened, become taut with resolve. There was a ferocity in his eyes that hadn't been there only minutes ago, before he had learned that a woman's life hung in the balance. Delicately. And dependent on him to save it.

He kept his voice soft but put steel behind it. "Tell me his name."

Chapter 2

"Need help?"

Drex set the empty cardboard box on the curb, turned, and had his first face-to-face with his nemesis.

If this was indeed Weston Graham, he was around five feet eight inches tall and, for a man of sixty-two, extraordinarily fit. His golf shirt hugged firm biceps and a trim waistline. He had a receding hairline, but his graying hair was long enough in back to be pulled into a blunt ponytail. His smile was very white and straight, friendly, and wreathed by a salt-and-pepper door knocker.

Drex swiped his dripping forehead with the ripped sleeve of his baggy t-shirt. "Thanks, but that's the last of them."

"I was hoping you'd say that. I only offered to be nice."

The two of them laughed.

"I'll take one of those beers, though," Drex said. "If you're offering."

His neighbor had crossed the connecting lawns with a cold bottle in each hand. He handed one to Drex. "Welcome to the neighborhood."

"Thanks."

They clinked bottles, and each took a drink. "Jasper Ford." He stuck out his right hand and they shook.

"Jasper," Drex said, as though hearing the name for the first time and committing it to memory, as though he hadn't had to wring it out of Gif and Mike, as though he hadn't spent the past week gleaning as much information on the man as he possibly could.

"I'm Drex Easton." He watched the man's eyes for a reaction to his name, but detected none.

Jasper indicated the pile of empty boxes Drex had stacked at the curb. "You've been hard at it for two days."

"It's been a chore to lug everything up those stairs. They're killers."

He chinned toward a steep exterior staircase that led up to an apartment above a garage that was large enough to house an eighteen-foot inboard. The structure was a good thirty yards behind the main house. Drex figured it had been positioned there to take advantage of the concealment provided by a massive live oak tree.

He squinted up through the branches and pretended to assess the apartment from a fresh perspective. "Moving in was worth the backache, though. It's like living in a tree house."

"I've never seen inside," Jasper said. "Nice?"

"Nice enough."

"How many rooms?"

"Only three, but all I need."

"You're by yourself, then?"

"Not even a goldfish." He grinned. "But, despite the ban on pets, I may get a cat. I spotted some mouse droppings in the kitchen area."

"I can see how a mouse could sneak in. The owners are snowbirds, down here only during the winter months."

"So Mr. Arnott told me. They come down the day after Thanksgiving, stay until the first of June."

"Frankly, when I learned the apartment had been rented out, I was concerned."

"How'd you hear about it?"

"I didn't. You showed up and started carting boxes upstairs."

Drex laughed. "And going through your mind was 'WTF?'"

By way of admission, the man smiled and gave a small shrug. "I have Arnott's number in case of an emergency, so I called him."

"I was an emergency?" Drex glanced down at his ragged shirt, dirty cargo shorts, and well-worn sneakers. "I can see where you might think so. You got one look at me and thought 'there goes the neighborhood.'" He flashed a grin. "I clean up okay, I promise."

Jasper Ford laughed with good nature. "Can't be too careful."

"That's my motto."

"Good fences make for good neighbors."

"Except that there's no fence." Drex looked across the uninterrupted expanse of grass between the two properties. Coming back to Jasper Ford's dark gaze, he said, "I'll confine my rude behavior to this side of the property line. You'll never know I'm here."

Jasper smiled, but before he could comment, his cell phone signaled a text. "Excuse me." He took the phone from his shirt pocket.

While he was reading the text, Drex arched his back in an overextended stretch that caused him to wince, and took another swallow of beer.

"My wife," Jasper said as he thumbed off his phone. "Her flight has been weather delayed. She's stuck at O'Hare."

"That's too bad."

"Happens a lot," he said somewhat absently as he glanced over his shoulder toward his house, then came back around to Drex. "How about some surf and turf?"

"Pardon?"

"I've got crab cakes ready for the pan. Steaks marinating. No sense in half of it going to waste."

"I couldn't impose."

"If it was going to be an imposition, I wouldn't have invited you."

"Well…" Scratching his unshaven cheek, Drex pretended to ponder it. "I haven't stocked the pantry or fridge yet. I've been subsisting on fast food."

Jasper chuckled. "I can do better than that. See you at sunset. We'll have drinks on the porch." He reached out and took Drex's beer bottle. "I'll toss this for you."

Drex stepped out of the shower and reached for his ringing cell phone, which he'd balanced on the rim of the sink. He looked to see who was calling, then clicked on. "Hey."

"How are you faring?" Mike asked.

"Right now, good. I'm standing naked and wet under a ceiling fan."

"Spare me."

"The fan squeaks, but this is the coolest I've been since I got here. Why didn't you tell me this apartment wasn't air-conditioned?"

"You didn't ask."

Once it had been decided among the three of them that Jasper Ford warranted further investigation, Drex flew to Charleston. He wasted no time in driving to Mount Pleasant and locating the Fords' home.

Google Earth hadn't done it justice. The two-story house was built of brick, painted white. Classically southern in design, a deep front porch ran the width of the façade, twin columns framing a glossy black front door with a brass knocker in the shape of a pineapple. The house was surrounded by a sprawling lawn and shaded by decades-old trees.

The residence looked lived in. Blooming flowers in all the beds. Thriving ferns on the porches. An American flag hanging from the eaves. Newspaper and mail delivery.

By contrast, the house next door looked less tended, and for the three nights Drex surveilled it, lights came on at the same time, went off at the same time. Timed to do so. No flowers, ferns, or mail.

He returned to Lexington, briefed Mike and Gif, and instructed Mike to find out who owned the property neighboring the Fords', which appeared to be a second home or otherwise infrequently occupied.

Mike did his due diligence, got a name and contact info off tax records.

Then Drex did his thing. He made a cold call to Mr. Arnott, who, with his wife, resided most of the year in Pennsylvania, but, upon retirement, had purchased the place in South Carolina to escape the cold and snow.

Drex, laying it on thick, told him of his situation, which was a complete fabrication. Then he got down to the heart of the matter. He was seeking temporary lodging in or near Charleston. During a scouting expedition to see what might be available, he'd crossed the Cooper River into Mount Pleasant, and as he was driving around getting the lay of the land, so to speak, he'd spotted the garage apartment. It was ideal: Secluded. Quiet. A "cabin in the woods," within the confines of a scenic and safe neighborhood.

The apartment would provide all the space he required. He would live there alone, no pets. He was a nonsmoker. And, in the bargain, he would keep an eye on the main house.

"Honestly, Mr. Arnott, if I'd been a burglar, I'd have chosen your house to break into. It's obvious that you're an absentee owner."

When Arnott hedged, Drex was tempted to play his FBI card. He didn't, fearing it would be tipped to Jasper Ford that he had a fed moving in next door to him. Instead he provided Arnott several fictitious references, all written by Gif, whom Arnott actually called to confirm his high recommendation. Mike also got a call to verify the reference letter signed by him. Between them, they convinced

Mr. Arnott that Drex Easton was a man of sound mind, good character, and everything he claimed to be.

Arnott agreed to lease him the apartment for the requested three months, although Drex would be there for only two weeks—his allotted vacation time. Only Mike and Gif would know how his time away was being utilized. Until he had a major breakthrough, he was keeping everyone else in the dark.

Besides, asking Arnott for a three-month lease lent credibility to his story and made him seem like a stabler, more responsible tenant. He paid the full amount of rent up front.

"Besides no AC, how is it?" Mike asked now. "Are you moved in?"

From the open bathroom door, Drex could see practically the entire apartment, and virtually every square inch of it was empty, as had been most of the boxes he'd carted up the stairs for the benefit of his audience next door. The apartment had come furnished, though sparsely. He'd brought only the essentials needed to keep himself clothed and groomed. He'd brought a coffeemaker, but he hadn't lied about a steady diet of fast food.

"All settled in," he told Mike. "My laptop is on the kitchen table. My pistol is between the mattress and box spring."

"In other words, it's the same as your place here," Mike said. "And you've lived here for how long?"

"Is there a reason for this call? If so, get to it. Because I don't want to be late for my date."

"In two days' time you've already lined up a *girl*?" Mike said. "When you said 'fully cocked,' you really meant it? I'll have to check my charts, but I think this might be a record."

"There's no girl, and cut the bullshit. Is Gif with you? Put me on speaker." When Drex could tell that Mike had switched over, he said, "Jasper Ford invited me over for dinner tonight."

After a second or two of stunned silence, Mike and Gif exclaimed their surprise.

"Here I have my high-powered binocs focused, all set up to spy on him, and he comes over today with a cold beer and a handshake, welcoming me to the neighborhood. I'm glad he made the first move. That saved me from having to devise a way to put me in his path and make his acquaintance."

He gave them a run-down of their conversation. "It was casual, friendly, but definitely an appraisal. When he saw me moving in, he called Arnott to check me out."

"Paranoid, you think?" Gif asked.

"Or just a watchful property owner, cautious of strangers," Mike said. "Anybody in that kind of neighborhood would be."

"It could be either," Drex said. "I should have a better feel for him after our dinner."

"What about the missus?" Mike asked.

It had been a worry to them that, although Drex had spotted Jasper coming and going over the past two days, he hadn't seen any sign of his wife. "He told me that she's been out of town, which I hope is the truth and that she's still alive. While we were talking, he did receive a text ostensibly from her." He told them about the delayed flight.

"Why Chicago?" Gif asked.

"He didn't say. But he did say that her being delayed happens a lot, indicating that she flies often."

"Makes sense," Mike said. "She was in the travel business."

"Yes, *was*," Drex said. Mike had discovered that the sale of Shafer Travel, Inc., had been the source of Mrs. Ford's mega bucks. "Question is, why is she still frequently on the go?"

When no answer was forthcoming, Drex said, "I'll feel better when I can confirm she's still with us. Maybe I'll get a lot of questions answered tonight. Speaking of…" He glanced out the window. The sun was sinking. "I've got to go now, get dressed, make a run to the liquor store."

"What for?"

"It wouldn't be neighborly to show up for dinner empty-handed."

As he signed off, he was thinking how neighborly it had been of Jasper to bring him a beer and then offer to toss the bottle for him.

However, wouldn't it have been more neighborly to let Drex finish drinking the beer? But no, Jasper Ford had wanted that bottle back.

"White for the crab cakes. Red for the steaks." Drex held up the bottles of wine in turn as he approached the screened porch where Jasper was sitting in a rocking chair beneath a twirling ceiling fan.

He got up and held open the screen door. "You didn't have to do that, but thank you." He took the bottles from Drex. "How about a drink first?"

"What are you having?" Drex motioned toward the highball glass on the wicker table next to the rocking chair.

"Bourbon on the rocks."

"Water?"

"No."

Drex grinned. "Perfect."

"Have a seat." Jasper put the white wine in the mini fridge beneath the built-in bar and poured Drex's drink. As he handed it to him, he said, "You do clean up okay."

Drex raised his glass in a quasi toast. "I try." He'd shaved, but had left a scruff. He'd worn casual slacks and a button-up shirt, the shirttail out. Docksiders, no socks.

Jasper resumed his seat in the rocker and sipped from his drink. "So, you're a writer."

Drex pretended to strangle on his sip of whiskey and looked at his host with surprise.

"Your literary agent was one of the references you gave Arnott."

"Oh! For a second there, I thought you were a mind-reader." Looking abashed, he said, "I'm trying to be a writer. Can't claim the title yet. I haven't published."

"Your agent told Arnott that you have real potential."

He waved that off. "All agents say that about their clients."

"She must believe it or she wouldn't be representing you."

"He."

"Sorry?"

"My agent is a he."

"Oh. My mistake."

My ass, Drex thought. That had been a test.

"Are you writing full-time?"

"Lately I have been."

"How do you support yourself?"

"Frugally." Jasper gave the expected laugh. Drex said, "My dad died a couple of years ago and left me a small inheritance. Nothing to boast about, but it's keeping a roof over my head while I work on the book."

"Fiction or non?"

"Fiction. Civil War novel."

Jasper raised his eyebrows, encouraging him to continue.

"I don't want to bore you," Drex said.

"I'm not bored."

"Well," Drex said, taking a deep breath, "the protagonist takes a sort of Forrest Gump journey through the conflict, from Bull Run to Appomattox. He grapples with divided loyalties, his moral compass, mortal fear during battle. That kind of thing."

"Sounds interesting."

Drex smiled as though he realized that was a platitude, but appreciated it all the same. "My agent likes the story, and said my research was factually sound. But he felt the narrative lacked color. It needed more heart, he said. Soul."

"So you came down here to get color, heart, and soul."

"I hope to soak up some while working on the second draft. And," he said, stretching out both his legs and the word, "I needed to get away from the distractions of the everyday grind."

"Like a wife?"

"Not anymore."

"Divorced?"

"Thank God."

"You sound bitter. What happened?"

"She accused me of cheating."

"Did you?"

Drex looked at him and cocked an eyebrow, but didn't answer. Instead he sipped his bourbon. It was a smooth, expensive one. "The divorce cost me dear and taught me a hard lesson."

"You'll never cheat again."

"I'll never marry again."

"Ah, never say never," Jasper said, shaking his index finger at him. "After the loss of my first wife, I grieved for her and stayed single for a long time. Thirty years, in fact."

"Man, that's loyalty. How'd she die?"

Looking Drex straight in the eye, he said, "In pain." He held the stare for a beat, then finished his bourbon in one shot, stood, and headed for the kitchen. "How do you like your steak?"

The medium rare rib eye had been seasoned and grilled to perfection. Jasper apologized for serving the meal in the casual dining room, rather than the more formal one, but the table was set a lot fancier than Drex was used to, and he confessed as much.

While they ate, Drex probed his host for more personal information, but in a manner he hoped would seem natural. "This house is really something."

"Thank you."

"You hire a professional decorator?"

"Only to consult. Talia knew what she wanted."

"Talia? That's your wife's name? Pretty." He glanced around. "She has good taste."

"She has great taste."

"Expensive taste?"

Jasper only smiled at that, but didn't respond.

Drex took a sip of the Cabernet he'd brought, blotted his mouth, and then picked up his utensils and cut into his steak again. "You seem to do all right," he said, applying his knife to the meat. "What's your line of work?"

"I work at enjoying the fruits of my labors."

Drex stopped chewing and looked across at Jasper to gauge whether or not he was joking. Jasper's expression didn't change. He didn't even blink. Drex swallowed and laughed out loud. "Lucky you. You retired early?"

"Several years ago."

"From what? Must've been a healthy business."

"I created some software that proved to be lucrative."

Or did you accumulate a fortune by rooking women out of theirs?

That's what Drex was thinking when Jasper smiled at him congenially and said, "I have lemon sorbet for dessert."

Drex declined the sorbet. And since it was obvious that Jasper didn't want to elaborate on his former field of endeavor, Drex let the subject drop. He also declined to have coffee, not wanting to outstay his welcome.

Although he offered to help with the cleanup, Jasper refused.

As Drex was about to leave, he mentioned that the apartment didn't have air-conditioning. Jasper insisted on lending him a box fan. He fetched it from his garage and told Drex to keep it for as long as he needed it.

"Thanks. Thanks for everything." Drex extended his hand.

As they shook, Jasper said, "Talia texted that she should be home by midnight. We're taking a boat out tomorrow afternoon. Not too far offshore. Just puttering around. Why don't you join us?"

Drex was anxious to meet his wife, gauge her, but didn't want to appear too eager. "Nice of you to offer, but it's been days since I looked at my manuscript. The move-in and all. I really should work tomorrow."

"You can't take off a Sunday? I'm sure the Lord would understand."

Drex pretended to have been persuaded. Jasper gave him the name of the marina and the number of the slip. "Meet us there around noon. We'll go ahead and get things ready. Come hungry. We'll have a picnic lunch on board."

"Sounds great." Drex thanked him again for the evening and carried the box fan across the lawn and up the stairs.

He began undressing by reaching under his loose shirttail and removing the holster from his waistband at the small of his back. Call him a cynic, but surf and turf had seemed a little over the top for a first visit even if the meal hadn't originally been prepared with him in mind.

Fifteen minutes later, he was stripped down to his underwear, the fan was on high, all the lights were off, and he was at the window watching through binoculars as Jasper went about cleaning up. When he was done, he locked the doors and turned out the lights. A few moments later an upstairs light came on. Minutes after, that light was also extinguished.

He hadn't waited up for his wife. Talia.

Drex repositioned the fan so it would be blowing across the bed. He lay down on his back and stacked his hands on his chest. But, tired as he was, he was still awake when he heard a car. He returned to the window that offered the most advantageous view of the Fords' house.

Turning into the driveway was a late-model BMW sedan. Drex checked his wristwatch. Mrs. Ford had overshot her ETA by twenty-seven minutes. She must have opened the garage door with a remote. She drove in, and the door went down.

Drex never distinguished more of her than a shadowy form, but by the lights being turned on, then off, he tracked her progress through the house. The last light to go out was behind a shade in a small upstairs window. He presumed it was a bathroom. Drex stayed at the window for several minutes more, but the house remained dark.

He returned to bed but lay awake, his mind troubled with thoughts of Talia Ford, lying beside her husband. When she got into bed with him, had she whispered good night, kissed his cheek, snuggled against him, reached for him, and initiated lovemaking? The thought of it made Drex ill.

At least she was alive. But for how long? Because if Jasper was the man Drex suspected him of being, his wife's days were numbered. If Jasper Ford was the man Drex had first come to know by the name of Weston Graham, then this woman would be the next of many whom Jasper had befriended, wooed, and robbed of millions before they disappeared without a trace. Drex was convinced that he had disposed of those women.

How'd she die?

In pain.

The words, Jasper's implacable doll-like stare when he spoke them, had made the hair on the back of Drex's neck stand on end. In that moment, it had felt as though Jasper was baiting him.

Drex hadn't taken the bait, but he'd wanted to.

He had wanted to lunge across the short distance separating them, grab the man—the good cook, the perfect host, the friendly neighbor—by the throat, and demand to know if he was the psychopathic cocksucker who had killed his mother.

Chapter 3

The vessel moored in the designated slip wasn't just a boat, but a yacht. It wasn't the largest in the marina, but it held its own among them, being impressively sleek and shiny. Drex felt like he should be wearing white pants and a blue blazer, maybe with a jaunty pocket handkerchief, and have a hat with gold braid and a shiny black brim.

Instead, he was in khaki shorts, a chambray shirt, and baseball cap.

Jasper waved to him from the aft deck. The woman beside him called down, "Ahoy, Drex. You're just in time for Champagne." She hefted a magnum by the neck.

He gave her his best smile and started up the ramp. "I'd settle for a beer."

"We have that, too."

A decade younger than her husband, she was very pretty in the soft and—what was the word Gif had used? Naïve? She had that dash of girlish naïveté that a con man would target. Her hair was blond, short, and artfully tousled. She was dressed in white capri pants and a bright pink sleeveless top with a scooped neckline that showed off a deep cleavage. The best that money could buy, Drex guessed.

As he joined them on deck, he and Jasper shook hands. "Have trouble finding us?"

"None at all." He took in the yacht, then divided a look between Jasper and his wife, landing on Jasper. "You're a lucky bastard. This is some beauty you have here." Then he leaned in, adding, "The boat's not bad looking, either."

All three of them laughed. Mrs. Ford flattened a hand against the swell of her breasts, the diamonds on her fingers flashing rainbows in the sunlight. "Why, thank you. Jasper warned me that you were a charmer. I'm so glad you joined us today, even though I understand we're dragging you away from your work."

"Thank you for the invitation, and it didn't take much arm-twisting to get me here. A writer looks for any excuse not to write."

"I would be completely daunted by the prospect of writing a book," she said.

"I'm completely daunted by it, too, Talia. I'm sorry, is it okay if I call you Talia?"

She and Jasper looked surprised, then both began laughing. She said, "You could call me Talia if that was my name. I'm Elaine. Elaine Conner."

Taken aback, Drex was about to stammer an apology when Jasper looked beyond him and smiled. "*Here's* Talia."

Drex did an about-face.

A woman dressed all in white was coming up the steps that led from the galley, a tray of canapés balanced on her right palm. Hearing her name, she tilted her head back and looked up through the hatch, straight at Drex.

His stomach dropped like an anchor, because, in that instant, he knew: *I'm so fucked.*

As Talia cleared the doorway onto the deck, the tall stranger stepped forward. "You could use a hand." He relieved her of the tray.

"Thank you." The sun was behind him. She shielded her eyes against the glare to better see him. The bill of his cap cast his eyes in shadow, but his bristly jaw and smile were visible. He didn't appear to be quite as "rough around the edges" as Jasper had described. "You must be our new neighbor."

"Guilty."

Jasper placed an arm across her shoulders. "Talia, this is Drex Easton. Drex, my wife."

"Pleased to meet you, Drex." She proffered her hand. He was holding the tray in his left, so his right hand was free to shake hers. It was a firm handshake, but not a bone-cruncher.

"Pleased to meet you, too, Talia."

"Jasper told me about the pleasant dinner you had together."

"It's a shame you missed it. Your husband is an outstanding cook."

"Which works out well, because I'm dreadful."

"This doesn't look dreadful." He nodded down at the array of hors d'oeuvres on the tray.

"The deli," she whispered.

"But the rémoulade for the shrimp salad is homemade," Jasper said. "I whipped it up this morning."

"And I recommend it highly," she said.

Elaine got their attention by clapping her hands. "Gather 'round. I insist on everyone having at least one glass of Champagne." She had filled four flutes and placed them on a cocktail table. "This is an occasion. We've made a new friend. Welcome, Drex."

"Thank you. I'm glad to be here."

Although he was the outsider, he looked at ease as he carried the tray to the table and set it in the center, then held out a chair for Elaine before seating himself.

"You forgot your hat, Talia." Jasper came up behind her and placed her wide-brimmed straw hat on her head.

"Thank you. It wouldn't have taken long for me to miss it."

"Wise girl," Elaine said to Drex. "She avoids sun exposure. Too late for me."

"You acquire a gorgeous tan. I freckle," Talia said.

"She's practically a vampire," Jasper said.

Affronted and embarrassed by his insensitive remark, she looked at the newcomer of the group, who was sitting directly across the table from her. He had slid on a pair of sunglasses, but she could tell that he was looking into her face, as though seeking the referred-to freckles.

What could have become an awkward moment was saved by Elaine, who prompted them to raise their glasses. She made a toast to everyone's good health then turned her attention to Drex and began plying him with questions.

Jasper spoke quietly to her. "I believe I embarrassed you with the vampire comment. I'm sorry."

"No harm done."

He patted her hand, then turned toward the other two and joined their conversation. Talia was content to let it flow around her without being required to either lead it or participate to any great extent. The tedious hours she'd spent in O'Hare, the bumpy flight to Charleston, then the drive home from the airport had left her exhausted. Jasper didn't wake up when she got into bed, for which she'd been relieved. It was his wont to ask for detailed accounts of her trips.

Over breakfast, she had suggested that she sit out today's excursion. "You and Elaine go without me. Enjoy yourselves. I'll be perfectly happy to stay behind and lounge all day."

"We've had this planned for days. Elaine will be disappointed if you don't come. Besides, I've invited a fourth."

That's when he'd told her about the man who'd moved into the garage apartment.

"Is it even livable?" she'd asked.

"He seems to think so. But I doubt his standards are very high."

"Why do you say that?"

"I'll let you form your own opinion. He's rough around the edges, but I will credit him with knowing which fork to use for each course, and the two bottles of wine he brought were passable."

"If you weren't that taken with him, why did you invite him to come along today?"

"Curiosity."

Drex Easton was more refined than Jasper had led her to believe, but then Jasper *did* have very high standards. Gauging by Elaine's body language, which had her leaning toward the writer across the armrest of her chair, she found him magnetic.

He seemed unfazed by her avid interest, answering her barrage of questions with humor but, Talia noticed, little elaboration. He was self-deprecating and unaffected.

But when he glanced across the table and shot her a smile, Talia wondered if perhaps he was exercising reverse psychology. Maybe his seeming disinterest in making a good first impression was a calculated attempt to make one.

Not so long ago, she would have accepted his open and friendly nature for what it was, rather than to look for duplicity. Jasper was more disinclined to take people at face value. She supposed that tendency of his was wearing off on her.

They finished the remainder of the Champagne, then Jasper pushed back his chair and stood. "Shall we get underway? Or would you rather serve lunch first, Elaine?"

"Let's go out a way and anchor for lunch."

Jasper saluted her. "After you, captain." He bent down and peeped beneath the brim of Talia's hat. "You don't mind if I play first mate, do you?"

"I know you can't wait to get your hands on the wheel. Go."

He pecked her cheek with his lips. To Drex he said, "Beer and soft drinks are in the fridge in the galley. Help yourself."

"Thanks. I'm good for now."

Jasper followed Elaine into the wheelhouse and closed the door behind them. The absence of Elaine's chatter was immediately noticeable. Drex was the first to remark on it. "Has Elaine ever met a stranger?"

Talia laughed. "Not since I've known her."

"Which is for how long?"

"A few years."

"How'd you come to meet?"

"She and her husband frequently cruised down here from Delaware. After he died, she decided to move here. She and I met when she joined the country club."

He gave a look around. "I assumed the yacht belonged to you and Jasper."

"No, it's Elaine's."

"Does she pilot it herself?"

"Usually only out of the marina."

"That takes some maneuvering skills."

"According to her, the late Mr. Conner was an avid boatman. He taught her how to pilot in case there was ever an emergency and she had to take over for him. She's coaching Jasper. Once we clear the buoys, she lets him have the wheel."

"He seemed eager to be at the helm."

"He loves boats and all things aquatic."

"What about you?"

"I enjoy our outings, but I don't have a passion for the water."

"No? What turns you on?"

Possibly she was reading innuendo into the question when none was intended. Otherwise it bordered on being inappropriate. Since they were going to be trapped on a boat together for hours, she chose to make a joke of it rather than an issue.

"Nutella," she said. "I eat it with a spoon straight from the jar."

He laughed.

The lighthearted mood had been reestablished. Feeling more

comfortable, she settled in her chair, tucking her right foot beneath her hips. She motioned toward his cap. "Did you go to Tennessee?"

"No. A buddy of mine is an alum and gung-ho fan. We went camping last summer, and I came home with his cap mixed up in my stuff. I never gave it back." He grinned. "It's ragged. I doubt he's missed it."

She smiled, then looked away, distracted by another boat passing them as it entered the marina. She waved to those onboard, and they waved back. But once the boat was past them, she again got the feeling that Drex Easton was studying her, and when she turned back to him, she caught him at it. "What?"

He pointed toward her empty glass. "You passed on a refill of Champagne. Can I go below and get you something else?"

"You shouldn't be waiting on me. You're the guest."

"But you didn't invite me. Jasper did. You probably would have preferred not having to entertain today. You got in late last night."

She tilted her head inquisitively.

"I heard your car when you pulled into the driveway."

"I'm sorry I disturbed you."

"You didn't. I wasn't asleep. I haven't slept through the night since I moved in."

"A new place takes some getting used to. Give it a few more nights."

"I don't think a few more nights are going to improve the lumpy mattress. The fan Jasper loaned me helped with the heat."

"He lent you a fan?"

"His generosity knows no bounds."

She smiled. Then, to her chagrin, she yawned. "Forgive me. The truth is, I didn't get a full night's sleep, either, and the Champagne has made me drowsy."

"Then I'll shut up and let you doze. Or would you rather I leave you in peace and...relocate?"

When he smiled in a certain way, an attractive dimple appeared in his right cheek behind the piratical scruff. She figured he knew that dimple was attractive and doubted he would relocate if she took him up on his offer.

"You may stay," she said.

"Ah, good. I'm drowsy, too. And after two days of moving in, it feels good to sit and do nothing." He slouched deeper into his chair, pulled the brim of his cap down to the top of his sunglasses, and linked his fingers over his lap. No rings. A sizeable but unadorned wristwatch with a black leather band.

His hands were large and long-fingered, with plump veins criss-crossing the backs of them. His sleeves were rolled up to midway between wrist bone and elbow. Even though he appeared relaxed, she sensed tensile strength in his limbs.

She looked away and followed a solitary cloud drifting between them and the horizon. A minute passed. He didn't move. The silence between them began to feel ponderous. She searched for something to say. "Drex is an unusual name."

He flinched and sat up straighter. "Sorry? I was about to nod off."

"No you weren't."

The moment the words were out, she wished she could call them back. Too late now, however. Above his sunglasses, one of his eyebrows arched to form a question mark.

With a trace of challenge in her tone, she said, "You were staring at me. I could see your eyes through your sunglasses."

He thumped the arm of his chair with his fist. "Damn! Busted." He shot her that smile again. "I *was* staring at you."

"Why?"

"Welllll, if I told the absolute, swear-on-the-Bible truth, Jasper would probably sew me up in a tow sack and pitch me overboard."

Talia couldn't help it. She laughed. He was a shameless flirt, and, since he made no secret of it, it was harmless. "Like the Count of Monte Cristo."

"My favorite book," he said.

"Oh? Why?"

He thought about it for a moment. "He was committed."

"To getting revenge."

He bobbed his chin. "He let nothing stop him, not even imprisonment. He was patient. He did his homework. He pulled off the best undercover guise ever. Got his man." He paused and then grinned wickedly. "And woman."

"His enemy's wife."

He sat up straight and leaned forward with his forearms crossed on the tabletop. "I called Jasper a lucky bastard when I mistook Elaine for his wife."

"You no longer think he's lucky?"

He didn't answer immediately. Then, "I think he won the Powerball. Twice. At least."

The dimple had disappeared, and so had the mischievous smile. Of a sudden, the flirting didn't seem quite so harmless.

Chapter 4

Elaine chose that moment to open the wheelhouse door and poke her head out. "Hold onto your hats and watch to see that those flutes don't slide off the table. We've cleared the marina, and Jasper's about to give it the throttle." She ducked back inside. The yacht gathered speed and moved out into open water.

Elaine had interrupted an uncomfortable moment. But Talia thought perhaps she had imagined the intensity in Drex's tone, because now his teasing grin was back.

"Why was I staring at you? I was contemplating. Here I am a wordsmith, but I'll be damned if I can think of an adjective that accurately captures the color of your hair. When I saw you coming up the stairs, I thought 'russet.'"

"Adequate."

"Adequate but lacking nuance."

"You need nuance?"

"Yes. Because when you got in the sunlight, I saw that your hair is shot through with strands of gold and copper. So what word would I use to describe it?"

"Why would you need a word? Why would you be describing

me? Unless you're planning to use me as a character in your book."

"Oh, God no! I think far too highly of you to do that."

Her laughter was followed by a comfortable silence as they stared out across the chop. He resumed the conversation by asking what had taken her to Chicago.

"I went to assess a hotel." Reading his puzzled expression, she smiled. "It's a prototype. New concept. Very minimalist. I tried it on for size."

"What for?"

"It's a long story."

He spread his arms. "I've got nowhere to go."

"Okay, but remember you asked."

"Fire at will."

"I was trying out the hotel for my clientele."

"Clientele?"

"My parents had a travel agency. I started working in the office when I was in high school. When I graduated college, I was made manager, and they semi-retired. Then Dad died, followed by my mother a year and a half later. I was their only child and heir. Shafer Travel, Inc., became mine."

"That sounded like the expurgated version. Go on."

"Well, I expanded the business, first by opening an office in Savannah, and then another in Birmingham. Those did well. I paid off the business loan that got those up and running, then took out another loan to open two more offices, one in Dallas, the other in Charlotte."

"Wow," he said. "This at a time when most people started booking everything travel-related online."

"Most people, yes. But when even the best travel agencies began cutting back on personnel and services offered, a market was created for white glove service. My agencies responded, and began catering to clients who didn't need to, or wish to, shop online for the cheapest airfare or haggle over a room rate."

"You stopped booking bus tours to see fall foliage?"

"And started booking private jets to see the seven wonders of the world. Word spread about our specialized service."

"Millionaires talk."

She smiled. "Before too long, Shafer Travel got the attention of a company that has dozens of agencies nationwide. It didn't look kindly on the competition mine were giving them." She raised her shoulders. "They made me an offer I couldn't refuse."

"You sold out."

"Lock, stock, and barrel."

"Congratulations."

"Thank you."

"So if you no longer have the business, why were you trying out the hotel in Chicago?"

"Are you sure you want to hear all this?"

"I don't know. How much more inept and underachieving am I going to feel when you're finished?" The dimple reappeared.

She tented her fingers and tapped them against her lips as she regarded him thoughtfully. "I don't quite trust you."

"I'm sorry?"

"Your self-denigration. I think you use it to disarm people so they'll form a lower opinion of you than they should."

He placed his hand over his heart. "What a relief. Here I thought my inadequacies were real. I'm glad to learn they're faked."

She didn't laugh as he obviously expected her to. Rather, she continued to wonder why he downplayed the shrewdness she detected in the eyes behind the dark lenses. Not that his psychology was of any consequence to her, she reminded herself. She went on with her story, but only because he motioned for her to do so.

"I discovered I wasn't cut out to retire at the age of thirty-two," she said. "Inside of a month, I was bored. So when I began getting calls from former clients, complaining about the lack of attention and personal service they were receiving, I agreed to handle their travel arrangements, everything from the time they left their front door until they returned. Down to the most minute detail."

"You do this for fun? Goodwill?"

"No, for a percentage of how much they spend on the trip."

"Ah!" He grinned. "I doubt I could afford you."

"Few can," she admitted. "That limits the number of clients I cater to. I get to keep my toe in, but only to the extent I want."

"Still giving the big boys competition?"

"I'm an...irritant. Especially to the company that bought me out."

He barked a laugh. "I'll bet. You're keeping the big spenders under your wing." He flopped back against the chair cushion. "For ingenuity alone, I'd give you a five-star rating."

His flattery made her feel good in a way it probably shouldn't. She experienced a warmth she wanted to bask in.

"How did you like the minimalist prototype?" he asked.

Glad to be pulled back on track, she said, "There were an over-abundance of outlets in which to plug in devices."

"But?"

"The room was sterile. No personality or character. No—"

"Ambiance?"

"Good word."

"Whew! Maybe I have promise as a writer after all."

She gave him an arch look before continuing. "Everything was so high tech, it took me fifteen minutes to figure out how to turn on the lights and keep them on. I'm not particularly fond of baroque or chintz, but I do like a chair that conforms to the human body, one that I can actually sit in."

"You won't be recommending the place."

"No. My clients appreciate having their travel streamlined, and having plenty of electrical outlets for their gadgets, but they also in-sist on creature comforts."

"I'm a creature who likes his comforts."

"Then why did you move into that tiny space with no air-conditioning and a lumpy mattress?"

"I hadn't suffered enough yet. To be a good writer, one must suffer."

"Self-flagellation?"

"I haven't tried it yet, but I'm almost to that point."

They shared a smile, then he asked, "When you go on these research trips, does Jasper ever go along?"

"Not that often. Only if I'm looking at something a bit more exotic than a hotel for the business traveler."

"Do you ever go overseas?"

"I go two or three times a year. Jasper, never."

"Why not? I'd think those would be the trips he'd want to take."

"He doesn't like the long flights."

"I see."

She sensed there was more to his dismissive comment than the mere two words. "What?"

"Nothing."

"What?"

"Well, I think Jasper must be the most secure man I've ever met to let you go traveling the world on your own and be okay with it."

"I didn't ask his permission, so it's not as though he *lets* me," she said coolly. "And I didn't say he was okay with it."

"Then he's not?"

"He is, but he keeps track of my itinerary."

"So he knows where you are at any given time."

"Yes." Minutes earlier, she'd been thinking how glad she was to have avoided one of Jasper's debriefings late last night. Now, she was defending his husbandly concern. "It only makes sense. It's a safety precaution."

"Me? I'd want to put a chip in your ear."

Again Drex's grin lightened the tenor of the conversation and relieved the tension inside her chest that had begun to collect. She had disliked having to justify Jasper's vigilance over her schedule.

Drex looked toward the wheelhouse. "How long have you two been together?"

"Together, a year and a half. Married, eleven months."

"That was a short courtship."

"Relatively."

"He must have swept you off your feet as soon as you met. How did you?"

"You wouldn't believe it."

He came back around to her. "Oh, no. Don't tell me you found each other online."

"Well, in a sense, but not on a match-up service. We corresponded by email for several weeks before we met in person."

His eyebrows bobbed above his sunglasses. "Do tell."

She laughed. "It's not at all salacious. He'd booked a trip—domestic—through our office in Savannah. When he returned, he had a complaint about one of the hotels we'd booked him into, and wanted to take up the issue with the top dog."

"That would be you."

"He was given my email address. I looked into his complaint, and found that it had merit. I got him a full refund for that night. He was impressed by the excellent service."

"And proceeded to email you flowery compliments for weeks."

"Then gave me flowers for real."

"Smoooooth. What did the card say?"

"There wasn't a card. He drove from Savannah to Charleston to deliver the bouquet in person."

He whistled softly. "Even smoother."

"It was a change from being asked out via text."

"The suave move worked, and here you are. Happ'ly ever after."

She looked down at her wedding band and turned it around on her finger. "Here I am." Her soft comment was followed by a ding. She raised her head and looked across the table. "Is that your phone?"

"Yeah." Looking resentful of the interruption, he stretched out his leg and dug into the front pocket of his shorts for his phone. He looked at the readout. "I set myself a reminder. I'm supposed to call my agent. But can I get cell service out here?"

"It extends offshore for ten or fifteen miles."

"Then I'd better make the call. He's expecting it."

He was about to stand when she motioned him back into his chair and got up herself. "I'll go inside."

"No, stay here. I'll go forward. Once he gets wound up, he tends to ramble."

"It would be hard for you to hear above the wind. Besides, I need to make myself useful."

Drex was reluctant to end their private conversation. He watched her until she was inside before he tapped in the number. It was answered immediately. "Sheriff's office, Deputy Gray speaking."

"Agent Easton. Did you locate the file?"

"Yes, sir."

Early that morning, Drex had called the Monroe County sheriff's office in Key West, Florida, figuring that whoever was working the undesirable Sunday morning shift would be junior in rank. A more senior officer wouldn't be as impressed to be speaking with a federal agent and would have given Drex a lot more hassle.

As good fortune would have it, Gray was just such a rookie.

In their earlier conversation Drex had told him that his field office in Lexington was investigating a missing person case. "Single, affluent, middle-aged woman. It's almost certain a kidnaping. One of our data analysts determined that some of the particulars of this disappearance are similar to a case your department investigated a few years back."

There was no such active case in Lexington, but there was a cold case in Key West, where Marian Harris had disappeared, abandoning her yacht in a private harbor and leaving her bank accounts empty.

It could be sheer coincidence that within hours of meeting Jasper Ford, Drex had been invited to go out on a boat with him. The man might never have spent a day of his life in Key West. But Drex had played a hunch and called the sheriff's department that morning anyway.

He was glad he'd had that foresight, and unapologetic for lying about an investigation in Lexington, because, since talking to Deputy Gray this morning, he'd learned from Talia that Jasper had a passion for being on the water and at the helm of a yacht.

Gray had asked for a few hours to locate the file. Drex had told him he would call back at a designated time. It wasn't the most ideal time to talk, but Gray was due to go off duty soon, and, besides that, Drex was eager to hear anything the deputy could tell him.

"What have you got for me? And you'll have to speak up. I'm outdoors."

"This case was before I joined the department. In between performing my other duties, I've been reviewing it, so I have a general grasp. It would help if I knew what you're looking for, specifically."

"In particular, I'm seeking information on one of Ms. Harris's acquaintances. A Daniel Knolls." Drex spelled the last name.

He could hear Gray tapping on a keyboard. "After she went missing, Knolls was interrogated and released. He owned up to staying overnight on her yacht on several occasions. But other people did, too. Their relationship was platonic, not romantic. He was never considered a suspect. He cooperated fully with investigators."

Drex already knew all that. Daniel Knolls had cooperated fully, then he'd bolted. He had vacated his apartment and had left no forwarding address. So far, Daniel Knolls hadn't been heard of again. No credit card charges. No activity on the Social Security number attributed to him. No passport. Taken at face value, he had ceased to exist within two weeks of Marian Harris's disappearance.

Drex looked toward the wheelhouse. He could see Jasper silhouetted behind the wheel. "Is there a photograph of Knolls in the file?"

"One."

Drex knew the picture. The quality was lousy. A merging of smiling people whooping it up on the deck of Marian Harris's yacht. Blurred figures backlit by a blazing setting sun. It could have been Drex himself standing there in the background, face averted from the camera.

He said, "Can you scan that photo and send it to the email address I gave you this morning?"

"Of course, sir."

"Is there anything new on the case? Any recent info on Knolls?"

"Let's see. Says here he was sought for questioning after Marian Harris's body was discovered, but he—"

"Excuse me, *what?*" He plugged his free ear with this index finger. "Did you say her body was discovered?"

"Yes, sir."

Drex's heart began to pound. None of the previous victims had ever been found. "When was this? Where?"

"Give me a sec here, please."

It took more than a sec. Drex thought his head would explode before the deputy said, "Okay. Here's the skinny. A construction crew in Collier County was dredging a creek so they could replace old bridge abutments with new ones. Backhoe dug up a box."

"Box?"

"Like a shipping crate. Wood. Dimensions were six by three by four feet. Lid was nailed shut. The remains were inside."

"When was this?"

"Uh...Only three months ago. FBI was given a heads-up. Everything was sent to an Agent Rud...rud..."

"Rudkowski."

"That's it."

That son of a bitch. Drex removed his ball cap, put his elbow on the table, and rested his forehead in his palm. The Champagne was churning hotly in his stomach. "The remains were positively identified as Marian Harris?"

"Using dental records."

"Cause of death?"

"Suffocation." Then, "Oh Jesus."

"What?"

The boat was slowing down. They would be anchoring soon. Through the glass walls enclosing the lounge area, Drex could see Elaine and Talia laughing together as they set the dining table for lunch.

Drex said, "Gray, you still there? What?"

He heard the deputy swallow. "Man, this is grim."

"Tell me."

"There was blood inside the crate. On the underside of the lid. Streaks of it, like claw marks. Appears the vic was buried alive."

Chapter 5

———◦◦◦———

Gif shared Drex's horror. "Buried alive?"

As soon as Drex had returned from the yacht cruise, he'd showered off the salt spray as well as the taint of Jasper Ford. He'd parked himself in front of the borrowed fan and placed a three-way call to Gif and Mike. They'd been waiting to hear about his afternoon excursion, but the news about Marian Harris was unexpected. It had rocked them, just as it had Drex.

"A minute after hearing that, I had to sit down across the table from him and eat chilled watercress soup and shrimp salad with his homemade rémoulade."

"Mild or spicy?"

"Fuck, Mike," Drex said. "That's crass, even for you."

"You're right. Sorry. I'm deflecting my guilt. How did I miss that her body had been discovered?"

"Don't beat yourself up," Gif said. "It really wouldn't have done us any good to know before today."

"At the time she was found, she'd been missing for almost two years," Drex said. "A widow, no children. Most of her friends in Key West were snowbirds, vacationers, jet-setters from the U.S. and abroad. Word eventually would have gotten around to them, I'm sure, but I doubt there was a groundswell of reaction. Local news in southern Florida may have made the recovery of her remains a headline. 'Authorities hope the discovery will provide clues into the Key West's woman's kidnaping and apparent murder.' Then, on to weather and sports.

"I don't know if there was a memorial service or observance of any sort. But it didn't warrant national news coverage, so it was easily overlooked, Mike."

Marian Harris's fate was upsetting to Mike and Gif, but, because of his mother, it affected Drex in ways they couldn't relate to.

He didn't have any substantial memories of her, only infinitesimal snatches of recollection lurking in the dark corners of his memory. But they were meaningless because he couldn't fit them into any context. He had no points of reference. By the time he was old enough to retain memories, she had been long absent from his life.

When he reached an age to become aware of and curious about this deficiency and had asked to see a picture of his mother, his dad had claimed not to have one. Then, as now, Drex figured that he'd been lying, or, if telling the truth, it was because he'd destroyed any pictures of his ex-wife.

Their separation had been bitter, absolute, and permanent. His father even went so far as to have his and Drex's names legally changed so that, even if she had rethought her decision and wanted to reconcile, she wouldn't have been able to find them. Though Drex didn't learn of that until years later.

In his early teens, when he was going through a rebellious phase, he'd demanded to know how he could contact her. His father had refused to provide him with any information, describing their severance as an extraction and an exorcism.

The only picture Drex had of her was the one that had been circulated by the Los Angeles PD when she went missing, and he hadn't seen it until years after the fact when no one was still actively looking for her.

It was then that he had assumed the search. He didn't really expect to find his mother living somewhere in obscurity. He had reconciled that she'd been killed and that her remains had been left where they were unlikely ever to be found.

No, he didn't begin searching for his mother. Rather for the man responsible for her disappearance. He had vowed not to stop until he found him. And he wouldn't.

However, from the outset of his quest, he had avoided speculating on his mother's manner of death. But after what he'd heard today about Marian Harris, to imagine the woman who'd birthed him suffering a similar fate, to envision how horrific her end might have been, made him break a sweat despite his recent shower and the whirring fan.

Plowing his fingers through his damp hair, he left his chair and went to stand by the window. The Fords had returned home only a few minutes behind him. He hadn't seen either of them since. There was no sign of them now.

Were they upstairs or down? Sharing a room? A bed? A kiss? Was he caressing Talia with the same hands that had nailed shut that shipping crate with a breathing Marian Harris inside?

He inhaled deeply through his nose, exhaled through his mouth, whispering, "He buried that woman alive."

"You say that like it means something," Gif said. "I mean more than the obvious."

Drex said, "We've been on the hunt for a con man who kills his victim solely to eliminate a witness. After learning about Marian, what's obvious to me now is that this guy is more than that. He likes the killing."

"Thrill kills?" Mike asked.

"Maybe not that extreme," Drex said thoughtfully. "Close, though. He could be evolving into that."

"His version of middle-age crazy?"

"You're joking, Gif, but that makes a weird kind of sense. He's getting older. He watches the news. He sees the new generation of

degenerates outdoing him. To compete, he's got to up his game."
He cursed softly. "Which means I do. I've got to rearrange my
thinking, start looking for traits in Jasper that—"

"You don't know that your neighbor is Knolls," Mike said. "Or
Weston Graham, or whatever the hell his real name is."

"It's him. I know it."

"No, you *don't*, Drex."

He was annoyed by his cohort's denial of what he felt—knew—
in his bones, in his gut. "Did you get the picture?"

Drex had asked the deputy in Key West to send the party shot to
a dummy email account to which none of the three could be linked.

"Yeah," Mike replied. "I magnified it and compared the guy in
the background to Ford's South Carolina driver's license picture.
There's no resemblance."

"I trust my gut more than I do photography. Look more closely."

"Drex—"

"Blow that picture up to the size of a fucking football field.
Count every pore on the bastard's face if you have to. It's him."

Quietly, Gif said, "You want it to be him."

"All right, yes!" Drex fired back, in an angry hiss. "I want it to
be him."

Staring at the Fords' house was only making him crazy. He went
to the fridge, got a bottle of water, and returned with it to the chair.
Neither of the other two spoke.

After taking a long drink and calming down a degree or two, he
said, "Find out everything you can about Elaine Conner."

He told them what he had learned about her through conversation. "The yacht is named *Laney Belle*, her husband's pet name for
her. It's registered in Dover, Delaware, where he hailed from. I get a
sense that he was older and had old money, but I'm guessing. She's
an attractive, rich widow."

"Our guy's type."

"That occurred to me," Drex said. "Although Elaine is more
bubbly than the others. More self-assured and less needy. Gregari-

ous. Life of the party. But he's very courtly toward her, and she eats it up."

"His wife isn't jealous?" Gif asked.

"If she is, I didn't pick up on it. She and Elaine come across as good friends."

"What's she like?"

"I just told you, Mike. Bubbly."

"Not her. Talia Ford."

"Shafer. I learned today that she goes by her professional name."

Mike, who had no regard for political correctness, huffed, "Women these days."

Gif repeated Mike's question. "What's she like?"

I took her tray, she took my breath. Her eyes are the color of wood smoke and just as hypnotic. A smile I wanted to eat.

He cleared his throat. "She's damn smart, I'll say that. Told me the history of her company. Inherited, but she expanded it, sold it, and then trumped the buyer. I was intimidated."

"A ball-breaker doesn't sound like our man's type."

"She's not a ball-breaker."

"Huh. By the way she was flaunting her success—"

"She wasn't *flaunting*," Drex said, making his irritation plain. "Why don't you get a clue, Mike?"

"About what?"

"Societal shifts."

"What?"

"Never mind. You're hopeless."

Gif interceded. "Drex, I think what Mike is clumsily and stupidly—"

"Hey!"

"—trying to get out of you is your sense of Jasper Ford's wife."

"I just told you," Drex said. "For a woman her age—"

"She's thirty-four."

Mike and his research. He would know her birthday, too. "Okay, then. She's accomplished a hell of a lot in her thirty-four years."

"She attractive?"

"You could say so, sure. All his victims have been. I thought you were looking for Shafer Travel ads from back before she sold it. No luck?"

"Found the ads," Mike said, "but they featured a family crest–looking logo, no photos of her. I did find some pictures of her on Google, but none that good or that recent. The business has social media accounts, but they're also under the logo. If she has personal accounts, they're private." After a portentous pause, he continued. "I did scare up a slick business journal that did a feature article on her shortly after she sold out. There was a picture. Close-up. Professional photographer. The piece was published a few years ago, but I doubt she's gone to seed since then."

Gif said, "Come on, Drex, level with us. One could say that she's several notches above 'attractive.' Or was that magazine photo air-brushed?"

"I doubt it was," Drex mumbled. A trickle of sweat slid down over his ribs. "She's a looker, okay? What of it?"

"What of it is, you like to look," Gif said.

"I confess. But this lady is married, remember?"

"Gif and I remember fine," Mike said. "Question is, do you?"

No one said anything. Drex wasn't about to defend himself when he hadn't done anything inappropriate. Unless lusting counted.

It was Gif, in his mediating role, who asked, "What are they like together, as a couple?"

"Comfortable. For all the attention he showered on Elaine, he was solicitous to Talia."

"Were they affectionate?"

"A kiss on her cheek. His hands were on her shoulders when he gave her a turn at the wheel. She kissed the back of his hand when he served her chocolate mousse. I think she must be a chocoholic. She eats Nutella straight from the jar."

"So do I," Mike said.

"Yeah, but I doubt she finishes the jar in one sitting," Drex said. He knew sure as hell that Mike wouldn't look like Talia licking the spoon clean. Which Drex had fantasized. In detail. In slow motion. With sound effects.

Gif asked, "You didn't get a sense that she was afraid of him?"

"Not in the slightest."

There had been that moment when she'd looked down at her wedding band and turned it around her finger. *And here I am.* She'd spoken so softly, the words were almost inaudible above the wind. Her expression had been, what? Not fearful. Not wary. Wistful?

Maybe. Or maybe that was the emotion Drex had wanted to see. His pals would probably conclude that, so he didn't mention it. Instead, he pitched his idea. "I don't know if or when I'll be with them again to observe. Elaine mentioned another get-together soon, but that could mean tomorrow or a month from now. The only way I'll learn what they're like alone together is if I plant a bug."

"I'm a freaking genius," Mike said around a groan. "I knew you were going to say that."

"Drex, you can't," Gif said. "Rudkowski would shit."

"It'll be good for him. I'll bet he's been backed up for years."

"This is nothing to joke about."

"You're telling me. Rudkowski has known about the discovery of Marian Harris's remains for three months. Did he inform me? No."

"For your own good."

"I'll decide what's for my own good. And what would be for my own good right now would be to eavesdrop on the couple next door."

Mike harrumphed, his way of saying that it was a foregone conclusion that Drex would break the rules and do it, and that trying to dissuade him was pointless.

Gif wasn't ready to give in. "If you're caught—"

"I'll take my chances. It's worth the risk. It was before. But now, knowing what he did to Marian Harris? Yeah. It's worth the risk."

"Are you sure, Drex?"

He said, "If it's him—"

"Big if."

"—and if we nail him—"

"An even bigger if," Mike said.

"—then it'll be *more* than worth it."

"No matter the personal cost to you?" Gif said.

"No matter the personal cost to me." In the ensuing silence, he felt the weight of their disapproval. "Guys, he has victimized eight women. Eight that we know of. My mother may not have been his first. Don't think about the consequences to me. Think about those women. Think about Marian Harris trying to claw her way out of that crate."

"We get it, Drex," Gif said. "But you'll be breaking the law."

"I'm aware. But you won't be. If I'm caught, I'll take full responsibility. You have my word on it."

"That's not what concerns me," Gif said.

"Well, it concerns me big time," Drex said. "I won't let you two be blamed. Not by Rudkowski or anyone."

After a lengthy silence, Mike heaved a heavy sigh and asked Drex if he needed any equipment shipped to him.

"No. I brought it with me."

"So this idea didn't just pop into your head."

Drex didn't respond.

"How do you plan to plant it?" Gif asked. "Where inside the house? When?"

"All TBD. I'll keep you posted."

He hung up before they could try further to talk him out of it.

———

The eyeglasses Drex wore were a prop. So was the ream of typing paper on the kitchen table next to his computer. Alongside the stack of blank sheets were the couple hundred pages of rubber-banded manuscript that had been typed by a woman in his office. Her name was Pam something. The text had been taken directly from a historical paperback novel set during the Civil War.

When he approached Pam with the request, she'd regarded him dubiously. "What do you want it for?"

"Something I'm working on."

She quirked an eyebrow. "You can't share?"

"Not yet."

She'd thumbed through the yellowed pages of the paperback. "What about typos? Does it have to be perfect?"

"No. In fact, a mistake here or there would be good. I'll be marking it up."

The single mother of two had a deadbeat ex. She'd agreed to do the transcription for three dollars a page. When she delivered it, Drex had given her a hug and a fifty-dollar bonus.

He marked up the pages with red pencil, dog-eared some of the sheets, dripped coffee over several, left puckered water rings on others.

Now, his setup looked very "writerly," should anyone be surreptitiously observing, which he sensed someone was.

While seated at his computer as though working on his book, he was actually reading additional material excavated by Mike. Marian Harris's parish church had held a memorial mass. After the forensic pathologist had completed his examination and turned his findings over to the authorities, her remains were cremated and placed in a vault in the church cemetery.

Although her will had specified allocations for various charities, there was nothing in the coffers to bequeath. The only asset not liquidated prior to her disappearance had been her yacht. As stipulated in her will, it was sold at auction, the proceeds gifted to the parish.

Drex hadn't asked Mike to research all that, but he was grateful to him for doing so. Marian Harris hadn't been confined forever in that shipping crate. Drex took some comfort in that.

But not much.

He wanted the son of a bitch who'd done that to her. With an instinct that was almost feral, he felt he had found him.

Throughout the evening, lights in the house across the lawn came on and went off. Shadows moved across window shades. Drex watched Jasper make himself a sandwich. He ate it at the kitchen table while perusing the Sunday newspaper. He saw Talia switch on a light as she entered a room upstairs.

He got only a glance before she shut the door behind her, but he saw that her hair was messily piled on top of her head, and that she had changed out of the oversize white linen shirt and wide-legged pants she'd worn on the cruise.

When they were on deck, and the wind had struck her just right, it had blown aside the fabric of her shirt, affording Drex a glimpse of a white tank top with skinny straps, a fragile-looking collarbone, an oh-so-slight suggestion of cleavage above the snug tank.

Nothing had actually been revealed. Which had been as frustrating as hell. Also as erotic. He'd wanted to unwrap her and explore the tantalizing terrain his imagination had mapped out.

Evening descended into night. Shortly after ten o'clock, he set aside his eyeglasses, folded up his computer, and turned out the lights inside the apartment. But he stayed at the window. He watched and waited until the house across the way remained dark for half an hour.

As he slipped out of the apartment and down the exterior staircase, his pistol was a reassuring pressure against the small of his back.

Jasper, sitting in the deep shadows of his screened porch, watched Drex ease through the door of the apartment, close it silently behind himself, and quickly descend the stairs. In total darkness. Even though there was a light fixture mounted on the exterior wall at both the top and bottom of the steep stairs, which Drex had referred to as killers.

He reached the ground without mishap. He didn't go to his car. Instead, he made a hard right turn and moved along the far side of the garage and eventually out of Jasper's view. Moments later, he reappeared from behind the garage at the opposite corner.

Jasper didn't move or do anything else that would give away his presence, watching as Drex continued along the back boundary of his lawn, moving parallel to the house, staying in sight except for those seconds when he was swallowed by a deep shadow or blocked from view by a tree trunk.

And, one of those times, he didn't reappear. He remained behind the trunk of the largest tree on the property.

Jasper lunged from his chair and barreled through the screen door. With long, rapid strides, he covered the distance between him and the tree. He almost collided with Drex has he stepped out from behind it. Jasper clicked on the flashlight he'd brought with him and aimed it directly into Drex's face. "What are you doing?"

Drex rocked back on his heels. "Jesus, Jasper. You scared the shit out of me."

He smiled his boyish smile. It had made Elaine's heart go pitter-pat. It made Jasper suspect that it was artificial and aptly employed whenever it suited him.

Currently it was meant to distract him when Drex reached behind his back with his right hand. He raised his left to shield his eyes from the flashlight's beam. "I thought you were probably in bed by now."

"I ask again, what are you doing out here?"

"Look, man, I'm sorry. I—"

"What have you got?" Jasper directed the light down, and leaned around to try to see what Drex was concealing behind his back.

Drex took a hasty step backward.

"What's in your hand? Let me see." Jasper thrust out his left hand, palm up.

Drex hesitated, then brought his hand from around his back and dropped a dead mouse into Jasper's palm. Jasper yanked his hand back. The mouse fell to the ground.

"I would have waited till morning to throw him out, but he was stinking up the apartment."

Jasper reigned in his temper as well as his rapid breathing. "Where were you taking it?"

"That community dumpster in the next block? I thought I'd throw him in that. Save him rotting in our trash cans at the curb. I guess I should have gone the long way, used the street. I opted for the shortcut across your yard. I'm sorry as hell I bothered you."

"I didn't know it was you," he lied. "All I saw was a tall, dark figure," Jasper said, forcing a smile. "If you take a shortcut again, you should identify yourself."

"I didn't think I'd be seen."

"Oh, I'm always watching."

They held each other's gaze for several beats, then Drex bent down and picked up the lifeless mouse by the tail. Holding it between them, he gave a jocular shrug. "Guess I won't need a cat, after all."

Jasper chuckled.

"Well, good night." Drex started off.

Jasper let him get only a few yards away before calling out, "Hold it."

He turned.

"Take this." Jasper walked forward and passed him the flashlight.

"Thanks. There wasn't one in the apartment."

Jasper smiled. "What are neighbors for?"

When Drex returned from depositing the mouse in the dumpster, he took his third shower of the day and went to bed, pulling the sheet only to his waist. The fan, aimed directly at him, hummed from the side of the bed.

His mission that night had been to get a different perspective of the layout of the Fords' house, in an attempt to figure out a way to get inside. From behind the tree, he'd been using the zoom on his phone's camera to try to spot security devices on windows and doors. When Jasper had burst from the house like a man possessed, he'd had no choice but to brazen it out.

Fortunately, he'd thought to take along the dead mouse as his excuse for being in Jasper's backyard, should he be caught. He didn't believe Jasper had bought the excuse entirely. But they'd played out the scene as though he had. It hadn't been easy for Drex, makebelieving with a man whose heart and mind were darker than he'd initially thought.

He still didn't know how he would breach the castle, but he had come away knowing that Jasper was vigilant to an extraordinary degree. Meaning that Drex would be damned lucky to succeed in planting just one bug. He wished he could plant one in every room.

But even if he could manage that, there were some areas he'd rather not infiltrate. Mainly the bedroom shared by Jasper and Talia. He didn't think he could stomach listening in on an intimate conversation or, God forbid, lovemaking.

He believed that Jasper was the man he sought. Which meant that Jasper's rich, successful wife was in jeopardy. But until every element of doubt had been erased, until Drex had irrefutable proof that Talia was living with a man who had buried another woman alive, he couldn't risk warning her.

He wouldn't call in the cavalry with Rudkowski leading the charge. That would spell certain disaster. Rudkowski, who didn't know the definition of finesse, would bungle it, give them away, and then God knew what Jasper would do. It chilled Drex to think of it. He was dealing with a personality that had a very sharp tipping point, one who was in control... until he wasn't.

His short-term goal was clear: maintain his cover while keeping Talia safe from the man she lived with. He would do whatever he could to prevent her from becoming victim number nine and meeting a fate like Marian Harris's. He was committed to protecting her life, regardless of how she looked.

But she looked like Talia Shafer, and he would be lying not only to his friends but also to himself if he didn't admit that her appeal upped his level of commitment to spare her life. If Jasper Ford was who he suspected, seeing him brought to justice would no longer be sufficient or satisfying. Drex wanted to engage in mortal hand-to-hand combat. He wanted to eviscerate him.

Of course he acknowledged that such macho thinking was juvenile, stupid, and dangerous. If he went at Jasper Ford for any reason other than getting justice for eight women, he would be in hock with Rudkowski for the rest of his life.

Beyond that, allowing emotions to call the shots was a recipe for disaster. Emotions messed with a man's mind. They either weakened his resolve or made him so determined, he grew reckless. One misstep, one reflexive reaction or unplanned remark could expose his playacting. Because Jasper would be watching. A single mistake, no matter how slight, could lead to failure. Worse, it could lead to Talia's death.

Sure as hell, Weston Graham, aka Daniel Knolls, aka Jasper Ford would be at the top of his game, staying cool, playing it smart.

So must Drex be.

But, God, that was going to be difficult when he couldn't rid his mind of Talia's brandy-colored hair, the skin that tended to freckle, the gray eyes that bespoke intelligence and goodwill, but also hinted at an irresistible elusiveness.

The loose-fitting clothes she had worn on the yacht hadn't been provocative or revealing, but Drex had imagined the shape inside them to be compact and sweet. When she'd talked about desiring chairs that conformed to the human body, he'd desired to have her human body conforming to his, her bottom nestling against his middle, seeking the perfect fit, finding—

Christ!

He slid his hand beneath the sheet. He was hot. He was hard. He was going to hell for coveting his neighbor's wife. He would burn for committing whatever the biblical term was for the sin of sexual self-gratification.

He wasn't deterred.

Chapter 6

—⊰◉⊱—

Bill Rudkowski entered his office carrying a sixteen-ounce thermal container of coffee in one hand, his briefcase in the other, and the imperishable chip on his shoulder.

He wasn't overly fond of mornings in general, but he downright despised Mondays. He greeted his assistant with a brusque nod. "Anything?"

"Everything needing your attention is on your desk."

"I can hardly wait."

"Guessing by your glower, I'm thinking your team lost yesterday."

"They suck." He entered his private office and kicked the door shut with his heel.

On his desk was more paperwork than he wanted to tackle before he'd finished his coffee. Once fortified with caffeine, and resigned to it being the beginning of another week, he started working his way through the pile.

He sorted the callback messages according to levels of urgency, scrawled his illegible signature on documents requiring it, and scanned updates on several active cases. When done, he spun his chair around to his computer and booted up.

The third email in his in box drew his attention immediately because of the name in the subject line. Marian Harris.

A case number followed her name. There was an attachment. The brief message in the body of the email read: *I thought you might want to see this again, too.* It was signed by an individual he had never heard of, a Deputy Randall Gray. His official contact info was that of the sheriff's department, Monroe County, Florida, but he had included his cell phone number.

Rudkowski opened the attachment. He recognized the photograph as the one taken aboard Marian Harris's yacht during a cocktail party at sunset. Following her disappearance several months later, everyone in the snapshot had been identified, tracked down, and interviewed by Key West PD, the sheriff's office, and/or FBI agents.

Rudkowski, who had closely monitored the case, had requested colleagues in south Florida to keep him in the loop of their investigation, since the Harris woman's mysterious disappearance bore similarities to other unsolved missing person cases with which he was familiar.

The case cooled and then went cold. Two years, give or take, had passed.

He had heard nothing further until her body was discovered, roughly three months ago. It had been a grisly find. Because of the swampy environment in which she'd been buried, her body was badly decomposed. It had yielded no clues as to who had nailed her inside the crate. The bloody claw marks on the inside of the lid indicated the unsub was a sicko of the lowest order.

While authorities in Florida were investigating there, Rudkowski rounded up a team of agents and used every criminal database, domestic and abroad, to search for a connection between Marian Harris and perps known to have buried their victims alive.

A distressing number of known suspects were still at large. Some remained unidentified. Of those who had been captured and convicted, a number of them were deceased. Several had been executed for their crimes, one had been killed by another inmate during a prison riot, others had died of natural causes while incarcerated. Which left those living out their remaining days behind bars. Rudkowski saw to it that all among that number were questioned.

One had actually confessed to Marian Harris's abduction and murder, but he was a schizophrenic and habitual confessor, who liked to brag about gory atrocities he hadn't committed. He had, in fact, been incarcerated in San Quentin when the Florida woman disappeared.

Of those questioned who denied ever having heard of Marian Harris, there wasn't any incriminating evidence to indicate otherwise. None could be linked to her.

The investigation again had stalled.

Rudkowski wondered why he'd been sent the familiar photograph now without a note of explanation. If newfound evidence had regenerated the investigation, why wasn't there an accompanying brief bringing him up to speed?

He closed the attachment and went back to the email. His gaze snagged on the last word of the brief message. *Too.* I.e., in addition to. Also.

His Monday morning tanked.

Muttering foul epithets, he snatched up the receiver of his desk phone and told his assistant to get Deputy Gray on the line. Then he waited, drumming his fingers on his desktop until the call was put through.

"Gray?"

"Yes, sir, Agent Rudkowski. Good morning."

Like hell it was. "I'm calling about the photograph you emailed me last night."

"Yes, sir?"

"Has there been a development in the Marian Harris case that I'm unaware of?"

"No, sir. Well, I don't believe so."

"You just emailed me this on a whim? Out of the blue? Why?"

"Well, because your name came up during a conversation I had with Special Agent Easton. I assured him that you had been notified when Marian Harris's remains were discovered. Your contact info was on the last communiqué between the FBI and our department, so I had your email address."

Rudkowski was seeing red, but it wasn't the deputy's fault, so he kept his voice as level as possible. "When did this conversation take place?"

"With Agent Easton? Yesterday."

"Did he say what had prompted him to call your department?"

"He said that, like you, he specializes in missing persons cases."

"Um-huh."

"He was calling specifically about the missing person case in Lexington. I'm sure you've heard about it."

"Over the weekend, I unplugged from the office and just now came in. I haven't seen anything about it."

"Well, Easton said there are similarities to Marian Harris. He wanted to compare the cases."

"Of course."

"He asked me to access the case file on Harris and give him an update. I asked for a few hours, because I had other stuff to do, but I had it all in front of me when he called back."

"I'm sure he appreciated that."

"I guess, but...I don't think he knew her remains had been found. He seemed upset when I told him about her being buried alive and all. Y'all must not work that closely together, or else he would have known."

"No, we don't work closely together at all," Rudkowski said, straining the words through his clenched teeth.

"He asked me to email him the picture. Later, I got to thinking that if he was investigating this new case, you might be in on it, too, being in the same state and all. That's why I sent the picture to you."

"Good thinking, deputy. Thank you. I'll give Easton a call. Do you have his cell number in front of you?"

"It's a private number, sir. Blocked. You know, because of all the classified and undercover work he does."

Rudkowski closed his eyes and rubbed the sockets, which had begun to throb. "Of course. I forgot. Never mind. I've got his private number here in my data bank. I can look it up. Thanks again."

"Sure."

Rudkowski dropped the telephone receiver back into the cradle, picked up his cell phone, and pulled up the last cell number he had for Easton. He called it. Got his voice mail. No surprise there. The jackass wasn't about to answer if he saw the name Rudkowski in the LED, especially if he was up to something.

Rudkowski pushed back his desk chair and marched to the door of his office, yanked it open, and barked to his assistant, "Call the SAC in Lexington."

She raised her eyebrows and, under her breath, said, "Must be Easton."

"Verify that they have a local missing person. Woman, probably middle-aged and well heeled. Then call Easton's office. He's not answering his cell, and I want to talk to him. Now. No excuses. If someone else there answers, have them drag him to the phone."

He went back into his office and slammed the door.

He could hear his assistant's muffled voice as she placed the ordered calls. He fumed. Maybe he should have told Easton about the gruesome discovery in Florida, but, dammit, this is precisely why he hadn't. He'd known Easton wouldn't leave it alone.

He'd been a thorn in Rudkowski's side for years, ever since he'd shown up in Santa Barbara, uninvited and without sanction, and had poked his nose into Rudkowski's investigation into a disappearance and probable kidnap case.

Easton had been young, idealistic, determined, clever, and passionate, as though designed to make Rudkowski appear old, jaded, lackadaisical, dumb, and indifferent.

To Rudkowski, Drex Easton didn't represent a righteous crusader, but rather an accusatory finger pointing out his inadequacies. He was a recurring rash. A major pain in the ass.

Only once had Rudkowski gotten the best of him, but it had been an empty victory, which ultimately had made him look petty and Easton self-sacrificial.

His assistant opened the door, but only by a crack in which her face appeared, as though she feared he might throw something at her.

"No missing person case this week in or around Lexington, except for a man in his eighties. They put out a silver alert. He had sneaked out of his retirement home and was found a few hours later doing tequila shots and ogling the waitresses at a Hooters."

Rudkowski had figured the missing person case was a hoax used by Easton to light a fire under the deputy in Florida. "You reach Easton?"

"He's on vacation."

"Excuse me?"

"He's on—?"

"I heard you," he barked. "Since when?"

"He cleared out midday last Friday."

"For how long?"

"Two weeks."

"Where did he go?"

"He didn't say. Nobody knows."

Chapter 7

K nock-knock?"

Talia came from the kitchen onto the enclosed porch, a dish-towel slung over one shoulder. She smiled at Drex, who stood on the step on the other side of the screen door. "Hi. You're early."

He looked at his watch. "I thought I was ten minutes late. Wasn't the invitation for six?"

"Six-thirty."

"Oh. Sorry. I'll come back."

"Don't be silly. Come on in." She went over and pushed the door open for him. "Jasper had to make a quick run to the store. I forgot to get buns."

Drex knew Jasper wasn't in the house, which is why he had arrived early. He'd already been showered and dressed when he saw Jasper backing his car out of their driveway. He'd pushed his bare feet into his docksiders, forewent grooming his hair, picked up the box of cupcakes he'd bought earlier at the bakery, dashed down the perilous stairs, and crossed the lawn in a gait that wasn't quite a jog, but close.

As he stepped inside, he handed Talia the bakery box.

"What's this?"

"I told Jasper I'd bring dessert."

Jasper had come over in the early afternoon to extend the invitation. Drex had seen him coming, and, by the time Jasper had climbed the stairs, Drex appeared to be an absentminded writer, unaware of everything except his manuscript. He pretended to emerge from a creative fog and had accepted the invitation, but only on the condition that he provide the sweets.

Talia raised the box's lid. "Cupcakes! Great! Dibs on one of the chocolate ones."

"I'll flip you for the second one."

She smiled at him, her eyes shifting up to his hair. He scrubbed his knuckles across the crown of his head and gave an abashed grin. "Is it a mess? Sorry. Hazards of my trade."

"Mussed hair and what else?"

"Forgetting my hair is mussed."

She scrutinized him for a moment as though unsure what to make of him, then nodded toward the bar. "Help yourself. I'll take these into the kitchen."

"What can I mix for you?"

"I already have a glass of wine."

She went into the kitchen, leaving him alone, and presenting him with an ideal opportunity to plant the listening device. The room transmitter weighed practically nothing, but he was as aware of it in his pants pocket as he would have been of a boulder.

Talia and Jasper spent a lot of time on their porch, sitting side by side in twin rocking chairs. He would like to be privy to those conversations, but the environment wasn't an ideal place to hide the electronic transmitter. It would be susceptible to humidity and dust. Inside the house would be less corrosive and better for clearer reception.

He poured himself a bourbon on the rocks and took it with him as he wandered over to the open door of the kitchen and looked in. "Ah. You *can* cook."

Talia shot him a glance over her shoulder from where she stood at the range. "I can boil water. Which is what I'm doing for corn on the cob."

He went inside and walked over to her. Three ears of corn, still in their husks, lay on the counter. "They're better cooked in the microwave."

She turned toward him and slid the towel off her shoulder. "Jasper wouldn't hear of it."

"Jasper isn't here." He set his drink on the counter. "Where's your microwave?"

She pointed to where it fit inside the cabinetry. "Are you sure about this? These are all we have, so if you ruin them—"

"I won't. Observe and learn. Step one. Pick ripe ears of corn off stalks in field. Oh, done that already."

She laughed.

"Step two, place ears of corn into microwave."

"Shucks and all? Without washing them or anything?"

"As demonstrated." He used flourishing motions like a magician to place the ears of corn in the oven. "Close door."

"That's step three?"

"No. That's the second part of step two."

"I see," she said with a seriousness belied by the smile she couldn't contain.

"Step three is to set the timer to cook on high for four minutes for each ear of corn."

She counted on her fingers. "Twelve minutes."

"Very good, sous chef. Maybe you should be writing this down."

She tapped her temple. "Taking notes."

"Good. Because you'll want to remember."

"Says you."

"Trust me."

"Not as far as I can throw you."

This time her serious tone wasn't phony, and it took Drex aback. His teasing smile collapsed. "Why not?"

She ducked her head and gave it a small shake. "Never mind."

"No. I'd like to know why you said that."

Raising her chin, she looked him straight in the eye. "You're way too cool."

"Way too cool for what?"

"Way too cool to be real."

"Oh, I'm real, Talia." He spoke in a low and vibrating tone that coincided with him dropping his gaze to her mouth. She didn't step back, but her breath caught and held.

The moment lasted for only a heartbeat, then he looked back into her eyes and resumed the ribbing manner. "I'm real *hungry*. Let's get cooking." He set the timer on the microwave and dusted his hands.

"Now what?" she asked.

She tried to sound as jocular as he but didn't quite manage it. He hadn't touched her, but his closeness had shaken her, and the male animal in him wanted to purr with satisfaction.

But he wasn't there to seduce her. He didn't want her to become even more mistrustful of him than she'd already admitted to being. He needed her to be relaxed around him. Comfortable and chummy and chatty. He needed her to talk about her husband, so he could determine if Jasper Ford, seeming law-abiding suburban-ite who had run a husbandly errand, was in actuality the twisted fuck who had buried Marian Harris alive.

So he tamped down the surge of testosterone and reclaimed his drink. Raising it in a toast, he said, "Now, I drink my bourbon, and you drink your wine while you anticipate the best corn on the cob you've ever eaten."

She peered dubiously through the microwave window at the ears of corn rotating inside, then shrugged. "Okay. How about out on the porch?"

Following her from the kitchen, he tried not to fixate on how nicely her light denim skirt molded to her bottom. From those enticing curves it flared out and stopped short of her knees by several inches.

Her top was a black, body-hugging, stretchy thing with arm-holes cut high enough to reveal a lot of shoulder. He spied a few freckles beneath the strands of hair that had escaped her topknot and curled against her neck.

He wanted to give all of it a thorough, hands-on inspection.

She sat down in the rocker that he knew to be hers from having spied on her and Jasper. He was about to take the other chair, but hesitated. "Should I save this for Jasper?"

She motioned him into the chair and took a sip of wine. As they settled into their seats, she asked, "Did you write today?"

"For several hours."

"You were at it for a long while last night." He gave her a quizzical look; she looked embarrassed. "Your shades were up and the lights were on. I saw you sitting at the computer."

He groaned. "I didn't do anything uncouth or indecent, did I?"

She gave a soft laugh. "Not that I saw."

He thought about what he'd done in his bed inspired by fantasies of her, and it wasn't entirely faked when he swiped his brow with the back of his hand as though greatly relieved. "Whew."

"I think writing must be harder work than most people realize."

"I can't speak for other writers, but for me, it's damn hard. I did a run on the beach this afternoon just to work the kinks out."

"Muscles tend to kink after sitting at a computer for long stretches of time."

"True, but I was referring to the kinks in my plot."

"Oh," she said, laughing. "Did the run work them out?"

"After a couple of miles, some of them smoothed out a little."

"Good."

He extended his legs in front of him and crossed his ankles. "What about your work? Are you off again any time soon?"

"Next week. In the meantime, I'm pulling together an itinerary for a client who wants to take his entire family to Africa for a month-long tour. First class all the way. Several countries, game preserves, Victoria Falls, Cape Town, photo safaris in the bush."

"Sounds scary."

"I don't send my clients anyplace that I deem unsafe."

"No, the scary part would be traveling for a month with family."

"Eight adults, eleven children."

He shuddered. "Terrifying."

She laughed, then turned more serious and looked into her glass of wine as she ran her index finger around the rim. "Jasper told me that you're divorced. Any children?"

"No."

She said nothing for a time, then, in a lighter tone, "He also told me about your encounter last night."

"Next time, I'll phone ahead before I come prowling across your backyard. When Jasper came barging around that tree, I thought I was a goner."

"The poor mouse was."

"Yeah. He must've gone peacefully, though. Saved me from having to trap him. Or get a cat."

She tilted her head and took him in from his hair to the scuffed toes of his shoes. "You don't strike me as a cat person."

"I'm not. But I'm not a mouse person, either."

She smiled.

"Which are you?" he asked. "Cat person or dog person?"

"I'm fonder of dogs."

"I haven't seen one around."

"Jasper is allergic."

"Too bad." He turned more toward her, tipped his head to one side, and gave her the same assessing treatment she'd given him. Nodding toward her glass of wine, he said, "Red over white?"

"Yes."

"Tropical climes or cold?"

"I was brought up in Charleston."

"Tropical then."

"Right."

"*Star Wars* or *Star Trek*?"

"*Star Wars*."

He stroked his chin. "Let's see, what else? I already know chocolate over vanilla. Land over sea."

"My turn. I know very little about you, not even the basics. You don't talk much about yourself."

He spread his arms wide. "My life is an open book." He glanced across the lawn toward the apartment. "So to speak."

"Will your novel reveal aspects of you?"

"Undoubtedly. It'll be subconscious, but some of me will probably sneak in there."

"Then in order for me to know you better, I'll have to read it."

He arched an eyebrow. "You want to know me better?"

Realizing she'd stepped into a trap of her own making, she repositioned herself in the rocker as though reestablishing boundaries. She took a sip of wine. "Yesterday on the boat, you were stingy with your answers to Elaine's questions."

"Hard to get a word in edgewise when talking to Elaine." He hoped that would put her onto another track. It didn't.

"See? That's a perfect example of how you deflect any discussion about yourself. Why?"

He raised his shoulders. "There's nothing interesting to tell."

"I don't believe you, Drex."

"Believe it. Even I am bored with me."

She smiled at his quip, but she wasn't dissuaded. "Let's begin with where you grew up."

"If I told you, you wouldn't believe me."

"You were raised by wolves."

He laughed. "Not quite. But actually, the guess isn't too far off."

She raised her wine stem to her mouth and took another sip, holding his gaze, letting him know with her eyes alone that she was going to persist until he told her.

He weighed the risks, thought *to hell with it*. He would go for broke. "Alaska."

She lowered her wineglass, her surprise evident. "You were born there?"

"No. We moved up there before I turned three. I stayed through high school."

"It's a long way from there to here."

He snuffled a laugh. "Longer than you can imagine."

"I wasn't talking about the geographic distance."

He met her gaze. "Neither was I." Their stare held, and he was the first to look away. He shook the remaining ice cubes, drained the bourbon, and set his glass on the table. He thought that would be the end of it, but Talia wasn't finished yet.

"Where did you live?" she asked. "The town."

"Nowhere you ever heard of, and never for very long in any one place. We were migratory."

"What did your parents do for a living?"

"My dad worked on the pipeline. That's why we moved a lot. We lived in some places so remote, I'm not sure they were on the map."

"Life couldn't have been easy."

"Wasn't. Hard work. Long hours. Isolation."

She looked at him as though expecting him to continue and expand on that. When he didn't, she said, "Was there anything to recommend that lifestyle?"

He gave her a wry grin. "For dad? Hard work. Long hours. Isolation. And the pay was good."

"He left you an inheritance. Jasper told me."

He drew his feet in and leaned toward her. Squinting one eye, he said, "It seems I've been the topic of a lot of conversations between you and Jasper. Any particular reason why?"

"No. Just curious."

"Huh. I rarely arouse that much curiosity in people."

She squirmed in her seat, raised her wineglass as though to drink from it, then changed her mind. "Based on your description of your upbringing, it sounds like a very male-dominated environment."

"It was."

"Your mother was okay with that? With the frequent moves, the isolation?"

He gave her a long look before saying quietly, "My mother never set foot in Alaska."

Her lips parted with surprise, and she seemed about to ask another question, when Jasper's voice came from behind them. "The minute my back was turned."

Chapter 8

Jasper's voice startled Talia. What was left of the wine in her glass sloshed as she left the rocking chair to meet her husband halfway. Although Jasper's tone hadn't been one hundred percent teasing, she responded as though it had been.

"You caught us red-handed." She took the grocery sack from him and kissed his cheek. "Thank you for making the run."

"You're welcome." He returned her kiss. Then, "Drex," he said, smiling and motioning toward the empty highball glass on the table. "Looks like you need a refill."

"I wouldn't say no to one. Let me pour yours while I'm at it."

"Thank you." Just then the microwave dinged. Jasper turned toward the kitchen. "What's that?"

Talia laughed. "It's called a microwave. Great invention. Not the abomination you've called it."

"That's a matter of opinion."

"Well, you'll be able to form another opinion soon. Drex has cooked the corn."

Drex poured Jasper and himself each a bourbon, then joined him and Talia in the kitchen, where they were making final preparations for the meal. With the same amount of fanfare as he had used to put the corn in the microwave, he pulled on a pair of oven mitts and demonstrated how to get the ears out of the husks.

"Whack off the end with the silk." He severed it from the cob with one hard chop with a butcher knife and had a bloodthirsty desire to plunge it into Jasper's heart. "Hold it upside down by the stalk. Annnnnd, out it slides, clean as a whistle."

Talia applauded. "I'll get the butter."

She set the small dining table on the porch and placed lit citronella candles around. Jasper grilled the burger patties on a smoker that probably cost more than Drex's car.

Jasper kept one eye on the burger patties, the other on Drex, following his every move, which made Drex wonder if he'd given away his increased antagonism. He decided to test the waters. Drink in one hand, the other in his front pants pocket, he strolled over and joined his host at the grill.

Wielding his spatula, Jasper flipped the patties. "That was quite a trick with the corn. Where'd you learn it?"

"A friend showed me. He's a—"

"Foodie?"

Thinking of Mike's bulk, Drex laughed. "No. That suggests a refined pallet. This guy will eat anything."

"Has he taught you any other tricks?"

"Nope. My culinary skills end there. That smells great, by the way," he said of the sizzling meat. "You obviously have the knack."

"Was the UPS delivery for you or Arnott?"

Drex gave him a sharp look.

"I saw the truck as it pulled into the drive."

"Huh." Drex swirled the ice cubes in his glass. "I ordered a box fan. I would have returned yours tonight when I came over, but I had a handful of cupcakes."

"You didn't need to buy a fan. Ours was yours to use for as long as you needed it."

"Thanks for that, but I'm beginning to feel like a mooch. In fact, I'd like to treat you and Talia to dinner. Don't panic. We'll go out. I don't think you'd enjoy a dining experience at my kitchen table."

Jasper smiled. "Don't feel like you must pay us back."

"I want to do it. But I'll need you to suggest some good local restaurants. I haven't tested any yet, and I don't trust online ratings."

"I'll jot down some of our favorites."

"I'd like to include Elaine." Drex paused before adding, "If that's all right with you."

Jasper turned his head and gave him a bland look. "Why wouldn't it be all right with me?"

Again, Drex's pause was calculated. He glanced over at Talia, who was fiddling with a vase of flowers she'd set in the center of the table. When he came back to Jasper, he said, "Just wanting to make sure I wasn't setting up an awkward situation."

"For whom? I'm not following."

Like hell you aren't. "I thought maybe you and Elaine…?" Drex raised his eyebrows.

"Are just friends."

Ignoring Jasper's icy tone, Drex broke a wide grin. "Great. I thought so, but, you know." He gave Jasper a light sock on the shoulder. A man-to-man, "we understand each other" tap. "Provide me that list of favorite restaurants and we'll double date."

Talia approached with a platter for the burger patties. Without taking his eyes off Drex, Jasper said, "Perfect timing, darling." Then he leaned over and kissed her solidly on the mouth, a stamp of ownership.

When he ended the kiss, Talia turned away, appearing flustered and surprised by the sudden amorous display. Drex gathered it wasn't something Jasper often did, and that he'd done it now for his benefit, not Talia's.

I get the point, you son of a bitch.

Recovering quickly, and showing admirable poise, Talia graciously invited them to take their seats at the table. They assembled their burgers according to personal preferences. When they were ready to eat, Talia noticed that she'd forgotten the skewers for the corn.

"I'll get them." Drex shot from his chair. "I spotted them on the counter."

Before either she or Jasper could stop him, he was already through the kitchen door. He swept the skewers off the counter into his palm, then glanced through the open door onto the porch. Jasper and Talia were debating the merits of ketchup over mustard. She laughed at something he said. They clinked wineglasses above one of the flickering candles.

Drex dropped to one knee, bent down toward the baseboard beneath the cabinetry, and felt along the seam connecting them.

"Looking for something?"

Drex tensed, then swiveled around and smiled as he came to his feet. "Found it." He held up a skewer. "One had rolled off the counter and under the cabinet." He took the skewer to the sink and rinsed it off.

Staring hard at Drex, Jasper stood blocking the doorway for what seemed to be an eternity, then his smile returned. He stood aside and motioned for Drex to go ahead of him. "I hope the corn hasn't gotten cold. I'm eager to sink my teeth in."

————

"I think he was talking about my neck, not the corn."

After returning from dinner, Drex had lowered all the window shades in the apartment. Half an hour later, he'd turned off the lights as though he'd gone to bed. He put in the call to Mike and Gif and immediately told them what they'd been standing by to hear: He had succeeded in planting the bug, and it was working. "I listened in as they cleaned up the kitchen."

Dual sighs had expressed their relief.

"How was it?" Mike asked now. "The corn on the cob."

"So scrumptious it pissed him off."

"He said that?" Gif asked.

"No, but I could tell."

Jasper had become even more piqued when Talia all but swooned as she licked melted butter from her fingertips and declared that Drex had delivered as promised. Her husband's genial expression never changed, but as the evening progressed, his dialogue became more terse, and his smiles began to look forced.

"Even if he's not Weston Graham, I don't like him," Drex said. "He has this air of superiority. All-knowing. I admit that it amuses me to prick with him."

"You're amused. He's controlled and all-knowing, which, by the way, you've told us are characteristics of serial killers. This quasi-friendship is making me nervous," Gif said.

"I've got to play it as I see it, guys. If I went in and tried to match him in a chest-thumping contest, he would have nothing to do with me. Instead, he's intrigued. Talia told me as much. He keeps having me back because he hasn't figured me out yet."

"God forbid he does."

"Cheer up, Mike. If I go missing, you'll know where to start looking."

"That's not funny," Gif said. "Do you go armed on these dinner dates?"

"He's not going to engage in a shootout. That's not his style."

"Nevertheless," said Gif, the guru of practicality.

"Tonight was the first time my weapon and badge stayed home. All I had with me was the transmitter. Keeping it concealed was worry enough."

He'd told them that he'd taken advantage of Jasper's absence by arriving early, but he hadn't said much about the private conversation that he and Talia had shared. He had revealed more to her than he should have, perhaps. But talking about himself might have earned him her trust, which was necessary if he was ever going to get her to open up about Jasper.

It had been risky to tell her the truth about his upbringing, rather than inventing one. But what he'd described might have sounded to her more fiction than fact. If she relayed it to Jasper, he might dismiss it as pure fabrication.

Even if Jasper accepted it as truth, it was unlikely he would ever draw a parallel between Drex Easton, would-be author next door, and the toddler who'd been whisked off to Alaska by his father after his mother's abandonment. Drex wasn't even certain she had ever told Weston Graham about her previous marriage. He might never have known of Drex's existence. His mother's perfidy then might well be protecting Drex from exposure now.

"So," Gif said, "what's your second impression of them?"

"Nothing they said or did triggered an alarm. They acted like a married couple."

Mike said, "Since neither of us has experience with matrimony, could you be a little more descriptive?"

"They're familiar. She brushed a crumb of hamburger bun off his beard. He flicked away a mosquito that landed on her arm. Like that."

"Were they affectionate?"

"To an extent."

"To what extent?"

"Look, Gif, if you want me to talk dirty to you, you'll have to pay me sixty bucks a minute."

"You don't have to bite my head off. Just give me a for-instance."

Drex swore under his breath. "Okay. For instance, when Jasper returned from his errand, she thanked him with a wifely kiss on the cheek, and he repaid it." *Then he kissed her on the mouth. Hard. And, swear to God, I believe he did it to see how I would react.* But he didn't tell Gif and Mike that because they would want to know how he had reacted.

"Did you get the night vision binoculars?"

"They were delivered today. Along with a new box fan. Good thing I added the fan to the order. Jasper mentioned seeing the UPS truck."

"Like he wanted to know what you'd had delivered?"

"That was my take. I explained it away by telling him about the fan. Returning his gives me a reason to go back to their house at least once again. And I invited them out to dinner, along with Elaine."

"When?"

"Soon as I can swing it. I tried not to sound too eager. Mike, what have you learned about Elaine?"

"Mr. Conner of Delaware was husband number two."

"What happened to number one?"

"Marriage fizzled early on. No substantial funds to divide. He remarried before she did. Mr. Conner was an older widower, pillar-of-the-community type, died of cancer. They were married for thirteen years."

"Kids?"

"Not together. He had one son, who was killed in a car wreck on his twenty-first birthday. Lost his son before his wife died."

"So Elaine inherited everything?"

"Right," Mike said. "But the net worth isn't as staggering as we estimated. She's rich. She'll never have to clip coupons. But she's not über-wealthy. Nowhere close to Marian Harris or Pixie, or to most of the others, now I think about it."

"How do her assets compare to Talia Shafer's?"

"Exactly which assets are you referring to?"

"Back off, Gif," Drex snapped. "I'm working here, not pining over a married woman. Don't start with that crap again."

"Is it crap?" Mike said. "Her name comes up, you act like you've been goosed with a cattle prod."

"No, I don't."

"Make that two cattle prods," he continued. "Why is that? Why so touchy?"

"I'm not touchy."

"I stand corrected. More like hot under the collar."

"I am not."

"You are."

"If I'm hot," Drex said, "it's because there's no AC in this fucking apartment. And every once in a while, I catch a lingering whiff of dead rodent. All I do all day is pretend to be writing a book, which entails sitting in a kitchen chair till my ass goes numb."

"I suppose that could explain your bad mood." That from Gif.

"I'm not in a bad mood."

"Well, whatever," Mike said. "What I'm about to tell you isn't going to improve it."

Drex pinched the bridge of his nose, only now realizing how exhausted he was. The unrelenting tension—guarding against making a mistake that would give him away, the constant observing and being under observation, not to mention lying by omission to his friends—was taking a toll on him physically.

Fatigue had no place is this undertaking. Shaking it off, he took a deep breath. "What now?"

Mike said, "That woman you got to type your faux manuscript?"

Drex had been prepared to hear much worse. "Pam? What about her?"

"She called me today. Said you'd given her my number."

"I did."

"Why?"

"Because for obvious reasons I didn't want to give her mine. I told her that if something urgent came up in the office and she needed to reach me, you were my go-to person."

"Well, something came up in your office."

Drex's heart bumped, but he didn't ask. He waited Mike out.

"Rudkowski called there, looking for you."

"*What?*"

"Three times, after his assistant put in the initial call. He worked his way up the chain of command, demanding to know where you were and how he could reach you."

"Shit!"

"This Pam thought I should know so I could inform you. She offered to help in any way she could if you were in a jam and needed her to cover for you. She asked me to tell you that. Made me promise I would. She seemed earnest."

"She's earnestly man-hungry," Drex said absently as he tried to process this news about Rudkowski. "She wants a stepdaddy for her two kids. Maybe she thought the project I gave her was an inroad to...something."

"Is it?"

"Hell no," he replied with impatience. Then, "Did Rudkowski try to reach either of you?"

"Not yet," Gif said. "But Mike gave me a heads-up, and I dodged calls for the rest of the day."

"That'll work for only so long," Drex said. "If he doesn't show up at your desk himself, he'll dispatch someone. If you're asked—when you're asked—you haven't seen me, didn't know my vacation plans."

"The regular drill," Gif said. "Play dumb."

"Which he won't believe," Mike remarked.

"Play it for as long as you can get away with it," Drex said. "Stick to your day duties, but it's red-alert time, boys."

"What's worrisome—" Gif began.

"Is the timing of the asshole wanting to talk to me today."

"That's what rattled Mike and me," Gif said. "How long has it been since you two had any contact?"

"Not long enough."

Drex came out of his chair and went over to the window. He pulled the edge of the shade away from the framework, creating a crack just wide enough to focus the new binoculars on the house across the way.

Gif said, "I don't think Rudkowski's call is a bizarre coincidence."

"But what roused him?" Mike asked.

"Must've been that deputy in Florida," Drex said. "Rudkowski's name was in the case file. Gray sounded green, eager to help. If he was doing some kind of follow-up and couldn't reach me, he'd likely contact Rudkowski."

Mike sighed. "If you're right, you need to destroy the phone you used when you called him."

"Already have. It's on the bottom of the Atlantic. After talking to him, I threw it out the porthole in the head." Thinking of the yacht reminded him. "Any progress on that picture, Mike?"

"A team of photo experts in Bombay are working on it for me. I've got TV dinners in my freezer that are older than them, and I don't understand a damn thing they do, but they're good. I passed along what you said about wanting to see the pores on his face."

They fell into a thoughtful silence, then Gif said, "We know your impressions of the couple next door. What do you think their impressions are of you?"

"While they were cleaning up the kitchen, he commented on my attire."

"Your attire?"

"That's the word he used. He said I dressed like a frat boy on his way to a keg bust."

They chuckled. Gif asked, "What did she say?"

"That they were almost out of dishwashing soap."

"Nothing more about you?"

"That was it. They finished up, turned out the downstairs lights. I think they've called it a night." He didn't want to think about them in bed together doing anything except sleeping. Or even that.

The optimistic Gif said, "Well, you've made some progress."

Mike, ever Eeyore, said, "You've only got ten more days to determine whether or not it's him."

"It's him."

"You want—"

"It's him, Gif. He smiles, he's pleasant, but open a vein and ice water would pour out of it. He's abnormally vigilant. Like last night. It was like he was waiting and watching to see if I would venture onto his property. Who notices when a UPS truck is on the block and where it stops?"

"I do," said Gif.

Mike snorted with disdain.

Drex continued. "He doesn't give me access to anything he's touched."

"Like what?"

Only now did he share with them the business about the beer bottle. "It was a neighborly gesture, but why would he take back the beer when I hadn't drunk but half of it? He didn't want me to have that bottle with his prints on it."

"But our unsub is a ghost. Nobody has his prints. Nobody even knows who he is. These women up and disappeared, but there's never been a crime scene."

"Until Marian Harris's body was found," Drex said. "Less than one hundred days ago. That's bound to have fueled his innate paranoia and put him on edge."

"But forensics didn't yield anything."

"We know that, Gif, but he doesn't."

Mike made a grunting sound acknowledging Drex's point. "That niggling doubt would make him wary of anyone moving in next door."

"Exactly."

Gif wasn't convinced. "I don't know. That's all conjecture. We've gotta get something solid."

"I'm aware of that," Drex said. "Mike, in any of the disappearance cases, was there any evidence with handwriting on it? Not the victim's. Not a named someone's. Handwriting that investigators never attached to a specific person. Could be anything. A note, shopping list, receipt. Anything."

"I'll have to check it out."

"Do. I asked Jasper for a list of recommended restaurants. He told me he'd jot some down. He—Hold on. What the hell's this?"

"What?" Gif had needlessly lowered his voice to a whisper.

"While we've been talking, I've been trying out my new binoculars. Jasper just walked into their kitchen."

"A midnight snack," Mike said.

"In the dark?" Drex said. "He hasn't turned on any lights. He's using his phone's flashlight."

"That's weird."

"Maybe not," Drex said.

"Why? What's he doing?"

Drex blew out his breath. "He went straight to the spot where he caught me crouching down."

"Oh, shit," Gif groaned.

Mike muttered something more profane.

Drex watched Jasper go down on one knee and bend toward the floor until his head almost touched it. He shone the light along the baseboard and underneath the cabinet. "He's looking for it. Feeling around."

"He didn't buy your lost skewer excuse."

"We are royally screwed," Mike said.

Drex lowered the binoculars and grinned into the darkness. "We would be if that's where I had planted the bug."

Chapter 9

———◆———

Talia?"

She raised her head from reading off her tablet and looked across the breakfast table at Jasper. "Sorry. I was catching up on the news."

He was staring thoughtfully into his coffee cup. "When I got back from the store last night, you and Drex were so engrossed in your conversation, neither of you realized I was there until I spoke. What were you talking about?"

"His boyhood in Alaska."

Jasper looked at her and sputtered a laugh. "Alaska?"

"Of all places."

"Anchorage?"

She shook her head. "Remote, off-the-map spots. Another cup of coffee?"

"No thank you."

She left the table to make herself a refill using the fancy machine she'd given Jasper for Christmas. It had taken her weeks to learn how to operate it, and she was still intimidated by the technology. While she waited for it to go through the brewing process, she filled Jasper in on what Drex had told her about his upbringing.

He said, "Sounds very rugged and romantic."

"Or bleak."

"It strikes me as a woeful tale spun by an aspiring novelist who's creating a rakish persona for himself, fashioning himself after Jack London or Ernest Hemingway."

She returned to the table and curled a leg beneath her as she sat down. "You think he made it up?"

"Talia, it reeks of hogwash."

She laughed, sipped her coffee, picked up the one remaining bite of cupcake on her plate, and held it out for Jasper. "Last chance, or it's all mine."

"I wouldn't dream of depriving you."

She popped the bite into her mouth. "Ummm. Chocolate cupcake. The breakfast of champions." She washed down the cake with another sip of coffee. As she returned her cup to the saucer, she said, "If Drex is lying to impress, why hasn't he regaled us with stories of derring-do in the wilds of Alaska? He does the opposite. When it comes to talking about himself, he artfully changes topics."

Jasper said, "One wonders why."

"Apparently *you* wonder why."

"You don't? You've been taken in by the dimple?"

She frowned with exasperation. "Please. Give me some credit. I see through his practiced charm, and I've told him so." She moistened the tip of her finger and used it to collect the remaining crumbs on her plate, then licked them off, the action giving her time to formulate an opinion.

As she moved aside the empty plate, she said, "I think the basics of the childhood he described are probably true, but he might have embellished them for dramatic effect."

"That's what bothers me. Why would he want to create an effect?"

"For his own amusement?" she said, raising a shoulder. "Or, as you said, to make his biography more colorful and adventuresome, a marketable background a publisher would jump at."

"I hope that's all his evasiveness amounts to."

She crossed her arms on the edge of the table and leaned forward. "So what if he stretches the truth a bit? Why does that concern you so much?"

"I'm amazed that it doesn't concern you." He gestured toward the garage apartment. "Without notice, a stranger moves in next door. He's unknown even to the Arnotts, yet he's living practically in the shadow of our home. The day we met, he told me he'd come to the area to soak up color and soul for his novel. Doesn't that imply that he would be out and about, observing and experiencing the culture? Instead, he rarely leaves the apartment."

"He's absorbed in the writing."

"Is he? Perhaps. But I get the feeling that he's not as devil-may-care as he wants us to believe."

She looked down and studied the wood grain in the tabletop. "In all honesty, I get that impression, too."

"Then we'd be wise not to believe everything he tells us and to be guarded about what we tell him. Don't you agree?"

"Yes." Then, lifting her gaze back to his, she said, "On the other hand, we could be overanalyzing and becoming paranoid when there's no cause to be. Maybe Drex was merely testing his storytelling ability last night. He wanted to see if he could weave an engaging history for himself and make me believe it."

"Possibly. After all, when you boil it down, fiction writers are glorified liars, aren't they?"

"I wouldn't put it quite like that."

He didn't ask how she would put it. Seeming to have closed the discussion to his satisfaction, he got up and carried his dirty dishes to the sink. It rather irked her to be dismissed, but she let the subject drop. She didn't want to engage in an argument where she would be placed in the position of defending Drex, whom she didn't know and who was possibly the blatant liar Jasper suspected him of being.

However, as Drex had described to her that period of his life, he had appeared to be telling the truth. There had been no teasing glint in his eyes or devilish smile to suggest either a white lie or a whopper.

My mother never set foot in Alaska. When he'd said that, his eyes, his whole demeanor, had conveyed stark, heartbreaking reality. "He grew up without his mother."

"Pardon?"

Caught musing out loud, she repeated, "He grew up without his mother."

"She died?"

"I don't know. That's when you barged in. I'm left with a cliffhanger."

"Regrettable. The unknown facets of Drex Easton are the ones I wish I knew."

He folded the dishtowel he'd used and draped it over the edge of the sink, then lifted his gym bag off the floor and slid the strap onto his shoulder. "All right with you if I hang around the club after my workout? I may stay and have lunch there."

"I could meet you."

"I thought you planned to work on the African trip for your client."

"Those plans are flexible."

"Better to leave them in place. I'm not sure when I'll want to eat." Her expression must have revealed her letdown. In a crisp voice, he asked, "Is that a problem, Talia?"

It was a problem that she must be made to print out an itinerary to leave with him whenever she went out of town, but that he got piqued if she asked about his plans for an afternoon.

She replied with comparable curtness. "No problem."

He moved to stand behind her chair, placed his hands on her shoulders, leaned down, and whispered in her ear. "Instead of lunch, how about I take my favorite girl out for dinner tonight?"

She was being placated, and it angered her. She was inclined to shrug his massaging hands off her shoulders. But, for the sake of marital harmony, she smiled back at him. "Your favorite girl would enjoy that."

He kissed her behind the ear. "I had better stay on my toes. Because I think our new neighbor spun that sad tale about his boyhood in order to woo you."

"Don't be ridiculous."

"It's not at all ridiculous. I believe you're too smart to fall for his adolescent seduction, but I also believe he's ballsy enough to try."

As he was about to pull away, she reached up and placed her hand on his arm. "If you're seriously worried about Drex's integrity and intentions, we don't have to continue being sociable."

"I've already obligated us to at least one more dinner. A double date with him and Elaine."

"Elaine?" she exclaimed. She came around in her chair and faced him. "This is the first I've heard of it."

"He extended the invitation last night."

"And you accepted? Jasper, Elaine—"

"It's okay. He more or less asked my permission to make a move on her. He thought she and I might be carrying on illicitly." Jasper winked at her. "Funny, isn't it?"

Drex thought, *Not that fuckin' funny.*

He pushed back his chair and went over to the window in time to see Jasper's car backing out of their drive. Through the surveillance receiver, he could hear Talia moving around the kitchen. Cabinet doors being shut. Water running. The sun's glare on the windowpanes prevented him from seeing her. He wondered what she'd worn down to breakfast.

"Jesus." He was becoming a peeping Tom. He pushed the heels of his hands into his eye sockets in an attempt to blind himself against envisioning her in some kind of soft sleepwear, disheveled and barefoot, hair in tangles, eyes drowsy.

Before dawn, he'd been awakened by an erotic dream featuring her. Images of her were unformed and ephemeral. He could feel more than he could see, but the sensations were intense. He woke up painfully aroused, the sheets saturated with sweat despite the gale powered by the new fan blowing across him.

He was out of sorts and troubled despite last night's success.

When he'd told Mike and Gif that Jasper's search for the transmitter was futile, that he was looking in the wrong place, they'd congratulated him on his ingeniousness.

"He thought he had me," he'd said, "but he's the one who got hoodwinked." When Jasper had come up empty-handed, Drex had felt like shouting at him across the lawn, *Gotcha, sucker!*

"He gave himself away," Drex told them. "Who goes looking for hidden surveillance after having a neighbor over for burgers? Nobody, that's who. I'm telling you, he's our man."

Mike and Gif had pressed him to tell them how he'd achieved hiding the bug, and where. He'd refused. "For me alone to know. It's my crime. If caught, only I will take the fall."

At that point, Gif, in his reasonable way, had resumed his argument that Drex should notify Rudkowski. "What you're doing is high-risk, Drex. You might give yourself away and not even be aware of it until it's too late. If not Rudkowski, alert somebody to what you're doing. Think of the additional resources that—"

"No, Gif. I tried that once, and it backfired. Big time. Remember?"

"Vividly," Mike grumbled.

"Okay, then. Before I involve Rudkowski this time, I'm gonna have the suspect hogtied and squealing confessions."

Gif sighed in defeat. "In the meantime—"

"I'll watch my back."

"Better yet, don't turn it to him."

After ending the call, Drex had gone to bed, but hadn't slept that long or well before the dream woke him. Giving up on going back to sleep, he'd gotten up, made coffee, and, restless and edgy, turned on the receiver and waited to hear something from the house next door.

Jasper had come downstairs first and cooked himself breakfast. Drex could hear a TV news show in the background, pans clanking, coffee beans grinding. Finally, Talia joined him. She'd told Jasper good morning in a voice slightly hoarse from sleep. Drex had imagined them exchanging a hug, a pat on the rump, a light kiss. That was as far as he'd let his imagination run.

Then for close to an hour, he'd listened to their breakfast dialogue. For the most part, it was inconsequential. She reminded Jasper that he needed to consult an arborist about one of their trees. His tailor had called; the clothes he'd had altered were ready to be picked up. He made polite inquiries about the family who were off to Africa, but he didn't sound that interested in Talia's answers.

There were also stretches of companionable silence.

Drex hadn't sat up and taken notice until Jasper had asked her, from out of nowhere, what she and he had talked about last night while alone. His heart had skipped a beat, not because the question made him anxious, but because he wanted to hear how Talia would respond.

He told himself it didn't matter. Lately, he was lying to himself a lot.

It came as no surprise that Jasper was leery of him. But Jasper hadn't emphasized to Talia just how mistrustful, had he? He hadn't told her that he had gone downstairs in the dark to search for a listening device that he suspected Drex of planting.

Had he omitted mention of that because he hadn't wanted to appear comically foolish? Or because he couldn't explain to her why such a notion would even enter his mind?

Drex was already aware of Jasper's suspicion, but it was helpful to learn the extent of it.

Talia also harbored doubts about his honesty, but she'd given him the benefit of the doubt, seeming more inclined to think he was exaggerating rather than outright lying. She'd also sounded sympathetic when she spoke of his mother.

After that, the tone of their conversation changed, subtly but noticeably. Having it piped into his ears through the headset seemed to have amplified the silent subtext as well as their spoken words. He wished he could have watched their expressions during that exchange, to gauge whether the testiness he'd sensed between them was real or imagined.

After Jasper left the house, there was no point in eavesdropping. Drex stored away the audio surveillance gear, booted up his laptop, and began rereading the information he had collected over the years about the eight women who had disappeared. If the material were converted to hard copy, the contents would fill a moving van.

Today, he applied what he now knew or sensed about Jasper Ford, searching for a connection to his victims. Had one of the women been a gourmet cook? Had one favored the bourbon Jasper drank? Had one shared his preference for Dijon mustard over ketchup? One small thing, previously overlooked, could be the link Drex was desperate to find, especially now that he feared his culprit had an even darker side.

Was it invisible to his victims until it was too late? Had his victims sensed it but ignored it? What had made them susceptible? What had made Talia susceptible?

He was still dwelling on that question several hours later when there came a knock.

He sat with his hand cupped over his mouth, absorbed in whatever was on his computer screen. When she tapped on the doorjamb, he came out of his chair so abruptly, it went over backward and landed on the hardwood floor with a loud clack.

"Mercy." Talia pressed her hand against her thumping chest. It would be hard to say which had startled her most: his sudden reaction, or seeing him shirtless and barefoot, wearing only a pair of cargo shorts. Flustered, she said, "I didn't mean to scare you."

"I scare easily."

She doubted that. A man with reflexes that lightning quick would have little to fear.

He righted the chair, closed his laptop, and came over to the door. She asked, "What are you most afraid of?"

"Failure."

She'd been teasing, but he hadn't paused to think about it, and he'd answered so unequivocally, she knew he was serious. Feeling awkward and rethinking the wisdom of coming over, she said, "Should I have called ahead?"

"You don't have my number."

"Oh. Right."

He smiled. "If you've come to borrow a cup of sugar, I'm all out."

"Oh. Well then . . . " She heaved a sigh and turned as though to leave.

He chuckled. "What's up?"

She came back around and glanced beyond him at the setup on the table. "I don't want to pull you away from your work."

"Please. Rescue me."

"I'm not bothering you?"

He looked on the verge of saying something, but apparently thought better of it. To this point they'd been talking through the screen door. "Want to come in?"

"Only to be nosy."

He grinned and unlatched the lock.

"I've never been up here," she said as she stepped inside.

"I doubt you'll think the view is worth the climb up those stairs."

She stood in the center of the room and pivoted to make a complete circle. When she came back to him, he grimaced and reached up to rub the back of his neck.

"I know," he said. "It's not even—what's the term?"

"Shabby chic?"

"This is shabby shit."

She laughed. "It has potential. With a can of paint and…"

"A hundred thousand dollars."

They shared another smile. She gestured behind her toward the window. "The tree is lovely, though. The moss seems to have been draped by a decorator."

"Yeah. It gives me something to stare at while I daydream." He wasn't staring at the Spanish moss in the tree, however. He was looking into her eyes. Abruptly he said, "Excuse me a sec."

He went around her and into the bedroom, pushing the door partially closed. She walked over to the window. He didn't exactly live in the shadow of their house as Jasper had said, but through the branches of the tree, she could see the back of it almost in its entirety. Screened porch, kitchen windows, the windows of the master bedroom upstairs. Since the Arnotts' departure in June, she hadn't had to concern herself with keeping the window treatments closed at night. She realized the need to now.

Hearing him reenter the main room, she turned. He'd put on a faded t-shirt and his docksiders, but she didn't comment on the change, because it would make them each mindful that she'd caught him bare-chested and wearing a pair of shorts that hung tenuously from his sharp hipbones. It seemed best to pretend she hadn't noticed.

The t-shirt was faded. His chin was bristly. He had bed-head, the saddle brown strands even more unruly than they'd been the night before. But his eyes—agate in color and ringed in black like those of a tiger—looked anything but sleepy as they focused on her.

"I didn't know you wore glasses," she said.

He took them off and, with a puzzled expression, inspected them. "Who put those there?"

She laughed.

He set the horn-rims on the table next to his laptop. "What's Jasper up to this morning?"

"He went to our country club."

"He's a golfer?"

"No. The club has an Olympic-size pool. He swims laps. A serious number of laps."

"Every day?"

"Unless it's lightning and they close the pool."

"Huh. That explains his well-defined traps. You swim, too?"

"No."

He snapped his fingers. "Your aversion to sun exposure and water."

"Right. I can stay afloat, but I don't really get anywhere."

"So what do you do for exercise?"

"Spin class. Stationary bike."

"Ah. That explains your well-defined..." He stopped, looked away from her, tipped his head down and scratched his eyebrow with his thumb. Then said, "Would you like something to drink?"

"Sure." She said it brightly, maybe a bit too brightly, because she was wondering what of hers he found well-defined and why he'd changed his mind about telling her.

The kitchen was open to the rest of the room, demarcated only by a rectangle of vinyl flooring. The handle on the refrigerator door was loose and rattled when he pulled on it. "Water, Diet Coke, beer."

"What are you having?"

He looked at her over his shoulder. "Wanna play hooky and have a beer?"

She raised her eyebrows in a yes.

He uncapped two bottles and brought them over. They clinked bottles before drinking. The beer went down cold and bitter. "Playing hooky is fun."

He studied her for a second, then snuffled.

"What?"

"Be truthful now," he said. "You've never played hooky a day in your life."

She ducked her head. "My parents had great expectations."

"You sought their approval."

"Yes, but I was stricter on myself than they were on me."

"No naughtiness? Not ever?"

"Not *often*."

"Hmm. I see potential here. Stick around," he drawled. "I can corrupt you in no time at all."

"Jasper said you'd be ballsy enough to try."

"He said I'm ballsy?"

"He did."

"Remind me to thank him."

He saluted her with his beer bottle, and she saluted him back, then walked over to the table. She set her index finger on the blank top sheet of a stack of paper that had seen wear and tear. "Your manuscript?"

"Or a pile of manure. Hard to differentiate."

"I doubt it's that bad."

"Trust me."

"Is this your only copy?"

"Only hard copy. I back up each day's work on two thumb drives."

She ran her finger up the curled corners of the sheets. "I don't suppose you'd let me take a peek."

"Absolutely not."

"I'll give you an honest assessment."

"I already have an honest assessment. Mine. It sucks."

"Then a second opinion could be beneficial."

He shook his head. "Not yet."

Jasper was patently suspicious of Drex. Her reservations weren't that steep, but she admitted to being intrigued by his reticence. Reading his book, even though it was fiction, could provide insight into the man behind the disarming dimple. But even as she had asked to read it, she'd known with near certainty that he would refuse. She didn't try to persuade him. Rather, she said, "I Googled you this morning."

His brow arched eloquently. "I've fantasized being Googled by a beautiful woman."

Without acknowledging either the compliment or the innuendo, she set her bottle of beer on the table and crossed her arms over her middle. "Another joke, another deflection. Aren't you going to ask me why I plundered the Internet in search of information on you?"

"I'm not that vain." Then he seemed to reconsider. "Well, I guess I am. What about me sent you plundering?"

"Is Drex Easton a *nom de plume* or your real name?"

He formed a slow grin. "You didn't find anything, did you?"

She didn't admit it, but her silence confirmed his guess, and his grin widened.

"I told you last night, Talia. Even I'm bored with me."

"Is it your real name?"

"Yes. Given to me by my dad."

She hesitated, then asked softly, "What happened to your mother?"

"I haven't the faintest."

She flinched. "What do you mean?"

"Exactly what I said. It's the God's truth, and that's all I'm going to say on the subject."

"Why the secrecy?"

He set down his beer bottle hard enough to make a thump against the tabletop. "What difference does my past make to you? Or, for that matter, my present and future?"

"Because of Elaine."

Chapter 10

⸺◆⸺

Drex seemed taken aback by her answer, which wasn't the whole truth, but it had moved them off the track that she'd been following—his past. It was the one subject that made him restive and annoyed.

Now, his forehead wrinkled with perplexity. "Elaine? Am I missing something?"

"Jasper told me you planned to invite her to dinner."

He raised his shoulders in a silent *So?*

"I'm not sure...That is, I hope..." She stopped, pushed her fingers through her hair, and said, "I'm botching this."

He placed his hands on his hips and tilted his head slightly. An attitude of impatient waiting.

She took a deep breath. "In the time I've known Elaine, she's had a string of romantic disappointments. A man expresses interest, she tends to become infatuated very quickly and then falls hard, only to discover that he was less attracted to her than to her—"

He held up a hand. "I get it. You want to protect her from a man like me who has no visible means of support and is looking for a rich…" In search of an appropriate word, he twirled his hand. "Patroness?"

"I've insulted you."

"No shit."

"That wasn't my intention, Drex. It's just that Jasper and I have become very fond of Elaine. Because she's innately affectionate and generous, she sets herself up to be taken advantage of. We don't want to see her hurt."

"By a snake like me."

She blew out a breath. "Insulted *and* angered."

He didn't say anything.

"I'm sorry. I shouldn't have interfered." She turned to go, but he hooked his hand in the bend of her elbow and gently brought her back around.

"Look, taking Elaine to dinner seems like an appropriate way to thank her for her hospitality on Sunday. That's my only agenda. Okay?"

She looked up at him with chagrin. "Now I feel small."

He let several seconds lapse, then placed his hand flat on the top of her head before drawing it toward his chest to measure her height against his collarbone. "You are small."

With him looking down on her, and her looking up at him, they smiled at each other. Smiles that didn't show teeth. Small, olive branch–extending smiles that faded with continuance and, as they aged, assumed a different, uncertain, and unsettling nature, until they didn't count as smiles at all.

He was the first to speak. Huskily. "What night?"

"What?"

He cleared his throat. "What night would be best for you and Jasper? You say, then I'll check with Elaine. And, yes, she gave me her number. But, no, I didn't ask for it."

Talia figured she deserved that dig. "Thursday?"

"Perfect. What are you in the mood for?"

"Oh!" She thumped her forehead with the heel of her hand.

"That's the reason I came over. Jasper told me that you had requested a list of good restaurants. He asked me to compile one for you."

She took a sheet of notepaper from the front pocket of her jeans and passed it to him. "These are within a reasonable driving distance. They're all reliably good. I prefer the Italian."

Without even glancing at the list, he said, "Italian it is."

She began backing away from him toward the door. With a flick of her hand toward the table, she said, "Thanks for the beer. I don't remember when I last drank one."

"See? You're already halfway to being corrupted. A cupcake for breakfast. Beer for lunch."

She laughed and moved toward the door. He got there first and opened it for her. She stepped out onto the landing, where she halted and came back around, standing in the wedge between the threshold and screen door he held open. "How did you know I had a cupcake for breakfast?"

His parted his lips to speak, but nothing came out.

"Drex? How did you know that?"

Again, he hesitated before raising his free hand and whisking the pad of his thumb across her cheek near the corner of her mouth, then holding his thumb up to where she could see. "Chocolate icing."

Following Talia's visit, the afternoon dragged on torturously. Drex almost wished she hadn't come. Almost. Because now he couldn't escape seeing her in this tacky room. She'd stood there. She'd touched that. Her voice and laughter echoed off the ugly wallpaper. Her scent permeated the stuffy air.

He tried to immerse himself in the case files, but having studied them for years, he knew their contents almost by heart. By reading the first few words of a sentence, he already knew its ending. The material held his attention for only minutes at a time before his mind drifted to something Talia had said or done.

At dusk, he gave up, shut down shop at his computer, and went for a run through the neighborhood. As he was returning, the Fords were backing out of their driveway in Jasper's car. Both waved to him.

He smiled and waved back, when what he felt like doing was to drive his fist through the windshield. Despite the difference in their ages, he had to admit they made a striking pair.

Before showering, he carted Jasper's box fan down the staircase and to the door of their screened porch, where he left it outside. He used a corner of it to anchor a note of thanks he'd written on a sheet of typing paper. He added the name of the restaurant where he'd made a reservation. *Thursday night. 7:30. Party of four.*

Elaine had accepted his invitation. It would worry Talia to know how exuberant her acceptance had been.

He watched a detective show on his laptop while eating his dinner of frozen pizza. The apartment's antique oven had given it an old grease-smoke taste. He didn't finish it. He wasn't hungry anyway.

He didn't go out, fearing that Talia and Jasper would come home during his absence, and he would miss an informative conversation.

Ten o'clock came, and they still hadn't returned. Ready to climb the walls, he called Mike and Gif. "They're still out, but I thought I'd go ahead and report the day's events."

He started by relating the breakfast table conversation and concluded by saying, "Jasper's nursing suspicion of me, but hasn't come after me with a hatchet."

"Yet," Mike said.

Drex asked if there had been anything out of Rudkowski. Not a peep.

"Which is a good thing," Gif said.

"Or not," Mike intoned. "If we'd heard rumblings, at least we'd know what he was up to."

Drex agreed. "It'll be eating at him that I inquired about Marian Harris, and then left for a two-week vacation to an unknown destination. He'll be looking for me. I'm on borrowed time here."

He cited the little he had to show for the time he'd already spent in residence and, pursuant to that, finally worked his way around to telling them about Talia's visit. "She just appeared, took me completely off-guard."

He told them about scrambling to close his laptop before she could see what was on the screen, making himself decent, and ensuring that his pistol, ID, and night vision binoculars were out of sight. "Fortunately I'd already put away the surveillance equipment."

Mike gave a grunt. "She came uninvited?"

"Like I said. She was hand-delivering a list of good local restaurants. I had hoped to get a sampling of Jasper's handwriting. Instead, Talia brought over a typewritten list she had compiled. At his request."

"How long did she stay?"

"Hmm, ten, twelve minutes." At least twice that long.

"What all did you talk about?" Gif asked.

"She asked to read my manuscript. I told her no way in hell. Words to that effect. Then she started in on me, asking about my past. I turned the tables on her and asked why she should care."

"Why *should* she care?" Mike asked.

"She's afraid her friend will develop a crush on me."

"Her friend Elaine?"

"Yeah. Talia was mother-henning. I set her straight on why I asked Elaine to dinner." He gave them the basic info, skimmed over the details.

He skimmed over a lot. He didn't describe to them Talia's old, holey jeans and how perfectly they fit her well-defined buns. Did they really need to know what her high, round B-cups did for a plain white t-shirt? He didn't mention the beer. For sure as hell he didn't tell them about lifting the speck of chocolate off her face with his thumb and wishing he could have licked it off and then stayed to tease the corner of her lips until they parted for him.

Because he didn't go into any of that, he couldn't account for the solemn silence that ensued when he finished. "Guys? Have you nodded off?"

Mike asked, "You at your computer?"

"No. In the bedroom."

"I just sent you an email. Call us back after you've looked at it."

He disconnected before Drex could say anything more.

He rolled up and off the bed, went into the main room, and opened his laptop. The subject line of Mike's email was empty, nor was there any content in the body of it. It had an attachment.

Drex opened it, and his heart blipped with excitement when the photograph taken aboard Marian Harris's yacht came up full screen. The boys in Bombay were geniuses and worth every penny they charged. The picture had been clarified and enhanced, and the quality was far better than Drex could have hoped for.

He zoomed in on the figure of the man he suspected was Jasper Ford. "Damn!" He'd hoped for a *voilá!*, for an unmistakable image of the man living next door.

But the improved color density had sharpened the contrast between the brilliant sunset and the male figure silhouetted against it. His features remained dark and indiscernible. His hair wasn't a sleek ponytail, but a wreath of frizzy curls. The nose in profile? It could possibly be Jasper's, but Drex couldn't swear to it, and, besides, he could have had rhinoplasty. Even a slight alteration could make a significant difference in his appearance.

He studied the close-up for several minutes before admitting that if there was something new and revelatory to see, he was missing it.

He returned the photo to its original size, sat back in his chair, and took it in as a whole, wondering what it was in particular that Mike and Gif had wanted him to see. Little of the yacht itself was visible in the picture, and Drex didn't see anything of consequence from what was shown. The enhancement hadn't changed Marian Harris's image that dramatically. There was nothing to see in the background except for the blazing sky.

The partygoers? The doctored chromaticity had deepened some hues, lightened others, making it easier to delineate forms within the mishmash of faces and limbs. Individuals were now distinguishable. One in particular on the fringe of the crowd caught Drex's eye because of a slender shaft of light shining on her hair and—

And matching it to the golds and reds that threaded through the sunset.

He sat perfectly still for a long time because he was too sickened to move. He could only stare at the face, which was out of focus, but dreamworthy, unquestionably lovely, and indisputably identifiable.

He got his *voilá!*, after all.

Chapter 11

Starting from the time he received that initial call from Deputy Gray in Key West, it took Rudkowski three days to find the hotel.

During that seventy-two hours, he'd pulled together every resource at his disposal in an attempt to tree Drex Easton without causing too much of a stir. He wanted to keep the higher-ups unaware that Easton was at it again.

The son of a bitch.

Rudkowski was tempted to let him move forward without intervention. Why not sit back in his La-Z-Boy, overdose on ESPN, and allow Easton to self-destruct? Rudkowski's life would be simpler once Easton was completely wiped off the landscape.

But in the process of destroying himself, Easton would create a shit storm. Some of it was bound to blow back on Rudkowski. He wasn't one of those rah-rah, diehard agents who thought the FBI was an exalted company of which he was fortunate to be a member. He wasn't a blindly loyal disciple of the bureau.

He was, however, fanatically devoted to his pension.

He didn't give Easton the satisfaction of calling Mike Mallory or Gifford Lewis, demanding to know where the hell he was and what he was up to. His cronies would report straight back to him that Rudkowski was on the warpath, and Easton would get a kick out of that. Even more, he would enjoy knowing that, so far, he was winning this current game of hide-and-seek.

But Rudkowski had agents surreptitiously keeping a close watch on Mallory and Lewis. For the past three days, they had reported for work as usual. After office hours, each had gone directly home. Neither was married, both lived alone, they seemed not to have any social life or any friends except for each other and Easton. On the surface they appeared to be the two biggest dullards on the face of the earth.

Rudkowski wasn't fooled. He sensed that behind the closed doors of their drab apartments, they toiled into the wee hours, diligently working underground for their ringleader, Easton.

Rudkowski would continue to have their activities monitored, although he knew it was futile. Neither of the men was likely to make a slip-up, and neither would betray Drex Easton, not even if his life depended on it.

Rudkowski knew that because there had been a time when their lives had depended on it, and neither had caved.

Twice over the course of the past three days, Rudkowski had called Deputy Gray in Key West to inquire if he had heard anything more from Easton. He hadn't. Rudkowski pulled rank and got a sergeant in the sheriff's department down there to see if he could retrieve the telephone number that had called there twice on Sunday, the calls several hours apart. It took a while, but the sergeant came through and passed the number along to Rudkowski.

It was a short-lived victory, because when Rudkowski called the number, he got a recording telling him that the call couldn't be completed as dialed. Unsurprising, really, considering the savvy bastard he was dealing with. Easton would have destroyed that phone within minutes of speaking with Gray.

Miracles did happen, however. Rudkowski's shrinking belief in them was fully restored just that morning soon after he had arrived at his office. Another agent who'd been helping him on his search popped in. "You still on Easton's tail?"

"What have you got?"

"That last cell number you had for him?"

"No longer good."

"Not any more, but it was nine days ago. He sent a text from it."

"To who?"

"Mike Mallory."

"Shocker. From where?"

"A chain hotel in Lexington. I got the address."

Rudkowski signed out for the remainder of the day and recruited another agent to drive him the seventy-something miles from Louisville to Lexington. When they reached their destination, Rudkowski left the second agent waiting in the car, preferring to handle this interview alone.

When the double automatic doors opened, a group of uniformed men and women filed past him pulling roll-aboards toward a waiting van. Flight crew, Rudkowski figured. Their departure left the lobby empty.

The receptionist greeted him as he approached the check-in desk. "Good afternoon, sir."

"Hi." He produced his badge and gave the young woman time to read his name on his ID. "It's pronounced just like it's spelled, short *u*. I need to speak to the manager, please."

"She's at lunch. She left me in charge."

He leaned across the counter and read her name tag. "Ms. Li?"

"Yes, sir."

"I'm here to ask about a guest—"

"Special Agent Easton?"

Rudkowski scowled. "How'd you know?"

"Because he's the only FBI agent I've checked in." She beamed a smile. "He'd be hard to forget anyway, because he was so nice."

Rudkowski wanted to grind his teeth. "Yeah. Hell of a guy."

"Are you—"

He cut her off. "I'll ask the questions, Ms. Li. If you don't mind."

Her warm smile turned cooler. She bobbed her head.

"How many nights did he stay?"

"He didn't."

"He checked in but didn't stay?"

"They were here for only a couple of hours. But Mr. Easton paid for a full day."

"'They'? Did he bring a woman?"

"Nothing like that," she said, her lips pursing primly. "He was here for a meeting with two associates."

"Mallory and Lewis?"

"I didn't get their names."

"Was one of them a fat guy, face like a bulldog?"

Seeming to be offended by the description, she said, "He was…heavyset. Not a handsome man."

"Not handsome and nice like Agent Easton."

She didn't say anything to that, only looked at him with unblinking eyes.

He asked, "What about the third man?"

"I don't remember him very well."

Gif Lewis, Rudkowski thought. That guy faded into the woodwork. Rudkowski worried his lower lip between his teeth. "Easton used a credit card?"

She answered with a curt nod. "He reviewed the bill to make certain I had added the minibar charges. Plus the cake."

"Cake?"

"He called down and asked me to have room service deliver—"

"*Cake?*"

"Yes."

No more "sir," he noticed. Not that he cared about her opinion of him, but he added a bit of saccharine to his next question, because it was the most important one. "Ms. Li, after settling the bill with the additional charges, did Easton happen to tell you where he was going from here? Did he make a reservation at one of your chain's other hotels?"

"No. But he left something for you."

"For me?"

"That's what I was trying to ask you at the start before you interrupted. I was about to ask if you had come to pick up the envelope. Mr. Easton said that you might be coming by for it within a few days. Honestly, I was about to give up on you. Wait just a moment, please."

She disappeared into an office and returned shortly with a letter-size envelope. "Here you are."

He plucked it from her hand. "Thanks."

"I've already been thanked. By Mr. Easton. I was happy to provide the service for him." She turned her back on him and went back into the office.

Rudkowski stalked across the lobby and through the double doors, waiting until he was outside to rip open the envelope and pull out the single sheet of hotel stationery. In the center of it was printed: *Hey there, Rudkowski. Kiss my ass.*

Chapter 12

———◦◉◦———

Stroking her cheek to remove the speck of chocolate icing had been one thing. Licking it off his thumb had been another. If Drex had stopped at the former, and hadn't done the latter, she would have forgotten the incident by now. Probably. Maybe. But because he had done it, she was still thinking about it two days later. With each replay of the scene in her mind, the scintillation was magnified. As was her unease over it.

Because it hadn't been a reflexive action that could be laughed off. He hadn't noisily smacked his lips or wisecracked about her chocolate addiction. It wasn't wittiness that had simmered in his eyes as they'd held her gaze. Nothing like that.

No, licking it off his thumb had been provocative. Which compelled her to report it to Jasper.

But she hadn't.

She hadn't told him later that afternoon when he returned from the country club, or during their dinner out that evening, or when they'd come home to find that Drex had brought back their fan, along with a note regarding tonight's reservation.

On any of those occasions she could have mentioned the incident to Jasper in an offhanded manner, made light of it, and given it no significance. But she hadn't slipped it into a conversation, and now too much time had passed, during which it had acquired significance.

Of late, there had been a mounting tension between Jasper and her, made even worse because neither of them acknowledged it. Telling him about the incident with Drex might force them to expose problems within the marriage, which, to this point, neither had been willing to do.

In any case, telling Jasper about it now would feel like a confession. He would want to know why she was just now getting around to informing him of it when they were an hour away from joining the man for a double date. She didn't want to get into anything with him just before leaving for their evening out.

As predicted, Elaine was as giddy as a coed who'd been invited to the prom by the varsity captain. She'd called Talia within minutes of Drex's inviting her and had recounted word for word all he'd said, speaking as though every sentence ended in a pair of exclamation marks. Over the course of the past two days, she had called Talia no fewer than a dozen times in a dither over what she should wear tonight.

Meanwhile, Talia hadn't seen or heard from Drex since leaving him on his doorstep. Without taking time even to say goodbye, she'd gotten the hell out of there. Several times, she had noticed that his car wasn't in the driveway, but hadn't caught sight of him leaving or returning. When she casually asked Jasper if he'd crossed paths with him, he'd said with disinterest, "No."

Now, soaking in a bubble bath, chin-deep in scented suds, Talia wondered if Drex shared her disquiet over the incident. If he had dwelled on those few moments as much as she had, he might regret what he'd done and could well be embarrassed when he saw her tonight. Would it make for an awkward situation?

No. There wouldn't be any awkwardness because she wouldn't

allow there to be. She would treat him as she had before: friendly, but with boundaries clearly drawn.

She was probably making far too much out of it anyway.

Having resolved that, she climbed out of the tub and proceeded to dress for the evening. She and Jasper had offered to pick up Elaine at seven. At fifteen minutes to, Talia checked her reflection in the mirror one last time, picked up her handbag, and, as she emerged from her dressing room, called to Jasper, "I'm ready."

Elaine lived in a classy community of townhouses, Georgian in design, which afforded owners ample and pricey square footage, but zero lot lines. Talia parked at the curb and went up the walkway connecting the sidewalk to Elaine's front door, which was made private from the street by an iron picket fence lined with shrubbery.

Within seconds of Talia's ringing the bell, Elaine opened the door and exclaimed, "Oh my God, you look stunning!"

"Thank you. So do you."

"It's new." Elaine pinched up the full skirt of her dress and curtsied.

"It's lovely."

"I can't do slinky anymore," she said wistfully, eyeing Talia up and down. "Is Jasper parking the car? Come in, come in so the mosquitoes don't eat us alive. Drex, will you please tend bar?"

Talia drew up short just as she stepped across the threshold and spotted him lounging on the sofa. A great cat, having feasted on a fresh kill and lazing in the sun, couldn't have appeared more satiated and indolent as he unfolded himself and stood up. "Hello, Talia."

He was wearing dress slacks and a necktie, but the tie had been loosened, his collar button undone. She hadn't yet braced herself to look him in the eye for the first time since last she saw him and was so taken off guard to find him here that the first words out of her mouth sounded like an accusation. "I thought you were meeting us at the restaurant."

"He called and asked if he could come by early," Elaine said. "And look what he brought me!" She pointed to the coffee table on which lay a rubber-banded manuscript.

"He had a copy made and asked me to read it and give him an honest assessment, which I swore I would do."

Talia's gaze moved from the manuscript back up to Drex. His smile was smug, his eyes glinting with insinuation, and she was certain he shifted them ever so subtly to the spot near her mouth that he'd touched with his thumb.

Before she gave in to the temptation to cross the room and slap him as hard as she could, she turned her back to him and addressed Elaine. "I'm sure he'll benefit from your opinion."

"He already has. He bounced several titles off me, and we decided on one just before you got here. Am I at liberty to tell her, Drex?"

"I'd rather keep it between us for now."

Taking in the scene, Talia noticed that Elaine's high-heeled sandals were lying on their sides in front of the sofa. Drex's suit jacket was folded over the arm of a chair. Two half-filled highball glasses were on the coffee table. A gas fire flickered in the fireplace. It lent a romantic ambiance, but wasn't radiating any heat.

Talia's cheeks, however, were. She was furious over the way he had played her. It was an insult that he had asked Elaine to read his manuscript when he had soundly rejected her offer to do so. He was also playing Elaine in the very manner that Talia had warned him against.

"What's keeping Jasper?" Elaine asked.

Talia hid her anger behind a rueful smile. "He sends his regrets."

"He's not coming? Why?"

"I would have notified you, but I didn't know myself until we were due to leave. He waited until the last minute to tell me so I wouldn't cancel on you. He insisted I come on. Besides, the plan was for us to drive you tonight. He didn't want to stand you up. As it turns out..." She let the statement go unfinished except for a one-shoulder shrug and a backward nod toward Drex.

He said, "Why isn't Jasper coming?"

She turned around to face him. "Tummy issues."

"A bug?"

"The oysters he had for lunch."

Elaine said, "I used to warn my husband against eating them raw."

Neither Drex nor Talia contributed anything to that. He was still looking at her as though they shared an inside joke. A naughty inside joke. Spending an evening in his company would be intolerable.

"I hate to bail on you, too," she said to Elaine. "But I really feel I should go home and make certain that Jasper is all right."

Elaine stepped forward and hooked arms with her. "Nonsense. You know how men are when they're sick. They're either pitiful and want their mommy or they're ornery. I believe Jasper would fall into the second category. Besides, I'm not about to let you waste that knockout dress. Drex, you don't mind escorting both of us, do you?"

The dimple appeared. "It'll be my pleasure. And I would hate to waste one of the desserts I took the liberty of pre-ordering."

"Oooh, what?" Elaine said.

"Chocolate soufflé."

The sly look he gave Talia set her teeth on edge.

He walked over to the bar, turned to her, and arched his brow. "Can I pour you a nice red wine?"

Ungently she tossed her handbag into the nearest chair. "No. Vodka martini. Dry. Straight up."

He wanted to kill her.

But first, he wanted to fuck her.

No, he wanted to fuck her, then torment her, then kill her.

Drex had been experiencing these violent urges ever since he'd seen her in that photograph taken aboard Marian Harris's yacht, separated from Jasper Ford by several yards, but *there*. The two of them.

"All that bullshit about the client complaint, the email exchange, the hand-delivered roses, was just that: bullshit," he'd told Mike and Gif when he'd recovered from the shock and was composed enough to call them.

"You're sure it's her?" Mike had asked. "I mean, Gif and me thought so, but we're going only by pictures. You've been up close and personal."

They didn't know how up close, how personal. "It's her."

"So what do you think?" Mike had asked. "Is she her husband's next victim, or his accomplice?"

"Hell I know," Drex had muttered in reply.

After seeing her and Jasper in such close proximity on the yacht's deck, when they weren't even supposed to have known each other at the time, he had methodically reviewed each of his own encounters with Talia, assessing them in a new light. Especially her unannounced visit to his grubby living quarters.

Providing him a list of restaurants had been an acceptable excuse for her coming over, but it was just as likely that Jasper had sent her on a fact-finding mission. If she had come to his door wearing a see-through negligee, it couldn't have looked any sexier than her jeans and t-shirt. But maybe that downplayed wardrobe had been calculated to make the visit seem neighborly and innocent.

Was the speck of icing an accidental and unnoticed leftover from breakfast, or had she dabbed it on deliberately, placing it in a spot that couldn't possibly escape his notice? A spot that had made his loins achy and tight.

The question about her culpability hung there unanswered until

Mike said, "Drex, let me pose a question that might simplify and clarify your thinking."

"Shoot."

"If she's in the dark about her husband and his past misdeeds, why did she lie to you about how they hooked up?"

The three of them had pondered the question in silence.

It was Drex who finally spoke, grumbling, "Here I've been losing sleep from worrying about her safety."

And here he was now, topping off Elaine's wineglass with the last of their second bottle. He'd never endured such a long dinner in his life. It was torture. From the instant Talia had come through Elaine's front door, he'd been baiting her, and it had worked. She had flung her small purse into the armchair as though throwing down a spiked gauntlet.

Inside that dress—which, by the way, *was* a slinky knockout worn with no detectable undergarments—she was steaming. Her entire body vibrated with indignation every time she looked at him, which wasn't often. In fact, for most of the dinner, she ignored him completely.

He wondered if her obvious ire had anything to do with that laden moment on his threshold, from which she had run like the apartment had burst into flames. Maybe his suggestive action had offended her.

But he figured her truculent mood tonight had more to do with Elaine, who was reacting to his courtly attention as forecast, which was exactly what Talia had wanted to guard against.

Elaine's effervescence made her impossible to dislike, but, as though sensing the strain between Talia and him, she'd appointed herself social chair of the trio and couldn't leave even the briefest silence alone. She filled any gap in the conversation with prattle. Drex responded as though delightfully entertained by every inanity, which fed Elaine's flirtatiousness, which fueled Talia's anger.

When they finished their entrées and were waiting for the soufflés to be served, Elaine excused herself to go to the ladies' room, leaving him alone with Talia for the first time that evening. She took her cell phone from her handbag and typed a text.

"To Jasper?"

She said a terse yes. While waiting for a reply, she took a slow visual survey of the drapery valance, the chandelier, the weave pattern of the tablecloth. She picked at her slender diamond bracelet as though discovering that it had been clasped around her wrist without her knowledge. She did not look at him.

"You seem out of sorts tonight."

She stopped inspecting her bracelet and looked across at him, but didn't say anything.

"Why are you in such a sulk? Missing Jasper?"

On the heels of his taunt, her phone dinged. She read the text, then clicked off.

"How's he doing?"

"Better."

"Puked it all up?"

"Drank a ginger ale." Then, with full-blown hostility, she said, "You really are a piece of work, aren't you?"

Drex didn't have time to respond because Elaine's return to the table coincided with the waiter delivering their soufflés.

They ate them, their conversation limited to comments about calories and how some foods were worth the splurge. They had coffee but didn't linger over it, and when Elaine suggested after-dinner drinks, Talia bowed out.

"I hate to cut the evening short," she lied. "Jasper says he's feeling better, but I really should get home to him."

Elaine had insisted that they all ride together to the restaurant, leaving Talia's car at the townhouse. When the restaurant valet brought around Drex's car, Elaine got in the front seat, as before. Talia sat in back.

Their positions were such that Drex could observe her in the rearview mirror. She kept her head turned toward the back seat window.

As they neared Elaine's neighborhood, she expressed regret that Jasper had missed such a luscious dinner. "If he's up to it, let's have a foursome lunch at the country club tomorrow."

Talia continued to stare out the window. "It will depend on how he feels in the morning. I'll have to let you know." She didn't sound at all enthusiastic about the prospect.

"I'll make a ressie for four in the hope that you can make it. Noonish? Or a bit later?"

Drex said, "Sorry, Elaine, but I have to decline."

"Oh, no."

"I'm stuck at a pivotal part of the novel and much in need of inspiration. I'm thinking of going in search of some."

"Where does a writer begin looking for inspiration?"

"Holy ground."

"Church?"

"Hemingway's house in Key West."

Talia's reaction was instantaneous. Her head came around. They locked eyes in the rearview mirror.

"Have you been there?" He addressed the question to her, but Elaine responded.

"My husband and I docked there. But only once. The vibe was a little too bohemian for him."

Drex acknowledged that with a nod but never took his eyes off Talia, who, after holding his stare for several seconds, had turned her head aside again. *Un-huh. No way,* he thought. He wasn't going to let the question go unanswered. "How about you, Talia?"

Without looking at him, she lowered her chin slightly. "I was there a couple of years ago."

"And?"

"And..." She raised a nearly bare shoulder. "It was all right."

"Just all right?"

"Not my worst destination, but not one of my favorites, either."

"What didn't you like? The food? The nightlife? What?"

With discernible impatience, she said, "Nothing I could put my finger on."

"Hmm. Did you tour Hemingway's house?"

"No, but I'm not surprised that you plan to."

"Why's that?"

She met his gaze in the mirror. "Jasper theorized that you want to create a professional image for yourself that's reminiscent of Jack London or Hemingway."

"Jasper devoted that much thought to me and my aspirations?"

"He made the comment after I told him about your upbringing in Alaska."

"Alaska?" Elaine chirped. "How fascinating."

"Not really," Drex said.

"I've never known anyone from there. You must tell me all about it. Come in for a nightcap?"

He pulled the car to the curb in front of her townhouse, put it in park, but left it running. "If I'm going to Florida, I'll need to get up early tomorrow and start making arrangements. Rain check?"

"Of course. Besides, you probably should follow Talia home."

He glanced back at her. "I planned to."

"I wouldn't dream of inconveniencing you. Besides, I'm a big girl." She got out of the car and shut the back door.

By the time Drex alighted and had come around to open the passenger door for Elaine, Talia was impatiently bouncing her key fob in her palm. "Thank you for dinner, Drex. It was lovely." Her drop-dead glare put her sincerity in doubt. "Good night, Elaine." She leaned in and air-kissed Elaine's cheek. "I'll be in touch."

"Give Jasper my regards. Promise to call me tomorrow and let me know how he's doing."

"Yes, I will." Without another word or glance at Drex, she turned and started walking toward her car, her high heels tapping the sidewalk with a marching cadence.

Elaine gave his shoulder a nudge. "I don't care how big a girl she is, I can tell she's upset. She hasn't been herself all evening. Make sure she gets home safely."

"After I walk you to your door."

"Nonsense. It's all of twenty steps."

"You sure?"

"Go. I think she must be more worried about Jasper than she's letting on."

He gave a grim smile at the unintended irony. "I'm sure you're right." He kissed Elaine lightly on the cheek and bid her good night, then quickly got back into his car and peeled away from the curb in pursuit of Talia's taillights.

Once he caught up with her, he stayed close and pulled into his driveway seconds after she pulled into hers. She opened the garage door remotely and lowered it as soon as her rear bumper cleared the opening.

Drex got out of his car and went around to open the trunk. He took out a duffel bag, closed the trunk, then headed up the path toward the garage apartment.

"How was the evening?"

Startled, he whipped around. Jasper was sitting in the dark on the screened porch, idly rocking in his chair. Drex gave him his good-neighbor smile. "You were missed. Feeling better?"

"Much."

"Bad oysters, Talia said."

"Must've been. Did you like the restaurant?"

"Superb. Thanks for the recommendation."

A light came on. Talia appeared as a silhouette in the open doorway between the kitchen and porch. She looked at Drex but didn't say anything. Jasper turned to her and extended his hand. She went to him and linked her fingers with his.

The gesture spoke volumes, the message was clear: We're a pair, a united front.

Drex covered a yawn with his hand and hitched his chin toward the staircase. "Well...I'm bushed. Good night."

Jasper responded with a good night.

Talia said nothing.

Drex climbed the staircase. The screen door was unlocked, but he used his key on the solid one. Inside, he crossed the living area in darkness, went into the bedroom, and switched on the lamp on the rickety nightstand. Then he returned to the bedroom door and shut it, preventing prying eyes from seeing him unzip the duffel he'd retrieved from his trunk. He took from it his laptop, binoculars, the audio surveillance equipment, FBI ID, and pistol.

Since connecting Talia to Jasper in Key West, he'd taken these items along whenever he went out. As a precaution. Just in case someone came searching the apartment. Someone to whom a locked door wouldn't be a deterrent.

And if someone did come snooping, he wanted to know it.

So he'd taken another precaution.

He picked up the lamp by its base and lowered it to the side of the bed where he had sprinkled talcum onto the floor, but not so much that it would be noticeable unless one was looking.

"Huh."

Between the time he'd left for his dinner and now, the powder had been smeared, as though someone had knelt at the side of the bed, perhaps to look beneath it or between the mattress and box spring.

He set the lamp back on the nightstand and switched it out, picked up the binoculars, opened the bedroom door, and went into the living room. At the window, he focused on the house next door. There were no lights on inside, but that didn't mean that he wasn't being watched.

Jasper had never intended to make that dinner date. He'd had other plans for the evening.

Drex huffed a soft laugh. "Bad oysters my ass."

Chapter 13

Talia never touched the latte.

She had bought it only to rent a table, which were in short supply. The coffee shop was an offshoot of the ground floor lobby of the multistoried medical building. This morning the place was crowded; the baristas were bustling to fill orders.

Talia surmised that countless patients had come here following medical procedures or examinations, the outcomes of which were either cause for celebration or cause for an immediate reevaluation of one's priorities.

At a table near hers, a young couple was laughing into a cell phone, sharing obviously happy news on FaceTime. Also nearby was an older couple. The woman was crying softly into a tissue while the man sat with shoulders slumped, his features haggard, his eyes glazed with despair.

Talia's emotions fit somewhere in between. She wasn't happy, but she refused to let hopelessness set in.

"Talia?"

She raised her head. Drex Easton was standing over her.

"I thought it was you. I spotted you from..." He paused in jerking his thumb over his shoulder in the direction of the lobby and leaned down to take a closer look at her. "What's the matter?"

She bowed her head again and pressed her fingertips against her forehead. He was the last person she would wish to bump into right now. She simply wasn't up to dealing with him. Rather than engage at all, she chose to retreat. She picked up her handbag and stood. "I was just about to leave. You can have the table."

But as she moved away, he closed his hand around her biceps, stopping her. "What's wrong?"

"Nothing."

"Don't say nothing. Something. Are you sick? Did Jasper have a contagious bug after all?"

"No. I'm fine."

"You don't look fine."

"Let go of my arm."

"Talia—"

"Let go." She pulled her arm free.

He reached for her again.

"Everything okay here?"

Talia hadn't noticed the approach of the other man until he was right there with them. He divided a concerned look between her and Drex, landing on Drex, a frown of stern disapproval forming between his eyebrows. She then became aware that other customers had stopped what they were doing to observe them.

Drex said, "Yeah, pal, everything's cool."

The man didn't excuse himself or back down, but continued to glower at Drex with suspicion.

Drex glowered back. "I *said*, everything's cool."

Ignoring him, the man looked at her, asking softly, "Ma'am?"

She swallowed. "Everything's fine." Her smile was wobbly and unconvincing, so she added, "I'm was upset, am upset, about… about…"

"About her dad's diagnosis," Drex said. "They're close."

Talia marveled at the ease with which he lied. Going back to the stranger, she said, "I appreciate your concern. Truly. But I'm fine. I just needed some air."

"Sure, honey." Drex shot the man a dirty look as he brushed past him, then, cupping her elbow, maneuvered her out of the coffee shop.

He guided her across the lobby to a seating area that was sectioned off by a row of potted plants. They lent some privacy, but Talia didn't want privacy with Drex. Nothing good had come of the times when they had been alone; Jasper seemed not to like it, and, besides, Drex's smarmy behavior of the night before was still fresh in her mind.

He motioned for her to sit down on one of the padded benches. She shook her head. "I have to go."

He looked at her with consternation. "You're upset."

"I wasn't until you intruded."

He just stood there, an imposing presence she couldn't go around without creating another scene. She plopped down on the bench. He perched on the edge of another that faced hers. She moved her knees aside so they wouldn't be so close to touching his.

"What's going on?" he asked.

"Nothing. You're making way too much of—"

"Something's wrong. I can tell."

"How can you tell? You don't know me well enough to gauge my moods. You don't know me at all."

In a sudden move, he leaned forward and said with heat, "And that's eating at me. A lot."

The change in his bearing was discomfiting. She reclined back to compensate for his nearness. "Why should it? If my whole world is caving in, what business is it of yours?"

"Is your whole world caving in?"

"No!" she exclaimed.

"Then why were you sitting there, staring into your coffee so morosely?"

"Morosely?"

"Till I looked it up, I didn't know what it meant, either."

"I know what it means, and so do you."

"All right then, what made you morose?"

"Lord," she said, huffing a breath. "You're not going to let it go, are you?"

By way of an answer, he folded his arms over his chest and settled on the bench as though in it for the long haul.

She closed her eyes briefly, then, resigned, said, "I had just come from the dentist. Top floor." She raised her hand to indicate the stories above them. "I was still a bit woozy from the chill pill they gave me. I thought a latte would perk me up before I started the drive home."

Gingerly she touched the side of her face. "The numbing began to wear off. I wasn't feeling all that great. Then you show up and make a spectacle of me." She paused, took a breath, and narrowed her eyes on him. "Don't ever grab me like that again."

"I didn't grab you."

She gave him a withering look.

He raked his fingers through his hair, turned his head aside and looked at the yellowing leaves on the nearest ficus tree, then came back to her. "I didn't mean for it to be a grab. I didn't mean to make a spectacle of you. I apologize."

He appeared to mean it. "Apology accepted." After a short silence, she said, "I thought you were going to Florida."

"I thought so, too. That was until I checked the airfares this morning."

She gave him a wan smile.

"Hemingway's house is still on my bucket list," he said, "but I may not make it down there until I publish."

"I'll keep an eye out for discount fares and alert you to them."

"Definitely a benefit to having the MVP of travel agents living next door."

The grin he flashed was too attractive, too rakish, too...too everything.

She looked away from him toward the bank of elevators where a car had just opened up. A group flowed out, another filed in. The building was full of people, yet they had the seating area to themselves, making it feel as though they were alone.

It occurred to her then what an odd coincidence it was that he had turned up here.

She regarded him with misgiving. "What are you doing here, Drex?"

"Downtown, you mean?"

"I mean in this building. Why are you here?"

"I was in search of the main library. Got turned around. Saw the sign for the coffee shop, came in for a shot of espresso and to get my bearings." He dismissed all that with a shrug, then his eyes sharpened on her face. "Still feeling woozy? You gonna be okay?"

"The latte worked."

"You didn't drink it. Not one sip."

It disconcerted her that he had noticed. It made her uneasy to wonder what else he might have observed that would be much more consequential. "I should go." She slid the strap of her handbag onto her shoulder and stood.

So did he. "Did the dentist give you any pain pills?"

"A prescription. But I doubt I'll need it. It was just a filling."

"Get the pills. Take one before you need it. Head off the pain."

"I think all I really need is a nap." She moved away. "See you around, Drex."

"Where's your car?"

"Parking garage."

"This building?"

"Third level."

"I could escort—"

"No, thanks." She raised her hand in a halfhearted wave, then turned and walked quickly toward the elevators.

Drex watched her progress across the lobby.

He wasn't the only one who did.

From his vantage point on the bench facing Talia's, Drex had looked beyond her shoulder and spotted the do-gooder in the coffee shop. He had claimed a table just the other side of the glass wall, which gave him a view of the seating area. For the duration of Talia and Drex's conversation, the guy had been eyeing them as though poised to rush to her rescue if necessary. It galled Drex no end.

Now, while the good Samaritan was watching Talia board the elevator, Drex ducked into the fire exit door that opened into the seating area. Leaping over the treads two or three at a time, he took the stairs down to the third level of the parking garage.

It smelled of motor oil, gasoline, and rubber. It was ill-lighted. The ceiling was low and foreboding. It could have been a parking garage in any city, anywhere in the world. Except that in this one, Talia Shafer was leaning against the driver's door of her car, crying.

Not wanting to frighten her, Drex made sure she heard him approaching. She came around quickly, and, upon seeing him, anger shimmered in her eyes along with unshed tears. "What are you doing here?"

"I told you. I was looking for the public library, got turned around—"

"You're lying!"

"So are you," he fired back, taking a step closer to her. "There aren't any dentists on the top floor. It's devoted to gynecology and obstetrics."

Seeming to deflate, she clamped her lower lip between her teeth and turned her head away. A tear escaped and rolled down her cheek all the way to her jawline, where she wiped it off.

Drex swallowed the knot in his throat. He didn't want to know, but had to ask, "Are you pregnant?"

She shook her head, then said a husky no.

Relief made his knees go weak, although five minutes ago, he wouldn't have credited that physical phenomenon. Then, a worse thought struck him. "Is something…" Awkwardly, he motioned toward her middle. "Wrong?"

"No." When he looked at her doubtfully, she repeated *no*. "And even if there were, I certainly wouldn't discuss it with you." She rubbed her fists across her eyes, bolstered herself by standing up straighter, and looked directly into his face. "You followed me here. I know you did. Tell me why."

"I was a butthole last night."

He stopped there, and, when he didn't continue, she said, "Are you waiting for an argument from me? If so, you're waiting in vain."

He gave her a wry half smile. "I saw you leave your house. I followed you in the hope of getting an opportunity to apologize."

"For beguiling Elaine?"

"For all of it. The manuscript, the smirks, the innuendos, the setup. I staged a scene for you to walk into and draw a conclusion."

"Well, I did."

"I know."

She gazed at him with bewilderment. "But why did you do it?"

"To see if you'd be jealous."

She took swift breath, then, lowering her head, stared at the gritty, oil-stained concrete between their feet. "I can't be jealous, Drex. I'm married."

"Yeah, I know. It's all I think about. You being married. You being married to him."

She raised her head and looked into his eyes. "You don't have cause, or the right, to think about it."

"But I do." He extended his arm and braced his hand against the roof of her car. He pressed his forehead against his biceps and expelled a long breath. "I think about it all the goddamn time, and it's making me crazy."

For the longest time neither of them moved. They scarcely breathed. Did she share his fear that something as negligible as a blink could cause a cataclysm from which they could never recover or escape? He couldn't read her thoughts. All he had to go on was her stillness.

Until finally, he heard her hair brush against her shoulder as she turned her head toward him. "I'm sorry, Drex," she murmured. "I don't know what to say."

He lifted his head from his arm and turned it toward her. Their faces inches apart, he focused on her mouth as she added, "I don't know what you expect me to say."

"Don't say anything." By the time the last whispered syllable had passed his lips, they were brushing hers.

She yanked her head back. He slid his hand off the roof of the car and raised both in surrender as he stepped away and continued to back up. "Out of line. Way out of line. I'm sorry."

He turned and took several steps away before he stopped and came back around. He looked at her for a count of five. "Bloody hell," he growled. "If I'm going to be sorry, I'm damn well going to make it count."

He covered the same distance in half the number of strides. When he reached her, he took her face between his hands, tilted it, and kissed her. But good. Without sweetness or timidity. Deeply. Boldly. Sexily. Pouring into the kiss all the frustration, anger, and lust she had aroused in him.

Then he released her abruptly, turned, and walked away.

He made it into the elevator and rode it down to the next level of the garage where he'd parked. But as soon as he alighted, he placed his back to the concrete block wall and knocked his head against it hard enough to hurt.

What the hell was he doing?

When he'd seen Talia backing her car out of her driveway, he'd given no conscious thought to following her. He'd just reacted. Fortunately, he'd planned on going out later, so the items he had begun taking with him whenever he left were already zipped into the duffel bag. He'd had the presence of mind to grab it before he'd bolted from the apartment, nearly breaking his neck getting down that blasted staircase, certainly breaking speed limits to catch up to her and then to keep her car in sight.

He hadn't planned on her knowing that he was tracking her. Between her getting into the elevator to go up and when she came back down, forty-seven minutes had elapsed. Forty-seven minutes during which he'd examined his motives for acting so rashly.

After a heated debate with himself, he concluded that he wasn't simply a man obsessed with a woman but that this additional surveillance was justified. She was as much a suspect now as Jasper. He needed to know where she went, whom she saw, and why.

Right?

Right.

So he'd continued to amble back and forth across the lobby, keeping a close watch on everyone the elevators disgorged, and trying not to attract the attention of the rent-a-cops posted at all the building's entrances.

When Talia reappeared, he'd ignored the bump his heart gave. From across the lobby, he'd monitored her activity in the coffee shop. After several minutes passed, he decided that no one was joining her. She hadn't consulted her cell phone. She hadn't glanced around periodically in anticipation of someone's arrival. Rather she sat alone, looking forlorn and in need of a friend.

He was good at that, too, he'd reminded himself. Role-playing. Wasn't that one of his best honed skills?

So into the coffee shop he'd gone.

But at that point, he'd known he was kidding himself. Her apparent anguish had taken precedence over her being a suspect in at least one capital crime. The more he saw of her, the looser his grip on objectivity became, until, as of now, it was virtually nonexistent. He'd gone so far as to admit his crazed obsession to her.

Aw, well. It was too late to rethink it. Too late for a do-over. He couldn't take back any of it. He didn't want to take back the kiss.

He pushed himself away from the wall and started down the

ramp toward his parking spot. As his car came into sight, he drew up short. *"Shit!"*

Standing in the deep shadows, the do-gooder from the coffee shop was leaning against the hood of his car, obviously lying in wait.

Anger propelling him, Drex didn't break stride but walked straight up to him and demanded, "What the fuck, Gif?"

Chapter 14

Drex sat slumped in the driver's seat of his car. For as long as he could, he withstood the weight of Gif's stare from the passenger side, then turned to him. *"What?"*

Gif the unflappable said, "You have to ask?"

"Why were you tailing me?"

"Why were you tailing her?"

"Surveillance."

"Surveillance?"

"Surely you're familiar with the word. Derived from the French—"

"Drex—"

"—verb—"

"Drex," Gif repeated, putting some oomph behind it.

He lapsed into angry silence and stewed, then snidely asked, "Did you and Mike toss a coin to see who would be the monitor, and you won? Or did you lose?"

"He and I discussed who should come and decided that—"

"You're a sneakier spy."

"Indubitably."

Drex scoffed. "Hate to break it to you, buddy, but you're slipping. The first rule of working undercover is to stay the hell undercover. Don't let the tailee know that he's being tailed. In the coffee shop, what the hell were you thinking?"

"That I should intervene."

"Why?"

"Because of the lady's apparent distress."

"I didn't cause her distress."

Gif conveyed his doubt by raising his eyebrows.

"I didn't," Drex said.

"Okay, but your manhandling wasn't helping."

"I didn't manhandle her."

Again the eyebrows went up.

Drex ignored them. "From now on, stay invisible, or you may forget how to."

Gif gave him a rare, and somewhat smug, smile. "I had the veal Milanese and a glass of Brunello."

Drex stared at him as though struck dumb, then shook his head with incredulity. "I never saw you."

"You weren't supposed to."

"How did you even know where we were having dinner?"

"I got here yesterday afternoon, parked down the block from your apartment, and waited until you came out, so spit-and-polished you could've been a groom. I followed." He shrugged as though it had been too easy. "The dinner seemed to go okay."

"If you don't count the smoke coming from Talia's ears." He explained about the manuscript. "That ticked her off. She didn't like me schmoozing Elaine, either. She sees me as an opportunist who'll prey on Elaine's affections and her bankroll."

"Now there's an irony."

"Tell me," he said. "Anyway, as I'm sure you saw, I followed Talia home, but didn't talk to her after parting company at Elaine's. Jasper was on the porch. We exchanged good nights."

"Why wasn't he at the dinner?"

Drex explained but stopped short of sharing his certainty that the untimely illness had been a fabrication devised to give Jasper an ideal opportunity to search the garage apartment. Informing his partners of that would only contribute to their distress. They were already discontented over something, or Gif wouldn't be here.

If they had issues with either him or the situation, they should have aired them, talked them over with him, rather than to go about checking up on him so underhandedly. He didn't like it. Not one bit.

"Why, Gif?"

"Why what?"

Drex gave him a droll look. "Something has your noses out of joint, or you wouldn't be here."

Gif grimaced as though troubled by intestinal gas. "That dinner date you arranged worried us."

"How come?"

"You were reluctant to talk about it."

True. He hadn't elaborated on the plans for the date because he didn't want his cohorts questioning his reasons for setting it up. Which indeed had been questionable. But Gif could sense an evasion and sniff out a lie from a mile away, so his straightforward answer came as no surprise to Drex.

He felt a mix of admiration and agitation. "It pisses me off that you two appointed yourselves my babysitters. Did you come to see if I was behaving myself? What are you going to do? Put me in timeout? Am I grounded?"

"Don't get riled."

"I'm already riled."

"Then I had just as well lay it out there."

"Do."

"Did you arrange this dinner just so you could spend more time with her?"

"Yes! So I could spend more time with her and *her husband*. Who we believe to be a serial killer. Isn't that why I'm here?"

Gif raised his hand in a peacekeeping gesture. "We just wanted to make sure that your eye was still on the target and not on... something else."

"And now you can be sure. Go home."

Gif tugged on his earlobe. "The wasn't the only reason for my coming."

"What else?"

"Not what, who."

"Rudkowski?"

"He's got a periscope up Mike's ass."

Drex cursed under his breath. "Well, that's just fabulous. How far up it?"

"He showed up at Mike's office yesterday morning all bluster and self-importance. Hauled Mike away from his desk and into a conference room. He grilled him about the meeting we had in the hotel. Remember the enchanting Ms. Li?"

Drex couldn't help but chuckle. "She delivered my note to Rudkowski?"

Gif didn't see the humor in it. "I think you're missing the point here."

Sighing, Drex pressed his thumb and middle finger into his eye sockets and rubbed them. He was suddenly very tired. "I get your point. Rudkowski isn't just following up on my mysterious vacation, he's micromanaging a pursuit."

"Precisely."

"I saw this coming and warned you of it. If he failed to find me, he'd come after you. I advised you to be on alert."

"Agents are watching us, night and day. We've pretended not to notice. But coming to Mike's workplace, putting him through the wringer? That takes Rudkowski's zeal to a new level." He studied Drex for a moment. "You left him a bread-crumb trail to follow to that hotel."

"You and Mike urged me to contact him."

"Through official channels, Drex. Making him the butt of a joke isn't what we had in mind."

Drex put up no defense. He figured he deserved this particular hand-slapping. "Rudkowski found the hotel by tracking the text sent from my old phone?"

"Isn't that how you planned it?"

He shrugged, as good as an admission.

"Rudkowski went to the hotel in person," Gif said. "Conversed with Ms. Li."

"I made certain she would remember me. The birthday cake and all."

"Likely she would have remembered you even without that."

"She's new on the job. Eager to accommodate."

"Nevertheless, I doubt she would have been quite so accommodating had you not been quite so suave." He paused. Then, "What did the note to Rudkowski say, anyway?" Drex told him, and Gif smiled in spite of himself. "I would have paid good money to see his expression when he read it. But it would have been nice for you to let Mike and me in on the joke before it was sprung."

Drex shook his head. "This way, you can truthfully claim ignorance and innocence."

"Makes no difference what we claim. We could take a blood oath, and Rudkowski still wouldn't believe us."

"Probably not. But, on the plus side, your consciences remain clear." He shot Gif a grin, but Gif wasn't in a jesting frame of mind.

"This is serious, Drex."

He dropped the grin. "Yeah, I know."

"You don't know the worst of it."

"There's more?"

"Rudkowski didn't stop with the grilling. He alleged that Mike had tampered with evidence, stolen classified documents, breached secure email accounts. He reeled off a laundry list of offenses."

"Shit."

"Right. On and on."

"How did Mike respond?"

"By bending over backward to cooperate. He surrendered his work computer for Rudkowski's flunkies to tear into."

"There's nothing on it relating to any of this."

"No, but Rudkowski threatened to get a search warrant for his apartment and to seize everything it in, from roof to basement."

Drex steepled his fingers and tapped them against his forehead. "He can't get a warrant based on a hunch. A judge would ask for cause, and Rudkowski doesn't have it."

"He would cite our history. Your obsession. Our loyalty to you. The—"

"Okay, okay. It's worrisome, but Mike will take care of it."

"He already has. When we first heard that the sleeping giant had been awakened by that deputy down in Florida, Mike took the precaution of emptying everything off his hard drives, then destroyed them."

"What about you?"

"Rudkowski considers me less of a problem than Mike. I'm not the computer genius. But immediately after Mike tipped me, I got out of Dodge before Rudkowski could ambush me, too. I took a week's worth of personal days."

"With what excuse?"

"Hemorrhoidectomy."

"You have hemorrhoids?"

"That's why I used it. My superiors may be skeptical, but who's going to ask to see proof of the necessity?"

Drex chuckled again.

"It's still no laughing matter," Gif said. "I left my workspace and apartment clean as a whistle. They can turn them inside out and won't find anything. But as long as you and I are off the grid, Rudkowski is going to plow on."

"No doubt."

Gif hesitated, then said, "You could still put in a call to him—"

"No."

"Okay then, skip Rudkowski and alert one of his higher-ups."

"Who would either throw it back to Rudkowski or send someone else down here to check it out, who would probably screw up, then we'd be blown, and Jasper would get away."

"If you explained the delicacy of the situation—"

"Not doing it, Gif. Not yet."

Gif relented. "All right. But please stop pricking with Rudkowski. Because whether we succeed or fail at getting Ford, Rudkowski isn't going to forget your making him look foolish. He doesn't think your pranks are funny." He paused for effect. "What really has Mike and me worried—"

"We're back to that?"

"We're afraid that one of these days, one of your inside jokes is going to blow up in your face."

Sobered by his friend's tone, Drex thoughtfully scraped his thumb across his stubbled chin, repeating quietly, "One of these days."

"Or has one already backfired?"

When Gif looked at someone the way he was looking at Drex now, it cut through bullshit like a cleaver. He was referring to Talia, of course. Drex answered as truthfully as he could. "I don't know."

"I think you do."

Drex faced forward and laid his head against the headrest, inwardly cursing Gif and his damn uncanny ability to read people.

A long silence ensued, then Gif said, "Why *her*? You could go back to Lexington tonight and, with a crook of your finger, have that pretty hotel receptionist at your beck and call."

Drex rolled his head to the side to look at Gif. "You think she's pretty? And enchanting? Why don't you go back to Lexington? When's the last time you got laid? Oh, no, wait. You've been too busy keeping tabs on my sex life to have one of your own."

"Don't do that. Don't try to turn the tables here. Mike and I have stuck our necks out for you—"

"You can quit at any time."

"That's it on a nail's head, Drex." The uncharacteristic volume of his voice was indication of his anger. "We don't want to quit. We're all in. We made our choices, and they've cost us huge. But now, when we're close to a payoff, it could all go to hell because of your hard-on for the suspect's wife."

"We don't know that she's complicit."

"We don't know that she isn't."

Although he knew Gif was right, it was infuriating to be scolded like a kid caught with his hand inside his pants. "You can relax. Nothing has happened." Gif didn't back down. Hell, for all Drex knew, Gif had been standing within a yard of them when he'd kissed Talia. He amended his denial, muttering, "Nothing much."

"Doesn't matter," Gif said. "If you only *want* something to happen, you're compromised."

"Hell I am. There's a gulf of difference between thinking on something and acting on it."

"Your dinner date—"

"Was an attempt to learn more about her. Is she friend or foe? Guilty as hell or pure as the driven snow? Would she be appalled to learn of her husband's crimes, or did she snicker from the sidelines while he was nailing shut that box on Marian Harris? I've asked myself those questions a thousand times."

"Mike and I get that."

"Then why'd you hustle down here to check on me?"

"To make certain that you hadn't lost perspective."

"I haven't."

"No?"

"No."

Gif looked at him and said nothing for a time, then, "What were you two talking about while hiding behind the ficus trees?"

"If you were able to see us, we weren't hiding, were we? But, as to what we were talking about, I tried to get out of her why she was upset."

"And?"

"Something female."

"Oh. That narrows it down to about a million different things. Could you be more specific?"

"I tried. She wasn't having it." Losing patience with the inquisition, he said, "Anything else? Did you save the best for last?"

"In fact I did." Gif's eyes narrowed a fraction. "I have to ask. What was predominantly on your mind when you whisked her out of the coffee shop? Were you trying to determine if she's Ford's accomplice, or were you wishing she wasn't his wife?"

Damn him. Leave it to Gif to strike straight to the heart of the matter. It was a question Drex dared not answer. He didn't know how he would answer even if he were inclined to. Gif was right: His attraction to Talia was a hazard. But knowing that didn't stop him from wanting her. His better judgment, integrity, and resolve were tested every time he got near her.

However, he wasn't going to discuss this personal conflict with Gif. It was his problem to solve, and he would work through it alone, without Mike's bullying or Gif's counsel.

He said, "Earlier, you mentioned a blood oath. Have you ever taken one?"

Gif shook his head.

"Well, I have." He thrust his arm across the console and held his hand palm up where Gif could see the thin scar that spanned it.

"I swore to my dad that I would get the son of a bitch who stole my mother from him and then killed her. He never recovered. He'd been dead on the inside for decades before he took his final breath." He stabbed the console with his index finger. "I will—I *am*—going to get the fucker responsible for their mutual destruction."

"No matter if—"

Drex cut him off. "I've said it, Gif. I've sworn it. No more questions."

Chapter 15

———⊶◉⊶———

Elaine bobbed her head to the waiter in thanks for the cosmopolitan he set in front of her, then smiled at her companion, who was seated opposite her at the low, round cocktail table. "I'm glad you called."

Jasper said, "I felt terrible about missing last night's dinner. I know how much you had looked forward to it."

"It wasn't the same without you."

"Come now."

She giggled. "It was a lovely evening, but you were missed."

"Thank you." He raised his bourbon highball to her, then took a sip. "Since I couldn't make lunch today, either, I didn't want you to think I was avoiding you."

"It never occurred to me to think that. The important thing is that you're feeling better. Was it ghastly?"

"I'll be avoiding oysters for a while."

"Poor baby." She sipped from her martini glass. "What's Talia up to this afternoon?"

"Absolutely nothing. She had an appointment earlier today. When she got home, she excused herself and went upstairs to take a nap."

"Was she all right?"

He leaned forward and whispered, "I think she might be a bit hung over from last night."

Elaine grinned knowingly. "It wouldn't surprise me. She's not a heavy drinker, or as conditioned as I am. We killed two bottles of wine over dinner, and, before that, Drex gave her a generous pour on a vodka martini."

Jasper's teeth clenched, but he smiled. "Drex was tending bar?"

"I hosted a happy hour."

"I thought Drex was going to meet you and Talia at the restaurant."

"That was the original plan, but he called and asked if he could come a bit early and bring his manuscript."

"Whatever for?"

"He left it with me to read. Talia didn't tell you?"

"We didn't talk much after she came in. I was up, but still queasy. She shooed me back to bed and slept in the guest room in case I had a virus and not food poisoning." He took unnecessary care readjusting the coaster under his glass. "Odd that Drex asked you to read his book. He's been so protective of it."

"I was flabbergasted! Delighted, but flabbergasted. I'm hardly qualified to critique it."

"I'm sure he asked because you showed such interest in the subject matter and writing process."

"I guess. But if he asked anyone among us to take a look at it, I'd have thought it would be Talia."

He sipped his bourbon, then asked with nonchalance, "Why's that?"

"She's so much brainier. I'm not the intellectual that she is."

He *tsk*ed. "You don't give yourself enough credit. Besides, I doubt Drex's novel is that complex and literary."

"Between you and me, it isn't. I read a few chapters before going to sleep last night, and a few more over my morning coffee. I'm surprised that it isn't…hmm…what's the word? Heftier?"

"Heftier will do. But in what way isn't it hefty?"

"I don't know how to explain it. He's so..."

Jasper tilted his head. "So...?"

"Well, manly."

"The book doesn't reflect his manliness?"

"You're goading me," she said, pretending to slap his hand. "But the truth is, no, it doesn't shout masculinity. I mean, it does, but not to the extent...Oh, I don't know what I mean."

"You expected a book written by him to read differently."

"Yes. It's not as meaty as I thought it would be." She seemed embarrassed to have expressed her opinion and tried to laugh it off. "But who am I to say? It's light fare. Fast paced. Overall, it's enjoyable reading, and that's what I'll tell him when he asks for my feedback. As I said, I'm no critic. Far be it from me to dampen his ambitions, and I wouldn't hurt his feelings for the world."

"Which may be why he asked you to read the novel instead of Talia. She would have been candid in pointing out its weaknesses."

"No doubt you're right, and that would not have set well. Already they rub each other the wrong way."

As she drained her glass, she dribbled a bit on her chin and was now dabbing at it with her napkin. Otherwise she might have noticed that Jasper's right eye ticked in reaction to her last statement.

"Hold that thought," he said and signaled the waiter for another round.

Elaine demurred. "I really shouldn't have two."

"I agree." He gave her a sly wink. "Three minimum."

"You are *bad*."

"My dear," he said silkily, "you have no idea." Then he motioned for her to pick up where she had left off. "You were saying something about Talia and Drex rubbing each other the wrong way?"

"It's probably just me, but—"

"No, I've also noticed it."

She sat forward, her bosom nearly knocking over her empty

martini glass. "You have? I thought I was imagining it. The minute she arrived last night, I sensed the antagonism, and it only got thicker as the night wore on."

"He must have said or done something to offend her."

"I don't think so. He was his charming self."

The waiter arrived with fresh drinks. As soon as he walked away, Jasper asked, "How do you explain this hostility between them?"

"They weren't hostile, exactly. Just not comfortable with each other like they'd been that day on the yacht. Remember, they talked for a long time out on the deck. I thought maybe something had happened that I was unaware of. A disagreement of some kind."

"Not to my knowledge. In fact, we hadn't seen Drex for a couple of days leading up to last night."

"Hmm." She gave an elaborate shrug. "Who can explain why we like some people and detest others? Although Talia's aversion is understandable if you compare Drex to you. You're polished and sophisticated. He's—"

"Manly."

She gave a gusty laugh. "That's not at all what I meant to imply. If Talia weren't in the picture, you'd have dozens of women lined up at your back door bearing casseroles, and I would be leading the charge. You know I adore you."

He placed his hand to his chest and humbly tipped his head.

Smiling at him, she sipped her drink, but as she lowered her glass, her smile became a thoughtful frown. "It's unlike Talia to be snippy. Even with someone she doesn't particularly like."

"Talia? Snippy?"

"I know, right? But on the drive from the restaurant back to my house, she got really short with Drex."

"What provoked it?"

"I have no idea. We were talking about Key West."

With great care, Jasper set his highball glass on the table, then left his fingers cupping the rim and turned the glass idly. "How did that come up?"

"Drex wants to visit Hemingway's house. He asked if we'd been there. It was a casual conversation. And then it wasn't. I'm not sure at what point it went downhill or why it did." She sipped at the ice crystals floating on the surface of her drink. "I think his questions began to pester her."

"Questions?"

"Basic ones that a prospective tourist would ask a travel agent. He kept at it even though she made it clear she didn't want to talk business."

"She didn't want to talk about Key West."

Noticing his shift in tone, Elaine's gaze sharpened on him. "Oh? Why?"

"It's a private matter. Not something that Talia is comfortable talking about, even with me. All I'll say is that she had a client who became a close friend. But the relationship ended abruptly." He paused before adding, "And badly."

"I'm sorry."

"It was a while ago but remains a sensitive topic with her. I trust you'll never bring it up again."

"Of course, Jasper." She picked up her glass and raised it to him. "On the subject of Key West, I'll be as silent as a grave."

Jasper could barely contain an eruption of laughter.

—◦—

"Jasper?"

Talia flipped on the kitchen light and was greeted by a startling sight. Dressed in pajamas, Jasper was crouched on the floor, running his hand along the baseboard beneath the cabinet. "What on earth are you doing?"

He came to his feet, dusting his hands. "I dropped an ice cube." He shaded his eyes against the overhead light. "Please switch that off. I think we're being watched."

"Watched?"

"Turn off the light, Talia."

She didn't appreciate his imperious tone but did as asked, then waited for him to explain his bizarre behavior.

He asked, "Have you been asleep all afternoon and evening?"

"No, I woke up to an empty house. I found the note you left on my dressing table. You and Elaine must have been enjoying yourselves. Your get-together for drinks extended into the dinner hour." She looked at the clock on the stove. "And beyond."

"I called to invite you to join us. Your phone went to voice mail."

"Oh. Right," she said with chagrin. "I silenced it when I lay down and forgot to turn it back on."

"Assuming you were asleep, I left you in peace rather than call on the house phone."

She nodded absently. "How was Elaine?"

"Enlightening. Did you skip dinner?"

"No. After reading your note, I ate a peanut butter sandwich and went back to bed. When did you get home?"

"An hour ago. Give or take."

"I didn't hear you."

"You were virtually unconscious."

She must've been. She felt as though she were coming out of a coma and discovering that while she'd been out, everything had gone awry. Nothing felt right or familiar, in particular this disjointed conversation with Jasper. He was prowling the room, stopping at every window to look outside.

She shook her head to try to clear the lingering cobwebs. "Are you going to tell me what's going on? What did you mean when you said we're being watched? Watched by whom?"

"By Drex."

Her heart gave a telltale bump. She'd returned home from their encounter in the parking garage shaken to her core by what he'd professed, by the kiss. She'd taken a mild sedative in the hope of sleeping off the conflicting emotions that assailed her. They'd run the gamut from fury—*how dare he?*—to shame. Even now, she felt the tingling, throbbing effects of that kiss.

She looked in the direction of the garage apartment and remembered standing at the living area window, looking through the branches of the live oak, and realizing that the rooms on the back of their house were open to his view. "Why would you think he's watching us?"

"Let's sit." There was enough ambient light for them to see their way around. They sat adjacent to each other at the dining table. "I think Drex Easton is a fraud at best. At worst…doesn't bear thinking."

"Jasper—"

"Hear me out."

Her heart was beating abnormally fast. Her hands had turned cold and clammy, made even more noticeable when Jasper reached for her right one and clasped it between his.

He said, "Elaine told me she's reading Drex's book, and that it's dreadful."

"She said that?"

"She put it a bit more kindly."

"Does she intend to tell him that?"

"Elaine wouldn't be that blunt. Even if she were, I don't think he gives a damn about her opinion or anyone else's. I don't think he's a writer at all."

"But he works at it. I've seen him. So have you."

He gave his head a hard shake. "He's pretending. He's only posing to be a writer until he finds someone, specifically a woman of Elaine's ilk, to support him."

While she didn't want to believe it, she herself had virtually accused Drex of having those intentions. "He has been tight-lipped about his work."

"About everything."

"But why a writer? If he's going for seduction, there are occupations much more fascinating and exhilarating."

"But not as easy to emulate. It's one occupation where he doesn't have to exhibit any notable skills. All he has to do is sit on his ass all day."

"I've seen him working. The day I went over to give him the list of restaurants, he was immersed in something on his computer."

"Are you sure it was his novel?"

"He said it was."

"Did you see what was on the monitor?"

"No. He closed the laptop."

"He could have been immersed in pornography. Online poker. Anything." He looked down at the hand he held in his. "Speaking of that day, Talia, did anything improper happen while you were over there?"

"No."

He lifted his gaze to hers. It was an effort for her to stare back without blinking. She could practically feel the brush of Drex's thumb against the corner of her mouth.

"The reason I ask," Jasper said, "is because Elaine also told me there was a strain between Drex and you last night, a hostility that became more palpable as the evening progressed. Was she imagining that?"

"No."

He looked at her as though expecting her to elaborate.

"I'm thirsty." Withdrawing her hand, she got up and went to the fridge. "Would you like a bottle of water?"

"No thank you."

She returned to the table with one, twisted off the cap, and took a drink.

"Talia? How do you explain this tension between you and Drex?"

"He brought up Key West. Not in a random way, either. And he wouldn't drop the subject."

"Yes, I know."

She jerked to attention.

"I heard all about it from Elaine. Nothing of it from you. Why didn't you tell me this the moment you got home last night?"

"Because whenever the subject of Marian arises, we both become upset. Drex's persistence unnerved me, but, in hindsight, I believe he only mentioned Key West in the context of wanting to visit the Hemingway house. Nothing more."

Jasper sat as still as a stone, but he wasn't as contained as he seemed. She could hear each deep inhale through his nose, each exhale. "I'm not so sure. Elaine said he pestered you with questions."

"I told him I didn't particularly like the place, he prodded me to tell him why. Rapid-fire questions. It was as though..."

"What?"

"It felt like he was trying to spark a reaction, make me blurt out something."

"Do you think he knows something about Marian?"

"No. Maybe, Jasper." She withdrew her hand from his and used it to rub her forehead. "I don't know."

"He's living next door, Talia," he hissed. "I should have known about this immediately."

"I didn't tell you because I predicted you would respond exactly as you are. You're jumping to a conclusion that has no real basis. You've mistrusted Drex from the start."

"As it turns out, with good reason."

"We don't know that!" she exclaimed in a stage whisper. "His mention of Key West triggered a response from me, and he noticed. I tried to shoot the topic down."

"But he persisted."

"Only to be obnoxious. Honestly, I think that's all there was to it."

And she did. Because this morning Drex had dismissed the idea of going there any time soon, and there hadn't seemed to be an ulterior motive to his mentioning it. In fact, she'd started the exchange by asking about his proposed trip.

But she couldn't tell Jasper about that conversation without telling him that Drex had followed her to the medical building. Knowing about that would reinforce his suspicion.

He'd been ruminating and now said, "Key West came up toward the conclusion of the evening. Elaine picked up on antagonistic vibes as soon as you arrived at her townhouse."

"I had told him about Elaine's history with men, of her falling hard and getting hurt. I warned him against romancing her. Last night, he flaunted that he was doing just that. He was positively oily."

"How did Elaine respond?"

"As expected. She was eating out of his hand."

Elaine's receptiveness to his flirtation came as no surprise. What Talia couldn't reconcile was the man she'd been with this morning and the Casanova of last night, who had irritated her no end.

Now, however, it seemed like a caricature, a part overplayed, and which had led to nothing. Because if he had so much as kissed Elaine before she'd arrived at the townhouse, Elaine would have found an opportunity by now to describe it to her with enthusiasm and in minute detail.

No, he hadn't kissed Elaine. He had wasted the romantic staging in Elaine's living room and, instead, had kissed her in a parking garage, a setting hardly conducive to romance. He might have been role-playing last night, but there hadn't been any artifice in his manner this morning. He'd been all too real. Every aspect of him. His anguish. *It's making me crazy.* Certainly his desire. *I'm damn well going to make it count.*

And he had. With fervency and finesse, he had penetrated more than her mouth. He had tapped into a deep-seated loneliness she hadn't realized was so acute until his own raw need had roused it and caused within her a strong tug of yearning. She could never be alone with him again.

"After today, I won't have anything to do with him."

"After *today?*"

She flinched at the sound of Jasper's voice and, too late, realized her slip. "Now that I've slept on it," she said. "Until Drex moves out, we'll keep our distance. Problem solved."

"Is it? I'm not as ready as you are to dismiss the Key West thing as a coincidence. The way Elaine described his interest, it seemed excessive."

"Did she pick up on your concern? Can I expect a call from her tomorrow, asking for the lowdown?"

"I told her it was a private and sensitive matter, and asked her never to mention it again. She promised not to."

Talia groaned.

"What?"

"Elaine loves intrigue. All you've done is entice her. She'll demand the lowdown."

"If she brings it up, shrug it off. Give her a drink, and tell her I made too much of it."

"Which you are."

He looked through the window. No lights were on inside the garage apartment. It was an indistinct dark form among the shadows. "We'll keep our distance from him," Jasper said. "If he's merely the man next door, he'll get the message and stop making overtures. If he's more than that, he'll make a nuisance of himself. That's when we'll know."

"We won't *know*."

"Strongly suspect, then. If he continues to come around, it will confirm my suspicion, and we'll be forced to take some drastic measures."

Alarmed, she said, "Like what?"

He patted her hand. "We'll wait and see. In the meantime, I've taken the precaution of changing the alarm code."

"That's unnecessary, Jasper. You're overreacting."

"Better safe than sorry. The new code is our anniversary date numerically, except backward. Got it?"

"Yes." She recited the sequence.

"Good. Don't forget it." He pushed back his chair and stood. "For now, let's go to bed."

"You go. I slept most of the day away. I think I'll read for a while. Maybe watch a movie."

"Then I'll say good night." He bent down and kissed her cheek, but as he moved away, she reached for his hand.

"Wait. There's something else. Something you should know." She wished he weren't standing over her. Looking up at him at an awkward angle made this all the more difficult. "I have a confession."

"Regarding Drex?"

"Yes." Her voice came out husky. She wet her lips. "He...he..."

"What?"

She lowered her head, took a deep breath, and, in a nanosecond, reversed her previous decision. "You asked if anything happened that day when I went over to his apartment."

"Anything improper."

"It wasn't improper, but something did happen. I offered to read his manuscript. He declined. No, not declined. Refused. Outright."

"Probably because he feared exposure as an imposter."

"Possibly. But the point is, when I arrived at Elaine's townhouse last night, found him there, learned that he had given her his manuscript to read, I behaved childishly. I was insulted that he had solicited her opinion over mine. That was the source of the tension."

"He rejected you, but was paying court to Elaine. You were jealous."

"Resentful, at least. I told you it was childish."

"But not a stoning offense," he said, chucking her under the chin.

Despite the playful gesture, his choice of words was troubling. In some cultures, one stoning offense was adultery.

"Remember to keep the lights off in the rooms within sight of his apartment."

He was almost through the door when she stopped him again. "I think I'll go to Atlanta for a few days."

The spur-of-the-moment decision was made almost simultaneous to her declaring it. Jasper turned. His face was in shadow, but she sensed that his expression was inquisitive, if not suspicious.

She said, "That new boutique hotel I told you about? It sounds like something my clients would flock to. I think I'll go and see if it lives up to the hype."

He said nothing for an interminable time, then, "Ordinarily you plan your business trips well in advance. The suddenness of this one is uncustomary, but it's in perfect keeping with your mood of late."

"My mood?"

"You haven't been yourself, Talia."

Tartly, she said, "Neither have you, Jasper."

"Me? In what way?"

"Not in a way I can put my finger on. But something."

He retraced his steps back to her. "Is the honeymoon over?"

"I could ask you the same."

"Why would you?"

"Because I suspect you're having an affair with Elaine." There, she'd said it.

"Don't be ridiculous."

"That's what every cheating partner says when accused."

"You're being preposterous. I am *not* sleeping with Elaine. Good God."

His denial didn't prompt her to back down or withdraw the allegation. She held his self-righteous glare.

Sounding frustrated, he said, "I'm not having an affair, but you're right. We need to get back on an even keel. A change of scenery would do us good. I'll come with you to Atlanta."

"Come with me?"

"Is that such an outrageous notion?"

"No, not at all. You're always welcome to come along, but you rarely do. I can't remember the last time you did."

"I've read about this place, and it does sound special. It poached a superstar chef away from a New York restaurant. We'll have each other to ourselves. No Elaine chattering a mile a minute. No bothersome neighbor," he said shooting a glance out the back window. "I don't see a downside to us enjoying time to ourselves."

The downside was that she would prefer to spend those several days alone. She needed time to think about the implications of her doctor's visit this morning and to reflect on the destabilizing events that had taken place since Sunday when she'd gone yachting on the *Laney Belle* and met Drex Easton.

She also needed to isolate a reason for the vague uneasiness that had plagued her for several months now. A premonition of doom was her constant companion, and that was a complete turnaround from the optimist outlook she'd always had. She'd arrived at no explanation for this gradual but inexorable reversal, but if the erosion of her marriage was the cause, that was reason enough to spend quality time with Jasper and try to get them back on track.

She smiled up at him. "That sounds lovely."

"Make the reservation."

"When do you want to go?"

He stroked her cheek, pushed back a strand of her hair, and curled his hand around her throat. "Tomorrow."

Chapter 16

⚜

Long after Jasper's final word, "Tomorrow," Drex sat, staring through the darkness at nothing. Like a prizefighter who'd received a knockout jab and had made a hard landing, it took a while for him to come around.

But when at last he did, it was with a jolt of furious energy. He whipped off the headset, picked up his cell phone, and placed a call.

Gif answered sleepily. "I didn't think you were speaking to me."

"Where are you staying?"

Gif gave him the name of the motel.

"What room?"

"You're coming now?"

"As soon as I can get there."

"Has something happened?"

"It's them."

"It's them?" He sounded wide awake now. "How do you know?"

"The bug. I was listening. Heard a lot."

Gif processed that. "You said 'them.' Her, too?"

Drex unlocked his jaw enough to say, "Her, too."

He dressed in darkness, added the surveillance equipment to the duffel bag, and took it with him. He felt his way down the staircase, then scurried along the far side of the garage to the back. Peering around the rear corner of the building, he halfway expected to see Jasper charging across the lawn after him as before.

He watched and waited, remaining so still he could feel the blood pumping through his veins, hear his heartbeat thudding against his eardrums. Supercharged by adrenaline and anger, remaining motionless was torture. But he stayed as he was for five long minutes. The Ford house remained dark.

"Sleep tight," he whispered as he slipped into the darkness.

He picked his way through the green belt that buffered the Arnott property from the street behind it. It was a moonless night. The atmosphere was laden with humidity. A light mist felt like cobwebs against his face. When he reached the street, he struck out at a dead run and covered the mile to the nearest convenience store in under six minutes.

There, mindful of security cameras, he pulled the hood of his windbreaker over his head, shuffled up to the counter, and asked the cashier if he could use his phone to call for a taxi. "My battery's drained." Never looking up from his hot rod magazine, the guy slid his cell phone across the counter.

It took twice as long for the taxi to get to the convenience store as it did to cover the distance to the motel. Drex asked to be dropped off at an apartment complex across the freeway from it. He paid the driver in cash, waited for him to get out of sight, then crossed the road to the motel.

Gif had texted him the room number. It was on the ground floor. Drex rapped softly on the door, heard the bolt, the chain, then Gif opened the door a crack. Moving aside to let Drex in, he said, "I didn't dress up." He was in boxers, a white t-shirt, black socks. He secured the door, then went over to the dresser, pulled a can of beer from the plastic webbing, and extended it to Drex.

"I could use a belt of whiskey."

"No whiskey."

"Then never mind." Drex took off his windbreaker, pulled a chair from beneath the table for two in front of the window, and sat down. He propped his elbows on his knees and used all ten fingers to hold back his hair. The adrenaline was wearing off.

Gif sat on the edge of the unmade bed. "I didn't hear your car."

"I left it at the apartment so they wouldn't know I was gone." He explained how he'd gotten there.

Gif asked, "You sure you weren't tailed?"

"Of course I'm sure. I made sure."

Gif looked him over and noticed that his clothes were damp. "Is it raining?"

Drex raised his head. "You want a weather report?"

Gif opened his mouth as though to retort, but thought better of it and closed his mouth with an audible click of teeth.

Drex said a few choice words directed toward himself. He took a deep breath, let it out. "I'm sorry, man."

"Doesn't matter."

"Yeah, it does. I'm sorry. Thanks for being here."

Gif bobbed his head, then took a sudden interest in the loose cuticle on his thumb. "You're sure she's in on it?"

"Hear for yourself."

Drex took the receiver/recorder from the canvas duffel, connected it to the audio feed of the headset, and passed it to Gif. "I think you'll find the conversation telling."

He left Gif to listen and went into the bathroom. He used the toilet and splashed cold water on his face. He gave his image in the mirror a look of sheer disgust. "Even now, you'd fuck her if given the chance, wouldn't you? Dumb bastard." He tossed the towel onto the floor and opened the door.

Gif was still listening, but his expression didn't give away his opinion of what he was hearing. Drex returned to his chair at the table and used a new burner phone to call Mike.

He answered with a growl. "Who's this?"

"Is this phone secure?"

"It goes through about five rerouters. Should be okay."

"Were you asleep?"

"No. I'm watching the people who're watching me."

"Gif filled me in on Rudkowski. I'm sorry as hell, Mike. When we started this, you gave me fair warning that you wouldn't help me dig my own grave or climb in with me."

"That's what I said, but I didn't mean it." He snorted what passed for a laugh. "Actually, it's kinda fun. They're out there in their van, eating cold pizza and scratching their balls. I had a pork loin with all the trimmings. Bottle of wine. I've got all the comforts of home. Still have my toys, too."

"They haven't served a search warrant?"

"Rudkowski is blowing smoke. He knows the chance of finding anything on my computers is nil. If he made good on his threat to search, he'd be left with nothing to show for it. He wouldn't be stupid enough to go through with it, because he'd never live down being made such a fool of."

"But you've still got a team watching you."

"Not cowboys. Old guys they wouldn't trust with any other duty."

"Could you get away without getting caught?"

"Skip out?"

"Skip town."

"Sure. But that's all the excuse Rudkowski would need to put a noose around my neck. And if he did, I'd be no good to you. So why would I want to skip?"

"We have them."

That he announced it without inflection or fanfare gave it more impact than if he'd shouted it with glee. Continuing in that manner, he gave Mike a broad-strokes version of what had taken place.

When he finished, Mike said, "So, her, too, huh?"

"Yeah."

For once Mike showed that he had a human side after all. He didn't follow with *I told you so.* "Okay. So now what?"

"Stand by. Gif is listening to the conversation now. We'll get back to you."

Drex had a few questions for Google. By the time he'd gotten the info he needed, Gif was removing the headset. Drex looked at him expectantly.

"Not to dash cold water on this, Drex, but it's a long way from a smoking gun or signed confession. It was illegally obtained, which makes it inadmissible in—"

"I know all that."

"Rudkowski would cook us and serve us in Quantico's cafeteria."

"Mike referenced a noose."

"Neither appeals to me." Gif fiddled with the headset as he mulled over this new development. "Do you think he's doing Elaine Conner?"

"I don't know, but it wouldn't surprise me. They're chummy."

"The Ford marriage sounds wobbly, if not rocky."

"Doesn't mean they aren't partners in crime. Or at least they were when they killed Marian Harris."

"But did they?" Gif brandished the headset. "This isn't solid enough to issue them a parking ticket. Nobody, not the FBI, *nobody* would touch it. In fact, if we pass this along as evidence or even probable cause, any law officer in the land would laugh his ass off and then arrest us for violation of the privacy act."

"Which is why we must proceed as we have been. On our own. Under the radar."

Gif grimaced and tossed the headset onto the bed. "Drex—"

"Get Mike on the phone. Please."

When they were on speaker, Drex addressed Mike. "Tomorrow the lovely couple next door are going on a getaway to Atlanta. I need you to find out the name of a new boutique hotel that poached a chef from a restaurant in New York. If you can—"

"The Lotus."

"What?"

"That's the hotel. I read an online article about the chef."

Gif and Drex looked at each other and, in spite of the grim circumstances, smiled.

"Okay. Thanks," Drex said. "Can you get there by tomorrow afternoon?"

"To Atlanta?"

"Don't ask like that. Ever been there?"

"No."

"It's nice."

"It's nice where I am."

"You can't leave a trail, which means you can't fly. You'll have to drive."

"How far is it?"

"Far. Google says almost four hundred miles." Mike grumbled something unintelligible. Drex said, "I'm not in the mood to argue about it, Mike. It's six hours in the car. You can snack all the way. Will you do it or not? If not, good night."

After a brief silence, Mike said, "What do I do when I get there?"

"Check into The Lotus. Make a reservation tonight."

"It's costly."

"I'll pay."

"It's the weekend. What if it's booked up?" Gif asked.

"Child's play," Mike said. "I'll hack their system and cancel somebody's reservation." He paused. "I don't suppose you're sending me there to sample the five-star cuisine."

"I'm sending you there to keep tabs on the Fords."

"Are you nuts?" Gif exclaimed. "He couldn't fade into the woodwork if they had a sequoia growing in the hotel lobby."

"He's not your typical undercover operative, no," Drex said. "He's obese and ugly—"

"I'm still here," Mike said.

"—which is why no one would take him for a spy."

Drex wanted Mike in Atlanta, but not only for the reason stated. He also wanted him out of Lexington. If the shit went down, he didn't want Mike to be within Rudkowski's reach. Eventually he would corral them, but Drex didn't want to make it easy for him.

Gif, in his reasonable manner, suggested that he be sent to Atlanta instead. "I'm already in a neighboring state."

"Yes, but Charleston is roughly a hundred and fifty miles farther. I checked. Besides, if Talia saw you, she might remember you from the coffee shop."

"He's unmemorable," Mike said. "And what's that about the coffee shop?"

"We'll tell you later," Drex said, impatience mounting. "Mike, can Sammy get you an untraceable car by morning?"

"With one phone call."

Sammy—Drex wasn't sure which alias was his real last name— was a mechanic who could make a rattletrap run like a Porsche. Early in Mike's career with the bureau, he had been in on the sting that busted Sammy for transporting stolen merchandise across state lines.

Sammy had served time, but, by the time of his release, Mike was working with Drex and had seen the advantages of cultivating a relationship with a guy like Sammy, someone who was only a little crooked. They'd used Sammy and his larcenous automotive know-how more than a few times.

"The tricky part will be making the swap," Mike said. "But Sammy is creative."

"Leave as early as possible," Drex said. "I'd like you in place by check-in time."

"I'll be missed when I don't show up for work."

"Hold on, you two," Gif said. "Please. This plan has pitfalls I can see from here."

After a few more minutes of back-and-forthing, Drex called an end to it, saying, "Either you're in or out, guys. If you want out, no hard feelings. But tell me now or shut up."

Neither said anything.

After a moment, Drex resumed. "Mike, I don't know for sure how long they're staying. You'll have to find that out somehow. I'll need to know when they're on their way back. "

Gif looked around his motel room. "In the meantime, what's my job?"

"Hang around until, or if, I need you for backup, and then come running."

"What'll you be doing?" Gif asked.

"Tearing their fucking house apart."

Mike and Gif put up another argument that lasted for half an hour. But Drex was resolute. While the Fords were whiling away a few days in the luxury hotel, he would have access to their house, ergo to their lives.

He was going to search exhaustively until he found something that linked them to Marian Harris. The photo taken on her yacht wasn't indicting. The authorities in Florida had used it to identify Jasper, aka Daniel Knolls, when Marian first went missing. He'd been interviewed by police and subsequently released.

Drex now wondered if Talia had also been questioned. He made a mental note to follow up with Deputy Gray.

He relegated that to the back burner of his mind and concentrated on what today might hold in store. His cohorts begged him to reconsider going inside the Fords' home. They cited that it was a crime. They enumerated the obstacles he'd likely confront. Security alarm. Nanny cams.

"Hell, this freako might've booby-trapped the place," Mike said.

"I wouldn't put it past him," Drex said. "I'll be careful."

"Say you get in without any trouble, and it turns out to be a gold mine of evidence," Gif said. "What good is it going to do us? Anything you find will be inadmissible."

"Anything I find will justify my killing him."

That had shut them up.

After signing off with Mike, Gif packed his things in preparation of moving to another motel. "With a credit card no one knows I have," he assured Drex.

The two of them left together in Gif's car. Dawn was just about to break, but the difference between it and the night was negligible. The overcast was solid. Precipitation alternated between an all-out rain and a mist now heavy enough to make windshield wipers necessary.

Drex directed Gif to the convenience store. "Let me out there. I'll go the rest of the way on foot."

"You sure?"

"I don't want my nosy neighbors to see you dropping me off." Gif pulled over. Drex said, "Call me with your new location."

"As soon as I'm checked in."

Drex reached for the door handle, but Gif said suddenly, "Listen, Drex. I gave you some grief about her, but I had started hoping, for your sake, that we were wrong."

Drex didn't react except to say a brusque "I'll be in touch." He got out, shut the door, and tapped the roof of the car twice. Only as Gif was driving away did he murmur, "Thanks, buddy."

He went into the twenty-four-hour store. A different cashier was on duty. He made his purchase, then set out for the apartment. He was skirting the green belt, looking for a place to cut through that wasn't too overgrown, when he spotted a lone runner on the street, coming from the opposing direction, taking form in the mist.

She must have seen him at about the same time as he saw her because she slowed her pace to a walk. She looked toward the other side of the street, as though considering crossing it to avoid him. But then she squared her shoulders and continued toward him.

He stopped where he was, forcing her to close the distance between them. But he took small satisfaction in that, because, even though he was cold with rage over how thoroughly he'd been duped, the sight of her up close made him hot and hard. Her tights and top were wet from sweat as well as from the elements. They conformed to her like a coat of paint, revealing the shapeliness of her legs, the perfection of her breasts, the small points of her nipples.

Her eyes were the color of the cloudy sky. Like the mist, they held mysteries. Her ponytail hung heavy and damp against the back of her neck. A bead of water dripped off a loose strand of hair at the side of her face and rolled down her cheek like yesterday morning's tear.

Which he'd fallen for. Like a lovesick kid. Like a damned idiot.

He suppressed a rush of renewed anger and said, "You're out early. Couldn't sleep?"

"Thunder woke me up."

"It hasn't thundered."

"Then it must've been something else."

"Must've been." He looked her over, making her aware that he was aware of every curve, dip, distension. "No spin class today?"

"They weren't open yet."

"You could've waited."

"I wanted to get an early start on the day. So did you, apparently." She indicated the grocery sack.

"I needed milk."

"Why didn't you drive?"

"I needed exercise."

"What's that?" She pointed at the duffel bag.

It hung against his side by the shoulder strap. He patted it. "That? That's my bag of tricks."

"I can see you're going to be obtuse."

"Obtuse. Ranks right up there with morose."

She shot him a look of annoyance and gestured as though to say she needed to be on her way. "Have a nice day." She tried to go around him. He sidestepped to block her. "Please let me by."

"Did you tell him?"

"Tell who what?"

He gave her a smile that was insolent and, he hoped, infuriating. "Your husband, Talia. Did you tell Jasper about the kiss?"

Another squaring of shoulders. "Yes."

"Yeah?"

"Of course I told him."

"And what was his reaction?"

"The same as mine."

"Oh, I doubt that."

She read the innuendo in his drawling tone and the snicker that accompanied it. "Go to hell." She tried to move past him, but he blocked her again. "Cut it out, Drex!"

"Jasper was upset?"

"No, not upset. Outraged that you would dare."

"Really? Then why didn't he barge up the stairs, kick in my door, and tear me apart limb by limb?"

"Because he isn't governed by animal impulses."

"Neither am I. If I were, we would have done a hell of a lot more than kiss."

She slapped him. Hard. It smarted like hell, but he only laughed. "You didn't tell him, did you?"

"Stay away from me." She nudged him with her elbow as she went past and took off running.

He turned to watch her, saying under his breath, "Liar."

She stopped and came back around. "What did you say?"

He didn't answer.

Raising her voice she repeated the question, enunciating each word.

By contrast he leaned forward and spoke in a whisper just loud enough for her to hear. "I said 'pants on fire.'"

Chapter 17

Following his three-way call with Drex and Gif, Mike had been unable to sleep. He lay on his bed and stared at the ceiling until daylight, then got up, showered, and dressed without any readjustment of his morning routine.

However, for what he was about to do, he did not have a method for mentally preparing himself.

His breakfast consisted of two toasted bagels with cream cheese and smoked salmon, a bowl of strawberries floating in heavy cream, and three cups of coffee with three teaspoons of sugar each.

Thus stoked, he was as ready as he was ever going to be.

But as he held his cell phone in his palm, he was once again gripped by indecision. For the next few minutes, he did some tough soul searching, telling himself that he could still change his mind.

Ultimately, however, he determined that he was doing the right thing. Without further deliberation, which could produce more doubt, he placed the dreaded call.

A gravelly voice answered. "Rudkowski."

"It's Mike Mallory."

As though waiting for a taunt, Rudkowski didn't say anything.

Had he been shocked speechless? Or was he rigging up a way to record the call? Mike figured both.

Finally Rudkowski said, "And?"

"I think you're an asshole of the most rectal sort."

"You interrupted my breakfast to tell me that?"

"No, I just thought you should know up front what I think of you, in case you didn't know already."

"I had more than an inkling. Now if that's all, my oatmeal is getting cold."

"That ballyhoo you raised about a search warrant? All you achieved was to make me look like a victim of your peevishness and make you look like a douche."

"A matter of opinion."

"It's unanimous. Even the agents you have watching my house would agree. You won't risk a search because you know you won't find anything."

"Maybe I'll get a warrant and maybe I won't. But whatever I decide about that, I'm keeping you under a microscope until I know what's going on. Your crony Gif took time off to have hemorrhoids removed. Really? Hemorrhoids? Nobody in his office remembers complaints of such."

"It's hardly something he would discuss with coworkers over lunch."

"Don't even try to cover for him. His sudden need for surgery coincides with your ringleader's vacation. Vacation," he repeated with scorn. "I know Easton is up to something. You three musketeers are playing with fire, and you're all going to get burned. Again."

Rudkowski had given him an opening. He took it. "That's why I called you." He let that hover to be certain he had Rudkowski's undivided attention. "Drex *is* up to something. And this time, I think he's..." He paused, took a deep breath. "What he's about to do could have serious repercussions. For all of us, but especially for him."

"What's he about to do? Where is he?"

"Un-huh. Before I tell you anything, we've got to strike a bargain."

"No bargain."

"Then enjoy your oatmeal."

"Wait! All right. What kind of bargain?"

"Drex gets a scolding, nothing more. You've got to promise me that you won't come down hard on him. He hasn't done anything yet. He's only talked about it."

"I promise."

Mike laughed. "You agreed way too fast, Rudkowski. You think I'd trust that?"

"I give you my word."

"Like that counts for shit. I want it in writing."

Rudkowski thought it over. "I'll be as lenient as I can be. That's the best I can offer. It's not just me you've got to worry about, you know."

"But your influence—"

"Will only go so far. They don't call it a *bureau* for nothing. I've got to account to my higher-ups here in Louisville."

Mike knew that to be the truth. "I guess that'll have to be good enough."

"Do we have a deal?"

"Yes. But I want witnesses to my voluntary surrender of information. I'll turn over everything I have, but not before getting your sign-off on it, plus passes for Drex, Gif, and me."

"Easton won't thank you."

"That's what kept me awake last night. He'll be pissed. But I hope I can convince him that he still has my loyalty. We share a commitment to getting this guy and putting him away."

Rudkowski scoffed. "'This guy.' Nobody has proved there is a guy."

"There's a guy. You just don't want to think so because you haven't identified and captured him yourself. While he's out there rooking and killing women, you'll shuffle paper and look busy until the day you can retire."

"While Easton is a man of action."

He said it derisively, but Mike smiled. "You're making my argument for me, Rudkowski. You've always put your resentment of Drex ahead of getting the bad guy. This creep is real, and I hope to God Drex eventually nails him." He hesitated.

"But this time feels different, and it spooks me. I've felt it from the start, but new information has recently come to light. We're talking about one sick dude, not just a con man. Gif has had a bad feeling, too, and we told Drex we did."

"But he thinks he's smarter than everybody."

"He's definitely smarter than you," Mike said. "But he's also single-minded and hardheaded. In typical Drex mode, he's latched on to this intel and is running with it. I'm scared he's running toward a cliff at full throttle, and, if he goes over, he'll crash land. I told him that I wouldn't help him dig his own grave. Or mine, either. And I'm not getting any younger." He paused, cleared his throat. "I love him like a kid brother. But this time the stakes for stepping out of line are just too damn high."

"You're doing the right and responsible thing."

Reverting to his customary snarl, Mike rebuked him. "Don't sound so goddamn pious, Rudkowkski. You've already peed down your leg over this. Relish the moment. Have your field day. But I'm not feeling a bit good about what I'm doing. I'm betraying my best friend, even if it is for his own good."

Rudkowski had the good sense not to offer another platitude.

Mike took a deep breath and sounded like a bellows when he exhaled it. "Shit, let's get this done. We'll meet at my office. I like the idea of having witnesses who like me better than you."

"When?"

"I'll leave now. Before I change my mind." He glanced at his wall clock. "I usually don't head to work this early. Will your watchdogs let me out of my driveway?"

"I'll call them. See you soon."

They disconnected. Five minutes later, Mike placed another call. Drex answered after the first ring. "Did it work?"

"Like a charm," Mike said. "I'm on my way to Atlanta. Sammy said to tell you hi."

———

Drex called Gif to report their success. "Mike must have laid it on thick, because Rudkowski fell for it. Imagine when he showed up at Mike's office ready to get the goods."

He told Gif that Mike had given Rudkowski just enough time to call the men watching his house and then had raised his garage door so they could see his car and think that he was about to leave as planned.

He'd carried out an armful of files—filled with back issues of epicurean magazines—and placed them in the passenger seat. He'd then gone back into the house and carried out a box—with back issues of *Wine Spectator*—which he placed in the back seat.

He'd gone inside the house again…and out the back door. He'd walked through the houses behind his. Sammy had been waiting on the next street in a standard gray car that looked like every other make and model of standard gray car.

"Motor was running," Drex told Gif. "Mike got in. They were off."

"I wonder how long it took before those agents realized he'd split?"

"I don't know, but whenever Rudkowski learned about it, he would've combusted."

"I get the feeling that this escape plan wasn't hatched by Mike."

Drex snuffled. "I know you advised me to stop pricking with Rudkowski, but—"

"But you can't resist a chance to get his goat."

"The important thing is, Mike is out from under his thumb."

"What if they canvass the neighborhood? Somebody could have noticed Sammy and remember the car."

"We took that into account. Sammy drove Mike to a picnic area a few miles outside of town where he'd left another car. Mike preferred the gray sedan, but Sammy argued that it might not be as *standard* as it looked."

"Hot?"

"Mike didn't ask. Anyway, he's Atlanta bound in a midnight blue minivan."

The summary had taken longer than was necessary to relay the facts. They were dancing around the subject that overrode all others. Gif seemed as reluctant to bring it up as Drex was to address it.

Gif gave in first. "Have you seen them stirring this morning?"

"No." Since Gif had asked about "them," collectively, it wasn't exactly a lie of omission that Drex didn't tell him about his dawn encounter with Talia. "But I listened in on their breakfast. Jasper told her he was going to let his meal settle and then go to the club for a swim. She asked if he was packed. He said he would pack when he got back from the club, leading me to think they're not leaving until this afternoon."

"Could be they're going to drive."

"No, they agreed they could get by without checking luggage. Delta has direct flights at three forty-six and five-nineteen. I'm thinking they'll be on one of those, but we won't know which until they leave the house. Any time past two o'clock would put them in a tight squeeze to make the three forty-six."

"Are they driving themselves?"

"They didn't say, but I'll call you as they're leaving. Be ready to move. I want you stationed at the airport, near security to confirm that they go through."

"Without her seeing me."

"Without her seeing you."

"And you?"

"I'll follow them in my car as far as the airport to make sure that's where they're headed. If they take another direction, I'll continue following until you can catch up with me. If they do go to the airport, I'll let you know to watch for them, then I'll circle around, come back here, and—"

"Break and enter."

"With any luck I won't have to break anything." Gif didn't respond to the quip. Drex sighed. "Don't start again."

"It's risky, Drex. Why take such a chance?"

"Because we've established that legal channels are closed, and I don't know any other way."

"Okay. But you don't have to go it alone. After I see them off, why don't I join the search? Another pair of eyes and hands would halve the time it will take."

"Nope. It's my plan, so my neck is the only one on the block. Besides, if I'm caught, I'll need you to rush in waving your badge and getting me out of hock with the local cops."

"I'd rather you not get caught."

"Goes without saying."

"What are you doing now?"

He was doing what he'd been doing since his exchange with Talia at dawn: wishing that Jasper *had* rushed up the stairs and kicked in his door. He wished Jasper *had* tried tearing him limb from limb. He would have demonstrated to him and his lying wife what animal impulses unleashed looked like.

But to Gif he said, "Killing time till they leave."

⸻

He paced. He sat. He eavesdropped on the Fords' intermittent conversations as they came and went from the kitchen, but nothing substantive had come from those exchanges. If Talia had told Jasper about seeing him that morning, and what had been said, she'd done so outside his hearing. The climate between the two of them seemed to have warmed from what it had been the night before.

It gave Drex no pleasure to speculate on what had brought that about.

At 10:05, Jasper left the house alone. He returned at 12:36.

Knowing that they could be leaving at any time soon after that, Drex posted himself at the window and began an uninterrupted vigil. At 2:07, his phone buzzed. He answered. Gif said, "The five nineteen flight?"

"Looks like. Stand by."

Three o'clock rolled around. Three fifteen arrived, and still there was no sign of them. By 3:22, with Drex on the verge of imploding, Jasper's car backed out of the garage.

Drex called Gif. "They're rolling."

"Car service?"

"He's driving."

"On it."

They clicked off. Drex watched to see which way the car turned out of the driveway, then waited at the door and counted slowly to fifty before bounding down the stairs.

He didn't pick up their tail until he reached a major thoroughfare and saw their car stopped at a traffic light. Several cars were between them. He slowed down to let more pass him to create a safer barrier without blocking them from sight. He followed them across the bridge into Charleston, then north on the freeway toward the airport.

Jasper stayed within the speed limit and stuck to the outside lane, making him easy to follow. When Jasper signaled to take the airport exit off the freeway, Drex called Gif. "Looks like it's a go. You in place?"

"Trying not to make myself conspicuous to ATF."

"We're here. Hang on." Staying a discreet distance behind Jasper, Drex followed him toward the parking garages and reported to Gif when Jasper entered the short-term one directly across the street from the terminal. "They should be coming your way in a matter of minutes."

"Roger that. Eyes peeled."

"I'm on my way back to the house."

He decided to go in through the screened porch, the obvious reason being that it couldn't be seen from the street. But, also, that was the area of the house with which he was most familiar.

The latch on the screen door didn't present a challenge. He pulled on a pair of latex gloves and had the flimsy lock busted within seconds. The lock on the solid back door took longer to pick, but he managed it easily enough. Then, with Mike's foreboding about booby traps in mind, he held his breath and pushed open the door. The alarm began to beep. He punched in the new code as he'd heard Talia recite it the night before.

The beeping ceased.

He closed the door. Moving from window to window in the kitchen, he scanned various sections of the property, looking for a sign that he'd been spotted. But there was no movement except for rainwater dripping from the eaves and causing ripples in the puddles beneath.

Satisfied that he'd gotten inside without detection, he let out his breath, and that exhalation was the only sound in the house. The silence was absolute. No ticking clock or hum of an electrical appliance, no gentle whirring of air passing through a vent. Nothing.

Adding to the eeriness of the silence was the gloom. Blinds and shutters had been left open, but the dreary day had created a premature dusk. The light that did leak into the house was so feeble, Drex had to give his eyes time to adjust to the dimness.

When Mike had recovered the real estate listing for the house, he'd printed out the included floor plan. Drex had familiarized himself with it so, even though he'd only been in a few of the downstair rooms, he knew the layout of the house. He made his way from the kitchen, through the formal dining room, and into the two-story foyer where the main staircase curved gracefully upward to the second floor.

He had decided to begin upstairs, do a general walk-through to see what each room consisted of and determine what it might yield, then search the spaces one by one in order of priority.

He climbed the stairs to the landing. Extending from it was a wide hallway, and midway down it, a set of double doors. He pushed them open and stepped into the master suite. Moving his gaze from left to right, he took in the entire room, mentally cataloguing the furnishings. The bed was positioned even with the double doorway and directly in front of him. He walked over and stood at the foot of it.

They'd left it made, decorative throw pillows attractively placed. Identical night tables bracketed the upholstered headboard. The items on them indicated who slept on which side of the bed. On Jasper's were a lamp and alarm clock only. On Talia's were a matching lamp and alarm clock, but also a crystal tray holding several pieces of jewelry, which she must have removed just before climbing into bed. Drex recognized the bracelet and a pair of gold hoop earrings that she'd worn to dinner on Thursday night.

A crystal pump bottle contained what appeared to be hand lotion. He told himself not to, but he rounded the end of the bed, leaned down, and sniffed. It was her fragrance, and it caused a twinge of longing. He cursed himself for being a damn fool.

Not allowing himself to dwell on the evidence of marital domesticity, he rapidly looked through the drawers of her night table. A hardcover fiction book, a paperback travel book on Norway, a box of personalized stationery in the name of Talia Shafer. Not Ford. That gave him a small sense of satisfaction.

The drawers contained nothing remarkable or intensely personal. Thank God. He couldn't have borne that. But maybe Jasper kept the sex toys in his nightstand.

Drex moved to that side of the bed and opened the drawers one by one. He didn't find items used for sexual enhancement or kinky bedroom antics. He didn't find anything. Nothing. Nada. The drawers were empty. He tapped on the back of the piece to see if it was false. It seemed solid, and the inside dimensions of the drawer matched those of the outside.

He looked under the bed. No doubt Jasper would find that highly amusing. There was nothing there.

Next he went to a chest of drawers. The first drawer he opened attested that it was Jasper's. Undershorts—an expensive name brand—were folded and lined up in rows that a seasoned valet would have been challenged to match in terms of straightness. The sock drawer was the same. In one drawer, the arrangement of silk pocket handkerchiefs looked like a canvas of modern art.

Drex was tempted to upend each drawer on the floor, if for no other reason than to make a mess in Jasper's pristine environment. He decided to wait until he had finished his overview, but damned if he wasn't going to start with this drawer of fancy hankies.

Jasper's closet looked like a men's store on Rodeo Drive. Impeccable. Every garment was perfectly hung with an inch of space in between. Shirts, pants, jackets were grouped by color. His shoes were aligned as though he'd used a ruler to make sure the toes didn't extend beyond the edge of the shelf.

Had Jasper arranged everything with such precision so he would know if somebody had touched his things?

Drex was pondering that when his cell phone vibrated, startling him and causing him to jump. He pulled the phone from his jeans pocket and answered in an unnecessary whisper. It was Gif.

"They didn't show."

"What?"

"They didn't show."

"What's that mean?"

Gif made a sound of impatience. "They didn't check in or go through security."

"You must have missed them."

"No, I didn't. Security is in plain sight."

"But I saw him drive into the garage."

"That may be, but they're not on that flight. I pretended to be running late and asked a ticket agent if I had time to make it. She told me the door of the plane had already been closed. It's probably taxiing as we speak."

Drex checked his watch and figured that Gif was right. His mind was careening, trying to process this. "Talia's in the travel industry. She must have some kind of escort service that bypasses regular security."

"I guess that's possible."

"What else could it be?"

"Private plane?" Gif ventured.

"They wouldn't have used public parking."

"Right."

"Can you get to the garage, check to see if their car is still there?"

"Sure, but it'll take me a minute."

"Stay on the line."

"Okay. But, Drex, if they changed their minds and are on their way home, you've got to get out of there."

"Way ahead of you." He pulled the double doors closed as he left the bedroom and hit the staircase at a run. The gloaming had turned darker but he was disinclined to turn on his flashlight. The flashlight on loan from Jasper.

Gif asked, "Have you disturbed anything?"

"No, I was saving that. Are you at the garage yet?"

Gif was puffing. "Almost. What's he drive?"

"Black Mercedes SUV. Shit!"

"What was that?"

"I bumped into a corner of the dining table. Why would they have changed their minds? Goddammit! I thought I'd have days of free access to this house."

Gif was growing shorter of breath. "Plans made on short notice get changed, canceled."

"But they were talking about it this morning. The weather forecast for Atlanta. What they should pack. How casual or dressy did they want to be. They went on for a full five minutes about—"

"Okay, I'm in the garage. Which way?"

Drex had come to a dead standstill in the center of the kitchen and repeated in his head what he'd heard himself say.

"Drex? When he turned in, did he go left or right?"

"They talked about the trip. At length. Both last night and this morning."

He pivoted toward the stove. After a second's hesitation, he went over to it and stuck his fingers in the narrow crack between it and the cabinetry where he'd placed the tiny transmitter while waxing poetic about the best way to cook corn on the cob.

It wasn't there.

He fell back a step, took several breaths, tried again, wedging his fingers in as far as they would go, but he knew where he had attached the bug, and it wasn't there.

"Drex!" Gif shouted in his hear. "Left or right?"

"Doesn't matter. You're not going to find their car."

"What? Why?"

"Hold on." He walked over to the spot where he had let Jasper catch him crouched in front of the cabinetry. He knelt down now and ran his hand along the baseboard.

And came up with the transmitter.

"Drex? Are you out of there yet? What is going on?"

"Jasper moved the transmitter."

"What? He couldn't have. He didn't know where it was."

"He found it. And, as an inside joke, he put it right where I had pretended to hide it that night." He gave a mirthless laugh. "We overheard exactly what they wanted us to hear."

"Son of a bitch."

"In spades," Drex said. "We've been played."

Chapter 18

Gif was yelling in his ear, being a hard-ass coach, drilling him. "Get out of that house. Vacate the apartment, too. *Hurry.*"

He'd needed the drilling to knock him out of the momentary stupor he'd lapsed into upon realizing that he'd been duped.

"I'll be in touch."

He disconnected. With Gif's urgent instructions ringing in his ear, he launched himself off the floor. On his way out, he reset the alarm and locked the back door, leaving both as they'd been. He straightened the lock on the screen door so one couldn't tell simply by looking that it was damaged.

Then he ran like hell to the garage apartment. Precipitation had made the stairs treacherous, but he charged up them and into the apartment. No sooner had he closed the door behind himself than he heard the siren.

"You have got to be fucking kidding!"

He stood in the center of the room, heart booming, lungs laboring, mentally shuffling through options and discarding them until he was down to only one.

In a flurry of motion, he felt for the wall switch behind him and flipped on the overhead light. Blinking against the sudden bright-ness, he peeled off the latex gloves and stuffed them into the pocket of his windbreaker, exchanging them for his pistol. He shucked the windbreaker and threw it aside where it landed carelessly in the ratty easy chair.

With pistol in one hand, he unbuttoned his jeans with the other, then pogoed on alternate legs toward the bedroom, pulling off his jeans as he went. He left them on the floor and switched on the lamp. His duffel bag was on the bed. He returned his pistol to it and took out his computer and the stained original manuscript—bless Pam's heart. He carried them into the living area and hur-riedly staged his workspace.

Out on the street, flashing lights created fuzzy streaks of color in the mist. The siren wailed down as the police car wheeled into the Fords' driveway and came to a jerky stop. Both doors opened.

Drex rushed back into the bedroom, stripped off his shirt, put on the fake eyeglasses, toed off his shoes, and grabbed the duffel by the strap. As he did, he spotted his FBI ID wallet lying at the bot-tom of the canvas bag.

He stopped to consider. He could use it now and, damn, it was tempting. But if he did, he would be blown. He couldn't revert to being the hapless writer *cum* gigolo. It was a dilly of an ace, but if he played it too early, he stood to lose the big pot: Jasper Ford.

He zipped up the duffel bag and shoved it into the closet. He then dashed into the living area and took a beer from the fridge. He twisted off the cap and poured half down the sink, then took the bottle with him to the table where he set it beside his laptop. He dropped into the chair, dry scrubbed the sweat off his face, and tried to appear tormented by writer's block.

As it turned out, he had plenty of time to catch his breath. It was five minutes before he heard them clumping up the stairs. He let them get halfway up, then scraped back his chair and ambled over to the door, arriving at the screen door the same time they did.

Looking back at him was a pair of patrol officers, the patches on their uniform sleeves designating the Mount Pleasant police department. Young. Crisp. And looking surprised to be greeted by a man in just his underwear.

Drex pretended to realize only then his state of undress and looked abashed. "Sorry, guys. What's going on?"

"What's your name?" officer number one asked.

"Drex Easton."

"You live here?"

Drex shot the room behind him a deprecating glance. "It's a roof. I've rented it for three months." He explained about the Arnotts. "Do you want to come in or..." He let the invitation trail to nothing.

But they took him up on it, came inside, and looked around.

"You live here alone?" number two asked.

"Yes."

"What's that?" Number one pointed to the manuscript.

"First novel."

"You're a writer?"

Grimacing, Drex said, "Not according to the heap of rejection letters."

Number one chuckled. Number two asked, "Do you know the people in the house across the way?"

"The Fords? Sure. We've hung out."

"Their security alarm went off."

Feigning puzzlement, Drex looked toward the house. "I didn't hear it. When was this?"

"Twenty minutes ago, give or take," officer number one told him. "Siren didn't sound. It cut off with the warning beeps. But Mr. Ford has an app on his phone that signals him when the alarm is activated. Since nobody was authorized to go in, like a cleaning lady or something, he called us."

Drex nodded understanding but held his tongue.

Number two asked, "Have you seen anybody around the neighborhood who looks like they don't belong?"

"Besides me?" Number one thought that was funny, too. Number two, not so much. Good cop/bad cop. Drex turned serious. "I haven't seen hide nor hair of anybody, and I've been here all day. Well, except for a few minutes early this morning. I went out for milk. What did he take?"

"Who?"

"The burglar."

"Nothing, looks like. No sign of a break-in."

"Huh. Wonder what set off the alarm. Or maybe that app on Jasper's phone is faulty."

"Could be. Because the alarm reset itself."

Drex rolled his eyes. "Technology, right?"

The two young officers looked at each other and seemed to come to the tacit conclusion that he was harmless. Number two said, "If you see or hear anything peculiar, please notify the department."

"Sure thing."

Number one wished him good luck with his novel.

"Thanks. I need it."

They thanked him for his time, said their good nights, and trooped down the stairs. A minute later, they backed out of the Fords' driveway and were on their way.

Drex drained the bottle of beer, then picked up his windbreaker from off the chair and fished his cell phone from the pocket.

Gif was beside himself. "I've called you a dozen times."

"I had company." He told him about his visitors. "If they'd arrived sixty seconds sooner, they would have caught me beating my way back up here. If I'd made a run for it when I first heard their siren, they could have seen me fleeing. False alarm."

"Close call. You need to get out of there. And I mean the apartment."

"Have you heard from Mike?"

"He got to the fancy hotel. I told him not to expect the Fords and brought him into the loop. He's standing by, waiting to see what you want him to do."

"I don't have a fucking clue."

"You need to clear out. This room has two beds. You can bunk here tonight. We'll discuss options."

"See you in a few."

―――

When he showed up at the motel without his belongings, Gif greeted him with exasperation. "Where's your stuff?"

"I didn't clear out."

"We agreed—"

"I didn't agree."

"You didn't disagree, either."

"I'm hungry. A mile back I passed a place." Drex turned around and headed for his car. He'd left the engine running. Gif pulled the motel room door shut and followed.

On the way to the restaurant, Gif said, "While I was waiting on you, I took the liberty of calling Mike."

"Did you interrupt his five-course, prix fixe dinner?"

"He canceled his reservation."

"Excuse me?"

"I know. Shocked me too. He was in his room, working."

"Doing what?"

"If the Fords left the airport in the vehicle they arrived in, it would show up on surveillance camera video."

"That would only prove they left. Wouldn't tell us where they were going."

"Mike's going to look into it anyway."

The seafood shack was outlined in turquoise and pink neon, and had a sign with a fish jumping out of a skillet. The shrimp was hot out of the deep fryer, and the beer was icy cold. They ate in silence for several minutes before Gif again raised the subject of Drex leaving the apartment.

Drex hadn't had a change of heart. "If they return to their

house, it'll look better if I'm still there, carrying on as though nothing happened. I replaced the transmitter where Jasper had left it. That'll be the first thing he checks. He will suspect that it was me who triggered the alarm, but he can't prove it."

"Unless he has nanny cams."

"Even if he had me on video stealing Talia's jewelry, would he drag the police in?" He shook his head. "No. He doesn't want involvement with the police."

"He got them involved tonight."

"Only to let me know that he's on to me. I'm sure he got a good chuckle out of that. But it was a tactical error."

"How so?"

"Why would he play hide-and-seek if he didn't have something to hide?"

Gif thought on that and conceded with a nod. "But what if they've vamoosed, and we never lay eyes on them again?"

Drex tried not to give in to the dejection that thought induced. To come away from this exercise with nothing to show for it would be a disappointing defeat. Even more crushing would be to think of Talia on an escapade with Jasper, the two of them laughing at him, crowing over how effortless it had been to gull him.

"If they've flown the coop," he said to Gif, "it won't matter if I've moved out or not, will it? He'll have vanished. We'll be back where we started, except that I'll be out three months rent on that rat hole."

Sensitive to his mood, Gif let the subject drop. They finished their meal, split the tab with a twenty each, and were sipping second beers when Drex's phone vibrated. "Must be Mike." He answered.

Straightaway Mike asked, "Where are you?"

"A restaurant. Just finished dinner."

"Gif there?"

"I'm looking at him."

"Have you seen any news?"

"No."

"Start moving."

Responding to Mike's no-nonsense timbre, Drex scooted out of the booth and motioned for Gif to follow. As they wended their way through tables of diners, he asked Mike, "What's up?"

"The yacht that belongs to the Conner woman, the *Laney Belle*, right?"

"Right. What about it?"

"Well, around nightfall a Coast Guard cruiser came upon a capsized dingy belonging to it."

"What?"

"The *Laney Belle* was located adrift about a half mile away. Nobody was on board."

"*What?*"

"And that ain't the worst of it."

Drex stopped so suddenly, Gif bumped into him from behind.

"A body has washed up on shore," Mike said.

Drex's shrimp and beer threatened to come up. "Whose body?"

"Name hasn't been released. All they're saying is...Drex, it's a woman."

Chapter 19

———◈———

Tossing his cell phone to Gif, who fumbled it before securing it, Drex said, "Talk to Mike. Ask him where we need to go."

He shouldered past the cluster of people waiting for tables, made it to the exit, and, once outside, broke into a run. Gif jogged along behind, Drex's phone to his ear. By the time they were fastening their seat belts, Mike had explained to Gif the nature of the emergency and given him the name of the marina near where the woman's body had been discovered.

"Mike said the fastest route to take—"

"I know how to get there." Drex sped from the restaurant's parking lot, tires squealing as he executed a shallow U-turn onto the thoroughfare. "Put the phone on speaker."

Gif did. Mike asked Drex what he wanted him to do.

"Be honest with me." Drex's fingers flexed and contracted on the steering wheel. "If the dead woman has been identified, and you're withholding that, I'll cut your heart out."

"I swear, Drex. They haven't released her name."

Drex forced himself to calm down, push personal considerations aside, and think pragmatically. "Pack up. Leave your car—"

"Sammy's car."

"Sammy's car. We'll square up with him later." He checked the clock on the dashboard. It was going on nine o'clock. "I think the last flight from Atlanta to Charleston is at—"

"Ten twenty-nine. I already booked a seat."

"Good man."

"Figured you'd want me there. Where should I go when I arrive?"

"Hell if I know. I haven't thought that far ahead."

"I'll text when I'm on the ground."

"Any sign that Rudkowski is on your tail?"

"None."

"Do you have another phone?"

"Charged and ready."

"I'm gonna switch, too. You and Gif trade numbers."

Gif clicked off the speaker while he and Mike sorted out the new phone numbers.

Drex concentrated on driving. He wove in and out of traffic, cursing motorists who went too slow. Gif held onto the strap above the passenger window but had the discretion not to comment on Drex's speed and chancy maneuvering.

As they neared the general vicinity of the marina, it became apparent that access to it had already been restricted. Some streets had been cordoned off. On those remaining open, traffic was being redirected by officers with flashlights and reflective vests. Seeing that one was about to signal him to make an unwanted turn, Drex whipped into the parking lot of a strip center where the shops were closed for the night and announced they would go the rest of the way on foot.

"There may be barricades," Gif said.

"Keep your badge handy."

"Do you intend to muscle your way in?"

"Only if I have to."

"If you do, Rudkowski will—"

"Keep your badge handy." Drex put a lid on Gif's arguments. They would be reasonable. He would encourage prudence. He would advise that they tread carefully.

Drex didn't want to hear it.

They made it to the base of the pier without being challenged. Drex indicated a roped-off area where the media had been shepherded. "Go mingle with the news crews. See if you can learn anything beyond what Mike has told us."

"Where will you be?"

"Up there." He motioned toward the elevated pier. "Look for me at the railing."

He climbed the steps. The pier was crowded with spectators, but they were unexpectedly subdued. Drex made his way through them until he reached the wood railing and saw what they were looking at on the beach below.

EMTs were lifting a body bag from the packed sand onto a gurney. Once transferred, it was strapped down. The gurney was carried to an ambulance and placed inside. The doors were shut with a sound that had a finality to it. The ambulance drove away down the beach.

As though watching the last scene of a sad movie, the crowd remained still and hushed before gradually beginning to disperse, talking quietly among themselves, posing questions of each other, speculating, philosophizing about the fragility of life.

"Drex."

The soft-spoken voice brought him around to Gif. "It's not official yet," he said, "but they're all but certain it's Elaine Conner."

Drex felt as though his breastbone would crack and his chest cave in. From anguish over Elaine. And guilt-ridden relief that it wasn't Talia. He turned back to the railing, braced his hands on the weathered wood, and bent double, taking deep breaths through his mouth.

Gif let him have a full minute before continuing. "People in the marina saw the yacht leaving the harbor, wondered why anybody

would be going out in weather like this. According to several witnesses, there, uh, there was a man at the wheel."

"Jasper."

"Unidentified."

"It was Jasper." Drex took one last deep breath and stood up
straight. "While he had us looking the other way, he must have
come straight here from the airport and boarded the yacht." Turning only his head, he looked sternly at Gif. His friend knew the
question he wanted to ask, but he couldn't work up enough
courage.

Gif raised his shoulders, looking apologetic. "It's unknown if
anyone else besides the man and Elaine were onboard."

What went unspoken was that the last time Talia was seen, she
had been in the company of her husband, but whether as a victim
or an accomplice remained unknown. As though following Drex's
thoughts, Gif said, "The authorities have had no indication of another casualty, so the search is being referred to as a rescue, not a
recovery."

Drex stared out across the water. "They may find Talia, or her
body," he said in a voice scratchy with emotion. "But if they search
till Doomsday, they won't find a trace of him." He pushed off the
railing, turned, and started walking with determination toward the
steps leading down. "The fucker can swim."

He was pleased with his new appearance.

True, Howard Clement wasn't as dashing as Jasper Ford, husband to Talia Shafer, friend to Elaine Conner, member in good
standing of an exclusive country club, snappy dresser, and connois-
seur of fine wine and cuisine.

But his new look and persona would do. He would never be recognized among the crowd of gawkers on the pier who watched as
Elaine became a headline, her life reduced to a sound bite.

However, that was more notoriety than most people got. When looked at that way, Jasper had done her a favor. He had attained for her in death the attention she craved in life.

Her exuberance had been annoying at times, especially when his investment advice paid off in large dividends. On those occasions the two of them celebrated privately. Often Elaine had urged him to let Talia join in. He had refused.

"She's a conservative investor and would never dare to take the gambles you do, Elaine." Elaine had preened over that.

He didn't have a one hundred percent accuracy rate, of course. Whenever his advice resulted in a loss, Elaine had accepted it philosophically, patted his cheek, told him she loved him anyway, then had asked where she should next put her money.

He would trot out inch-thick analyses of various investment opportunities in the US as well as in foreign markets. He would excite her with projections, then dampen that excitement by enumerating the risks. He'd enticed her with estimated yields, but cautioned her to give serious consideration to the volatility of international trade in an unstable diplomatic climate.

Her attention span had been that of a gnat. She'd been easily confused by the vernacular and eventually overwhelmed by the volume of information. "Oh, just pick one and handle it for me."

Actually, it had been almost too easy. He'd grown a bit bored with her. Ever cheerful and optimistic, she'd rarely challenged anything he proposed.

That was up until tonight. He had called and told her about a squabble between Talia and him that had culminated in the cancellation of a getaway. He'd asked if Elaine would meet him on the *Laney Belle*. "I need a stiff drink and a good friend."

He'd been assured that she would gladly provide both.

She'd welcomed him aboard with a sympathetic hug and an open bottle of bourbon. But when he suggested that they take a short cruise, she had balked. The weather wasn't ideal, she'd said. They couldn't sightsee with the mist so heavy, and the forecast was for conditions to worsen, not improve. She would rather err on the side of safety and keep the *Laney Belle* snug in the marina.

On and on, she'd whined, whined, whined until he'd wanted to strangle her. She hadn't given in until he announced—irritably—that his coming to her for consolation after his quarrel with Talia had been a bad idea, that he was leaving.

"Oh, all right. But only for a little while."

He'd promised to make it quick. That was a promise she had forced him to break.

He'd persuaded her to let him pilot the boat out of the marina because she'd had several drinks. He'd seen to it that she had two more before suggesting that they give the dinghy a test run.

"Tonight? Talia would scalp me if I let you do that."

"That's the point," he'd said, giving her a conspiratorial wink. "She would never allow it. She's afraid of the water, you know. Let's misbehave and do it while she's not looking."

Elaine had been unable to resist the thought of misbehavior.

She'd giggled through the process of getting the dinghy into the water and climbing in. There had been a litany of "ooopsy-daisies" and hilarity over her tipsiness. She'd squealed like a little girl whenever the dinghy was rocked by a swell, and she'd been laughing when a wave sloshed into the boat and knocked her off balance.

She'd stopped laughing when he shoved her overboard. Ocean water had filled her mouth, silencing her scream as she went under. He'd gone in seconds after her and had hooked his elbow around her neck from behind as she'd struggled to the surface.

It was a lifesaver's maneuver, which she'd relaxed against, until realizing that he wasn't keeping her afloat, but holding her under. Then she'd begun to fight. He'd promised to make it quick, but she hadn't allowed it. It had seemed to take for bloody ever for her to die.

He'd let go and pushed away from her, swum back to the dinghy, and hung onto the side of it until he'd regained his breath. Once recovered, he'd peeled off his clothes. He'd practiced doing this in shallower swells. It was harder to accomplish than he had counted on, and took more time, but eventually he was down to his Speedo.

He'd sent his shoes adrift and made a tear in his shirt before letting it go. Then he'd tied his remaining garments together and attached them to a fire extinguisher he'd taken from a cabinet on the yacht. He'd placed it in the dinghy while Elaine was pouring another round. The heavy canister sent his bundle of clothing to the depths.

The hardest part of the whole ordeal had been to overturn the dinghy, which, clearly, had been designed *not* to capsize.

Then he'd swum. He'd estimated that it would take him at least an hour to reach the shoreline, although he couldn't be precise about how far the dinghy had drifted from the yacht. He'd rested periodically but pushed himself.

He was twelve minutes off on his timing, but had missed his destination by only thirty yards. As he'd walked to where he'd left the car, he'd watched the tide erase his footprints almost as soon as they were formed.

The car was a heap that he'd bought months ago off a we-tote-the-note lot. He'd paid in cash and had the title made out to Howard Clement. He hadn't bothered to register it. He'd scraped off the VIN number. He was confident it could never be traced to him.

He had parked it in a clump of scrubby palmetto with a lacy overlay of kelp that had washed onto the beach. In the unlikely event that his tire tracks were ever detected, they would be difficult to imprint. He'd pulled on the pair of latex gloves, which he'd carried folded inside his swimsuit, then reached for the magnetic box he'd secreted beneath the car and used the fob inside to open the trunk. He'd lifted out the roll-aboard he had ostensibly packed for a getaway, but which actually contained everything he needed to undergo a metamorphosis.

The backseat of the car served as his chrysalis.

When he'd emerged an hour later, gone were the ponytail and

door knocker. He'd shaved his head, leaving only a ring of hair on the lower third. He covered the tan line on his scalp with a khaki Gilligan hat.

He'd dressed in a pair of unshapely cargo shorts and a loud Hawaiian print shirt he'd bought in Key West two and a half years ago, when he'd determined that his next target would be the lovely Talia Shafer who lived in Charleston, a city that attracted thousands of tourists wearing ungodly attire. He'd padded the front of the shirt to simulate middle-age spread. He slid his feet into a pair of rubber flip-flops. He'd chosen eyeglasses that were nondescript and could be purchased for a few dollars in just about any retail outlet.

When he'd looked at himself in the rearview mirror, he'd laughed out loud. Not even his wife, not even the woman he'd just drowned, would recognize him.

He replaced everything he'd used in the roll-aboard for disposal later. Before closing it, he took out a wallet, an old and well-used one that he'd bought at a flea market, and checked to make sure the necessities were there. The driver's license had been issued in Georgia, the photo taken after disposing of the fuzzy wig he'd worn as Marian Harris's shy money manager, Daniel Knolls, and before he grew out his hair and beard to become Jasper Ford.

He had a credit card in the name of Howard R. Clement. The card was over a year old and had just enough charges on it to remain active. The wallet also contained the modest amount of currency that Jasper Ford had withdrawn from an ATM three days ago. He'd put the wallet in the back pocket of his shorts.

Last, from a zippered pocket in the lining of the suitcase, he'd taken a small velvet drawstring bag and transferred it to the front pocket of his cargo shorts, sealing it inside with the Velcro strips attached to the fabric. He'd patted the pocket with affection and smiled.

As of tonight, his collection had a new addition.

After locking the roll-aboard into the trunk, he'd driven off the beach. His initial plan had been to head straight up the coast, perhaps traveling as far as Myrtle Beach tonight, where he would get a room and lay low for several days, at least until the hubbub had died down and the search for him and Elaine was discontinued.

Then he would return and choreograph Talia's suicide. Acquaintances would conclude that she'd been led to it by grief over the deaths of her good friend and husband, whose body, regrettably, had never been recovered.

It had been a very workable plan. But as Howard Clement had been chugging along a major thoroughfare in his clunker, a convoy of emergency vehicles had forced him and other motorists to pull onto the shoulder so they could pass. They had been headed in the direction of the shore and the marina.

Could it possibly be? he'd asked himself.

Over the course of his illustrious career, he had never made a spontaneous decision. Never. But this one time, he had yielded to temptation. Acting on impulse, he had changed his route.

———◦———

Now, as he gazed down at the body on the beach, he supposed it had been Elaine's fake tits, acting as flotation devices, that had caused her body to wash ashore so soon. He had reckoned on it taking a day or so, if indeed it ever did.

But there she lay, faceup, covered with a yellow plastic sheet. A police helicopter flew over. Its downwash flipped back a corner of the sheet to reveal her hand. No one except Jasper seemed to notice.

"Jesus, you just never know, do you?"

Jasper turned. Standing close behind him was a gum-smacking redneck wearing jean cut-offs, combat boots, and a tank top featuring a coiled cobra with dripping fangs. Revolting. "Sorry?"

"When you get up in the morning, you don't figure on it being your last."

"You're right there, buddy," said Howard, in the nasally twang of his newly assumed persona.

He turned away from the redneck and watched with mounting pleasure as the activity on the beach increased. The audience of onlookers on the pier expanded. Jasper delighted in the comments he overheard.

If they only knew who they were rubbing shoulders with, he thought.

He had been on the pier for over an hour when he was jostled along with others near him who were being elbowed out of the way by a man plowing his way to the railing.

Drex.

Jasper experienced a jolt of alarm.

But he soon realized that Drex wasn't looking for him. He was fixated on what was taking place on the beach. He'd made it just in time to catch the final act: that of the body being carted away.

Once the ambulance was gone, Jasper allowed himself to be shuffled along with the crowd as it vacated the pier. A bottleneck formed at the steps. Jasper waited his turn, then flip-flopped down. But he didn't go far, because Drex had stayed behind, gazing out across the water, hands gripping the railing, his body as taut as a bowstring.

Which confirmed what Jasper had suspected all along. He wasn't who he claimed to be, and he wasn't writing a novel. One didn't bug one's neighbor's house unless one had a reason for doing so. And now this drowning death had left him obviously upset, which was disproportionate to how long he'd known Elaine.

From the start, the timing of his arrival to the neighborhood had made Jasper uneasy because it had coincided so closely—mere months—with the discovery of Marian Harris's remains.

That had come as a shock. One evening he had returned home from an errand to find Talia in her study, crying her heart out.

"Remember I told you about my friend Marian who lived in Key West?"

"Of course. The one who went missing a couple of years ago."

"I just heard from a mutual friend," Talia had said as she blotted up tears. "They found her remains buried in a shipping crate. It was horrible."

It certainly had been horrible news to him. None of the others had ever been found. This was an unwelcome first, and it had rattled him. He was brilliant. He didn't make mistakes. But he would be a fool to ignore the possibility that he *might*.

He wouldn't commit a major gaffe. No, the oversight would be something minor, inane, ridiculous, something that, because of its sheer triviality, a genius like him would never think to avoid.

That evening, while Talia was mourning the grisly death of her friend, he had resolved that the time had come for Jasper Ford to evaporate.

His marriage to Lyndsay had been brief, but rife with drama. After her, he'd sworn to remain a bachelor and, for thirty years, he had. Then, ill-advisedly as it turned out, he'd experimented with matrimony again. The intimacy of the union, inside the bedroom and out, spawned risks he hadn't foreseen when he'd asked for Talia's hand. Choosing her in particular had been a miscalculation. He would have been better off selecting a bubblehead like Elaine.

Talia was far too perceptive. He had sensed her gradually increasing mistrust, which had resulted in last night's accusation of an affair. He had never slept with Elaine, but that Talia sensed *something* amiss was his cue that it was time to bid farewell to Jasper Ford.

But how to go about it had presented him with a unique problem: He had two women to dispose of this time. He couldn't leave either Talia or Elaine alive to search for him. He was confident that he was up to the challenge of their termination, but the solution had to be well thought out, methodically planned, and precisely executed.

But then Drex's unexpected appearance had thrust Jasper's strategy into overdrive. He'd sowed seeds of doubt about their neighbor in Talia's mind, hoping to thwart any interaction between them until he could formulate another plan.

Then—bless her!—Talia's mention of a getaway had opened up an opportunity.

Even better, he could broadcast it using the transmitter that Drex had planted. Talk about a backfire. It had been too delicious.

He'd acted quickly, but efficiently, and so far everything had gone splendidly.

But now here Drex was, playing fly in the ointment again.

Jasper risked making himself conspicuous by loitering near the pier, but within minutes another man joined Drex. They talked briefly, then, in a decisive manner, Drex turned away from the railing. The two of them strode along the pier and descended the steps in a hurry. They walked past him without giving him a second glance.

Jasper dismissed the other man as a sidekick.

But he was struck by Drex's unfamiliar demeanor. No jaunty gait, no dimpled smile. This Drex was no aw-shucks wannabe. There was an intensity about him, an angry determination in his bearing. It couldn't be mistaken. It definitely couldn't be dismissed.

And with that thought, the freshly cut hair on the back of Jasper's neck stood on end.

Drex Easton was him.

Jasper had been feeling him for years, an unknown entity who was invisible, but whose presence he felt. A shadow. Untouchable, but *there*. More often than he wanted to admit, he would sense him like a ghostly waft of cool air. He would awaken and imagine a menacing presence hovering over him while he slept. Sometimes, in a crowd, he would whip around suddenly in the hope—and fear— that he would spot him, that he would be able to pick him out in a sea of unknowns.

He never did, but he knew he existed. He knew he was corporeal and not just an inhabitant of nightmares and premonitions. He was real and on Jasper's trail with the unflagging purpose of a bloodhound and the fervor of a pilgrim, undeterred by time or distance or failure.

But how did one combat someone unseen? It would be like fencing in absolute blackout. He couldn't strike out without giving away his position. He couldn't beat him at his own game because he didn't know who he was, what he looked like, or his name.

Until now.

Chapter 20

Talia had been home for no longer than fifteen minutes before she was curled up in an oversize upholstered chair and sipping a glass of wine. The compact, first-floor room tucked under the staircase had a desk where she conducted her business, but she'd also furnished it with comfortable pieces, making it as much her retreat as her workplace.

She was enjoying the peacefulness it afforded when the doorbell rang.

Disgruntled by the interruption and mystified as to who would be on her doorstep this late on a Saturday night, she set aside her glass of wine, made her way to the front door, and looked through the peephole.

The two men looking back at her were strangers. With misgiving, she called through the door, "Can I help you?"

"Mrs. Ford?"

"Yes."

"I'm Dave Locke, this is Ed Menundez. We're detectives with the Charleston Police Department." Each held up a badge where she could see it. "Can we please speak with you?"

"The police department?"

"We'd like to speak with you, please."

She hesitated for a moment then disengaged the alarm, flipped the deadbolt, and opened the door. Dividing a look of perplexity between the two, she asked, "Speak with me about what?"

"May we come in?"

"What's happened?"

"May we?"

She gave Locke a vague nod of assent and stepped aside. She realized then that she'd left her shoes in front of her easy chair. The marble floor of the entry was cold against her bare feet. She shut the door and turned to the men, repeating, "What's happened?"

"Are you here alone?" Locke, evidently the spokesman of the duo, was tall and thin, with a pleasant bearing and eyes that drooped at the outer corners.

"Yes."

"Mr. Ford?"

"He's in Atlanta." The first panicked thought that entered her mind was that there had been a plane crash. "His flight . . . ?"

"No, this isn't about a flight."

"Then please tell me why you're here."

"Are you acquainted with Elaine Conner?"

She swallowed, nodded, and replied, "Very well. She's a good friend of mine."

"We gathered that, because your name showed up numerous times in her recent calls log."

"You have Elaine's phone?"

"We discovered it on her yacht."

"I'm sorry, I don't understand. What were you doing on Elaine's yacht? Is she all right?" But even as she asked, she knew. Her eyes widened with alarm. "Has there been an accident?"

Locke extended his hand, but came short of actually touching her. "Mrs. Ford, the body of a woman was discovered on the beach tonight, washed ashore. We believe it's Elaine Conner."

Talia gaped at them with disbelief, then covered her mouth and backed into one of the straight chairs flanking the console table. She bumped against the leg of it, rocking a crystal vase so hard it would have fallen off if Menundez hadn't reacted quickly enough to stabilize it.

Locke was still talking. Talia had to focus on each word in order to comprehend what he was saying. "…ask if you knew how to contact Mrs. Conner's next of kin."

Talia wanted to wake up from this awful dream before it became any worse, but try as she might to force herself awake, the scene remained real, palpable, harsh. Her feet were freezing. Her ears were buzzing. Two heralds of dreadful news were looking down on her, awaiting a response.

"She…" She stopped, drew in two quick breaths, and tried again. "Elaine doesn't have any living relatives. No next of kin."

"Then we may need to impose on you."

"Impose on me?"

"To take a look at a sketch and verify that it's her."

Talia stared up at them, but was too benumbed to speak. This could not be happening.

Locke said, "The coroner will make a positive ID, but it would be helpful if you could identify her from a sketch. We should be receiving it shortly." He motioned to the iPad his partner held at his side.

Shakily, Talia stood up. "I'm going to get my shoes."

"I'll get them for you," Locke said. She got the impression it wasn't an offer out of kindness.

"I left them in my study. The room behind the stairs. My phone is on the end table. Please bring that, too."

He left her with Menundez, who was younger, stockier, and more all-business. He wasn't merely looking at her. He was scrutinizing her. To break the strained silence she asked him if it was still raining.

"Off and on," he said.

Locke returned with her requested phone. Awkwardly he passed her one shoe at a time. She put them on, then, feeling only slightly steadier, stood.

"Better?" Locke asked.

"I'm fine."

She knew she should probably ask if they would like to move into the living room and sit while they waited for the expected email, but inviting them to do so would make this visit seem even more official, and she was resistant to doing that.

Speaking in a low voice one would use to calm an anxious animal, Locke told her the time the 911 call had come in and the approximate location of where the body had washed ashore.

"Where the pier is?" she said. "That's near the marina where Elaine's yacht is moored."

"It left the marina a little after seven this evening."

"She took it out alone?"

"Would that be unusual?"

"Yes. She was adept at piloting it, but conscientious and careful. It wouldn't be like her to take it out on a night like tonight, especially by herself. Maybe she loaned it to someone. Or it could have been stolen."

"Mrs. Conner was onboard. Investigators have talked to several people who corroborate having seen her on deck."

"Investigators?" She looked at Menundez, whose expression remained disturbingly impassive, then came back to Locke. "Do you think the woman found on the beach was the victim of a crime?"

"We don't know yet. Several agencies are looking into it. Isle of Palms PD called us in to assist. A Coast Guard patrol discovered the dinghy."

"Dinghy?"

He told her that it had been found capsized.

"That makes no sense. Why in the world would Elaine get into the dinghy, after dark, in this weather?"

"Questions we'd like answered," he said.

They seemed to expect her to provide the answers. "There must have been an emergency onboard. Did Elaine call in an SOS or send some kind of distress signal?"

"No, ma'am."

"That yacht is equipped with state-of-the-art technology. She's bragged to me about it. At the first sign of trouble, she would have sent out an alert." Locke just looked back at her, saying nothing. With emphasis, she said, "There must be a mistake. It can't be her. Who discovered the body?" Locke told her. "Oh. How awful for the little boy."

"When his dad realized what it was, he made sure the kid didn't see it."

She tried to connect Elaine and her effervescent personality to a lifeless body washed ashore. It was impossible. "I don't believe it's Elaine."

Locke gave her a nod that could have been interpreted any number of ways, but she interpreted it to mean that he disagreed.

They all heard the beep signaling that the email had come in. Menundez opened the cover on his iPad, accessed his email, then gave Locke a nod.

Locke turned to her. "Can you give it a look?"

Talia tried to distance herself from the surreal situation, to withdraw emotionally, to become an observer rather than a participant, believing that watching from outside herself was the only way she would get through this.

"Do I need to prepare myself for what I'm about to see?"

"Are you asking if the face is disfigured?"

"Yes, that's what I'm asking."

"No. No blood, nothing like that."

She took a deep breath, then nodded, and Menundez held the tablet out to where she could see the screen.

The face as captured by the sketch artist showed no signs of trauma. But it was definitely a rendition of Elaine's face without her vitality and animation.

The detectives must have known from her reaction what the answer was, but Locke asked quietly, "Is that Elaine Conner?"

Talia nodded, spoke a raspy yes, then said, "Excuse me, please." She didn't wait for permission.

She went into the powder room, the nearest bathroom, and bent over the toilet. She retched. Hard. Repeatedly. But she hadn't eaten since breakfast, so nothing came up. The bout left her feeling wrung out and trembly.

She cupped water from the faucet with her hand and rinsed her mouth out, then used a guest towel to bathe her face with cold water. She raked back her hair with her fingers, then rejoined the detectives.

Locke said, "Can we get you something, Mrs. Ford? A drink of water?"

She understood then that their business with her wasn't finished. They weren't offering condolences and bowing out with an apology for having ruined her night. They had come to her with questions that needed answers.

She wanted to cover her head and weep over the loss of her friend with the infectious laugh and *joie de vivre*. Instead, she wearily offered the detectives coffee.

"Coffee would be good," Locke said.

"Coffee, thanks," Menundez said.

She led them into the kitchen, then stood before the elaborate coffeemaker and stared at it, dazed, as though it were the control panel on a NASA spaceship. She couldn't remember which buttons to push or in what sequence.

Noticing, Menundez stepped in. "I have one like it. Allow me?"

"Thank you." He took over for her. Maybe he wasn't an automaton after all.

She put a kettle on the stove to boil water for tea for herself, then sent Jasper a text asking him to call her as soon as possible. When she saw Locke looking at her quizzically, she said, "I texted Jasper."

"Have you heard from him?"

"No, but I didn't expect to. We had a late dinner reservation."

Simultaneously she and the detective looked at the clock on the microwave. It was almost eleven-thirty. "If he doesn't call soon, I'll try to reach him through the hotel switchboard. He'll be very upset. Elaine was his friend, too."

"Yes, mutual friends told us that they had drinks together yesterday at the country club."

"And stayed for dinner." Although she had voiced her suspicion of an affair to Jasper, she felt a need now to set the record straight: Their date yesterday hadn't been behind her back. "I didn't feel well last evening. Rather than join them, I stayed in and slept through dinner."

Locke nodded thanks to his partner, who had passed him a cup of coffee. He blew across the top of it. "Why didn't you go to Atlanta? Was it a business trip for Mr. Ford?"

"No. He's retired." Becoming increasingly uncomfortable with the tenor of his questions, she turned her back to him, opened a cabinet, and took down a box of chamomile tea. "The trip was to have been a getaway. I made it as far as the airport, then began feeling queasy. I begged off but insisted that Jasper go ahead without me. It's a new hotel. Jasper is a gourmet. He looked forward to trying out the chef."

"What new hotel?"

"The Lotus."

Menundez left his freshly brewed cup of coffee on the counter, stepped out of the kitchen into the dining room, and got on his cell phone.

"Did you get over it?"

Talia had watched the other detective leave and could now hear him speaking quietly into his phone. She turned back to Locke. "Pardon?"

"The queasiness."

"It comes and goes."

"Nothing serious, I hope."

She shook her head. "I had some dental work done yesterday morning. The prescribed pain pills must not have agreed with me."

"You were sleeping them off last night while your husband and Mrs. Conner were at the country club."

"I thought I had slept them off. I guess I didn't. The upset recurred today."

Locke set his unfinished coffee on the table. "Do you have an explanation for the house alarm going off this afternoon?"

She followed the direction of his gaze to the control box on the wall next to the back door. "The alarm went off?"

"Not the siren. It was shut off during the warning beeps with time to spare. Strange, because no one was at home."

She shook her head in confusion. "When was this?"

Menundez returned in time to hear her question. "Five oh-seven," he said. "Patrolmen were dispatched. Saw no sign of a break-in."

"A glitch in the system, you think?" Locke asked.

Menundez said, "Or else someone who knew the code was here."

If they'd been speaking in a foreign language, Talia couldn't be more confounded. "Like who?"

"We hoped you could tell us," Menundez said.

"I'm sorry. I know nothing about the alarm going off, so I can't explain why it did."

"Quite a coincidence that cops have come to your house twice in one day," Locke remarked.

Disquieted by the way the two were regarding her, she folded her arms over her middle, even knowing how defensive it looked. "Why are you asking me all these questions?"

"We have to eliminate every possibility."

"Possibility of what?"

She had addressed the question to Locke, but Menundez answered. "The possibility that Mrs. Conner's death wasn't an accident caused by misjudgment on her part. The possibility that foul play was involved."

Before Talia could process that, Locke asked, "Did you walk your husband into the airport, see him off?"

It took several seconds for his seemingly unrelated inquiry to sink in. "No. No, we said our goodbyes in the parking garage. Why?"

"Because some of the people we've talked to who saw the *Laney Belle* leave the marina said that a man was steering her, not Mrs. Conner."

Talia hugged her middle a little tighter.

Locke continued. "We were also told that Mrs. Conner often allowed your husband to pilot the boat."

"That's true," Talia said, "but it couldn't have been Jasper this evening."

"Had Mrs. Conner ever invited anyone else to take the wheel?"

"Not to my knowledge, but that doesn't mean that she didn't."

"You two were close friends."

"Yes."

"Were you acquainted with all her other friends?"

"Many of them."

"Male friends?"

"Some."

"If she had a new man in her life, would she have told you?"

"More than likely," she said huskily.

"Has she taken a romantic interest in someone recently?"

Willing herself not to glance toward the apartment across the way, she gave her head a brisk shake.

"She wasn't seeing anyone?"

"In the way you're implying, I don't believe so."

The two detectives looked at each other, then back at her. Menundez said, "Mrs. Ford, is it possible that your husband changed his mind about going to Atlanta at the last minute?"

"He would have notified me. He would have been home hours ago."

"Unless he was onboard the *Laney Belle* with Elaine Conner," Locke said.

"That's an offensive implication, Detective Locke."

"The implications to you are more dire than marital unfaithfulness. If your husband was on the yacht, and there was an emergency, an accident, he could have suffered an injury. As we speak, search-and-rescue teams are out looking for him, or his—"

The kettle screeched. Talia nearly jumped out of her skin. She turned quickly and lifted it off the burner. In the process she sloshed some of the boiling water onto her hand. She cried out. The detectives lurched forward, ready to lend assistance, but she warded them off.

"I'm fine. It's fine." She tucked her scalded hand into her opposite armpit. "You believe that Jasper is either in need of rescue or already dead? Is that what you're saying?"

Their grim expressions confirmed it.

"You're wrong. If he were going out on the water with Elaine tonight, he would have told me."

"Did they take the yacht out together often?"

"Not often. But there have been occasions." She wet her lips. "Were you given a description of the man who was with her?"

"Not a very good one. No one actually saw him board the yacht. It was a gloomy dusk. The mist limited visibility. One witness said the man he saw in the wheelhouse was wearing a baseball cap. Other than that—"

"Baseball cap?"

At her startled reaction, Locke and his partner came to attention. Locke said, "That's been confirmed. A baseball cap was found on the yacht."

Talia wilted against the edge of the countertop. "Orange, with a white capital letter T?"

"University of Tennessee," Locke said.

She covered her face with her hands.

"Does your husband own a cap like that?"

She shook her head, said *no* into her moist palms, then lowered her hands. Her throat seized. She had to swallow several times. "No. But our neighbor does."

"Next door?"

"He rents the garage apartment behind the house next door."

Menundez said to Locke, "The patrolmen who responded to the call about the alarm talked to that guy."

Locke asked Talia, "Was he acquainted with Mrs. Conner?"

"Jasper and I introduced them."

"What's his name?"

Menundez was hurriedly swiping the screen of his phone. "I've got it here."

"My name is Drex Easton."

Startled, the three of them turned as one. He was standing in the open doorway between the screened porch and kitchen. How had he opened it without their hearing him? He was wearing the same dark suit he'd worn the night he escorted Elaine and her to dinner. The same shirt and tie.

But an altogether different countenance.

His right hand was raised and open to show a small leather wallet with a clear plastic window and a gold badge. His eyes zeroed in on Talia's. "FBI Special Agent Drex Easton."

Chapter 21

———⊷◉⊶———

Rudkowski was sprawled on his hotel room bed, watching without much interest the dirty movie on the room's flat screen, nursing his third scotch, and wondering how a man who weighed almost three fifty could vanish into thin air. It had been some trick, but Mike Mallory had managed it, and Rudkowski was made to look like a fool. Again.

His cell phone rang. He spilled half his whiskey in his haste to mute the bump-and-grind sound track and answer his phone. "Rudkowski."

"It's Deputy Gray."

"Who?"

"In Key West. We talked a few days ago."

"Oh, yeah, yeah." Rudkowski sank back onto his pillow. "Make this quick, please. I've got a situation here."

"I'm sorry to bother you, but I'm trying to reach Agent Easton, and, like the time before, he didn't leave me his number this morning. It was my oversight. I should have made sure—"

"Hold it. This morning? You talked to Easton this morning?"

"Well, yesterday morning, officially."

While Rudkowski had been licking his wounds and swilling cheap scotch, midnight had slipped past him. "Okay. Yesterday morning. Did he say where he was calling from?"

"Well, no, sir, but he can't on account of him being—"

"Undercover."

"Yes, sir."

"Why was he calling you?"

"Same as before. The Marian Harris case."

"Specifically?"

"He asked if a Talia Shafer had been questioned during the investigation into Harris's disappearance."

Rudkowski rolled over and picked up the notepad and pen on the nightstand. "Spell the names, please. And who is she?"

The deputy gave him the spellings. "She was in the photograph of the party scene on the boat."

"So were dozens of other people. What was Easton's particular interest in her?"

"He couldn't disclose that, because it's—"

"Classified."

"Yes, sir. I thought you would know what his interest was."

What he didn't know about Easton's recent activities would fill the fucking Superdome. "Was this Talia Shafer considered a person of interest in the Harris case?"

"No, sir. Agent Easton asked if there were any notes taken during her interview, but it was just basic stuff. Date and time. Names of the officers who talked to her. Nothing came of it, nothing to follow up on. Agent Easton thanked me for checking, and that was it."

Rudkowski figured that he'd had too much to drink. He was having trouble connecting the dots. "So, if that was it, why are you trying to reach Easton now?"

"Because about an hour ago, our department got a call from Charleston PD."

"South Carolina?"

"Right."

Rudkowski listened with shrinking patience as the deputy related what he knew about the death of an Elaine Conner.

"They haven't ruled out that it was an accident, but they're leaning toward foul play. A man was with her on the yacht. He's unaccounted for. Anyhow, one of the investigators up there remembered reading about our case down here and was struck by the similarities."

"Rich lady. Snazzy boat."

"Yes, sir. So they called our department to compare notes. I thought Agent Easton would want to look into this Charleston case, too."

"I'm sure he will. I'll tell him—"

"Especially since Talia Shafer is from there."

Rudkowski froze in the process of raising his glass to his mouth. "Say again, deputy."

"Talia Shafer lives in Charleston. At least she did. I'm not sure Agent Easton knows that. This incident in Charleston occurred only a few hours after he called me, asking about her. It's a crazy coincidence."

"Not so crazy," Rudkowski said, speaking too softly for Gray to hear.

"I figured he would want to know about this new case, if he doesn't already. Since I can't reach him, will you see to it that he gets the message?"

Rudkowski clicked off the TV and swung his legs over the side of the bed. "You can count on it, Deputy Gray. In fact, I'm going to deliver it personally."

Chapter 22

Talia was immobilized by Drex's stare as two men eddied around him into the kitchen and introduced themselves to the detectives. Drex walked toward her, crowding into her personal space before he stopped. "Surprise."

"You're *FBI?*"

"The writing thing wasn't working out."

A cavalcade of recollections flashed through her mind. Her involuntary reactions to his deceptive charm, her nervous retreat from his apartment, her anguish over what had taken place in the garage of the medical building, the ambiguities she'd wrestled with, the times she had defended him against Jasper's reservations. All that crystalized into hatred.

Softly but emphatically, she said, "Go straight to hell."

"You tried that already." He spread his arms. "I'm still here, and you're up shit creek."

He held for a beat, then turned away from her and shook hands with Locke and Menundez. "I apologize for crashing your party, but I believe you'll welcome our intrusion. We can shed a lot of light on your investigation. Excuse me, Mike."

He nudged the enormous man aside and knelt down to reach beneath the cabinet. When he straightened up, he held out his hand to show the detectives the object in his palm.

"What is that?" Talia asked.

Drex turned to her. "Commonly called a bug. I've been using it to eavesdrop on you and Jasper."

"You bugged our home?"

"You say that like you didn't know it was there."

"I didn't! Isn't that illegal?"

She asked the group at large, but it was Drex who said, "It's not as illegal as kidnaping, conspiracy to commit murder, and murder, which is what you and Jasper stand to be indicted for, so if I were you, I wouldn't split hairs on legalities."

He wasn't teasing. He wasn't baiting her as he'd done in Elaine's living room. This wasn't playacting. He was serious, and the import of what he had alleged stole her breath. "What are you talking about?"

"We'll get to it. First, meet Agent Mike Mallory, who put me on to you and Jasper."

"A pleasure."

His response was so droll, Talia couldn't tell if it applied to the introduction or to the service he'd performed for Drex.

Drex pointed to the other man. "Agent Gif Lewis. He—"

"You're the man from the coffee shop," she said. "I remember you."

"That's a first," the heavy man said under his breath.

Gif Lewis acknowledged her with a polite nod. "Mrs. Ford."

Feeling stung and betrayed, she said, "But you seemed so nice. I truly believed you were trying to help."

"I was. Drex was coming on a little strong."

"He does that." She shifted her gaze to Drex, wondering if his fellow agents knew how strongly he had come on to her in the parking garage. He was still watching her with cool contempt, as though she were responsible for his actions, for the kiss. He didn't look away from her until Locke addressed him.

"You said you could shed light?"

Drex seemed to shake off whatever else he was thinking and got down to the matter at hand. "Has anybody checked Elaine Conner's financial portfolio, her bank accounts?"

"It was on another team's to-do list," Menundez said.

"Let me tell you what they'll find." Drex formed an O with his fingers and thumb. "Zero. Zilch. He cleans them out. He kills them. He vanishes."

"You can't mean Jasper."

Drex ignored Talia's outcry and said to his cohorts, "Take these gentlemen into the living area and start briefing them. We'll be there in a minute."

Locke looked uncertain about leaving her alone with Drex, but Menundez fell into step behind Drex's men. Locke followed. She waited until they were out of earshot before she launched into Drex. "You've been spying on us?"

"Most of it was boring. I didn't bug your bedroom."

"You bastard."

"But I make damn good corn on the cob."

Incensed, she spun away from him. "I want to hear what they're saying."

"Wait. Did you burn your hand?"

She looked back at him, wondering how he knew.

"The kettle whistled. You cried out."

"Never mind my hand." She placed it behind her back. "I want to know what's going on. First Elaine..." Grief, exhaustion, dismay, fear, and another dozen emotions avalanched and overwhelmed her. Hot tears filled her eyes. Her voice cracked. "I *hate* you."

"Let me see your hand."

She didn't move, so he went to her and reached behind her back. His touch wasn't rough, but still she flinched as he took hold of her hand. He examined the red splotch on the back of it, then pulled her over to the sink, turned on the cold water tap, and guided her hand beneath the stream. "Don't move."

She wanted to tell him to fuck off, but the cold water brought instant relief, so she stayed. He got ice cubes from the dispenser in the door of the refrigerator and returned with them. Placing his hand beneath hers, palm to palm, he supported it while gently rubbing the ice cubes across the burn.

She stared at their joined hands as the water spilled over them, became hypnotized by the slow circles he drew on the back of her hand with the ice cubes. "Don't be nice to me," she said, her voice hoarse. "You're ruining my life."

"You ruined your life the day you went in cahoots with Jasper, whom I first came to know as Weston Graham."

"I don't know what you're talking about. None of it."

His eyes bored into hers. "Where is he, Talia?"

"Atlanta. If you were listening in, you no doubt heard us laying plans last night. He and I—"

"He's not in Atlanta. He never went. He never intended to."

"You're trying to trick me like you've been doing since I met you." She tried to pull her hand away, but he curled his fingers up, linking them with hers and keeping her in place.

"Listen to me." His voice was low and emphatic. "All those questions the detectives put to you about Jasper, where he was tonight, and so forth? They already knew the answers. And your answers didn't mesh with what they know for fact.

"Local police, the sheriff's office, state police. They've got resources. Mike has even better resources. We've all been busy trying to determine Jasper's whereabouts ever since Elaine's body washed ashore and witnesses claimed that a man was at the helm of her yacht."

"Wearing a baseball cap that belongs to *you*."

"I didn't realize it was missing until Locke mentioned it. I'm certain that Jasper took it from the apartment the night we went out to dinner."

She opened her mouth to protest, but he cut her off with a hard shake of his head. "We'll argue the finer points later. What's important to your future, short-term and long-range, is to stop lying. Now."

"I'm not lying."

His jaw tensed angrily. "You lied to those detectives about a damn dental appointment and disagreeable pain pills. If you'll lie about something that trivial, you'll lie about something large."

She lowered her head. "That was a fib, not a significant lie."

She could feel his angry breathing against the crown of her head. "You've lied about plenty that *is* significant, Talia. Confirmed by the airlines: Jasper wasn't on that flight, nor any other Delta flight, private plane, or another carrier. Confirmed by TSA: His boarding pass was never scanned. He wasn't on their security cameras. Confirmed by the Lotus Hotel: He didn't check in or show up for your dinner reservation. All of which you told those detectives that he did." He put his finger beneath her chin and tipped her head up, forcing her to look directly into his incisive eyes. "Where. Is. He?"

"If he's not at The Lotus Hotel in Atlanta, then I. Don't. Know."

He held her stare for several seconds, then dropped the remnants of the ice cubes into the sink and turned off the faucet. They shared a dishtowel to dry their hands. "Do you want to put some salve on that burn?"

"I think it's okay."

He motioned her toward the living area. "Remember, I gave you a chance."

Mike, Gif, and the two detectives had drawn chairs up to the coffee table and were huddled around it, intent. As Drex and Talia entered the room, Locke was saying, "But no bodies were ever discovered?"

Drex said, "Not until Marian Harris."

Talia stopped in her tracks. "Marian?"

"Your friend Marian Harris." Drex pointed at the sofa. "Have a seat."

"I'll stand."

"Suit yourself, but this is going to take a while." In order to join the group, he pulled a chair over to the table, took off his jacket, and hung it on the back before sitting down. As he loosened his necktie, he asked Mike, "Have you worked forward or backward?"

"Forward. Starting with—"

"Lyndsay Cummings," Drex said. "The first we know of."

"Right." Mike shifted in his chair. "We'd just got to the Harris woman."

"Please don't refer to her like that," Talia said. "She was my friend."

Drex crossed his arms over his chest and leaned back in his chair. "You and Jasper talked at length about Marian last night. My 'excessive' interest in Key West had you both skittish."

"Did you bring up Key West only to bait me?"

"Yes. And guess what? You bit."

He turned to the detectives. "During her conversation with her husband about it, Talia admitted to getting upset over any mention of Key West and/or Marian Harris." He recapped what he'd overheard.

"This is a direct quote that refers to me. Jasper asks, 'Do you think he knows something about Marian?' Talia replies, 'No. Maybe, Jasper. I don't know.' Jasper, anxious and insistent. 'He's living next door, Talia. I should have known about this immediately.'

"They go on like that for about ten minutes. Neither confessed to nailing her inside a shipping crate, but it was a telling discussion. On the heels of it, they made plans to leave town. It's recorded. You can listen if you want."

Talia was looking at him with horror. "Jasper thought you were on a fishing expedition, that *you* might have nailed Marian inside that shipping crate." She turned to the other men. "Jasper didn't completely trust him from the start. He thought he was a phony.

"He became even more suspicious when Drex expressed his interest—which *was* excessive—in Key West. Out of the bug's range, Jasper theorized that the discovery of Marian's body might have made the culprit nervous, that he was going around to former acquaintances of hers and testing their reactions to any mention of her or Key West." Looking back at Drex, she said, "If he sounded skittish, it was because he didn't want happening to me what had happened to Marian."

She had grown heated. Drex remained cool. "The culprit did get nervous, all right. Because he feared I knew that he had bilked Marian, then killed her."

"Jasper didn't even know her!"

Drex lunged forward, almost coming out of his chair. "You two met through her."

"No, we didn't. I told you how we met."

He sat back. "Share with the detectives. Mike and Gif already know the story."

Talking rapidly, in stops and starts, she told Locke and Menundez a condensed version.

When she finished, Drex said, "It's awfully sweet, but it's a lie."

Mike addressed the two detectives. "Our guy had hooked his other ladies using online match-up services."

"That's not how he and I met," Talia said.

"Right enough," Drex said. "You were introduced by Marian Harris."

"Jasper and I didn't meet until months after Marian's disappearance."

Drex motioned to Mike, who withdrew the party photo from a file he'd brought in with him. Drex got up and walked over to the sofa, where Talia had changed her mind about sitting down. He held the picture out to her. "Ever seen this?"

"Yes. It was the last known picture taken of Marian. After her disappearance, the police interviewed everyone who was at that party, me included."

He looked at the photograph as though giving it a fresh assessment. "You're not exactly in on the merriment. How come you're out there on the fringes all by yourself?"

"I didn't know any of the other guests."

He cocked his head to one side, indicating doubt.

She said, "I went to Key West to check out a hotel. Marian was a good client. I called her to see if she and I could have lunch. She said what good fortune it was that I was in town. She was hosting a party that night and insisted that I attend."

"You didn't know anyone else there?"

"I just said that."

"You didn't mix and mingle?"

"Since I was the outsider, Marian introduced me to several people."

"What about him?" He pointed out the blurred figure silhouetted against the sunset. "Did she introduce you to him?"

She squinted. "Possibly."

"What's his name?"

"I don't know."

"Daniel Knolls."

"If we were introduced, I don't remember him."

He leaned down to her and whispered, "You're sleeping with him."

She recoiled. "That's not Jasper!"

He passed the picture to Locke, who looked at it and passed it to his partner. It made its way back to Mike, who replaced it in the file. Drex returned to his chair and gave Talia a long look. She stared back with defiance and hostility. "Say you're as honest as Abe, telling the truth—"

"I am."

"Haven't you been struck by the similarities between Elaine Conner and Marian Harris?"

He could tell by the wariness in her eyes that she had. He let that question simmer, then said, "You told the detectives that you and Jasper parted company in the airport parking garage."

"We did."

"You told Jasper that you didn't feel up to going, but urged him to go without you. You kissed goodbye and waved each other off."

She nodded, but only after a nanosecond of hesitation, which Drex made mental note to pursue later.

He said, "You drove Jasper's car out of the airport."

"Yes."

"She did," Menundez said. "I got texted a security cam freeze frame."

Mike had that, too, but Drex didn't reveal that. The local cops didn't need to be apprised of Mike's hacking talents, lest some rule-bending was soon called for. To Talia, he said, "The camera got you, but if someone was inside the trunk of your car, Jasper for instance, he would have gotten away unseen."

"Uh, Easton. He took a taxi." Menundez held up his cell phone. "They texted me the video. Shows clear that he never went inside the airport. They're checking with the taxi company to see where it dropped him."

Mike had obtained that information more than an hour ago. Drex had only used the ploy about escaping in the car trunk to see how Talia would react when she learned that Jasper truly had run out on her.

Looking stunned, she asked quietly, "May I see that video, please?" Menundez handed her his phone. Stoically she watched the brief segment of video, then passed the phone back. "Thank you."

Drex got up again, walked over to the sofa, and, this time, sat down beside her. Close beside her. Close enough to feel her trembling. "Talia, it's not too late for you to talk to us. I don't know what Jasper told you, or promised you, but it appears that he's abandoned you to take the fall."

"For what?"

"Elaine's murder."

"It hasn't been established that she was murdered. There could have been an accident. He could be out there in the water, waiting to be rescued."

"The man who swims miles every day?"

"He could be hurt."

"He could also be safely on shore and changing his appearance as we speak. The next time you see him, you won't recognize him as the man you share a bed with. You didn't recognize him as the man at Marian's party, but that was him, going by the name of Daniel Knolls. Marian was his most recent victim before Elaine, but there were a lot of others before he met you. He doesn't deserve your loyalty. One last time, where is he?"

"I don't know." Her voice was so husky, it was barely audible.

He stayed as he was, peering deeply into her eyes. They were watery, but she never looked away.

Sighing regret, Drex stood up and motioned for the other men to follow him. They withdrew as far as the entryway. They were still within Talia's sight, but Drex spoke so that she couldn't overhear.

He posed a question to the group at large. "What do you think?"

Locke said, "Since we first broke the news to her about the body on the beach, she's seemed distraught and unaware of her husband's activities." He looked over at his partner.

Menundez shrugged. "I don't know. I flip-flop."

Drex looked at Gif. "What's your verdict?"

"We've laid a lot on her. I abstain."

Drex gave him a sour look. "Mike? Your take?"

Mike addressed the detectives. "How much do you know about her? You know she's not hurting financially?"

"We haven't been given figures," Locke said, "but word is that she's worth a bundle."

"Well, up to this point, me, Gif, and Drex have been agonizing. Was she going to be this asshole's next victim? Or was she in on his fleecing scheme?" He raised one beefy shoulder. "She's still breathing. Elaine Conner is in the morgue. Which is answer enough for me."

"Victim or accomplice," Drex said, "we've reached a stalemate with her."

He looked into the living room, where Talia sat, hands clasped in her lap, rocking back and forth, staring vacantly into space. She looked frail and afraid. But he thought of how hot and cute she had looked when she'd paid him the surprise visit to the apartment. That could have been calculated. It had worked. He'd wanted what was inside those ragged jeans.

This sad victim could also be a pose that appealed to another instinct. He wanted to be her protector, to hold her, reassure her, comfort her over the tragic loss of her friend. His susceptibility made him mad at her, but absolutely furious with himself.

He turned back to the other men. "I'm thinking a night spent in the detention center might make her more forthcoming."

Chapter 23

Drex's suggestion caused Locke to wince. "We don't have anything to hold her on."

"Seriously, Drex?" Gif said in a stage whisper. "Jail?"

"It would be a short night," he argued. "Only a few hours. Just long enough to convince her that we're not messing around."

"One major discrepancy is gnawing at me," Gif said. "The audio surveillance." He told the detectives about Jasper's finding the transmitter and moving it. Looking back to Drex, he said, "If he knew you were eavesdropping, why did he talk about Marian Harris at all?"

"Because he can't help himself from bragging about killing her and getting away with it." He turned to the two detectives. "I've been after him for a long time, but having spent time with him and learning the unspeakable circumstances of Marian Harris's murder, it's evident to me that he has the characteristic ego of a serial killer. He doesn't want to be caught, but his ego compels him to flaunt how smart he is."

With chagrin, he added, "Much as I hate to admit it, he outsmarted me this time. He said just enough. Stopped just shy of a confession. He knew that a defense lawyer would shred the recording in court, even if it were admissible, which it isn't. Jasper used it to get me running in the wrong direction, and now he's laughing up his sleeve."

"I guess you're right," Gif said, and the rest nodded in grudging agreement.

Drex asked the group, "So what's it to be?"

"If we mention jail, she'll lawyer up," Menundez said.

"Shit." Drex dragged his hand down his face. "You're right. In which case, our involvement would become known. Sooner or later, if not already, the FBI will get in on this investigation. There's a resident office here, right?"

Locke nodded.

"Good men and women, I'm sure, but I would rather continue operating independently if at all possible."

"We could use their help, Drex," Gif said.

"True, but here's my thought. Jasper knows that I'm screwing with him, but he doesn't know why. I could be a crook trying to poach his territory. I could be a gigolo after his hot wife. I could be a cop trying to nail his murderous ass. As long as he's unsure, we have an edge."

"How's that?" Locke asked.

"Because I don't think he'll be able to stand not knowing. I don't think he'll go too far afield without either dismissing me because I'm no real threat, or dispatching me because I am. But if I'm at the epicenter of a bureau investigation, he won't risk sticking around. He'll leave me to the devil and vanish."

Mike said, "I predict he'll vanish if you put his wife in lockup. As you told her, he'll turn his back and let her take the fall."

Drex scowled. "Thanks for those words of wisdom, Mike."

"I'm just saying—"

"And you're right," he snapped. "I just don't trust her not to take off, and we can't strap on an ankle bracelet."

"Good God, no," Gif said.

Looking troubled, Locke said, "How about this? No lockup, but make it clear to her that she's not to go anywhere. Get Mount Pleasant PD to send over a policewoman to stay inside the house with her."

"With us right next door, that would be overkill," Drex said. "Besides, someone shows up in a uniform, she'll clam up even tighter until she can summon a lawyer. Gif, Mike, and I'll take turns standing watch till morning."

"She won't like it," Locke said.

"I don't give a fuck what she likes." Drex thought on it, then added, "But having a couple of patrolmen outside wouldn't be a bad idea. They'd be two extra sets of eyes for us and give her peace of mind."

"How will I explain the three of you to them?" Locke asked.

Drex shrugged. "Tell them the truth, but emphasize that we're undercover and that if they tell anybody we're here, even within their own department, we'll cut out their tongues."

"In other words, use subtlety and tact," Gif said.

"I'll get on it." Menundez took out his phone, but before placing the call, he read another text. "You were right, Easton. Local FBI is now assisting," he told the group, then continued reading. "Word got out how similar our case is to Marian Harris's. Tomorrow, an agent familiar with that investigation is flying in to talk to Mrs. Ford."

Mike groaned.

"Rudkowski?" Drex asked Menundez.

"How'd you know?"

Gif, Mike, and Drex exchanged looks of disgust. Drex said, "He's a blowhard. All mouth. No brains. The three of us took personal days, using phony excuses, just to follow this lead on Jasper Ford before Rudkowski could barge in and muck it up. Mike eluded him yesterday, made him look like an ass, which isn't difficult to do. He won't be happy to see us."

"Who has seniority?" Locke asked.

"He does. In years, not know-how. What time is he due?"

"Around ten. Wants to interview Mrs. Ford right away."

"They say where?" Mike asked.

Menundez shook his head.

"Find out and let us know the location," Drex said. "We'll have her there." Seeing the consternation registered by Mike and Gif, he said, "It was only a matter of time, guys. We're lucky he didn't run us to ground before now."

———✦———

Talia had remained seated on the sofa. When the group of men broke up, the two detectives came over to her and expressed their condolences regarding Elaine. "I'm sorry we had to put you through that identification procedure," Locke said.

"You were only doing your job."

He thanked her for her cooperation then said, "We're still relying on your cooperation, Mrs. Ford. Please don't leave town."

"I have no intention of going anywhere until my husband is accounted for."

He nodded and gave her his business card. Menundez also passed her his.

Locke said, "Call either of us if you think of anything that could be useful to the investigation."

Although Drex's arguments were damning, she wasn't ready to concede that it had been Jasper onboard the yacht with Elaine. "Are they still searching for the man?"

"Yes, ma'am. We'll notify you if there's something to report."

"Please. No matter how bad the news may be."

He gave her a bland smile. "Try to get some rest. We'll see you tomorrow."

Menundez nodded a quasi goodbye, then followed Locke out, leaving her alone with Drex and his partners.

Gif said, "I'll take first shift."

Talia shot to her feet. "What do you mean first *shift*?" She walked over to Drex. "You're my jailers now?"

"Protectors."

She scoffed at that. "I feel less safe with you than with anybody."

"Then you'll be relieved to know that two police officers will be parked on the street. If you feel unsafe, you can signal them for help, and they'll come running."

"Am I allowed to go upstairs to my room? Alone."

Ignoring her snideness, he said, "Of course. In fact I recommend it. Tomorrow doesn't promise to be your best day. Get some sleep if you can. See you in the morning."

He turned away and walked from the room, the large man lumbering behind him. Gif passed her his business card. "That's my cell number. Text me if you need anything during the night."

She took the card but was still looking at the arched opening through which Drex had left. "Does he always wear that gun?" She'd seen the holster clipped to his belt at the small of his back.

"While on duty."

"Is he a good guy or bad guy?"

"Depends on who's asking."

She looked at Gif. "*I'm* asking. Can I trust him?"

"You can trust his commitment to catching Weston Graham."

"You mean Jasper?"

"To Drex he'll always be Weston Graham."

"Why?"

"You'll have to ask Drex." He backed away. "I'll be in the kitchen."

He left her. She turned toward the staircase, which, in her exhausted state, looked as daunting as Everest. Using the bannister for support, she climbed it slowly.

She got into the bath but sat beneath the shower and rested her head on her raised knees. From the detectives' arrival until now, she'd been required to function with some level of composure and reasonableness.

Now that she was alone, the reality of her circumstances crashed down on her. Elaine was dead. Jasper was a multifaceted mystery. And she? She was trapped in a mercurial situation that defied her attempts to grasp it.

As the water pounded over her, she wept. Hard. Copiously. In wracking sobs. When the water ran cool, she got out and pulled on an old pair of cotton pajamas that she hadn't worn since her marriage. The printed fabric, baggy bottoms, and loose-fitting top had been designed for comfort, not seduction.

She left the master bedroom in favor of the guest room across the hall. She got into bed and lay motionless in the darkness, staring at the ceiling.

Where was Jasper? If it was true that he hadn't gone to Atlanta, why hadn't she heard from him? If he had survived the accident that killed Elaine, was he struggling to hold on until he was rescued? Or was he dead? Why had he gone to Elaine tonight? Which of them had suggested that they take the yacht out? Why were they in the dinghy? What had he done?

She had cried her eyes dry over Elaine, but, as she was assailed by unthinkable possibilities about her husband, they stung with the need to cry more. Questions swirled through her mind like a swarm of fireflies, blinking on, blinking off before she could arrive at an answer.

When the door opened, she knew who it was before he spoke. "You didn't get your tea."

She pushed herself up onto her elbows. "What?"

"I noticed the tea bag in an otherwise empty mug on the counter. You burned your hand when you lifted the kettle off the stove and never got your chamomile."

She switched on the bedside lamp. He held the steaming mug in one hand. A fat accordion file was secured in the crook of his other arm. He came into the room without invitation, but she was too depleted to put up an argument. He set the mug on the nightstand and laid the file on the foot of the bed.

"What's that?"

"Some light reading in case you can't sleep. But beware. If you start on it, I doubt you'll sleep at all."

"Thanks for the tea."

To her annoyance, he drew an armchair over to the side of the bed and sat down.

"Don't feel like you have to stay."

He didn't bother to acknowledge the hint that he leave. He asked how her hand was.

"Hardly stings anymore."

"Good."

Still, he didn't go. He spread his knees and clasped his hands between them. Head down, addressing the floor, he said, "I'm sick about Elaine. You have every reason to doubt my sincerity, but I mean it, Talia. I had my eyes on Jasper. On you. But I should have seen this coming. Warned her. Something."

"She wouldn't have believed you, especially if you had warned her off Jasper."

"Probably not. But I should have made an attempt. A word of caution might not have saved her, but I wouldn't feel so rotten about failing her." He sat up straight and looked at her directly. "Were they having an affair?"

"You were listening. You heard me ask, you heard Jasper deny it."

"I heard you ask and heard him deny it. But were you asking for my benefit, or yours? Were you playing to the bug, or did you really nurse suspicions about the nature of their relationship?"

"It didn't know anything about that damn bug! And I don't know whether or not to believe Jasper's denial. What I *do* know is that I would rather have Elaine alive and cheating with my husband than lying dead in the morgue." Her voice cracked. "Can we postpone talking about this please? At least until morning?"

"All right," he said with surprising empathy. "For whatever it's worth, I liked her. A lot, in fact."

"She was impossible not to like. I'll miss her...her..."

"Verve and vivacity."

She gave him a weak smile. "Good words. Maybe you should have become a writer."

"In my next life."

After a long stretch of silence that grew awkward for her, he looked around with curiosity, taking in the bedroom, which she had left intentionally uncluttered for the convenience of overnight guests.

But no guests had ever used the room. Jasper wasn't keen on inviting friends to stay over for a weekend or holiday. He'd never given her a satisfactory reason why, always brushing off her protest with something like, "I prefer having you all to myself." She'd never pressed the issue, and instead had visited out-of-town friends when she went on business trips.

As she had visited Marian when she made the trip to Key West. On the heels of that thought, she said, "I don't remember meeting that man in the party picture. If it was Jasper, I didn't know it."

He hiked an eyebrow.

"I'm telling you the truth. I didn't pick him out that night as someone I'd like to get to know."

"Maybe. But I'm certain he picked you out that night."

"What do you mean?"

"We'll circle back to that. Tomorrow. There's a lot of ground to cover tomorrow."

Miffed by his reticence, she said, "All the more reason for us to say our good nights now."

"Why are you sleeping in here? Why not in the master?"

"I didn't want you spying on me. You can't see into this room from your living room window."

"Fair comeback."

His wry smile gave her a hint of the dimple, and that irritated her. "You don't know fair from foul, Drex. You accuse me of lying, when that's all you've been doing."

"And now you know why."

"In the line of duty, I suppose."

"Yes. What's your excuse?"

She let it drop, too tired to fight back.

He motioned down to the mug. "Drink your tea while it's hot."

"It hasn't steeped long enough."

"What was the doctor's appointment about?"

The swift change in topic was tactical, intended to take her off-guard, and it did. "That's personal."

"So's murder."

"Don't bully me. Haven't I had enough to deal with tonight?" She reached for the mug of tea, but her hand was unsteady.

He took the mug from her. "You're going to scald yourself again."

"As if you care."

"I do care, goddammit!"

"That's not what you told your buddies!" Perhaps she had a reserve of fight left in her, after all. "I have excellent hearing and, clear as a bell, I heard exactly the regard you give my feelings, my likes and dislikes."

He looked about to defend himself, but she raised her hand to stop him. "Never mind." With a weary sigh, she pressed her head deeper into the pillow and looked at the ceiling. "Leave me alone, Drex. If you want to know about my appointment with the gynecologist, I'm sure one of your friends will unearth the information for you, even if it breaches ethics."

"Mike's already offered. I told him no."

She shifted her gaze back to him.

"I would rather you volunteer it," he said.

She didn't see what harm could come from him knowing. If she confided this, maybe she would win a measure of trust, which she feared she might need in the days to come.

"I would like to have a child. Jasper asked for time to adjust to the idea of parenthood at his age. But I'm not getting any younger, either. Biological clock. All that. So I had eggs harvested to be frozen until he...until the time was right to have IVF."

Drex didn't move, speak, blink.

"When you approached me in the coffee shop, I had just received the disappointing news that some of the eggs—and the number wasn't abundant to begin with—weren't robust. Which means much lower odds for success, should we decide even to try fertilization."

She was looking down at her fingers as they pleated the edge of the counterpane. His hand came into her range of vision. He was holding out the cup of tea with the handle toward her. She took it from him, sipped. The tea had grown tepid, but she continued to take small drinks of it. It gave her something to do besides look at him.

Since becoming involved with Jasper, she hadn't been alone with many men, but certainly with no one who unsettled her as Drex did. He posed an indefinable, but very real, threat. She'd felt it from the moment she met him. Instinct had cautioned her to Keep Away, not out of fear that he would endanger her intentionally, but as though she were getting too close to open flame. The light source that attracts the moth isn't responsible for its innate heat, nor can it be blamed for the moth's compulsion to fly into it.

While confident in every other circumstance of her life, when near Drex, she felt unsure and self-conscious. He made her aware of everything about herself. As now. She could feel every inch of her skin inside the soft pajamas, everywhere the cotton conformed to her shape, every place it abraded her with no more friction than a warm breath.

She was even more keenly aware of him. He had taken off his necktie. His collar button was undone, his shirt cuffs rolled back, his shirttail pulled out. At best, his hair had been finger combed. The dishevelment only made him more attractive. She flashed back to the sight of his bare chest and abdomen and the dusting of hair that tapered to a strip that disappeared into his low-slung waistband.

This awareness of him created a pressure against her chest, which she wanted to shove away . . . but also to hug tightly.

"One more question and I'll let you go to sleep," he said. "Why didn't you kiss goodbye?"

Her head came up. She met his gaze. She exhaled through her mouth. "What?"

"You and Jasper didn't kiss goodbye at the airport, did you? And the reason you didn't go on that trip had nothing to do with an attack of queasiness. Jasper picked a fight on the way to the airport, didn't he?"

"No."

"Talia."

She returned the mug the nightstand, threw off the covers, and tried to get up. He placed his hands on her shoulders. She resisted, but his eyes held her more imperatively than his hands.

"Jasper picked a fight," he said quietly but with intensity. "You quarreled. You didn't kiss goodbye and wave him off, did you? That was a lie."

She glared at him, breathing hard, but she would die before admitting that he was right.

"What was the fight about? You wanted IVF, he didn't?"

She shook her head. "I hadn't even told him I was having the harvesting procedure. I still haven't."

"Why not?"

"An opportunity hasn't presented itself."

"Bullshit. You've had plenty of opportunities to tell him. You haven't because you're afraid he'll be relieved, and his relief will break your heart."

"I'm not talking about this with you. It's personal. Furthermore, it's irrelevant."

"Is it?"

"Yes."

"Okay, so what did you quarrel about on the way to the airport?"

"It was a spat, over *nothing*. Nothing important."

"It was important enough for you to nix a romantic getaway."

"I wish I had it to do over again."

"Well, you don't!"

The incisiveness of his tone shut her down. She turned her head aside. He took hold of her chin and brought it back around. "Who started the quarrel?"

She pushed his hand away from her face. "I don't remember."

"Yes you do."

"What difference does it make?"

"A monumental difference. It was Jasper, right?"

She remained stubbornly silent.

He was just as stubbornly persistent. "Right?"

"All right, yes! He got angry."

"At what?"

"At me."

"Over what?"

"Over you!"

He recoiled and dropped his hands from her shoulders, then sat very still. "What about me?"

She reached for the mug of tea, changed her mind, and let her hand fall back onto the bed. She wet her lips. "While we were driving to the airport, Jasper picked up where he had left off the night before. He went on and on about how you couldn't be trusted. I came to your defense. Erroneously, as it turns out." She paused and took a swift breath to stave off a sob. "I should have listened when Jasper said you weren't who you claimed to be. You've been lying all along. Everything has been a lie. You played us. Jasper. Elaine. Me."

She jerked the covers back up and patted them into place, getting them just the way she wanted before looking at him. "Either arrest me and haul me to jail, or get out of here and leave me alone."

She rolled onto her side and faced away from him.

She kept her eyes squeezed shut. For the longest time he didn't move, but eventually she felt the shift of air when he stood. He switched out the lamp. In the darkness, she sensed him bending over her.

He whispered, "The kiss wasn't a lie." His fingers threaded through her hair and rearranged it on the pillow.

Then he left the room, closing the door softly behind him.

Chapter 24

In the kitchen, Gif was sitting at the table eating a bowl of cereal. "I helped myself," he said to Drex, crunching.

"I'm sure she won't mind."

"What did you help yourself to?"

Drex, who was on his way to the back door, stopped, turned, and gave his associate a berating look.

Unfazed, Gif spooned another bite into his mouth. "I go to the bathroom, come back. You're nowhere to be seen. I texted you. No reply. Texted Mike. He said you hadn't shown over there. You weren't in any of the rooms downstairs, so—"

"You've made your point."

Gif polished off the cereal in two slurping spoonfuls, then pushed the bowl aside. "Is that why you maneuvered this situation? You got the detectives out of here so you could tuck her in?"

"That's not why."

"'I'm thinking a night spent in the detention center,'" Gif quoted and gave an eye roll. "As if."

"Thanks for putting up the arguments against it. They made my suggestion more credible."

"I've worked with you long enough to know when you're manipulating someone."

"This way they went away thinking it had been their idea to leave her in our charge."

"Oh, I get why you did it. Just don't try to manipulate Mike and me."

"You're too smart for me."

"Question is," Gif said, and shot a glance toward the ceiling, "is she too smart for you?"

Drex backed up against the counter and crossed his arms. Staring at the toes of his shoes, he replied, "I don't know, Gif."

"Mike thinks she is."

"He's made that abundantly clear, but he mistrusts all women."

"And all men."

"And all men," Drex said around a chuckle. Then, back to serious, he said, "I took her a cup of tea, that's all. She looked weepy and vulnerable. I took advantage and tried to worm something out of her."

"To what avail?"

"Zip. She's either genuinely shaken by Elaine's death and mystified by Jasper's vanishing act—"

"Or?"

"Or she's a damn good con."

"She would have learned from the master."

"That's what I can't discount," he said, no joy in his tone. "So, tomorrow morning, you and Mike will deliver her to Rudkowski."

"Where will you be?"

"Making myself scarce."

Gif shook his head. "Drex—"

"Don't start, Gif. If I get anywhere near him, I had just as well cut off my dick now and deny him the pleasure."

Gif's silence indicated that he concurred. "What about Mike and me? What do you want us to do after dropping her off?"

"Has to be your decision, and each of you has to make up

his own mind, independent of the other and me. I can't ask you, nor do I expect you, to stick with me on this. You know the shit storm this is going to raise. Don't underestimate Rudkowski. We did before."

"This isn't like that."

"No, it's worse. Sleep on it. Sleep on it good." He pushed away from the counter and moved toward the door.

"Drex?"

He came back around.

"While Mike and I contemplate whether or not to stick with you or throw ourselves on Rudkowski's mercy, it would help if we knew how you were going to deal with her if it turns out that she's her husband's partner in crime."

The question was an insult. Damned if he was going to answer. "Mike will relieve you in a couple of hours."

The following morning when Talia entered the kitchen, the three men were gathered around the dining table, so deep into their discussion that she'd been there for a while before they noticed her.

When they did, they fell silent and stared, no doubt taken aback by her appearance. She'd pulled a robe on over her pajamas, but hadn't taken the time to groom herself before coming down.

Gif pushed back his chair and stood. "Good morning. Can I get you some coffee?"

The aroma of freshly ground beans was thick in the room, as was the yeasty scent of doughnuts. A box of them was in the center of the table. Gif nudged it in her general direction.

"Mike went out for them," he said. "Help yourself."

Disregarding Gif's offers, she walked straight to the table and thumped the thick file in front of Drex, nearly upsetting the cup of coffee in front of him. "I couldn't sleep, so I followed your suggestion to do some light reading."

He reached for the back of the chair that Gif had vacated and motioned her into it. "Get her some coffee, please, Gif."

She sat down in the proffered chair, not having taken her eyes off Drex since she'd come into the room. There were dark crescents under his eyes. He hadn't slept, either.

Gif set a cup of coffee within her reach, asked if she needed anything to go in it, and she shook her head. Drex took a chocolate-covered doughnut from the box, placed it on a paper napkin, and slid it over to her.

Ignoring the coffee and doughnut, she gestured at the bulging file. "You believe that Jasper had something to do with these women who went missing?"

He folded his forearms on the table, leaned upon them, and talked for half an hour virtually uninterrupted. Occasionally he asked Mike to verify a date or place. Gif elaborated when invited to. Otherwise, her attention stayed riveted on Drex, and his on her.

"He made himself fit into the lifestyle of an oil heiress in Tulsa. By those who knew Pixie, Herb Watkins was described as having short black hair, a goatee, and liked Native American art, for which Pixie had a passion.

"For Marian, he adopted frizzy hair, probably permed, because he knew it would be reminiscent of her hippie stage and that she would find that appealing.

"Then he spotted you at her party. Learned you were very well off. Saw you as a prospect. Through Marian and his own research, he learned everything he could about you. He probably followed you, Talia. Logged where you went, where you ate, what you drank, where you shopped.

"He deduced that, as a world traveler, you would be attracted to a sophisticated gentleman who would hand-deliver flowers even if it meant driving one hundred and fifty miles. Classy dresser. Gourmet cook. A man who appreciated expensive bourbon, all the finer things in life. Goodbye Daniel Knolls and his frizz, hello Jasper Ford with the cosmopolitan ponytail."

When he finished, she looked at each of the men in turn. Their expressions were grave. All too apparent was the depth of their conviction that Jasper was the man they sought. She didn't deny the allegations, didn't defend her husband, because to do so would be tantamount to accepting the horrific implication that he was indeed their culprit.

Drex asked if Marian had ever confided to her anything about her friend Daniel Knolls.

"No."

"Nothing?"

"She was a proud and private woman. If in fact the two of them had met online, she might not have wanted it known."

"That fits," Drex said. "He doesn't want a woman who would be open about it and, by talking about it, put someone on to him. If not for Mike's memory, he wouldn't have found the thread."

"Must have been a boon when you introduced him to Elaine Conner," Mike said. "He didn't have to work quite so hard."

She bowed her head and massaged her brow. "Before coming downstairs I called Detective Locke. They're certain that Elaine and the man onboard the yacht got into the dinghy together. His identity and fate are still unknown."

"I know his identity," Drex said. "It was Jasper, and he swam ashore. I'd bet my life on it."

She wanted not to believe it. She wanted to hear from Jasper that he had changed his travel plans, had gone somewhere else, and, after spending a remorseful and restless night, was on his way home for a reconciliation.

She wanted to rewind the clock to when they were newlyweds and she didn't harbor a single doubt as to his character. Or, if what these federal agents believed to be true, she would wish to revert to the life she'd had before meeting him.

But time couldn't be reversed. This was her here-and-now, and she must face this calamity head-on.

She looked at Drex. "Say that's true, that it was Jasper on the yacht with Elaine. How did he get to the marina? Locke told me that the taxi he took from the airport dropped him at a hotel out near there."

"He didn't check in," Mike said.

Locke had also told her that. "According to Locke, Jasper instructed the taxi driver to let him out a distance from the entry. I can't fathom why."

"To avoid security cameras," Drex said. "He had left a car either on the hotel property or somewhere in the vicinity. He drove it back to Isle of Palms, to a predetermined spot on one of the beaches. Remote. A place that would be dark as soon as the sun went down, but within reasonable walking distance of the marina.

"He went there on foot, chose his time, and managed to board the *Laney Belle* without being seen. If anyone had happened to see him, they would describe a man wearing an orange baseball cap, not a man with a gray ponytail."

"Locke said that Elaine's neighbors at the townhouse had seen her leaving it, alone, at around five-thirty. I suppose she and Jasper had a date to meet on the yacht."

"Not necessarily," Drex said. "He may have called her, told her that the two of you had squabbled, and asked if he could nurse his misery, or anger, on the yacht. Something like that."

"She would have dropped what she was doing to lend him a shoulder."

"He would have counted on that."

"But Elaine would have been disinclined to take the boat out in bad weather."

"Jasper appealed to her spirit of adventure. Or sweet-talked her. 'Please, Elaine. The ocean air will clear my head.' Once in open water, he convinced her that there was a malfunction of equipment, or an emergency onboard that spelled peril for them if they didn't abandon ship. Somehow he persuaded her to get into the dinghy."

"Without her cell phone? Or his?"

"Negligible," he said without forethought. "He would have

come up with something. The weather was interfering with cell service. They were out of service range. If she questioned him about the phones, providing a logical answer would have been easy. After he killed her—we won't know until after the autopsy by what method—he swam to shore."

"Clothed?"

"Possibly. But maybe after dispatching Elaine, he stripped down and used something to sink his clothes. He had a change waiting for him in the car on shore. I'd wager that those articles of clothing would be nothing like what the Jasper you know would wear."

Gif said, "He was probably long gone by the time Elaine Conner's body was discovered."

Talia wanted to clamp her hands over her ears and hear no more. But she had to hear it, had to deal with it, had to prepare herself for accepting the unimaginable. "Everything you've said is plausible. But every bit of it is assumption."

Drex conceded that with a nod.

"You could be completely wrong."

"Yes."

"Then how can you theorize with such certainty that it happened that way?"

"Because that's how I would have done it."

The statement caused her breath to catch. All along she had intuited that there was more to Drex Easton than he let on, that he was shrewder than he pretended to be, not nearly as laid-back, that there was a dark side camouflaged by the dimple.

But she had miscalculated just how much intensity he concealed with his superficial posturing. He was a man on a mission. One had to respect his commitment. But it also filled her with foreboding.

"How long have you been after him?"

"Long time."

"Since—?"

"Seems forever."

"And you won't stop until you catch him, will you?"

"Never doubt it."

She gestured at the file lying on the tabletop between them. "And if Jasper proves not to be him?"

"He is, Talia. He is."

His tone left no doubt of that, either.

Chapter 25

Talia, when you left the airport where did you go?" Drex asked.

"I came home."

"At ten o'clock."

"Was it?"

Mike said, "Ten oh-three to be exact."

"How can you be exact?" she asked.

"I was about to board a flight."

Drex took up the explanation. "Mike was in Atlanta, waiting on you and Jasper to show up at The Lotus."

"So he could spy on us?"

"Yes," he replied without apology. "But when we learned that you and Jasper never got on the flight, and that a body had washed ashore, plans changed quickly. Gif and I went straight to the marina. We got there in time to see Elaine's body taken away. From the marina, we came to the apartment and were on the phone with Mike giving him an update when you drove into your driveway."

"At ten oh-three," the large man repeated.

She ignored him. "When I got home, there weren't any lights on inside the garage apartment. But then, if you were spying on me, there wouldn't have been, would there?"

"No. Spying is easier with the lights off."

"Don't make fun of me."

"I'm not. None of this is fun or funny, Talia. Do you want to hear the rest?"

Tamping down her humiliation and anger, she bobbed her head.

"Gif and I were debating what to do about you when Locke and Menundez showed up. The transmitter was too far away to pick up what they were saying until you moved into the kitchen. For all we knew, they'd come to arrest you. We know now they asked you to make an ID."

"If you already know all that, why are you bringing it up?"

"The time gap. Surveillance cameras show you leaving the airport at four forty-seven."

"Eight," Mike said.

Drex gave him a frown but corrected himself. "Four forty-eight. Talia, where were you between then and ten o'clock?"

"Does it matter?"

"It'll matter to Locke, Menundez, and every other investigator on this case, county, state, and federal, including our own Bill Rudkowski."

Mike said, "It'll matter a lot if, during that five hours, you hooked back up with your husband, say on the beach, where you were flashing a light so he would know where to make landfall after ensuring that Elaine Conner was no longer breathing."

Talia was developing a tremendous dislike for this man, and hoped that the drop-dead look she gave him conveyed as much. She went back Drex. "From the airport I drove downtown."

"And did what?"

"Walked around."

"Such a nice night for a stroll," Mike said. "In the drizzle and rain and all."

"I was unmindful of the weather."

None of the men took issue, but they were regarding her with patent doubt.

"Where did you walk?" Drex asked.

"Along Bay Street. I went into a restaurant and lingered."

"Lingered, why?"

"There was no rush to get home. I believed Jasper had gone to Atlanta."

The men looked at one another and seemed to conclude that her answer was at least credible, if not truthful.

"Where did you park downtown?" Gif asked.

"I got lucky and found an empty parallel spot on one of the side streets."

"Fucking lucky, I'd say," Mike muttered.

Her temper snapped. "I've had it with you and your snide editorials. If you want to accuse me of lying, do it. If not, stop with the mumbling, all right?"

Drex patted the air in a *calm down* gesture and suggested that Mike dispense with his remarks unless they were pertinent. He asked Talia for the name of the restaurant. She told him.

"The waiter will remember me. I had two glasses of wine and ordered dinner. But I didn't have an appetite and never touched the plate. The waiter noticed and asked if the food wasn't to my liking. He offered to bring me something else. I declined, tipped him well, and left."

"Did you pay with a credit card?"

"Yes."

Drex turned to Gif. "Relay all that to Locke. Their guys can do the fact-checking."

Gif left the room to make the call. Drex glanced at the clock. "Menundez texted that Rudkowski is going to interview you downtown at police headquarters." He looked her over, taking in her dishabille. "You'll need to be ready in twenty minutes or so in order for Mike and Gif to get you there by ten o'clock." He pushed back his chair and stood.

"Aren't you coming with us?"

"No."

"Why?"

"I've got other things to do."

She stood up. "Such as?"

"Such as going after your husband without being hamstrung by red tape. Good luck."

"Wait. What's going to happen with this Rudkowski?"

He shrugged. "I don't know."

"Guess," she said tartly.

"Well, if I were to guess, he'll spend most of today taking turns grilling you hard, then leaving you alone for long stretches of time to search your conscience, to ruminate on and perhaps reassess your position. Don't say a word unless a lawyer is with you."

"You're worried about my welfare?"

"No, I'm worried about testimony being tossed out because it was obtained without counsel present. Rudkowski may claim you as the feds' own, but if Locke is also allowed to interrogate you, he'll be the good cop. Menundez is young and yet to prove himself, so you can probably count on him to be tougher. But you probably won't see anyone familiar. Except your lawyer. I hope you have a good one."

"What about them?" She indicated Mike, who was inspecting what was left of the doughnut selection, and Gif, who'd just returned and announced that Rudkowski's plane had landed.

In answer to her question, Drex said, "The three of us are out of Rudkowski's favor and unsure what form his payback will take. Could be a slap on the wrist, or much harsher discipline. Mike and Gif have volunteered to face his wrath and that of the bureau, giving me a head start tracking down your lawfully wedded husband."

"Who could be dead!"

"He isn't."

"You don't know that."

"Yes, I do. Furthermore, so do you, Talia."

"I know no such thing."

"Come on. You don't believe for a second that he's foundering out there in the ocean, praying for rescue. Know how we know? Tell her, Gif."

The other man said, "If you thought that your husband was in a struggle to survive a watery grave, you would be hysterical."

Drex rounded the table and bore down on her so that she had to grab hold of the back of her chair to maintain her balance. "Hysterical. As in out of your mind. Frantic. You'd be tearing at your hair and raising hell with the Coast Guard, with every damn body, to *find* him, *save* my husband." He leaned in closer, and added softly, "You haven't."

She angled away from him, but he only made a countermove to keep his face within inches of hers. "When you were told there was a man at the helm of Elaine's boat, and I was ruled out, it was no mystery to you who it was. Which leaves Mike, Gif, and me, and all the other cops working this case, with only two possible conclusions.

"One, you knew who the man was all along because you two conspired to kill Elaine. Or," he said, slapping his palm against the file lying on the table, "you believe Jasper Ford is the latest incarnation of our man. You believe he harmed these eight women. Now nine. He befriended them, robbed them, killed them, and disposed of them."

She hiccupped a sob. "I don't want to believe it."

"But you do, don't you?"

Drex was stirring her long-held, secret fear that she didn't really know her husband. Ambiguities and uncertainties, which she had staved off, rationalized, chalked up to an illicit affair, and even taken blame for, were now closing in on her. They were so cruel and frightening, she tried to keep them at bay. "What evidence do you have against him?"

"Not a frigging bit."

"Then—"

"But answer me this. Do you honestly believe they're going to find Jasper or his body? In a dire emergency, would your water-savvy husband have left a vessel as tricked out as that yacht? Even if their phones weren't working, even if all fail-safe systems *had* failed, he wouldn't have swapped that yacht for a damn dinghy.

"Do you actually expect him to come staggering through that door battered and bruised, embrace you, and give you an account of a harrowing experience? No. You don't. You strike none of us as a lady who's waiting in desperation for her missing and feared-dead husband to return."

He jabbed the space between them with his index finger. "He took Elaine on that excursion with the intention of killing her. And he did. Deny it till hell freezes, but you know it, and so do we."

Pressured by her own doubt, feeling the weight of their vile allegations, she hugged her elbows and sank into the chair.

Her failure to respond immediately, along with her self-protective body language, spoke volumes to Drex. Now was the time to apply the thumbscrews. He said to Gif, "Call the PD. Stall them."

"How?"

"Shit, I don't know. Try to get Locke. He's tenderhearted. Tell him she's not feeling well, that we can't get her out of the bathroom, something. Ask him to pacify Rudkowski. Say that we'll have her there soon. Ish. An hour at the outside."

"Will it be an hour at the outside?"

"Remains to be seen." Gif left the kitchen to do as instructed. Drex motioned at the box of doughnuts and said to Mike, "Take those to the officers posted outside."

"I already took them a box of their own when I brought these."

"Then ask them if they need a bathroom break. Water. Sodas. Tell them Mrs. Ford is currently indisposed, but we're working on her."

"Rudkowski won't hold out forever."

"Neither will Mrs. Ford if she knows what's good for her."

That roused her. She straightened her hunched shoulders and looked up at him. He said, "They're champing at the bit to interrogate you. And make no mistake, that's what today will be. One long, grueling interrogation. I suggest you be thinking of what you're going to say."

"I need time to—"

"You've had time, Talia. I gave you time last night. You're out of time."

"Allow me to absorb all this. Please."

Drex considered, then said to Mike, "Buy me a few minutes with those guys outside."

Mike limited his opinion to a harrumph and a scowl then left through the door connecting to the garage. They heard the automated door going up. Drex resumed his seat at the table. He stared at her until she squirmed and asked, "What?"

"You're using up your minutes."

She raised her hands in a gesture of helplessness. "It's all so much." She looked at the file. "So horrendous. I don't know where to start."

He got up from his chair and dragged it over near to hers. He straddled it backward so they were facing each other. He met her gaze directly and waited. Waited longer. Then said, "This will come as no surprise. I've wanted you since I first laid eyes on you."

Her lips separated, but she didn't say anything.

"When we were alone on the deck of Elaine's yacht, I was staring at you, all right. Engaging in polite conversation, but in my mind all your layers of white clothing were dissolving, and I was seeing you naked and on your back in an unmade bed. During your surprise visit to the garage apartment, I honestly don't know how I kept my hands off you. Touching your face was all I allowed myself, and it was torture. I still taste that kiss, your mouth. I want to taste you all over. I want to—"

He broke off, dropped his head forward, and finished in a rough voice. "I want to do it all." Then he raised his head, and, in a soft but insistent voice, said, "But if you fucking lie to me now, I'll see to it that you go to prison for a long, long time."

She swallowed. Faintly, she said, "Everything I've told you is the truth. I swear it. How Jasper—that's the only name I've known him by. How we met, all of it, true, Drex. Elaine was my friend. Marian. How you could think that I would…"

She had to swallow again, then recovered and faced him with a small measure of defiance. "I have fibbed to you about inconsequential things. But I am not a criminal. I never conspired to hurt anyone."

"Okay. Okay. That still leaves us with this. The man you're married to is a serial killer. I've been after him for years. I've crawled inside his twisted brain, put myself in his place, and it's a hellish, diabolical place to be. I loathe it. I detest it. I don't want to live the rest of my life inside his fucked-up head.

"Until I moved next door and met him face-to-face, he was a phantom. Vapor. No more tangible than fog and just as impossible to capture. I feared I never would. But now I know he's human."

He raised his hand and squeezed it into a fist. "He's flesh and blood. He eats and drinks. He puts on his pants one leg at a time. He sweats. He's real, and he lives among us. I can touch him, and I'm going to catch him." He paused and inhaled deeply. "Where could he be, Talia?"

"I don't know. I swear I don't."

"Hometown?"

"He claimed none. He told me his parents were itinerant workers."

"Where?"

"I got the impression of southern California. But I don't know if he told me that, or if that was conjecture on my part."

"His parents' names?"

"He wouldn't talk about them. He said he'd risen above his

roots, and didn't want to revisit the past. Ever. And, anyway, they were both deceased."

"No family?"

"None."

"Old friends?"

"No."

"Convenient." He had expected as much. "Did he mention past relationships, former marriages?"

"He was married once, a long time ago. She died."

"She didn't die. He killed her. Her name was Lyndsay Cummings."

Talia glanced at the file. "She was the first of the eight?"

"First that we know of." He wiped his damp upper lip with the side of his index finger. "Did he ever talk about her and their marriage?"

"He said the memories were too painful."

"No doubt."

She rested her hand on top of the file, staring at it. "No bodies were ever discovered, Drex."

"Which doesn't mean they weren't killed. What it does mean is that we haven't had forensic evidence that could connect the disappearance of one woman to another, and then to another, establishing a pattern that would ultimately point us to an individual. Not until Marian Harris, that is."

She pressed her fingertips to her lips. "He couldn't have done that."

He didn't argue with her, but she gained some breathing room when Gif returned. "A message from Rudkowski. He says we either deliver the material witness within half an hour or he's coming here after her, and woe be to us."

"Shit!"

"Locke's patting his hand, but you know Rudkowski. Where's Mike?"

"Hand-patting the patrolmen outside."

"How long are you willing to wait, Drex?"

"Five more minutes."

Gif divided a look between him and Talia, took in the seating arrangement, and must have concluded that Drex was putting on the full court press. He said, "I'll check to see if there's anything I can do to further Mike's cause." He left by way of the garage door.

"You heard," Drex said. "You've got five. So think and talk fast. What did Jasper bring into the marriage?"

"Sorry?"

"Possessions, Talia."

"I don't understand what you're asking."

"The guys I profile are sociopaths, and they share characteristics. No conscience. Above the rules. They're smug and have overblown egos."

"I overheard you describing that to the detectives last night."

He nodded. "They're also compulsive collectors."

"Collectors?"

"They take souvenirs."

He watched her face as she reasoned out what he was saying. Her gaze dropped to the file. "What were they missing?"

"We don't know, and that's been damn frustrating. None of the women had the same body type, no common feature like blue eyes, crooked teeth, long hair, short hair, a beauty mark. They were physically different, and lived different lifestyles. No common hobby.

"Nothing alike except healthy bank accounts that were emptied within days of their disappearances. He could collect safe deposit box keys, ballpoint pens, locks of hair, fingernails. We don't know. But I would bet my career that there's something he takes from them. And saves. And takes out on occasion and fondles. Possibly masturbates."

She looked nauseated at the thought.

"Does he have a safe, sealed packing box, tool box, tackle box, anything that he asked you not to open?"

She was shaking her head before he finished. "He told me he had sold everything when he moved to Savannah."

"From Florida."

"He said Minnesota. He told me he no longer needed heavy clothing and cold weather gear, so he had disposed of everything."

"A logical lie. But didn't he have any personal items? Photographs? Memorabilia? Stamp collection? Coins? A cigar box of postcards?"

"Nothing, Drex."

He looked at his wristwatch. "*Think*, Talia."

"He had his car, his clothes, some cookbooks."

He shot to his feet. "Where are they?"

"They're *cookbooks*."

"Where are they?"

But by the time he had repeated the question, he had remembered the shelf above the stove. He went over to it and picked one of the books at random. It was a two-year-old edition with a glossy cover. The spine was unbent. The pages were so new and unused, some stuck together. He remarked on its newness.

"When we met, he hadn't been a foodie for long," she said. "It was a hobby he began after his retirement."

"Books are good hiding places. I'll have Gif tear into them." She seemed on the verge of protesting, and he pounced on that.

"Do you *want* him caught, Talia?"

The file held her interest for a ponderous moment, then she looked up at him. "If he did what you allege, then, yes, of course. Those women deserve justice."

He said nothing, just looked at her.

"You don't believe I'm sincere?"

"You married him, Talia, and shared all that the state of matrimony implies. I think you'll have a difficult time convincing Rudkowski, et al., that you never felt something was off about your husband."

"I felt he kept secrets," she said softly and with reluctance. "More lately than at first. I attributed it to an affair."

"Had you ever accused him prior to night before last?"

"No."

"You showed your hand with that accusation. You're lucky he went after Elaine first. When I came tearing down here to South Carolina, I thought I was rushing in to save *you*. You're loaded. All of us figured you were next. But you weren't."

"You sound disappointed."

"No, I just want you to understand what that means to you. If the authorities don't find his body, and they won't, they'll keep their eye on you. They may not call you a suspect, but there'll always be that shadow of doubt as to what you knew or didn't know, what your level of participation was, if you had any compliance whatsoever."

"I didn't!"

"Okay."

"You don't believe me," she exclaimed. "What do I have to do to prove I'm innocent?"

"Die."

She slumped against the back of her chair and looked at him with incredulity over his bluntness.

He said, "If you turn up dead, the authorities will reason that he killed you to shut you up, whether or not you were culpable. If you go on living, untouched, there'll forever be that question mark beside your name."

She looked around her, taking in various perspectives of the room as though it had become alien territory. When she came back to him, she said, "I realized this last night, although I didn't want to acknowledge it."

"Realized what?"

"That no matter how this ends, I'll never regain the life I lived before. Will I?" He didn't say anything, but she got the message. She nodded, then straightened her spine and asked, "Will they hold me in jail?"

"I don't know."

"If it were up to you?"

"It won't be. Not entirely."

"If it were. Entirely."

"I would rather have your full cooperation with the investigation. I'd want your input, your gut instinct, your recollections, your unconditional help in catching him."

"What if I offered my unconditional help?"

"That would go a long way with them."

She looked down at her lap in which her hands rested. "You're good at this, aren't you?"

"At what?"

"Manipulation. Bending people to your will."

"Yes. I'm very good at it. But I'm not trying to manipulate you. I'm telling you like it is."

"Why should I trust that that's true?"

He couldn't come up with an answer. "The clock is ticking, Talia."

She looked at him with appeal. "Are you a good guy?"

"I could tell you I am. I could cross my heart and hope to die. Swear to my goodness on a stack of Bibles. But you'd be crazy to take my word for it."

"Who was Weston Graham to you?"

The question took him aback, but he answered without pause. "Not was, *is*."

"Who is he to you?"

"The man who killed my mother. Lyndsay Cummings." She registered wordless shock. He let it sink in before adding, "That's why I want him, Talia. I want to see him burn. And whether that makes me a good guy or a bad one, I really don't give a shit."

He was aware of the seconds passing as she stared into his eyes. Finally she said, "I offer my unconditional help."

He pushed out of the chair. "I'm sure they'll be glad to have it."

"I don't offer it to them. I offer it to you."

Mike, Gif, and the two young cops trooped single file up the exterior stairs to the apartment. The patrolmen took turns using the bathroom, then Mike and Gif doled out bottles of water from the refrigerator. They raided the cabinet and found an unopened box of Nutter Butters, which the cops took with thanks. The four trooped single file down the staircase. Mike and Gif waved the officers back to their squad car and started toward the house.

As they crossed the lawn, Gif admired the rear perspective of the Ford's house. "Pretty place, isn't it? Makes me question my life choices."

"Not me. All this grass to mow? No thanks."

"Do you have one aesthetic inclination, Mike?"

He thought on it. "I like my steak tartare garnished with fresh parsley."

Gif laughed, but as they got closer to the screened porch, he lowered his voice and asked, "What do you think they're talking about?"

"He's trying to squeeze as much information out of her as he can before she lawyers up."

"You think she's dirty, don't you?"

"Dirty or not, she's dangerous."

"Dangerous how?"

"To Drex," Mike grumbled. "His head is under her skirt. That makes a man stupid."

"About that, I think we should back off."

Mike stopped and turned to him. "Back off?"

"Stop nagging him about it."

"Let him screw her and pretend not to notice?"

"That's right, Mike. It's not our business."

"Since when?"

"Since he hasn't screwed her already. When have you known him not to when he wanted to?"

Reading between the lines of what Gif had said, Mike grunted a sound to express his contempt for the frailties of human beings since the fall of Adam, then continued on without further comment.

They went in through the back porch. The kitchen was empty. The two looked at each other. Gif called, "Drex?"

The name echoed throughout the house. Mike elbowed past Gif and went as fast as his waddle allowed into the dining room and then beyond into the living area. "Check upstairs."

Gif mounted the staircase in a run. He checked all the rooms—empty rooms—before coming back down and shaking his head at Mike, who was returning from an inspection of all the first floor rooms. "Damn!" he said, wheezing. "It's a friggin' curse, being right all the time."

Gif stepped past him. "What's this?"

On the dining table was a cookbook with a note in Drex's handwriting lying on top of it. Gif read it aloud. "Tear apart all the cookbooks. Hiding place for souvenirs?"

In addition to the cookbook was a manila envelope with a brass clasp. Drex had written on the envelope: *Special Agent Rudkowski, congratulations. You're getting your heart's desire.*

Mike and Gif looked at each other with dread. Gif unfastened the clasp and shook out the contents of the envelope.

It was the wallet containing Drex's badge and ID.

A sheet of notepaper drifted out along with it. On it was written: *P.S. I'm keeping my gun and the girl.*

Chapter 26

H is *resignation?*" Locke exclaimed.

Gif and Mike regretted having to lay this on the detective, who seemed like a conscientious cop and overall nice guy. They had anticipated the disbelief he expressed. It matched their own.

Gif said, "There's more." He then read aloud the last line of Drex's note.

"You're telling me he left and took Mrs. Ford with him?"

"Looks like."

"The two of them just up and left?"

"Looks like."

"Where would they have gone?"

"Your guess is as good as ours," Gif said. "Last we saw of them, he was trying to wear her down, and I think making progress. Maybe he thought if he got her alone—"

"He gave up his authority to do that when he surrendered his badge. Which car did they take?"

"They didn't. All four are still here. Hers, her husband's, Drex's, and mine."

"They left on foot?"

"Unless they sprouted wings."

"How in hell did they manage it? *Why?*"

"I'm sure there's a logical explanation."

"There is," Locke said, speaking with more vexation than they'd heard from him before. "Easton is either harboring a material witness who requested him to do so or he's kidnaped her, and I lean toward the latter."

"Drex wouldn't force or coerce her to go with him. I'm certain of that." Gif looked over at Mike, who gave him a telling look back, and Gif amended his statement. "Fairly certain."

Locke said, "Last night that woman was afraid of him."

"She was apprehensive of all of us, not just Drex." Gif didn't share that Drex had spent a good half hour in a bedroom alone with her. "But he has impressed upon her that it's her missing husband she should be scared of."

Locke heaved a sigh. "On that, I'm afraid Easton is right. Following the autopsy, the coroner ruled Elaine Conner's death a homicide. She didn't drown; she was choked to death."

Gif received the news without comment. Mike muttered a string of obscenities. Neither took pleasure in having foretold her fate.

Locke was saying, "When your call came in, I had my phone in my hand about to call Easton with this update. We don't know that the perp was Jasper Ford—"

"We do."

"The search-and-rescue for him is still on."

"You won't find him."

"Well, right now I need to locate his wife," Locke said with asperity. "She is key to this investigation. Pass this latest info along to Easton. He's bound to come to his senses and bring her back before anyone else notices that they're gone."

"We've called his phone a dozen times," Gif said. "He isn't answering."

"Do you have Mrs. Ford's number? If not, I do. I'll call her."

"Won't do you any good. We've tried it. Out of service."

Locke said, "He would've removed the battery so it can't be used to lead us to her."

"In all probability."

"That's not something an innocent person does, Agent Lewis."

"An innocent person would if they were frightened enough of a guilty person. If we can't track her phone, neither can Ford. To us, to Drex, he isn't *missing*. He's *at large*. The difference in terminology is significant."

"It hasn't been established that he was the man on the yacht. "

"Who else could it have been?"

"Anybody."

"You don't believe that. Fingerprints?"

"We lifted them from the wheel. But even if we match them to Ford's, he had steered the boat many times. The circuit solicitor would tell us to try again."

"Who?" Gif asked.

"DA. That's what they call them in South Carolina," Mike explained. He'd been listening on speaker, but until now hadn't spoken. "Locke, if you need something on Ford to take to the prosecutor, get a warrant to search this house, inside out."

"We tried," Locke said. "Judge declined to issue one. Ford hasn't been positively identified as the man on the yacht. Mrs. Ford's alibi checks out. The waiter remembers her just like she said. There's no probable cause. But maybe, now that she's made herself scarce, I'll go back to him. Press it."

Gif could tell that Locke was beginning to feel the pressure of what this turnabout with Talia meant to him. He would get a lot of departmental backlash for losing a material witness and possible suspect.

In addition to that, Rudkowski was going to blow a gasket. He would require appeasement, and the only appeasement that would satisfy him would be to have Drex's head served on a platter.

Above all, Locke was confounded by what Drex had done, which to the detective would seem outlandish. It didn't fit his code of professional conduct or conform to the rules of law enforcement.

Gif took pity. "Detective, listen. Drex isn't playing a dirty trick on you, although it may feel like that. I guarantee that somehow he'll make it up to you. Menundez, too. Believe me, he wouldn't have surrendered his badge unless he was convinced that it was the best, maybe only, course of action left to him. Something compelled him to whisk Talia out of here, or he wouldn't have done it.

"Don't make the mistake of discrediting him, or questioning his commitment to capturing the serial criminal we acquainted you with last night. Drex has never been this close to getting him, and he won't squander the chance. He'll go for broke. He'll go to any lengths, even if it means his own downfall."

With reluctance, and what sounded like grudging respect, the detective said, "I sensed all that. The guy's passionate. But you've worked with him for a long time. I just met him. Has he ever done anything this out of line before?"

Gif looked over at Mike, who gave a shrug that said Locke would hear of Drex's shenanigans sooner or later. Gif said, "I'm sure Agent Rudkowski will be all too glad to fill you in."

"I'll relay this latest news to him on our way there."

Gif started. "You're coming here?"

"Rudkowski had already made up his mind not to wait on Easton to deliver Mrs. Ford. He was coming to the house to question her. After I break this news to him—"

"Duck when you tell him," Mike said.

"—he'll want to begin the search for her where she was last seen. How will he react to Easton's resignation?"

"With glee. And he'll want to kill him for pulling this stunt. I'm glad it's you, not me, who has to tell him. Good luck. We'll see you when you get here." Gif clicked off.

"Poor guy."

Mike had his back to the room, looking out the front window.

In a low rumble, and a rare show of empathy, he said, "Chalk up another victim to this son of a bitch."

"Number nine."

"Shit, Gif."

He sighed. "Yeah. And we have no way of knowing how many we've missed."

"I don't want to think about it."

Gif said, "I'll text Drex about the coroner's ruling. It won't come as a shock. He already knew." He sent the text to the last cell number he had for Drex, not knowing if that phone was still in existence.

The news about Elaine Conner had cast a pall over him and Mike. They maintained a lengthy silence, then Mike snorted with his customary disdain. "Those two uniforms are searching the bushes across the street." They had asked the two young officers who'd been guarding the house to take a look around the immediate neighborhood for a sign of Drex and Talia. "Do they really think they're going to find them in the thicket?"

It was a rhetorical question, which Gif didn't bother answering. Mike turned away from the window and posed another. "How the hell did they disappear in such a short amount of time on foot? Even for Drex, it was slick as owl shit."

"She knows the neighborhood, and you can bet he has committed it to memory in the time he's been here. He got to my motel the other night by jogging to a local mini-mart and calling Uber. I dropped him back there the next morning."

"Should we drive over, check it out?"

"He wouldn't use the same location, and I doubt he'd use the same method."

"I don't think so, either," Mike said. "I only suggested it because I've got nothing else."

Gif did some rough calculation in his head. "When I came through the kitchen, they were nose-to-nose in conversation."

"Was she still in her pajamas?"

"Yes, but they had a good ten, twelve minutes after I joined you," Gif said.

"Enough time for them to make their getaway while we were waiting for peeing cops and fetching Nutter Butters. Jesus," Mike said, ridiculing his own gullibility. "How did he talk you into leaving him alone with her?"

"He didn't. I volunteered to check on you."

"You only thought you volunteered," Mike said. "You were manipulated."

Gif shot him a grim smile. "And here just last night, he told me that we were too smart for him."

"Not this morning, we weren't."

"What worries me?" Gif said, idly scratching his frowning forehead. "This time he might have been too smart for his own good."

"Worries me, too," Mike said. "I told you the woman was a hazard to Drex's thinking. He's off to God knows where with her, which, mark my words, will lead to nothing good. Not only that, he's left us to Rudkowski."

Gif's gaze shifted to the cookbook still on the dining table. "He also left us with an assignment."

The envelope addressed to Rudkowski was waiting for him on the dining table. He fingered the mocking note from Drex as he glared at the two young police officers who'd served as guards the night before.

"Where are they?"

His bellow made one of the officers jump. "We don't know, sir. We've been combing the neighborhood. A lady down the street knows Mrs. Ford, but she—"

"Not them," Rudkowski barked. "Mallory and Lewis."

"Oh. They left. About—" The officer consulted his partner, who said, "Twenty minutes ago. About."

Rudkowski looked over at Locke. "You told them we were on our way?"

"Lewis said they would see us when we got here."

Rudkowski walked a tight circle, holding onto his temper by a thread. When he came back around to the young policemen, he asked, "Did they happen to say where they were going?"

"To meet you."

"What car did they leave in?"

"Must've been Lewis's. He was driving."

"Did you happen to get a license plate number?"

"No, sir, b-but why would we?"

Menundez stepped forward. "Signals got mixed is all."

Rudkowski's blood pressure spiked. "After everything I told you on the drive here about this trio, you think mixed signals is the reason Mallory and Lewis have also flown the coop?"

Locke came to his younger partner's defense. "They may have heard from Easton and had to leave in a hurry. Before we jump to conclusions, why don't you call them?"

Rudkowski snapped his fingers. "Good idea. Why don't *you*?"

Locke bobbed his head at Menundez. As the younger detective moved away to follow the directive, he shot Rudkowski a look of contempt, which Rudkowski ignored. "You two," he said to the uniformed officers, "get back to what you were doing, which was precious little."

"Do you want us to call our department or the FBI, get more officers—"

"No," Rudkowski said. "For the time being, I want to keep this under wraps."

He didn't want to appear more of a buffoon than he already did. He'd jumped the chain and placed a call to the SAC of the field office in Columbia, asking him to call him back on a matter of some urgency. He didn't know whether to look forward to speaking with him and alerting him to Easton's latest chicanery or to fear the flak he himself would catch for being outwitted again.

Left alone now with Locke, he said, "Show me around."

"We don't have a warrant yet."

"We have a material witness who has skipped out to avoid being questioned."

"That hasn't been ascertained."

"She ran off dressed in pajamas. Wouldn't you say that indicates flight?"

"Or coercion," Locke said.

"Which Easton is more than capable of, and, ethically, he's not above it. But there were four other men on this property. If he was forcing her, why didn't she scream bloody murder? There's no sign of a tussle. No, detective, she left of her own volition. Now show me around."

They went upstairs. From the master bedroom window, Locke pointed out the garage apartment. "There's a window behind that oak. Easton had a good vantage point. He could surveil them without being seen."

Rudkowski snorted. "If you call window-peeping and illegal bugging surveillance."

Locke turned tight-jawed but didn't comment.

They walked through the rooms on both floors, finding nothing of particular interest. They concluded the tour in a small room behind the main staircase. "Mrs. Ford's study," Locke explained. "When she came to the door for us last night, she left her shoes in here. I came to get them for her."

"Do you extend that kind of courtesy to every murder suspect?"

"We didn't know then that it was a murder. She wasn't a suspect."

"Well, it was, and now she is."

Menundez joined them. "I called the numbers I have for Mallory and Lewis. They go to voice mail."

"Um-huh. You still think signals got mixed?" Rudkowski huffed a sardonic laugh. "Apparently you haven't absorbed what I've told you. Easton is Peter Pan. Lewis and Mallory are the lost boys. They weren't always. They were good agents. Lewis has always been a nerd, but Mallory actually did field work before he turned to blubber.

"Then the two started working with Easton. He recruited them with flattery, told them he needed men with their individual and unique skills. He's corrupted them. They have no families, no social life, no nothing. Their world revolves around him. They would walk through fire for him. They *have*."

"Because they believe in what he's doing," Menundez said. "It seemed to me that they're every bit as committed as Easton."

The young detective's admiration of the three inflamed Rudkowski. "Committed to breaking rules, yes."

"Sir, regardless of their methods, the perp is real. They've gleaned a lot of—"

"Save it, Menundez," Rudkowski snapped. "For years Easton's been piecing together a scenario and molding it to fit an imaginary bogeyman." He spread his arms at his sides. "He doesn't even have the bodies to prove the women are dead."

In contrast to his shout, Locke's voice was low. "The Harris woman in Key West is dead. You can't deny the parallels between her case and Elaine Conner."

"That photo, right? With the fuzzy-haired guy in the background? And in the foreground—as has recently been brought to my attention—Talia Shafer Ford. We can't confirm that the man in the picture is Jasper, but we can sure as hell tell it's her. Two friends of hers, both rich, both dead.

"I'm not saying that the Marian Harris case and this one aren't connected. I'm saying these two aren't connected to any of Easton's others. What's the common denominator here, fellas?" He snapped his fingers several times as though to hurry them to provide an answer.

"Talia Shafer. Maybe her old man drowned after killing the Conner woman. Maybe a shark got him. Or maybe he escaped and left her holding the bag. However it happened, she was in on it."

"I'm not convinced of that, Agent Rudkowski," Locke said.

"Well, if we get a search warrant for this house, maybe we'll dig up something that will convince you. Twist that judge's arm. Send those rookies outside home. They're useless. Easton is long gone."

"His car is still here."

"He's long gone," he repeated. "Even after everything I've told you, it still hasn't sunk in, has it? You've never come up against somebody like him, and, in your career, you probably never will again."

He divided a look between them, but ended on Menundez. "Keep in mind that his preoccupation is psychopaths." He stabbed his temple with the tip of his index finger. "He thinks like they do. He's cunning, unprincipled, egotistical, and relentless."

He let that hover, then said, "Find him, you'll find your suspect. You'll have all the help you need from the bureau. I look forward to reading Easton's eloquent resignation letter to the SAC in Columbia. He'll be pleased. Easton has built a reputation for himself through the rank and file. He's been a blight on the FBI for more than a decade."

He moved to the doorway. "Call the judge back and tell him we need that warrant. While we're waiting on it, we can grab some lunch." He turned to go, then stopped and came back around. "Does Mrs. Ford look like her picture? Young? Fair of face and form?"

The two detectives consulted each other with an exchanged look, then Locke spoke for both of them. "You could say."

Rudkowski snuffled. "Easton's got the devil's own luck with pussy."

Drex sensed that Talia was about to utter a sound of protest over Rudkowski's vulgarity. He stopped it by placing his finger lengthwise over her lips. Even the slightest sound, an intake of breath, could have given away their hiding place.

Chapter 27

———◈———

It had been agony to remain perfectly still and silent for the duration of Rudkowski's conversation with the pair of detectives, especially when listening to the harsh things he'd said about Gif and Mike.

Drex was glad to hear his stamping footsteps moving out of the study and down the hall. As soon as he was out of earshot, Menundez said something under his breath in Spanish. Locke asked him for a translation. What he'd said was unflattering to Rudkowski and his ancestry, but less of an insult than the jerk deserved.

The two detectives remained in the study while Locke called the judge, who must have been unavailable. The detective said, "Tell him there's been a development. Ask him to call me back. Thank you."

After a pause, Menundez asked, "Where do you think they went?"

"You'll have to be more specific."

"Mallory and Lewis."

"On a mission for Easton."

"That's what I think, too. What about him and her?"

Locke said, "Maybe she tried to escape, and he had to chase after her."

"Is that what you really think?"

"Hell, no."

"Easton's got balls. Gotta give him that. Would you have the nerve to pull something like he's doing?"

"No."

"I admire the guy."

"Don't let Rudkowski overhear that."

"What an asshole. Even after what we now know about Easton and his team, I would choose them over that guy to lead the charge or cover my back."

"Easton called him a blowhard. That description doesn't come close."

"How'd he make it into the FBI and manage to stay on?"

"Must've been a nephew," Locke said. "I'll get the search warrant for him, but, between you and me, I think it's a waste of time."

"How's that?"

"If Jasper Ford *is* Easton's guy, and he's as canny as Easton says, he wouldn't have left anything incriminating behind. He never has before."

"Maybe he did, and the investigators missed it."

"But Easton wouldn't have." Following Menundez's unintelligible agreement, Locke said, "We'd better rejoin Rudkowski."

"Do we really have to eat with the guy?"

"We're his ride."

Menundez continued to mouth about it. Their voices faded as they left the room.

Tension ebbed out of Talia. "Close one," Drex whispered.

"I'm not cut out for adventures like this."

"Me neither. I'm too tall. I'm getting a crick in my neck." He'd had to keep his head lowered in order to fit beneath the ceiling.

"How's the bump?"

"I'll live." He'd banged his head as they'd squeezed into the small space. "You could have warned me about the low ceiling."

"There wasn't time."

"Sure there was. We had maybe a second and a half to spare."

Inside the enclosure, it was pitch black dark. He couldn't see her, but he felt the silent laugh that caused her breasts to shift against his chest, then resettle in the hollow between his ribs. They were soft, unbound, and enduring this forced alignment with them had been both agony and bliss.

Except for pressing his finger against Talia's lips, he hadn't dared to move. He estimated that two hours had elapsed since her offer of unconditional help had launched him into action. Through the back porch screen he'd seen his partners marching up the stairs to the apartment, the two young patrolmen trailing them.

"I've got to get you out of here," he'd told her. "Now. Before they come back. They'll try to stop me, and they would be right to."

He'd gnawed on the problem as he watched the quartet disappear into the apartment. How could he and Talia leave, either from the back or front of the house, without being seen? Taking any of the cars would result in a chase.

Then he'd remembered something from the floor plan he'd studied before breaking in the first time. "There's a sizeable unlabeled space beneath the stairs," he said to Talia. "Storage closet?"

"Safe room."

"Where's it accessed?"

"My study."

"Who knows about it?"

"Jasper and me."

"Well, unless he's in it, that's where we're going, and we've gotta be quick."

They had rifled a kitchen utility drawer to find a pen, some notepaper, and an envelope. After seeing why he'd requested them, Talia had exclaimed, "You can't resign!"

"We'll discuss it later." He'd hastily assembled the items on the dining table, then hustled her down the hallway and into her study, where he'd drawn up short. "Where is it?"

She stood her ground. "Drex, you can't throw away your career."

"I'm not. I'm fulfilling it. How do we get into the safe room?"

Through the window, he'd seen that Mike and Gif had parted company with the officers and were making their way across the expansive lawn toward the house. "Talia? It's gotta be now."

She'd hesitated, searching his eyes, then went over to a built-in bookcase and reached between two books. With a metallic click, a section of shelving had popped out a few inches. Drex had propelled her toward it. "Is it ventilated?"

"Yes."

"Get in." He'd taken one last glance out the window. His partners were approaching the porch.

Talia had slipped into the space. He crowded in behind her. "How do I shut us in?"

She'd turned to face him, reached around him, and pulled the door closed with a handle that had been digging into his right kidney ever since. Both being breathless by then, he'd asked in a whisper if she was all right.

"A little claustrophobic."

"Close your eyes."

"I'm thinking about Marian."

He'd put his lips to her ear. "Don't. Just close your eyes. Breathe."

They'd said no more after that because footsteps were heard thudding upstairs and others approaching the room from the hallway. Judging by the heavy tread, it had been Mike who'd come looking for them in the study. They'd held their breath until they heard him head back down the hallway toward the front of the house, where he and Gif had discovered the items left on the dining table.

Drex still felt a twinge of conscience for hoodwinking them, but they could never be held accountable for something they didn't know about. He would beg their forgiveness later.

He and Talia had remained sealed in darkness. He, too, had spent some of that time dwelling on Marian Harris's final minutes. Hours? Who knew how long she had struggled to free herself, to survive.

That was justification enough for what he was doing. It was rash, unadvisable, and irreversible. No apology or rationale would be adequate to pacify either the FBI or the local authorities. But he was prepared to live with the consequences of his action. Whether or not he was wrong about the others, Marian Harris was dead, and now Elaine Conner. He would die before letting Talia be added to their number.

To call this a safe *room* was inaccurate. It was no larger than a telephone booth. They couldn't change positions without risking making a sound. The slightest bump, thud, or scrape would carry through the walls and give them away. Because they couldn't be sure who was inside the house at any given time, they'd had to remain perfectly still.

Time crawled. Sounds reached them, but they were indistinct and not always identifiable. Occasionally they'd caught a word or two spoken by someone in the front rooms, but then there would be stretches when their light breathing was the only sound.

During one of those silences, Talia had whispered, "How long do we have to stay?"

"Longer."

She'd sighed but hadn't complained.

At that point he hadn't known whether or not his partners were still in the house or perhaps had returned to the garage apartment. They could have posted the two young cops to stand guard duty inside. He'd felt it prudent to stay put.

Then Rudkowski had made his grand entrance. Drex had sensed his arrival even before he could be heard chewing out the patrolmen for letting Mike and Gif leave. Learning that they had gotten clear before Rudkowski descended on them had made Drex smile.

Talia and he had tensed when Rudkowski and Locke came into the study. It had put additional strain on their already strained muscles, but Drex was glad he had gotten to hear the game plan.

Of course he'd wanted to rip out Rudkowski's jugular with his teeth over the crude comment, not because it was an insult to him, but to Talia. It had made him feel better, knowing that Locke and Menundez had accurately sized him up. They hadn't even wanted to share a meal with him.

After their footsteps had faded to nothingness, Talia whispered. "Have they gone?"

"Let's give them a few more minutes before chancing it."

"Chance sneaking out?"

"Chance searching the house before they return with the warrant."

"Oh. Then what?"

"*Then* we chance sneaking out."

"Will we be able to?"

"That's the hope. We're not out of the woods yet."

When she gave a small nod, her hair brushed against his cheek. He thought strands of it got caught in his scruff.

"I was afraid my stomach was going to growl," she said.

"You should have eaten your doughnut."

"It was a matter of principle not to touch it."

"Because I'd given it to you?"

"Exactly."

"Next time, you'll know better than to let pride get in your way."

"Next time." With those words, she drooped, as though the prospect of what they still faced sapped her strength. "I'm scared, Drex."

"Fear is healthy."

"It's draining. Exhausting. I'm so tired."

"Lean against me."

She did.

God, he was going to die. "Just a few more minutes, then you can stretch."

"No, I meant I'm so tired of living the way I have been."

"How's that?"

She took time to choose her word. "Watchfully. For a while now, I've treaded very carefully around Jasper."

He thought on that. "I want to hear about it. Everything. Later. When we're out of here. All right?"

Again she nodded. Again he thought strands of her hair were caught in his whiskers, and the thought of that alone, in addition to their proximity, sent heat rushing to his center.

He tried to stay focused. "Say it out loud. 'All right.'"

"All right. I'll explain later. For now, I'll just say thank you."

"What did I do? Other than cram you into a closet."

"You forced me to acknowledge what I had intuited about Jasper but refused to accept. I feel unburdened, liberated from my own denial, by your browbeating. I realize you were only doing your job, but you have my gratitude anyway."

"Talia." He bent his head lower and nuzzled her just below her ear. "This isn't only doing my job." He caught the lobe of her ear between his teeth.

She stirred and whimpered his name. He followed the soft expulsion of breath to its source, her parted lips, and covered them with his. Her mouth was hot and wet and receptive when he pressed his tongue inside.

Unlike when he'd kissed her before, this time she didn't turn her head aside and angle away. Instead she leaned into the kiss, not just with her mouth but with her body.

They shifted instinctually, matching up parts that had been created to complement each other. Still, it was a tease to what it could be. He had believed there wasn't room enough to reposition themselves, but he discovered there was, as he curved his arm around her waist.

In doing so, his elbow knocked against the wall. The giveaway sound would have alarmed him earlier, but now he disregarded it and focused only on splaying his hand over Talia's ass and pulling her closer, up, onto him. She responded by arching up even higher until—God!—the fit stole their breath. Until then they hadn't broken the mad kiss, but they did now, gasping in unison.

A heartbeat later, their mouths fused, and, again they were governed by carnal instinct. His palm followed her shape from her waist to the top of her thigh, caressing bare skin that felt like warm silk against his hand, although he didn't even remember sliding it inside her pajama bottoms.

He couldn't say when she had raised her hand to his head, yet her fingers were imbedded in his hair, urgently tugging on it to pull him closer.

Beneath his circling thumb, her nipple was hard, but how had he found it beneath her pajama top? He didn't know, but he loved the feel of it, of her, of her excitement, and knowing he had kindled it.

He hadn't thought to thrust against the welcoming V between her thighs, but he was, and it was killing him not to be inside her.

These incredible sensations coalesced in an instant of clarity, and he realized that if he didn't stop now, there would be no stopping.

He lifted his mouth away from her hungry kiss and clasped her head between his hands. "Talia, Talia." With his forehead pressed to hers, he kept repeating her name on gusts of breath until she stilled against him. "God knows I want to," he groaned. "But I can't. Not under his roof."

He let go of her, fumbled behind his back for that son of a bitching handle, and flipped it up. The wall popped open behind him. He ducked his head and stumbled backward out of the enclosure and into the room. Reaching for her hand, he guided her out of their hiding place.

The house was silent and, he sensed, empty save for the two of them. It was another gray day. The blinds were partially shut. The room was dim. He thought it was probably best that they couldn't see each other clearly. She couldn't have missed his erection. He'd never been this hard without having a woman under him or straddling him or sucking him.

In her dishevelment, Talia had never looked so sexy. Her lips plump and damp. Hair a mess. One side of her shapeless robe was hanging off her shoulder. Her nipples were peaked beneath her pajama top. She looked ravishing. Ravish*ed*. If only. Jesus, was he *crazy*?

No. He'd been right to stop.

"I had to," he said, his voice hoarse. "I would never have gotten over being with you here. In *his* house."

She swallowed with apparent difficulty and drew her robe back into place, then crossed her arms over her front. "I understand. I do. I probably would have hated myself afterward, too. I shouldn't have let it go that far."

He scrubbed his hands over his face.

"Right. And besides all that, I've placed us in a serious situation. It's not too late for you to change your mind. You could stay here, wait for Locke and company, tell them that I had talked you into splitting but then you saw the light."

"No. I'm going with you."

"I have your trust now?"

"It was hard-earned, but yes."

He took a deep breath, dropped his head forward, and for several seconds stared at the floor. When he raised his head, he spoke with unmitigated gravity. "Also trust this, Talia. If given an opportunity to kill him, I'm going to."

"I hope so," she said gruffly. "Because if you don't, he will surely kill me."

Chapter 28

As Drex had gathered, there was no one inside the house, but a police unit was parked at the curb with two officers keeping watch.

"I hope Rudkowski didn't want fast food for lunch," he whispered as he turned away from the window. "No lights, no unnecessary sound, and we've got to make these minutes count. Where should we start? I've already searched the master bedroom."

"When?"

"Yesterday after you left for the airport."

"It was you who set off the alarm."

"Thought I was so clever to know the new code. Jasper laid that trap for me. Were you aware of the app on his phone?"

"App?"

"Never mind. Doesn't matter now." He thought for a moment. "Any other spaces like that safe room?"

"No. Until today, there's never been cause to use it."

"Whatever Jasper's trophies are, they're small, easily hidden, and he would keep them close to him, not where you would have better access. Where does he spend most of his time?"

She led him upstairs to a room at the end of the hallway. It was similar in proportion to her study. It was furnished with a desk and computer, a leather recliner, and a wall-mounted flat-screen TV. Like any ol' man cave. Except that it was sterile, a stage setting lacking enough props to make it look lived in.

The hardwood floor was bare of carpet or rugs. Drex didn't have time to see if any of the planks were loose, but he didn't detect any cracks that would suggest a hidey-hole underneath. And, anyway, Jasper wouldn't be that mundane.

He pulled the chair from beneath the desk and powered up the computer. "Do you know his password?"

Talia gave it to him. He typed it in. "If he gave you his password, we won't find anything. Is this the only computer he has?"

"That I know of."

Drex accessed Jasper's email. Talia identified the names she recognized, most of whom were vendors they used for various services or acquaintances from the country club.

"Friends of Jasper's?"

"Sometimes he plays doubles tennis and will have lunch with the group afterward. That's about the extent of it. He's not a mingler."

He'd had several exchanges with Elaine, but they didn't amount to anything. The most recent email from her had come in on yesterday morning, the day of her death. She'd thanked him for drinks and dinner the night before. There was no mention of an evening excursion on her yacht.

Drex went to the history of websites Jasper had visited. Most were for foodies or wine enthusiasts. Nothing exotic or noteworthy.

He was shutting down the computer when, from behind him, Talia said, "Drex, our picture is missing." She was looking down on a round cocktail table next to the recliner. "Jasper made a ceremony of putting our wedding photo on that table the day we moved in."

"Touching."

"I thought so at the time."

"Who had the picture framed, you or him?"

"I did. Why?"

"It could be significant that he took it with him. His souvenirs would be stashed in something portable, like a picture frame. Unless he hid his collection inside the walls for retrieval later."

"If he'd torn into walls, I would have known."

"When you were having the house decorated?"

"We didn't make structural changes."

"While you were out of town? He never had any 'repair' done, anything like that?"

"Not to my knowledge."

"Any other pictures?"

"Of me. None of him."

"Figures. The only one I know of in existence was the one taken on Marian's yacht. I doubt he knew he was in the shot."

He asked Talia to check the front of the house. Keeping out of sight, she peered through the louvered blinds. "They're still there. Just sitting. No other cars on the street."

Drex, who'd been surveying the Spartan room, noted all the bare shelves. "He doesn't like clutter, does he?" he asked wryly. "DVDs? Books? Coffee mugs with funny sayings?"

"I told you, he didn't bring much with him."

"Yeah, but who doesn't have *stuff*?" Then he realized that he didn't. Mike and Gif were on him all the time about how barren his apartment was. Shaking off the thought that he had anything in common with Jasper, he asked Talia where the attic access was.

"In the garage. A ladder pulls down from the ceiling."

"No time for that."

"I need to put some clothes on," she reminded him.

He nodded. "Wear something dark. Nothing fancy. Comfy."

"Can I bring some things with me?"

"If you pack them in a bag you can carry in one hand or on your shoulder. Go. I'll finish in here."

She rushed out. Aware of the clock, Drex checked the closet but found only a couple of tennis racquets and a pair of swimming flippers, all hanging from the rod by specialized hooks. He tapped the back wall of the closet. It didn't sound particularly hollow, and even if it were, he didn't have any way to tear into it. There was nothing on the closet floor, not even a pair of sneakers past their prime.

In frustration over the shortage of time, he gave the room one last scan, then crossed the hall and entered the master suite. Since Talia hadn't slept in here last night, everything appeared to be exactly as it had been when he'd searched it yesterday. The crystal tray holding Talia's jewelry was still on her nightstand.

On the outside chance that Jasper had returned undetected, Drex checked his night table drawers again. All were still empty. Underwear, socks, the artistically folded handkerchiefs—nothing had been disturbed in the bureau. Nor had anything in the closet.

Staring into it, Drex muttered, "Fucking whack job."

"What's that?" Talia had moved up behind him.

"I was saying this looks exactly like my closet."

She laughed, but it lacked mirth. "When we first married, I teased him about being such a stickler for order." She ran her hand along the sleeves of the jackets so precisely hung. Drex figured she enjoyed disturbing the perfection. "Actually I'm surprised he was willing to leave this wardrobe behind," she said. "He's so particular about it. He changes it frequently. Almost everything is custom made. He keeps his tailor in business."

"Custom made for Jasper Ford. Another of his incarnations wore blue jeans, flannel shirts, and cowboy boots. He went horseback riding and fly fishing."

"How do you know all that?"

"I know a lot more. What I know right now is that we've got to get the hell out of here."

"How do you propose we do it?"

"I have a route out the back."

"They could see us."

"They're guarding against someone coming in, not going out." While talking, he'd been tapping in Gif's cell number.

He answered immediately. "Well, well. We'd about given up on you."

"I need you to come pick us up."

"Us? So she's still with you?"

"Yes. Remember how to get to the mini-mart?"

"Sure."

"How long will it take you to get there?"

"About forty-five seconds."

Drex thought about it, then chuckled. "Who figured it out?"

"Mike. Said you had to be inside the house because a woman couldn't possibly have dressed that fast."

Talia had changed into jeans, a black t-shirt, and a rain jacket with a hood. A small bag hung from her shoulder. "You'd be surprised," Drex said and winked at her. "We'll meet you at the mini-mart."

"You don't have to go there. We're on the next street. Where you and Talia had a four-minute chat that morning after I let you out at the mini-mart."

"You sly dog."

"Don't get caught."

They clicked off. Drex motioned to Talia's bag. "I hope you chose well. I don't know when you'll be able to come back."

She walked over to the nightstand and worked her wedding ring off her finger. With a plink, it landed on the crystal tray. "I'll never come back."

———◆———

As they exited through the kitchen door onto the screened porch, Drex paused to set the alarm.

"Why are you doing that?"

"To piss off Rudkowski when he comes back."

"He'll know you've been in here."

"That's the beauty of it."

"What's with the two of you?"

"Long story. I'll tell you sometime."

He wasn't as confident of making an escape unseen as he'd made out to be to Talia, but it had begun to rain harder. That helped. Plus he had cut through the lawn and the green belt enough times to know what areas of the back of the property were visible from the street in front.

Gif's sedan was parked where he'd said it would be. He and Talia scrambled into the back seat, shaking off rainwater. "In the nick of time," Gif said. "A convoy of squad cars just went through that intersection behind us." He headed in the opposite direction. "Where to?"

"Just away," Drex said. "Let me think."

"We got a room at a suite hotel," Mike said. "Within minutes of checking in, I figured out you'd never left the house. Where did you hide?"

Drex told them.

Mike grumbled, "Should've remembered that space from the floor plan."

As though sparked by that comment, Talia spoke for the first time. "I've remembered something." She turned on the seat toward Drex. "Were you watching us that day before we went to the airport?"

"Like a hawk."

"Jasper went to the country club to swim that morning."

"He left at ten something."

"The time isn't so important. Did you see him return?"

"I saw him pull into the garage, around—"

"But you didn't see *him*?"

"Only the car."

"I don't think he came back with his gym bag."

"Maybe he left it in the trunk of his car."

"He didn't. I was with him when he loaded our suitcases for the airport. The bag wasn't there." She leaned forward and said to Gif, "Do you know where the country club is?"

"No, but I can take directions."

She told him the first turn to take, then said to Drex, "I have the code to his locker. He left his wristwatch in it once. I was at the club having lunch with a couple of girlfriends. He called and asked me to retrieve his watch. He didn't trust the attendant with the code to his locker, so he gave it to me, then alerted the attendant that I would need brief access when no one was in there."

"He might have changed the code since then." That from Mike.

Talia said, "It's worth a try."

"How will you get into the men's locker room?" Drex asked.

"Can't you tell that I'm on the verge of a meltdown, worried sick over what's become of my husband, frantic over the failure of the authorities to find him? Possibly there's something in his locker that would prove helpful to the search. Who's going to deny me access?"

Mike harrumphed his opinion of the plan. Gif raised his eyebrows in the mirror. Drex grinned. "I'm rubbing off on you."

"God help us," Mike grumbled.

⸻❖⸻

She insisted on going in alone. "If we all go, it'll look like a parade and call attention."

"Not all of us have to go. Just me," Drex said. "If I'm with you, and someone denies you access, all I have to do is flash my—" He broke off.

Talia gave him an arch look.

Gif offered to go in with her. "If the occasion calls for it, I'll use my badge."

"Since you're not stupid enough to have surrendered it," Mike said, turning his head to glower at Drex. "Still, somebody should go with her."

She addressed the back of Mike's head. "So I won't skip out on you?"

"Just sayin'. Somebody should go."

By the time they'd reached the country club, it had been decided that Gif would accompany her into the clubhouse. As she got out at the entrance, Drex wished her good luck and squeezed her hand. He waved off the valet and took Gif's place behind the wheel. "I'll park over there." He pointed out an area of the lot.

Talia was recognized by staff, but all seemed shocked to see her looking so bedraggled. Her trek through the green belt in the rain had contributed to the overall impression of a woman in desperation.

The attendant on duty at the desk outside the men's locker room seemed downright alarmed. "Mrs. Ford?"

"Hi, Todd. It is Todd, isn't it?"

"Yes, ma'am." He was young. Gauging by his physique, he availed himself of the club's weight room often and for hours at a time. "Any word about Mr. Ford?"

"No. Which is why I'm here. Is anyone in there?"

"In the—?"

"The locker room, the locker room." With impatience she thumped the countertop in beat with her words. "I need to go in there." For good measure, she made her voice thready. "I want to check my husband's locker. Maybe something he left in it will—"

"It was empty."

"What?" Talia said with genuine dismay.

"Two detectives already came."

"When?"

Todd scrunched up is face. "About an hour ago, I guess. They had the club manager open your husband's locker. It was empty. Saw inside it myself."

She opened her mouth to speak, but Gif stepped forward and laid a cautioning hand on her shoulder. "They explained that to her, Todd. Or tried to. Sergeants Locke and Menundez?"

"I never got their—"

"Was Special Agent Rudkowski with them?"

"The third guy? I think he was their boss."

"Yes, he thinks so, too. They assured Mrs. Ford that her husband's locker was empty, but she's, uh, terribly distraught, as you can imagine. She insisted on checking it for herself. I volunteered to bring her."

"You're a detective, too?"

"Police chaplain."

"Oh."

"If it wouldn't be too much trouble..."

"Well, sure. Sure." The young attendant gave Gif a reassuring wink. "Of course you can go in, Mrs. Ford," he said, speaking to her as though she were deranged. "I don't think anyone's in there. Weather's keeping the golfers in the card room. But let me double-check. I'll be right back."

Gif commended her performance. Talia commended his. But as they left the country club, dejection settled over all four of them. Feeling dispirited down to his bones, Drex gave the responsibility of driving back to Gif, leaving him free to concentrate.

The abbreviated search of the house hadn't yielded anything. The trip to the country club had been a bust. He had nothing to work with. Nothing. As before. As always. Jasper had left nothing behind to come back for. Except Talia.

He'd taken only a wedding photo and...and what?

He stirred, stilled, stirred again. "Talia, you and Jasper took roll-aboard suitcases to the airport, correct?"

"Yes."

"One each?"

"Yes. To carry on."

"Did you pack for him, or see what he packed?"

"No. By the time he came home from the club, I'd finished packing. I left our room to him and went down to the study to catch up on emails and business-related calls. I worked right up until time to leave for the airport."

"Mike, in that security video showing Jasper getting into the taxi?"

"Yeah?"

"He had his roll-aboard with him, right?" Drex thought he remembered correctly, but he wanted to check Mike's computerized memory to be sure.

"He placed it in the back seat with him."

Drex resettled, turned his head, and stared out the rain-streaked car window. Jasper had left behind a custom-tailored wardrobe and took with him only what he could pack into a roll-aboard. He fit his whole life into a piece of carry-on luggage. With the tip of his finger, Drex followed a rivulet of rainwater as it trickled down the outside of the glass.

What had he packed into that roll-aboard? Where was it now?

Gif drove them to the suite motel where he and Mike were already checked in. Gif pulled under the porte cochere. Mike said to Gif, "I've got this, Reverend Lewis." He turned to Drex. "Every suite has two bedrooms."

Drex didn't rise to the bait. "Then it works out even."

Mike shot a look at Talia, then squeezed himself out of the passenger door and lumbered into the lobby.

"Understating the obvious," she said to Drex, "he doesn't like me."

"Don't take it personally. He doesn't like anybody."

A few minutes later Mike returned and passed a card key to Drex. "Not that you asked, but we brought all your stuff from the garage apartment."

"Thanks."

"We didn't figure you'd be returning for it," Gif said.

In a lame attempt to lighten the mood, Drex said, "I miss the place already." No one reacted.

Gif said, "What about your car?"

"Temporarily abandoned. They may impound it. I don't know. Don't care. I'll worry about that after…After."

Gif parked. They all got out. Mike said, "Here's ours. Yours." He pointed to another of the suites, facing his and Gif's from across a gravel courtyard dotted with dwarf palmettos.

"I'll see Talia in, then come and get my things," Drex said.

Without further discussion, he walked Talia to their door, unlocked it, and told her he would be back within a few minutes. "Keep the chain on." Looking as downcast as he felt, she nodded.

He waited until he heard her secure the lock then, heedless of the rain, strode across the courtyard and rapped on the door. Gif opened it. Drex went past him and made a beeline to Mike, who was sprawled in a chair in the living room looking not dissimilar to Jabba the Hut.

"Cut it out, Mike."

"What?"

"Give me a fucking break. You know what."

"All right." Mike raised his hands as though in surrender.

"I mean it," Drex said, stressing the words.

"Be nice or take my leave?"

"I couldn't have phrased it any better. I need *you*. But I don't need your shit. The situation is bad enough without it. Be nice. Or leave."

Mike raised his hands higher. "I said, all right."

Drex backed away. Now that the air had been cleared between them, he said, "Rudkowski has probably already blacklisted you. Do you think you can hack the autopsy report on Elaine?"

"Won't have to." Mike nodded toward Gif. "He bullshitted it out of somebody in the coroner's office."

"Email it to me, please, Gif."

"Sure," Gif said.

Drex spotted a stack of cookbooks on one of the living area end tables. "I see you got my message. Start digging into them."

"They don't look used enough to hold secrets," Gif said.

"Maybe not, but check anyhow."

"In the meantime, what are you going to do?"

They both looked toward Mike as though expecting an innuendo involving Talia. He raised both hands again. "What? This is me, being nice. Besides, that setup was so easy it was beneath me."

Drex actually gave him a grudging smile as he lifted his duffel bag off the sofa. "I'm going to my room to think."

"About what?"

"About what I would do now if I were Jasper."

Chapter 29

Talia released the chain and opened the door. She looked so forlorn that Drex asked her what the matter was.

"I'm sorry my brainstorm didn't pay off."

"Most brainstorms don't. We celebrate the odd occasions when they do."

"Those odd occasions are what keep you going?"

"What keeps me going is that I haven't caught him yet."

"It's going to be more difficult now that you've resigned. Maybe if you appealed to Rudkowski, he would disregard what you did this morning."

"You heard him. Does he sound like a man to whom a *mea culpa* would make a dent?"

"No."

"However, I might attempt it except for the time it would cost."

"And you think time is of the essence, don't you?"

Not wanting to alarm her—yet—he hedged. "I need to shut myself off and think. Are you going to be all right for a while?"

"After the night and morning I've had? I need some downtime, too."

He gave a strand of her hair a tug then kept hold of it. "I wish I'd seen you in action in the locker room. Gif said you struck just the right note. Somewhere between a pit bull and pitiful."

"I'm out of my league."

He tucked the strand of hair behind her ear and rubbed the lobe he'd taken a bite of earlier. "I'm afraid I am, too."

"Why do you say that?"

He lowered his hand. "Jasper's been at this for three times longer than I've been chasing him. He's had more practice." He gave her a grim smile as he checked his watch. "We're regrouping at six o'clock. Gif's going to bring in dinner."

They climbed the stairs. The two bedrooms were separated by a short hallway, the shared bathroom between them. "I put my things in here." She pointed to the bedroom on the right. "I'll see you a little before six."

She turned away, but before she'd taken a single step, he reached for her and brought her around. He pulled her to him and wrapped his arms around her.

"I want to lie down with you so bad." He kissed the side of her neck. "But you wouldn't want to go where I've got to go now."

He hugged her tighter, then his arms relaxed and finally dropped to his sides. He left her, entered the darkened room, and closed the door behind him.

Gif had brought in Chinese. They divided the cartons and sat around the dining table to eat.

The cookbooks, Drex noted, had been ripped apart. Pages from them formed a snowbank in a corner of the room. Nodding toward it, Drex said, "Nothing?"

"Not a single notation," Gif replied. "And we went through each book page by page. Nothing glued into the backings. We turned up *nada*."

"Some of the recipes look good, though," Mike said. "I saved those."

"You can add that to the paper pile." Drex pointed his fork at the phony manuscript he'd set on the bar when he'd come in. It had been included in his belongings that Mike and Gif had brought from the garage apartment. "I won't be needing it anymore."

"Did you actually write all that?" Talia asked.

"I had it copied from a paperback book."

"Elaine told Jasper it wasn't very good."

"Pam will be crushed," Mike said as he polished off an egg roll.

Talia looked at Drex. "Pam?"

Drex shot Mike a warning look. "A woman at the office typed it for me. I never even read it, only messed up the pages to make them look authentic."

"You had me fooled," Talia said. "That day I came over to the apartment and asked…"

Becoming aware that Mike and Gif were listening with rabid interest, Drex said, "That was the point. To fool you."

After that, conversation lagged, and they focused on eating. When they were finished, they made quick work of cleaning up then chose their seats in the living area. Mike claimed the largest chair, Gif straddled one of the dining chairs, Talia curled up into a corner of the sofa. Drex perched on the opposite arm of it.

He had decided how he was going to call the meeting to order, despite how tough it would be on Talia. He had to be straightforward, perhaps even harsh, because it was essential to erase any lingering doubts in his partners' minds about her culpability.

"Talia?"

She took a breath and let it out slowly. "This is the 'I want to hear it all later,' isn't it?"

"Yes. Speaking for all three of us, we need it explained how you couldn't have known that you were married to a psychopath."

It was the opening Mike had been waiting for. "When I saw you in that picture taken at Marian Harris's party, that did it for me."

"And you haven't changed your mind," she said.

"Say you didn't meet your husband that night—"

"I didn't."

"—and that everything else you've told us is true, didn't he ever strike you as not quite right in the head?"

"I'd like to hear that myself," Gif said, quieter and less judgmental than Mike.

"Yes, I sensed something wasn't quite right," she said. "But I couldn't isolate what it was. You three think in terms of criminology and psychopaths every day. That's outside my realm. So, no," she said, addressing Mike, "it didn't pop into my mind one day that my husband was a serial killer."

"Okay," Drex said. "Take a breath. This isn't an inquisition. We're trying to analyze and understand him more than we are you. What first sparked your feeling that something was off?"

"It didn't spark. It came on gradually. Initially, I talked myself into believing that it was the difference in our ages. Three decades' difference."

"But you married him anyway," Drex said.

"The strangeness didn't start until *after* we married. Soon after, though, I began to notice oddities. For instance the way he phrased things. Words and expressions seemed to have a double meaning that escaped me. I felt particularly uneasy when we were alone, but I couldn't account for it. I thought it might have been hormonal. I was going through some procedures." She glanced at Drex. "But my uneasiness persisted. Over the past few months things he said and did became even stranger."

"Did this strangeness intensify around the time Marian's remains were discovered?" Drex asked.

Her brow furrowed. "Now that you mention it, yes. About that time."

"That fits," he said, getting nods of agreement from Mike and Gif. "That would have agitated him. Made him second-guess burying her alive."

"Maybe it wasn't his intention to," Gif said. "When he nailed shut that box, he mistakenly thought she was dead."

Mike jumped on that. "'Mistakenly' is the key word. A blunder like that is anathema to him. It would have set him off."

Drex had followed their exchange with interest, but he didn't want to address the particulars of it yet. "It would have set him off in either case. The discovery of that grave spoiled his perfect record."

Back to Talia, he said, "You went out to dinner together one night this week. I waved at you as you were leaving."

"Yes."

"You two seemed simpatico. All dressed up. Hubby taking his best girl to dinner."

"So you heard that conversation?"

He nodded.

She looked embarrassed. "The invitation surprised me. That was the first date night we'd had in weeks."

"He was playing to me?"

"He must have been. But what I thought was that he was trying to cover an affair."

Drex looked at his cohorts to gauge their opinions. Gif looked interested but as yet undecided. You could have cut Mike's skepticism with a knife.

Drex turned back to Talia. "What shape did his strange behavior take? What did he do to make you think something was really out of joint?"

"Nothing threatening or overtly weird. He never mistreated me. On the contrary, he was solicitous, often to an annoying degree. But sometimes, when he looked at me in a certain way, it would cause a chill to creep over me. I began making up excuses to avoid intimacy."

"How did he react?"

"Casually."

"Not violently?"

"Not at all. Just the opposite. He was indifferent."

She pulled one of the sofa's throw pillows into her lap and hugged it against her chest. A shield, Drex thought, against what she was still reluctant to admit.

"His indifference seemed abnormal," she said.

"It's all kinds of abnormal," Drex said, "because he is. Some of these guys can't function sexually unless it is violent. But Jasper isn't about sex. It's the mind fuck he gets off on. Except for my mother, his relationships with the women have been platonic." Mike and Gif looked like they'd been goosed. "Yes, I told Talia this morning, and I trust her not to reveal it to anyone else. But back to the point I was making. None of his other relationships have been characterized as love affairs."

Mike said, "Even the solicitations he put on the match-up websites didn't reference sex or romance. Only companionship."

Looking at Talia, Drex said, "For whatever it's worth, I doubt he was romantically involved with Elaine. I don't believe she would have betrayed you. However, to you, an affair was a logical explanation for his quirky behavior."

"Why was I the exception to his platonic relationships?" Talia asked.

"We'll come back to that," Drex said. "Go on with what you were telling us earlier. How did his strangeness manifest itself?"

"Small things, any one of which could have been overlooked, but collectively they bothered me. Like his obsession with his clothes, his closet."

For the benefit of the other two, Drex described it.

"He was fanatical about the fit of every garment," Talia continued. "He fussed over sleeve length, buttons, everything. I was never allowed to fold his laundry and store it. He had a 'system,' he said. I teased him about the way he lined up utensils in the kitchen drawer."

"He didn't laugh it off," Drex said.

"No, he took umbrage. His obsessions like that began to wear on me. Walking a fine line twenty-four/seven is exhausting. I started inventing reasons to go out of town. My business trips came to feel like escapes. I could only relax when I was away from him. Which should have told me something, shouldn't it?"

She asked it of all three men, letting her gaze light briefly on one before moving to the next, until she came back around to Drex. He said nothing, wanting to hear how she answered her own question.

"We're supposed to trust our fear. That's what we're told. I didn't. I rationalized it away or denied it altogether." She waited a beat, then added, "Until you moved in next door. Then everything changed."

Mike shifted in his seat. Gif cleared his throat. Drex didn't move, just continued to look into Talia's troubled eyes.

"Jasper was mistrustful of you right from the start, although you'd given him no reason to be. You'd even returned the fan he loaned you. I couldn't understand his aversion."

"He saw Drex as competition."

She nodded at Gif. "Male assertion, protecting his territory, that would have been understandable over time, and if Drex and I had given him reason to be jealous. But Drex has been here all of a week, and Jasper turned paranoid almost from the day he moved in."

"'Suspicion always haunts the guilty mind,'" Drex quoted.

"What?"

"Shakespeare," Mike said.

"But don't be too impressed," Drex said. "I only know that line because it applies to a mind like Jasper's." He held up his index finger. "*Except* that he feels only the suspicion, not the guilt. In his mind, whatever he does is sanctioned.

"Oh, he's subtle," he went on. "He doesn't pull the wings off houseflies or eviscerate kittens. Although he may have in his youth, or in secret now. But when he's 'working,' he assumes all the trappings of normalcy.

"He expresses remorse when it's called for. 'Shame about your dog getting hit by a car.' He apologizes for minor offenses like being late for an engagement or forgetting a birthday. He takes a small gift to a hostess. He invites a new neighbor over for dinner. Because that's what civilized people do.

"But he's role-playing. He's condescending. Behind his hand, he's snickering at everyone who falls for his act. He's had nine personas that I know of, but they all originated and were governed by the same distorted psyche, in which he's far superior to everyone else, and rules do not apply to him."

"I feel so stupid, so foolish."

"Don't, Talia. He played you brilliantly. 'Not tonight, honey'? Fine. He was the perfect gentleman about it. The epitome of consideration. Never got pissed off, never complained, ultimately stopped asking. Right?"

She gave a small, self-conscious nod.

"That fell right into step with the way he wanted your relationship to be. He mastered without being masterful. What wife would complain about such an ideal husband? That closet, those pristine drawers made you want to scream, but you didn't, because most wives would regard it a miracle if, for once, their slob of a husband picked up his dirty underwear from off the bathroom floor.

"Jasper deliberately used words and phrases that were disturbing, then contrasted them with utmost thoughtfulness. That kept you off balance. Made you... What was the word you used today? *Watchful.* That was the turn-on of all turn-ons to him. He sensed your mounting wariness. Nurturing it was his foreplay."

"Leading to what?"

"Killing."

"Nucking futs," Mike mouthed.

Distressed, she hugged the pillow closer. "I'll never forgive myself for not heeding my instincts and saying something, doing something, sharing my misgivings with Elaine. If I had, she might still be alive."

"And you would be dead."

After Drex's sobering declaration, a silence ensued. Then Gif said, "No doubt he would then have turned to Elaine for condolence."

"And snuffed her, too," Mike said.

"That's one of the points I want to broach with you," Drex said. "These circumstances were different from all the previous ones. This time there were two women. One, he married. Marian Harris was also a departure from the norm."

"In what way?" Gif asked.

Drex stood up and went over to the eating bar that separated the living area from the kitchenette. He planted his hands on the surface of it and used his arms as struts.

"I don't think he buried Marian alive by mistake. I think he had become bored with his routine and wanted to try something new. He challenged himself. He wanted to see if he could do it and get away with it. And so far he has.

"Talia represented another challenge. She wasn't middle aged, wasn't meek or insecure, wasn't an heiress. Not at all like her predecessors, she was much younger, more beautiful, and her fortune was self-made. Could he lure a woman like that? Or, better yet, the biggest coup of all, get her to marry him? He succeeded.

"He was introduced to Elaine. Independently, she wouldn't have been a challenge. But going for two? Two who knew each other, were friends, who saw each other frequently and could compare notes about him?

"Ah, that was a risk to beat all risks. Even riskier than leaving Marian to die on her own before someone heard her screams. The challenge of Talia and Elaine combined was too tempting to resist. Dare he try?" Drex dropped his head between his shoulders. "He did, and has accomplished half his goal."

No one behind him moved. No one spoke. Finally, Gif said, "This is his way of escalating."

"I believe so. It's his middle-age crazy we talked about. He's taking chances he's never taken before, and it scares me shitless." He paused, then said, "See if you can get Locke on the phone."

As Drex predicted, the other three in the room reacted to the request with a start. Before anyone could ask why or object, he said, "We need somebody inside, feeding us information, and keeping us updated. Rudkowski? Forget it. Lost cause. Do either of you have a contact in any of the FBI offices in South Carolina?"

They replied with shakes of their heads.

"So you can't call in any favors. Besides, you can bet that Rudkowski has by now soured them on all of us. Same goes for Charleston PD, sheriff's office, state police, Homeland Security. Every law enforcement agency."

"Locke is a member of that fraternity," Mike said.

"As well as Menundez," Talia said.

"Yes, but you heard them talking when they were alone in your study." He briefed Mike and Gif on what he and Talia had overheard from inside the safe room. "They saw through Rudkowski's bluster and neither likes him. Us, they admire. I believe Menundez would jump at the chance to assist."

"So why not call him instead?" Mike asked.

"Because Locke is more experienced, more mature, the deeper thinker, the less impulsive, the more senior guy, and, for all those reasons, that's who we need."

Gif hesitated, but took his phone out, went to his log of recent calls, and placed one to Locke. "Put it on speaker," Drex said, then pointed to a place on the bar, and that's where Gif set the phone. He scooted his chair closer to the bar and resumed his seat.

Mike stayed where he was. Talia moved to Drex's side. He turned his head toward her and spoke softly. "Sorry I had to put you through that."

"It was healthy for me, actually. Better than keeping it bottled up. I want him expunged, Drex."

"Me too."

She searched his eyes. "You put yourself through much worse, didn't you? In that dark room for hours with the door shut?"

"That's what they pay me for."

"They *did*."

He gave her a wan smile just as Locke answered with his name, sounding world-weary.

Drex addressed the phone and identified himself. "Can you talk to me without an audience?"

"Give me five minutes and call back."

"Nope. Now or never. Yes or no? I made off with your material witness. Don't you want to know why I called?"

"To negotiate a prisoner exchange?"

"All right, be an ass. Goodbye."

"Wait!" They heard muttered cursing, followed by a lengthy pause, some muffled sounds, then, "Okay, I'm alone. Why did you call?"

"Do you think Jasper Ford killed Elaine? And please don't give me the toe-the-department-line answer. Yes or no?"

"Yes."

"That's good news. Bad news is that you're never going to catch him by looking for him."

"How's that?"

"You're going through the routine. Airlines. Rental car companies. Hotel check-ins. Tell me I'm wrong."

Silence.

"What I thought," Drex said. "Listen to me. He is no longer Jasper Ford. He's somebody else. He's undergone so complete a transformation that you wouldn't know him if he walked up to you and grabbed you by the balls." He let Locke think on that, which the detective did without comment. Drex continued. "He left the airport with his roll-aboard. Did he leave it behind in the taxi?"

"No."

"Was it found on the yacht?"

"No."

"It was in the car."

"Mrs. Ford had his car."

Drex explained to the detective his theory that Jasper had left a spare car near the hotel where the taxi had dropped him. "An innocuous vehicle that can never be traced to him. He used it to get around that night. Inside it was that suitcase. Jasper swam ashore, but it was another person who left the beach."

"You're guessing."

Drex rubbed his forehead. "I went on a trip this afternoon, into this sick shit's head. He wanted everybody to think that Jasper Ford had been lost at sea. Do you agree?"

"Okay."

"He could not risk Jasper Ford ever being seen again. Jasper Ford had to cease to exist just like his previous incarnations did. He changed his appearance and his identity somewhere out there on the beach."

"Search parties have been combing the beaches—"

"You won't find so much as a gum wrapper. He's sanitary. Meticulous. Freakin' anal. He put everything back into the suitcase. What he did with it after that, I don't know. But it contained everything he needed to transform himself into someone else."

"All right, for the sake of argument—"

"I'm not being argumentative for the sake of argument, Locke," he said with heat. "I want to catch him, but I can't fly blind. I'm trying to impress upon you that if you want him, toss the handbook on police methodology into the nearest trash can." He took a breath. "But I'm listening. What was your argument?"

"If he did change his appearance, everything you said, we've already lost him. He's gone."

Drex looked over at Gif. "Gif said that this morning. He surmised that Jasper was probably long gone even before Elaine's body washed ashore. I didn't take issue with that supposition, because, at the time, I thought it likely. I don't any longer."

"Why not?" the detective asked.

"Because I put myself in Jasper's place, and came up with three reasons why I wouldn't leave the vicinity right away. First, if I had successfully pulled off a plan that intricate, it would be irresistible to me to enjoy it. It would be like skipping the fireworks after the championship win. He wants to bask in the glow of the fallout he's created. The last local newscast I saw, he's being described as a person of interest in Elaine's death."

"It was decided to hold back on naming him a suspect. We still can't put him on the yacht or in the dinghy. It's been tossed around that an unknown third party was aboard."

"If they follow that line of thinking, he'll get away. Locke, you've got to convince somebody that this isn't a man who woke up yesterday morning and decided to knock off a lady friend. It's not a love triangle gone south. Not even common thievery. He didn't act on impulse.

"I promise you that he's been plotting this for a while. Having talked to Talia about his recent behavior, I believe the discovery of Marian Harris's grave served as his catalyst."

"Detective?" Talia said.

"Mrs. Ford?" Locke exclaimed. "I didn't realize you were listening in. Are you all right?"

"If you're asking if I came with Drex by choice, yes. There was no coercion on his part." She paused. "But I feel badly about the awkward position I've placed you and Mr. Menundez in. Last night you treated me kindly through a difficult experience. Thank you."

"You're welcome," he said stiffly. "What do you think about Easton's conjectures?"

"I don't disagree with anything. In fact, he's opened my eyes to much that I chose not to see. With no offense intended toward your department or any law enforcement agency, I believe you should listen to him and act on his advice."

The detective sighed. "Easton, you said there were three reasons why you think he'd stick around. What's the second?"

"To kill Talia."

Drex's candor took Locke aback. He cleared his throat before asking her if Jasper had ever threatened her.

"No."

"Did you ever feel threatened by implication or—"

"No," she replied, interrupting him. "That's what makes it so terrifying to me now. He had some odd habits, but I didn't perceive them as aberrant characteristics or take them as the warning signs I should have."

"We don't have time for her to rehash what she's already told me about their relationship," Drex said. "Just take my word for it. He won't leave here with her still living. It would be untidy."

"He's right, detective," she said. "I've lived with Jasper. I know his habits. He won't leave me as a loose thread."

"To say nothing of her dough," Mike said.

"Who's that?" Locke asked.

"Mallory."

"So the gang's all there?"

"Hello," Gif said.

"You know you're all screwed," the detective said. "Rudkowski has vowed to see to it. Is it true that—"

"Look," Drex interrupted. "We'll sort all that out when we have to. Right now, we've got to figure out a way to draw Jasper into the open."

Locke said, "You didn't get to the third reason why you think he's still in the neighborhood."

"Ego."

Drex pushed himself off the bar and went to stand at one of the narrow windows on either side of the front door. He twirled the wand to open the blinds. "He knows I'm on to him. Doesn't make any difference to him whether or not I carry a badge, he knows I'm after him and, because of the trouble I went to with that impersonation of a writer, he must have some inkling of my determination to nail him.

"But he pulled a fast one on me. He plotted and executed a humdinger of a murder. He duped Talia. He had me chasing my tail. He somehow swayed Elaine. None of us saw it coming. *I* didn't see it coming, and I should have. He outsmarted me, and he'll want to rub my nose in it."

"Okay, but how?" Locke asked. "By killing Talia?"

That was the question that had tormented Drex that afternoon as he lay in the dark and focused on his quarry. If he were Jasper, would he want to dispatch Talia right away and be done with it? The game would be over. Where would the fun in that be?

"What I think," he said slowly, "is that he'll want me to worry about her, to fret over when and how he'll strike. He'll want to keep her on edge and afraid, too."

"You're contradicting yourself," Mike said grouchily. "You just argued that he wouldn't leave until he'd taken care of her."

"But not yet." Drex stared out into the rain. "In order to get my attention, to let me know that he's not done with me yet, that he's still pulling the strings, he'll strike swiftly. But he'll kill somebody else."

Locke exhaled loudly. "Oh, shit."

Chapter 30

Alerted by the detective's tone, Drex turned away from the window and looked at the phone lying on the bar. "What? Locke? What?"

Locke started backpedaling. "It's not his MO. Not at all."

Drex crossed to the bar and shouted toward the phone. "*What?*"

"A woman was found dead in Waterfront Park."

"Near the water, and you say it's not his MO? He's sending me a valentine. When did it happen?"

"First call came in less than an hour ago."

"How was she killed?"

"No visible wounds. No blood. No obvious weapon."

"Then why's she dead?"

"Her neck was broken. Looks like he killed her barehanded."

Drex plowed his fingers through his hair, then held them there, cupping the top of his head.

Locke said, "But you didn't hear any of this from me. Other detectives were assigned. It's their case—"

"Not anymore. It's mine." Drex pushed the phone toward Gif. "Get the details."

"He may not want to tell—"

"Then get them from someone else."

Gif picked up the phone and began talking to Locke.

Drex said to Mike, "Get on your laptop. It may already be on-line news. Get the buzz."

"That's what it'll be. Buzz."

"Get it anyway."

"Where are you going?"

"To bring the car around. Where's the key?"

While still talking to Locke, Gif fished the key fob from his pants pocket and tossed it toward Drex. But Talia's hand shot out and caught it in midair. "I'll drive," she said.

"You're staying here with Mike."

"Half an hour ago, you said you don't have any contacts in Charleston. You don't know your way around."

"We'll find our way."

"I'm going."

"You need to stay here."

"No, I need to do this. I *need* to do this."

He tried to stare her into compliance, but realized how unfair that would be. She had offered to help, and she needed to do something to assuage the guilt she felt over Elaine.

Mike huffed up behind them. "I got the exact location. I'm coming, too."

⸻

The four of them piled into Gif's car. Drex rode shotgun, the other two got in back. Talia was driving—speeding—toward the waterfront at the confluence of the Cooper River and the Atlantic, where the so-named park, the pier, and other attractions made the area a destination landmark of Charleston.

Gif filled them in on what Locke had told him. "Locke says CID is hopping."

"CID?" Talia asked.

"Criminal Investigations Division," the three men said in unison.

Gif continued, "Two back-to-back female homicide victims within twenty-four hours sent up red flags."

"No shit," Mike said.

"Have they identified the victim?" Drex asked.

"Sara Barker. Her purse was found beneath her, strap was still on her shoulder. Driver's license, credit cards, all there. Diamond wedding ring on her finger. It's believed she was attacked from behind as she was about to get into her car."

"Age?"

"Thirty-nine. Having dinner out with three girlfriends. Her husband was at home with their two children, boy, age nine, girl, six."

Drex clenched his fist and thumped his forehead with it. "Completely random victim. Something else he hasn't tried. Or, hell, maybe he has. Maybe he's killed dozens we don't know about, and I've only spotted the ones that fit a pattern."

"Which this one doesn't," Mike said. "So you don't know this was him."

"I know," Drex said. "He's showing off. Catch me if you can, asshole. That's what he's thinking."

Talia broke in. "I see an empty space in there." She pointed out the parking lot of a busy restaurant. "This may be as close as I can get, and we'll be inconspicuous here."

Drex nodded approval. She pulled into the parking lot and claimed the space. The instant she cut the engine, Drex reached for the passenger door handle.

"Drex, you can't go," Gif said. "Neither can Talia. Last thing Locke said, he warned me that Rudkowski would bulldoze his way into this, whether CPD liked it or not. If you're seen—"

"We're had." Drex cursed Gif's rational thinking and underscored the curses with additional ones because Gif was right.

Mike said, "You stay here. Gif and me will nose around and pick up what we can."

"Thanks all the same, Mike," Gif said, "but you're too much mass to go unnoticed."

Drex said, "He's right."

"No offense taken. I'll stay here in the nice, dry car, and update you off my laptop."

Drex asked Gif for Locke's phone number, which he supplied. Before he got out, he asked Drex if there was anything specific he wanted him to look for. "Rudkowski," Drex said.

"Goes without saying."

"You see him, shrink out of sight and come right back. Also keep your eyes and ears open for a calling card from Jasper."

"What do you mean?"

"He wants me to know it's him," Drex said. "He'll have left me a sign."

"Like what?"

"I don't know. It'll be something subtle. A inside joke between him and me."

<hr />

After Gif left, Drex called Locke. He could tell the detective was in a moving vehicle. "Where are you?"

"Menundez and I have been called to the scene of a homicide."

The way he said that was his way of signaling to Drex that he hadn't told Menundez about their previous conversation. "That's a boon to me," he said.

"It's not our investigation, but they wanted us to take a look, see if there may be a connection between this homicide and ours last night."

"Other than gender of the victim?"

"Yes. Something that would indicate the same perp."

"I already know it's the same perp. If you find evidence of it, call me immediately."

"I'll see how it goes."

It became plain that Locke wasn't going to talk where Menundez could overhear. Drex guessed it was as much for the younger man's protection as for Locke's own. Even though the honorable gesture was working against Drex right now, he admired the detective for not wishing to compromise a junior partner.

"All right. I'm reading you. But when you can give me more details—"

"No promises."

"Understood. But as a show of faith, I'll text you my phone number and our current location."

"How long will you be there?"

"Till we're not."

"How long will the phone number be good?"

"Till I don't answer."

"I've got to go," Locke said. "We're here."

The detective clicked off, and so did Drex. He sent the promised text immediately. Then, tapping the phone against his chin in frustration, he related to Talia and Mike what Locke had told him.

"Somebody might overlook a vital link. Dammit." He reached for the door handle and lifted it.

"Drex?" Talia exclaimed.

"I can't just sit here and do nothing," he said.

"You've got to, Drex," Mike said. "If you're caught intruding, you'll be shut down. Gif and me, too. Locke will be hung out to dry, because Rudkowski will know it was him who tipped you."

"I'm not going to let Locke catch the flak."

"That won't be your call. Do you want to cost him his job?"

Gripped by indecision, he kept the car door open but didn't get out. He looked at Talia, who said, "Mike is right." He cast a look over his shoulder at Mike, whose expression was more baleful than usual. Drex conceded the wisdom of discretion. "Okay, but I can't just sit. I'll keep to this parking lot. Stretch my legs. Clear my head."

He flipped up the hood of his rain jacket and got out.

———

With the intention of joining him, Talia reached for the driver's door handle, but from the back seat, Mike said, "Give him a few. He'll be all right. He gets like this."

She settled back into her seat. "It pains him, doesn't it? What he does."

"It's been known to. When it does, we—Gif and I—keep our distance, let him work through it. He eventually comes out of it."

"The Drex Easton I met—good Lord. It was a week ago today," she said, amazed by how much longer it seemed that he had been in her life. "That Drex was laid back and witty."

"That's a side of him, too. He can be a real cut-up."

She watched Drex disappear into the rain. He was walking shoulders hunched, his hands crammed into the pockets of his windbreaker. "How long has he been doing this?"

"Officially? Since he got his PhD in criminal psychology."

She looked back at Mike, who took up more than half of the back seat. Seeing her surprise, he tipped his head in the general direction Drex had gone. "Dr. Easton."

"I had no idea."

"He doesn't let on."

"I take it that he and Rudkowski go way back."

"Way back."

"They had a falling out?"

"No. That implies they were once allies. They started out like oil and water."

"Over what?"

"Rudkowski's ineptitude. It became readily apparent to Drex early on, out in California. Santa Barbara woman went missing."

"Never found."

Mike nodded. "Or her money. Anyhow, after that case, Rud-kowski relocated to Louisville. He hated like hell that Drex settled in Lexington. Being that close makes it easier for Drex to keep a fin-ger on Rudkowski's pulse, but it also makes it easier for Rudkowski to stay on top of Drex. And he does. Like chain mail."

"Which is why Drex works around him."

"Rudkowski is a joke and knows it. He's envious of Drex. Drex is smarter, a born leader, better looking, gets lots of girls."

He'd paused before the last phrase, and Talia understood that he'd tacked it on only to provoke her. She opted to be provoked. "Are you trying to put me in my place? To let me know where I stand with Drex? With you?"

He didn't say anything.

"You know, Mr. Mallory, in the past thirty-six hours my life has collapsed around me. It's in shambles, and I don't know if I'll ever be able to free myself of the wreckage, or even survive. So winning you over is not a priority. The truth is, I really don't care if I do or not."

She didn't flinch from his sharpened scrutiny, but it surprised her to see a twitch at the corner of his wide mouth that was as close to a smile as she'd ever seen from him. "After that speech, you're beginning to."

Drex chose then to return. He opened the passenger door and slid in. "It's really starting to come down. Did I miss anything?"

Talia glanced at Mike, then shook her head no.

Mike asked Drex if Locke had called him back yet. "No, but he probably—"

All three of them nearly jumped out of their skins when some-one rushed up to the passenger side of the car and knocked hard on the window. Menundez was looking in on them, his face a rain-streaked grimace.

Drex opened the door. "How'd you know where we were?"

"Locke sent me to get you."

Drex already had one leg out of the car. "What did you find?"

"Lewis."

Drex froze. "What? Gif?"

Menundez shot a look toward Talia, another toward Mike, before coming back to Drex. "The ambulance just left with him."

Chapter 31

———◆———

Speaking in stops and starts, Menundez told them that Gif had been discovered lying on the pavement. "He was in excruciating pain. Couldn't talk. Barely able to breath. Somebody called 911. By the time emergency services arrived, he was unconscious."

Drex grabbed the detective by the collar and all but hauled him into the car.

"Was he still alive?"

"I don't know. I swear, I don't."

"What happened to him?"

"Nobody knows. He was in the middle of a crowd. Just dropped. People around him thought maybe a heart attack or stroke. Locke stayed to question them. Sent me to tell you."

"Thanks."

Talia already had the motor running. As soon as Drex released his hold on Menundez, she peeled out of the parking space, leaving the detective where he stood.

She navigated the streets of downtown in the direction of University Hospital ER, where Menundez had told them Gif was being taken. She made only one wrong turn, going the wrong way down a one-way street. She dodged oncoming motorists who flashed their brights and honked, but she didn't ease up on the accelerator.

In the passenger seat, Drex was beside himself, taking all the blame for letting Gif go alone. She dropped him at the entrance to the ER. He bolted from the car and ran inside while she and Mike went in search of parking.

By the time they caught up with Drex, he was threatening the personnel at the admissions desk with demolition of the hospital if they didn't inform him of his friend's condition.

"At least tell me how seriously he was injured," he shouted at the woman, who must have been the one in charge. "Was he shot? Stabbed? Bleeding? *What?*"

Unfazed, she said, "There's nothing I can tell you, sir. You're welcome to take a seat in the waiting—"

"I'm not taking a seat!"

Talia and Mike flanked him, each hooking an arm through his and pulling him away. They wrestled him toward the waiting area where Mike pushed him into a chair and told him to get a grip.

"You're not the only one upset, you know. Losing it isn't helping."

Drex told him to back the eff off, then planted his elbows on his knees and buried his face his hands.

"Keep an eye on him," Mike said to Talia. "My badge will make that harpy more accommodating."

"Hold on." She caught him by the sleeve. "Flashing your badge might draw unwelcome attention to us."

She'd become aware of other people in the waiting area, who had diverted their attention from cell phones, magazines, and pamphlets about miracle drugs, and were now observing them with avid interest, as though the personal drama that had brought them to the ER tonight paled in comparison to Drex's.

Mike's glower made most go back to what they'd been doing.

Talia crouched in front of Drex and placed her hand on his knee. "Drex, do you still have my cell phone and the battery with you?"

He raised his head and looked at her as though she were speaking in tongues. When the words registered, he nodded. "Why?"

"Put the battery in." When he started shaking his head, she pressed his knee. "One call, then you can take it out again. Trust me. I've got this."

Either he did place his trust in her or he was too worried over Gif to argue, but he began doing as she asked. She left him under Mike's watch and returned to the admissions desk.

The woman took her sweet time sorting through a stack of forms, then, without even looking up from her task, said, "Yes?"

"Is Dr. Phillips in the hospital tonight? Andrew Phillips."

She looked up then. "He's chief of surgery."

"I know. Would it be possible for you to get a message to either him or his assistant?"

She sputtered as though Talia had told a good one. "I don't think so."

"I see. Well, thank you." She gave her a pleasant smile. "I'll call Margaret."

"Who's that?"

"Mrs. Andrew Phillips." Talia held her gaze. "Or, so I don't have to disturb her, if you think it's possible to reach someone on Dr. Phillips's staff, please ask them to call me. My name is Talia Shafer."

The woman shifted her stance as though her shoes had suddenly become too tight. "Like the children's foundation?"

"Exactly like that. Margaret serves on our board."

The woman thought it over, then, "What's your phone number?"

Talia recited it; the woman wrote it down. "Please convey that I'm in the ER waiting room, and that I'm very anxious to know the condition of a patient named Gif Lewis."

The woman gave her a sulky nod.

Talia returned to Drex. She sat in the chair beside his, took her phone from his listless hand, and checked to see that he'd restored the battery and turned it on. "We should know something soon."

"Your approach must've been more diplomatic than mine."

"I didn't use diplomacy. I pulled strings."

She could tell that he wasn't really engaged in what they were saying to each other. He was staring straight ahead, his eyes bleak, haunted. She placed her hand in his, sliding her palm against his, then linking their fingers. They didn't talk.

Across from them in a facing row of chairs, Mike was overflowing the seat of his, but he looked stalwart. Talia found herself judging him less harshly. He was a disagreeable grump, but a levelheaded and reliable friend. His outward display of worry was more contained than Drex's, but she could tell that it was just as deeply felt.

At one point, Drex looked over at him and said hoarsely, "Jesus, Mike."

"I know."

"I'm wishing for a heart attack."

Mike confessed that he was, too. "They're survivable."

After that, they lapsed into a somber silence, stirring only when a stout man, dressed in scrubs and sporting a white beard, pushed through a door and strode into the waiting area with the bearing of a commanding general. Or a chief surgeon at a major teaching hospital.

He glanced around and, spotting Talia, walked straight over. She stood up, Drex and Mike doing likewise. She said, "Andy, I didn't expect you! You could have sent an underling or just called me."

"Does this have anything to do with Jasper? Margaret and I were shocked to hear about it. Has there been any word?"

"Thank you for your concern. There's nothing new to report on

Jasper's disappearance, but indirectly that's why I'm here. One of the men on the investigative team was brought here by ambulance a short while ago."

"Lewis."

"Yes. What can you tell me?"

"I can tell you that he's alive."

She, Drex, and Mike all slumped with relief. "We're all very glad to hear that," she said. "Thank you, Andy." She made hasty introductions. "Mr. Lewis is more than simply their colleague, he's their very good friend. Naturally, they've been anxious to know his condition."

"And that woman over there wouldn't even tell us what had happened to him," Drex said.

The surgeon looked him up and down. "You must be the extremely rude and vituperative individual referred to by her."

That bounced off Drex. "Is Gif going to be all right?"

Talia knew Andrew Phillips to be kind, but he was also brusque. "Come with me."

Without further ado, he turned away. They followed him through the door from which he'd entered and headed toward a bank of elevators. He jabbed the up button. "Mr. Lewis presented with a lacerated liver that required immediate surgery."

Talia covered her mouth with her hand. "Heavens."

"Knife?" Drex asked as they boarded the elevator.

"Blunt trauma."

"He took a blow to the gut?" Mike asked.

The surgeon placed his fist in the wedge where his rib cage came together. "Right here. Vulnerable spot. Ask any boxer. You catch a blow there, you'll likely go to the mat. Hurts like a mother. Excuse me, Talia. Renders you unable to move, breathe. Blood pressure tanks. Here we are."

The surgeon alighted from the elevator first and led them to a much smaller waiting room, which was unoccupied. "Whoever hit him knew what he was doing," he said. "The blow was perfectly placed and done with harmful intent. I wouldn't rule out brass knuckles or some other object. In any case, it was hard enough to cause a sizeable tear. Good news, your friend got here before catastrophic blood loss, and he had an excellent trauma team working on him. The tear has been repaired. He seems overall healthy. Barring any complications, which aren't anticipated, he'll live."

While Mike and Talia expressed their relief, Drex turned away from them and placed one hand on the back of his neck, indicating to Talia that anxiety and tension had concentrated there. Likely he also needed a moment to suppress his emotions.

"When I got your call, they were closing him up," the surgeon was saying. "So if he's not already out of surgery, it shouldn't be much longer. I'll be sure someone lets you know."

Drex came around. "Can I see him?"

"He'll be in recovery ICU for several hours."

"Can I see him?" Drex repeated.

"He'll be out of it. But if you—"

"I do."

Dr. Phillips eyed him as though he warranted his reputation for rudeness, but also with respect for a man who didn't mince words. "I'll tell the staff to grant you a minute as soon as possible."

"Thank you. For everything. I mean it."

The surgeon acknowledged Drex's appreciation with a curt nod, then reached for Talia's hand and patted it. "This business with Jasper..." He let that trail. "Margaret and I are here for you, whenever."

"You certainly have been tonight. Thank you."

He gave her hand a final pat, turned to Drex and Mike, and said, "I have utmost respect for the FBI. Good luck to your friend." Then he left them as though already late to the next emergency.

"Friends in high places," Mike wheezed as he lowered his bulk onto an upholstered love seat.

Talia said, "I'm glad I could be of some use."

"Well, thanks," Mike said.

Drex didn't thank her verbally. He simply pulled her into a tight hug.

———✦———

Drex had paced miles, it seemed, before he was summoned by a nurse and told he could see Gif. He followed her to one of the ICU rooms, where she left him. Under the loose hospital gown, Gif looked fragile and pale and, if Drex didn't know better, dead. The rhythmic blinks and blips on the machines to which he was connected were reassurance that his systems were functioning.

When the nurse returned to escort him out, she emphasized that Gif was doing well, that his vitals were strong, and that she predicted a full recovery.

"Take good care of him," he said.

"I will."

"He'll complain, but don't listen. Do what's needed to get him well."

"I promise."

Drex hugged her tightly, too.

He relieved Mike and Talia of their concern immediately upon reentering the waiting room. "He looks poorly, but he's doing well. His condition has been upgraded to stable." They were on the verge of asking questions when his cell phone vibrated in his pocket. "Hold on. This may be Locke." He looked at his phone. "It is. He's sent a text."

Warning! Rudkowski here. On our way up.

Drex read it silently and then out loud. "Dammit." Gif's emergency had temporarily distracted him from the other crisis. This jerked him right back into the thick of it.

"He's still typing," he told Mike and Talia, then read the new message aloud. "'Take fire stairs. Look for M.'"

"Menundez," Mike said. "Go!" He shooed them toward the door.

Drex said, "I can't leave Gif."

"He'll never forgive you if you don't. Go!"

"What about Rudkowski?"

"I'll be the sacrificial lamb." Then, rubbing his hands over his extensive midsection, he said, "Sacrificial ox."

They hurried down the fire stairs to the ground floor. Menundez was waiting for them where the stairwell opened into a lobby. "How's Lewis?"

"Out of surgery and in ICU." Drex gave him a concise update. "I can't thank you enough for getting word to me."

"Sure, man." Menundez called their attention to the unusual amount of activity in the lobby. "As you can see, there's a large police presence."

"For us?" Drex asked.

"Busy night. Two assaults, one fatal, in the same area within hours of each other."

"Mike Mallory stayed behind to stall Rudkowski, but he'll be demanding to know where Talia and I are."

"Hear ya. Keep your heads down," the detective said, and started threading this way toward one of the entrances. Glancing around, he lowered his voice before continuing. "Rudkowski is an idiot. After this thing with Lewis, Locke brought me into the loop."

"You and he talked to witnesses who were near Gif when he went down?"

"Yeah, but didn't get much. Boatload of people had just gotten off one of the harbor tours. Word spread about the deadly assault of a woman. The crowd began migrating toward the scene of the crime. Lewis must've got caught up and swept along."

"No one saw the attack?"

He shook his head. "One guy we talked to said that at almost the same time Lewis dropped, he noticed a man making his way through the throng in a hurry. He didn't think anything about it at the time."

"Description?"

"He only saw him from the back, and all he remembers is that he had on a rain poncho. And it could have been just a man in a hurry. Security cameras may have picked him up. They're being checked."

"I'll appreciate any information you can pass along."

"You got it. Locke and me will do what we can to help."

"If you're called on it, I swear I won't let them hang you out to dry."

"Mr. Easton," he said grimly, "if it means catching Ford, I wouldn't mind if I was."

They were approaching an exit where two uniformed policemen were standing together, chewing the fat more than being vigilant. "Just keep walking," Menundez said out of the side of his mouth. "We'll be in touch."

He veered off and headed toward the officers, saying to them as he walked up, "Hey, guys. Menundez from CID. That second emergency near the wharf? It was an assault."

"Any connection to the homicide?"

"We don't know yet, but..."

That's all Drex and Talia heard before they cleared the door. At the first opportunity, Drex pulled her out from under the bright lights of the porte cochere and into the shadows of the building. There he stopped.

"I thought we were in a hurry," she said.

"Let's wait here for a minute or two, see if anybody follows us out."

"Police?"

"Jasper." Thinking out loud, he said, "He killed that woman for no other reason than to draw me out, get me to make myself visible, so he could follow me. Follow me to you. I didn't show, but he recognized Gif."

"But how? From where?"

"Hell I know. I can't figure that. Gif doesn't just fade into the woodwork. He becomes the woodwork. But Jasper picked him out of that crowd."

His eyes narrowed with wrath over what Jasper had done to Gif. "The calling card he left me was anything but subtle. If Jasper materialized in front of me right now, in any disguise, I swear to God I'd kill him."

After waiting for several minutes and seeing no one worthy of a second look, he took Talia's hand. Together they made their way to where she'd parked Gif's car. Drex asked for the key. "I'm driving."

"You may get lost."

"I hope I do. It would make a tail more noticeable."

Earlier that day, Jasper had bid Howard Clement a fond farewell. The man with a penchant for garishly printed shirts had served his purpose, but it had been time to assume another identity.

Tonight, as he'd moved among ordinary people looking very much like one of them, no one paid him any heed. Even if the woman he'd killed had seen him coming, she wouldn't have felt threatened. Had she seen him as she walked alone across the dark and deserted parking lot—such a stupid thing for her to do—she probably would have smiled and wished him a good evening before turning her back to him to unlock her car door.

But she hadn't seen him as he came out of the darkness and moved up behind her. The full nelson had taken her so unaware that she'd barely squeaked in surprise as he clamped his hands around her head like a vise, and forced it forward and down at such a steep angle that the vertebrae in her neck had snapped like twigs. Spine severed. She was dead. It had taken no time at all.

He'd left her where she fell and took a stroll out onto the wharf. It had been crawling with tourists who'd defied the inclement weather. He'd blended in. He'd walked all the way out to the end of it and stayed for several minutes to enjoy the view across the water. He had started back when he heard the first sirens' whoops and wails like trumpeters announcing his achievement. He'd wanted to stop in his tracks and take a bow.

Wanting to be near the crime scene as the curious began converging, he'd picked up his pace, but not enough to be noticed. A reasonably sized crowd had already collected and continued to grow. He'd meandered among families, teenagers groping each other, packs of rambunctious young men, all bunching together, ebbing toward the concentration of police activity.

Jasper hadn't cared to see the body. He'd seen it. He'd been on the lookout for Drex Easton.

He would come, just as he had to the beach. Of that Jasper had had no doubt. Easton would want either to confirm or rule out that this slaying was the handiwork of Jasper Ford. And Jasper had wanted him to know that it absolutely was.

Take that, Easton.

He'd wondered at what point Easton had initiated his chase? Jasper had been intuiting him for years, but he couldn't pinpoint the time he had first sensed him. The knowledge that he had a pursuer hadn't come to him in a jolt of awareness. It had been a seepage into his subconscious. When had it started? After Pixie? Before Loretta? Did Easton know of all his aliases, he wondered, going back all the way to Weston Graham?

How could he? Weston had existed thirty years ago. Easton would have been a boy.

He'd been speculating on how he had come to be the lodestar of Easton's vocation when he did a double take on a man in the crowd. He was as colorless as a person could possibly be, but Jasper had recognized him instantly as Easton's sidekick who'd been with him on the pier above the beach.

The man had been observing the scene and looking into each individual face with the same studied casualness that Jasper boasted himself capable of doing. In an instant he had realized that the man was looking for him. But for Jasper Ford, not his newly assumed identity.

Jasper had really wanted to find Easton. Find him, find Talia.

But this opportunity had been too fortuitous to pass up. The gift horse, so to speak.

Jasper had kept the man in sight and carefully stayed out of his. He'd bided his time, allowing the crowd to thicken until it had become difficult to wade through the newcomers asking what had happened and craning their necks in order to see.

Eventually he had worked his way around until he was walking directly toward the man. There was a cluster of people within touching distance of them, but no one noticed when Jasper socked the man hard.

Easton's pal went down without a sound. With all the jostling going on around them, no one noticed his collapse for a few precious moments, long enough for Jasper to put some distance between them. He kept moving, sometimes swimming upstream, sometimes being propelled by those around him.

But soon he heard the exclamations behind him, had felt the disturbance rippling outward from the spot where the man had dropped. Like everyone else, Jasper halted, turned to look back to see what this new source of commotion was.

His jab had been hard enough and so well placed that it would have incapacitated Easton's buddy. To what extent didn't matter much. Easton would get the message.

As he'd left the vicinity, he'd felt a groundswell of satisfaction inside his chest. It had been a productive night. Much more so than he'd counted on. He'd wished to mark his success, make it an occasion. But he'd foregone a celebration. He was bold, not reckless.

So he'd prudently returned to his car, added his newest trophy to the velvet bag, and zipped it back into an inside pocket of his tracksuit.

Driving away, he'd passed ambulances racing toward the scene of yet another emergency, a scene of havoc, another of his masterpieces.

He'd cruised through the city, in no particular hurry, on the hunt for new lodging.

Chapter 32

Drex took a roundabout route from the hospital. After twenty minutes of aimless driving and doubling back several times, he was convinced that they weren't being followed.

He considered switching hotels, but that would involve a check-in process he would rather avoid. He returned them to the suite they'd occupied that afternoon and, once inside, plopped into a chair and sent Mike a text. Seconds later, his phone rang, surprising him.

"I expected something more covert than a call."

"I'm all by my lonesome."

"Rudkowski?"

"Went apeshit when he learned that you two had ducked out. He threatened to arrest me. I double dog dared him. I hadn't absconded with a material witness, had I? I was keeping vigil over my friend who *could have died tonight*.

"Locke told him that he was being unreasonable. Talia's hotshot surgeon came to see what all the yelling was about, told Rudkowski to pipe down or he'd have security throw him out. Rudkowski told me to tell you that you were ruined, that he would see to it, then he left with Locke and Menundez. I think both of them are solid."

"Me too. Have you seen Gif?"

He hadn't, but he was receiving periodic updates that Gif was holding his own.

There had been no developments in the investigation into the homicide or the assault on Gif. "They're reviewing surveillance camera videos," Mike said, "but they have a lot more of them to look at. Out of Rudkowski's hearing, the detectives promised to keep us apprised. The coroner's report on the woman killed tonight is expected in the morning. Locke said he'd shoot it to us, along with the one on Elaine Conner."

"Jasper's got people working overtime tonight."

"He must be so proud," Mike returned drolly. "Anyhow, nothing more we can do tonight except wait."

"I feel guilty for having a bed and you don't," Drex said.

"I can sleep sitting up. Do most of the time anyway."

"Let me know if there's any change in Gif's condition. I'll come immediately."

"Okay."

"I mean it, Mike. *Any* change."

"Cross my overtaxed heart." With that he clicked off.

Drex looked over at Talia. "Did you hear any of that?"

"I got the gist."

"Talia." He paused in order to give his next words heft. "Thank you." She tipped her head inquisitively. "For pulling those strings. If you hadn't, we might still be in the dark about Gif. I'd still be losing my mind."

"I believe the lady at admissions thought you already had."

"I'm surprised she didn't send for the straitjacket squad."

They smiled at each other. Then he leaned his head back and dug the heels of his hands into his eye sockets. "God, how long has this day been?"

"Long."

He lowered his hands from his eyes and slapped his knees as he rolled up out of the chair. "I'm going to shower, unless you want the bathroom first."

"Go ahead."

He trudged up the stairs, went into his bedroom, and took off his windbreaker and shoes. He unclipped his holster from his belt and considered taking the pistol into the bathroom with him so it would be within reach. But he set it on the nightstand instead. When he went into the bathroom he noticed that Talia's bedroom door was closed.

By the time he'd undressed, the water in the shower was steaming. Flattening his hands on the wall above the taps and standing directly beneath the spray, he let it pound so hard against the back of his head and neck that it stung.

Then he was shocked into awareness of a softer, gentler touch between his shoulder blades. His head snapped up.

"No, stay as you were." Talia moved up behind him and pressed her body—all of it—against his. She rubbed her center against his ass. Her breasts sandwiched his spine.

"Oh, my God. Talia—"

"Stay as you are."

"But I want to see you. And it feels so good."

"To me, too." She rested her cheek against his back. "It feels good to be needed. Allow me to do this for you. Okay?"

He answered by saying nothing and staying as he was. She backed away only far enough to reach for something. It must have been the bottle of shower gel, because her hands were soapy when she applied them to the back of his neck.

Starting at the base and working up, she kneaded out the achiness, then slid her fingers into his hair and massaged his head. On their way back down, they gently pinched the tops of his ears and earlobes, then moved across his shoulders, squeezing the tension out of them.

He sighed a long, drawn out *ah*. "That felt great. Thanks."

"You're welcome."

"Can I turn around now?"

"No."

"When?"

"When I'm done."

"When will that be?"

"When I say when."

She got a refill of gel, then pressed her hands firmly against his back on either side of his spine, rubbing circles into his lats, working her way down until her hands were on his butt, creating deep depressions in his glutes with her fingers.

"Your muscles are tight," she said. "Relax."

"Relax? Are you serious? I'm dying here."

She laughed softly. "I don't think so."

Her thumbs became twin pressure points on the small of his back. They rode the bumpy path of his vertebrae all the way down to the cleft of his ass, then teased it with feather-light brushes that caused his breath to hitch.

"Damn, Talia. Now?"

"Not yet."

Again she withdrew to get more gel. *The bottle must be near empty by now*, he thought. Then all thought ceased as her arms came around him, and she covered his pecs with her hands.

"I like the hair," she whispered, tweaking it.

"Yeah?"

"Um-huh. Just the right amount."

After her thumbs glanced his nipples, her hands took a sinuous, crisscrossing, slippery course down his torso, over ribs and abdomen, past his navel, until her fingers slid down the channels above his thighs where they met at the base of his cock.

Christ. He didn't want to beg.

He didn't have to. Her hands took turns forming silky fists around him, one massaging upward and moving off, only to be outdone by its alternate that followed just behind. When he didn't think he could withstand any more, one hand didn't slide off at the tip. It stayed. Fingers dripping lather made teasing rotations around the crest, over it, again, as though testing its tautness, and then something wicked was done to the slit.

Through clenched teeth, he strangled out, *"When."*

He turned around and hauled her against him. He tried to pause and register all the incredible sensations that holding her wet and naked against him induced, but his brain was functioning on a more primitive tier.

He gathered up a handful of her hair and pulled her head back, tilting her face up to his. He looked into her eyes, then covered her mouth with his. It was a ravenous kiss. He couldn't get enough of her, and she was as hungry.

He skimmed her breast with his palm, then claimed it, reshaping it, lifting it as he lowered his head and took her nipple into his mouth. With each tug, she whimpered in pleasure and clasped his head to hold him to her.

He skimmed her front, marveling over the feminine curves and hollows, the incredible softness of her skin. Briefly he entangled his fingers in the hair between her thighs, then parted the soft flesh beneath.

She was slick and pliant around the fingers he pressed into her. When he began stroking, her head dropped forward against his chest. He felt the scrape of her teeth against his pec. With urgency, she reached down and closed her hand around his erection.

"Talia," he gasped, pushing her hand aside and withdrawing his fingers from her. "This is going to be some fever-pitch fucking. If we attempt it in this shower, we'll be the next two patients in the emergency room. Let's get in bed."

Dazed, she nodded.

He gave himself a fifteen-second rinse, turned off the taps, and helped her out of the stall. He yanked a towel off the bar and handed it to her, then took one for himself. They haphazardly dried themselves as they stumbled into one of the bedrooms. His, he thought, although he didn't know for sure and didn't care. It had a bed.

He flung back the covers, then sat down on the edge, placed his hands on her bottom, and pulled her between his spread legs. Leaning into her, he rubbed his face against her breasts, touched his tongue to her nipples, flicked it over the occasional freckle and imagined it melting in his mouth like a speck of raw sugar. He nuzzled her middle and swirled his tongue over her navel. Moving lower, he breathed out through his lips into the damp curls.

She spoke his name in a husky whisper.

He turned her and guided her down until she was lying on her back, arms at her sides, hands at shoulder level, palms up. Taking her up on the invitation he saw in the unresisting pose, as well as the look in her smoky eyes, he knelt, opened her thighs, and kissed her with utmost intimacy, his tongue doing as his fingers had minutes earlier. He took tender love bites, applied gentle suction, tantalized her with erotic play, and only then exposed that most vulnerable spot.

Her body jerked in reaction to the first sweep of his tongue, then she began moving in response to and in anticipation of each fluid caress. They increased in frequency, the carnal friction intensifying with each one until she was arching up for more, then more, and more, until an orgasm seized her. He stayed with her, whisking his lips against her, murmuring her name, until the final aftershock shuddered through her and she lay still.

He levered himself up and above her—and was shocked to see tears sliding down her temples into her hair. She reached for him, grabbing at him until their mouths were melded and he had pushed into her.

But he went only far enough to secure himself just inside. There he waited, wanting to commit to memory this moment of feeling her around him for the first time. Then he continued pressing into her until he was solidly imbedded.

She hugged him to her tightly, and it was fantastic, but he had to move or he was going to die. He buried his face in her hair. "If I get too rough, slow me, stop me. I want…I want…Oh, God…"

The mating instinct took over. In spite of his best intentions, his strokes became faster and stronger. A slight shift in his position enabled him to reach deeper, and he did. God, did he.

"Don't hold back," Talia said on a near sob, lifting his head from the crook of her neck so she could look into his face.

He kissed her again and continued kissing her until he couldn't focus on anything except the orgasm that rocked her and caused her to bow her back and clench around him. That was his undoing. Grafted to her, he came in a burst of light.

Drowsily she said, "Moving to the bed was a good idea."

"One the best I've had lately. I might have irreparably injured us in that shower stall."

"It would have been worth it."

He hitched an eyebrow. "Yeah?"

"Hmm," she said, stretching luxuriantly.

She lay on her back but was angled slightly toward him. He was lying on his side, propped on one elbow, extremely attentive to her nakedness, but seemingly blasé toward his own.

Of course he had no call to be self-conscious. He was lean and long limbed, muscled but not bulky, clouded with lovely brown hair in all the right places.

Against her, it all felt wonderful.

"Can you get drunk on sex?" she asked.

"I could get drunk on you."

"I feel as though I'm on display."

Drex gave her a lazy smile. "I'm feasting my eyes, all right."

"Your tiger eyes."

"Tiger eyes?"

"That's what they remind me of."

He leaned down and licked the slope of her breast. "Hear me purring?"

She laughed and sank her fingers into his unruly hair. "I heard you growling. Several times." She pulled him toward her for a kiss. It was lazy, unhurried, and delicious.

When they finally broke apart, he resumed his position and continued his survey of her terrain by touching her nipple with his fingertip. "I'm going to have to coin some new adjectives to describe color...." His caress had caused her nipple to tighten. "...and texture."

His hand moved down the center of her torso, his fingers barely grazing her skin. When he reached her mound, he feathered the hair. "But some things defy description."

"You don't need descriptive words. You're not a writer."

"Hmm." Preoccupied with what his fingers were doing, he said, "I may take it up just for the research." He angled his head back and took her in, his gaze moving from her tousled hair to the tips of her toes. "You are gorgeous, Talia Shafer."

"I was going to say the same about you." She scrubbed his bristly jaw line with her knuckles, smoothed his sun-glinted eyebrows with her index finger, then trailed it down his cheek and dipped it into his dimple. He deepened it for her by smiling, and she laughed lightly.

It felt so good, so right to be with him like this, she was reluctant to bring into the open something that had been needling her. She reached for his hand and drew it up to the center of her chest, holding it between her breasts, but not provocatively. She traced the network of veins on the back of it. "Drex, what we just did was amazing."

"On a scale of one to ten?"

She smiled, but he must have sensed that she wasn't teasing, that what she had to say was serious, because he pulled the covers up over them before resettling beside her and intertwining their legs.

"I don't want to spoil this," she said. "But I must ask."

He brows drew together. "What?"

"You talked tonight about Jasper playing an inside joke on you."

"Something to let me know that he'd gotten the best of me."

She shifted her gaze back to his hand and ran her finger along the ridge of his knuckles. "Did you sleep with his wife to get the best of him?"

He became so still that she feared she had ruined something precious, and that the memory she would be left with was of him being highly offended and storming from the bed, the suite, her life.

But after a ponderous silence, he said, "Look at me." She did. He said, "No. Believe me, wanting you in my bed has been no joke, inside or otherwise. Mike, Gif, and I had words. They lectured me like maiden aunts about letting my dick do my thinking. They cited the conflict of interest this—" he said, sawing his hand between them, "—would create. You see the effect of all their wise counsel."

He turned the hand she held against her chest and linked their fingers. "If I had wanted to use you to taunt Jasper, that's what I would have done. Taunted. I would have let him *think* that we had slept together or planned to at our first opportunity."

He studied their clasped hands. "You probably won't believe me, but I swear, for all my tomcatting, I've never been with a married woman. You're my first adultery, and I wouldn't break my personal moral code just to score points against Jasper."

"But you were unfaithful to your wife."

"No, I wasn't."

"You told Jasper—"

"I've never had a wife to cheat on."

Her head went back an inch. "What?"

"I've never been married."

She was stunned by the joy that spread through her from knowing that. "No one special enough to make you stop tomcatting?"

"No time or inclination to let anything special develop. Besides, I wouldn't drag a good woman into my particular hell."

"Into that dark place you have to go?"

He nodded. "Hazard of the trade."

"You didn't drag me into it this afternoon. In fact you shut me out."

"Because it's hardly conducive to foreplay, and I was hoping to get lucky."

She smiled, but didn't let him flirt her away from the subject. "Mike and I talked."

"Oh, great. Did he go into his maiden aunt persona?"

"A little. Dr. Easton."

She recapped her conversation with Mike. When she finished, Drex said, "I started looking for Weston Graham long before I earned my doctorate."

"When you learned he had killed your mother? How did that come about?"

"Are you sure you want to hear that?"

"Yes. I'd like to know."

"You accept that Weston Graham and Jasper Ford are one and the same?"

"You've convinced me. No, actually, *he's* convinced me with his actions over the past two days."

He reflected for a moment, then said, "Although I'm not certain he launched his career with my mother, I suspect it. Maybe he hadn't consciously mapped out woman killing as a career path. But after he'd rid himself of her and walked away unscathed, he recognized his talent and saw a future in exploiting it."

She scooted closer to him and laid her hand on his chest. "I saw her picture in your files. She was lovely."

"I have no memory of her."

"How old were you when she went missing?"

"Around ten, I think. But my dad had moved the two of us to Alaska years before that."

"Tell me about it."

He took a deep breath, rubbed his legs against hers, readjusted his head on the pillow. "A lot of it I've had to piece together because Dad wouldn't talk about it. Never. But what I gather is that she abandoned us to be with Weston Graham."

"She abandoned you, too?"

"I don't know if she did so without a second thought, or if Dad was unbending on keeping me with him. He cut me off from her. Completely." He told her about the name change. "That's why I wasn't afraid to use my name with Jasper. I knew he wouldn't recognize it."

"Wasn't that a rather spiteful thing for your dad to do?"

"No doubt spite was his motivation. He made it impossible for her to find us. But it was fortuitous, because it also prevented Weston from locating us after he'd disposed of her. We might have been two of those loose threads you referred to earlier.

"I knew none of this at the time, understand," he said. "My first clear recollections are of living in Alaska, and it was always just Dad and me."

"What you described to me, all the moving around, et cetera?"

"All true."

"It must've been a lonely life for you."

He admitted as much by giving her a rueful smile. "On the other hand, I didn't know anything different. Not until I got older and saw that other dads actually talked over mealtimes. They laughed and joshed with their kids. They had male buddies they hung out with to drink beer and watch ball games. They had women they slept with. Our house was devoid of anything feminine. I began to notice the touches that my friends' houses had that ours didn't. It was the...the appealing *something* that a woman emanates."

He fell silent for a moment, then said, "My mother's desertion robbed Dad of all that enjoyment, of all joy. She stole his soul. Then Weston stole from her."

"She had money?"

"What seemed like a lot at the time. It was modest by today's standards. After her, Weston, with a new identity, set his sights much higher. But when she went missing, and investigators began digging into her life, it was discovered that all her assets, which she'd inherited from her parents, had miraculously disappeared along with her."

"How did your father learn of it?"

"It made the newspapers. I didn't know he'd saved them until later. But I remember when the change came over him. He'd never been a hard drinker, but he started drinking heavily at night, every night, long into the night. He became even more taciturn than normal. I didn't ask him what the matter was, I think out of fear of what he would tell me. But even if I had asked, he wouldn't have told me. She had been eradicated from my life."

"But your dad still loved her. He was bereaved."

"I see that now. I didn't then. Years later, when I was old enough to read up on her disappearance, I matched the timing of it to that dark period when Dad really shut down."

"And you were around ten years old? That must have been an awful time for you."

"In one respect, it was beneficial. That's when I learned to be sociable. I stayed over at friends' houses a lot. Their parents must've felt sorry for me. They took me in, saw that I was well fed. Anyway, over time, Dad stopped drinking and went back to being more himself. Which was still a level of bereavement. He grieved for my mother, for everything about her, until the day he died."

"When was that?"

"I was in my first year of college in Missoula. I was summoned home. He'd had a stroke, which didn't kill him right away."

"Did you make it home in time to be with him?"

"That's when he shared the story of my mother. He'd secretly kept all the newspaper write-ups about her disappearance. He told me about Weston Graham, who was sought as the prime suspect but never captured. Her disappearance remains a cold case of the LAPD."

He raised his right hand to within inches of her face. "See the scar?" A faint white line bisected his palm. "While my dad lay dying, I cut both our palms, pressed them together, and took a blood oath to get the bastard." Wryly, he added, "It's taken one hell of a long time. All my adult life. And I'm still working on it."

With gruffness in his voice, he continued. "I wouldn't trade for those last minutes with Dad, though. When I made that vow, he cried. It was the most naked emotion I'd ever seen from him. Ever. In my life. It was the closest he and I ever came to having a genuine father-son relationship. He died later that day."

She took his hand and kissed the palm, openmouthed. "He loved you very much."

He looked at her with doubt.

"Perhaps he took you away to spite or to wound your mother, but maybe he saw Weston for what he was and feared for you."

"Maybe," he said grudgingly. "That has occurred to me."

"Drex, if he hadn't loved you and wanted you with him, he could have dumped you anywhere along the way, and at any time. It couldn't have been easy for a single man working on the pipeline to rear a child alone."

"He felt an obligation to me, maybe. But he had lost the will to live."

"Then why didn't he kill himself and be done with it? Leave you to your own devices?" She raised her eyebrows in question.

He gave her a hard look, but he didn't say anything.

"He loved you. Believe it." She settled close to him again. "How do you feel toward your mother?"

"I vacillate between deep resentment over her letting me go and sorrow for the fate she must've suffered. Fair to say that I'm con-flicted?"

"Fair to say."

They lay quietly for several minutes, then he placed his forearm across his eyes and moaned.

"What?"

"I finally got you naked in bed. I should be talking dirty to you, not blathering all this maudlin crap."

"You can still talk dirty." She slid her hand beneath the sheet. It took only one stroke to bring him erect. She laughed. "Well, that didn't take long."

"I told you a sad story. Are you doing this out of pity?"

"I don't think anyone would pity a man so well endowed."

He flashed a grin that would have done the devil proud.

"But even if it is out of pity, do you want me to stop?" she teased.

"Hell, no. Have at it."

She rolled onto him and began dropping kisses on his chest.

"Talia?"

"Don't bother me, I'm busy."

"I just want to ask—"

"Later."

She opened her thighs and guided him in. He hissed swear words as she slowly sank down onto him and began rocking. He grunted with pleasure. "And I thought the first time was good." He angled himself up in order to reach her breasts. His mouth was hot and avid, and left her nipples wet with loving.

When he lay back, he gripped her hips between his hands and coaxed her, coached her, cajoled her in the raunchiest language. Several minutes later, on short puffs of breath, he said, "Have at it. That's what I said. But, sweetheart...God a'mighty."

He slid his hand between them. His revolving thumb worked its magic, and half a minute later, she lay sated atop his heaving chest.

When she had regained her breath, she whispered, "You were saying?"

"Hmm?"

"Before I had my way with you, you were about to ask me something."

"Oh. Never mind."

"No, ask."

He combed his fingers through her hair and rearranged it on her shoulders.

"I remember you doing that last night when you came up to the guest room."

"I couldn't keep myself from touching you. I'd have rather put my hands inside those ugly pajamas, but I settled for stroking your hair."

"It was nice. The kind of touch I needed then. What were you going to ask?"

He hesitated. "When we were in the shower, you said it was nice to be needed. You practically asked permission to give me the best damn hand job ever."

"Really?"

"Don't get me off the subject. What I'm wondering is... You don't have to tell me. You owe me no explanation. I just—"

"Jasper neither invited or welcomed attention like that. He didn't... He never said, 'Have at it.'"

He didn't respond immediately, and when he did, it wasn't to pursue the topic of her relationship with Jasper. "I probably could have said something a little more romantic."

"It was romantic to me."

He tipped her head up. His eyes moved over her face, taking in every feature. He ran his thumb along her lower lip. "Sleepy?"

"I'm having trouble keeping my eyes open."

"Let's go to sleep." His reach was long enough to turn off the lamp on the night table.

Talia was about to move off him, but he wrapped his arms around her, one under her bottom, the other just below her shoulders. He raised his head and pecked a kiss, then left his lips against hers. "Stay here."

"Like this?"

"Just like this." He dabbed the corner of her mouth with the tip of his tongue. "I'm not ready to leave you yet."

"I may get heavy."

"I may snore."

She returned her cheek to his chest and closed her eyes, feeling more languid and safe than she could ever remember feeling. "You thought my pajamas were ugly?"

He answered with a soft snore.

Chapter 33

At some point during the wee hours, Drex had disengaged from Talia, moved her off him, and turned her onto her side so they could spoon. He woke up with his arm tingling from having gone to sleep supporting her head. He checked the clock on the night table and was surprised by the time. He hadn't planned to sleep that long. It would be daylight soon.

As tempting as it was to stay snuggled with Talia, he had thinking to do.

He eased his arm from beneath her head and scooted off the bed without waking her. He took only his phone and pistol with him as he tiptoed from the bedroom and into the bathroom. Five minutes later, he emerged, showered and dressed in the clothes he'd worn the day before and which had remained on the bathroom floor all night.

Downstairs, he brewed a cup of coffee, then sent Mike a text asking for an update on Gif. Mike called him back. Keeping his voice low, Drex answered on the first ring. "How's he doing?"

"I got to see him around four-thirty. He had woken up, but was still under the influence. Wanted to know what had happened to him."

"He didn't remember?"

"Remembered a throng of people. He was making his way through as best he could toward the cordoned-off crime scene. Next thing he knew, he was on the ground, in pain like none other, paralyzed. Couldn't even breathe."

"He never saw his attacker?"

"He wasn't looking for one."

"Right," Drex said. "Did you get any sleep?"

"Couple of hours. You?"

"Some."

"Talia okay?"

"She's still asleep."

The unasked question hovered between them. Drex chose to ignore it. "Have you heard from Locke?"

"Check your email. He sent the coroner's reports about ten minutes ago."

"I haven't turned on my laptop yet. I'll get to them as soon as we hang up."

"No surprises in the one on Elaine Conner. The woman last night? He came up behind her, probably caught her in a nelson, snapped her spinal column, C-six."

"Jesus."

"Tell me."

Drex said, "What worries me most is the cheekiness of it. He killed that woman and hung around."

"In the hope that you would show."

"No doubt, but staying in the vicinity is out of his norm. He's done it twice now within twenty-four hours. Takes balls."

"No, it doesn't," Mike said. "It takes a psychopath. He's accelerating."

"Spiraling at the speed of a tornado."

"Because you've come too close."

"He's taunting me. These two dead women are his red cape."

"We've got to put this cocksucker out of commission, Drex."

"I know. But listen, Mike, you can't come back here."

"I already figured that."

"Beyond the chance of leading Rudkowski to Talia and me, I need you to stay with Gif."

"Figured that, too. At least through today to make sure he's on the mend."

"Are you okay with hanging out there?"

"I'm better off than Gif."

"I know, but—"

"Did you hug a nurse?"

"What?"

"A nurse. Gray hair, smiling eyes?"

Drex remembered her now. "She promised to take good care of Gif."

"Well, she must've enjoyed that hug. Since you aren't here, she's taken me under her wing. Fetched me a pillow and blanket last night. This morning, she brought me a washcloth and towel. I took a sponge bath in the men's room. There's a large cafeteria. I've got my laptop and charger. I'll be doing for you here what I'd be doing for you there. I'm fine. So long as Rudkowski leaves me alone, but I doubt he'll make another scene like he did last night."

"Thanks, Mike. I'll stay in touch. Let me know if you see an opportunity for me to talk to Gif."

"Will do."

They disconnected. Drex made himself another cup of coffee and set up his laptop on the eating bar. He opened the email from Locke, whose message was: *No connection between the two homicides except gender and birthdays in April. You still think it's him?*

"You bet your ass I do." But Drex knew he would need more than, "*I* feel *him*," to convince the law enforcement community that the man who was missing and feared lost at sea was on dry land, alive and well and lethal.

He opened the first attachment in the email, which was the coroner's report on Elaine Conner. He read it word for word. As

Mike had said, it didn't contain much that Locke hadn't already shared with them.

The report on Sara Barker, the woman murdered last night, was difficult for Drex to read. It was a heinously wasteful act. Jasper being his most self-indulgent.

After going through the report once, Drex left the bar and wandered into the living area, where he turned on the television. Network morning shows were in full swing. During the brief break-in for the local station, a story was aired about Sara Barker's murder. A spokeswoman for the family described her friend as a giving, loving person. "Who would do such an unspeakable thing?"

"Who indeed?" asked the young female reporter, looking straight into the camera, affecting a tragic tone and expression.

"The same man who buried a woman alive," Drex replied.

When the reporter began chatting energetically with the weatherman, Drex muted the TV and returned to the bar. He pulled up the report on Elaine Conner again. "Come on, Elaine. You loved to talk. Talk to me. Tell me what I'm missing."

It had to be here: Weston/Jasper's trademark, initial, stamp, signature. *Something*. What the hell was it?

He read the report again out loud, as though speaking the words would sharpen their definitions and make them revelatory.

And then he read a word, and, as soon as his mouth formed it, his mind slammed on the brakes. Returning to the beginning of the sentence, he read up to that word, and stopped on it again.

His hands got clammy. His heartbeat sped up. But before he let himself become too excited, he went back to the report on Sara Barker. He scrolled through the various forms until he found the one he sought. He magnified it to make the print larger on his monitor. And there it was. The same word. In a seemingly innocuous notation in the autopsy report.

He broke out in goose bumps.

In his haste to get up, he knocked the barstool over backward. He mounted the stairs two at a time and painfully banged his shoulder against the doorframe as he barged through it and into the bedroom.

"Talia!" He rounded the bed and sat down on the side she was facing as she slept. "Talia." He shook her shoulder.

She roused and blinked up at him, then smiled sleepily. "Good morning."

He placed his hands on her shoulders, as much to stabilize himself as to focus her. "Tell me again about Jasper's wardrobe being custom-made, keeping his tailor busy."

She struggled to sit up, dragging the sheet up over her breasts and pushing her hair off her face. "What? Has something happened?"

"You said he fussed over things, like buttons."

"Yes. He recently had his tailor replace buttons that he called 'outmoded.'"

Drex's gut clenched. "He did?"

"No more than a week ago. He had old buttons swapped out for new ones on several pieces."

Drex held still and let it sink in, then released her and sat back on his bent knee. Staring into near space, he said quietly, "He takes a button." Coming back to Talia, he looked into her gaze, from which all sleepiness had disappeared. "He takes a button."

Getting off the bed, he paced the length of it. "He's collected them. He puts them on garments he has custom made and wears them in plain sight of everybody. His trophies are on display, no one suspecting they came off the bodies of women he killed. That's his joke on us dumb slobs."

He ran his hand over the top of his head, then down the back of his neck. It was still difficult for him to breathe evenly. His heart was racing, and not from climbing the stairs at the pace he had.

"How did you come to this conclusion?" Talia spoke softly as though not to derail his train of thought or interrupt the flow of deductive reasoning.

"In the coroner's report on Elaine, he described her body as it was on the beach. The position it was lying in. So forth. She was fully clothed. A black, low-heeled sandal was on her right foot. The left one was missing. She was dressed in black capri pants and a light blue shirt. The coroner noted that a button on the shirt cuff was missing.

"The woman last night was wearing a skirt with decorative buttons down the left side. Here," he said, running his hand along the side of his thigh. "According to the autopsy report, which included photographs of her clothing, the last button in the row was missing."

Talia processed all that. "How does this help you?"

"It links the two homicides, Elaine's and Sara Barker's. It's a telltale signature that I never had before, because there has never been a corpse before. Until Marian Harris." He gave Talia a sharp look, then left the bedroom and clambered down the stairs, snatched his phone up off the bar, and called Mike. When he answered, Drex said, "He takes a button."

"Come again?"

Sputtering in his haste to get it out, Drex told him of his discovery.

"Possible coincidence," Mike said.

"It's possible for me to be voted pope, but how likely is it? Did that deputy in Key West send you the coroner's report on Marian Harris?"

"We never asked for it."

"Shit! You're right. Gray—that's his name—mentioned the decomposition of the remains. I was focused on the atrocity, and then on getting that party pic enhanced. I'll call him now. If Marian was clothed when the creep buried her, forensics would have a description of the garments, even if they were partially disintegrated. The report would include the detail of a missing button."

"You hope."

"I hope. But this feels right, Mike. If we can connect Marian's murder to these most recent two, Rudkowski can't deny that we're chasing a serial killer. If he does, we'll jump the chain."

"But you've still got to prove that Jasper Ford is the creep."

"One step at a time. This is a leap. Stay handy. I'm putting in a call to that deputy now."

Talia came downstairs as he was rifling through his duffel bag looking for the cell phone that had Gray's phone number logged. Her hair was still wet from the shower. She smelled of the gel, the scent of which would forever call to mind that erotic experience.

As she walked past him on her way into the kitchen, he said, "By the way, good morning back," and leaned over for a quick kiss on the mouth, then resumed replacing a battery in the cell phone.

Talia said, "Jasper had his buttons switched out recently so he could take all of the trophy ones with him when he disappeared."

"That's my theory. They're small, portable."

"When he moves on, he'll have them sewn onto other clothes, adding the newest two."

"He would, but he's not going to move on, Talia." He clicked on the back of the phone. "He's not getting away this time."

He pulled up the number of the sheriff's office in Key West and hoped to God Gray was on duty. When the main line was answered, he asked for him and, while he waited, watched Talia make herself a cup of coffee. Her hands were shaky. When she turned to face him, he said, "You okay?"

Her smile was tentative. "Yes. It's just that this pushes it beyond speculation. It's become very real."

"I know." He went over to her and stroked her face. "I'm sorry."

She covered his hand with hers, holding it against her cheek. "Don't be sorry. Don't be sorry at all." He gave her another tender kiss, then righted the barstool and guided her onto it.

"This is Deputy Gray."

Drex jerked his attention back to the phone call. "Gray, it's Special Agent Easton."

After a brief silence that teemed with resentment, the young deputy said, "Agent Rudkowski called me about half an hour ago. He told me all about you and what you've done. I can't talk to you."

"Deputy—"

"Sorry."

"Gray! Don't hang up. Listen. I need—"

"I can't talk to you." He was emphatic, but spoke in an undertone, as though afraid of being overheard. "I've been warned by the *FBI* not to talk to you, or send anything to you. Rudkowski also reported all this to my sergeant, who is furious."

"Okay. Busted. I manipulated you, and my tactics have been questionable."

"Questionable? Did you really run off with a material witness?"

"Yes, in order to try and save her life. I don't want her to meet a fate similar to Marian Harris's. Which is why I'm calling. I think I've found a link between—"

"You're not hearing me, Easton. You have no authorization. I can't help you."

"All I'm asking is that you send me the coroner's report on Marian Harris."

"That report is exempt from public disclosure because the criminal investigation is ongoing."

"That sounds memorized."

"It was. Rudkowski suggested it, so I'd have a reply if you had the gall to contact me again."

Drex spat out an expletive, but he forced himself to remain calm. Being overbearing wasn't going to work on Gray, who had been cowed by pressure coming at him from all sides. At any other time, Drex would feel bad for having exploited the green officer's initial willingness to help.

He said, "All right. I understand your reluctance to send it to me. Instead, send it to Agent Mallory. Remember him? You sent him—"

"Rudkowski said I wasn't to feed him anything, either. Or somebody named Lewis. He said you three have formed a league of your own. That you're impeding two homicide investigations. He also told me that this isn't the first time you've pulled illegal and unethical stunts."

Drex pinched the bridge of his nose. "Will you at least read through that report, and then let me ask you some questions pertaining to it?"

"I. Can't. Talk. To. You."

"I'm not asking you to *talk*. A simple yes or no. In fact, you don't even have to speak. You could cough. Once for yes, twice for no."

"Rudkowski said you'd turn it into a game of some kind or another."

"I'll limit it to one question. *One*. That's all. Will you do that much?"

"Sorry, no."

"Lives are at risk, Deputy Gray."

"Rudkowski told me you'd say that, too. He said you're—"

"I'm...?"

"Delusional."

"Do you think so?" The deputy remained silent. Drex said, "I suppose you were also instructed to pass along this phone number if I called, so Rudkowski can use it to locate me."

Drex heard him swallow hard. "I'm sorry, Easton," he said and hung up.

"Michael Mallory?"

Mike was in the process of trying to hack the police report on last night's murder of Sara Barker. He looked up, expecting to see someone on the hospital staff. Instead, facing him were two uniformed sheriff's deputies, one of each gender.

He closed his laptop. "That's me."

"We'd like to ask you some questions."

"Check with detectives Locke and Menundez, Charleston PD. They know all about it. The man attacked last night at Waterfront is my friend. I have their permission to keep vigil."

"Maybe. But it was an FBI Agent Rudkowski who told us where to start looking for you."

Mike didn't like the sound of that. "Well, you found me."

"Do you know a Sammy Markson? Also known as—"

"I know all Sammy's aliases."

"So you do know him?"

"I helped put him away for his first stint."

"A few days ago, did you drive a vehicle provided by him from Lexington, Kentucky, to Atlanta?" The woman deputy consulted her small notepad. She read off the make, model, and license plate number of the minivan. "Blue in color."

Mike scowled. "Why're you asking?"

"Did you?"

He mulishly held his tongue.

"If you're unwilling to answer," said the male deputy, "we'll have to take you in for further questioning."

"First, you need to tell me what for, and, if you're taking me in for an interrogation, once we get there, you must provide me with legal counsel before I say a word."

"This is an informal interview," the woman said.

Mike snorted. "We all know there's no such thing. What's your probable cause for hassling me?"

The two looked at each other and seemed to come to an agreement. The woman said, "Last night, Sammy Markson was arrested and charged with several counts of grand theft auto."

That little shit. He was cutting deals with the Fayette County, Kentucky, sheriff's department.

Mike had notified Sammy that he was coming to Charleston and that he had left the minivan at the Atlanta airport for retrieval at a later date. It had seemed the decent thing to do. He could now kick himself.

The male deputy said, "Markson provided your name as someone who would vouch for him."

"Vouch that he's guilty or vouch that he's innocent?"

"He didn't specify. Which is our probable cause for hassling you."

Mike gave a grunt of contempt. "Sammy would sell out his own mother."

"He did. Late last night. Let's go, Mr. Mallory."

"Wait, my friend is—"

"Agent Rudkowski is being kept apprised of Lewis's condition. By last report, he's stable. You'll be notified if he takes a downturn."

Mike saw no point in arguing with these two, who were merely carrying out their orders. His fight was with Rudkowski. He heaved himself off the love seat and tucked his laptop under his arm. Just then, his cell phone chimed. "May I?"

Again the pair silently consulted each other. The man came back to him. "Make it quick."

He answered. Drex said, "Rudkowski got to the deputy in Key West. He's clammed up, and there was no cracking him. We've lost that resource."

Mike sighed. "That's the good news."

Drex pitched the phone onto the bar, where it landed with an unheeded clatter. But even before that display of temper, Talia knew that Mike had relayed something Drex hadn't wanted to hear.

With a sinking feeling, she said, "Bad news about Gif? Please say no."

"No, he's still doing okay."

"Then what?"

When Drex had awakened her and told her about his breakthrough, he'd been humming like an overloaded electrical circuit. The call to the deputy in Florida had dimmed the wattage. But this call to Mike had taken all the sizzle out of him.

"In terms of helping, Gif was lost to me as of last night. Now Mike's been hamstrung. If I didn't know better, I'd think Fate was working against us. Dammit!" He picked up his coffee cup and hefted it like a baseball pitcher on the mound. He even looked at the far wall as though gauging the distance.

Before he could pitch it, she walked over, took the cup from him, and set it back down on the bar. "What's happened with Mike?"

He gave her a run-down, after which she asked, "*Was* the car stolen?"

"Probably."

"Did Mike know?"

"He didn't ask. Sammy won't incriminate him because he'll want him as a future ally, which it appears he'll need. But the point is, Mike is mired in this now and unavailable to me."

"What can I do?"

He was about to reply when one of his cell phones rang. He looked at the readout. "Locke." He answered and put it on speaker so she could listen in. "Morning."

Locke said, "You're still answering this number."

"For the time being. Did you hear about Mike?"

"No. What about him?"

"Long story, and it will keep. What's up?"

"Remember me telling you that one of the people we talked to last night noticed a man walking away from where Lewis fell?"

"Witness said he seemed to be in a hurry."

"We've isolated him on two security cameras."

Drex glanced over at Talia. "Jasper?"

"Since we never met him, and you say he'll have altered his appearance, we don't know. We need you to take a look."

"Absolutely. I've got a breakthrough for you, too."

"What?"

"I want to confirm it first. Soon. Now."

"Is Mrs. Ford still with you?"

"Hello, detective," she said. "I'm here."

"Good morning, Mrs. Ford. Are you all right?"

Drex said, "You know, every time you talk to her when she's in my company, the first thing you ask is if she's all right. It's beginning to hurt my feelings, in addition to pissing me off."

"Well, is she?"

"I'm fine," she said. "Where should we meet you?"

"Not here at the department."

"Rudkowski is still in residence?" Drex asked.

"We suggested he relocate to the FBI office. He says his business is with us."

"I doubt the local agents would welcome him."

"Anyway, we're stuck with him. Menundez and I will come to you."

Drex laughed shortly. "I don't think so."

"You told me where I could find you last night, and good thing you did."

"Yeah, but this could be a trap baited with a bogus security camera video."

"It isn't. But I wish I had thought of doing that yesterday."

Drex looked at Talia, who gave a quasi-shrug of consent.

"Okay," he said. "But I have a favor to ask. Two favors."

Sounding put out, the detective said, "I'm already doing you a favor."

"These are small ones, and nothing compromising." He asked him to call Deputy Gray in Key West. "Request the coroner's report on Marian Harris."

"I already did. Yesterday. It was emailed."

"Good man!"

"It relates to your breakthrough?"

"If I'm guessing right."

"I'll forward it to you."

As eager as he was to see that report, Drex scotched that idea. Emails left a trail. He needed Locke working for him on the inside. If the detective was called on abetting him, he would lose that vital connection to the cases. "Print it out and bring it with you."

"Why don't you just tell me what you're looking for?"

"No need to get you excited if I'm wrong. Besides, I want to see it for myself."

The detective sighed with exasperation. "What's the second favor?"

"Food. A couple of breakfast sandwiches."

"Okay. Where are you?"

Drex told him the name of the suite hotel and the street it was on.

"We'll be there in twenty minutes."

"Oh, Locke." Drex stopped the detective before he could disconnect. Holding Talia's gaze, he said, "Talia goes by Shafer."

Chapter 34

Drex opened the door to their knock. "That was twenty-five minutes."

"There was a long line at the drive-through." Menundez came inside and passed a carryout sack to Talia, who set it on the dining table.

"What was your breakthrough?" Locke asked.

Drex said, "Let's see that report from Florida."

The four of them gathered around the table. Menundez withdrew from his breast pocket a sheaf of documents that had been paperclipped and folded together. He passed them to Drex, who hastily thumbed through them.

Talia scooted closer to him so she, too, could read the report, which described in detail the contents of the wooden crate as the coroner had first examined it where it had been unearthed. There was no mention of a button. Fighting disappointment, Drex shuffled through the other documents until he found the autopsy report.

He scanned it so rapidly, it was Talia who saw the notation first and pointed it out to him. Under his breath, he exclaimed with a bit of anticlimactic wonder, "Damn. It's actually there."

"Documenting that you were right," she whispered.

Smiling at her, he mentally did a fist pump, but then realized what he was celebrating. "Hell of a thing to be glad about, though."

Beneath the table, she placed her hand on his thigh.

Locke made a sound of impatience. "I hate to interrupt your private moment, but can we please be filled in?"

"Have either of you read this?" Without waiting for them to answer, Drex turned the report around and stabbed the notation. "Missing button."

Locke immediately made the connection. He blinked across at Drex. "Both Conner and Barker had a button missing from their clothing."

"That's his souvenir," Drex said. "That's the connecting link I haven't had before now."

Menundez beamed.

Locke was less elated. "It supports your hypothesis of a serial killer, but it doesn't prove that he's Jasper Ford."

"I realize that, which dims my jubilation a bit," Drex admitted. "Without concrete proof, this similarity could still be dismissed as a coincidence. Maybe the security video will help."

He took a bite of the sandwich Talia had unwrapped and passed to him. Noticing the detectives' sudden and obvious dejection, he stopped chewing, swallowed, and said, "What?"

"The video doesn't help us, but I'll show it to you anyway." Locke opened the laptop and turned it around so Drex and Talia could see the freeze-framed shot. "This is the guy we were curious about."

The form Locke pointed out to them was draped in a plastic souvenir-shop rain poncho and looked like a ghostly blob. Only a portion of his face was visible. Drex said, "I don't even recognize Gif in this shot."

"Here's Gif. We had to zoom to find him."

The individual in question was walking toward Gif.

"His body type is wrong," Talia said. "He's too tall and thin. I don't believe it's Jasper."

"It isn't," Locke said glumly. "The witness we talked to last night picked him out of this freeze-frame early this morning. He recognized the poncho. Turns out that the poncho man was picked up on several cameras, not just two. One on a nearby parking lot showed him with his wife and three kids climbing into an SUV. Car tag was clear as a bell. Menundez followed up."

The younger detective picked up from there. "We got a home address from his car registration. A couple of uniforms were dispatched to screen him. He admitted to being in that mob. He'd gotten separated from his family as they disembarked the tour boat. He was anxious to catch up with them. Except for those few minutes when they were separated, he was with his family all evening on an outing planned weeks ago."

Drex pushed his half-eaten sandwich aside. "So he really was just a man in a hurry."

"Looks like," Locke said. "Which leaves us with pretty much nothing."

"The search of our house yesterday must have yielded Jasper's fingerprints," Talia said.

"But we don't have those of Daniel Knolls or any of his previous personas," Drex said. "There's nothing to match." After a short silence, he asked if Rudkowski had been told about their went-nowhere lead on the poncho man.

Locke nodded with unconcealed distaste.

"His reaction?" Drex asked.

Menundez was at the ready to tell him. "He called you delusional and paranoid, and said that you'd made Jasper Ford a suspect only so you could get a shot at his wife." The young detective glanced in Talia's general direction. "Sorry."

"No apology necessary," she said. "I couldn't care less about that horrid man's opinion."

Drex didn't comment except to murmur an epithet directed at Rudkowski.

"There's something else," Locke said.

Drex sighed and leaned back in his chair. "Let's have it."

"This morning some guys fishing just off shore hauled in a man's shoe." Locke looked at Talia. "It matches the description you gave us of what your husband was wearing when you last saw him. Size ten, brown loafer with tassel." Going back to Drex, he added, "Rescue teams, including the Coast Guard, are inclined to think that's all they'll find of him."

"Sort of shoots down my theory that he's still alive, doesn't it?"

"If nothing else turns up by dark tonight, they're calling off the search."

"Shouldn't his wife have been notified of that?" Talia said.

"Attempts have been made. No one has been able to reach you," Locke reminded her, sliding a look toward Drex. He let that settle, then said, "There's more."

"Jesus," Drex said. "I don't know how much more good news I can stand."

Locke gave him a grim smile. "Both Elaine Conner's and Ms. Shafer's financial portfolios are—"

"Let me guess," Drex interrupted. "Intact. No recent activity. No sizeable withdrawals. Every cent accounted for."

Locke shrugged. "I guess if he's playing dead, he can't be cleaning out bank accounts. Either he's prepared to wait for things to blow over before he cashes in, or he's sacrificing the money altogether in order to avoid capture."

"Priceless." Drex laughed, but without humor. "You're right, of course, but he also knew that I would look to see if money was missing. That's why he left it alone."

Leaning forward again, he addressed the other three earnestly. "Don't you see? Jasper knew what I would allege, because that's been his MO. He made certain that I would be proved wrong. More than anything he wants me discredited and humiliated."

He caught the two detectives exchanging a telling look and groaned, "What else?"

"We saved the best for last." Locke withdrew a sheet of folded paper from the breast pocket of his sport jacket and laid it, still folded, on the table. "It's a warrant for your arrest."

"What?" Talia exclaimed.

"The deputy in Key West ratted you out for calling him this morning. Rudkowski wasted no time. He insisted. Our hands were tied."

Drex flipped back the folds and scanned the warrant. "CID detectives were sent to handle this piddling misdemeanor shit?"

"Rudkowski figured that we would see you before anyone else could find you."

"I can't believe it," Talia said.

"I can," Drex said. "The man's pettiness knows no bounds. He'll put his one-sided rivalry above catching a man who would walk up behind a defenseless woman and break her neck."

"Can he put you in jail?" Talia said.

Locke answered for Drex. "We don't have to be in any rush to get him there."

"Thanks for that." Drex stood up and began to roam restlessly. "The thing is, the resentful jerk has effectively hobbled me. *Now,* when a single hour could make all the difference. Jasper may decide that Talia's fortune and/or her life aren't worth the risk of being captured. He'll choose to disappear as he has before.

"Or, he could decide that he's enjoying this killing spree and continue it in a frenzy until he's finally treed. He would actually get off on that kind of notoriety. I guarantee you that wherever he is, he's watching all the TV stories about the woman he killed last night. He's feeling very proud of himself. The celebrity status fuels his ego, and when he's good and stoked, he'll act again."

"Let's hope not."

"You're not listening, Locke." Drex returned to the table and, bracing on his hands, leaned in. "He's beyond *hope.* Remember the Chi Omega sorority house? Bundy killed those girls, and minutes later attacked another only a few blocks away. Jasper is thumbing his nose at us in that same fashion. He proved it last night. He committed a random murder for no other reason except that he felt like it and wanted to yank my chain. The attack on Gif had to be spontaneous, because there's no way he could have planned it.

"That kind of footloose violence may not make you nervous, but it scares the crap out of me. If he kills somebody else, you, Menundez, Rudkowski may be able to sleep nights, but I won't.

"And if he says to hell with it, leaves the area, gets away, I'll never get another crack at him, because now he knows me. From now on, he'll be looking for me over his shoulder and will see me coming."

He gave a hard shake of his head. "This is the time. We've got to stop him now. We've got to catch him plying his trade. We've got to catch him with those goddamn souvenir buttons in his possession."

"Okay. I get it," Locke said, returning some of Drex's ire. "But you've been trying for years. We've been at it for two days. Any ideas?"

Drex yielded to the detective's frustration. It matched his own. "No."

Pushing away from the table, he walked through the living area to the far side of it and shoved open the panels of drapery. Outside, it continued to drizzle. For days now the skies had refused to clear. However, if it were sunny, Drex would resent it. The dreariness befitted the circumstances.

Behind him, Talia explained to the detectives the situation Mike was in. In cop-speak they answered her questions about the investigation into Sara Barker's murder.

Drex listened to the conversation with one ear, latching onto key words, but tuning out the minutiae. Most of it was irrelevant, anyway. They weren't going to apprehend Jasper using textbook police procedure.

In order to catch him, one couldn't think like a cop. One had to think like *him*.

He asked himself if he were Jasper, if he were in Jasper's situation, what would he do? What ploy would he use? A switchback? A prank? An irony? What would be the ultimate joke?

In a blinding instant, he had an inspiration.

He returned to the table, got on Locke's laptop, pulled up the freeze-frame, and was immediately annoyed by its limitations. "Is the rest of the video on here?"

The question caught Locke in mid-sentence. He fell silent and looked at Drex, who continued with impatience, "The minutes leading up to and right after Gif was attacked. Are they on this laptop?"

"No. The video was jerky. Hard to tell up from down, so I just downloaded that freeze-frame. The whole of it is back at the department."

"I need to see it. Right now. Have someone email it."

Neither detective moved, their reluctance evident.

"What?" Drex said. "Earlier you offered to email it to me yourself."

"That was before this." Locke flicked his hand at the arrest warrant. "We could get into real Dutch by sending you evidence now."

"Okay, then sneak me into the department. Let me watch it there."

"Sneak you in? We're supposed to be delivering you to Rudkowski. If we don't, we're sunk."

"I get it, guys. But, God, this timing sucks." He socked his palm with the other fist. "Jasper is escalating. Rudkowski is wound up like a top. Incredible. I have two enemies, and they want the same thing, which is to shut me down."

"Discredited and humiliated," Talia said, repeating the words he'd spoken minutes ago.

But hearing them now stopped him in his tracks. Slowly, softly, he said, "They want the same thing. They want me bested."

A plan began to take shape. He grabbed hold of it before it could evaporate. Even as it formed and became clearer, he began appealing to the detectives. "Sneak me into the police department. Let me watch the video *before* my showdown with Rudkowski."

"What do you expect to see on it?" Menundez asked.

"You were looking for somebody who was moving through the crowd in a hurry. Maybe we should watch for someone who wasn't in such a hurry." That didn't seem consequential enough to convince them, but that was all Drex was willing to tell them at this point.

"Let me watch the video, then no more favors, I swear. Please." He looked at his watch. "But decide. I need the face-off with Rudkowski to happen soon. Before he does something stupid."

"Like put you in jail," Locke said. "As soon as he sees you, that's what he'll do."

"Then it's up to me to convince him otherwise." He split a look between the two. "Cuff me if you want, just let me see the video. Do we have a deal?"

"Yes," Menundez said.

And simultaneously Locke said, "No."

"Fifteen minutes," Drex pleaded.

Locke wavered. "We've got to deliver Rudkowski something." He looked at Talia. "He's still hot to question you. That may pacify him for fifteen minutes."

Drex turned to her. She asked, "Will it help you?"

"Honestly, I can't guarantee that it will."

She smiled and raised her shoulders. "He'll track me down sooner or later. I had just as well get it over with."

When Drex moved, it was as though he'd been spurred. He reached for Talia's hand and pulled her up and out of her chair. "We'll get our stuff and be right back."

Responding to his haste, Talia shot up the stairs, Drex right behind her.

When they reached the landing, she pulled him into the bedroom and slammed the door shut. "What's your plan?"

"Time's short. I can't lay it all out for you now."

"You mean you won't."

"That's right, I won't. Listen," he said before she could argue. "Did that recovered shoe or the untouched bank accounts convince you that Jasper is dead?"

"No."

"No. If he wants to continue his illustrious career, he can't afford to leave us alive. I don't want him sneaking up on either of us like he did on Gif and Sara Barker. I've got to draw him out."

"I understand that, but how—"

"The less you know—"

"Stop that! Tell me."

He shook his head. "This has to be my thing."

"Well, in case it's slipped your mind, it's also *my* thing."

Immediately repentant, he said, "Of course. I'm sorry. That was a dumb thing to say. I made it your thing, didn't I?"

She gripped his upper arms and shook him slightly. "No, *Jasper* did. I'll never get back the year I spent with him, but I'll be damned before I'll let him control one more day of my life. Not if I can help it."

"Help by trusting me."

"I have to trust *myself*, Drex." She flattened her hand against her chest. "I didn't trust my instincts before. For all the reasons I've tried to explain, I suppressed my misgiving and lived with a man who is innately evil. Now, every instinct I have is screaming for me to trust you. But am I in denial again because of my sexual attraction to you? You say you're a good guy, but you operate outside the law. So do I doubt my instincts, or trust them?"

"Trust them." He cupped her face. "My methods are dodgy. I bend rules. I break them. But I'm a good guy."

"Those dodgy methods scare me."

"I understand. But remember what scares me most? I told you that day you came up to the apartment."

"Failure."

"Failure. Failure to catch him."

There was a hard rap on the door, and Locke shouted through it, "Easton!"

"Be right there," he shouted back. Then in a whisper, "My worst fear is that Jasper will slip through my fingers, that it will be generally accepted that he drowned, that I'm a crackpot, that the missing button connection is bunk. Then, when nobody's looking for him any longer, he'll come back to finish you. I've got to end this, Talia, and I've got to end it now. You can doubt my methods, but don't doubt my purpose."

She looked deeply into his eyes, then nodded, and said huskily, "I do trust in that."

He aligned his forehead with hers and whispered a heartfelt thank you, then said, "Sexual attraction, huh?" He pulled her to him and kissed her deeply, his hand on her bottom, pulling her close. She dug her fingers into his hair. The brevity of the kiss only heightened the passion behind it.

"Easton!"

Drex ignored the banging on the door but broke the kiss. "One last thing. Rudkowski will try to browbeat you."

"I can handle him."

"I have no doubt." Her gave her a parting kiss, then turned her about and pushed her toward the door. "Show yourself before Locke has a coronary."

Chapter 35

Locke walked Talia downstairs. Drex asked for a minute in the bathroom. He shut the door and called Mike.

"Who's this?"

"Me. Forgive my whisper. I've locked myself in the bathroom. Any news of Gif?"

"Your swooner at the hospital called me about half an hour ago. They're moving him into a private room."

"That's great news."

"I thought so." He passed along Gif's hospital room number. "I haven't been able to go see him, though."

"They're still holding you at the sheriff's office?"

"They're fiddle-farting around. I'm going to kill Sammy."

"Can't you talk your way out of there?"

"Working on it. I was trying to give an ex-con a break by renting a car from him. How was I to know that it was stolen? Live and learn. That's my story, and I'm sticking to it."

"Doesn't look good that you skipped town and left Rudkowski dangling."

"Our signals got crossed. His word against mine. And the agents who were guarding my house hate him and love the homemade lasagna I took them, so I'm betting they'll back me. In any case, these guys here have got nothing to hold me on, because Sammy, who fears my murderous wrath, swears that I was oblivious. They'll have to release me, in time."

"Any estimate on when that might be?"

"Why?"

"Well, speaking of Rudkowski…" In a rapid clip, overriding Mike's numerous attempts to interrupt, Drex updated him on the recent setbacks, ending with his arrest. "They don't have a choice but to take me in."

"That ass-wipe Rudkowski."

"True. But I need you to do something for me besides name-calling."

"Like what?"

Drex made his request. Mike's response was, "Have you lost your fucking mind?"

"I don't have time to explain why, or to argue with you about it. I've already overextended Locke's patience. I need a yes or no."

"You realize that if I do this, it can't be undone."

"Nine murders can't be undone."

There was a knock at the door. "Now, Easton."

"You gotta tell me, Mike," Drex whispered. "Will you do it?"

"It's your funeral."

When Mike said that, in that particular grumble, Drex knew he had him. "Thanks. Later."

He clicked off, snapped up the lock, and opened the door.

Locke was on the threshold. "Who were you talking to?"

He replied with a wide grin. "The hospital. Gif's being moved out of ICU into a private room."

Locke took the phone from him. He went to recent calls and pulled up the last number. "That's Mallory's number."

"Okay, so I skipped a step. I called Mike, who told me the news that he got from the hospital."

"You're giving me the runaround."

Drex sighed, looked away, came back to him. "I called Mike to ask if he would bail me out."

"What did he say?"

"You want it straight and unfiltered?"

"That would be a welcome change."

"He asked if I'd lost my fucking mind."

Drex asked if they could take Gif's car so Talia wouldn't be stranded. Locke agreed on the condition that Drex would go with him. Talia would ride with Menundez.

When they arrived at the police department, Locke parked in a designated slot. They reunited with Talia and Menundez at an entrance for personnel. Before they went in, Locke turned to Drex. "You carrying?"

"Yes."

"You're not planning to shoot him, are you?"

"Rudkowski? Hadn't planned to."

"That's too bad. But I can't let you go inside with a weapon. Give it to Menundez."

Knowing it would be pointless to argue, Drex passed the detective his pistol, saying, "Escort Talia to Rudkowski. Keep him occupied long enough for me to view that video."

Locke intervened. "You know, typically, the apprehended don't give the orders."

"You agreed to give me fifteen minutes," Drex said.

"I didn't agree to anything."

"I need to see that video before I see Rudkowski."

"You're not going to talk him out of the arrest."

"Don't underestimate my powers of persuasion."

Locke remained dubious, but he said to Menundez, "Text me which room you're in. Fifteen minutes or less, we'll be up."

Before they separated, Drex reached for Talia's hand and squeezed it. "Give him hell." She smiled and squeezed back.

Locke led Drex into a room that had a modicum of privacy. He accessed an available computer and downloaded the security camera video. Drex had noted earlier the time burn-in on the freeze-frame. He fast-forwarded to it, then backed up three minutes from there and started playing. To Drex's disappointment, the images were no more distinct on this larger monitor than they had been on Locke's laptop.

"Warned you it was lousy," Locke remarked as he watched over Drex's shoulder.

It was. Drex paused and restarted it frequently, zoomed in on still frames, zoomed out, fast-forwarded and rewound so often that Locke said, "I'm getting motion sick."

"Me too. I could do with a Coke. Got one around here?"

"Forget it. I'm not leaving you alone."

"I wouldn't cut out on you. Scout's honor."

"You've got ten more minutes. I've got calls to return."

Locke walked a short distance away, but still in sight, and got on his phone. Drex paused the video at a certain point and leaned in closer to the monitor to study one of the frozen images. He backed it up, saw the same individual. He fast-forwarded, but slowly, watching even more closely.

Locke returned. "Time," he said.

Drex pushed back his chair and stood up. "Thanks."

"Hold it. Did you catch something I should see?"

"Rudkowski's waiting."

"Look," Locke said with irritation, "you can continue bullshitting, or you can clue me to your plan."

"Plan?"

Locke gave a sigh of exasperation. "Easton, I admire you more than I like you. I think you're smart, and I think you're earnest. Menundez has a man crush on you. You appeal to his cowboy-cop ideal. When Rudkowski told us about you, the things you've done in the name of 'duty,' I thought at first that he had to be lying."

"All this to say...?"

"I would rather have you at my back, even without a badge, than that guy with one. But I've got to know the plan you're hatching."

Drex thought too much of Locke's integrity to continue pretending. "In your situation I would feel the same frustration. But I'm reluctant to discuss a plan that isn't even close to hatching. It's still embryonic."

"I could help, field ideas."

"When the time is right."

Still looking vexed, Locke said, "Have you ever met the SAC in Columbia? The one Rudkowski is reporting to?"

"No."

"Doesn't matter. Jump the chain. Call him directly. Explain this grudge match between you and Rudkowski."

"Who has painted me to be a nut case. Even if I could get through to the SAC, by the time I convinced him that I wasn't delusional and paranoid it could be too late."

"All right, how about this? I'll take you in to see our chief. He's a reasonable man, and he's had two women murdered in the past two nights. He wants the culprit. Bounce your idea...Why not?" he asked when Drex began shaking is head.

"Because, as reasonable as he may be, he'll toe the line. While he's trying to figure out what to do with me, time is running out."

"Maybe it already has. By now, Jasper Ford may be long gone."

"Do you honestly think that? If you do, say so."

"No. I think he's alive and unraveling just like you say."

"Okay then. This is the game-winning three-point shot at the buzzer, and I don't need my own damn team trying to block it."

"That's my point, we're not a team."

"We are," Drex said. "I swear."

Uncertainty in his eyes, the detective asked quietly, "Can you make the shot?"

"I don't know. I hope so, but I'm nursing no illusions. If I fail, it'll be spectacular. But it will be my own throat I've cut. *Only* mine."

"That's just it," Locke said. "If you're put out of commission for good, it'll be a hell of a waste of talent and guts. I want you to win. I just wish you would play by the rule book."

"I can't."

"Why not?"

"Because *he* doesn't."

"Don't play dumb, Mrs. Ford. Don't act like you didn't know that I wanted to talk to you. You are a material witness in a felony case involving the kidnap and murder of Elaine Conner, as well as the unexplained disappearance of your husband."

Talia's only previous exposure to Special Agent Rudkowksi had been the dialogue she'd overheard while hiding in the safe room with Drex. Her opinion hadn't improved upon meeting him. Since he'd entered the interrogation room where Menundez had ensconced her, Rudkowski had been railing at her, virtually without taking a breath.

As he continued to rant, she kept her expression as aloof as possible, her gaze steady on him. She wasn't accustomed to the cops-and-robbers environment, much less to being shouted at. Her failure to react with fear and trembling had roused him to become increasingly loud.

Menundez said now, "Ease up, Rudkowski. She's not a suspect."

"I'll determine that."

Talia seized her first opportunity to get a word in edgewise. "Agent Rudkowski, I'm well aware of the seriousness of the crimes."

"Are you? Then why have you hampered the investigation by avoiding this interview? You also tampered with evidence."

"I did no such thing. When I left my house before you served the search warrant, I took nothing from it except a couple of changes of clothing and some toiletries."

"Your husband's cookbooks. Menundez here says they filled that shelf above the stove. That shelf was conspicuously empty."

"I didn't take the cookbooks."

"Then it was Easton."

"He had nothing with him when we left the house. Not even his personal belongings."

"Then his cronies made off with them. How come? What did they do with them?"

Since Jasper's cookbooks had turned out to be a disappointing false lead, and therefore irrelevant, she saw no point in either denying the action or defending it. But Rudkowski's yammering about them was keeping him preoccupied, which was what Drex needed her to do.

The agent propped his hip on the corner of the table, crowding her in an obvious attempt to be intimidating. "What tactic did Easton use to get you to pull a vanishing act with him?"

"No tactic."

"Come on. He's a con man. Did he schmooze you with his boyish charm? Hate to be the one to break it to you, but you wouldn't be the first to fall for it, you know."

"He convinced me that my husband is a career criminal and, given the opportunity, would very likely try to kill me."

He scoffed. "You believed that?"

"If I had a grain of doubt, it was dispelled last night when Jasper killed that woman and critically injured Mr. Lewis."

"Those crimes have not been attributed to Jasper Ford. They're relative to nothing. Alleging that your husband was involved is just another of Easton's wild hares. Had your husband ever met Gif Lewis?"

"Not to my knowledge."

"Then how did he recognize him to attack?"

Drex had been unable to explain that. She refrained from answering.

Rudkowski cupped his ear. "Come again? I didn't catch that," he mocked.

"See what I'm getting at, Mrs. Ford? Easton makes up stuff to support his crazy notions. His claims of a serial killer have no basis, and never have." He poked his index finger against his temple. "He's nuts. He's obsessed with a bogeyman of his own invention."

She leaned away from him and gave him an unhurried once-over. "Then why are you so unstrung?"

He blinked. "Pardon?"

"I don't understand your agitation. If you believe that Drex is a mental case, why haven't you dismissed his wild hares as such, and gone on about your business?"

"Because he's impeding my investigation."

"Excuse me," she said coolly, "but from my perspective, it seems you've contributed very little to the investigation of Elaine Conner's murder and the search for my husband, whether he's dead or alive, innocent or guilty. By contrast, you've spent a great deal of time pursuing Drex and deriding him at every opportunity. If anyone has an obsession, Special Agent Rudkowski, it appears to be *you*."

Menundez snickered.

Rudkowski's whole body inflated with indignation. His forehead broke a greasy sweat. He pushed off the table and, placing his hands on his knees, bent down until his face was level with hers. "You had better watch it, Mrs. Ford, or Shafer, or whatever you choose to be called. I'll put you in lockup until you decide to cooperate."

"How could I possibly be more cooperative? I came here of my own volition."

"But you haven't answered my question."

"Which one?"

Rudkowski returned to his full height. "Where is Easton?"

With a pleasant smile, she said, "Right behind you."

Chapter 36

Drex had arrived in time to overhear Talia's putdown of Rudkowski. Based on his apparent choler, she had effectively fired him up to his pressure-cooker state. From the threshold, he said, "You sound out of sorts, Bill. We could hear you from the end of the hall."

Locke nudged Drex into the room and closed the door behind them. He asked Menundez if he'd shared with Rudkowski the autopsy report on Marian Harris.

"Not yet. I saved Easton the honor." The younger detective produced the report and passed it to Drex. "I circled the notation in red."

"Thanks."

Rudkowski shouldered between them and snatched the printout from Drex. "You're under arrest. I'm considering booking her, too."

Talia uttered a sound of dismay. "What for?"

"Leaving official custody without permission. Obstruction of justice."

Locke and Menundez began protesting, but Drex talked over

them. "You're not going to arrest Talia," he said. "Stop being a jackass and read that."

With impatience, Rudkowski slid on a pair of reading glasses and homed in on the marked spot. "A button was missing off her blouse. So what?"

"So..." Locke proficiently explained its relevance. "This links that Florida cold case to our two here." Menundez also had printouts of the other two reports and showed Rudkowski the notations about the missing buttons.

Rudkowski removed his glasses and said, "Well, it's a commonality that warrants further investigation. But it could also be a coincidence."

"Our chief of police doesn't think it is," Locke said. "Neither does the sheriff's office, the state police, or the local FBI agents working the Elaine Conner case, or the SAC in Columbia."

Rudkowski said, "You went over my head and talked to him before bringing this to me?"

"We couldn't find you," Menundez said, deadpan. "You must've been in the john."

Before Rudkowski could form a comeback, Drex again held up a hand that signaled for quiet. "Locke, with your permission, I'd like to speak to Rudkowski alone, please."

Rudkowski huffed. "So you can crow, I suppose."

"I don't consider the murders of three women something to crow about," Drex said evenly.

"Oh, you've gone sentimental? Must be the influence of your new girlfriend here."

Talia stepped forward as though to whale into him. Drex put out an arm to hold her back. "You're a small-minded weasel, Bill. Ask anybody. And there's a lot of bad blood between you and me. For once, put it aside. While you're standing here tossing out insults to a woman who outclasses you by about a thousand times, and trying to get the best of me, a serial killer remains at large."

"Even if that were so," Rudkowski said, "it's none of your concern, is it? You're over, remember?" He held the printouts directly in front of Drex's face and shook them. "By the way, this constitutes theft of a document pursuant to an active federal investigation. I can add that to your other offenses."

Drex pushed the papers away from his face. "I didn't steal that report, Locke obtained it. As per usual, you're missing the big picture. Let's talk about it, man to man."

"Sure, we can talk, but I'm immune to you. Nothing you say will change my mind."

Drex turned to the other three and motioned toward the door. "Maybe I can make him see sense, and he'll tear up that arrest warrant."

"Not going to happen," Rudkowski said.

Drex ignored him and appealed to Locke. "Give me a few minutes with him."

Locke said, "God knows you're good at talking people into doing what they don't want to do." He motioned Menundez and Talia out.

She looked at Drex with concern. He bobbed his chin in reassurance. Still looking uncertain and worried, she left with Menundez. Locke hung back. "You'll have won some favor and faith by coming here of your own volition. Don't screw it up."

"Duly noted."

Locke left them. Drex closed the door and turned to Rudkowski, who confronted him, one eye squinted, his head tilted. "You want to parley?"

"Only because all other options have been exhausted. Much as it pains me to ask anything of you, can we declare a truce?"

"What are you trying to pull? One of your pranks?"

"No."

"One of your switcheroos that you find so funny and cute?"

"Not this time. I swear."

Rudkowski snorted.

"Hear me out, Bill." Drex pulled a chair from beneath the table.

"Seat?" Rudkowski looked at the chair as though it might be a clown's collapsible prop, but he sat down in it. Drex took the chair across from him.

Rudkowski said, "Let's hear it."

"Give me back my badge."

Rudkowski's expression went blank. "Where's the punch line?"

"No punch line."

"That's got to be a joke."

"No joke."

"It's the funniest thing I've heard in a decade." Then he did guffaw. "Even if I gave it back, it's worthless now."

"I need it for a day, one day, twenty-four hours. Then..." Drex raised his hands in surrender. "You can have me."

"I already have you."

Drex took a breath. "You saw those autopsy reports. Do you understand what they signify?"

"You think I'm too dense to grasp their significance?"

"I wasn't implying that. I only meant—"

"You implied that you, Dr. Easton, are smarter than me."

"Than I," Drex said under his breath.

Rudkowski glared at him with malice. "You're over and out. For good. When is that going to sink in? Maybe while you're in jail. You'll have plenty of time to reflect."

"I'll sign a confession, Bill. In blood."

"I like that idea."

"Tomorrow."

Rudkowski scraped back his chair. "Stay here till someone comes to book you."

"Wait. Please. Please," Drex repeated and held out his hand as though to keep him in his seat.

Rudkowski hesitated, then resettled.

Drex tried another tactic. "I'm this close to him." He made an inch with his thumb and index finger. "He's close."

"You know that?"

"I feel it."

"Do you think that what you *feel* is going to fly with a prosecutor? You have no *proof* that such a person even exists. That business with the buttons? Circumstantial."

"I realize that. But it's more than I've had on prior cases. He thinks he's outsmarted us. He hasn't. We're smarter. He's tripped up and doesn't even know it. This is our one chance to get him."

"By him you mean Ford? His bloated body will drift ashore one of these days."

"Could, but I don't think so. Give me twenty-four hours, with a badge. If I don't produce him, I've failed. You can lock me up and laugh your ass off. You can publicly ridicule me."

He paused to let Rudkowski savor the appetizing thought of that. "But, if I succeed, and we nail the son of a bitch, it's even better for you."

"How do you figure?"

"You get all the credit."

"What about you?"

"I take none."

"You take none?"

"I'll stipulate it in writing."

"Nothing you write down will be worth the paper it's written on."

"I'll email it. Emails are forever."

"Not yours. You've got Mallory to rig them for you." He shot Drex a smug smile. "Your friend Gif is temporarily safe from arrest, but the fat man is already being held at the sheriff's office."

"Thanks to you. But they're not going to book him for a crime committed by a repeat offender out of state."

"With a phone call from me, they'll book him for obstruction in this state."

Drex said, "Fine. Play hardball. Call now. Have Mike booked. You know what he'll do? He'll use his one phone call to speak to the SAC in Columbia. He'll reiterate everything Locke has already told him. He'll emphasize how crucial that coroner's report in Florida is to these homicide cases here, and how you, for no other reason than to spite me, delayed our access to it. He'll soon see that you've been more of an impediment to this investigation than Mike or I have been.

"At the very least, he'll have the agents in the resident office here check you out, and you'd fare even worse. They would want to know why you're not over there, lending assistance, instead of over here in the PD, distracting hardworking detectives from their two murder investigations."

He paused. "Bill. Think. Wouldn't you rather give me one more day of freedom than wind up looking bad? Stupid, spiteful, and bad?"

"You're bluffing."

"You think so?" Drex shrugged. "Then call my bluff." He let the dare stand, then added, "The only reason I haven't called that SAC myself is because I wanted to stay under the radar."

"So you wouldn't be jailed."

"Well, that. I grudgingly admit it. But I wanted to keep a low profile because you know what these departments are like. When it comes to leaks, they're sieves. I've been holding my breath, afraid word would leak to the media that we've tied these local cases to the one in Florida. If that got out, and Ford heard it, his ego would mushroom. He would—"

Drex stopped talking and looked hard at Rudkowski, whose complexion had taken on a rosier hue. "What?"

Rudkowski stayed stubbornly silent.

"*What?*" Drex stared him down, then lunged from his chair and leaned over the table. "Tell me you haven't talked to the media."

Rudkowski puffed up defensively. "I've agreed to grant an interview."

"Oh, God no! When?"

"At noon."

Drex swung around to look at the wall clock. "That's only ten minutes from now."

"Which is why we need to wrap this up. Anything else?"

"Bill, you can't give that interview."

"Why shouldn't I?"

"Who did you talk to?"

"A reporter named Kelly Conroe. She contacted me," Rudkowski said, boasting.

Drex recalled the reporter he'd seen that morning reporting on Sara Barker's murder. Pretty, perky, articulate, earnest. She'd struck him as eager. Someone who played to the camera, who would take the story and run with it.

Rudkowski was still talking. "Somebody here gave her my name as a spokesperson for the FBI. Which leaves you out, doesn't it?"

"Get back to her, Bill," Drex said. "Ask her to sit on the story until tomorrow."

"Why would I want to do that?"

"For the reasons I spelled out."

"Ford's mushrooming ego? I can't even say that with a straight face." He stood up. "I'm meeting her downstairs. Stay put until Locke comes for you."

"Christ." Drex turned his back, lowered his head, massaged his nape. "This is a nightmare." Coming back around quickly, he said, "Okay, let this Kelly Whatever record the interview, but ask her to hold it until the late news tonight."

"That's not the way a news operation operates."

As he headed toward the door, Drex caught him by the arm and whipped him around. "I beg you to reconsider."

"Let go of me." He tried to break free of Drex's grasp, but Drex held on. "Twenty-four hours."

"Let go, or I'll have you held on an assault charge."

"Charge me with whatever the fuck you want," Drex shouted. "I'll face the judge and plead guilty to anything you throw at me. Tomorrow. But I need today."

Rudkowski worked his arm free. "Your plans for today are an arraignment." He turned and opened the door.

Drex charged after him, bumping into Locke, who was on the other side of the threshold. He caught Drex in a bear hug, which Drex tried to escape with the fury of a madman. Locke ordered him to calm down. Drex only struggled harder to go after Rudkowski.

When Rudkowski reached the corner of an intersecting hallway, he glanced over his shoulder and shot Drex a triumphant grin.

"Don't do it, Bill!"

Rudkowski went out of sight around the corner.

Drex's head dropped forward. "The bastard's really going to do it."

The detective backed him against the wall and propped him there, keeping his hands on his shoulders. "If I release you, are you going to do something crazy?"

Drex shook his bowed head.

Gradually Locke eased his hold, then lowered his hands. "I take it you got nowhere."

"He wouldn't budge."

"Did you really expect him to?"

"No."

"I'm sorry it didn't go better for you."

Drex raised his head, winked, and flashed a grin. "It went perfect."

Chapter 37

Jasper had learned on the morning news the name of Drex Easton's buddy whom he'd assaulted. Gifford Lewis was in guarded condition, but expected to survive the seemingly random and unwarranted attack.

"It was neither random nor unwarranted," Jasper argued with the motel room TV.

Lewis was a ten-second mention. Much more to-do was made of the woman who'd been fatally attacked without any apparent motive. The reporter droned on and on about what a wonderful person Sara Barker had been. There were heartrending pictures of her surrounded by her children and husband, all smiling sunnily.

Jasper noted that a victim of unprovoked violence was never remembered as being a wretched reprobate, a cheat and liar, a subhuman leech on society whom the world was well rid of. They were always eulogized as self-sacrificing saints.

"Call me cynical."

After watching the broadcasts, he spent the remainder of the morning making preparations to leave Charleston. But as noon approached, he grew eager to hear more about the havoc he'd wrought.

He tuned in just as the news was coming on the air. One of the anchors said, "Our own Kelly Conroe is coming to us live with an interview with a lead investigator. She files this exclusive report. Kelly, what's the latest?"

The blond reporter's mouth was a slash of carmine lipstick, which, in Jasper's opinion, was an unpleasing distraction.

"I'm here with FBI Special Agent William Rudkowski, who is assisting local authorities with their investigation into the murder of Elaine Conner, whose body washed ashore the night before last."

The camera shot widened to include a man who appeared to be in his late fifties, nothing remarkable about his appearance, although his stance indicated the bellicose attitude of a man who thought highly of himself, probably as overcompensation for insecurities and shortcomings.

The reporter asked him to explain the FBI's involvement.

"The Conner case captured my attention because circumstances surrounding it bear a striking resemblance to a two-year-old homicide case in Key West, Florida. We're examining the similarities. If it's determined that the two cases are related, it will represent a major breakthrough and move us closer to identifying and apprehending a serial perpetrator, to whom the disappearances of at least nine women are attributed."

The reporter asked him to expand on what the similarities between the cases were, and asked if any new evidence had been discovered. "I can't comment on an ongoing investigation," he said. "At this time, all I'll say is that this individual is under the delusion that he's outsmarted us. He hasn't. We're smarter. He has left us a distinct signature. He's tripped up, and doesn't even realize it."

The claim didn't rattle Jasper in the least. It was poppycock. If there had been any evidence connecting him to Marian Harris, Drex's wannabe-writer charade would have been unnecessary.

Agents would have stormed Jasper's house and placed him under arrest.

Having heard enough of the blather, he was about to switch off the TV when the reporter said, "You've taken a man into custody this morning. Drex Easton, who holds a doctorate in criminal psychology. What's his connection to these cases, and what charges is he facing?"

Drex had a doctorate? He was *in custody*?

One of the anchors cut to the heart of the matter. "He's said to have become recently acquainted with Elaine Conner, Jasper Ford, and Ford's wife, Talia Shafer. Is he considered a suspect in Conner's murder?"

"No," the agent replied. "But Easton has, over the course of many years, hindered other FBI investigations by interfering without authority. From the night Ford went missing and Mrs. Conner was killed, Easton has prevented Ford's wife from cooperating with the investigation. He was arrested this morning. Together they were brought in for questioning. He's being arraigned this afternoon, facing state charges of tampering with evidence and obstruction of justice. Similar federal charges are pending."

It appeared to Jasper that the agent wished to say more. Jasper wanted to hear more, but his curiosity went ungratified. The reporter thanked the FBI agent and turned to face the camera, which zoomed in on her.

"Easton's involvement with the key parties, which has led to his arrest, is a surprising twist in a case that already has authorities baffled."

"Kelly, what's the status of the search for Mr. Ford?" asked one of the anchors.

"Ongoing. However, there has been a development." She went on to relate that fishermen had reeled in one of his shoes. "It's looking more and more likely that he drowned. I haven't received confirmation, but the word is that the search for him will be suspended after today."

She wrapped up, and they returned to the studio. Jasper muted the television but stared at the miming heads for a full minute, trying to assimilate the shocking news that Drex Easton was to be arraigned later today.

What a well-deserved comedown! He wouldn't be so cocky when standing before a judge, would he? He wouldn't be glib and disarming. The court would not go all aflutter over the dimple that Elaine had found so dashing. Drex Easton, humbled to the level of a common criminal, would be a sight to behold.

Not that Jasper would go anywhere near that courthouse.

In his current incarnation, the chances of being recognized were slim to none. But it would be foolish to risk exposure when he was so close to being free and clear of this venture and ready to move on to his next.

He turned off the TV and wiped down the remote. Everything else in the room he had already thoroughly sterilized. His suitcase was packed except for the last two items to go into it. It lay open on the end of the bed. He'd hung the Do Not Disturb card on the outside doorknob to ward off the housekeeper, both while he remained and after he was gone.

Watching the noon news had been the last item on his agenda before taking his departure. He confessed that the half-hour delay had been a trifle self-indulgent, but he couldn't resist watching all the reports about himself, and he had enjoyed them immensely. He could leave Charleston feeling very proud.

Although it did stick in his craw that he was leaving with a major ambition unfulfilled: killing Talia. He had never before abandoned a project without completing it, and it galled him to do so now.

He was undeterred, of course. He would kill her. But the risk of doing so presently was too great. He would wait for several months, perhaps for as long as a year. Which, now that he thought on it, wouldn't be at all bad. The anticipation of ending her life, especially when she believed him dead, would ferment in his imagination like a fine wine. He could spend idle days fantasizing it.

He wondered if she and Drex had consummated their grubby, base lust for each other? Of course they had. No doubt that's what they'd been doing while she was supposed to have been cooperating with the police investigation. Jasper didn't care a whit if they'd screwed like rabbits. He only wished the two of them knew how utterly indifferent he was to it.

It also nagged him that he had to leave without learning what had drawn Drex's attention to him in the first place. *Over the course of many years* suggested that for most of Drex's adult life he had nursed an obsession so consuming that he had bucked the FBI in order to indulge it.

Jasper couldn't help but wonder what had instigated that fixation. Had it been a particular episode, an individual, or had Easton simply been born with a righteous zeal to seek justice for those who couldn't obtain it for themselves?

He would like to have had those questions answered. Strictly out of curiosity. He wasn't afraid that Drex and his fancy PhD would one day close in on him. Whatever authority Drex had possessed previously he'd been stripped of. He'd overstepped, flouted rules, and now was up to his neck in criminal charges. Jasper would love to be inside that courtroom when Drex had to answer for them.

But no. It would be unwise to tempt fate. He would leave as planned. Talia and Drex could play out the rest of their plebeian, romantic melodrama without him.

It wasn't as though he wished to be the star of it.

New challenges awaited him. He was off to meet them. The FBI was moving closer to identifying and apprehending a serial perpetrator? He had left a signature? He'd been outsmarted? That was a laugh. Who did they think they were dealing with?

"I'm not an amateur, you know. Just ask her."

He looked behind him at the dead woman on the bed. She lay facedown, her head at an odd angle to her shoulders. The back of her dress had ridden up, revealing thick thighs, lumpy with cellulite.

Stupid cow. He'd needed refuge and hadn't wanted to press his luck by checking into a hotel. She'd been so trusting. But then, why wouldn't she be? He had appeared harmless.

He loathed the idea of touching her again, but he tamped down his revulsion and used a tiny pair of manicure scissors to clip the threads securing a button to the neckline of her dress just above the zipper. Holding it by the eyelet, he twirled the small, fabric-covered sphere. What clever way could he sport it, he wondered.

He didn't have to decide now. He could take his time and be creative, as he'd had to be with some of the buttons already in his collection. But he never failed to come up with an ingenious way in which to hide them in plain sight.

He replaced the scissors in his leather manicure set, zipped it up, and placed it in his suitcase, then removed the velvet pouch from the inside pocket. Over the past two days, he had increased his collection from an even dozen to fifteen buttons. The FBI had underestimated his achievements by six women, proof that their agents weren't as brilliant as that moron on TV had boasted. Jasper's nimble mind could run circles around Dr. Easton's.

Indeed, it had, hadn't it?

He worked open the pursed top of the velvet bag and was about to drop the new addition into it when, yielding to an irresistible urge, he dumped the contents onto the top of the dresser. The hectic pace of the past few days had prevented him from looking at his souvenirs arrayed like this.

He wondered if the FBI's "striking similarities" and "signature" were the missing buttons. Had Easton made that connection? Jasper didn't see that it mattered, except that it caused another, sharper pang of regret that there wasn't a button from Talia. That would have been the best prize of all.

But he really must get over that disappointment. He couldn't allow himself to be detained by it. For the time being—and only for the time being—Talia was beyond his reach. Accept it.

He soothed his irritation by separating the buttons so he could admire them independently and reminisce on how he'd come by each one. There were three pearls, but each of a different size. Two were made of tortoiseshell. Four of various shapes and textures were solid black. The matte white one had adorned the skirt of the woman he'd killed last night. Naturally, all the brass ones looked somewhat military. One silver disk had a finish as smooth as satin. And, now, this cloth one.

He took a moment to appreciate its uniqueness, then it went first into the pouch. One by one he added the others, each joining the collection with a satisfying clink. He was about to pull the drawstring closed when something struck him as odd. He paused to consider, then upended the bag and spread out the buttons again. He counted them. Recounted. Meticulously, he grouped them into rows of five.

He hadn't miscounted. One of the rows was short a button.

With his heart knocking and a sweat breaking out over his shaved head, he squeezed the velvet pouch to see if one of the smaller buttons had become trapped by an inside seam. He didn't feel anything, but to be sure, he turned the bag inside out.

He searched among the magazines stacked on top of the dresser. He felt along the bottom of the television set, thinking that perhaps one had slid beneath it. He pushed aside the ice bucket and plastic wrapped glasses.

It wasn't on the dresser. He dropped to his knees, looked under the bed, the desk, the dresser. He crawled across the floor, madly skimming his hands over the carpet.

He stood up, breathing as though he'd swum miles. Starbursts of red exploded behind his eyes. Twin freight trains roared through his ears.

One of his trophies was missing.

Chapter 38

After his face-off with Rudkowski, which had produced the desired result, Drex powwowed with Locke, Menundez, and Talia in the interrogation room.

"You wanted him to blab all that on TV?" Locke asked.

"In the hope of luring Jasper to the courthouse for my arraignment. Once he learns I'm being publicly disgraced, I don't think he can stand to miss it."

"That's your plan?" The detective looked skeptical.

"Do you have an alternative?" When no one spoke, Drex said, "The first step worked, and it was crucial. While Rudkowski is busy being a TV star, let's take another look at that security video."

"I'm supposed to be booking you," Locke said.

"A minute or two isn't going to matter."

Grudgingly, the detective did as asked. Drex sat down at the small table. The other three gathered around to watch the video.

"As I play it, keep an eye on this person and watch how he navigates." Drex pointed to a blurred figure on the monitor. "See? He walks right past Gif, then turns and comes back. It's hard to tell with all the jostling and shoving, but I think that on that second pass, they bump shoulders. That could have been when he struck."

"How could he have done it that quickly, and without anyone noticing?" Talia asked.

"Someone did." Drex paused the video. "Now here, five seconds later, Gif has disappeared. We know that he was on the ground. A minute after that, here's the same individual, standing a few yards away, watching. EMTs arrive. He makes a slow circuit of the area."

He fast-forwarded, picking up the person at various spots around the perimeter of the camera's range. "Once Gif had been taken away—" He fast-forwarded before pausing the video again. "—he reappears briefly here before being swallowed up by the crowd. That's his back," he said, pointing.

"I don't know," Locke said, frowning. "Looks to me like just another curious bystander. There were dozens of them milling around."

"But only a very few came into such close contact with Gif mere seconds before he went down. Appearing to be a curious bystander would be good cover. He didn't make himself conspicuous by running, or even rushing to get away."

"The height is right," Talia said. "He's a little thicker in the middle than Jasper."

"He padded his clothing."

"Even with that," she said, "I couldn't swear that it's him."

"Sorry, Easton, but I don't think so, either." Menundez was squinting at the screen. "In fact, to me, your suspect looks like a woman."

Drex turned away from the screen to face the three of them and gave a sly smile. "The perfect disguise. No one was looking for a woman. No one would suspect an older woman of committing an unprovoked attack like Gif suffered. Sara Barker would have turned her back to her without reservation."

"Son of a gun," Locke whispered.

Menundez said something in Spanish that Drex figured was a bit more explicit.

Talia just looked at him, her lips parted in astonishment.

Drex asked Locke if he could round up some men within the department whom he trusted. "Who can keep their eyes open and mouths shut. Have them take a look at this video, then ask if they'd be willing to loiter around the courthouse this afternoon and be on the lookout? Best I can tell by this video, he was dressed in a generic, dark-colored tracksuit that would be appropriate for either sex. Short-haired wig."

"He might have changed identities again."

"He might have," Drex said. "But it's a damn good ruse, the kind of joke that Jasper would eat up, and it worked well for him last night."

Locke said, "I'll do the recruiting while Menundez is booking you."

———————

Over Rudkowski's protests, the detectives hadn't put Drex in lockup to await his arraignment, but had remanded him to the interrogation room with a stern warning not to betray their trust by trying to sneak out.

He gave them his promise, but they'd posted an officer outside the door anyway. Rudkowski was too busy fielding calls from media outlets to closely monitor Drex's preferential treatment. Had he, he would have created a ruckus.

Drex's phone had been confiscated along with his other personal belongings, but he was allowed to borrow Talia's to put in a call to Gif.

When Gif answered, Drex said, "Man, it's good to hear your voice."

"Drex, have you lost your fucking mind?"

"I see you've talked to Mike."

"We just hung up. Sheriff's office finally released him, and he's on his way to you. He called from an Uber car and filled me in. Said you played Rudkowski like a fiddle."

"With Mike's help. He tipped that reporter for me, anonymously. The stealth only made her more determined to seek out Rudkowski for comment. I knew he would jump at a chance to denounce me on TV. While appearing to try and talk him out of it, I spoon-fed him what I wanted Jasper to hear. He even quoted me directly. Let's hope it works to draw Jasper out."

"I understand your reasoning, but, Drex, you let the genie out of the bottle. You stand accused of breaking the law of the land."

"I did break the law of the land."

"But now the world knows it."

"Worth it, Gif, if we nail him."

"Are you in lockup?"

"An interrogation room. With visitation rights." Across from him Talia sat, unsmiling.

"How will you plead?"

"Not guilty. I'm not going to make it easy on Rudkowski. I've met with my court-appointed counsel. He's old and tired, but knows the ropes. He told me we lucked out on the assigned prosecutor, who's green, lazy, and none too bright. I was booked on misdemeanor state charges. Even if it goes to trial, which I doubt, I'll probably get off with a fine and probation."

"Rudkowski won't settle for that. He'll file federal charges and see to it that you do time. You know he will. Furthermore—"

"Gif, if you want to tell me how crazy I am, you'll have to get in line. But what I did, I did out of desperation, not insanity. Now, enough of that. How are you doing? Are you in pain?"

"They gave me one of those self-dispensing things."

"Good drugs?"

"Not good enough."

"Jesus, Gif. I'll never forgive myself for sending you to wander around alone last night, knowing that whack job—"

"Don't try to get off the subject."

"I'm not."

"Sure you are. I recognize the tactic. What does Talia think about what you've done?"

Drex looked over at her, where she sat, her brow knit with consternation. Her arms were folded across her middle, providing a shelf for her delectable breasts. Although, clearly, allure wasn't her intention.

"She's so mad at me, her freckles are about to combust."

"Why's she mad?"

"She says I'm setting a trap with myself as bait."

"Well, you are."

"Listen, Gif, all this talk is wearing you out. I can hear it in your voice. You need to rest. Don't worry about anything."

"That sounds like a brush-off."

"It is." Although Gif did sound out of steam, his voice having gone thin.

"I hate this, Drex. When you need me most, I'm laid up here, useless. I want to help, to be doing *something*."

"You're healing. That's a big something. Get well enough to lay into me the next time we see each other."

"When will that be?"

"Uncertain. Depends on whether or not I'm granted bail. Rudkowski will argue that I'm a flight risk."

"You are."

"Yeah, but maybe the judge will rule in favor of a flight risk over a buffoon."

"You're joking, but you could go to jail. After all these years, everything you've sacrificed to this, I can't stand to think of it ending with you behind bars."

"You're not going to cry, are you?"

"Maybe."

Drex smiled, but his voice was husky with emotion when he said, "You've been true blue, Gif. Thanks."

He disconnected, stared into the near distance for several seconds, then shook off his melancholia and passed Talia her phone. "Somebody was beeping in."

She pulled up the number. "Third time today. I don't recognize the number. Solicitation, no doubt." She set aside her phone and reached for his hands, drawing them across the table toward her. "Drex—"

"We've been over it," he said, interrupting what he knew would be another round of arguments, all reasonable, none he cared to go through again. "You're not to get anywhere near that courthouse. If you show up in the courtroom—"

"What will you do?" she challenged.

"It's what *he'll* do that should worry you."

"It does," she exclaimed softly. "I worry about you. You've made yourself a target. Even your best friends don't understand why."

"Yeah, they do. They argue, but they understand."

She turned his hand palm up. "You and your damn sense of honor." She lifted his hand to her mouth and kissed the self-inflicted scar. "But I wouldn't like you nearly as well if you didn't hold to it."

"Life's crammed with cruel ironies like that." He reached for a strand of her hair and rubbed it between his thumb and fingers. "I came down here in search of my nemesis, and discovered you. You were an unexpected lightning strike, Talia Shafer."

"So were you, Drex Easton."

"That last time...?" He arched his brow suggestively. "I liked the way you woke me up."

"I thought you would never notice."

He snuffled a laugh. "When a man is sleeping with a woman on top of him, and his cock starts being squeezed in that particular way, he tends to notice. Just so you know."

She ducked her head coyly. "I'll tuck that away for future reference."

"I didn't know how much I liked slow, sleepy sex."

"That was my first time for it."

"Mine, too. Which is why I didn't know how much I liked it." His gaze took a lazy tour down her front. "I had a particularly depraved encore planned for us."

"Oh?"

"Hmm. Hell of a one."

She reached across and poked her finger into his dimple. "Give me a hint."

He turned his cheek toward her hand and captured her finger between his teeth. "It was going to start out tame enough, but would end up with you seeing God and screaming my name."

"The imagination runs wild."

He gave a rueful grin. "Sadly, it'll have to keep. I'm off to the slammer."

"Don't make light of it."

"I don't," he said solemnly. "Come here." They leaned toward each other across the small table and brushed lips.

Mike chose that moment to barrel in. Seeing that he had interrupted a private moment, he halted, but only for a second before coming into the room and closing the door. "Met Menundez in the hall. He got this from the trunk of Gif's car." He dropped Drex's duffel bag on the floor.

"My suit is rolled up in it. I wanted to appear in court looking a bit more respectable."

"Locke's given you ten minutes to change before heading downtown."

"Did you get Gif's key back from Menundez?"

Mike held up the fob.

"You and Talia go back to the hotel. We didn't officially check out. See if you can get our rooms back."

"What do we do there?" Mike asked.

"Wait for word."

"You're to babysit me," Talia said sweetly.

Drex gave her a droll look, then went back to Mike. "Await word. With luck, you'll be able to bail me out before dinnertime."

"Okay, but fair warning. If Rudkowski gets another bee up his butt, I'm not going to talk him into throwing me in the clink, like a certain dumbass we know. I'm getting the hell gone from Dodge."

"Noted. Now beat it, you two, so I can change."

He went to the door and pulled it open. As Talia drew even with him, he said, "Don't forget to turn off your phone. Mike will take the battery out for you."

"As soon as I check my messages." She looked at him with a combination of vexation and anxiety. There were a thousand things Drex wanted to say to her, but the cop posted outside the door was within hearing distance. She went out into the hallway without a further goodbye.

As Mike approached him, Drex put out a hand and, speaking for Mike's ears alone, said, "If I'm incarcerated and Jasper remains at large, he'll come after Talia. She'll need a bodyguard, Mike."

"That speech of mine about getting gone?" He batted it down with his large paw. "I won't go anywhere without taking her with me."

"Thanks. You're a friend."

"Yeah, yeah," he grumbled, "and of all my bad habits, you're by far the worst."

Drex closed the door after him, squatted down, and unzipped his duffel. He took from it his suit and dress shirt. They were hopelessly wrinkled but would have to do. He forewent a tie. He was just about to start stripping down when the door opened and Talia burst in, Mike behind her.

She was brandishing her cell phone. "The call that was beeping in? The number I didn't recognize that had called three times? It was Mr. Singh."

"Who the hell—"

"Jasper's tailor."

Chapter 39

Talia's words tripped over each other in her haste to get them out. "He'd called twice before. This time he left a voice mail. He was asking about a button."

"What about it?"

"His accent is thick, hard to understand, but he was calling to make certain that I had found it."

"Found it?"

She shook her head, indicating that she was in the dark, too. "I'm going to call him back. I knew you'd want to hear."

"Get him," he said to her then stuck his head out the door and told the cop in the hallway to summon Locke and Men- undez.

"They'll be back for you in ten minutes."

"Tell them to come *now*."

"They'll ask why."

"Tell them I'm escaping."

He slammed the door. Talia had placed the return call. She, Mike, and he listened breathlessly at the series of rings before Singh answered with the name of his shop. "How may I help you?" As

Talia had warned, his accent was thick. Being on speaker amplified it and made it even more difficult to understand.

"Mr. Singh, it's Talia Shafer. Mrs. Ford."

"Mrs. Ford," he said in apparent relief. "You found the button?"

"I'm not . . . No. I'm sorry, Mr. Singh. I don't know what you're referring to."

"The button I stupidly failed to return to Mr. Ford along with the others."

The door swung open. Locke and Menundez rushed in, looking harried and put out. Mike shushed them before they could barrage them with questions. In a low voice, and with an economy of words, he informed them of what was going on.

Singh's manners were faultless, his deference admirable, but impatience was driving Drex nearly out of his skin. Eventually, with Talia's tactful prodding, the tailor related his story.

The short of it was that Jasper had asked him to save all the buttons that he'd replaced. Mr. Singh had put them in an envelope, sealed it, and had given it to Jasper when he'd picked up the clothes.

The following day, which would have been Saturday, the day the Fords were to have gone to Atlanta, Mr. Singh had been sweeping up his shop at closing time and had found one of the buttons on the floor.

"Behind the counter," he said woefully. "It was my terrible mistake. I must have dropped it when I was placing them in the envelope."

He continued lamenting and apologizing until Talia diplomatically coaxed him back on track. "Where is the button now, Mr. Singh?"

Immediately after making the "unfortunate discovery," he had called Mr. Ford, but got his voice mail. He'd left a message of profuse apology, but Mr. Ford hadn't responded. The next morning, Singh heard the news about his disappearance. He'd been anguishing ever since. Believing that Talia would want the button, especially now that it would have greater sentimental value if

Mr. Ford was never found, he'd gone to their home earlier today to return it personally.

"But no one was there, so I dropped the envelope with it inside into your mail slot."

Menundez high-fived the air in front of him. Locke blew a gust of breath up toward his forehead. Mike harrumphed in satisfaction. Drex closed his eyes and hoped to God he wasn't dreaming. The squeeze Talia gave his hand assured him that he wasn't.

"Mrs. Ford?"

"Yes, yes, Mr. Singh, I'm here and overwhelmed by your kindness. I can't thank you enough for calling me. I will be very happy to get the button back."

As he launched into another litany of apology, Drex motioned for her to get a description of the button. To do so, she took Singh off speaker.

The four men huddled. Drex said, "If Jasper asked to have those buttons back, they must've been his trophies. This is one of them." He gave the group at large a broad grin. "Let's go."

"Hold on," Locke said. "In under half an hour, you've got to appear in court."

"And you have got to be kidding!" Drex shouted. "I want my hands on that damn button!"

With reasonable calm, Mike said, "I'll go get it."

"I'll go with him." Talia had ended the call. "I recognize it immediately from Mr. Singh's description. Brass, round, with an embossed anchor. It was the single button on a navy blue blazer. One of Jasper's favorite jackets."

"An anchor. Nautical motif," Drex said. "Jesus. If it matches a button found in Marian Harris's makeshift coffin, it'll be hard evidence, not circumstantial." He turned back to Locke, but the detective was shaking his head.

"We're taking you to be arraigned."

Talia laid a hand on Drex's arm. "Mike and I will get it and bring it to you. Even if you're in jail."

He had no choice. "Okay. As evidence goes, it's compromised," he said to Mike. "But treat it like evidence. Safeguard it. No matter what happens to me at the courthouse, that button needs to be turned over to the FBI."

"You got it."

Drex gave Talia a meaningful look, but because they had an audience, neither said anything. With an uncustomary show of gallantry, Mike opened the door and stood aside for her to go ahead of him, then both walked quickly down the hallway.

Locke asked Drex if he still wanted to change clothes.

Drex nodded. "I won't take long."

"Five minutes."

It took him only two. He hoisted the duffel back to his shoulder and opened the door. "I'm ready," he informed the cop on guard.

"Locke said for you to cool your heels until he comes to get you."

Drex backed into the room and closed the door.

How long would it take for Mike and Talia to reach her house? He mentally mapped out their route and tried to establish an ETA. He had every confidence in them. He was less trustful of Fate. He wanted to be handy if it intervened, and he had to ward it off. And, damn it, selfishly, he wanted to be there to claim the treasure he'd spent years seeking.

But not for the world would he miss snaring Jasper. The hell of it was, he couldn't prepare for what would go down at the courthouse. Whatever unfolded was out of his hands and entirely up to Jasper. His capture could be uneventful or explosive. There was no way of knowing.

But a worse possibility was that nothing at all would happen. Weston Graham would have eluded him, likely forever.

Whether he succeeded or failed, he was ready to get on with it. The uncertainty, coupled with needing to be two places at once, was making him nuts. Psyched up and pumped full of restless energy, he made endless circuits of the meager square footage until finally the door opened and Locke motioned him out.

"What took so long?"

"That reporter who interviewed Rudkowski called me. She wants a sound bite from you when we get to the courthouse."

"Anything I said would have to be censored."

They made their way through the building. Menundez was waiting for them in the car, engine running. Once underway, Drex asked if their men were in place.

"Loitering around in plainclothes, as you asked," Locke told him.

"How many?"

"Six inside. One on each of the four sides of the building outside. They've all seen the video and know what to look for."

He would have to rely on their competence and Locke's discretion in choosing them. It all felt too loose, too much left up to Jasper. Damn! It was difficult to predict what he might do, and Drex really couldn't concentrate on it because his mind kept wandering back to that button.

"Do you have the autopsy report from Key West on your laptop?" he asked Locke, who nodded. "Can you pull it up?"

While the detective was doing so, Drex mused out loud. "There was always going to be something that tripped him up. Who would have thought a button?"

"Weirdo," Menundez editorialized from the driver's seat.

Locke passed his laptop back to Drex. "Here are all the photos we were sent. The clothing remnants they found in the crate look like a pile of rags. No loose or attached buttons are mentioned in the coroner's description of the crate's contents. Only that one was missing."

"Which means that when she was killed, Marian was wearing something with only one buttonhole."

"Like Jasper's blazer," Locke said.

"Like Jasper's blazer." On a sudden inspiration, Drex said, "Do you have the yacht party photo in your files?"

"Only the printouts your guys gave us, and they're back at the office."

"Damn." Then, "Let me borrow your phone, please. Gif wanted to help."

Locke passed him his phone. Drex tapped in Gif's number. He answered, groggy but conscious.

"You still want to be useful?"

"What do you need?"

"Do you have the yacht party photo on your phone?"

"Yes."

"If I'm remembering right, Marian is wearing a jacket."

"White. Summer weight, like linen."

"That's right," Drex said, remembering. "Zoom as closely as you can on the jacket's button."

"The button?"

"I'll fill you in later. Take a screen shot of the button. Good as you can get, and text it."

Gif came through in less time than it took for them to wait out a traffic light. It wasn't a clear or well-focused picture, but it was good enough.

Drex said, "Brass, round, with an embossed anchor."

Locke took his phone back so he could see for himself. "Well. I'll be damned."

Menundez grinned at Drex in the rearview mirror. "We have him."

"Not yet," Drex said. "We know it's him, but we still have to catch him."

Inexplicably, he felt that cheer was premature. Why? Him and his damned *whys*. He hated them, but he trusted them. There was always a reason for them.

He laid his head back against the seat of the car, closed his eyes, and looked for a distortion in this development. What didn't feel right? What was clouding this cause for celebration?

What did he know about Jasper? What did he surmise? How did Jasper fit the profile?

With the exactitude of a die-cast puzzle piece.

Drex's thoughts went back to the conversation he'd had with Talia when he'd described to her the common characteristics of serial killers.

No conscience. Overblown egos. They're smug. They're also collectors.

They take souvenirs.

He'd been absolutely certain that Jasper collected something from his victims, and that the collection would be his secret but most sacred possession. He'd emphasized to Talia that he would have a perverse affection for his souvenirs, that he would fondle the items, possibly derive sexual pleasure from them. He would treat those buttons like a cherished lover. He would never—

The realization slammed into Drex as though Jasper had sucker punched him as he had Gif.

Jasper would never, ever, under any circumstances, have left his collection in someone else's hands, not in the hands of a tailor.

"Oh, fuck, oh, *fuck*!" Drex sat up straight, banged the ceiling of the car with his fist, and yelled, "And I made sure he knew where I would be."

Talia had told Drex she would never come back to the house. At the time, she had meant it, but as Mike turned onto the street, she realized the impracticality of that statement. The house represented Jasper to her, and, therefore, she would never spend another night under this roof.

But there were things totally unrelated to him, her parents' effects, photo albums that chronicled her life with them and special friends, these things she would want to keep. Removing them was a project she didn't look forward to.

Now, however, she was eager to get inside.

Mike pulled into the driveway so sharply, one of the tires

bumped over the curb. "Where are the cops guarding the place?" he asked.

"Locke recalled them this morning when Drex and I went peaceably to the police station. And Jasper is considered either a corpse or a fugitive. No one expects him to return."

She popped the door handle, got out, and headed for the front door.

"Hold up." Mike squeezed himself out from behind the steering wheel. "If you open the door, it'll move the envelope. I need to take a picture of it as it was found."

"Without my remote, I can't open the garage. We'll have to go in through the back porch."

The latch on the screen door that Drex had broken was dangling loose, but the door leading into the kitchen was locked. Talia used her key. The alarm beeped when she pushed open the door.

Mike remarked that at least Rudkowski had had the courtesy to set the alarm when he left after searching the house.

"Locke, actually," Talia said. "He asked me for the code last night and had one of the guarding officers set it."

They quickly cut through the kitchen and dining room, into the wide foyer. A heap of mail lay on the floor just inside the door beneath the mail slot. "That has to be it on top," Talia said.

It was a standard white envelope without a letterhead, postage, or addressee. There was a noticeable lump in the center of it. Mike began taking pictures with his phone camera. "Do you have a sealable bag?"

Talia retraced her steps into the kitchen. She opened the door to the walk-in pantry and flipped on the light. She grabbed the box of ziplock bags from a shelf and returned with it to the living room.

"I have a variety of sizes. Is this one okay?"

Mike, who was in the process of texting, glanced up. "Fine. I'm sending these pictures to Locke. Drex will want to know we have it."

After sending the texts, he slid his phone into his breast pocket and took one of the bags from the box. Kneeling, without touching the envelope, he manipulated it into the bag and zipped it in. As he struggled to stand, he said, "Maybe we should take the blazer, too."

"Good idea. I'll get it. Unless it was confiscated when they searched yesterday."

"Let's check." Mike made to follow her upstairs. She said, "You stay."

Breathing hard from the exertion of coming to his feet after kneeling, he nodded. "Okay. I'm gonna get some water."

"In the fridge. I'll meet you in the kitchen."

She trotted up the stairs and walked quickly down the hallway, but when she reached the closed double doors of the master suite, she hesitated. She was averse to entering the toxic atmosphere of that room again. She didn't want to see the bed in which she had lain beside Jasper Ford, breathing the same air as he, vulnerable in her sleep.

But Drex was waiting for her.

Steeling herself, she pushed open the doors and was, for an instant, taken aback by the disarray. But then she remembered the search. The officers under Rudkowski's leadership hadn't done as much damage as they could have, she supposed, but things had been moved and slewed about.

Jasper would have been enraged over the present state of his handkerchief drawer.

His closet door stood ajar. She crossed to it and opened it wide. Garments had been pushed aside, sweater boxes opened and rifled through, shoes removed from the shelves and piled onto the floor. But it didn't appear that anything had been confiscated...except possibly the navy blazer.

Twice, she hastily sorted through the color-coordinated blue grouping of garments. The jacket wasn't there.

"Are you looking for this, Mrs. Ford?"

She spun around.

Jasper stood in the door opening. He was wearing the blazer.

Secure in its buttonhole was a single button. Brass, round, with an embossed anchor.

His smile was obscenely obsequious, his voice a perfect imitation of Mr. Singh's. "It wasn't lost at all."

Drex's outburst startled Menundez. He braked hard, forcing traffic around them to do the same. Tires screeched. Horns blared.

Above that additional clamor, Drex shouted to Locke, "Call Mike. Call Mike. Do it now. Tell him not to go to their house. Call Talia. It's a trap. Menundez, turn around. Head for Talia's house."

Locke looked at him with fury. "What the hell are you talking about? We're going to court."

"Jasper's not going there. Shit! I've got tell Mike." Drex lunged for Locke's phone, but the detective drew his hand back and kept it out of his reach. Beside himself, Drex shouted, "Menundez, turn the fucking car around!"

Realizing the more deranged he appeared, the less likely they were to listen to him, Drex forced himself to speak calmly. "Please. I know I lost it there for a sec, but you've got to listen to me."

"We *have* listened. That's why we're here. Everybody's in place. He's one of ours." Locke swept his hand toward a guy geared up in latex and a helmet holding up a tricked-out bicycle. He was looking at them with a cop's wariness.

Drex wanted to weep, wanted to tear at his hair, wanted Menundez to turn around!

"You've got to trust me one last time."

Locke's phone rang in his hand. Drex lurched forward again, trying to grab it. "Answer, answer, it might be them."

Locke clicked on. Rudkowski shouted through the speaker. "Where are you? They're about to call our case. Get that son of a bitch in here. *Now!*"

Drex didn't wait to hear any more. He reached for the back seat door handle.

"Don't do it!" Menundez shouted.

Drex turned his head and stared straight into the bore of the detective's pistol. "Shoot me then, just get to Talia's house." Rudkowski's screaming was acting like a power drill against his skull. "Hang up on that idiot and listen to me!"

Locke didn't move. Menundez didn't lower his pistol. Drex, his voice cracking, said, "I beg you. He set it up to kill her, and he will."

The two detectives looked at each other. Menundez continued to hold the pistol on him, but he tilted it down. Locke said into his phone, "We have an emergency," then clicked off, leaving Rudkowski raving. "You're sure?"

"Yes."

Locke, hearing Drex's conviction behind the single word, motioned for Menundez to get them underway. The younger man wasted no time. He popped a magnetic beacon on the roof of the car and, motioning frantically for other cars to move aside, cleaved a route through the logjam. At his first opening, he stamped on the accelerator.

"All right," Locke said, "you've got what you wanted. You had better have a damn good explanation for it."

"First, call Mike." The detective did so without argument. They all listened with mounting anxiety as Mike's phone rang several times without being answered.

Through clenched teeth, Drex said, "Please no, no."

"He's all right," Locke said. "He texted pictures. The envelope is there, right where the tailor said it would be."

"It may be there, but it wasn't a tailor who left it. Call Talia's phone."

Locke did. "Goes straight to voice mail."

"I told her to turn it off," Drex said in anguish. "Menundez, kick it up!"

Locke ordered Drex to calm down. "Why do you think Jasper is at their house?"

"He would never have left those buttons with a tailor. He wouldn't have left them with anybody. It was Jasper who called Talia and made her, all of us, believe in the fortuitous kindness of Mr. Singh."

Menundez swore.

Still skeptical, Locke said, "You thought you were right about the courthouse."

"A mistake I'll have to live with. Die with."

"We've skipped out on the court, on the prosecutor, Rudkowski. We're screwed and so are you if this turns out to be a bust. You had better pray to God you're right."

Heart in his throat, Drex said, "I pray to God I'm wrong."

Chapter 40

The man standing in the open bedroom doorway was barely recognizable to Talia as the groom with whom she had exchanged marriage vows. He had shaved his head and beard. Unlike the natty dresser he'd been, he had put the blazer on over a pair of dark cargo pants and a golf shirt, both of which were ill-fitting and sloppy.

But of course the blazer was only for effect, she realized now.

How had he gotten in without Mike intercepting him? Likely, he had already been inside the house when they'd arrived. He had let himself in, turned off the alarm, and reset it.

It sent shivers up her spine to think of him lying in wait, in anticipation of springing this perfectly laid trap.

Her heart was pounding, but she tried to appear unafraid. With as much composure as she could muster, she said, "Hello, Jasper. Since we parted ways at the airport, you've been awfully busy."

"I could say the same for you, sweetheart."

"Stop talking like that," she snapped. "You sound ridiculous."

"I agree wholeheartedly. But it worked to fool you."

His smile was backed by a condescension that was all too familiar. She wondered that it hadn't made her skin crawl all those months that she had spent with him, as it did now.

"Maybe you would like the voice of Daniel Knolls better." He switched from the Indian accent to a throaty rumble. "You don't remember me the night of Marian's party, do you?"

She didn't answer.

"Marian introduced us. You responded politely, but with disinterest." He strolled farther into the room. She moved backward an equal distance. Her caution seemed to amuse him.

He said, "I, on the other hand, took a great deal of interest in Marian's young, attractive, and very affluent friend. Marian had grown tiresome. I had already solicited for her replacement on an online dating service, but I never had to pursue it because you were such an ideal candidate. You virtually dropped from that blazing sunset sky and into my lap. That very night, I began contemplating Marian's demise."

Talia's shudder was involuntary.

He noticed it, though, and her revulsion seemed to please him. "In effect, Talia, you're to blame for Marian's ghastly end. Come to think of it, Elaine's, too. If not for your friendship with them, they would still be alive."

When she flinched, he said, "What's the matter, Talia? Can't take the chastening for getting your friends killed?"

"My friends are dead for only one reason. Because you are criminally insane."

"Who told you that? Dr. Easton?"

Even as she squared off with him, her mind was scrambling to think of a way to get around him, to go through him, to overpower and disable him until help arrived. Surely help would arrive! "Where is Mike?"

He laughed. "The tub of lard?"

"What have you done to him?"

"I've put him out of his misery. He was huffing and puffing like a steam engine before I choked the life out of him."

She couldn't withhold a mewl of anguish, but she held herself upright by sheer force of will. If she cracked in the slightest, she would shatter completely. If she did that, she was doomed. She probably was anyway, but she wasn't going to give Jasper the satisfaction of watching her fracture.

"Drex knows that I'm here."

"Unsurprising. You two have become nauseatingly attached. But he's at the courthouse, waiting for me to show up." He tapped his cheek as though in contemplation. "I must say, there was a brief period of time today when I actually entertained the notion of going there to witness his fall from grace."

"Dressed as a woman and wearing a wig?" Talia scoffed. "Drex picked you out of a surveillance camera video, Jasper, and he wasn't even challenged by its poor quality. You gave yourself away. You're not nearly as clever as you perceive yourself to be."

"Yet he's there while you're here, eager to get your hands on this." He fingered the button on the blazer.

"What was in the envelope?"

"A pebble," he said, grinning. "Evidence of nothing. I confess to having experienced a brief panic attack earlier today when I thought I'd lost this beauty." He rubbed the button again. "But then I remembered that it was the one button I didn't switch out. I wanted to have one to wear until the others could be incorporated into my new wardrobe, whatever it might be.

"I came out of the panic when I realized that this blazer, button intact, was in my suitcase the whole time. But the episode gave me an idea about how lure you back here. I really hated to leave with unfinished business between us."

No doubt the unfinished business meant the finish of her if she couldn't think of a way to escape him. "Drex knows about your silly button collection. He knows how you think. He'll figure out that the call from Mr. Singh was a trick. He'll come after me."

His lips formed a rueful moue. "Meaning no slight to you at all, dearest, but I think it's me he's after. He's been on the chase for a long time, hasn't he?"

"Since he was nineteen. That's when he learned that you had killed his mother."

He reacted with a start. "His *mother?*"

"Lyndsay Cummings."

"Well, well, what do you know?" He laughed. "He's the child? Lyndsay thought her ex-husband and son were a well-concealed secret, but I knew about them, of course. Just like I know about your little eggs stored in an ice tray."

She couldn't hide her shock, and it made him smirk. "I wonder what they do with the ova if they aren't used before the mother dies. Hmm." He waved off the thought. "Anyway, after I disposed of Lyndsay, I spent several months trying to pick up the trail of her ex-husband and the boy. I didn't want to live looking over my shoulder for the vengeful Cummings men."

"Drex's father legally changed their names so you couldn't find them."

"Did he? Well, no wonder Drex's name didn't ring a bell. In any case, I bored of tracking them."

"You didn't get bored, Jasper. You *failed*. Drex, on the other hand, was tenacious. He kept at it until he found you."

"Which only underscores what a sad, wasted existence his has been. To fritter away one's life in pursuit of vengeance for a mother who abandoned him?" He shook his head and *tsk*ed. "And the really pathetic thing? He's only begun."

"What do you mean?"

"I mean, Talia, that he'll have a real bloodlust for me after I kill you."

With no more warning than that, he rushed her.

Acting on instinct, she turned and tried to make it into the bathroom, where she could put a locked door between them. But she soon realized that turning her back to him was the worst thing she could have done. From behind, he enwrapped her in a hug that pinned her arms to her sides and made her neck susceptible to the arm he crooked beneath her chin.

"Let her go, or I will kill you."

Drex's voice!

Jasper swiveled around, hauling her with him.

Drex hadn't shouted. He'd made a controlled and imperative statement of fact. He certainly looked deadly enough. His tiger eyes were fixed on Jasper. In his outstretched hands, he cradled a handgun. It was aimed at a spot slightly above and behind her: Jasper's forehead.

Jasper said, "I'll snap her neck."

"The bullet will get there first."

"You're not going to kill me."

"You don't think?"

"You're restricted by code. FBI rules. Law and order."

"If you don't let her go, there's no code, no rule, no law, *nothing* that would stop me from blowing your brains out."

"You do that, you'll never know where your mother is buried."

Drex grimaced.

Jasper laughed. "Ah, I've presented you with a dilemma. You want to save Talia, which is romantic to the nth degree. But, if you kill me, you'll never know your mother's final resting place."

"You're right," Drex said, lowering the pistol. "I'll just shoot you in the leg instead."

He pulled the trigger. Jasper's body jerked. He cried out. When his leg buckled, he dragged Talia down with him. She used that nanosecond of weakness to lunge away from him.

He caught her by the hair and tried to jerk her backward.

Rapid gunfire erupted.

His grip on her hair was released so abruptly, she fell forward, landing hard on her knees, gasping for breath, deafened by the barrage.

Then Drex was there, kneeling beside her. He took her by the shoulders and gently pulled her into a sitting position. Her hearing was still muffled, but his lips were moving, asking repeatedly if she was all right.

Dumbly, she nodded.

He kissed her forehead, then eased her toward Menundez, who was at her other side, down on one knee. A number of uniformed officers had crowded into the open doorway. Locke was motioning them back, keeping them from entering the room.

She took all this in, but her gaze followed Drex as he walked over to where Jasper had collapsed. He had crumpled against his closet door, listing at a severe angle. He was bleeding from numerous wounds in his chest and abdomen.

Drex crouched in front of him.

———⬥———

With cold objectivity, Drex regarded the wounds he'd inflicted. The one in Jasper's thigh was the only one that had required some shooting skill. He'd had to make it count without hitting Talia.

The others, he'd gone for center of mass. They hadn't required careful aim to do fatal damage.

Had he felt any remorse for that, he only had to look into the black, fathomless eyes, from which not a single glimmer of a human soul had ever shone. He had only to think of the women who had suffered and died and been abandoned in ignominious graves.

He said, "You're already dead. You've got minutes, if that. Weston."

Jasper's lips formed a rictus of smug delight. "Your mother liked my name. Liked me. So much so that she gave you up to be with me." He gurgled a laugh. "You'll never find her, you know."

"Probably not. But that's not my heart's desire. This is."

Drex reached out and yanked hard on the button of the blazer. With a snap of threads, it came free. Drex bounced it in his palm. "So much for your collection."

Blood had filled Jasper's mouth and coated his teeth, making his grin grotesque. He was wheezing for each shallow breath, blowing bubbles of blood, but he forced himself to speak.

"I suppose that you'll open up my brain and study it, won't you, Dr. Easton? You'll want to know what made me tick. You could write a textbook about me." His laugh was a blood-sputtering travesty. "Probe my brain, slice and dice it, dig into it till the day you die. It will never tell you where to look for your mother."

Drex leaned in a little closer. "Your brain has absolutely zero value, Weston. It will cook in an incinerator and turn to ash. It will never be dissected and analyzed. You are nobody's idea of a specimen worth writing about. Know why?" He placed his lips against Jasper's ear. "You're too fucking ordinary."

Seconds later, he watched Weston Graham die an inglorious death, carrying that crushing insult into hell with him.

Talia wept with relief when she learned that Mike was alive.

Drex wanted to comfort her, but they were kept separated while being questioned by investigators from the Mount Pleasant police department. When it came his turn, Locke advised him to let him do most of the talking. Drex was happy to oblige. He was coming down off a bitch of an adrenaline surge.

Locke and Menundez explained to the investigators what had brought them rushing to the Ford residence. "We alerted your department to a possible crisis situation," Locke told them, "but we had a good head start and arrived ahead of everyone else."

Menundez explained how Jasper had come to be shot by a small-caliber pistol belonging to him. "I carry a spare in an ankle holster. I gave it to Easton before we entered the house."

Those interrogating them turned as one to regard Drex with suspicion. One asked Menundez, "He was booked today. You didn't think twice about giving him a weapon?"

"I only thought twice about taking his," Menundez replied.

Locke picked up. "We entered through the back porch and found Mallory lying prone on the kitchen floor. He was unconscious, not dead."

Indeed, Mike's eyes had fluttered open as Drex's fingers plowed the folds of fat beneath his chin in search of a pulse. Mike had pushed Drex away with one hand and pointed them upstairs with the other.

Locke said, "I stayed behind to call in medical help for Mallory and to apprise your guys of what was happening. I asked them to approach covertly. Easton and Menundez proceeded upstairs."

"What happened when you got up there?" The question was addressed to Drex.

"We heard their voices. Approached with caution. No sooner had I motioned to Menundez that I was going in than we heard him say that he was going to kill her. When I cleared the door, he had her in a headlock. I tried to talk him into letting her go. He didn't heed. I shot him in the leg."

"Tricky shot," a policeman remarked. "You must have had excellent marksmanship training somewhere."

"Alaska. A school buddy of mine."

"A hunter?"

"A hoodlum."

Just then, Locke was pulled away from the group by a uniformed officer. Drex and Menundez continued to answer questions. When Locke returned, he reported grimly that a woman's body had been discovered in a local motel. "It's estimated she's been dead for at least twelve hours. Cause of death, forcibly broken neck. A button is missing from her dress."

The news cast a greater pall over the already somber scene. The coroner came and went. Jasper's body was taken away, but not before a velvet pouch with a drawstring was found in one of the pockets of his cargo pants. It was placed in an evidence bag. To it, Drex added the brass button he'd ripped off.

The house was cleared of excess personnel, although there were still officers and investigators milling from room to room, carrying out various responsibilities. Drex found Talia in the living room, talking with Locke.

"We both need some air." Without waiting for permission, he motioned Talia off the sofa and took her by the arm.

Locke didn't protest, but he said to their retreating backs, "Don't go far."

They made their way through the kitchen, where Menundez was availing himself of the coffee machine. They crossed the lawn to the garage apartment and sat side by side on a lower step of the exterior staircase. The wood was damp from the recent weather, but the rain had stopped. For the first time in days, the sky was clear. Moonlight shone through the branches of the live oak tree, casting shadows.

They didn't talk for several minutes, only held each other. When she did angle away from him, she said, "Mike's going to be all right?"

"I talked to him by phone about half an hour ago. The nurses are drill sergeants, the doctors prepubescent idiots, they're giving him Jell-O and calling it food. He said that he's too fat to choke with bare hands, that anybody with half a brain should know that. He was at his grumpiest. In other words, doing well."

"Does Gif know?"

"I talked to him, too. Told him everything."

"What did he have to say about it?"

Drex knew what she was referring to, but he answered by saying, "That he's wanted to choke Mike himself many times."

She smiled, and he smiled back, but the aftermath of the crisis caught up with them simultaneously, and they kissed ravenously, clutching at each other, assuring themselves that the other was there, whole, alive.

Drex felt her tears on his cheeks, or was he the one crying? Taking her face between his hands, he said, "On the way here, I died a thousand deaths. When I heard your voice—"

"I know, I know," she said, laughing and crying at once. "I felt the same when I heard yours. Thank you for saving my life."

"I gunned him down in front of you, Talia. Are you...I wasn't sure how you would feel about that."

"Oh, God, Drex." She nestled closer to him. "Profound gratitude and relief that it's over. He's done. That's how I feel about it."

He bent his head over hers and kissed her crown.

"There they are."

Instantly, they separated and looked toward the house. Rudkowski was strutting toward them, Locke, Menundez, and another man, a stranger, trailing him.

"Jesus." Drex stood up and said to Rudkowski, "We don't have to do this now."

"Not up to you, is it?" Rudkowski marched to within a few feet of them, then stepped aside and motioned to the man Drex didn't know. "Read him his rights."

The man came forward, turned Drex around, and placed a pair of flex cuffs on his wrists as he Mirandized him.

"What are you doing?" Talia pushed past the stranger and confronted Rudkowski. "What is wrong with you?" She shoved him in the chest with both hands. "Jasper gave him no choice. He was about to kill me and would have if Drex hadn't acted. Menundez, tell him. If you and Drex hadn't—"

"I know all of that," Rudkowski said snidely. "I'm arresting him for obstruction of justice, tampering with—"

"Oh, for godsake!"

"—evidence, and impersonation of a federal agent."

"That's ridiculous. He only resigned in order to—"

"He didn't *resign* from anything," Rudkowski said. "That badge he so theatrically surrendered, no doubt to impress you with his self-sacrifice, is counterfeit. It will be submitted as evidence at his trial."

"Counterfeit?"

"Oh. Like you didn't know," he said with scorn.

She turned to Drex. "What is he talking about?"

Before Drex could speak, Rudkowski practically squealed, "He's a phony. He and his merry band are imposters. They only profess to be FBI agents, flashing around fake badges and IDs whenever the mood strikes."

She rounded on Rudkowski, then looked at Locke and Menundez.

Locke cleared his throat. "He, uh, had us convinced, too. Until Rudkowski told us different."

Rudkowski said, "I assumed you knew, Mrs. Ford. Which is why I came down so hard on you. I thought you'd gone along with him, never mind that he's a criminal. Most women do."

"'Criminal' is a pretty harsh word," Locke said.

"How about lawbreaker?" Rudkowski said. "Use whatever word you like. They all mean the same thing. He commits crimes. And since he's a repeat offender, and has already served time for the *same offense*, he won't get off so lightly this time. I'm going for the maximum sentence."

To Drex, it seemed an eternity that Talia stared at Rudkowski, unmoving, before she came slowly around to him. The instant she looked into his face, she saw the truth engraved there. Her disillusionment caused his heart to contract.

Speaking low, he said, "Five years ago, I served eight months of a two-year sentence in federal prison for impersonating an FBI agent. Mike and Gif got off on probation."

She placed her hand at the base of her throat, which already showed a bruise Jasper had inflicted. Drex knew he was bruising her almost as deeply now.

"He's run a great con," Rudkowski said.

Giving no regard to him, Drex said, "I used the badge, played the part, but never for self gain. Only as a means to capture Weston Graham."

In a faint voice, she said, "You never were with the FBI?"

"Mike and Gif were until..." He hitched his chin toward Rudkowski. "They were with the bureau when I went to them and sought their help."

"Because they were corruptible," Rudkowski said.

"Because of their particular skills," Drex said. "They assisted me—"

"Covertly and illegally."

"—because they believed in what I was doing. After my release from prison, they left the bureau and started working with me."

"As accomplices," Rudkowski said. "And by the way, the FBI was happy to be rid of them."

"Why don't you shut the fuck up?" Menundez muttered.

Talia seemed unaware of them. Her wounded gaze remained on Drex. "Is the doctorate another fake?"

"No."

"Then why didn't you just use it and join the FBI?"

"Because I didn't want to be fettered by procedure and bureaucracy."

"It was easier just to act the part?" she said.

"Not easier. More efficacious."

"Efficacious." She gave a bitter laugh. "Good word. A writer's word. You certainly had gullible me fooled. Drex the writer. Drex the federal agent. Drex the good guy," she finished huskily.

"I'm the same man, Talia."

"The same *con* man," Rudkowski said. "Let's go."

The stoic stranger, whom Drex took to be another agent, nudged him forward. He went without protest, but as he came even with Talia, he stopped. "Talia—"

"Anything you have to say, I don't want to hear. I'm not listening to any more of your lies," she said and turned her back to him.

Epilogue

———◦◉◦———

Drex read the discreet sign on the office door, summoned his courage, and pushed it open. Talia was seated at a desk, looking into a computer monitor. She turned her head with a smile of greeting in place. Upon seeing him, it dissolved.

He stepped into the office and closed the door.

The space was smart yet inviting. Vintage, arte-deco travel posters in matte black frames gave the light gray walls modish splashes of color. A Palladian window, virtually a wall in itself, overlooked a landscaped courtyard enclosed by ivy-covered brick walls, a burbling fountain in the center. The mix of chic and nostalgic created an environment that he would expect of her.

Her plain white shirt looked anything but plain on her. Sunlight coming through the window backlit her hair, creating a halo of red and gold.

She hadn't stood up to welcome him, but, since she hadn't yet picked up the crystal objet d'art on her desk and hurled it at him, he said, "I need help planning a trip."

"I only work with established clients."

"You came highly recommended."

"By whom?"

"Elaine Conner."

Looking pained, her gaze dropped a fraction.

He put his hands in his pants pockets and strolled over to one of the posters, studying the sleek lines of the artwork as he said, "I heard you escorted her body to Delaware."

"She stipulated in her will that she wanted to be buried there beside her husband."

"You saw to the dispersal of her estate to various charities."

"A while back, she had asked if I would be the executor. I agreed, of course, never guessing..."

When she trailed off, Drex said, "May she rest in peace."

After a respectful silence, Talia curtly changed the subject. "I heard you pled guilty."

He turned away from the poster and looked at her. "Who'd you hear that from?"

"Gif."

"He's recovered. Almost like new."

"Yes, I know," she said. "He stopped by to see me before going home to Lexington."

"Yeah? You two have a nice visit?"

"Very nice. He apologized."

"For what?"

She gave him a baleful look, which would have caused a less determined man to duck and run. He stayed.

Her desk was a sheet of gray-tinted glass supported by an iron base. Black. The same color as the high heel that was angrily tapping up and down against the floor beneath her chair, where she sat with legs crossed, providing him a six-inch view of thigh above the hemline of her narrow, black skirt.

"Where are you traveling to?"

Her question drew his gaze up from the scenery underneath the desk to her stormy eyes. "Pardon?"

"Where are you going on the trip that you came here to waste my time about?"

"Waste your time?" He thumbed toward the door. "You're open for business."

"To established clients."

"So you said."

She looked down at her wristwatch. Such a dainty wrist, with a sprinkling of golden freckles. "One of which is due here soon with his wife to discuss their African adventure."

"They haven't gone yet?"

"They had to postpone."

"Huh."

"So state your business, please."

"I told you. I'm planning—"

"You can't go on a trip!" she exclaimed, slapping her hand onto the glass desktop. "I know you were being sentenced today. Gif said—"

"You talked to Gif more than once?"

"He said you agreed to plead guilty if Rudkowski would lay off him and Mike."

He shrugged. "I was the corrupting influence. If not for me, they wouldn't have run afoul of the law."

"Rudkowski reluctantly agreed not to touch them, but tacked on several more charges against you. Horse poop, Mike called them."

"You've talked to Mike, too?"

"He said that with those additional indictments, you could face up to five years."

"I got two."

"Oh," she said on a catch of breath. The starch went out of her posture. She looked down.

"Suspended."

Her head snapped up. "What?"

"Surprised me, too. Sent Rudkowski into orbit. The judge read

the sentence, then suspended it because of extenuating circumstances."

"Which were?"

"Rudkowski being an incompetent asshole. I'm putting words in
the judge's mouth, but that was the essence of it. Additionally, I had
a lot of people who defended my questionable actions."

"Locke and Menundez, I'm sure."

"Them. Their chief. Plus the SAC in Columbia. People at my
workplace in Lexington put in a good word for me." He walked
over to the desk and picked up the crystal formation, studying it
from various angles, watching the rainbows it created as he turned
it one way, then another. "What is this supposed to be?"

"Nothing. Put it down. So the judge just let you off?"

"Uh-hum. What really worked in my favor, what his honor
found most compelling, was the affidavit you videotaped and sent
to him."

Standing suddenly, she grabbed the objet from him and returned it to the desktop with a decisive *thunk*. "You were never
supposed to know about that! Mike swore to me that—"

"Mike swore. Gif said. Just how often do you and those two
busybodies put your heads together? What all have you talked
about?"

"For one thing, your *work*."

"Work?"

"Foolish me. Because of the indictments against you, I was worried that you might be fired from your job. I wondered if you were
financially able to pay your legal fees. As it turns out, my concern
was misplaced."

"Which one of the blabbermouths told you?"

"You sold a patent when you were twenty years old? *Twenty*? For
millions?"

"I didn't do anything for it. It fell into my lap. Literally. When I
was sorting through Dad's stuff after he died, I upended a drawer,
and all these engineering drawings fell out. Scores of them. I didn't

even know what they were, had to ask someone. He had designed a thingamajig that went on a doodad that would improve the performance of a piece of machinery."

"A piece of machinery essential to the construction and maintenance of the Alaskan pipeline. And about a hundred other industries. Shipping. Forestry. Earth moving."

"I didn't know that when I filed the patent. I didn't have a clue what Dad had been doing all those long, dark nights when he shut himself off in his bedroom. He was the engineer, not me. I never even made a prototype of the thing."

"You didn't have to."

"No. While I was still at Missoula, manufacturing companies started calling me, wanting to buy the patent. I negotiated for months and sold to the highest bidder. To this day, I'm unclear as to what the gizmo does." He raised his hands. "Wasn't my field of interest. I carried on with what I wanted to do, got my doctorate, and went to work at the security company where I'm still employed."

"Coaching mega-conglomerates on how to screen potential employees so they don't hire embezzlers, pirates, spies, and such."

"Every day a criminal thinks up a new way to be one. It's a constant learning curve. I get paid for trying to outwit the outlaws. It's a great gig. I love the work."

"A gig." She placed her hands on her hips. "You're a major shareholder in a company that has eight branches nationwide."

He was going to kill Mike and Gif. "I go to the office every day, eat lunch in the campus cafeteria, and, just like everybody else, take my two weeks' vacation."

"Two weeks at a time. About six times a year."

"Every employee gets—"

"Stop it, Drex." She blew out a gust of breath in exasperation. "'How much more inept and underachieving am I going to feel?'" she said, quoting him from the day they had met. "And to think I felt sorry for you, a struggling writer living in that ratty apartment."

"Well, if it makes you feel any better, the one in Lexington is about that ratty. I've been preoccupied for the past fifteen, twenty years."

Her annoyance plain, she gnawed her inner cheek. "Why couldn't I find anything about you, the whiz kid, on the Internet?"

"I filed the patent under an LLC. Once it sold, the LLC was dissolved. I've conducted my other business behind blinds like that. I didn't want my name floating around out there in case Weston Graham ever got wind of it."

She assimilated all that and seemed to find it a satisfactory answer. "Is impersonating a federal agent still your hobby?"

"I was sternly admonished by the judge to give that up for good. But I was done with it anyway. Because *he's* done. It's over. Your words, Talia."

"What else don't I know about you? Are there other surprises in store?"

She was entitled to be angry. He wasn't. But a man could only take so much before becoming riled. "No," he said. "And I must say that you're very well informed for someone who, the last time I saw you, told me that you didn't want to hear anything I had to say, and, since then, hasn't answered or responded to a single call. Or email. Or text. Nothing!" He ended on a shout.

She matched it. "What would you have said?"

"I would have asked you to forgive me."

"Never!"

"Fine! Don't forgive me. Will you fuck me?"

Her lips parted. A soft breath puffed out.

He backed down and lowered his volume. "Sorry. I'd be more romantic, but that takes more patience than I've got right now." He moved aside the crystal thing so he could lean toward her.

"I have no right to ask. I never did. You were married, and I was deceiving you with every word and deed. But any time I've been near you since I first saw you coming up the hatchway of that boat,

I've wanted to claim you in a way that's...hell, almost primitive. And I honestly don't know how much longer I can stand here looking at you without acting on that impulse."

Later they would argue over who had moved first in order to get around the desk. After a brief but mad round of kissing and a wrestling match to pull out shirttails, unbutton plackets, get his knotted necktie over his head, and unhook her bra, they were against the wall, hands competing to cover the most bare skin in the least amount of time.

"Is that courtyard public?" he asked.

Reaching far to her right, Talia groped the surface of a small table and came up with a remote. She pressed a button, then dropped the device to the floor.

Drex turned his head, saw the shade silently lowering over the window, and said, "I need to get one of those."

She grabbed his hair with both hands and brought him back around to her. He began rubbing openmouthed kisses down her throat, across her chest, over her breasts. Pecking at her nipple, he asked, "What time are your clients due?"

"You're not the only liar. No one's due. But we should probably lock the door. You never know who will just wander in uninvited."

"Don't go anywhere."

On the short trip to the door and back, he worked open the button on his waistband and unzipped. Talia was bent over squirming out of her skirt. When she straightened up, he was stunned by the sight. Between her thighs was a V of material the same color as her skin, too sheer and pale to hide what was underneath.

"Damn."

He'd said he wanted to claim her. Physically, without question. But as much as that, he wanted an understanding reached, a pact made, a possession consecrated, and he wanted it *now*.

He went to her and lifted her onto him. The coupling was swift and absolute, the stroking urgent and unrestrained. They pushed and pulled against each other, with each other. When they came, it was together, with groans of gratification and sighs that spoke volumes without words.

They sealed it with a deep, ardent, soul-melding kiss.

He sat on the floor with his back to the wall, Talia lying across his lap. She lightly scratched her nails over his scruffy chin and cheeks. "I'm reading *The Count of Monte Cristo* again."

He traced the waistband of her panties from hipbone to hipbone, a tantalizing caress for both of them. "Have I told you how much I like these?"

"About a dozen times. And stop trying to distract me from the subject."

"I'm absorbed in this subject." His fingers drew lazy designs on the sheer fabric.

To get his attention, she rose up and bit his lower lip. "I wanted to kill you, you know."

"That came across."

"But I've ached to see you. I want to tell you all about me. I want to know all about you."

"There'll be time for that. We have a lot to talk out, and we will. That is, if you want you and I to be a 'we.'"

"I thought I'd spent the last few minutes proving that I do. Either that, or I'm just really slutty."

"I adore you really slutty. Take this sorry excuse for panties, for instance."

"You're incorrigible." Her scold was meaningless; her smile packed a thousand watts.

A sassy side of her was emerging now that she was no longer living under Jasper's influence, and Drex loved it. She probably didn't even realize until after he was gone how subtly he had suppressed aspects of her personality.

Drex had learned from Mike and Gif that she was completely

out of the house and that it was up for sale. They'd told him that she had withstood with remarkable aplomb the tsunami of media coverage generated by the exposure of Jasper's history. Loyal clients and friends had rallied around her, protecting her, lending unflagging support until the hubbub eventually ebbed. He saw no reason to bring all that up now. He would wait for her to introduce the subject.

However, he did ask where she was living.

"I'm leasing a townhouse while deciding on something more permanent. I needed a place to work, though, so I rented this office."

"Do you have an extra key for that townhouse?"

"I'll see if I can scare one up." She snuggled against him, burrowing her nose in his chest hair. "Where are you going on your trip?"

"Alaska."

She tipped her head back and looked up at him.

He fiddled with a strand of her hair. "Because of the buttons, all those cold cases are being revisited. Eventually one of the buttons could be connected to my mother. If it is, and I get it back, I'll put it in a hermetically sealed box, take it up to Alaska, and bury it there next to Dad."

"I think he would like that," she said, her voice rough with emotion.

"In the meantime, I thought I'd go up, plant a tree, add a headstone, something that would represent closure to me."

"The fulfillment of your oath."

"That sounds so lofty, but I guess, yeah. I would like for you to go with me."

She kissed her fingertip and pressed it to his lips. "If you would like me to, I will."

He sank his fingers into her hair and massaged her scalp, while his other hand drifted back and forth across her breasts. "I want to volunteer."

"For what?"

"To be the sperm donor when you thaw those eggs out."

She rubbed her cheek against his pec. "You already have been."

Both of his hands fell still. "What?"

"One of my eggs that wasn't harvested proved to be more robust than those that were."

His gaze moved down to the feminine landscape that had entranced him minutes earlier, then came back up to meet her eyes.

Shyly she said, "We were both a bit primitive that night." Drex just looked at her. After a time, she asked, "Are you ever going to blink?"

He did.

Then he pulled her into a hug, and they did something they had never done together: They laughed, out loud, and long.

Praise for MUDBOUND

"A compelling family tragedy, a confluence of romantic attraction and racial hatred that eventually falls like an avalanche . . . The last third of the book is downright breathless."

—*The Washington Post Book World*

"[A] supremely readable debut novel . . . *Mudbound* is packed with drama. Pick it up, then pass it on."

—*People*, Critics Choice, 4-star review

"*Mudbound* argues for humanity and equality, while highlighting the effects of war . . . [The] mixture of the predictable and the unpredictable will keep readers turning the pages . . . It feels like a classic tragedy, whirling toward a climax. [An] ambitious first novel." —*The Dallas Morning News*

"By the end of the very short first chapter, I was completely hooked . . . [*Mudbound* is] so carefully considered and so full of weight . . . This is a book in which love and rage cohabit. This is a book that made me cry." —*Minneapolis Star Tribune*

"[A] tremendous gift, a story that challenges the 1950s textbook version of our history and leaves its readers completely in the thrall of her characters . . . *Mudbound* may well become a staple of syllabi for courses in Southern literature."

—*Paste* magazine, 4-star review

"Does an excellent job of capturing the impacts of racism both casual and deliberate." —*The Denver Post*

"[An] impressive first novel . . . Jordan is an author to watch."

—*Rocky Mountain News*

"This is storytelling at the height of its powers: the ache of wrongs not yet made right, the fierce attendance of history made as real as rain, as true as this minute. Hillary Jordan writes with the force of a Delta storm. Her characters walked straight out of 1940s Mississippi and into the part of my brain where sympathy and anger and love reside, leaving my heart racing. They are with me still." —Barbara Kingsolver

"Is it too early to say, after just one book, that here's a voice that will echo for years to come? . . . Jordan picks at the scabs of racial inequality that will perhaps never fully heal and brings just enough heartbreak to this intimate, universal tale, just enough suspense, to leave us contemplating how the lives and motives of these vivid characters might have been different." —*San Antonio Express-News*

"This book packs an emotional wallop that will engage adult and adolescent readers . . . The six narrators here have enough time and space to develop a complicated set of relationships. The fault lines among them converge into a crackling gunpoint confrontation, a stunning scene that ranks as my personal favorite of this year." —*The Cleveland Plain Dealer*

"Refusing to turn the page is not an option. Jordan is able to make her painful subject matter irresistible by putting the breath of life in these people." —*Richmond Times-Dispatch*

"Jordan has an uncanny knack for nailing the voices of characters she has no business knowing, but know them she does. *Mudbound* also reminds us of the sacrifices made by all soldiers, and how the home front isn't always as appreciative as it should be." —MSNBC.com, Can't Miss column

"Luminous . . . The power of *Mudbound* is that the characters speak directly to the reader. And they will stay with you long after you put the book down."   —*Jackson Free Press*

"A page-turning read that conveys a serious message without preaching."   —*The Observer* (U.K.)

"*Mudbound* dramatizes the human cost of unthinking hatred . . . That [she] makes a hopeful ending seem possible, after the violence and injustice that precede it, is a tribute to the novel's voices . . . The characters live in the novel as individuals, black and white, which gives *Mudbound* its impact."
                      —*The Atlanta Journal-Constitution*

"If Hillary Jordan's new book, *Mudbound,* is ever made into a movie, the odds are very good that it will end up on the short list for an Academy Award. Not just because of the quality of Jordan's writing . . . but also because she tackles some of this country's most enduring and well-trodden emotional and historical territory."   —*Albany Times Union*

"The recognition [Jordan]'s received for the work has been nothing short of sparkling . . . *Mudbound* is as much a tale of racism as it is the transcending powers of love and friendship."
                      —*Austin American-Statesman*

"Full of rich details and dimensional, engaging characters, and it sucks readers in like quicksand from its opening scene."
                      —*Creative Loafing, Atlanta*

"[A] heart-rending debut novel . . . Jordan's beautiful, haunting prose makes it a seductive page-turner."   —*DailyCandy*

"A meticulous, moving narrative."   —*Texas Monthly*

"Jordan has crafted a story that shines . . . A good historical novel with a twist of an ending." —*The Oklahoman*

"This is one of the most extraordinary novels I've read all year . . . Set against the pull of the land—and of the lonely heart—the ensuing tragedy is both inevitable and heart shattering."

—*Dame* magazine

"Stunning and disturbing . . . A story of heroism, loyalty, respect and abiding love." —*Rocky Mount Telegram*

"No denying that readers in search of straightforward storytelling will be hooked." —*Memphis Flyer*

"Debut novelist Hillary Jordan has crafted an unforgettable tale of family loyalties, the spiraling after-effects of war and the unfathomable human behavior generated by racism."

—*BookPage*

"[A] beautiful debut . . . A superbly rendered depiction of the fury and terror wrought by racism." —*Publishers Weekly*

"[A] poignant and moving debut novel . . . Jordan faultlessly portrays the values of the 1940s as she builds to a stunning conclusion. Highly recommended."

—*Library Journal*, starred review

"*Mudbound* is a real page-turner—a tangle of history, tragedy, and romance powered by guilt, moral indignation, and a near chorus of unstoppable voices."

—Stewart O'Nan, author of *A Prayer for the Dying* and *Last Night at the Lobster*

MUDBOUND

A NOVEL BY

HILLARY JORDAN

ALGONQUIN BOOKS OF CHAPEL HILL.

2009

Published by
ALGONQUIN BOOKS OF CHAPEL HILL
Post Office Box 2225
Chapel Hill, North Carolina 27515-2225

a division of
WORKMAN PUBLISHING
225 Varick Street
New York, New York 10014

This is a work of fiction. While, as in all fiction, the literary perceptions and insights are based on experience, all names, characters, places, and incidents either are products of the author's imagination or are used fictitiously.

Library of Congress Cataloging-in-Publication Data
Jordan, Hillary, [date]
    Mudbound : a novel / by Hillary Jordan.—1st ed.
        p. cm.
    ISBN-13: 978-1-56512-569-8 (HC)
    1. Farm life—Mississippi—Fiction. 2. World War, 1939–1945—
Veterans—Fiction. 3. African American veterans—Fiction.
4. Race relations—Mississippi—Fiction. I. Title.

PS3610.O6556M83 2008
813'.6—dc22   2007044471

ISBN-13: 978-1-56512-677-0 (PB)

18 17 16 15 14 13 12 11

To Mother, Gay and Nana,
for the stories

If I could do it, I'd do no writing at all here. It would be photographs; the rest would be fragments of cloth, bits of cotton, lumps of earth, records of speech, pieces of wood and iron, phials of odors, plates of food and of excrement. . . .

A piece of the body torn out by the roots might be more to the point.

—JAMES AGEE, *Let Us Now Praise Famous Men*

I.

JAMIE

HENRY AND I DUG the hole seven feet deep. Any shallower and the corpse was liable to come rising up during the next big flood: *Howdy boys! Remember me?* The thought of it kept us digging even after the blisters on our palms had burst, re-formed and burst again. Every shovelful was an agony— the old man, getting in his last licks. Still, I was glad of the pain. It shoved away thought and memory.

When the hole got too deep for our shovels to reach bottom, I climbed down into it and kept digging while Henry paced and watched the sky. The soil was so wet from all the rain it was like digging into raw meat. I scraped it off the blade by hand, cursing at the delay. This was the first break we'd had in the weather in three days and could be our last chance for some while to get the body in the ground.

"Better hurry it up," Henry said.

I looked at the sky. The clouds overhead were the color of ash, but there was a vast black mass of them to the north, and it was headed our way. Fast.

"We're not gonna make it," I said.

"We will," he said.

That was Henry for you: absolutely certain that whatever he wanted to happen *would* happen. The body would get buried before the storm hit. The weather would dry out in time to resow the cotton. Next year would be a better year. His little brother would never betray him.

I dug faster, wincing with every stroke. I knew I could stop at any time and Henry would take my place without a word of complaint—never mind he had nearly fifty years on his bones to my twenty-nine. Out of pride or stubbornness or both, I kept digging. By the time he said, "All right, my turn," my muscles were on fire and I was wheezing like an engine full of old gas. When he pulled me up out of the hole, I gritted my teeth so I wouldn't cry out. My body still ached in a dozen places from all the kicks and blows, but Henry didn't know about that.

Henry could never know about that.

I knelt by the side of the hole and watched him dig. His face and hands were so caked with mud a passerby might have taken him for a Negro. No doubt I was just as filthy, but in my case the red hair would have given me away. My father's hair, copper spun so fine women's fingers itch to run through it. I've always hated it. It might as well be a pyre blazing on top of my head, shouting to the world that he's in me. Shouting it to me every time I look in the mirror.

Around four feet, Henry's blade hit something hard.

"What is it?" I asked.

"Piece of rock, I think."

But it wasn't rock, it was bone—a human skull, missing a

big chunk in back. "Damn," Henry said, holding it up to the light.

"What do we do now?"

"I don't know."

We both looked to the north. The black was growing, eating up the sky.

"We can't start over," I said. "It could be days before the rain lets up again."

"I don't like it," Henry said. "It's not right."

He kept digging anyway, using his hands, passing the bones up to me as he unearthed them: ribs, arms, pelvis. When he got to the lower legs, there was a clink of metal. He held up a tibia and I saw the crude, rusted iron shackle encircling the bone. A broken chain dangled from it.

"Jesus Christ," Henry said. "This is a slave's grave."

"You don't know that."

He picked up the broken skull. "See here? He was shot in the head. Must've been a runaway." Henry shook his head. "That settles it."

"Settles what?"

"We can't bury our father in a nigger's grave," Henry said. "There's nothing he'd have hated more. Now help me out of here." He extended one grimy hand.

"It could have been an escaped convict," I said. "A white man." It could have been, but I was betting it wasn't. Henry hesitated, and I said, "The penitentiary's what, just six or seven miles from here?"

"More like ten," he said. But he let his hand fall to his side.

"Come on," I said, holding out my own hand. "Take a break. I'll dig awhile." When he reached up and clasped it, I had to stop myself from smiling. Henry was right: there was nothing our father would have hated more.

HENRY WAS BACK to digging again when I saw Laura coming toward us, picking her way across the drowned fields with a bucket in each hand. I fished in my pocket for my handkerchief and used it to wipe some of the mud off my face. Vanity—that's another thing I got from my father.

"Laura's coming," I said.

"Pull me up," Henry said.

I grabbed his hands and pulled, grunting with the effort, dragging him over the lip of the grave. He struggled to his knees, breathing harshly. He bent his head and his hat came off, revealing a wide swath of pink skin on top. The sight of it gave me a sharp, unexpected pang. *He's getting old,* I thought. *I won't always have him.*

He looked up, searching for Laura. When his eyes found her they lit with emotions so private I was embarrassed to see them: longing, hope, a tinge of worry. "I'd better keep at it," I said, turning away and picking up the shovel. I half jumped, half slid down into the hole. It was deep enough now that I couldn't see out. Just as well.

"How's it coming?" I heard Laura say. As always, her voice coursed through me like cold, clear water. It was a voice that belonged rightfully to some ethereal creature, a siren or an angel, not to a middle-aged Mississippi farmwife.

"We're almost finished," said Henry. "Another foot or so will see it done."

"I've brought food and water," she said.

"Water!" Henry let out a bitter laugh. "That's just what we need, is more water." I heard the scrape of the dipper against the pail and the sound of him swallowing, then Laura's head appeared over the side of the hole. She handed the dipper down to me.

"Here," she said, "have a drink."

I gulped it down, wishing it were whiskey instead. I'd run out three days ago, just before the bridge flooded, cutting us off from town. I reckoned the river had gone down enough by now that I could have gotten across—if I hadn't been stuck in that damned hole.

I thanked her and handed the dipper back up to her, but Laura wasn't looking at me. Her eyes were fixed on the other side of the grave, where we'd laid the bones.

"Good Lord, are those human?" she said.

"It couldn't be helped," Henry said. "We were already four feet down when we found them."

I saw her lips twitch as her eyes took in the shackles and chains. She covered her mouth with her hand, then turned to Henry. "Make sure you move them so the children don't see," she said.

WHEN THE TOP of the grave was more than a foot over my head, I stopped digging. "Come take a look," I called out. "I think this is plenty deep."

Henry's face appeared above me, upside down. He nodded. "Yep. That should do it." I handed him the shovel, but when he tried to pull me up, it was no use. I was too far down, and our hands and the walls of the hole were too slick.

"I'll fetch the ladder," he said.

"Hurry."

I waited in the hole. Around me was mud, stinking and oozing. Overhead a rectangle of darkening gray. I stood with my neck bent back, listening for the returning squelch of Henry's boots, wondering what was taking him so goddamn long. *If something happened to him and Laura,* I thought, *no one would know I was here.* I clutched the edge of the hole and tried to pull myself up, but my fingers just slid through the mud.

Then I felt the first drops of rain hit my face. "Henry!" I yelled.

The rain was falling lightly now, but before long it would be a downpour. The water would start filling up the hole. I'd feel it creeping up my legs to my thighs. To my chest. To my neck. "Henry! Laura!"

I threw myself at the walls of the grave like a maddened bear in a pit. Part of me was outside myself, shaking my head at my own foolishness, but the man was powerless to help the bear. It wasn't the confinement; I'd spent hundreds of hours in cockpits with no problem at all. It was the water. During the war I'd avoided flying over the open ocean whenever I could, even if it meant facing flak from the ground. It was how I won all those medals for bravery: from being so scared of that vast, hungry blue that I drove straight into the thick of German antiaircraft fire.

I was yelling so hard I didn't hear Henry until he was standing right over me. "I'm here, Jamie! I'm here!" he shouted.

He lowered the ladder into the hole and I scrambled up it.
He tried to take hold of my arm, but I waved him off. I bent
over, my hands on my knees, trying to slow the tripping of my
heart.

"You all right?" he asked.

I didn't look at him, but I didn't have to. I knew his forehead
would be puckered and his mouth pursed—his "my brother,
the lunatic" look.

"I thought maybe you'd decided to leave me down there," I
said, with a forced laugh.

"Why would I do that?"

"I'm just kidding, Henry." I went and took up the ladder,
tucking it under one arm. "Come on, let's get this over with."

We hurried across the fields, stopping at the pump to wash
the mud off our hands and faces, then headed to the barn
to get the coffin. It was a sorry-looking thing, made of mis-
matched scrap wood, but it was the best we'd been able to do
with the materials we had. Henry frowned as he picked up one
end. "I wish to hell we'd been able to get to town," he said.

"Me too," I said, thinking of the whiskey.

We carried the coffin up onto the porch. When we went
past the open window Laura called out, "You'll want hot coffee
and a change of clothes before we bury him."

"No," said Henry. "There's no time. Storm's coming."

We took the coffin into the lean-to and set it on the rough
plank floor. Henry lifted the sheet to look at our father's face one
last time. Pappy's expression was tranquil. There was nothing

to show that his death was anything other than the natural, timely passing of an old man.

I lifted the feet and Henry took the head. "Gently now," he said.

"Right," I said, "we wouldn't want to hurt him."

"That's not the point," Henry snapped.

"Sorry, brother. I'm just tired."

With ludicrous care, we lowered the corpse into the coffin. Henry reached for the lid. "I'll finish up here," he said. "You go make sure Laura and the girls are ready."

"All right."

As I walked into the house I heard the hammer strike the first nail, a sweet and final sound. It made the children jump.

"What's that banging, Mama?" asked Amanda Leigh.

"That's your daddy, nailing Pappy's coffin shut," Laura said.

"Will it make him mad?" Bella's voice was a scared whisper.

Laura shot me a quick, fierce glance. "No, darling," she said. "Pappy's dead. He can't get mad at anyone ever again. Now, let's get you into your coats and boots. It's time to lay your grandfather to rest."

I was glad Henry wasn't there to hear the satisfaction in her voice.

LAURA

When I think of the farm, I think of mud. Limning my husband's fingernails and encrusting the children's knees and hair. Sucking at my feet like a greedy newborn on the breast. Marching in boot-shaped patches across the plank floors of the house. There was no defeating it. The mud coated everything. I dreamed in brown.

When it rained, as it often did, the yard turned into a thick gumbo, with the house floating in it like a soggy cracker. When the rains came hard, the river rose and swallowed the bridge that was the only way across. The world was on the other side of that bridge, the world of light bulbs and paved roads and shirts that stayed white. When the river rose, the world was lost to us and we to it.

One day slid into the next. My hands did what was necessary: pumping, churning, scouring, scraping. And cooking, always cooking. Snapping beans and the necks of chickens. Kneading dough, shucking corn and digging the eyes out of potatoes. No sooner was breakfast over and the mess cleaned up than it was time to start on dinner. After dinner came supper, then breakfast again the next morning.

Get up at first light. Go to the outhouse. Do your business, shivering in the winter, sweating in the summer, breathing through your mouth year-round. Steal the eggs from under the hens. Haul in wood from the pile and light the stove. Make the biscuits, slice the bacon and fry it up with the eggs and grits. Rouse your daughters from their bed, brush their teeth, guide arms into sleeves and feet into socks and boots. Take your youngest out to the porch and hold her up so she can clang the bell that will summon your husband from the fields and wake his hateful father in the lean-to next door. Feed them all and yourself. Scrub the iron skillet, the children's faces, the mud off the floors day after day while the old man sits and watches. He is always on you: "You better stir them greens, gal. You better sweep that floor now. Better teach them brats some manners. Wash them clothes. Feed them chickens. Fetch me my cane." His voice, clotted from smoking. His sly pale eyes with their hard black centers, on you.

He scared the children, especially my youngest, who was a little chubby.

"Come here, little piglet," he'd say to her.

She peered at him from behind my legs. At his long yellow teeth. At his bony yellow fingers with their thick curved nails like pieces of ancient horn.

"Come here and sit on my lap."

He had no interest in holding her or any other child, he just liked knowing she was afraid of him. When she wouldn't come, he told her she was too fat to sit on his lap anyway, she might break his bones. She started to cry, and I imagined that old

man in his coffin. Pictured the lid closing on his face, the box
being lowered into the hole. Heard the dirt striking the wood.

"Pappy," I said, smiling sweetly at him, "how about a nice
cup of coffee?"

BUT I MUST START at the beginning, if I can find it.
Beginnings are elusive things. Just when you think you have
hold of one, you look back and see another, earlier beginning,
and an earlier one before that. Even if you start with "Chapter
One: I Am Born," you still have the problem of antecedents,
of cause and effect. Why is young David fatherless? Because,
Dickens tells us, his father died of a delicate constitution. Yes,
but where did this mortal delicacy come from? Dickens doesn't
say, so we're left to speculate. A congenital defect, perhaps,
inherited from his mother, whose own mother had married beneath her to spite her cruel father, who'd been beaten as a child
by a nursemaid who was forced into service when her faithless
husband abandoned her for a woman he chanced to meet when
his carriage wheel broke in front of the milliner's where she'd
gone to have her hat trimmed. If we begin there, young David
is fatherless because his great-great-grandfather's nursemaid's
husband's future mistress's hat needed adornment.

By the same logic, my father-in-law was murdered because
I was born plain rather than pretty. That's one possible beginning. There are others: Because Henry saved Jamie from
drowning in the Great Mississippi Flood of 1927. Because
Pappy sold the land that should have been Henry's. Because

Jamie flew too many bombing missions in the war. Because a Negro named Ronsel Jackson shone too brightly. Because a man neglected his wife, and a father betrayed his son, and a mother exacted vengeance. I suppose the beginning depends on who's telling the story. No doubt the others would start somewhere different, but they'd still wind up at the same place in the end.

It's tempting to believe that what happened on the farm was inevitable; that in fact all the events of our lives are as predetermined as the moves in a game of tic-tac-toe: Start in the middle square and no one wins. Start in one of the corners and the game is yours. And if you don't start, if you let the other person start? You lose, simple as that.

The truth isn't so simple. Death may be inevitable, but love is not. Love, you have to choose.

I'll begin with that. With love.

THERE'S A LOT of talk in the Bible about cleaving. Men and women cleaving unto God. Husbands cleaving to wives. Bones cleaving to skin. Cleaving, we are to understand, is a good thing. The righteous cleave; the wicked do not.

On my wedding day, my mother—in a vague attempt to prepare me for the indignities of the marriage bed—told me to cleave to Henry no matter what. "It will hurt at first," she said, as she fastened her pearls around my neck. "But it will get easier in time."

Mother was only half-right.

I was a thirty-one-year-old virgin when I met Henry McAllan in the spring of 1939, a spinster well on my way to petrifaction. My world was small, and everything in it was known. I lived with my parents in the house where I'd been born. I slept in the room that had once been mine and my sisters' and was now mine alone. I taught English at a private school for boys, sang in the Calvary Episcopal Church choir, babysat my nieces and nephews. Monday nights I played bridge with my married friends.

I was never beautiful like my sisters. Fanny and Etta have the delicate blonde good looks of the Fairbairns, my mother's people, but I'm all Chappell: small and dark, with strong Gallic features and a full figure that was ill-suited to the flapper dresses and slim silhouettes of my youth. When my mother's friends came to visit, they remarked on the loveliness of my hands, the curliness of my hair, the cheerfulness of my disposition; I was that sort of young woman. And then one day—quite suddenly, it seemed to me—I was no longer young. Mother wept the night of my thirtieth birthday, after the dishes from the family party had been cleaned and put away and my brothers and sisters and their spouses and children had kissed me and gone home to their beds. The sound of her crying, muffled by a pillow or my father's shoulder perhaps, drifted down the hallway to my room, where I lay awake listening to the whippoorwills, cicadas and peepers speak to one another. *I am! I am!* they seemed to say.

"I am," I whispered. The words sounded hollow to my ears, as pointless as the frantic rubbings of a cricket in a matchbox. It was hours before I slept.

But when I woke the next morning I felt a kind of relief. I was no longer just unmarried; I was officially unmarriageable. Everyone could stop hoping and shift the weight of their attention elsewhere, to some other, worthier project, leaving me to get on with my life. I was a respected teacher, a beloved daughter, sister, niece and aunt. I would be content with that.

Would I have been, I wonder? Would I have found happiness there in the narrow, blank margins of the page, habitat of maiden aunts and childless schoolteachers? I can't say, because a little over a year later, Henry came into my life and pulled me squarely into the ink-filled center.

My brother Teddy brought him to dinner at our house one Sunday. Teddy worked as a civilian land appraiser for the Army Corps of Engineers, and Henry was his new boss. He was that rare and marvelous creature, a forty-one-year-old bachelor. He looked his age, mostly because of his hair, which was stark white. He wasn't an especially large man, but he had density. He walked with a noticeable limp which I later learned he'd gotten in the war, but it didn't detract from his air of confidence. His movements were slow and deliberate, as if his limbs were weighted, and it was a matter of great consequence where he placed them. His hands were strong-looking and finely made, and the nails wanted cutting. I was struck by their stillness, by the way they remained folded calmly in his lap or planted on either side of his plate, even when he talked politics. He spoke with the lovely garble of the Delta—like he had a mouthful of some rich, luscious dessert. He addressed most of his remarks to Teddy and my parents, but I felt his gray eyes on my face all through dinner, lighting there briefly, moving away and then returning again. I remember my skin prickling with heat and damp beneath my clothes, my hand trembling slightly when I reached for my water glass.

My mother, whose nose was ever attuned to the scent of male admiration, began wedging my feminine virtues into the conversation with excruciating frequency: "Oh, so you're a college graduate, Mr. McAllan? Laura went to college, you know. She got her teaching certificate from West Tennessee State. Yes, Mr. McAllan, we all play the piano, but Laura is by far the best musician in the family. She sings beautifully too, doesn't she Teddy? And you should taste her peach chess pie." And so on. I spent most of dinner staring at my plate. Every time I tried to retreat to the kitchen on some errand or another, Mother insisted on going herself or sending Teddy's wife, Eliza, who shot me sympathetic glances as she obeyed. Teddy's eyes were dancing; by the end of the meal he was choking back laughter, and I was ready to strangle him and my mother both.

When Henry took his leave of us, Mother invited him back the following Sunday. He looked at me before he agreed, a measuring look I did my best to meet with a polite smile.

In the week that followed, my mother could talk of little else but that charming Mr. McAllan: how soft-spoken he was, how gentlemanly and—highest praise of all from her—how he did not take wine with dinner. Daddy liked him too, but that was hardly a surprise given that Henry was a College Man. For my father, a retired history professor, there was no greater proof of a person's worth than a college education. The Son of God

Himself, come again in glory but lacking a diploma, would not have found favor with Daddy.

My parents' hopefulness grated on me. It threatened to kindle my own, and that, I couldn't allow. I told myself that Henry McAllan and his gentlemanly, scholarly ways had nothing to do with me. He was newly arrived in Memphis and had no other society; that was why he'd accepted Mother's invitation.

How pathetic my defenses were, and how paper-thin! They shredded easily enough the following Sunday, when Henry showed up with lilies for me as well as for my mother. After dinner he suggested we go for a walk. I took him to Overton Park. The dogwoods were blooming, and as we strolled beneath them the wind blew flurries of white petals down on our heads. It was like a scene out of the movies, with me as the unlikely heroine. Henry plucked a petal from my hair, his fingers lightly grazing my cheek.

"Pretty, aren't they?" he said.

"Yes, but sad."

"Why sad?"

"Because they remind us of Christ's suffering."

Henry's brows drew together, forming a deep vertical furrow between them. I could tell how much it bothered him, not knowing something, and I liked him for admitting his ignorance rather than pretending to know as so many men would have done. I showed him the marks like bloody nail holes on each of the four petals.

"Ah," he said, and took my hand.

He held it all the way back to my house, and when we got

there he asked me to a performance of *The Chocolate Soldier* at the Memphis Open Air Theatre the following Saturday. The female members of my family mobilized to beautify me for the occasion. Mother took me to Lowenstein's department store and bought me a new dress with a frothy white collar and puffed sleeves. On Saturday morning my sisters came to the house with pots of color for my cheeks and eyes, and lipsticks in every shade of red and pink, testing them out on me with the swift, high-handed authority of master chefs choosing seasonings for the sauce. When I was plucked, painted and powdered to their satisfaction, they held a mirror to my face, presenting me with my own reflection like a gift. I looked strange to myself and told them so.

"Just wait till Henry sees you," laughed Fanny.

When he came to pick me up, Henry merely told me that I looked nice. But later that day he kissed me for the first time, taking my face in his hands as naturally and familiarly as if it were a favorite hat or a shaving bowl he'd owned for years. Never before had a man kissed me with that degree of possession, either of himself or of me, and it thrilled me.

Henry had all the self-confidence that I lacked. He was certain of an astonishing number of things: Packards are the best-made American cars. Meat ought not to be eaten rare. Irving Berlin's "God Bless America" should be the national anthem instead of "The Star-Spangled Banner," which is too difficult to sing. The Yankees will win the World Series. There will be another Great War in Europe, and the United States would do well to stay out of it. Blue is your color, Laura.

I wore blue. Gradually, over the course of the next several months, I unspooled my life for him. I told him about my favorite students, my summer jobs as a camp counselor in Myrtle Beach and my family, down to the second and third cousins. I spoke of my two years at college, how I'd loved Dickens and the Brontës and hated Melville and mathematics. Henry listened with grave attention to everything I chose to share with him, nodding from time to time to indicate his approval. I soon found myself looking for those nods, making mental notes on when they were bestowed and withheld, and inevitably, presenting him with the version of myself that seemed most likely to elicit them. This wasn't a deliberate exercise of feminine wiles on my part. I was unused to male admiration and knew only that I wanted more of it, and all that came with it.

And there was so much that came with it. Having a beau — my mother's word, which she used at every possible opportunity—gave me cachet among my friends and relations that I'd never before enjoyed. I became prettier and more interesting, worthier somehow of every good thing.

How lovely you look today, my dear, they would say. And, *I declare, you're positively glowing!* And, *Come and sit by me, Laura, and tell me all about this Mr. McAllan of yours.*

I wasn't at all sure that he was my Mr. McAllan, but as spring turned to summer and Henry's attentions showed no sign of slacking, I began to allow myself to hope that he might be. He took me to restaurants and the picture show, for walks along the Mississippi and day trips to the surrounding countryside, where he pointed out features of the land and the farms we passed. He was very knowledgeable about crops, livestock and such. When I remarked on it, he told me he'd grown up on a farm.

"Do your parents still live there?" I asked.

"No. They sold the place after the '27 flood."

I heard the wistfulness in his voice but put it down to nostalgia. I didn't think to ask if he was interested in farming his own land someday. Henry was a College Man, a successful engineer with a job that allowed him to live in Memphis—the center of civilization. Why in the world would he want to scratch out a living as a farmer?

"MY BROTHER'S COMING UP from Oxford this weekend," Henry announced one day in July. "I'd like for him to meet you."

For *him* to meet *me*. My heart fluttered. Jamie was Henry's favorite sibling. Henry spoke of him often, with a mixture of fondness and exasperation that made me smile. Jamie was at Ole Miss studying fine arts ("a subject of no practical use whatever") and modeling men's clothing on the side ("an undignified occupation for a man"). He wanted to be an actor ("that's no way to support a family") and spent all his spare time doing thespian productions ("he just likes the attention"). Yet despite these criticisms, it was obvious that Henry adored his little brother. Something quickened in his eyes whenever he talked about Jamie, and his hands, normally so impassive, rose from his sides to make large, swooping shapes in the air. That he wanted Jamie to meet me surely meant that he was considering a more permanent attachment between us. Out of long habit, I tried to stifle the thought, but it stayed stubbornly alive in my mind. That night, as I peeled the potatoes for supper, I imagined Henry's proposal, pictured him kneeling before me in the parlor, his face earnest and slightly worried—what if I didn't accept him? As I made my narrow bed the next morning, I envisioned myself smoothing the covers of a double bed with a white, candlewick-patterned spread and two pillows bearing the imprints of two heads. In class the next day, as I quizzed my boys on prepositional phrases, I pictured a child with Henry's gray eyes staring up at me from a wicker bassinet. These visions bloomed in my mind like exotic flowers, opulent and jewel-toned, undoing years of strict pruning of my desires.

The Saturday I was to meet Jamie I dressed with extra care, wearing the navy linen suit I knew Henry liked and sitting patiently while my mother tortured my unruly hair into an upswept do worthy of a magazine advertisement. Henry picked me up and we drove to the station to meet his brother's train. As we stood in the flow of disembarking passengers, I scanned the crowd for a younger copy of Henry. But the young man who came bounding up to us looked nothing like him. I studied the two of them as they embraced: one weathered and solid, the other tall, fair and lanky, with hair the color of a newly minted penny. After a time they clapped each other on the back, as men will do to break the intimacy of such a moment, then pulled apart and searched each other's face.

"You look good, brother," said Jamie. "The Tennessee air seems to agree with you. Or is it something else?"

He turned to me then, grinning widely. He was beautiful; there was no other word for him. He had fine, sharp features and skin so translucent I could see the small veins in his temples. His eyes were the pale green of beryl stones and seemed lit from the inside. He was just twenty-two then, nine years younger than myself and nineteen years younger than Henry.

"This is Miss Chappell," said Henry. "My brother, Jamie."

"Pleased to meet you," I managed.

"The pleasure's mine," he said, taking my offered hand and kissing the back of it with exaggerated gallantry.

Henry rolled his eyes. "My brother thinks he's a character in one of his plays."

"Ah, but which one?" Jamie said, raising a forefinger in the air. "Hamlet? Faust? Prince Hal? What do you think, Miss Chappell?"

I blurted out the first thing that came into my head. "Actually, I think you're more of a Puck."

I was rewarded with a dazzling smile. "Dear lady, thou speakest aright, I *am* that merry wanderer of the night."

"Who's Puck?" asked Henry.

Jamie shook his head in mock despair. "Lord, what fools these mortals be," he said.

I saw Henry's lips tighten. I suddenly felt sorry for him, standing there in his brother's shadow. "Puck's a kind of mischievous sprite," I said. "A troublemaker."

"A hobgoblin," Jamie said contritely. "Forgive me, brother, I'm only trying to impress her."

Henry put his arm around me. "Laura's not the impressionable type."

"Good for her!" Jamie said. "Now why don't you two show me this fine city of yours?"

We took him to the Peabody Hotel, which had the best restaurant in Memphis and a swing band on weekends. At Jamie's insistence we ordered a bottle of champagne. I'd had it only once before, at my brother Pearce's wedding, and I was light-headed after one glass. When the band started up, Jamie asked Henry if he could have a dance with me (Henry didn't dance, that night or any other, because of his limp). We whirled round and round to Duke Ellington, Benny Goodman and Tommy Dorsey, music I'd heard on the radio and danced to in the parlor with my brothers and young nephews. How different this was, and how exhilarating! I was aware of Henry's eyes following us, and others' too—women's eyes, watching me enviously. It was a novel sensation for me, and I couldn't help but revel in it. After several numbers, Jamie escorted me back to our table and excused himself. I sat down, flushed and out of breath.

"You look especially pretty tonight," Henry said.

"Thank you."

"Jamie has that effect on girls. They sparkle for him." His expression was bland, his tone matter-of-fact. If he was jealous of his brother, I couldn't detect it. "He likes you, I can tell," he added.

"I'm sure he doesn't dislike anyone."

"Well, at least not anyone in a skirt," Henry said, with a wry smile. "Look." He gestured toward the dance floor, and I saw Jamie with a willowy brunette in his arms. She was wearing a satin dress with a low-cut back, and Jamie's hand rested on her bare skin. As she followed him effortlessly through a series of complicated turns and dips, I realized what a clumsy partner I must have been. I wanted to cover my face with my hands; I knew everything I felt was there for Henry to see. My envy and embarrassment. My foolish yearning.

I stood up. I don't know what I would have said to him, because at that moment he rose and took my hand. "It's late," he said, "and I know you have church in the morning. Come on, I'll take you home."

He was so gentle, so kind. I felt a rush of shame. But later, as I lay sleepless in my bed, it occurred to me that what I'd shown Henry so nakedly wasn't new to him. He must have seen it before, must have felt it himself a hundred times in Jamie's presence: a longing for a brightness that would never be his.

JAMIE RETURNED TO Oxford, and I put him out of my thoughts. I was no fool; I knew a man like him could never desire a woman like me. It was marvel enough that Henry desired me. I can't say whether I was truly in love with him then; I was so grateful to him that it dwarfed everything else. He was my rescuer from life in the margins, from the pity, scorn and crabbed kindness that are the portion of old maids. I should say, he was my potential rescuer. I was by no means sure of him, and for good reason.

One night at choir practice, I looked up from my hymnal and saw him watching me from one of the rear pews, his face solemn with intent. *This is it,* I thought. *He's going to propose.*

Somehow I got through the rest of the practice, though the director had to chide me twice for missing my entrance. In the choir room afterward, as I unbuttoned my robe with clumsy fingers, I had a sudden vision of Henry's hands undoing the buttons of my nightgown on our wedding night. I wondered what it would be like to lie with him, to have him touch my body as intimately as though it were his own flesh. My sister Etta, who was a registered nurse, had told me about the sexual act when I turned twenty-one. Her explanation was strictly factual; she never once referred to her own relations with her husband, Jack, but I gathered from her private smile that the marriage bed was not an altogether unpleasant place.

Henry was waiting for me outside the church, leaning against his car in his familiar white shirt, gray pants and gray fedora. That was all he ever wore. Clothes didn't matter to him, and his were often ill-fitting—pants drooping at the waist, hems dragging in the dirt, sleeves too long or too short. I laugh now when I think of the feelings his wardrobe aroused in me. I practically throbbed with the desire to sew for him.

"Hello, my dear," he said. And then, "I've come to say goodbye."

Goodbye. The word billowed in the space between us before settling around me in soft black folds.

"They're building a new airfield in Alabama, and they want me to oversee the project. I'll be gone for several months, possibly longer."

"I see," I said.

I waited for him to say something more: How he would miss me. How he would write to me. How he hoped I'd be here when he returned. But he said nothing, and as the silence stretched on I felt myself fill with self-loathing. I was not meant for marriage and children and the rest of it. These things were not for me, had never been for me. I'd been a fool to think otherwise.

I felt myself receding from him, and from myself too, our images shrinking in my mind's eye. I heard him offer to give me a lift home. Heard myself decline politely, telling him I needed the fresh air, then wish him the best of luck in Alabama. Saw him lean toward me. Saw myself turn my head so his kiss found my cheek instead of my lips. Watched as I walked away from him, my back as straight as pride could make it.

Mother pounced on me as soon as I came in the door. "Henry stopped by earlier," she said. "Did he find you at church?"

I nodded.

"He seemed eager to speak with you."

It was hard to look at her face, to see the hope trembling just beneath the surface of her bright smile. "Henry's going away," I said. "He doesn't know for how long."

"Is that . . . all he said?"

"Yes, that's all." I started up the stairs to my room.

"He'll be back," she called out after me. "I know he will."

I turned and looked down at her, so lovely in her distress. One pale, slender hand lay on the banister. The other clenched the fabric of her skirt, crumpling it.

"Oh, Laura," she said, with a telltale quaver.

"Don't you dare cry, Mother."

She didn't. It must have been a Herculean effort. My mother

weeps over anything at all: dead butterflies, curdled sauce. "I'm so sorry, darling," she said.

My legs went suddenly boneless. I sank down onto the top step and put my head on my knees. I heard the creak of her footsteps and felt her sit beside me. Her arm went around me, and her lips touched my hair. "We won't speak of him," she said. "We won't mention his name ever again."

She kept her promise, and she must have passed the word to the rest of the family, because no one said a thing about Henry, not even my sisters. They were just overly kind, all of them, complimenting me more often than I deserved and concocting ways to keep me busy. I was in great demand as a dinner guest, bridge partner and shopping companion. Outwardly I was cheerful, and after a time they began to treat me normally again, believing I was over it. I wasn't. I was furious — with myself, with Henry. With the cruel natural order that had made me simultaneously undesirable to men and unable to feel complete without one. I saw that my former contentment had been a lie. This was the truth at the core of my existence: this yawning emptiness, scantily clad in rage. It had been there all along. Henry had merely been the one who'd shown it to me.

I didn't hear from him for nearly two months. And then one day, I came home to find my mother waiting anxiously in the foyer. "Henry McAllan's come back," she said. "He's in the parlor. Here, your hair's mussed, let me fix it for you."

"I'll see him as I am," I said, lifting my chin.

I regretted that little bit of defiance as soon as I laid eyes on him. Henry looked tan and fit, more handsome than he ever had. Why hadn't I at least put on some lipstick? No — that was foolishness. This man had led me on, then abandoned me. I hadn't gotten so much as a postcard from him in all these weeks. What did I care whether I looked pretty for him?

"Laura, it's good to see you," he said. "How have you been?"

"Just fine. And you?"

"I've missed you," he said.

I was silent. Henry came and took my hands in his. My palms were damp, but his were cool and dry.

"I had to be sure of my feelings," he said. "But now I am. I love you, and I want you to be my wife. Will you marry me."

And there it was, just like that: the question I'd thought I would never hear. Granted, the scene didn't play out quite like I'd pictured it. Henry wasn't kneeling, and the question had actually come out as more of a statement. If he felt any worry over my answer, he hid it well. That stung a little. How dared he be so sure of himself, after such a long absence? Did he think he could simply walk back into my house and claim me like a forgotten coat? And yet, beside the enormity of his wanting me, my anger seemed a paltry thing. If Henry was certain of me, I told myself, it was because that was his way. *Meat should not be eaten rare. Blue is your color. Will you marry me.*

As I looked into his frank gray eyes, I had a sudden, unbidden image of Jamie grinning down at me as he'd spun me around the ballroom of the Peabody. Henry was neither dashing nor romantic; like me, he was made of sturdier, plainer stuff. But he loved me, and I knew that he would provide for me and be true to me and give me children who were strong and bright. And for all of that, I could certainly love him in return.

"Yes, Henry," I said. "I will marry you."

He nodded his head once, then he kissed me, opening my mouth with his thumb and putting his tongue inside. I clamped my mouth shut, more out of surprise than anything; it had been years since I'd been French-kissed, and his tongue felt foreign, thick and strange. Henry let out a little grunt, and I realized I'd bitten him.

"I'm sorry," I stammered. "I didn't know you were going to do that."

He didn't speak. He merely reopened my mouth and kissed me again exactly the same as before. This time I accepted his invasion without protest, and that seemed to satisfy him, because after a few minutes he left me to go and speak to Daddy.

WE WERE MARRIED six weeks later in a simple Episcopal ceremony. Jamie was the best man. When Henry brought him to the house he greeted me with a bear hug and a dozen pink roses.

"Sweet Laura," he said. "I'm so glad Henry finally came to his senses. I told him he was an idiot if he didn't marry you."

Jamie had spoiled me for the rest of the McAllans, whom I met for the first time two days before the wedding. From the moment they arrived it was clear they felt superior to us Chappells, who (it must be said) had French blood on my father's side and a Union general on my mother's. I didn't see much of Henry's father that weekend—Pappy and the other men were off doing whatever men do when there's a wedding on—but I spent enough time with the McAllan women to know we'd never be close, as I'd naïvely hoped. Henry's mother was cold, haughty and full of opinions, most of them negative, about everyone and everything. His two sisters, Eboline and Thalia, were former Cotton Queens of Greenville who'd married into money and made sure everybody knew it. The day before the wedding my mother gave a luncheon for the ladies of both families, and Fanny asked them whether they'd gone to college.

Thalia arched her perfectly plucked brows and said, "What good is college to a woman? I confess I can't see the need for it."

"Unless of course you're poor, or plain," said Eboline.

She gave a little laugh, and Thalia giggled with her. My sisters and I looked at each other uncertainly. Had Henry not told them we were all college girls? Surely they didn't know, Fanny said to me later; surely the slight had been unintentional. But I knew better.

Still, not even Henry's disagreeable relations could dampen the happiness I felt on my wedding day. We honeymooned in Charleston, then returned to a little house Henry had rented for us on Evergreen Street, not far from where my parents lived. And so my time of cleaving began. I loved the smallness of domestic life, the sense of belonging it gave me. I was Henry's now. Yielding to him—cooking the foods he liked, washing and ironing his shirts, waiting for him to come home to me each day—was what I'd been put on the earth to do. And then Amanda Leigh was born in November of 1940, followed two years later by Isabelle, and I became theirs more utterly even than I was their father's.

It would be six years into my marriage before I remembered that cleave has a second meaning, which is "to divide with a blow, as with an axe."

JAMIE

IN THE DREAM I'm alone on the roof of Eboline's old house in Greenville, watching the water rise. Usually I'm ten, but sometimes I'm grown and once I was an old man. I straddle the peak of the roof, my legs hanging down on either side. Snatched objects race toward and then around me, churning in the current. A chinaberry tree. A crystal chandelier. A dead cow. I try to guess which side of the house each item will be steered to by the water. The four-poster bed with its tail of mosquito netting will go to the left. The outhouse will go to the right, along with Mr. Wilhoit's Stutz Bearcat. The stakes of the game are high: every time I guess wrong the water rises another foot. When it reaches my ankles I draw my knees up as much as I can without losing my balance. I jockey the house, riding it north into the oncoming flood while the water urges me on in its terrible voice. I don't speak its language but I know what it's saying: It wants me. Not because I have any significance, but because it wants everything. Who am I, a skinny kid in torn britches, to deny it?

When the river takes me I don't try to swim or stay afloat. I open my eyes and my mouth and let the water fill me up. I feel my lungs spasm but there's no pain, and I stop being afraid. The current carries me along. I'm flotsam, and I understand that flotsam is all I've ever been.

Something glows in the murk ahead of me, getting brighter as I get closer to it. The light hurts my eyes. *Has a star fallen in the river?* I wonder. *Has the river swallowed everything, even the sky?* Five rays emanate from the star's center. They're moving back and forth, like they're seeking something. As I pass by them I see that they're fingers, and that what I thought was a star is a big white hand. I don't want it to find me. I'm part of the river now.

And then I'm not. I feel a sharp pain in my head and am yanked up, back onto the roof, or into a boat—the dream varies. But the hand is always Henry's, and it's always holding a bloody hank of my hair.

More than a thousand people died in that flood. I survived it, because of Henry. I wasn't alone on Eboline's roof, she and my parents were there with me, along with her husband, Virgil, and their maid, Dessie. The water didn't come and take me, I fell into it. I fell into it because I stood up. I stood up because I saw Henry approaching in the boat, coming to rescue us.

Because of Henry. So much of who I am and what I've done is because of Henry. My earliest memory is of meeting him for the first time. My mother was holding me, rocking me, and then she handed me to a large, white-haired stranger. I was afraid, and then I wasn't—that's all I remember. The way Mama always told it, I started to pitch a fit, but when Henry held me up in front of him and said, "Hello, little brother," I stopped crying at once and stuck my fingers in his mouth. I, who howled like a red Indian whenever my father or any other male tried to pick me up, went meekly into my brother's hands. I was one and a half. He was twenty-one and just returned from the Great War.

Because of Henry, I grew up hating Huns. Huns had tried to kill him in a forest somewhere in France. They'd given him his limp and his white hair. They'd taken things from him too—I didn't know what exactly but I could sense his lack of them. He never talked about the war. Pappy was always prodding him about it, wanting to know how many men Henry had killed and how he'd killed them. "Was it more than ten? More than fifty?" Pappy would ask. "Did you get any with your bayonet, or did you shoot em all from a distance?"

But Henry would never say. The only time I ever heard him refer to the war was on my eighth birthday. He came home for the weekend and took me deer hunting. It was my first time getting to carry an actual weapon (if you can call a Daisy Model 25 BB gun an actual weapon) and I was bursting with manly pride. I didn't manage to hit anything besides a few trees, but Henry brought down an eight-point buck. It wasn't a clean kill. When we got to where the buck had fallen we found it still alive, struggling futilely to get up. Splintered bone poked out of a wound in its thigh. Its eyes were wild and uncomprehending.

Henry passed a hand over his face, then gripped my shoulder hard. "If you ever have to be a soldier," he said, "promise me you'll try and get up to the sky. They say battle is a lot cleaner up there."

I promised. Then he knelt and cut its throat.

From that day on, whenever the crop dusters flew over our farm, I pretended I was the pilot. Only it wasn't boll weevils I was killing, it was Huns. I must have shot down hundreds of German aces in my imagination, sitting in the topmost branches of the sweet gum tree behind our house.

But if Henry sparked my desire to fly, Lindbergh ignited it with his solo flight across the Atlantic. It was less than a month after the flood. Greenville and our farm were still under ten feet of water, so we were staying with my aunt and uncle in Carthage. The house was full, and I was stuck sleeping in a three-quarter bed in the attic with my cousins Albin and Avery, strapping bullies with pimply faces and buckteeth. Crammed between the two of them, I dreamed of the flood: the guessing game, the voice of the water, the big white hand. My moaning woke them, and they punched and kicked me awake, calling me a pansy and a titty baby. But not even their threats—to smother me, to throw me out the window, to stake me out over an anthill and pour molasses in my eyes—could stop the flood from coming to get me in my sleep. It came almost every night, and I always gave in to it. That was the part I dreaded: the part where I just let the water have me. It seemed a shameful weakness, the kind my brother would never give in to, even in a dream. Henry would fight with everything he had, and when his last bit of strength was gone he'd fight some more—like I hadn't done. At least, I was pretty sure I hadn't. That was the hell of it, I had no memory of what had happened between the time I fell in the water and when Henry pulled me out. All I had was the dream, which seemed to confirm my worst fears about myself. As the days passed and it kept recurring, I became more and more convinced it was true. I'd given myself willingly to the water, and would do it again if I had the chance.

I started refusing to take baths. Albin and Avery added "pig boy" to the list of endearments they had for me, and Pappy whipped my butt bloody with a switch, yelling that he wouldn't have a son who went around stinking like a nigger. Finally my mother threatened to bathe me herself if I wouldn't. The thought of Mama seeing me naked was enough to send me straightaway into the tub, though I never filled it more than a few inches.

It was during this time that stories about Lindbergh started to crop up in the papers and on the radio. He was going after the twenty-five-thousand-dollar Orteig Prize, offered by a Frenchman named Raymond Orteig to the first aviator to fly nonstop from New York to Paris, or vice versa. The purse had been up for grabs since 1919. A bunch of pilots had tried to win it. All of them had failed, and six had died trying.

Lindbergh would be the one to make it, I was positive. So what if he was younger and greener than the other pilots who'd tried? He was a god—fearless, immortal. There was no way he would fail. My confidence wasn't shared by the local papers, which dubbed him "the Flying Fool" for attempting it without a copilot. I told myself they were the fools.

The day of the flight, our entire family gathered around

the radio and listened to the reports of Lindbergh's progress. His plane was sighted over New England, then Newfoundland. Then he vanished, for sixteen of the longest hours of my life.

"He's dead," Albin taunted. "He fell asleep, and his plane crashed into the ocean."

"He did not!" I said. "Lindy would never fall asleep while he was flying."

"Maybe he got lost," said Avery.

"Yeah," said Albin, "maybe he was just too stupid to find his way."

This was a reference to the fact that I'd gotten lost a few days before. The two of them were supposed to take me fishing, but they'd led me in circles and then disappeared snickering into the woods. I was unfamiliar with the country around Carthage and it took me three hours to find my way back to the house, by which time my mother was out of her mind with worry. Albin and Avery had gotten a whipping, but that didn't make me feel any better. They'd bested me again.

They wouldn't this time. Lindbergh would show them. He would win for both of us.

And of course, he did. "The Flying Fool" became "the Lone Eagle," and Lindy's triumph became mine. Even my cousins cheered when he landed safely at Le Bourget Field. It was impossible not to feel proud of what he'd done. Impossible not to want to be like him.

That night after supper, I went outside and lay on the wet grass and stared up at the sky. It was twilight—that impossible shade of purple-blue that only lasts a few minutes before dulling into ordinary dark. I wanted to dive up into that blue and lose myself in it. I remember thinking there was nothing bad up there. No muck or stink or killing brown water. No ugliness or hate. Just blue and gray and ten thousand shades in between, all of them beautiful.

I would be a pilot like Lindbergh. I would have great adventures and perform acts of daring and defend my country, and it would be glorious. And I would be a god.

Fifteen years later the Army granted my wish. And it was not. And I was not.

RONSEL

THEY CALLED US "Eleanor Roosevelt's niggers." They said we wouldn't fight, that we'd turn tail and run the minute we got into real combat. They said we didn't have the discipline to make good soldiers. That we didn't have brains enough to man tanks. That we were inclined by nature to all kind of wickedness—lying, stealing, raping white women. They said we could see better than white GIs in the dark because we were closer to the beasts. When we were in Wimbourne an English gal I never laid eyes on before came up and patted me right on the butt. I asked her what she was doing and she said, "Checking to see if you've got a tail."

"Why would you think that?" I said.

She said the white GIs had been telling all the English girls that Negroes were more monkey than human.

We slept in separate barracks, ate in separate mess halls, shit in separate latrines. We even had us a separate blood supply—God forbid any wounded white boys would end up with Negro blood in their veins.

They gave us the dregs of everything, including officers. Our lieutenants were mostly Southerners who'd washed out in some other post. Drunkards, yellow bellies, bigoted no-count crackers who couldn't have led their way out of a one-room shack in broad daylight. Putting them over black troops was the Army's way of punishing them. They had nothing but contempt for us and they made sure we knew it. At the Officers' Club they liked to sing "We're dreaming of a white battalion" to the tune of "White Christmas." We heard about it from the colored staff, who had to wait on their sorry white asses while they sang it.

If they'd all been like that I probably would've ended up fertilizing some farmer's field in France or Belgium, along with every other man in my unit. Lucky for us we had a few good white officers. The ones out of West Point were mostly fair and decent, and our CO always treated us respectful.

"They say you're not as clean as other people," he told us. "There's a simple answer to that. Make damn sure you're cleaner than anybody else you ever saw in your life, especially all those white bastards out there. Make your uniforms look neater than theirs. Make your boots shine brighter."

And that's exactly what we did. We aimed to make the 761st the best tank battalion in the whole Army.

We trained hard, first at Camp Claiborne, then at Camp Hood. There were five men to a tank, each with his own job to do, but we all had to learn each other's jobs too. I was the driver, had a feel for it from the very first day. Funny how many of us farm boys ended up in the driver's seat. Reckon if you can get a mule to go where you want it to, you can steer a Sherman tank.

We spent a lot of time at the range, shooting all kind of weapons—.45s, machine guns, cannons. We went on maneuvers in the Kisatchie National Forest and did combat simulations with live ammo. We knew they were testing our courage and we passed with flying colors. Hell, most of us were more scared of getting snakebit than getting hit by a bullet. Some of the water moccasins they had down there were ten feet long, and that's no lie.

In July of '42 we got our first black lieutenants. There were only three of them but we all walked with our heads a little bit higher after that, at least on the base. Off base, in the towns where we took our liberty, we walked real careful. In Killeen they put up a big sign for us at the end of Main Street: NIGGERS HAVE TO LEAVE THIS TOWN BY 9 PM. The paint was blood red in case we missed the point. Killeen didn't have a colored section, only about half of them little towns did. The one in Alexandria near Camp Claiborne was typical—nothing to it but a falling-down movie theater and two shabby juke joints. Wasn't no place to buy anything or set and eat a meal. The rest of the town was off limits to us. If the MPs or the local law caught you in the white part of town they'd beat the shit out of you.

Our uniforms didn't mean a damn to the local white citizens. Not that I expected them to, but my buddies from up north and out west were thunderstruck by the way we were treated. Reading about Jim Crow in the paper is a mighty different thing from having a civilian bus driver wave a pistol in your face and tell you to get your coon hide off the bus to make room for a fat white farmer. They just couldn't understand it, no matter how many times we tried to explain it to them. You got to go along to get along, we told them, got to humble down and play shut-mouthed when you around white folks, but a lot of them just couldn't do it. There was this Yankee private in Fort Knox, that's where most of the guys in the battalion did their basic training. He got into an argument with a white storekeeper who wouldn't sell him a pack of smokes and ended up tied with a rope to the fender of a car and dragged up and down the street. That was just one killing, out of dozens we heard about.

The longer I spent around guys from other parts of the country, the madder I got myself. Here we were, about to risk our lives for people who hated us as bad as they hated the Krauts or the Japs, and maybe even worse. The Army didn't do nothing to protect us from the locals. When local cops beat up colored GIs, the Army looked the other way. When the bodies of dead black soldiers turned up outside of camp, the MPs didn't even try to find out who did it. It didn't take a genius to see why. The beatings, the lousy food and whatall, the piss-poor officers—they all added up to one thing. The Army wanted us to fail.

WE TRAINED FOR two long years. By the summer of '44, we'd about gave up hope that they were ever going to let us fight. According to the *Courier* there were over a hundred thousand of us serving overseas, but only one colored unit in combat. The rest were peeling potatoes, digging trenches and cleaning latrines.

But then, in August, word came down that General Patton had sent for us. He'd seen us on maneuvers at Kisatchie and wanted us to fight at the head of his Third Army. Damn, we were proud! Here was our chance to show the world something it'd never seen before. To hell with God and country, we'd fight for our people and our own self-respect.

We left Camp Hood in late August. I ain't never been so glad to see the back of a place. Only thing I'd miss about that hellhole was Mallie Simpson, she was a schoolteacher I kept company with in Killeen. Mallie was considerable older than me. She might've been thirty even, I never asked and didn't care. She was a tiny little gal with a big full-bellied laugh. She knew things the girls back home didn't have the first idea about, things to do with what my daddy calls "nature activity." Some weekends we didn't hardly leave her bed, except to go to the package store. Mallie liked her gin. She drank it straight up, one shot at a time, downing it in one gulp. She used to say a half-full glass of gin was a invitation to the devil. Seemed to me there was plenty of devilment going on with the glasses being empty, but I wasn't complaining. I said goodbye to her with real sadness. I reckoned it'd be a long while before I had another woman—from what I'd heard, Europe had nothing but white people in it.

But I reckoned wrong. There were plenty of white people over there all right, but they weren't like the ones back home. Wasn't no hate in them. In England, where we spent our first month, some of the folks had never seen a black man before and they were curious more than anything. Once they figured out we were just like everybody else, that's how they treated us. The gals too. The first time a white gal asked me to dance I about fell out of the box.

"Go on," whispered my buddy Jimmy, he was from Los Angeles.

"Jimmy," I said, "you must be plumb out of your mind."

"If you don't I will," he said, so I went on and danced with her. I can't say I enjoyed it much, not that first time anyway. I was sweating so bad I might as well to been chopping cotton. I hardly even looked at her, I was too busy watching every white guy in the place. Meantime my hand was on her waist and her hand was wrapped around my sweaty neck. I kept my arms as stiff as I could but the dance floor was crowded and her body kept on bumping up against mine.

"What's the matter," she asked me after awhile, "don't you like me?" Her eyes were full of puzzlement. That's when it hit me: She didn't care that I was colored. To her I was just a man who was acting like a damn fool. I pulled her close.

"Course I like you," I said. "I think you just about the prettiest gal I ever laid eyes on."

We didn't stay in their country long, but I'll always be grateful to those English folks for how they welcomed us. First time in my life I ever felt like a man first and a black man second.

In October they finally sent us over to where the fighting was, in France. We crossed the Channel and landed at Omaha Beach. We couldn't believe the mess we seen there. Sunken ships, blasted tanks, jeeps, gliders and trucks. No bodies, but we could see them in our heads just the same, sprawled all over the sand. Up till then we'd thought of our country, and ourselves, as unbeatable. On that beach we came face-to-face with the fact that we weren't, and it hit us all hard.

Normandy stayed with us during the four-hundred-mile trip east to the front. It took us six days to get there, to this little town called Saint-Nicholas-de-Port. We could hear the battle going on a few miles away but they didn't send us in. We waited there for three more days, edgy as cats. Then one afternoon we got the order to man all guns. A bunch of MPs in jeeps mounted with machine guns rolled up and parked themselves around our tanks. Then a single jeep came screeching up. A three-star general hopped out of it and got up onto the hood of a half-track. When I seen his ivory-handled pistols I knew I was looking at Ole Blood and Guts himself.

"Men," he said, "you're the first Negro tankers to ever fight in the American Army. I'd have never asked for you if you weren't the best. I have nothing but the best in my Army. I don't give a damn what color you are as long as you go up there and kill those Kraut sonsabitches."

Gave me a shock when I heard his voice, it was as high-pitched as a woman's. I reckon that's why he cussed so much—he didn't want nobody to take him for a sissy.

"Everybody's got their eyes on you and is expecting great things from you," he went on. "Most of all, your race is counting on you. Don't let them down, and damn you, don't let me down! They say it's patriotic to die for your country. Well, let's see how many patriots we can make out of those German bastards."

Course we'd all heard the scuttlebutt about Patton. How he'd hauled off and hit a sick GI at a hospital in Italy. How he was crazy as a coot and hated colored people besides. I don't care what anybody says, that man was a real soldier, and he took us when nobody else thought we were worth a damn. I'd have gone to hell and back for him, and I think every one of us Panthers felt the same. That's what we called ourselves: the 761st Black Panther Battalion. Our motto was "Come Out Fighting." That day at Saint-Nicolas-de-Port they were just words on a flag, but we were about to find out what they meant.

A TANK CREW's like a small family. With five of you in there day after day, ain't no choice but to get close. After awhile you move like five fingers on a hand. A guy says, *Do this,* and before he can even get the words out it's already done.

We didn't take baths, wasn't no time for them and it was too damn cold besides, and I mean to tell you the smell in that tank could get ripe. One time we were in the middle of battle and our cannoneer, a big awkward guy from Oklahoma named Warren Weeks, got the runs. There he was, squatting over his upturned helmet, grunting and firing away at the German Panzers. The air was so foul I almost lost my breakfast.

Sergeant Cleve hollered out, "Goddamn, Weeks! We oughta load you in the gun and fire you at the Jerries, they'd surrender in no time."

We all about busted our guts laughing. The next day an armor-piercing shell blew most of Warren's head off. His blood and brains went all over me and the other guys, and all over the white walls. Why the Army decided to make the walls white I could never understand. That day they were red but we kept right on fighting, wearing pieces of Warren, till the sun went down and the firing stopped. I don't remember what battle that was, it was somewhere in Belgium—Bastogne maybe, or Tillet. I got to where I didn't know what time it was or what day of the week. There was just the fighting, on and on, the crack of rifles and the *ack ack ack* of machine guns, bazookas firing, shells and mines exploding, men screaming and groaning and dying. And every day knowing you could be next, it could be your blood spattered all over your buddies.

Sometimes the shelling was so ferocious guys from the infantry would beg to get in the tank with us. Sometimes we let them, depending. Once we were parked up on a rise and this white GI with no helmet on came running up to us. Ain't nothing worse for a foot soldier than losing your helmet in battle.

"Hey, you fellas got room for one more?" he yelled.

Sergeant Cleve yelled back, "Where you from, boy?"

"Baton Rouge, Louisiana!"

We all started hooting and laughing. We knew what that meant.

"Sorry, cracker," said Sarge, "we full up today."

"I got some hooch I took off a dead Jerry," said the soldier. He pulled a nice-sized silver flask out of his jacket and held it up. "This stuff'll peel the paint off a barn, sure enough. You can have it if you let me in."

Sarge cocked an eyebrow and looked around at all of us.

"I'm a Baptist, myself," I said.

"Me, too," said Sam.

Sarge hollered, "You want us to burn in hell, boy?"

"Course not, sir!"

"Cause you know drinking's a sin."

We all had plenty of reasons to hate crackers but Sarge hated them more than all of us put together. Word was he had a sister who was raped by a bunch of white boys in Tuscaloosa, that's where he was from.

"Please!" begged the soldier. "Just let me in!"

"Get lost, cracker!"

Reckon that soldier died that day. Reckon I should've felt bad about it but I didn't. I was so worn out it was hard to feel much of anything.

I didn't talk about none of that when I wrote home. Even if the censors would've let it through, I didn't want to fret Mama and Daddy. Instead I told them what snow felt like and how nice the locals were treating us (leaving out a few details about the French girls). I told them about the funny food they had over there and the glittery dress Lena Horne wore when she came and sang to us at the USO. Daddy wrote back with news from home: The skeeters were bad this year. Ruel and Marlon had grown two whole inches. Lilly May sang a solo in church. The mule got into the cockleburs again.

Mississippi felt far, far away.

LAURA

December 7, 1941, changed everything for all of us. Within a few days of the attack on Pearl Harbor, Jamie and both of my brothers had enlisted. Teddy stayed with the Engineers, Pearce joined the Marines and Jamie signed up for pilot training with the Air Corps. He wanted to be an ace, but the Army had other plans for him. They made him a bomber pilot, teaching him to fly the giant B-24s called Liberators. He trained for two years before leaving for England. My brothers were already overseas by then, Teddy in France and Pearce in the Pacific.

I stayed in Memphis, worrying about them all, while Henry traveled around the South building bases and airfields for the Army. He remained a civilian; as a wounded veteran of the Great War he was exempt from the draft, for which I was grateful. I didn't mind his absences once I got used to them. I soon realized they made me more interesting to him when he was home. Besides, I had Amanda Leigh for company, and then Isabelle in February of '43. The two of them were as different as they could be. Amanda was Henry's child: quiet, serious-minded, self-contained. Isabelle was something else altogether. From the day she was born she wanted to be held all of the time and would start wailing as soon as I laid her in her crib. Her demanding nature exasperated Henry, but for me her sweetness more than made up for it.

I was bewitched by both of them, and by the beauty of ordinary life, which went on despite the war and seemed all the more precious because of it. When I wasn't changing diapers and weeding my victory garden, I was rolling bandages and sewing for the Red Cross. My sisters, cousins and I organized drives for scrap metal and for silk and nylon stockings, which the Army turned into powder bags. It was a frightening and sorrowful time, but it was also exhilarating. For the first time in our lives, we had a purpose greater than ourselves.

Our family was luckier than many. I lost two cousins and an uncle, but my brothers survived. Pearce was wounded in the thigh and sent home before the fighting turned savage in the Pacific, and Teddy returned safe and sound in the fall of '45. Jamie lost a finger to frostbite but was otherwise unharmed. He didn't come home after he was discharged, but stayed in Europe — to travel, he said, and see the place from the ground for a change. This baffled Henry, who was convinced there was something wrong with him, something he wasn't telling us about. Jamie's letters were breezy and carefree, full of witty descriptions of the places he'd seen and the people he'd met. Henry thought they had a forced quality, but I didn't see it. I thought it was natural Jamie would want to enjoy his freedom after four years of being told where to go and what to do.

Those months after the war were jubilant ones for us and for the whole country. We'd pulled together and been victorious. Our men were home, and we had sugar, coffee and gasoline again. Henry was spending more time in Memphis, and I was hoping to get pregnant. I was thirty-seven; I wanted to give him a son while I still could.

I never saw the axe blow coming. The downstroke came that Christmas. As we usually did, we spent Christmas Eve with my people in Memphis, then drove down to Greenville the next morning. Eboline and her husband, Virgil, hosted a grand family dinner every year in their fancy house on Washington Street. How I hated those trips! Eboline never failed to make me feel dull and unfashionable, or her children to make mine cry. This year would be even worse than usual, because Thalia and her family were driving down from Virginia. The two sisters together were Regan and Goneril to my hapless Cordelia.

When we pulled up at Eboline's, Henry's father came and met us at the car. Pappy had been living with Eboline since Mother McAllan died in the fall of '43. One look at his grim face and we knew something was wrong.

"Well," he said to Henry by way of greeting, "that stuck-up husband of your sister's has gone and killed himself."

"Good God," Henry said. "When?"

"Sometime last night, after we'd all gone to bed. Eboline found the body a little while ago."

"Where?"

"In the attic. He hanged himself," Pappy said. "Merry Christmas."

"Did he leave a note saying why?" I asked.

Pappy pulled a sheet of paper from his pocket and handed it to me. The ink had run where someone's tears had fallen on it. It was addressed to "My darling wife." In a quavering hand, Virgil confessed to Eboline that he'd lost the bulk of their money in a confidence scheme involving a Bolivian silver mine and the rest on a horse named Barclay's Bravado. He said he was ending his life because he couldn't bear the thought of telling her. (Later, when I was better acquainted with my father-in-law, I would wonder if what Virgil really couldn't bear was the thought of spending one more night under the same roof as Pappy.)

Eboline wouldn't leave her bed, even to soothe her children. That job fell to me, along with most of the cooking for a house full of people; Henry had kept the maid on for the time being, but he'd had to let the gardener and cook go. I did what I could. As much as I disliked Eboline, I couldn't help feeling terribly sorry for her.

After the funeral, the girls and I drove home to Memphis while Henry stayed on to help his sister sort out her affairs. He would just be a few days, he said. But a few days turned into a week, then two. The situation was complicated, he told me on the phone. He needed more time to settle things.

He took the train home in mid-January. He was cheerful, almost ebullient, and unusually passionate that night in our bed. Afterward he threaded his fingers through mine and cleared his throat.

"Honey, by the way," he said.

I braced myself. That particular phrase, coming out of Henry's mouth, could lead to anything at all, I never knew what: *Honey, by the way, we're out of mustard, could you pick some up at the store? Honey, by the way, I had a car accident this morning.*

Or in this case, "Honey, by the way, I bought a farm in Mississippi. We'll be moving there in two weeks."

The farm, he went on to tell me, was located forty miles from Greenville, near a little town I'd never heard of called Marietta. We'd live in town, in a house he'd rented for us there, and he'd drive to the farm every day to work.

"Is this because of Eboline?" I asked, when I could speak calmly.

"Partly," he said, giving my hand a squeeze. "Virgil's estate is a mess. It'll take months to untangle, and I need to be close by." I must have given him a dubious look. "Eboline and the children are all alone now," he said, his voice rising a little. "It's my duty to help them."

"What about your father?" I asked. Meaning, can't he help them?

"Eboline can't be expected to look after him now. Pappy will have to come and live with us." Henry paused, then added, "He'll be driving the truck up next week."

"What truck?"

"The pickup truck I bought to use on the farm. We'll need it to move the furniture. We won't be able to take everything at once, but I can make a second trip when we're settled."

Settled. In rural Mississippi. In two weeks' time.

"I bought a tractor too," he said. "A John Deere Model B. It's one hell of a machine—you won't believe how fast it can get a field plowed. I'll be able to farm a hundred and twenty acres by myself. Imagine that!"

When I said nothing, Henry propped himself up on one elbow and peered down at my face. "You're mighty quiet," he said.

"I'm mighty surprised."

He gave me a puzzled frown. "But you knew I always intended to have my own farm someday."

"No, Henry. I had no idea."

"I'm sure I must have mentioned it."

"No, you never did."

"Well," he said, "I'm telling you now."

Just like that, my life was overturned. Henry didn't ask me how I felt about leaving my home of thirty-seven years and moving with his cantankerous father in tow to a hick town in the middle of Mississippi, and I didn't tell him. This was his territory, as the children and the kitchen and the church were mine, and we were careful not to trespass in each other's territories. When it was absolutely necessary we did it discreetly, on the furthermost borders.

MOTHER CRIED WHEN I told her we were leaving, but it was hardly the squall I'd expected. It was more of a light summer shower, quickly over, followed by admonitions to buck up and make the best of it. Daddy merely sighed. "Well," he said,

"I guess we've had you with us longer than we had any right to expect." This was what happened to daughters, their expressions seemed to say. You raised them, and if you were lucky they found husbands who might then take them off anywhere at all, and it was not only to be expected, but borne cheerfully.

I tried to be cheerful, but it was hard. Every day I said good-bye to some beloved person or thing. The porch swing of my parents' house, where Billy Escue had given me my first real kiss the night of my seventeenth birthday. My own little house on Evergreen Street, with its lace curtains and flowered wallpaper. The roaring of the lions at the nearby zoo, which had made me uneasy when we first moved in but now provided a familiar punctuation to my days. The light at my church, which fell in shafts of brilliant color upon the upturned faces of the congregation.

My own family's faces I could hardly bear to look at. My mother and sisters, with their high Fairbairn foreheads and surprised blue eyes. My father, with his wide, kind smile and sloping nose that never could hold up his spectacles properly.

"It'll be an adventure," said Daddy.

"It's not that far away," said Etta.

"There are bound to be nice people there," said Mother.

"I'm sure you're right," I told them.

But I didn't believe a word of it. Marietta was a Delta town; its population—a grand total of four hundred and twelve souls, as I later learned—would consist mostly of farmers, wives of farmers and children of farmers, half of whom were probably Negroes and all of whom were undoubtedly Baptists. We would be miles from civilization among bumpkins who drank grape juice at church every Sunday and talked of nothing but the weather and the crops.

And as if that weren't bad enough, Pappy would be there with us. I'd never spent much time around my father-in-law, a blessing I didn't fully appreciate until that last week in Memphis, when I was forced to spend all day every day alone with him while Henry was at work. Pappy was sour, bossy and vain. His pants had to be creased, his handkerchiefs folded a certain way, his shirts starched. He changed them twice a day, not that they were ever soiled by anything but spilled food; he exerted himself only to roll cigarettes and instruct me on how to pack. I dug up some books I thought he'd like, hoping to distract him, but he waved them away contemptuously. Reading was a waste of time, he said, and education was for prigs and sissies. I wondered how he'd ever managed to produce two sons like Henry and Jamie. I hoped that once we got to Marietta, he'd be spending his days with Henry at the farm, leaving the house to me and the girls.

The house was the only bright spot in this otherwise bleak picture. Henry had rented it from a couple who'd lost their son in the war and were moving out west. He described it as a two-story antebellum with four bedrooms, a wraparound porch and, most enticing to me, a fig tree. I've always been crazy for figs. As I wrapped dishes in newspaper and boxed up lamps and books and linens, I spent many not entirely unpleasant moments picturing myself walking out my back door, plucking the ripe fruit from the branches and eating it unrinsed, like a greedy child. I imagined the pies and minces I would make, the preserves I would lay in for the winter. I said nothing of this to Henry; I wasn't about to give him the satisfaction. But every night at supper, he'd bring up some pleasing detail about the house that he'd neglected to mention before. Had he told me it had a modern electric stove? Did I know it was just three blocks from the elementary school where Amanda Leigh would start first grade the following year?

"That's nice, Henry," I would reply noncommittally.

The day of our departure, we rose before dawn. Teddy and Pearce came and helped Henry load the truck with our furniture, including my most prized possession—an 1859 Steiff upright piano with a rosewood case carved in the Eastlake style. It had belonged to my grandmother, who'd taught me to play. I'd just started giving lessons to Amanda Leigh.

Daddy arrived as I was making my last check of the house. I was surprised to see him; we'd said our goodbyes the night before. He brought biscuits from Mother and a crock of her apple butter. The eight of us ate the hot biscuits standing in the mostly empty living room, shivering in the chill, licking our sticky fingers between bites. When we were done my father and brothers walked us out to the car. Daddy shook Pappy's hand, then Henry's, then hugged the children. At last he turned to me.

Softly, in a voice meant for my ears alone, he said, "When you were a year old and you came down with rubella, the doctor told us you were likely to die of it. Said he didn't expect you'd live another forty-eight hours. Your mother was frantic, but I told her that doctor didn't know what he was talking about. Our Laura's a fighter, I said, and she's going to be just fine. I never doubted it, not for one minute, then or since. You keep that in your pocket and take it out when you need it, hear?"

Swallowing the lump in my throat, I nodded and embraced him. Then I hugged my brothers one last time.

"Well," Henry said, "the day's getting on."

"You take good care of my three girls," Daddy said.

"I will. They're my three girls too."

The children and I sang as we left Memphis. They sat beside me in the front seat of the DeSoto. Henry, Pappy, and all our belongings were in the truck in front of us. The Mississippi River was a vast, indifferent presence on our right.

"You've got to ac-cent-tchu-ate the positive," we sang, but the words felt as foolish and empty as I did.

It was nearing dusk when we turned onto Tupelo Lane. This, I knew, was the name of our street, and I felt a little ripple of excitement each time Henry slowed down. Finally he pulled the truck over and stopped, and I saw the house: a charming old place much as he'd described, but with many agreeable particulars he'd neglected to mention—probably because, being Henry, he hadn't noticed them in the first place. There was a large pecan tree in the front yard, and one side of the house was entirely covered in wisteria, like a nubby green cloak. In the spring, when it bloomed, its perfume would carry us down into sleep every night, and in the summer the lawn would be dotted with fallen purple blossoms. There were two bay windows on either side of the front door, and under them, clumps of mature azalea bushes.

"You didn't tell me we had azaleas, Henry," I chided him when I'd gotten the girls bundled up and out of the car.

"So we do," he said with a smile. I could tell he was feeling pleased with himself. I didn't begrudge him that. The house was truly lovely.

Amanda Leigh sneezed. She was leaning heavily against my leg, and her sister was half-asleep in my arms. Both of them had head colds. "The children are done in," I said. "Let's get them in the house."

"The key should be under the mat," he said.

As we started up the walk, the porch light went on and the front door opened. A man stepped out onto the porch. He was huge, with hunched shoulders like a bear's. A small woman came up behind him, peering from around his shoulder.

"Who are you?" he said. His tone wasn't friendly.

"We're the McAllans," Henry replied. "The new tenants of this house. Who are you?"

The man widened his stance, crossing his arms over his chest. "Orris Stokes. The new owner of this house."

"New owner? I rented this place from George Suddeth just three weeks ago."

"Well, Suddeth sold me the house last week, and he didn't say nothing to me about any renters."

"Is that a fact," Henry said. "Looks like I need to refresh his memory."

"You won't find him. He left town three days ago."

"I gave him a hundred-dollar deposit!"

"I don't know nothing about that," Orris Stokes said.

"You get anything in writing?" Pappy asked Henry.

"No. We shook on the deal."

The old man spat into the street. "How a son of mine could be such a fool, I'll never know."

I watched my husband's face fill with the knowledge that he'd been cheated, and worse, that he was powerless to make it right. He turned to me. "I paid him a hundred dollars cash," he said, "right there in the living room of that house. Afterward I sat down to dinner with him and his wife. I showed her pictures of you and the girls."

"You'd best be getting on," said Orris Stokes. "Ain't nothing for you here."

"Mama, I have to tinkle," Amanda Leigh said in a child's loud whisper.

"Hush now," I said.

The woman moved then, coming out from behind her husband. She was a tiny bird-boned thing with freckled skin and small, fluttering hands. No steel in her, I thought, until I saw her chin. That chin—sharply pointed and jutting forward like a trowel—told a different story. I imagined Orris had felt the sting of her defiance on more than one occasion.

"I'm Alice Stokes," she said. "Why don't y'all come in and have a little supper before you go?"

"Now, Alice," said her husband.

She ignored him, addressing herself to me as if the three men weren't there. "We've got stew and cornbread. It ain't fancy but we'd be pleased to share it with you."

"Thank you," I said, before Henry could refuse. "We'd be most grateful."

The house was cheaply furnished and deserved better. The ceilings were high and the rooms spacious, with lovely period details. I couldn't help but imagine my own things in place of the Stokeses': my piano beside the bay window in the living room, my Victorian love seat in front of the hand-carved mantel in the parlor. As I sat down to supper at Alice's crude pine table, I thought how much better my own dining set would have looked beneath the ornate ceiling medallion.

Over supper we learned that Orris owned the local feed store. That perked Henry up a bit. The two of them talked livestock for a while, discussing the merits of various breeds of pigs—a subject on which Henry was astonishingly well versed. Then the talk turned to farm labor.

"Damn niggers," Orris said. "Moving up north, leaving folks with no way to make a crop. Ought to be a law against it."

"In my day we didn't let em leave," Pappy said. "And the ones that tried sneaking off in the middle of the night ended up sorry they had."

Orris nodded approvingly. "My brother has a farm down to Yazoo City. Do you know, last October he had cotton rotting in the fields because he couldn't find enough niggers to pick it? And the ones he did find were wanting two dollars and fifty cents per hundred pounds."

"Two-fifty per hundred!" Henry exclaimed. "At that rate

they'll put every planter in the Delta out of business. And then what'll they do, when there's nobody to hire them and give them a roof over their heads?"

"If you're expecting sense from a nigger, you're gonna be waiting a good long while," said Pappy.

"You mark my words," said Orris, "they're gonna be asking for even more this year, now the government's done away with the price controls."

"Damn niggers," said Pappy.

It was eight o'clock by the time we finished supper, and the children were nodding into their bowls. When Alice offered to let us stay the night, I accepted quickly; it was a two-hour drive to Eboline's in Greenville, and I wasn't about to chance our flimsy wartime tires on those pothole-filled roads in the dark. Henry and Orris both looked like they wanted to object, but neither of them did. The three men went outside to cover the furniture in the truck against the dew, while Alice cleaned up and I put the girls to bed. After I got them tucked in, I helped her make up the bed Henry and I would share.

"This is a big house," I said. "Is it just you and Mr. Stokes?"

"Yes," she said in a low, sad voice. "Diphtheria took Orris Jr. in the fall of '42, and our daughter Mary died of pneumonia last year. Your girls are sleeping in their beds."

"I'm sorry." I busied myself with the pillowcases, not knowing what else to say.

"I'm expecting," she confided shyly after a moment. "I haven't told Orris yet. I wanted to be sure it took."

"I hope you have a fine strong baby, Alice."

"So do I. I pray for it every night."

She left me then, wishing me a good sleep. I went to the window, which looked out over the backyard. I could see the promised fig tree, its branches naked of leaves but still graceful in the moonlight. *If he had just signed a lease,* I thought. *If he were just a different sort of man.* Henry was never good at reading people. He always assumed everybody was just like him: that they said what they meant and would do what they said.

When the door opened I didn't turn around. He walked up behind me and laid his hand on my shoulder. I hesitated, then reached up and touched it with my own. The skin on top was soft and papery. I felt a rush of tenderness for him, for his aging hands and his wounded pride. He kissed the top of my head, and I sighed and leaned into him. How could I wish him to be other than he was? To be hard and suspicious, like his father? I couldn't, and I felt ashamed of myself for having had such thoughts.

"We'll find another house," I said.

I felt him shake his head. "This was the only place for rent in town. It's all the returning soldiers, they've taken all the housing. We'll have to live out on the farm."

"What about one of the other towns nearby?" I asked.

"I've got no time to look elsewhere," he said. "I have to get the fields broken. I'm already starting a month late."

He stepped away from me. I heard the snap of the suitcase opening. "The farmhouse isn't much, but I know you'll make it nice," he said. "I'm going to brush my teeth now. Why don't you get into bed?"

There was a brief pause, then the door opened and shut. As his footsteps receded down the hall, I looked at the fig tree and thought of the fruit that would begin ripening there come summer. I wondered if Alice Stokes liked figs; if she would gather up the fruit eagerly or let it fall to the ground and rot.

IN THE MORNING we said goodbye to the Stokeses and headed to the general store to buy food, kerosene, buckets, candles and the other provisions we would need on the farm. That's when I learned there was no electricity or running water in the house.

"There's a pump in the front yard," Henry said, "and some kind of stove in the kitchen."

"A pump? There's no indoor plumbing?"

"No."

"What about the bathroom?" I said.

"There is no bathroom," he said, with a hint of impatience. "Just an outhouse."

Honey, by the way.

A stout-bodied woman in a man's checked shirt and overalls spoke from behind the counter. "You the new owners of the Conley place?"

"That's right," said Henry.

"You'll be wanting wood for that stove. I'm Rose Tricklebank, and this is my store, mine and my husband Bill's."

She stuck her hand out, and we all shook it in turn. She

had a strong, callused grip; I saw Henry's eyes widen when her hand grasped his. Yet for all her mannish ways, from the neck up Rose Tricklebank resembled nothing so much as the flower whose name she bore. She had a Cupid's-bow mouth and a round face surrounded by a mop of curly auburn hair. A cigarette tucked behind one ear spoiled the picture, but only a little.

"You'll want to stock up good on supplies today," she said. "Big storm's coming in tonight, could rain all week."

"Why should that matter?" Pappy asked.

"When it rains and that river rises, the Conley place can be cut off for days."

"It's the McAllan place now," Henry said.

After we paid, Rose hefted one of our boxes herself and carried it out to the car, over Henry's protests. She pulled two licorice ropes out of her pocket and handed them to Amanda Leigh and Isabelle. "I've got two girls of my own, and my Ruth Ann is about your age," she said to Amanda, tousling her hair. "She and Caroline are in school right now, but I hope you'll come back and visit us soon."

I promised we would, thinking it would be nice to have a friend in town, and some playmates for the girls. As soon as she was out of earshot, Henry muttered, "That woman acts like she thinks she's a man."

"Maybe she is a man, and her husband hasn't cottoned to it yet," Pappy said.

The two of them laughed. It irritated me. "Well, I like her," I said, "and I plan on visiting her once we get settled in."

Henry's brows went up. I wondered if he would forbid me

to see her, and what I would say if he did. But all he said was, "You'll have a whole lot to do on the farm."

THE FARM WAS about a twenty-minute drive from town, but it seemed longer because the road was so rutted and the view so monotonous. The land was flat and mostly featureless, as farmers will inevitably make it. Negroes dotted the fields, tilling the earth with mule-drawn plows. Without the green of crops to bring it alive, the land looked bleak, an ocean of unrelieved brown in which we'd been set adrift.

We crossed over a creaky bridge spanning a small river lined with cypresses and willows. Henry stuck his head out the window of the truck and shouted back at me, "This is it, honey! We're on our land now!"

I mustered a smile and a wave. To me, it looked no different from the other land we'd passed. There were brown fields and unpainted sharecroppers' shacks with dirt yards. Women who might have been any age from thirty to sixty hung laundry from sagging clotheslines while gaggles of dirty barefoot children watched listlessly from the porch. After a time we came to a shack that was larger than the others, though no less decrepit. It had a deserted air. The truck stopped in front of it, and Henry and his father got out.

"Why are we stopping?" I called out.

"We're here," Henry said.

Here was a long, rickety house with a warped tin roof and shuttered windows that had neither glass nor screens. Here was a porch that ran the length of the house, connecting it to a small lean-to. Here was a dirt yard with a pump in the middle of it, shaded by a large oak tree that had somehow managed to escape razing by the original steaders. Here was a barn, a pasture, a cotton house, a corncrib, a pig wallow, a chicken coop and an outhouse.

Here was our new home.

Amanda Leigh and Isabelle scrambled out of the car and ran around the yard, delighted with everything they saw. I followed, stepping up to my ankles in muck. It would be weeks before I learned that on a farm, you always look before you step, because you never know what you might be stepping in or on: a mud puddle, a pile of excrement, a rattlesnake.

"Will we have chickens, Daddy? And pigs?" Amanda Leigh asked. "Will we have a cow?"

"We sure will," Henry said. "You know what else?" He pointed back to the line of trees that marked the river. "See that river we crossed over? I bet it's full of catfish and crawdads."

There was some kind of structure on the river, about a mile away. Even from a distance I could tell it was much larger than the house. "What's that building?" I asked Henry.

"An old sawmill, dates back to before the Civil War. You and the girls stay out of there, it's liable to fall down any minute."

"It ain't the only thing," said Pappy, gesturing at the house. "That roof needs repairing, and them steps look rotten. And some of the shutters are missing, you better replace em quick or we're liable to freeze to death."

"We'll get the place fixed up," Henry said. "It'll be all right. You'll see."

He wasn't speaking to Pappy, but to me. *Make the best of it,* his eyes urged. *Don't shame me in front of my father and the girls.* I felt a stirring of anger. Of course I would make the best of it, for the children's sake if nothing else.

With the help of one of the tenants, a talkative light-skinned Negro named Hap Jackson, Henry unloaded the truck and moved the furniture in. I saw right away that we wouldn't be able to bring much more from Memphis. The house had just three rooms: a large main room that encompassed the kitchen and living area, and two bedrooms barely big enough to hold a bed and a chest of drawers each. There were no closets, just pegs hammered at intervals along the walls. Like the floors, the walls were rough plank, with gaps between the boards through which the wind and all manner of insects could enter freely. Every surface was filthy. I felt another surge of anger. How could Henry have brought us to such a place?

I wasn't the only one displeased with the accommodations. "Where am I gonna sleep?" demanded Pappy.

Henry looked at me. I shrugged. He had laid this egg all by himself; he could figure out how to hatch it.

"I guess we'll have to put you out in the lean-to," Henry said.

"I ain't sleeping out there. It don't even have a floor."

"I don't know where else to put you," Henry said. "There's no room in the house."

"There would be, if you got rid of that piano," Pappy said.

The piano just barely fit in one corner of the main room.

"If you got rid of that piano," Pappy said, "we could put a bed there."

"We could," Henry agreed.

"No," I said. "We need the piano. I'm teaching the girls to play, you know that. Besides, I don't want a bed in the middle of the living room."

"We could rig a curtain around it," Pappy said.

"True," Henry said.

They were both looking at me: Henry unhappily, his father wearing a smirk. Henry was going to agree. I could see it in his face, and so could Pappy.

"I need to speak to you in private," I said, looking at Henry. I went out onto the front porch. Henry followed, shutting the door behind him.

In a low voice, I said, "When you told me you were bringing me here, away from my people and everything I've ever known, I didn't say a word. When you informed me your father was coming to live with us, I went along. When Orris Stokes stood there and told you you'd been fleeced by that man you rented the house from, I kept my mouth shut. But I'm telling you now, Henry, we're not getting rid of that piano. It's the one civilized thing in this place, and I want it for the girls and myself, and we're keeping it. So you can just go back in there and tell your father he can sleep in the lean-to. Either that or he can sleep in the bed with you, because I am *not* staying here without my piano."

Henry was looking at me like I'd just sprouted antlers. I stared back, resisting the urge to drop my gaze.

"You're overtired," he said.

"No. I'm fine."

How my heart thumped as I waited him out! I'd never defied my husband so openly, or anyone else for that matter. It felt dangerous, heady. Inside the house I could hear the girls squabbling over something. Isabelle started crying, but I didn't take my eyes off Henry's.

"You'd better go to them," he said finally.

"And the piano?"

"I'll put a floor in the lean-to. Fix it up for him."

"Thank you, honey."

That night in our bed he took me hard, from behind, without any of the usual preliminaries. It hurt, but I didn't make a sound.

HENRY

WHEN I WAS SIX years old, my grandfather called me into the bedroom where he was dying. I didn't like to go in there—the room stank of sickness and old man, and the skeleton look of him scared me—but I was reared to be obedient so I went.

"Run outside and get a handful of dirt, then bring it back here," he said.

"What for?"

"Just do it." He waved one gnarled hand. "Go on now."

"Yes, sir."

I went and got the dirt. When I returned with it, he asked me what I was holding.

"Dirt," I said.

"That's right. Now give it to me."

He cupped his hands. They shook with palsy. I poured the dirt into them, trying not to spill any on the sheets.

"What am I holding?" he asked.

"Dirt."

"No."

"Earth?"

"No, boy. This is *land* I've got. Do you know why?" His eyebrows shot up. They were gray and bushy, tangled like wire.

I shook my head, not understanding.

"Because it's *mine*," he said. "One day this'll be your land, your farm. But in the meantime, to you and every other person who don't own it, it's just dirt. Here, take it on back outside before your mama catches you with it."

He poured it back into my hands. As I turned to leave, he grabbed ahold of my sleeve and fixed me with his rheumy eyes. "Remember this, boy. You can put your faith in a whole lot of things—in God, in money, in other people—but land's the only thing you can count on to be there tomorrow. It's the only thing that's really yours."

A week later he was dead, and his land passed to my mother. That land was where I grew to manhood, and though I left it at nineteen to see what lay outside its borders, I always knew I'd return to it someday. I knew it during the weeks I spent overseas with my face pressed in alien mud soaked in the blood of people not my own, and during the long months after, lying on my back in Army hospitals while my leg stank and throbbed and itched and finally healed. I knew it while I was a student up in Oxford, where the land doesn't lie flat, but heaves itself up and down like seawater. I knew it when I went to work for the Corps of Engineers, a job that took me many places that were strange to me, and some others that looked like home but weren't. Even when the flood came in '27, overrunning Greenville and destroying our house and that year's cotton crop, it never occurred to me that my father would do other than rebuild and replant. That land had been in my mother's family for nearly a hundred years. My great-great-grandfather and his slaves had cleared it, wresting it acre by acre from the seething mass of cane and brush that covered it. Rebuild and replant: that's what farmers do in the Delta.

My father did neither. He sold the farm in January of '28, nine months after the flood. I was living down to Vicksburg at the time and traveling a great deal for work. I didn't find out what he'd done till after it was too late.

"That damned river wiped me out," Pappy liked to tell people after he'd moved to town and started working for the railroad. "Never would've sold otherwise." ·

That was a lie, one of many that made up his story of himself. The truth was he walked away from that land gladly, because he feared and hated farming. Feared the weather and the floods, hated the work and the sweat and the long hours alone with his own thoughts. Even as a boy I saw how small he got when he looked at the sky, how he brushed the soil from his hands at the end of the day like it was dung. The flood was just an excuse to sell.

Took me nearly twenty years to save enough to buy my own land. There was the Depression to get through, and then the war. I had a wife and two children to provide for. I put by what I could and waited.

By V-J Day, I had the money. I figured I'd work one more year to give us a cushion and start looking for property the following summer. That would give me plenty of time to learn the land, purchase seed and equipment, find tenants and so on before the new planting season started in January. It would also give me time to work on my wife, who I knew would be reluctant to leave Memphis.

That's how it was supposed to be, nice and orderly, and it would have been if that good-for-nothing husband of Eboline's hadn't gone and hanged himself that Christmas. I never trusted my brother-in-law, or any man comfortable in a suit. Virgil was a great drinker and a great talker besides, and those are stains enough on anybody's character, but what sort of man ends his life with no thought for the shame and misfortune his actions will bring upon his family? He left my sister flat broke and my nephew and nieces fatherless. If he hadn't already been dead, I would have killed him myself.

Eboline and the children needed looking after, and there was no one to do it but me. As soon as we buried Virgil, I started searching for property nearby. There was nothing suitable for sale around Greenville, but I heard about a two-hundred-acre farm in Marietta, forty miles to the southeast. It belonged to a widow named Conley whose husband had died at Normandy. She had no sons to inherit the place and was eager to sell.

From the minute I set foot on the property, I had a good feeling about it. The land was completely cleared, with a small river running along the southern border. The soil was rich and black—Conley had had the sense to rotate his crops. The barn and cotton house looked sound, and there was a ramshackle house on the property that would serve me well as a camp, though it wouldn't do as a home for Laura and the girls.

The farm was everything I wanted. Mrs. Conley was asking ninety-five hundred for it—mostly, I reckoned, because I'd driven up in Eboline's Cadillac. I bargained her down to eighty-seven hundred, plus a hundred and fifty each for her cow and two mules.

I was a landowner at last. I could hardly wait to tell my wife.

But first, I had some things to take care of. Had to find us a rent house in town. Had to buy a tractor—I wasn't about to be a mule farmer like my father had been—and a truck. And I had to decide which tenants to keep on and which to put off. With the tractor I could farm more than half the acreage myself, so I'd only need three of the six tenants who were living there. I interviewed them all, checking their accounts of themselves against Conley's books, then asked the ones with the smallest yields per acre and the greatest talent for exaggeration to leave.

I kept on the Atwoods, the Cottrills, and the Jacksons. The Jacksons looked to be the best of the bunch, even though they were colored. They were share tenants, not sharecroppers, so they only paid me a quarter of their crop as opposed to half. You don't see many colored share tenants. Aren't many of them have the discipline to save for their own mule and equipment. But Hap Jackson wasn't your typical Negro. For one thing, he could read. The first time I met him, before he signed his contract, he asked to see his page in Conley's account book.

"Sure," I said, "I'll show it to you, but how will you know what it says?"

"I been reading going on seven years now," he said. "My

boy Ronsel learned me. I wasn't much good at it at first but he kept after me till I could get through Genesis and Exodus on my own. Teached me my numbers too. Yessuh, Ronsel's plenty smart. He's a sergeant in the Army. Fought under General Patton hisself, won him a whole bunch of medals over there. Reckon he'll be coming home any day now, yessuh."

I handed him the account book, as much to shut him up as anything. Underneath Hap's name, Conley had written, *A hardworking nigger who picks a clean bale.*

"Mr. Conley seemed to have a good opinion of you," I said.

Hap didn't answer. He was concentrating on the figures, running his finger down the columns. His lips moved as he read. He scowled and shook his head. "My wife was right," he said. "She was right all along."

"Right about what?"

"See here, where it says twenty bales next to my name? Mist Conley only paid me for eighteen. Told me that was all my cotton graded out to. Florence said he was cheating us, but I didn't want to believe her."

"You never saw this book before?"

"No suh. One time I asked Mist Conley to look in it, that was the first year we was here, and he got to hollering at me till it was a pity. Told me he'd put me off if I questioned his word again."

"Well I don't know, Hap. It says here he paid you for twenty."

"I ain't telling no part of a lie," he declared.

I believed him. A Negro is like a little child, when he tries to lie it's stamped on his face plain as day. Hap's face held nothing but honest frustration. Besides, I know it's common practice for planters to cheat their colored tenants. I don't hold with it myself. Whatever else the colored man may be, he's our brother. A younger brother, to be sure, undisciplined and driven by his appetites, but also kindly and tragic and humble before God. For good or ill, he's been given into our care. If we care for him badly or not at all, if we use our natural superiority to harm him, we're damned as surely as Cain.

"Tell you what, Hap," I said. "You stay on and I'll let you look in this account book any time you want. You can even come with me to the gin for the grading."

He gave me a measuring look and I saw that his eyes, which I'd thought were brown, were actually a muddy green. Between that and his light skin, I figured he must have had two white grandfathers. It explained a lot.

He was still looking at me. I raised my eyebrows, and he dropped his gaze. I was glad to see that. Smart is well and good, but I won't have a disrespectful nigger working for me.

"Thank you, Mist McAllan. That'd be just fine."

"Good, it's settled then," I said. "One more thing. I understand your wife and daughter don't do field work. Is that true?"

"Yessuh. Well, they help out at picking time but they don't do no plowing or chopping. Ain't no need for em to, me and my sons get along just fine without em. Florence is a granny midwife, she brings in a little extra thataway."

"But you could farm another five acres with them helping you in the fields," I said.

"I don't want no wife of mine chopping cotton, or Lilly May neither," he said. "Womenfolks ain't meant for that kind of labor."

I feel that way myself, but I'd never heard a Negro say so before. Most of them use their women harder than their mules. I've seen colored women out in the fields so big with child they could barely bend over to hoe the cotton. Of course, a colored woman is sturdier than a white woman to begin with.

Laura wouldn't have lasted a week in the fields, but I thought she'd make a fine farmwife once she got used to the idea. Shows you how smart I was.

SHE WAS AGAINST the move from the minute I told her about it. She didn't say so directly, but she didn't have to. I could tell from the way she started humming whenever I walked in the room. A woman will make her feelings known one way or another. Laura's way is with music: singing when she's content, humming when she isn't, whistling tunelessly when she's thinking a thing over and deciding whether to sing or hum about it.

The music got a lot less pleasant once we got to the farm. Slamming doors and banging pans, raising her voice to Pappy and me. Defying me. It was as if somebody had come in the night and stolen my sweet, biddable wife, leaving behind a shrew in her place. Everything I did or said was wrong. I knew she blamed me for losing that house in town, but was it my fault the girls got so sick? And the storm—I suppose that was my doing too?

It hit the middle of the night we arrived, making an ungodly racket on the tin roof. The girls' room was leaking, so we brought them into the bed with us. By morning they were both coughing and hot to the touch. They'd been sniffling for a few days but I hadn't thought much of it, kids are always catching something. The rain kept up all that day and the next, coming down in heavy sheets. Late that second afternoon I was out in the barn mending tack when Pappy came to fetch me.

"Your wife wants you," he said. "Your daughters are worse."

I hurried to the house. Amanda Leigh was coughing, high, cracking sounds like shots from a .22. Isabelle lay in the bed beside her, making a terrible wheezing noise with each indrawn breath. Their lips and fingernails were blue.

"It's whooping cough," Laura said. "Go and fetch the doctor at once. And tell your father to put a pot of water on to boil." I wanted to comfort her but her eyes stopped me. "Just go," she said.

I told Pappy to put the water on and ran out to the truck. The road was a muddy churn. Somehow I made it to the bridge without skidding off into a ditch. I heard the river before I saw it: a roar of pure power. The bridge was two feet underwater. I stood with the rain lashing my face and looked at the swollen brown water and cursed George Suddeth for a liar, and myself for a gullible fool. Never should have trusted him to begin with, that's what Pappy said, and I reckoned he was right. Still, it's a sorry world if you can't count on a man to keep his given word after you've sat at his table and broken bread with him.

It was on the way back to the house that I thought of Hap Jackson's wife, Florence. Hap had said she was a midwife, she might know something of children's ailments. Even if she didn't, she'd be able to help with the cooking and housework while Laura nursed the girls.

Florence herself answered my knock. I hadn't met her before, and her appearance took me aback. She was a tall, strapping Negress with sooty black skin and muscles ropy as a man's—an Amazon of her kind. I had to look up at her to talk to her. Woman must have been near to six feet tall.

"May I help you?" she said.

"I'm Henry McAllan."

She nodded. "How do. I'm Florence Jackson. If you looking for Hap, he's out in the shed, tending to the mule."

"Actually, I came to see you. My little girls, they're three and five, they've taken sick with whooping cough. I can't get to town because the bridge is washed out, and my wife . . ." *My wife is liable to kill me if I come home with no doctor and no help.*

"When they start the whooping?"

"This afternoon."

She shook her head. "They still catching then. I can give you some remedies to take to em but I can't go with you."

"I'll pay you," I said.

"I wouldn't be able to come home for three or four days at least. And then who gone look after my own family, and my mothers?"

"I'm asking you," I said.

As I locked eyes with her, I was struck by the sheer force of her. That force was banked now but I could sense it un-

derneath, ready to come alive at need. This wasn't your commonplace Negro vitality—the animal spirits they spend so
recklessly in music and fornication. This was a deep-running
fierceness that was almost warriorlike, if you can imagine a
colored farmwife in a flour-sack dress as a warrior.

Florence shifted, and I saw a girl of maybe nine or ten in the
room behind her, white to the elbows with flour from kneading
dough. Had to be the daughter, Lilly May. She was watching
us, waiting like I was for her mother's answer.

"I got to ask Hap," Florence said finally.

The girl ducked her head and went back to her kneading,
and I knew that Florence was lying. The decision was hers to
make, not Hap's, and she'd just made it.

"Please," I said. "My wife is afraid." I felt my face get hot as
she considered me. If she said no, I wouldn't ask her again. I
wouldn't stoop to beg a nigger for help. If she said no—

"All right then," she said. "Wait here while I get my
things."

"I'll wait in the truck."

A few minutes later she came out carrying a battered leather
case, a rolled-up bundle of clothes and an empty burlap bag.
She opened the passenger door and set the case and the clothes
inside.

"You got you any chickens yet?" she asked.

"No."

She closed the truck door and walked around to the chicken
coop on the side of the house, moving unhurriedly in spite of
the pouring rain. She stepped over the wire fence and tucked

the bag under one arm. Then she reached into the henhouse, pulled out a flapping bird and, with one sure twist of her big hands, wrung its neck. She put the chicken in the bag and walked back to the truck, still moving at that same steady, deliberate pace.

She opened the door. "Them girls gone need broth," she said, as she climbed inside. She didn't ask my permission, just got in like she had every right to sit in the cab with me. Under normal circumstances I wouldn't have stood for it, but I didn't dare ask her to ride in back.

FLORENCE

FIRST TIME I LAID eyes on Laura McAllan she was out of her head with mama worry. When that mama worry takes ahold of a woman you can't expect no sense from her. She'll do or say anything at all and you just better hope you ain't in her way. That's the Lord's doing right there. He made mothers to be like that on account of children need protecting and the men ain't around to do it most of the time. Something bad happen to a child, you can be sure his daddy gone be off somewhere else. Helping that child be up to the mama. But God never gives us a task without giving us the means to see it through. That mama worry come straight from Him, it make it so she can't help but look after that child. Every once in awhile you see a mother who ain't got it, who just don't care for her own baby that came out of her own body. And you try and get her to hold that baby and feed that baby but she won't have none of it. She just staring off, letting that baby lay there and cry, letting other people do for it. And you know that poor child gone grow up wrong-headed, if it grows up at all.

Laura McAllan was tending to them two sick little girls when I come in with her husband. One of em was bent over a pot of steaming water with a sheet over her head. The other one was just laying there in the bed making that awful whooping sound. When Miz McAllan looked up and seen us her eyes just about scorched us both to a crisp.

"Who's this, Henry? Where's the doctor?"

"The bridge is washed out," he said. "I couldn't get to town. This is Florence Jackson, she's a midwife. I thought she might be able to help."

"Do you see anybody giving birth here?" she said. "These children need a medical doctor, not some granny with a bag full of potions."

Just then the little one started gagging like they do when the whooping takes em real bad. I went right over to her. I turned that child onto her side and held her head over the bowl, but all that come out was some yellow bile. "I seen this with my own children," I told her. "We need to get some liquid down em. But first we got to clear some of that phlegm out."

She glared at me a minute, then said, "How?"

"We'll make em up some horehound tea, and we'll keep after em with the steam like you been doing. That was real good, making that steam for em."

Mist McAllan was just standing there dripping water all over the floor, looking like somebody stabbed him whenever one of them little girls coughed. Times like that, you got to give the men something to do. I asked him to go boil some more water.

"That tea'll draw the phlegm right on out of there," I told Miz McAllan. "Then once they get to breathing better we'll make em some chicken broth and put a little ground-up willow bark in it for the fever."

"I've got aspirin somewhere, if I can find it in all this mess."

"Don't fret yourself over it. Aspirin's made out of willow bark, they do the same work."

"I should have taken them to the doctor yesterday, as soon as they started coughing. If anything happens to them . . ."

"Listen to me," I said, "your girls gone be just fine. Jesus is watching over em and I'm here too, and ain't neither one of us going nowhere till they feeling better. Give em a week or so, they'll be right as rain, you'll see." I talked to her just like I talk to a laboring woman. Mothers need to hear them soothing words. They just as important as the medicines, sometimes even more.

"Thank you for coming," she said after awhile.

"You welcome."

After they had some tea and was quieted down some I went and started plucking the chicken I'd brought. I hadn't been in the house since the Conleys left and it was filthy from standing empty. Well, not altogether empty—plenty of creatures had been in and out of there. There was mouse droppings and snail tracks on the floor, cicada husks stuck to the walls and dirt all over everything. When Miz McAllan come in and seen me looking, I could tell she was ashamed.

"I haven't had time to clean," she said. "The children took sick as soon as we got here."

"We'll set it to rights, don't you worry."

Whole time I was plucking that chicken and cutting up the onions and carrots for the broth, that ole man was setting at the table watching me. Mist McAllan's father, that they called Pappy. He was a bald-headed fellow with hardly any meat on him, but he still had all his teeth—a whole mouthful of em, long and yellow as corn. His eyes was so pale they was hardly any color at all. There was something bout them eyes of his, gave me the willies whenever they was on me.

Mist McAllan had gone outside and Miz McAllan was back in the bedroom with the children, so it was just me and Pappy for a spell.

"Say, gal, I'm thirsty," he said. "Why don't you run on out to the pump and fetch me some water?"

"I got to finish this broth for the children," I said.

"That broth can do without you for a few minutes."

I had my back to him, didn't say nothing. Just lingered along, stirring that pot.

"Did you hear me, gal?" he said.

Now, my mama and daddy raised me up to be respectful to elderly folks and help em along, but I sure didn't want to fetch that water for that ole man. It was like my body got real heavy all of a sudden and didn't want to budge. Probably I would a made myself do it but then Miz McAllan come in and said, "Pappy, there's drinking water right there, in the pail by the sink. You ought to know, you pumped it yourself this morning."

He held his cup out to me without a word. Without a word

I took it and filled it from the pail. But before I turned around and gave it back to him I stuck my finger in it.

For supper I fried up some ham and taters they had and made biscuits and milk gravy. After I served em I started to make up a plate for myself to take out to the porch.

"Florence, you can go on home now," Miz McAllan said. "I'm sure you've got your own family to see to."

"Yes'm, I do," I said, "but I can't go home to em. It's like I told your husband when he come to fetch me. That whooping cough is catching, specially at the start like your girls is. They gone be contagious till the end of the week at least. If I went home now I could pass it to my own children, or to one of my mothers' babies."

"I ain't sleeping under the same roof as a nigger," Pappy said.

"Florence, why don't you go check on the girls?" Miz McAllan said.

I left the room but it was a small house and there wasn't nothing wrong with my ears.

"She ain't sleeping here," Pappy said.

"Well, we can't send her home to infect her own family," Miz McAllan said. "It wouldn't be right."

There was a good long pause, then Mist McAllan said, "No, it wouldn't be."

"Well then," Pappy said, "she can damn well sleep out in the barn with the rest of the animals."

"How could you suggest such a thing, in this cold?" Miz McAllan said.

"Niggers need to know their place," Pappy said.

"For the last few hours," she said, "her *place* has been by your granddaughters' bedside, doing everything she could to help them get better. Which is more than I can say for you."

"Now Laura," Mist McAllan said.

"We'll make up a pallet for her here, in the main room," Miz McAllan said. "Or you can sleep in here and we can put Florence out in the lean-to."

"And have her stinking up my room?"

"Fine then. We'll put her in here."

I heard a chair scrape.

"Where are you going?" Mist McAllan asked.

"To the privy," she said. "If that's all right with you."

The front door opened and then banged shut.

"I don't know what's gotten into your wife," Pappy said, "but you better get a handle on her right quick."

I listened hard, but if Mist McAllan said anything back I didn't hear it.

SLEPT FOUR NIGHTS in that house and by the end of em I'd a bet money there was gone be trouble in it. Soft citybred woman like Laura McAllan weren't meant for living in the Delta. Delta'll take a woman like that and suck all the sap out of her till there ain't nothing left but bone and grudge, against him that brung her here and the land that holds him and her with him. Henry McAllan was as landsick as any man I ever seen and I seen plenty of em, white and colored both. It's in their eyes, the way they look at the land like a woman they's itching for. White men already got her, they thinking, *You mine now, just you wait and see what I'm gone do to you.* Colored men ain't got her and ain't never gone get her but they dreaming bout her just the same, with every push of that plow and every chop of that hoe. White or colored, none of em got sense enough to see that she the one owns them. She takes their sweat and blood and the sweat and blood of their women and children and when she done took it all she takes their bodies too, churning and churning em up till they one and the same, them and her.

I knew she'd take me and Hap someday, and Ruel and Marlon and Lilly May. Only one she wasn't gone get was my eldest boy, Ronsel. He wasn't like his daddy and his brothers, he knowed farming was no way to raise hisself up in the world. Just had to look at me and Hap to see that. Spent our lives moving from farm to farm, hoping to find a better situation and a boss that wouldn't cheat us. Longest we ever stayed any-where was the Conley place, we'd been there going on seven years. Mist Conley cheated us some too but he was better than most of em. He let us put in a little vegetable patch of our own, and from time to time his wife gave us some of their old clothes and shoes. So when Miz Conley told us she'd up and sold the farm we was real anxious. You never know what you getting into with a new landlord.

"I wonder if this McAllan fellow ever farmed before," Hap fretted. "He's from up to Memphis. Bet he don't know the eating end of a mule from the crapping end."

"It don't matter," I told him. "We'll get by like we always do."

"He could put us off."

"He won't, not this close to planting time."

But he could a done it if he'd had a mind to, that was the plain truth. Landlords can do just about anything they want. I seen em put families off after the cotton was laid by and that family worked all spring and summer to make that crop for em. And if they say you owe em for furnishings you don't get nothing for your labor. Ain't nobody to make em do right by you. You might as well not even go to the sheriff, he gone take the boss man's side every time.

"Even if he wants us to stay," Hap said, "we still might have to move on, depending on what type a man he is."

"I don't care if he's the Dark Man hisself, I ain't moving if we don't have to. Took me this long to get the house fit to live in and the garden putting out decent tomatoes and greens. Besides, I can't just go off and leave my mothers." I had four mothers due in the next two months and one of em, little Renie Atwood, was just a baby herself. Couldn't nary one of em afford a doctor and I was the only granny midwife for miles around.

"You'll move if I say so," Hap said. "For the husband is the head of the wife, even as Christ is the head of the church."

"Only so long as he alive," I said. "For if the husband be dead the wife is loosed from his law. Says so in Romans."

Hap gave me a sharp look and I gave him one right back. He's never once laid a hand to me and I always speak my mind to him. Some men need to beat a woman to get her to do what they want, but not Hap. All he has to do is talk at you. You can start off clear on the other side of something, and then he'll get to talking, and talking some more, and before long you'll find yourself nodding and agreeing with him. That was how I started loving him, was through his words. Before I ever knowed the feel of his hands on me or the smell of him in the dark, I used to lay my head on his shoulder and close my eyes and let his words lift me up like water.

Henry McAllan turned out not to be the Dark Man after all, but wasn't no use telling that to my husband. "Do you know what that man is doing?" Hap said. "He's bringing in one of them infernal tractors! Using a machine to work his land instead of the hands God gave him, and putting three families off on account of it too."

"Who?"

"The Fikeses, the Byrds and the Stinnets."

That surprised me about the Fikeses and the Stinnets, on account of them being white. Lot of times a landlord'll put the colored families off first.

"But he's keeping us on," I said.

"Yes."

"Well, we can thank the Almighty for that."

Hap just shook his head. "It's devilry, plain and simple."

That night after supper he read to us from the Revelations. When he got to the part about the beast with seven heads and ten horns, and upon his horns ten crowns and upon his heads the name of blasphemy, I knowed he was talking bout that tractor.

THE REAL DEVIL was that ole man. When Miz McAllan asked me to keep house for her like I done for Miz Conley,

I almost said no on account of Pappy. But Lilly May needed a special kind of boot for her clubfoot and Ruel and Marlon needed new clothes, they was growing so fast they was about to split the seams of their old ones, and Hap was wanting a second mule so he could work more acres so he could save enough to buy his own land, so I said I'd do it. I worked for Laura McAllan Monday to Friday unless I had a birthing or a mother who needed looking in on. My midwifing came first, I told her that when I took the job. She didn't like it much but she said all right.

That ole man never gave her a minute's peace, or me neither. Just set there all day long finding fault with everything and everybody. When he was in the house I thought up chores to do outside and when he was out on the porch I worked in the house. Still, sometimes I had to be in the same room with him and no help for it. Like one time I had ironing to do, mostly his ironing, he wore Sunday clothes every day of the week. He was setting at the kitchen table like always, smoking and cleaning the dirt from under his fingernails with a buck knife. Cept he couldn't a been getting em too clean cause he was too busy eyeballing me.

"You better be careful, gal, or you're gonna burn them sheets," he said.

"Ain't never burnt nothing yet, Mist McAllan."

"See that you don't."

"Yessuh."

He admired the dirt on the tip of the knife awhile, then he said, "How come that son of yours ain't home from the war yet?"

"He ain't been discharged yet," I said.

"Guess they still need some more ditches dug over there, huh?"

"Ronsel ain't digging ditches," I said. "He's a tank commander. He fought in a whole lot of battles."

"That what he told you?"

"That what he done."

The ole man laughed. "That boy's pulling your leg, gal. Ain't no way the Army would turn a tank worth thousands of dollars over to a nigger. No, ditch digger's more like it. Course that don't sound as good as 'tank commander' when you're writing the folks back home."

"My son's a sergeant in the 761st Tank Battalion," I said. "That's the truth, whether you want to believe it or not."

He gave a loud snort. I answered the only way I could, by starching his sheets till they was as stiff and scratchy as raw planks.

LAURA

FAIR FIELDS. That's what Henry wanted to call the farm. He announced this to me and the children one day after church, clearing his throat first with the self-consciousness of a small-town politician about to unveil a new statue for the town square.

"I think it has a nice ring to it, without being too fancy," he said. "What do you girls think?"

"Fair Fields?" I said. "Mudbound is more like it."

"Mudbound! Mudbound!" the girls cried.

They couldn't stop laughing and saying the name. Mudbound stuck; I made sure of it. It was a petty form of revenge, but the only kind available to me at the time. I was never so angry as those first months on the farm, watching Henry be happy. Becoming a landowner had transformed him, bringing out a childlike eagerness I'd rarely seen in him. He would come in bursting with the exciting doings of his day: his decision to plant thirty acres in soybeans, his purchase of a fine sow from a neighbor, the new weed killer he'd read about in the *Progressive Farmer*. I listened, responding with as much en-

thusiasm as I could muster. I tried to shape my happiness out
of the fabric of his, like a good wife ought to, but his contentment tore at me. I would see him standing at the edge of the
fields with his hands in his pockets, looking out over the land
with fierce pride of possession, and think, *He's never looked at
me like that, not once.*

For the children's sakes, and for the sake of my marriage, I
hid my feelings, maintaining a desperate cheerfulness. Some
days I didn't even have to pretend. Days when the weather was
clear and mild, and the wind blew the smell of the outhouse
away from us rather than toward us. Days when the old man
went off with Henry, leaving the house to me, the girls and
Florence. I depended on her a great deal, and for far more than
housework, though I wouldn't have admitted it then. Each time
I heard her brisk knock on the back door, I felt a loosening in
myself, an unclenching. Some mornings I would hear Lilly
May's more hesitant rapping instead, and I would know that
Florence had been called away to another woman's house. Or
I'd open the door to find an agitated husband standing on my
porch, twisting his soiled straw hat in his hands, saying the
pains had started, could she come right now? Florence would
take her leather case and go, bustling with purpose and importance, leaving me alone with the girls and the old man. I
accepted these absences because I had no choice.

"I got to look after the mothers and the babies," she told me.
"I reckon that's why the Lawd put me on this earth."

She had four children of her own: Ronsel, her eldest, who
was still overseas with the Army; the twins, Marlon and Ruel,

shy, sturdy boys of twelve who worked in the fields with their father; and Lilly May, who was nine. There had been another boy, Landry, who'd died when he was only a few weeks old. Florence wore a leather pouch on a thong around her neck containing the dried remains of the caul in which he'd been born.

"A caul round a child mean he marked for Jesus," she told me. "Jesus seen the sign and taken Landry for His own self. But my son'll be watching over me from heaven, long as I wear his caul."

Like many Negroes, Florence was highly superstitious and full of well-meaning advice about supernatural matters. She urged me to burn my nail clippings and every strand of hair left in my brush to prevent my enemies from using them to hex me. When I assured her that wouldn't be necessary, as I had no enemies, she looked pointedly at Pappy across the room and replied that the Dark Man had many minions, and you had to be vigilant against them all the time. One day I smelled something rotten in the bedroom and found a broken egg in a saucer under the bed. It looked to have been there for at least a week. When I confronted Florence with it, she told me it was for warding off the evil eye.

"There are no evil eyes here," I said.

"Just cause you can't see em don't mean they ain't there."

"Florence, you're a Christian woman," I said. "How can you believe in all these curses and spirits?"

"They right there in the Bible. Cain was cursed for killing his brother. Womenfolks cursed on account of Eve listened to that ole snake. And we got the Holy Spirit in every one of us."

"That's not the same thing at all," I said.

She replied with a loud sniff. Later I saw her give the dish to Lilly May, who went and buried the egg at the base of the oak tree. Lord knows what that was supposed to accomplish.

There was no colored school during planting season, so Florence often brought Lilly May to work with her. She was a fey child, tall for her age, with purple-black skin like her mother's. The girls adored Lilly May, though she didn't talk much. She had a clubfoot, so she lacked Florence's slow heavy grace, but her voice more than made up for it. I've never heard anyone sing like that child. Her voice soared, and it took you along with it, and when it stopped and the last high, yearning note had shivered out, you ached for its passing and for your return to your own lonely, mortal sack of flesh. The first time I heard her, I was playing the piano and teaching the girls the words to "Amazing Grace" when Lilly May joined in from the front porch, where she was shelling peas. I've always prided myself on my singing voice, but when I heard hers, I was so humbled I was struck dumb. Her voice had no earthly clay in it, just a sure, sweet grace that was both a yielding and a promise. Anyone who believes that Negroes are not God's children never heard Lilly May Jackson sing to Him.

This is not to say that I thought of Florence and her family as equal to me and mine. I called her Florence and she called me Miz McAllan. She and Lilly May didn't use our outhouse, but did their business in the bushes out back. And when we sat down to the noon meal, the two of them ate outside on the porch.

• • •

EVEN WITH FLORENCE's help, I often felt overwhelmed: by the work and the heat, the mosquitoes and the mud, and most of all, the brutality of rural life. Like most city people, I'd had a ridiculous, goldenlit idea of the country. I'd pictured rain falling softly upon verdant fields, barefoot boys fishing with thistles dangling from their mouths, women quilting in cozy little log cabins while their men smoked corncob pipes on the porch. You have to get closer to the picture to see the wretched shacks scattered throughout those fields, where families clad in ragged flour-sack clothes sleep ten to a room on dirt floors; the hookworm rashes on the boys' feet and the hideous red pellagra scales on their hands and arms; the bruises on the faces of the women, and the rage and hopelessness in the eyes of the men.

Violence is part and parcel of country life. You're forever being assailed by dead things: dead mice, dead rabbits, dead possums, dead birds. You find them in the yard, crawling with maggots, and smell them rotting under the house. Then there are the creatures you kill for food: chickens, hogs, deer, quail, wild turkeys, catfish, rabbits, frogs and squirrels, which you pluck, skin, disembowel, debone and fry up in a pan.

I learned how to load and fire a shotgun, how to stitch up a bleeding wound, how to reach into the womb of a heaving sow to deliver a breached piglet. My hands did these things, but I was never easy in my mind. Life felt perilous, like anything at all might happen. At the end of March, several things did.

One night near to dawn, I woke to the sound of gunshots. I was alone with the children; Henry and Pappy had gone to

Greenville to help Eboline move into her new and considerably more humble abode—the big house on Washington Street had been sold to pay off Virgil's debts. I checked on the girls, but the shots hadn't wakened them. I went out to the porch and peered into the graydark. A half mile away, in the direction of the Atwood place, I saw a light moving. Then it stopped. Then, from that same direction, came two more gunshots. Thirty seconds later there was another. Then another. Then silence.

I must have stood on the porch for twenty minutes, hands clenched in a death grip around our shotgun. The sun rose. Finally I saw someone coming up the road. I tensed, but then I recognized Hap's slightly stooped gait. He was out of breath when he reached me. His clothes were covered with dirt, and he too was carrying a shotgun.

"Miz McAllan," he said. "Is your husband here?"

"No, he and Pappy went to Greenville. What's going on? Was that you firing your gun?"

"No, ma'am, it was Carl Atwood. He done shot his plow horse in the head."

"Good heavens! Why would he do that?"

"He been messing with that whiskey. Ain't no devilment a man won't get hisself into when he's full of drink."

"Please, Hap. Just tell me what happened."

"Well, Florence and I was asleep when we heard them first two gunshots. Both of us like to jump right out of our skins. I got up and looked out the window but I couldn't see nothing. Then we heard another two shots, sound like they coming from the Atwood place. I got my gun and went over there but I know them Atwoods is crazy so I snuck up on em. First thing I seen was that plow horse of Carl's, haring through the fields like the devil hisself was after it. I could hear Carl a-cussing that horse, hollering, 'You oughten not to done it, damn your hide!' Then here he come chasing after it with his shotgun. I could tell he'd been at the whiskey and I was afraid he was gone see me and shoot me too so I dropped down on the ground and laid there real still. He pointed the gun at that horse and bam! He missed again and fell over backwards. That horse let into whinnying, I could a swore it was laughing at him. Carl kept trying to get up and falling back down again, all the while just a-cussing that horse up and down. Finally he got up and aimed again and bam! This time that horse went down, wasn't twenty feet from where I was laying. Carl went over to it and said, 'Damn you to hell, horse, you oughten not to done it.' And then he pissed—begging your pardon Miz McAllan, I mean to say he done his business on that horse, right on its shot-up head, cussing and crying like a baby the whole time."

I hugged myself. "Is he still out there?" I asked.

"No, ma'am. He went on back home. Reckon he'll be sleeping it off most of the day."

Carl Atwood was my least favorite of all our tenants. He was a banty rooster of a man, spindly legged and sway backed, with little muddy eyes that crowded his nose on either side. His lips were dark red, like the gills of a bass, and his tongue was constantly darting out to moisten them. He was always polite to me, but there was a sly, avid quality about him that made me uneasy.

I looked in the direction of the Atwood place. Hap said, "You want me to stay here till Mist McAllan come back?"

As tempted as I was to say yes, I couldn't ask him to lose an entire day in the fields during planting season. "No, Hap," I said. "We'll be fine."

"Florence will be over in a little while. And I'll keep a sharp eye out for Carl."

"Thank you."

I spent the day pacing and looking anxiously out the windows. The Atwoods would have to go. As soon as Henry got home, I'd tell him so. I wouldn't have my children living near such a man.

Later that afternoon, I was at the pump getting water when I saw two figures coming up the road. They walked slowly and unsteadily, one leaning on the other. As they got closer I recognized Vera Atwood and one of her daughters. Vera was huge with child. Except for the jutting mound of her belly, she was little more than skin stretched over bone. One eye was swollen shut, and she had a split lip. The girl had the look of a frightened fawn. Her eyes were large, brown and wide-set, and her dark blonde hair wanted washing. I guessed her to be ten or eleven at most. This, then, wasn't the Atwood girl who'd had an out-of-wedlock baby in February. That child was fourteen, Florence had told me, and her baby had lived only a few days.

"Howdy, Miz McAllan," Vera called out. Her voice was soft and eerily childlike.

"Hello, Vera."

"This here's my youngest girl, Alma."

"How do you do, Alma," I said.

"How do," she replied, with a dip of her head. She had a long, elegant neck that looked incongruous sprouting from her ragged dress. Her face under the grime that covered it was fine-boned and sorrowful. I wondered if she ever smiled. If she ever had reason to.

"I come to speak with you woman to woman," Vera said. She swayed on her feet, and Alma staggered under the extra weight. The two of them looked ready to collapse right there in the yard.

I gestured to the chairs on the porch. "Please, come and sit."

As we made our way up the steps, Florence appeared in the doorway. "What you doing walking all this way, Miz Atwood?" she said. "I done told you, you got to stay off a your feet." Then Florence saw the state of Vera's face. She scowled and shook her head, but she held her tongue.

"Had to come," said Vera. "Got business with Miz McAllan."

I handed Florence the bucket. "Bring us a pitcher of water, will you?" I said. "And some of that shortbread I made yesterday. And keep an eye on Amanda Leigh for me."

"Yes'm."

Vera half sat, half lay in the chair with one hand curled over her upthrust belly. The faded fabric of her dress was stretched so taut I could see the nipple-like lump her navel made. I felt a wave of longing to have a child growing inside of me again. To be full to bursting with life.

"You wanna touch it?" she asked.

Embarrassed, I looked away. "No, thank you."

"You can if you want." When I hesitated, she said, "Go on. He's kicking now, you can feel it."

I went over to her. As I laid my palm against her belly, her scent enveloped me. Everyone smelled a little ripe on the farm, but Vera's odor was positively eye-watering. I stood there holding my breath and waited. For a long moment nothing happened. Then I felt two sharp kicks against my hand. I smiled, and Vera smiled back at me, and I saw the ghost of the girl she'd once been. A pretty girl, much like Alma.

"He's a feisty un," she said proudly.

"You think it's a boy?"

"I pray for it. I pray to God every day He's done sending me girls."

Florence brought out a tray with the food and drinks. Vera accepted a glass of water but waved the shortbread away. Alma looked to her mother for permission before taking a piece off the plate. I expected her to cram it in her mouth, but she nibbled at it delicately.

"Go on now," her mother said. "I need to have a word with Miz McAllan."

"There's a mockingbird's nest in that bush over there," I said.

Alma went obediently down the steps and over to the bush, and Florence went back in the house. Her footsteps didn't go far, though, and I knew she was listening.

"Your Alma's a good girl," I said.

"Thankee. You got two of your own, ain't you?"

"Yes. Isabelle's three and Amanda Leigh's five."

"I reckon they're good girls too. Reckon you'd do anything for em."

"Yes, of course I would."

Vera leaned forward. Her eyes seemed to leap out from her haggard face and grab hold of me. "Don't put us off then," she said.

"What?"

"I expect you're wanting to, on account of what Carl done last night."

"I don't know what you mean," I stammered.

"I seen that nigger walking this way earlier. I know he must a told you."

I nodded reluctantly.

"We ain't got nowhere to go if you put us off. Nobody'll hire us this late in the season."

"It's not up to me, Vera, it's up to my husband."

She laid a hand on her belly. "For this un's sake, and my other younguns', I'm asking you to keep us on."

"I'm telling you, it's not my decision."

"And if it was?"

If her eyes had accused me, I might have been able to look away from them, but they didn't. They just hoped, blindly and fiercely.

"I don't know, Vera," I said. "I have my own children to think about."

She stood up, stomach first, grunting with the effort. I stood too but didn't move to help her. I sensed she wouldn't have wanted it. "Carl never hurt nothing that weren't his own," she said. "It ain't his way. You tell that to your husband when you tell him the rest." She turned away. "Alma!" she called. "We got to be going now."

Alma came at once and helped her mother down the steps, and together they tottered across the yard to the road. I went inside. I needed to see my girls, badly. As I walked past Florence, she muttered, "That man gone burn in hell someday, but it won't be soon enough."

Amanda Leigh was reading quietly on the couch. I scooped her up and carried her into the bedroom where her sister was taking her nap. Isabelle's features looked blurred and insubstantial under the mosquito netting. I jerked it back, startling her awake, then sat down with Amanda on the bed and crushed them both to me, breathing in their little girl scent.

"What is it, Mama?" Amanda Leigh asked.

"Nothing, darling," I said. "Give your mother a kiss."

BAD NEWS IS about the only thing that travels fast in the country. I was giving Amanda Leigh her piano lesson when I heard the car pull up out front, followed by the sound of running feet. The door flew open and Henry came in, looking a little wild. "I stopped at the feed store and heard what happened," he said. "Are you all right?"

"We're fine, Henry."

The girls pelted over to him. "Daddy! Daddy!"

He knelt down and hugged them both so hard they squealed, then came over to me and took me in his arms. "I'm sorry, honey. I know you must have been scared. I'll go over there right now and tell the Atwoods they have to leave."

I hadn't known what I was going to say to him until that moment, when I found myself shaking my head. "Don't put them off," I said.

He stared at me as though I'd gone crazy. Which I undoubtedly had.

"Vera Atwood came by this morning, Henry. She's eight and a half months pregnant. If we put them off now, where would they go? How would they survive?"

A burst of harsh laughter came from the doorway. I looked up and saw Pappy standing there with a box of groceries. He came in and set them on the table. "Well ain't this a touching scene," he said. "Saint Laura, protector of women and children, begging her husband for mercy. Let me ask you this, gal. When Atwood decides to come after you, what are you gonna do then, huh?"

"He won't," I said.

"And how do you figure that?"

"Vera swore he wouldn't. She said he never hurt anything that wasn't his own."

The old man laughed again. Henry's jaw was tight as he looked at me. "This is farm business," he said.

"Honey, please. Just think it over."

"I'll go have a word with Carl tomorrow morning, see what he has to say for himself. That's all I'll promise."

"That's all I'm asking."

Henry walked toward the front door. "Next thing you know she'll be telling you what to plant," Pappy said.

"Shut up," Henry said.

I don't know who was more astonished, me or Pappy.

The next day at dinnertime, Henry told us about his meeting with Carl Atwood. Apparently the horse had gotten into the drying shed and had eaten all of Carl's tobacco. Which explained why the creature had gone so berserk, and why Carl had been so furious.

"I told him I'd keep him on through the harvest," Henry said. "But come October, they'll have to leave. A man who'll do that, who'll kill the hardworking creature that saves him from toil and puts food on his table, is a man who can't be trusted."

I thanked him and reached for his hand to give it a squeeze, but he pulled it away. "Now that Carl's got no plow horse," he said, "he'll have to use one of our mules and pay us a half share like the Cottrills. It'll mean extra money in our pocket. That's the main reason I'm keeping them on." His eyes met mine and held them. "There's no room for pity on a farm," he said.

"Yes, Henry. I understand."

I didn't understand, not at all, but I was about to go to school on the subject.

HAP

PRIDE GOETH BEFORE destruction, and a haughty spirit before a fall. Many's the time I'd sermoned on it. Many's the time I'd stood in front of a church or a tent full of people and praised the meek amongst em while warning the prideful their day of reckoning was coming sooner than they thought, oh yes, it was a-coming right quick and they would pay for their impudent ways. I should a been telling it to the mirror is what I should a been doing, if I'd a listened to my own preaching I wouldn't a ended up in such a mess. Ain't no doubt in my mind God had a hand in it. He was trying to instruct me whatall I'd been doing wrong and thinking wrong. He was saying, *Hap, you better humble down now, you been taking the blessings I've given you for granted. You been walking around thinking you better than some folks cause you ain't working on halves like they is. You been forgetting Who's in charge and who ain't. So here's what I'm gone do: I'm gone send a storm so big it rips the roof off the shed where you keep that mule you so proud of. Then I'm gone send hail big as walnuts down on that mule, making that mule crazy, making it break its leg trying to bust*

out of there. Then, just so you know for sure it's Me you deal-
ing with, the next morning after you put that mule down and
buried it and you up on the ladder trying to nail the roof back
onto the shed I'm gone let that weak top rung, the one you ain't
got around to fixing yet, I'm gone let it rot all the way through so
you fall off and break your own leg, and I'm gone send Florence
and Lilly May to a birthing and the twins out to the far end of
the field so you laying there half the day. That'll give you time
to think real hard on what I been trying to tell you.

A dead mule, a busted shed and a broke leg. That's what
pride'll get you.

I must a laid there two three hours, tried to drag myself to
the house but the pain was too bad. The sun climbed up in the
sky till it was right overhead. I closed my eyes against it and
when I opened em again there was a scowling red face hanging
over me with fire all around the edges of it, looked like a devil
face to me. I wondered if I was in hell. I must a said it out loud
cause the devil answered me.

"No, Hap," he said, "you're in Mississippi." He pulled back
some and I seen it was Henry McAllan. "I stopped by to see if
you had any storm damage."

If my leg hadn't a been hurting so bad I'd a laughed at that.
Yessuh, I guess you could say we had us a little damage.

He went and fetched Ruel and Marlon from the fields. When
they picked me up to carry me in the house I must a blacked
out cause the next thing I remember is waking up in the bed
with Florence leaning over me, tying something around my
neck.

"What you doing?" I said.

"Somebody must a worked a trick on you. We got to turn it back on em."

I looked down under my chin and seen one of her red flannel bags laying there full of God knew what, a lizard's tail or a fish eye or a nickel with a hole in it, no telling whatall she had in there. "You take that thing off a me," I told her, "I don't want none of your hoodoo devilment."

"You get well, you can take it off yourself."

"Damnit, woman!" I tried to lift myself up so I could get the bag off and pain lit out from my leg, felt like somebody taken a dull saw to it and was working it back and forth, back and forth.

"Hush now," Florence said. "You got to lay still till the doctor gets here."

"What doctor?"

"Doc Turpin. Mist McAllan went to town to fetch him."

"He won't come out here," I said. "You know that man don't like to treat colored folks."

"He will if Mist McAllan asks him to," Florence said. "Meantime I want you to drink some of this tea I made you, it'll help with the pain and the fever."

I swallowed a few spoonfuls but my belly wasn't having it and I brung it right back up again. The fellow sawing away at my leg picked up his pace and I went back out.

When I come to it was nighttime. Florence was sleeping in a chair next to the bed with a lit lantern by her feet. Her face looked beautiful and stern with the light shining up from underneath it. My wife ain't pretty in the average female way but

I like her looks just fine. Strong jaw, strong bones and a will to match em, oh yes, I seen that back when we was courting. My brothers Heck and Luther made fun of me for marrying her on account of her being taller than me and her skin being so dark. They was just like our daddy, never did think of nothing but nature affairs in choosing a woman. I tried to tell em, you don't wed a gal just to linger between her legs, there's a lot more to a married life than that, but they just laughed at me. Fools, both of em. A man can't prosper by hisself. Unless he can hold onto his wife and she holds onto him too, he won't never amount to nothing. Before I married Florence I told her, "I aim to make this a lifetime journey so if you ain't up for it just say so now and we'll stop right here."

And she said, "Let's go." So we went on and got married, that was back in '23.

She must a felt me thinking bout her cause her eyes opened. "You wasting kerosene," I said.

"I reckoned you was worth it." She reached over and felt my forehead. "You running a fever. Let's get a little food in you, then we'll try some more willowbark tea."

Her touch was gentle but I could tell by the hard set of her mouth she was vexed, and I could guess the reason for it.

"Doc Turpin never showed up, huh?" I said.

"No. Told Mist McAllan he'd try to come out tomorrow after he was done with his other patients."

I looked down at my leg. It was covered with a blanket and Florence had propped it up on a sack of cornmeal. I shifted a little and was sorry I had.

"He sent poppy juice for the pain," she said, holding up a

brown bottle. "I gave you some just before sundown. You want some more?"

"Not yet, we got to talk first. How bad is it?"

"The skin ain't broke, but still. It needs to be set by a doctor."

"I'd trust you to do it."

She shook her head. "If I did it wrong . . ." She didn't finish the thought but she didn't have to. A cripple can't make a crop, and a one-legged man ain't good for much of anything at all.

"What'd you tell Henry McAllan?" I said.

"Bout what?"

"Bout that mule."

"The truth. He could see for hisself it wasn't in the shed."

"And what did he say?"

"He asked if we'd be wanting to use one of his mules and I said what if we did for awhile. And he said then we'd have to pay him a half share instead of a quarter and I said but the fields is already broke. And he said but you still got to lay em off and fertilize and plant and if you using my mule to do it you got to pay me a full half. And I said we wouldn't be needing his mule, we'd get along just fine without it. And he said we'll see about that."

Meaning, if we couldn't get the seed in quick enough to suit him he'd make us use his mule anyway and charge us half our crop for it. Half a crop would hardly be enough to keep us all fed for a year, much less buy seed and fertilizer, much less buy us another mule. You got to have your own mule, elseways you lost. Working on halves there ain't nothing left over, end of the year come around and you got nothing in your pocket and nothing put by for the lean times. Start getting into debt with the boss, borrowing for this, borrowing for that, fore you know it he owns you. You working just to pay him back, and the harder you work the more you end up owing him.

"We ain't using Henry McAllan's mule," I said. Big words, but they was just words and we both knew it. Ruel and Marlon couldn't make a twenty-five-acre crop by themselves, they was strong hardworking boys but they was just twelve, hadn't come into their full growth yet. If Ronsel was home the three of em could a managed it, but it was too much work for two boys with no mule and I didn't have nearly enough put by for another one. Paid a hundred and thirty dollars for the one that died, reckoned on having him another ten twelve years at least.

"That's what I told him," Florence said. "I also told him I couldn't keep house for his wife no more cause I'd need to be out in the fields with the twins."

I opened my mouth to tell her no but she covered it up with her hand. "Hap, there ain't no other way and you know it. It won't kill me to do a little planting and chopping till you get to feeling better."

"I promised you I'd never ask you to do field work again."

"You ain't asking, I'm offering," she said.

"If I'd a just fixed that ladder."

"Ain't your fault," she said.

But it was my fault, for holding my head so high I couldn't see the rotted board right under my foot. Laying there in that bed, I never felt so low. The tears started to rise up and I shut my eyes to hold em in. Damned if I was gone let into eye-shedding in front of my wife.

BY THE TIME Doc Turpin finally showed up late the next day my leg was swole up bad. I'd been to him twice before, once when I got lockjaw from stepping on a rusty nail and the second time when Lilly May taken sick with lung fever. He wasn't from Marietta, he'd moved up from Florida bout five years ago, word was he was in the Klan down there. We didn't have the Klan in our part of Mississippi. They tried to come into Greenville back in '22 but Senator Percy ran em off. He was a real gentleman, Mr. Leroy Percy was, a good sort of white man. Doc Turpin was the other sort. He hated the colored race, just hated us for being alive on this earth. Problem was he was the only doctor anywhere around. You had to go all the way to Belzoni or Tchula for another doctor, either way it was a two-hour wagon ride. Sometimes you had to, depending on when you got sick. Doc Turpin only treated colored people on certain days of the week and it wasn't always the same. Time I had that lockjaw it was on a Monday and he said he couldn't see me till Wednesday, but when I took Lilly May to him it was a Friday and he told me it was my lucky day cause Friday was nigger day.

When Florence brung him in to me he told her to go wait in the other room. "Is there any way I can help you, doctor?" she asked.

"If I want something I'll tell you," he said.

I would a liked her to stay and I knew she wanted to but she

went on and left. Doc Turpin shut the door behind her and
came over to the bed. He was a fat fellow with yellow-brown
eyes and a funny little tilted-up nose, looked like it belonged
on a lady's face. "Well, boy," he said, "I heard you went and
broke your leg."

"Yessuh, I did."

"Henry McAllan sure does want to see you get well, so I
spose I'd better fix you up. You know how lucky you are to have
a landlord like Mr. McAllan?"

Seemed like every time I seen that man he was telling me
how lucky I was. I didn't feel too lucky right at that moment
but I nodded my head. He pulled the cover off a my leg and
whistled. "You sure did bust yourself up good. You been taking
that pain medicine I sent you?"

"Yessuh."

He poked my leg and I jumped. "When was the last time you
had some of it?" he said.

"Right after dinner, bout four five hours ago."

"Well, in that case, this is gonna hurt some." He reached
down into his bag and pulled out some pieces of wood and
some strips of cloth.

"Can't you give me some more medicine?" I said.

"Sure I can," he said, "but it won't take effect for another
fifteen or twenty minutes. And I don't have time to sit here and
wait on it. Mrs. Turpin's expecting me home for supper." He
handed me one of the pieces of wood, smaller than the others.
There were marks all over it in curved rows. "Put that between
your teeth," he said.

I put it in my mouth and clamped down on it. Sweat broke out all over me and I could smell my own fear, and if I could smell it I knew Doc Turpin could too. Couldn't do nothing bout that but I told myself I wasn't gone cry out, no matter what. God would see me through this like He seen me through so much else, if I just had faith in Him.

What time I am afraid, I will trust in Thee.

"Now, boy," he said, "I'd shut my eyes if I was you. And don't you move. Not if you want to keep that leg a yours." He winked at me and grabbed my leg by the knee and the ankle.

In God I will praise His word, in God I have put my trust. I will not fear what flesh can do unto me.

He pulled up sharp on my ankle and the pain come, pain so bad it made whatall I had before seem like stubbing a toe. I screamed into the stick.

Then nothing.

LAURA

WHEN HENRY TOLD ME Florence wouldn't be coming back, I felt something close to panic. It wasn't just her help around the house I'd miss, it was her company, her calm, womanly presence in my house. Yes, I had the children, and Henry in the evenings, but all three of them were unspeakably happy on the farm. Without Florence, I would be all alone with my anger, doubt and fear.

"It's only till July," Henry said. "Once the cotton's laid by, she should be able to come back."

July was three months away—an eternity. I spoke without thinking. "Can't we lend them one of our mules?"

As soon as the words were out of my mouth I regretted them. "Lend" is a dirty word for Henry, akin to the foulest profanity. He distrusts banks and pays cash for absolutely everything. At Mudbound he kept our money in a strongbox under the floorboards of our bedroom. I had no idea how much was in there, but he'd shown me where it was and told me the combination of the lock: 8-30-62, the date Confederate forces under the command of Robert E. Lee crushed the Union Army in the Battle of Richmond.

"No, we can't 'lend' them a mule," he snapped. "You don't just 'lend' somebody a mule. And I'll tell you something else, if Florence and those boys don't get that seed in real quick, they'll be using our mule all right, and paying us for the privilege."

"What do you mean?"

"Well, it's just like with the Atwoods. If they don't have a mule and they can't get the work done on time, they'll have to use one of ours. Which means they'll have to pay us a half share in cotton. It's hard luck for them, but good for us."

"We can't take advantage of them like that, Henry!"

His face reddened with outrage. "Take advantage? I'm about to let Hap Jackson use my stock to make his crop. A mule I paid good money for, that I'm still paying to keep fed. And you think I ought to let him use it for free? Maybe you think I should just give him that mule outright, on account of Hap being sick and all. Why don't we give him our car while we're at it? Hell, why don't we just give him this whole place?"

Sounded like a fine plan to me.

"I just think we owe it to them to help them, honey," I said. "After all, Hap hurt himself working for us, trying to repair our property."

"No. Hap hurt himself working for Hap. If he didn't repair that shed, *his* tools would rust, and *his* income would suffer for it. Farming's a business, Laura. And like any business, it carries risks. Hap understands that, and you need to understand it too."

"I do, but—"

"Let me put it another way," he said. "I sank everything we had into this place. Everything. We need to make some money this year. If we don't, *our* family's in trouble. Do you understand that?"

Like the Union Army at Richmond, I was utterly defeated. "Yes, Henry," I said.

He softened a little, gracious in victory. "Honey, I know this has been hard on you. We'll see about finding you a new maid just as soon as the planting's done. In the meantime, why don't you go to Greenville tomorrow and do a little shopping. Buy yourself a new hat and some Easter dresses for the girls. Take Eboline to lunch. Pappy and I can fend for ourselves for a day."

I didn't want a new hat, I didn't want to see Eboline and I especially didn't want a new maid. "All right, Henry," I said. "That sounds nice."

THE GIRLS AND I set out early the next morning. On the way I stopped at the Jacksons' to check on Hap and drop off some more food for them. I hadn't seen Florence since the day of the accident, and her haggard, unkempt appearance alarmed me.

"Hap's terrible sickly," she said. "His leg ain't healing straight and he been running a fever for three days now. I've tried everything but I can't get it to come down."

"Do you want us to get Doc Turpin back?"

"That devil! Never should a let him lay a hand on Hap in the first place. Half the colored folks who go to him end up sicker than they was before. If Hap loses his leg on account of that man . . ." She trailed off, no doubt contemplating various gruesome ends for Doc Turpin. My mind was racing in a different direction: If Hap lost his leg, I'd never get Florence back.

And so I went shopping in Greenville—not for hats and Easter dresses, but for a doctor willing to drive two hours each way to treat a colored tenant. It would have been easier to find an elephant with wings. The first two doctors I saw acted like I'd asked them to do my laundry. The third, an old man in his seventies, told me he didn't drive anymore. But as I turned to leave, he said, "There's Dr. Pearlman over on Clay Street. He might do it, he's a foreigner and a Jew. Or you could go to niggertown, they've got a doctor there."

I decided to take my chances with the Jewish foreigner, though I was unsure what to expect. Would he be competent? Would he try to cheat me? Would he even agree to treat a Negro? But my fears proved foolish. Dr. Pearlman seemed kindly and learned, and his office, though empty of patients, was well-kept. I'd barely finished explaining the situation to him before he was getting his bag and hurrying out the door. He followed me and the girls to Hap and Florence's house, where I paid him the very reasonable fee he asked and left him.

By the time we got home it was almost dark. Henry was waiting on the porch. "You girls must have bought out half of Greenville," he called out.

"Oh, we didn't find much," I said.

He walked over to the car. When he saw there were no packages, his eyebrows went up. "Didn't you get anything?"

"We got a doctor," said Amanda Leigh. "He talked funny."

"A doctor? Is somebody sick?"

I felt a flutter of nervousness. "Yes, Henry, it's Hap. His leg's not healing. The doctor was for him."

"That's what you spent your whole day doing?" he said. "Looking for a doctor for Hap Jackson?"

"I didn't set out to look for one. But there was a doctor's office right next to the dress shop, and I thought — "

"Amanda Leigh, take your sister in the house," said Henry.

They knew that tone and obeyed with alacrity, leaving me alone with him. Well, not quite alone; I saw the old man at the window, lapping up every word.

"Why didn't you come to me?" Henry asked. "Hap is my tenant, my responsibility. If he's sick, I need to know about it."

"I just happened to stop by their place on my way to town. And Florence said he'd gotten much worse, so I — "

"Did you think I wouldn't have taken care of it? That I wouldn't have gone and fetched Doc Turpin?"

He wasn't so much angry as hurt; I saw that suddenly. "No, honey, of course not," I said. "But Florence doesn't trust Doc Turpin, and since I was already in Greenville . . ."

"What do you mean, she doesn't trust him?"

"She said he didn't set Hap's leg properly."

"And you just took her word for that. The word of a colored midwife with a fifth-grade education over a medical doctor's."

Put like that, it sounded ridiculous. I had taken her word, unquestioningly. And yet, as I stood withering under the heat of my husband's gaze, I knew I'd do it again.

"Yes, Henry. I did."

"Well, I need you to do the same thing for me, your husband. To take my word for it that I'm going to do what's best for the tenants, and for you and the children. I need you to trust me, Laura." In a thick voice he added, "I never thought I'd have to ask you that."

He left me standing by the car. The sun had slipped below the horizon, and the temperature had dropped. I shivered and leaned against the hood of the DeSoto, grateful for its warmth.

HAP

WHEN I COME TO, Doc Turpin was gone and I was still alive, that was the good news. The bad news was my leg hurt like the dickens. It was all bandaged up so I couldn't see it, but I could feel it all right. Heat was coming off it and the skin felt dry and tight. That was a bad sign, I knew that from tending to mules.

"Doctor said you should get to feeling better in a day or two," Florence said.

But I didn't feel better, I felt worse and worse. The throbbing got real bad and I was in and out of sense. I remember faces floating over me, Florence's, the children's. My mama's, and she'd been laying in the clay going on twenty years. Then come a strange white man bending over me, a settle-aged man with a gray beard and one long eyebrow thick as a mustache.

"This is Doc Pearlman," Florence said. "He gone fix your leg."

He picked up my wrist and held it while he looked at his pocket watch. Then he shined a light in my eyes and put his eyeball right up next to mine and looked in there. "Your husband is in shock," he said, in a funny accent. He started shaking his head like he seen something that disgusted him, I reckoned he was mad on account of having to doctor a nigger. I didn't want no angry white man doctoring me and I told him so but he went ahead anyway and started taking the bandages off a my leg. I let into thrashing.

"Hold him still," he said to Florence.

She came and held my shoulders down. I tried to push her off me but I was too weak. I couldn't see what the doctor was doing and I had a bad feeling.

"Has he got a saw?" I asked her.

"No, Hap."

"Don't you let him cut my leg off. I know he's mad but don't you let him."

"You got to lay still now," Florence said.

The doctor bent down to me again, so close I could smell the pipeweed on his breath. "Your leg wasn't set properly, and it's in flames," he said.

"What?" I started fighting Florence again, trying to get up, but I might as well to been wrestling Goliath.

"Shh," she said. "It's just swole up is all. That's what's causing your fever."

"I'm going to make you sleep now," said the doctor. He put a little basket over my nose and mouth and dribbled some liquid on there. It had a sickly sweet smell.

"Please, Doc, I need my leg."

"Rest now, Mr. Jackson. And don't worry."

I tried to stay awake, but sleep was tugging, tugging. The

last thing I remember is him bending down to get something out of his bag. There was a little knitted cap on the back of his bald head, looked like a doily, and I wondered how he got it to stay on there. Then sleep took ahold of me and swallowed me up.

WHEN I WOKE UP it was morning and my leg still hurt, but less than before. This time I was glad of the pain till I remembered ole Waldo Murch and his arm that had to be took off back in '29. Waldo swore that arm still ached even though it wasn't there no more. I'd seen him myself plenty of times, rubbing at the air, and I wondered if it was that kind of imagine pain I was feeling. But I guess God must a decided He'd humbled me enough cause when I pulled the blanket off there was my leg, all bandaged and splinted up. I'm here to tell you, seeing you got two legs when you thought you was down to just one is a mighty glad feeling.

I could hear Florence moving around in the other room and I called out to her.

"I'm fixing your breakfast," she said. "Be right there."

She brung me a plate of brains and eggs. Soon as I smelled it my stomach let into growling, felt like I hadn't et in a week. "Take this first," she said, handing me a pill.

"What is it?"

"Pencil pills. They to keep away the infection. You got to take em twice a day till they all gone."

I swallowed the pill and tucked into the food. Florence put

her hand on my forehead. "Fever's down," she said. "You was plumb out of your head yesterday. Sure is a good thing that doctor showed up. Miz McAllan brung him all the way from Greenville."

"She went and fetched him by herself?"

"Yeah. Drove up in the car with him following her."

"When you see her, tell her we're much obliged."

She snorted. "You lucky you still got your leg after the job that butcher done on it. Doc Pearlman was considerable mad about it, I mean to tell you. Said Doc Turpin didn't deserve to be called a doctor."

"Reckon Doc Pearlman ain't from around here," I said.

"No, he's from somewhere over to Europe. Australia, I think he said."

"You mean Austria. That's the place Ronsel was where it snowed all the time."

Florence shrugged. "Whatever it's called, I'm mighty glad he ended up here instead of there."

"How long am I gone be laid up?"

"Eight to ten weeks, if there's no infection."

"Eight weeks! I can't lay here till June!"

She went on like I hadn't said a word. "Doc said we got to keep a sharp eye out for it. And you got to keep that leg real still. He's coming back on Monday to check on you, said if the swelling was down he'd make you a cast."

"How am I gone chop cotton in a cast? How am I gone preach on Sundays?"

"You ain't," Florence said. "The children and me gone do the chopping, and Junius Lee gone drive over from Tchula and do the preaching, and you gone keep your weight off a that leg like the doctor told you to. If you don't, you could wind up a cripple, or worse."

"And if I do and we have to go back to sharecropping, we'll never get out from under Henry McAllan."

"Can't worry bout that now," Florence said. "God'll see to that, one way or another. Meantime you gone do what the doctor told you."

"The contentions of a wife are a continual dropping," I said. "Proverbs 19:13."

"And a prudent wife is straight from the Lord," she shot back. "Proverbs 19:14."

Woman knows her Scripture, I'll give her that. Got no book-learning but there ain't nothing wrong with her memory.

"I better get out to the fields," she said. "Lilly May will be here if you need anything. You rest now."

Lingered along, lingered along. Laid in that bed knowing my wife was out doing my work for me. Couldn't even do my business without one of em helping me. I tried to put it off till Florence and the boys got home but one day I couldn't wait and I had to ask Lilly May to come help me with the pan. There's some things a daughter should never have to do for her daddy. Made me wish I'd a just crapped myself and set in it till Florence got home.

Meantime she and the twins was just about done in from working in the fields. Florence's hands was all blistered up and I seen her rubbing her back when she thought I wasn't looking.

She didn't complain though, nary a word, just went on and did what had to be done. They worked straight through, even on Sunday, and Florence don't hold with working on the Sabbath. They had to do it though. Had to get them fields planted before Henry McAllan decided to bring in his mule.

Monday rolled around and Doc Pearlman come back just like he said he would. He took the bandages off a my leg and looked at it. "Goot," he said, which I took to mean good. "The swelling is gone. We must make the cast now. For that I will need boiled water."

Florence sent Lilly May to do it. Meantime, Doc Pearlman was checking me all over, looking in my eyes and listening to my heart and wiggling my toes. He didn't seem to mind touching me. I wondered if all the white people in his country were like him.

"Florence says you from over to Austria," I said.

"Ya," he said. "My wife and I came here eight years ago."

Fore I could think what I was saying I said, "Our son Ronsel was there. He's a tanker, fought under General Patton."

"Then I'm grateful to him."

I shot a glance at Florence. She looked as fuddled as I was. Speaking real slow to be sure he understood me, I said, "Ronsel fought against Austrian folks."

He got a kindling look in his eye, made all the hairs on my arms stand straight up. "I hope he killed a great many of them," he said. Then he left the room to go wash his hands.

"Well, what do you make of that?" I said to Florence.

She shook her head. "All kind a crazy white people in the world."

THE RAIN CAME the next day, a big hard rain that packed the fields down tight as wax. Nothing we could do but set there and watch it and fret for two days till it finally cleared up. Florence and the children went back out to the fields, even Lilly May. Field work was hard for her with her bad foot and all but there wasn't no help for it.

I laid in the bed with my leg propped up, itching and cussing. Felt like I had a bunch of ants crawling around under my cast, looking for their next meal. There was no way to scratch either, the cast went all the way from my ankle to the top of my thigh.

I was weaving a basket out of a river birch trunk, trying to take my mind off the itching, when I heard a infernal noise and I looked out the window and seen Henry McAllan driving up on that tractor. He turned it off and got down.

"Hap?" he called out.

"Over here," I called back.

He come to the bedroom window and looked in. We howdyed and he asked how I was feeling.

"Whole lot better, thanks to that doctor Miz McAllan brung me," I said. "Sure am grateful to her for fetching him."

"I expect you are," he said. He lit a cigarette. "How much longer you gonna be in that cast?"

Behind him off in the distance I could see Florence and the children out plowing. I mean to tell you, setting there jawing with Henry McAllan while my family was toiling in the hot sun hurt me a lot worse than my leg. "Another month or so is all," I said.

"Is that a fact."

"Yessuh."

"You know, I broke my leg in the Great War. As I recollect, it was a couple of months before the cast came off, and longer than that before I could do any real work."

"I'm a fast healer, always have been," I said.

He took a drag off his cigarette. I waited, knowing what was coming. "The thing is, Hap, it's the second week of April," he said. "Y'all ought to be well into planting by now but you haven't even gotten your fields laid off."

"Soil has to be rebroke first on account of the rain."

"I'm aware of that. But if they were using a mule they'd be done in no time. As it is it'll be the end of the week before they even start fertilizing, much less getting that seed in the ground. There's just the three of them, Hap. I can't afford to wait any longer. You're a farmer, you understand that."

"It won't take that long. We got Lilly May helping too."

"A crippled little girl's not going to make the difference and you know it." He flicked his cigarette into the dirt. "You tell one of your boys to come fetch that mule after dinner today."

Then I looked on all the works that my hands had wrought, and on the labor that I had labored to do: and behold, all was vanity and vexation of spirit, and there was no profit under the sun.

"Yessuh," I said. The word stuck in my throat, but wasn't nothing else I could say. *That's it, Hap,* I told myself, *you a sharecropper again now, might as well get used to it.*

When Florence come in for dinner with the children I didn't even have to tell her, she took one look at my face and said, "He sending that mule, ain't he."

"Yeah. Starting this afternoon."

"Well," she said, "it'll make the plowing go faster anyway."

We set down to eat. It wasn't much of a meal, just fatback and grits one of the sisters from church had brung by earlier, but I said the blessing like always. When I was through Florence kept her head bent for a good long while. I knew what she was praying for. It was the same thing I'd been asking Him for every day since I fell off a that ladder: for Ronsel to come home and deliver us.

II.

LAURA

HENRY STAYED MAD at me, and he showed it by ignoring me in our bed. My husband was never an especially passionate man, but he'd always made love to me at least twice a week. In the first months of our marriage I'd felt awkward and reluctant (though I never refused him—I wouldn't have dreamed of it). But eventually we settled into an intimacy that was sweet and familiar, if not entirely fulfilling. He liked to do it at night, with one lamp on. At Mudbound it was one candle. That was his signal: the sound of the match head rasping against the striker. Joined with Henry, his body shuddering against mine, I felt very close to him and miles distant from him at the same time. He was experiencing sensations I wasn't, that much was plain to me, but I didn't expect ecstasy. I had no idea it was even possible for a woman. I hadn't always enjoyed Henry's lovemaking, but it made me feel like a true wife. I never realized how much I needed that until he turned away from me.

If my bed that April was cold, my days were hot, sweaty and grueling without Florence to help me. Henry hired Kester Cottrill's daughter Mattie Jane to come and clean for me, but she was slovenly and a chatterbox to boot, so after the first day I restricted her to laundry and other outdoor tasks. I saw Florence mostly from a distance, bent over a hoe, chopping out the weeds that threatened the tender cotton plants. Once I ran into her in town and started to complain about Mattie Jane. Florence gave me a look of incredulous scorn—*This is your idea of a problem?*—that shamed me into silence. I knew I should be grateful I wasn't spending twelve or more hours a day in the cotton fields, but it was poor consolation.

One Saturday at the end of April, the five of us went into town to do errands and have dinner at Dex's Diner, famed for its fried catfish and the sign outside that read:

JESUS LOVES YOU

MONDAY - FRIDAY 6:00-2:00

SATURDAYS 6:00-8:00

After we ate we stopped at Tricklebank's to get the week's provisions. Henry and Pappy lingered on the front porch with Orris Stokes and some other men, and the girls and I went inside to visit with the ladies. While I chatted with Rose, Amanda Leigh and Isabelle ran off to play with her two girls. Alice Stokes was there, radiantly pregnant, buying a length of poplin for a maternity dress. Wretched as I was, I couldn't bring myself to begrudge her happiness. We'd been chatting for a few minutes when a Negro soldier came in the back door. He was a tall young man with skin the color of strong tea. There were sergeant's stripes on his sleeves and a great many medals on his chest. He had a duffel bag slung over one broad shoulder.

"Howdy, Miz Tricklebank," he said. "Been a long time." His voice was sonorous and full of music. It rang out loudly in the confines of the store, startling the ladies.

"Is that you, Ronsel?" Rose said wonderingly.

He grinned. "Yes, ma'am, last time I looked."

So this was Florence's son. She'd told me all about him, of course. How smart he was, how handsome and brave. How he'd taken to book-learning like a fish to water. How he drew people to him like bees to honey, and so on. "Ain't just me talking mama nonsense," she'd declared. "Ronsel's got a shine to him, you'll see it the minute you lay eyes on him. The gals all want to be with him, and the men all want to be like him. They can't help it, they drawn to that shine."

I had thought it was mama nonsense, though I hadn't said so. What mother doesn't believe her firstborn son has more than his fair share of God's gifts? But when I saw Ronsel standing there in Tricklebank's, I understood exactly what she meant.

He dipped his head politely to me and the other ladies. "Afternoon," he said.

"Well, I declare," said Rose. "Aren't you grown up."

"How you been doing, Miz Tricklebank?"

"Getting along fine. You seen your folks yet?"

"No, ma'am," he said. "Bus just got in. I stopped to buy a few things for em."

I studied him as Rose helped him with his purchases. He

looked more like Hap, but he had Florence's way of filling up a room, and then some. You couldn't help but watch him; he had that kind of force. He glanced over at me curiously, and I realized he'd caught me staring. "I'm Mrs. McAllan," I said, a little embarrassed. "Your parents work on our farm."

"How do," he said. His eyes only met mine briefly, but in those few seconds I had the feeling I'd been thoroughly assessed.

"Do Hap and Florence know you're coming home?" I said.

"No, ma'am. I wanted to surprise em."

"Well, I know they'll be mighty glad to see you."

His forehead wrinkled in concern. "Are they all right?"

He didn't miss much, this son of Florence's. I hesitated, then told him about Hap's accident, emphasizing the positive. "He's using crutches now, and the doctor said he should be walking again by June."

"Thank God for that. He can't stand to be idle. He's probably driving Mama crazy, being underfoot all day."

Uneasily, I looked away from him. "What is it?" he asked.

I realized suddenly that the other women had gone dead silent and were watching us, making no effort at discretion. Some looked shocked, others hostile. Rose looked concerned, and her eyes held a warning.

I turned back to Ronsel. "Your parents lost their mule," I said, "and then we had a spell of bad weather. They're using our stock now. And your mother's working in the fields with your brothers."

His jaw tightened and his eyes turned cold. "Thank you for

telling me," he said. The ironic emphasis on the first two words was impossible to miss. I heard a sharp intake of breath from Alice Stokes.

"Excuse me," I said to Ronsel. "I have shopping to do."

As I walked away from him, I heard him say, "I'll come back for that cloth later, Miz Tricklebank. I better get on home now."

He paid Rose hurriedly and headed for the front door with his purchases and his duffel bag. Just before he reached the door, it opened and Pappy came in, followed by Orris Stokes and Doc Turpin. Ronsel stopped just short of running into them.

"Beg pardon," he said.

He tried to step around them, but Orris moved to stand in his way. "Well, looky here. A jig in uniform."

Ronsel's body went very still, and his eyes locked with Orris's. But then he dropped his gaze and said, "Sorry, suh. I wasn't paying attention."

"Where do you think you're going, boy?" said Doc Turpin.

"Just trying to get home to see my folks."

The door opened again, and Henry and a few other men came inside, crowding behind Pappy, Orris and Doc Turpin. All of them wore unfriendly expressions. I felt a flicker of fear.

"Honey," I called out to Henry, "this is Hap and Florence's son Ronsel, just returned from overseas."

"Well, that explains it then," drawled Pappy.

"Explains what?" said Ronsel.

"Why you're trying to leave by the front door. You must be confused as to your whereabouts."

"I ain't confused, suh."

"Oh, I think you are, boy," Pappy said. "I don't know what they let you do over there, but you're in Mississippi now. Niggers don't use the front here."

"Why don't you go out the back where you belong," said Orris.

"I think you'd better," said Henry. "Go on now."

It got very quiet. The air fairly crackled with hostility. I saw muscles tense and hands clench into fists. But if Ronsel was afraid, he didn't show it. He looked slowly around the store, meeting the eyes of every man and woman there, mine included. *Just go,* I pleaded with him silently. He let the moment drag out, waiting until just before the breaking point to speak.

"You know, suh, you're right," he said to Pappy. "We didn't go in the back over there, they put us right out in front. Right there on the front lines, face-to-face with the enemy. And that's where we stayed, the whole time we were there. The Jerries killed some of us, but in the end we kicked the hell out of em. Yessuh, we sure did."

With a nod to Rose, he turned and strode out the back door.

"Did you hear what he just said?" sputtered Pappy.

"Nigger like that ain't gonna last long around here," said Orris.

"Maybe we ought to teach him better manners," said Doc Turpin.

Things might have turned ugly, but Henry stepped forward and faced them, hands up and palms out. "No need for that. I'll have a word with his father."

For a moment I was afraid they wouldn't back down, but then Orris said, "See that you do, McAllan."

The men dispersed, and the tension lifted. I did my shopping and rounded up the girls, and we left Tricklebank's. On the way back to Mudbound, we came upon Ronsel walking down the middle of the road. He moved to one side to let us pass. As we went by him, I traded another glance with him through the open window of the car. His eyes were defiant, and they were shining.

RONSEL

HOME AGAIN, HOME AGAIN, jiggety-jig. Coon, spade, darky, nigger. Went off to fight for my country and came back to find it hadn't changed a bit. Black folks still riding in the back of the bus and coming in the back door, still picking the white folks' cotton and begging the white folks' pardon. Nevermind we'd answered their call and fought their war, to them we were still just niggers. And the black soldiers who'd died were just dead niggers.

Standing there in Tricklebank's, I knew exactly how much hot water I was in but I still couldn't shut my mouth long enough to keep myself from drowning. I was acting just like my buddy Jimmy back in our training days. I told him and told him he'd better humble down if he knew what was good for him, but Jimmy just shook his head and said he'd rather get beat up than act like a scared nigger. And he did get beat up, once in Louisiana and twice in Texas. The last time a bunch of local MPs roughed him up so bad he was in the infirmary for ten days, but Jimmy never did humble down. If we hadn't shipped out I think they might've killed him. When I told him that he just laughed and said, "I'd have liked to seen em try."

Jimmy would've been proud of me that day at Tricklebank's, but my daddy would've blistered my ears. All he knew was the Delta. He'd never walked down the street with his head held high, much less had folks lined up on either side cheering him and throwing flowers at him. The battles he'd fought were the kind nobody cheers you for winning, against sore feet and aching bones, too little rain or too much, heat and cotton worms and buried rocks that could break the blade of a plow. Ain't never a lull or a cease-fire. Win today, you got to get up tomorrow and fight the same battles all over again. Lose and you can lose everything. Only a fool fights a war with them kind of odds, or a man who ain't got no other choice.

Daddy had aged a considerable bit in the two years since I'd last seen him. There was white in his hair and new worry lines around his eyes. He'd lost weight he didn't need to lose too, Mama said that was since he broke his leg. But his voice was as strong and sure as ever. The day I got home I could hear it from way out in the yard, thanking God for the food they were about to eat and the sun He'd been sending lately to make the cotton grow, and for the health of all here present including the laying hens and the pregnant sow, and for watching over me wherever in creation I was. Which by that time was standing right in the doorway.

"Amen," I said.

For a minute nobody moved, they all just set there gawping at me like they didn't recognize me. "Well?" I said. "Ain't nobody gone offer me some supper?"

"Ronsel!" yelled Ruel, with Marlon a half second behind him like always.

Then they were up and hugging me, and Mama and Lilly May were kissing my face and carrying on about how big and handsome I was and asking me how was my trip and when did I get back to the States and how come I hadn't wrote to tell them I was on my way home. Finally Daddy hollered, "Quit fussing over him now and let him say hello to his father."

He was setting there with his leg propped up on a stool. He held out his arms and I went and gave him a big hug, then knelt down by him so he wouldn't have to look up at me.

"I knew you'd come," he said. "I prayed for it, and here you are."

"And here you are with your leg in a cast. How'd you manage to do that?"

"It's a long story. Why don't you set down and eat and I'll tell you all about it."

I couldn't help smiling. With my daddy, everything's a long story. I heaped my plate. There was salt pork and beans and pickled okra, with Mama's biscuits to sop up the juice.

"I used to daydream about these biscuits," I said. "I'd be setting on top of my tank eating my C rations—"

"What's a sea ration?" said Ruel.

"Is that some kind of fish?" said Marlon.

"C like the letter *C*, not like the ocean. It's Army food. I brought some home so you could try them. They're in my bag. Go on, you can look."

The twins ran over to my duffel bag, opening it and pulling everything out onto the floor. Still a couple of kids, though they were near as tall as me. Made me a little sad to watch them, so young and eager. I knew they wouldn't stay that way much longer.

"Anyway," I said to Mama, "I told all the guys about your biscuits. By the time the Jerries surrendered I had every man in the company dreaming of them, even the Yankee lieutenants."

"I dreamed about you," Mama said.

"What did you dream?"

She shook her head, running her hands up over her arms like she was cold.

"Tell me, Mama."

"It don't matter, none of it come true. You back with us now, safe and sound."

"Back where you belong," Daddy said.

AFTER DINNER THE two of us were having a jaw on the porch when we seen a truck coming down the road. It pulled up in our yard and Henry McAllan got out.

"Wonder what that man wants now?" said Daddy.

I got to my feet. "I reckon he wants to talk to me."

"Why in the world would Henry McAllan want to talk to you?" said Daddy.

I didn't answer. McAllan was already at the foot of the steps.

"Afternoon, Mist McAllan," said Daddy.

"Afternoon, Hap."

"Ronsel, this is our landlord. This here's my son Ronsel that I been telling you bout."

"We've met," said McAllan.

Daddy turned to me, worried now.

"I better speak with you alone, Hap," said McAllan.

"I ain't a child, sir," I said. "If you got something to say, you can say it to my face."

"All right then. Let me ask you a question. You planning on staying here and helping your father?"

"Yes, sir."

"Well, you're not helping him, acting like you did earlier at Tricklebank's. You're just helping yourself to a heap of trouble, and your family too."

"What'd you do?" asked Daddy.

"Nothing," I said. "Just tried to walk out the door is all."

"The front door," McAllan said, "and when my father and some other men objected to it he made a fine speech. Put us all in our place, didn't you?"

"Is that true?" said Daddy.

I nodded.

"Then I reckon you better apologize."

McAllan waited, his pale eyes fixed on me. I didn't have a choice and he knew it. He might as well to been God Almighty as far as we were concerned. I made myself say the words. "I'm sorry, Mr. McAllan."

"My father will want to hear it too."

"Ronsel will pay him a visit after church tomorrow," said Daddy. "Won't you, son?"

"Yes, Daddy."

"That's fine then," said McAllan. "Let me tell you something else, Ronsel. I don't hold with everything my father says, but he's right about one thing. You're back in Mississippi now, and you better start remembering it. I'm sure Hap would like to have you around here for a good long while."

"Yessuh, I would," said Daddy.

"Well then. Y'all enjoy your Saturday."

As he turned to leave, I said, "One more thing, sir."

"What?"

"We won't be needing that mule of yours much longer."

"How's that?"

"I aim to buy us one of our own just as soon as I can find a good one."

Daddy's jaw dropped. I heard a little gasp from inside the house and knew Mama was listening too. I'd wanted to buy it first and surprise them with it, but I wanted to knock Henry McAllan down a peg even more.

"Mules cost a lot of money," he said.

"I know what they cost."

McAllan looked at my father. "All right, Hap, you let me know when he finds one. In the meantime I'll rent you mine on a day-to-day basis. I'll just put it on your account and we can settle after the harvest."

"I'll settle with you in cash soon as I get that mule," I told him.

I could tell Henry McAllan didn't like that, not one bit. His voice had a sharp edge to it when he answered. "Like I said, Hap, I'll just put it on your account."

Daddy laid a hand on my arm. "Yessuh, that'll be fine," he said.

McAllan got in his truck and started up the engine. As he

was about to pull away, he called out, "Don't forget to stop by the house tomorrow, boy."

I watched the truck disappear into the falling dusk. The whippoorwills had started their pleading and the lightning bugs were winking in and out over the purpling fields. The land looked soft and welcoming, but I knew what a lie that was.

"No point in fighting em," said Daddy. "They just gone win every time."

"I ain't used to walking away from a fight. Not anymore."

"You better get used to it, son. For all our sakes."

WE FOUGHT FOR six months straight across France, Belgium, Luxembourg, Holland, Germany and Austria. With the different infantry battalions we were attached to, we killed thousands of German soldiers. It wasn't personal. The Jerries were the enemy, and while I tried to account for as many as I could, I didn't hate them. Not till the twenty-ninth of April 1945. That was the day we got to Dachau.

We didn't know what it was even, just that it was in our way. Nary one of us had ever heard of a concentration camp before. There'd been rumors floating around about Germans mistreating POWs, but we thought they were just tall tales meant to scare us into fighting harder.

By then I'd gotten my own tank command. Sam was my bow gunner. We were driving toward Munich a few miles ahead of the infantry when we caught the smell, a stink worse than anything I'd ever smelled in my life, and by that time I'd smelled plenty of corpses. About a mile later we came to a compound fenced all around by a concrete wall, looked like a regular military post from the outside. There was a big iron gate set in the wall with German writing on the top. Then we seen the people lined up in front of the gate, naked people with sticks for arms and legs. SS soldiers were walking up and down the lines, shooting them with machine guns. They were falling in waves, falling down dead right in front of us. Sam took out the soldiers while Captain Scott's tank busted down the gate.

Hundreds of people—if you can call skin scraped over a pile of bones a person—came staggering out of there. Their heads were shaved and they were filthy and covered with sores. Some of them ran off down the road but most of them were just walking around in a daze. Then they caught sight of this dead horse that'd been hit by a shell. It was like watching ants on a watermelon rind. They swarmed the carcass, ripping off pieces of it and eating them. It was horrible to see, horrible. I heard one of the guys retching behind me.

We followed the sound of gunshots to this big barnlike building. It was on fire and I could smell roasting flesh. We came around the corner and seen more SS soldiers shooting at people inside. The building was full of bodies stacked six foot high on top of one another, smoking and burning. Some of them were still alive and they were crawling over the dead ones, trying to get out. The SS soldiers were standing there just as calm as they could be, shooting anybody that moved.

We opened fire on those motherfuckers. Some of them ran and we got out of the tank and chased them down and shot them. I took out two myself, shooting them in the back as they were running away from me, and I felt nothing but glad.

I was walking back to my tank when a woman tottered over to me with her hands stretched out toward me. She had on a ragged striped shirt but she was naked from the waist down—that's the only way I could tell she was a woman. Her eyes were sunk way back in the sockets and she had sores all over her legs. She looked like a walking corpse. I started backing away from her but I stepped in a hole and fell and then she was on me, clutching me, jabbering nonstop in whatever language she spoke. I was pushing her away, yelling at her to get the fuck off me, when all the strength seemed to go out of her and she went limp. I laid there underneath her and stared up at the sky—such a pale pretty blue, like nothing bad had ever happened under it or ever could happen. Her weight on me was light as a blanket, so light she was hardly there at all. But then I felt the warmth of her body through my uniform. I ain't never been so ashamed of myself. It wasn't her fault if she seemed less than human, it was the fault of them that did this to her, and them that didn't raise a voice against it.

I sat up, trying to be careful. Her head was laying in my lap and she was looking up at me like I was her sweetheart, like the sight of me was everything she ever hoped for in this world. I rooted around in my pockets and found a chocolate bar. I unwrapped it and gave it to her. She sat up and crammed the whole thing in her mouth, like she was afraid I was going to change my mind and take it away from her. I felt a shadow on me and looked up and seen other prisoners surrounding us, dozens of them, ragged and stinking and pitiful. Some were talking and making eating motions with their hands and mouths, and some were just standing there quiet as ghosts. I was feeling around in my pockets to see what other food I had when the woman in my lap curled up into a ball, moaning and grabbing her stomach.

"What's the matter?" I said. "What's the matter with you?" But she just laid there jerking and moaning like she was gut-shot. It went on a long while and there wasn't nothing I could do. Finally she went still. I put my head on her chest and listened but I couldn't hear a heartbeat. Her eyes were wide and staring. They were blue, the same pale blue as the sky.

"Ronsel!"

I looked through the stick-thin legs of the prisoners and seen Sam walking toward me. Tears were running down his face. "Medic says not to feed em," he said. "Says it can kill em since they ain't eaten in so long."

I looked back down at her, the woman I'd just killed with a chocolate bar. I wondered what her name was and who her people were. I wondered whether anybody ever held her like I was doing, whether anybody ever stroked her hair. I hoped somebody did, before she came to this place.

I NEVER THOUGHT I'd miss it so much. I don't mean Nazi Germany, you'd have to be crazy to miss a place like that.

I mean who I was when I was over there. There I was a libera-
tor, a hero. In Mississippi I was just another nigger pushing a
plow. And the longer I stayed, the more that's all I was.

I was in town picking up some feed for the new mule when
I ran into Josie Hayes. Well, she was Josie Dupock now—she'd
gone and married Lem Dupock last September. Josie and me
used to walk out together before the war. I was real sweet on
her, even thought about marrying her. But when I joined up
she was so vexed with me she wouldn't see me or speak to me,
and I ended up leaving Marietta without saying goodbye to
her. I sent her a few letters but she never wrote back, and after
awhile I just let it go. So when I seen her there on Main Street,
I wasn't sure what to expect.

"Heard you was back," she said.

"Yeah. Got home about two months ago. How you been?"

"Been fine. I'm married now."

"Yeah, Daddy wrote and told me."

A silence came down between us. Time I knew Josie we
were always laughing and jollying. I used to tickle her till she
squealed but she never tried to get away, just wriggled and
giggled and if I stopped she'd tease me till I started up again.
She didn't look like she did much laughing now. She was still
a fine-looking gal but her eyes had hardened up, and I had a
good idea of why. Lem and me went to school together. He
was the kind always starting trouble and never ending up with
the blame, just setting off to the side smiling while the rest of
us were getting our butts switched. When we got older he was
always slipping around at the gals, had him two or three at a

time. Lem Dupock wouldn't never give a woman nothing but tears, I could've told Josie that a long time ago.

"Ain't seen you in church," I said.

"Ain't been there. Lem ain't the church-going kind."

I hesitated, then asked, "He treating you all right?"

"What's it to you, how he's treating me?"

Not a damn thing I could say to that. "Well," I said, "I'd best be getting on home, Josie. You take care of yourself."

I started to head back to the wagon but she grabbed ahold of my arm. "Don't go, Ronsel. I need to talk to you."

"What about?"

"Bout us."

"Ain't no us, Josie. You seen to that five years ago."

"Please. There's some things I want to say to you."

"I'm listening."

"Not here. Meet me tonight."

"Where?"

"My house. Lem's gone, he went down to Jackson. I ain't expecting him back till next week."

"I don't know, Josie," I said.

"Please."

I knew I shouldn't have gone over there but I went anyway. Ate the supper she fixed me and talked about old times. Let her tell me how sorry she was. Let her show me. Josie and me used to fool around some but we never laid down together. I'd imagined it plenty of times though, how it would feel to have her and to let her have me. Afterward we'd snuggle up and talk and laugh together, that was how I always pictured it.

It wasn't nothing like that. It was sad and lonesome during and stone quiet after. I thought Josie was asleep but then in a husky voice she said, "Where you gone to, Ronsel? Who you thinking bout?"

I didn't tell her the truth: that I was all the way to Germany, thinking about a white woman named Resl, and the man I was when I was with her.

HER FULL NAME was Theresia Huber, Resl was just a nickname. That surprised me at first, that the Germans would have nicknames like we did. Shows you how well the Army trained us not to think of them as human.

Resl's husband was a tanker too, he got killed at Strasbourg. That was one of the first things she asked me: "Vas you at Strasbourg?" I was glad I could tell her no. She had a six-year-old daughter, name of Maria, a shy little thing with dark blue eyes and hair white as cotton. That was how I met Resl in the first place, was through Maria. When we rolled into a town the women would send their children out to beg us for food. German or not, it was a hard thing watching hungry kids rooting around in garbage cans, so we always kept some extra rations in our mess kits. The day we got to Teisendorf there were more kids than usual swarming around our tanks. Maria was hanging back a little like she was afraid. I went over to her and asked her name. She didn't answer, I reckoned she didn't understand me, so I pointed at my chest and said "Ronsel" then pointed at hers. But she just stood there looking up at me

with eyes too big for her face. Child that age should've still had
baby fat in her cheeks but hers were hollowed out. I gave her
all my extra rations that day and the next. The third day she
took me by the hand and led me back to her house. Sam went
with me. We always went in pairs, just in case. Even though
the Jerries had surrendered, you could still run into trouble in
some of them little Bavarian towns — SS soldiers hiding out in
somebody's cellar, that kind of thing. But when we got to the
house all we found was Resl, waiting for us with hot soup and
a little old loaf of brown bread about the size of my hand. We
gave her our rations and told her we weren't hungry but she
kept on pushing the food at us. We could tell it was hurting her
feelings that we wouldn't eat so finally we had some. The soup
was mostly water with a few potatoes and onions floating in
it and the bread like to broke our teeth, but we made "mmm"
sounds and told her it was good.

"Goot!" she said. Then she smiled for the first time and my
breath caught. Resl was that sorrowful kind of pretty that's
even prettier than the happy kind. Some women get like that,
hard times just pares them down till all that's left is their
beauty. I'd seen it at home amongst my own people too but
somehow it was different over there, and not just because the
faces were white. Here was a woman who'd never wanted for a
thing in her life and now all of a sudden she had nothing — no
husband, no food, no hope. Well, not nothing, she had her
daughter and her pride, and those were the two things she
lived for.

Resl's English wasn't too good and I hardly spoke ten words

of German, but that don't matter between a man and a woman who understand each other. Up to that point I'd stayed away from the fräuleins—after whatall I seen at Dachau I just didn't want to mess with them—but plenty of the other guys had German sweethearts. Jimmy taken up with this gal, she wasn't even a fräulein, she was a frau, meaning a missus with a live husband. Jimmy met her up in Bissingen, the first town we occupied after the cease-fire, and when we left there to go to Teisendorf she followed after him. There were plenty of others like her too. I used to wonder what would make a woman want to transact herself that way, want to leave her husband and take up with a colored man who'd laid waste to her country and killed her people. But after knowing Resl awhile I started to understand it better. It wasn't just that she'd been without a man for two years and here I was giving her food and whatever else she wanted from me. That was part of it, sure, but there was more to it than that. The two of us had something in common. Her people were conquered and despised, just like mine were. And just like me, Resl was hungry to be treated like a human being.

I spent every spare minute I had at her house. With the money and provisions I gave her, she made dumplings and sauerkraut and rye bread, and sausage when we could get it. Every night after she put Maria to bed, Resl and me would set on the couch for a spell. Sometimes she'd talk in German in a low sad voice—remembering how things used to be, I guessed. Sometimes I'd tell her about the Delta: how the sky was so big it shrank you to nothing, and how in the summertime the lint from the cotton laid a fuzzy coat of white over everything in the house. Then after awhile I'd feel her tug at my hand and we'd go upstairs. I'd been with a fair number of women by that time, I never made a dog of myself like some of the guys but I'd had my share of romances. But I never felt nothing like I felt with Resl in the nights. She gave her whole self to me, didn't hold back, and before too long I didn't either. When I was on duty I'd be thinking about her the whole time, got to where I could smell her scent even when I wasn't with her. One time in the quiet after, she put her hand on my chest and whispered, "Mein Mann." I was happy to be her man and I told her so, but later I found out from Jimmy it also meant "my husband." That fretted me for a few days, till I made myself see the truth. The way we were together, we might as well to been man and wife.

So in September when most of the other guys took their discharges and headed home, I volunteered to stay in Teisendorf. Lot of greenhorns were coming over from the States to replace the guys who'd shipped out, and the Army needed seasoned men to show them the ropes. Jimmy and Sam told me I was crazy for staying, but I couldn't stand to leave Resl. First time I ever lied to my mama and daddy was when I wrote and told them the Army wasn't ready to let me go yet. I didn't like to do it but Daddy wouldn't have understood the truth. Me loving a white woman, he might've come around to that, though he would've told me I was a damn fool. But me not jumping at the first chance to come home—that, he never would've understood, not if he had a hundred years to think about it.

But then in March the Army gave me a choice: either re-enlist or ship out for the States. I wasn't about to sign up for four more years of soldiering so I took my discharge. Lot of tears over it but there wasn't nothing else I could do. I couldn't stay in Germany, and I damn sure couldn't bring Resl and Maria home with me. On the boat to New York I told myself it was just one of them things, just a wartime romance that was never meant to last, between two people who didn't have nobody else.

Till that night with Josie I even believed it.

FLORENCE

EVERY DAY I asked God, *Please send him home to us. Send him home whole and right in his mind. And if that's too much to ask of You just let him be right in his mind and not like my uncle Zeb, who come back from the Great War with all his parts but touched in the head.* One morning my mama and I went out to the yard and found all six of our hens laid out in a neat row with their necks wrung and Uncle Zeb laying sound asleep at the end of the row like he was number seven. Few weeks later he wandered off and we never laid eyes on him again.

Four years I prayed for my son to come home. The first two years we only seen him twice, that was when he was still in training in Louisiana and Texas. We was hoping he'd miss out on all the fighting but then in the summer of '44 they sent him over there, smack dab in the middle of it. Every now and then there'd be an article about his battalion in the *AFRO American* and Hap would read it out loud to me. Course by the time we got ahold of the paper it was usually a month old or more and Ronsel was long gone from wherever they was writing about.

Same with his letters, it took em forever to reach us. Whenever we got one I'd hold it in my hand and wonder if he was being shot at or lying somewhere bleeding or dead right at that moment, but the marks on the paper didn't tell me. And when the war was over and he didn't come home, them marks didn't tell me why. Ronsel was always after me to learn how to read but I don't see the point of it myself. Writing on a paper ain't flesh and blood under your roof.

But there's a old word that goes, "Be careful what you wish for or you might just get it." God answered all my prayers. He sent my son home safe and with enough money for a new mule too. We was back to working on a quarter share and I was keeping house again for Miz McAllan while Lilly May stayed home and looked after her father. (Well, I didn't exactly pray to keep Laura McAllan's house but I sure did like the extra money.) Hap was getting around good on his crutches, preaching again on Sundays and spinning his old dreams, talking bout getting a second mule and taking on more acres and saving up to buy his own land. Marlon and Ruel loved having their big brother back. They followed him around like puppies, pestering him for stories about the places he seen and the battles he was in. Oh yes, we all got our wishes, all on account of Ronsel, and all except for him.

What he wanted was to leave. He never said so—I didn't raise my children to be complainers—but I could tell he wasn't happy from the day he got home. At first I thought he was just vexed on account of that ugly business at Tricklebank's with ole Mist McAllan and them other no-count white men. Told myself he'd been away a long while and just needed to get hisself settled back in, but that didn't happen. He was jumpy and broody, and he twitched and moaned in his sleep. When he wasn't working in the fields he was writing letters to his Army friends or setting on the porch steps staring off at nothing. Didn't talk at mealtimes, wasn't chatting up the gals at church. That fretted me more than anything. What man don't want a woman's arms around him after he's just got done fighting a war?

Part of him was still fighting it, I knowed that from his sleep talk. I reckoned he seen some pretty terrible things over there and maybe done some too, things that wasn't setting easy with him. But I also knowed it wasn't just the war troubling him. It was the Delta, pressing in on him and squeezing the life right out of him. And we was too, by wanting him to stay.

Hap said that was hooey. Said I worried too much about Ronsel and always had. Maybe that was true and maybe not but I knowed my son and it wasn't like him to be so quiet. Four of my five children come peaceful into the world, but not Ronsel. When I was carrying him he squirmed all day and kicked all night. My aunt Sarah, she taught me midwifing, she said all that ruckus was a good sign, it meant the baby was healthy. "Well," I told her, "I sure am glad somebody's feeling good cause I'm plumb wore out." Then when I went into labor, Ronsel decided he was just gone stay put. I labored thirty-two hours with him. He like to tore me in two coming out and when he finally did he bout busted our ears with his squalling. Aunt Sarah didn't even have to turn him upside down and swat him, his lungs already knowed what to do.

After all that I thought I was gone have a devil baby on my hands but Ronsel was just as sweet as he could be. Strong too. Before he was even a year old he was walking. I'd set him on a pallet at the end of the row I was picking and here he'd come, toddling down that row, wanting my breast. He was always babbling and singing to hisself. His first word was *Ha!* and he said it fifty times a day, pointing at his foot or a cloud or a cotton worm, any little thing that caught his eye. By the time he was three he was talking up a storm, wanting to know everything bout everything. Come time to go to school he was always itching to go, and always hangdogging around during planting and picking time when school was closed. When he finished eighth grade his teacher come to see me, said Ronsel had a gift. Well, she wasn't telling me nothing I didn't already know. She said if we'd let him come in the afternoons she'd keep on teaching him. I had a wrangle with Hap over that, he wanted Ronsel helping him full-time in the fields. But I stood my ground, told Hap we had to let our son use whatall the Lord seen fit to give him, not just his strong back and his strong arms.

"You sure this is what you want?" Hap asked him.

"Yes, Daddy."

"You'll still have to help me till two o'clock every day and get all your chores done besides. Won't leave you no time for fishing or having fun."

"I don't mind," Ronsel said.

Hap just shook his head and let him go. And when the war come and Ronsel was hell-bent on joining the white man's army, Hap didn't understand that either but he let him.

When I looked at my children I could see me and Hap in all of em. And I loved my husband and myself too, and so I loved our children. But when I looked at Ronsel I seen something more, something me and Hap couldn't a gave him cause we ain't got it. A shine so bright it hurt your eyes sometimes but you still had to look at it.

I loved all my children, but I loved Ronsel the most. If that was a sin I reckoned God would forgive me for it, seeing as how He the one stacked the cards in the first place.

LAURA

THE COTTON BLOOMED at the end of May. It was magical, like being surrounded by thousands of little white fairies, shimmering in the sunlight. The blooms turned pink after a few days and fell off, revealing green bolls no bigger than my fingertip. They would ripen over the summer and burst open in August. My own time would come right around the new year. My morning sickness had started in early May, so I reckoned I was about two months pregnant.

I wanted to be certain before I told Henry. There was no obstetrician in Marietta, much less a hospital; most women had their babies at home with Doc Turpin. I had no intention of going that route if I could help it. I was about to ask Eboline for the name of her doctor in Greenville when I received a timely invitation from Pearce to attend Lucy's confirmation at Calvary at the end of June. Lucy was my goddaughter as well as my niece; of course I had to go. And while I was in Memphis, I would pay a visit to my old obstetrician, Dr. Brownlee.

Henry couldn't spare the time to accompany me, but he agreed to let me and the girls go for a week. Seven days in civilization! Seven days with no mud, no outhouse and no Pappy. It was a heady prospect. I would have a hot bath every day, twice a day if I wanted to. I would call people on the telephone and have afternoon tea at the Peabody and visit the Renoirs at the museum. I might even lie awake in bed at night and read a book by lamplight that didn't flicker.

Henry drove us to the train station. He went at his usual leisurely pace, slowing often to look at the farms we passed and compare the growth of their cotton, soybeans, and corn to ours. I wanted to tell him to hurry up or we'd miss the train, but I knew he couldn't help himself. Henry never had much use for nature in its untouched state. Forests didn't move him, nor mountains, nor even the sea, but show him a well-tended farm and he was breathless with excitement.

We arrived at the station with ten whole minutes to spare. Henry kissed the girls and exacted solemn promises from them to be good and mind me. Then he turned to me. "I'll miss you," he said. Time and the daily sight of his cotton thriving had thawed him considerably, though he was still touchy about his authority and had only just resumed our intimate relations in the last week.

"I wish you could come with us," I said.

As soon as the words were out of my mouth I realized they weren't true. I wanted some time away from him, not just from Pappy and the farm. I wondered if Henry suspected how I felt.

"You know I can't be away for that long, not this time of year," he said. "Besides, you girls will have more fun without me along."

"I'll write to you every day."

He bent and kissed me. "You just make sure and come back, hear? I couldn't do without you."

He said it lightly, with a smile, but I thought I detected a faint undercurrent of worry in his voice. I felt a twinge of guilt at that, but not nearly enough to make myself say, *I'm not going after all, not without you.*

The train ride seemed interminable to me. It was stiflingly hot, and the sooty air that blew through the open windows made me queasy. But to the children, who had never been on a train before, it was a grand adventure. My parents met us at the station, Daddy with a big hug and Mother with the expected flood of tears.

It was wonderful, after five months of exile, to be among my own people again. To stand in church and hear the voices of my family, young and old and in-between, ringing out on every side of me. To sit between my sisters on Etta's wicker glider and sip sweet tea while our children chased lightning bugs together in the slowgathering dusk. And best of all, to share my joyful news, once Dr. Brownlee had confirmed it, with all of them, and be the object of their tender fussing. At any other time, I might have padlocked myself to my old bed in my parents' house and thrown away the key rather than return to Mudbound. But within a few days, I began to want Henry: the groan of his weight settling onto the mattress beside me at night; the damp, heavy press of his arm across my waist; the rasp of his breathing as I fell asleep. I never felt more in love with my husband than when I was carrying his children.

I reckon that's the Lawd's doing—that's what Florence would have said.

The night before we were to return, just as I was about to turn off the bedside lamp, I heard a soft drumming of finger-nails on my door. My mother came in and sat on the edge of the bed, bringing the familiar smell of Shalimar with her. It was Daddy's favorite scent and she never wore any other, just like she never cut her hair because he liked it long. During the day she wore it pinned up, but now it hung like a girl's in a long silver plait down her back. She was seventy-one years old, and to me, as lovely as ever. And as maddeningly indirect.

"I've been thinking about your brother," she said.

"Pearce?" Pearce was the one of us she worried the most about, because he was entirely too serious and had married into money.

"No, Teddy," she said. Teddy was her favorite, though she'd always tried valiantly to hide the fact. Teddy was everybody's favorite. He was a natural clown; he didn't hesitate to spend his dignity, and we all loved him for it, even Pearce.

"What about him?"

"I was just about your age when I was carrying him, you know."

I'd heard the story many times: How she'd conceived at thir-ty-eight, after the doctor had told her she'd never have another child. How it had been the most trouble-free pregnancy and shortest labor of them all.

"The last baby came the easiest," I said, quoting the familiar ending to the story. "I hope it'll be the same for me."

"Except Teddy wasn't the last baby," my mother said in a low voice.

"What do you mean?"

"He was a twin. His little sister was stillborn ten minutes after him. She barely weighed four pounds."

"Oh, Mother. Does Teddy know?"

"No, and don't you ever tell him," she said. "I don't want it haunting him like it has me. I should have listened to the doctor, he warned me not to get pregnant again. He said I was too old, that my body couldn't take the strain, but I thought I knew better. And so that poor little child, your sister——" She broke off and looked down at her hands.

"Is that why you're telling me this?" I asked. "Because you're afraid for me?" She nodded. "But Mother, if you hadn't gotten pregnant again, you wouldn't have had Teddy. And how could any of us bear it without him? We couldn't."

She gave my hand a hard squeeze. "You just be extra careful not to strain yourself," she said. "Let Henry and your colored girl do for you, and if you feel tired, rest. You rest even if you aren't tired, for a couple of hours every afternoon. Promise me."

"I will, Mother, I promise. But you're worrying for nothing. I feel fine."

She reached out and stroked my hair just as she had when I was a child. I closed my eyes and let sleep take me, feeling utterly safe.

• • •

THE NEXT DAY, I returned to the farm, if not quite eagerly, then at least willingly. Henry was thrilled by my news. "This one will be a boy," he said. "I feel it in my bones."

I hoped his bones were right. Not that I didn't adore my girls, but I wanted the fiercer, less complicated love, unsullied by judgment and comparisons to one's own self, that my sisters had for their sons, and my brothers for their daughters.

"Well, one thing's for sure," said Florence, the day I told her I was pregnant. "You definitely carrying a male child."

"What makes you say that?"

"I've knowed for almost two months now. The signs are all there, plain as the nose on your face."

I ignored the implication that she'd known I was pregnant before I had. "What signs?" I asked.

"Well, you ain't had much morning sickness, that's one way you can tell it's a boy. And you craving meat and cheese more than sweets."

"I always do."

"Besides," she said, with a decisive wave of her hand, "the pillows on your bed are to the north."

"What difference does that make?"

The lift of her eyebrows sent a clear message: How could I possibly be so ignorant of such a universally known fact? "You'll see, six months from now," she said.

Things between the two of us were much the same as they had been, but she was noticeably stiffer around Pappy and, to a lesser extent, Henry. That was because of the trouble with Ronsel, I knew. We hadn't seen much of him since the day he'd come to apologize to the old man, and for Ronsel's sake I was glad. He and Pappy weren't oil and water, they were oil and flame. Best for all concerned if they stayed far apart.

Unfortunately I had no such option with respect to my father-in-law. He was constantly underfoot and more cantankerous than ever once Henry put him to work helping me and Florence around the house. Henry was always protective of me when I was pregnant, but this time he was positively Draconian: under no circumstances was I to risk any sort of exertion. Florence could do only so much in a day, so it fell to Pappy to help with the hauling, milking, churning and so on.

"You'd think a man would be allowed to enjoy the fruits of his labor in his old age," he said. "You'd think his family wouldn't put him to work like a nigger."

"It's only for a little while, Pappy," I said. "Just to make sure you have a healthy grandchild."

He snorted. "Just what I need. Another granddaughter."

JULY SPED BY. The weather got hotter and the cotton grew. I wasn't showing much yet, but I could feel the baby's presence inside of me, a tiny spark I fed with prayers and whispered exhortations to grow and be well. My pregnancy had completely healed the breach between Henry and me, unraveling our anger and knitting us back together again. We began to talk about what we would do when the baby was born. There was no question of our staying on the farm with an infant. Henry promised we'd look for a house to rent right after the harvest. If necessary, he said, we'd live in one of the neighboring towns, Tchula or Belzoni, even though it would mean a longer drive for him. The thought of being in a real house again was exhilarating. I began to feel a certain wistful nostalgia for Mudbound—now that I knew I was leaving it—and even occasionally to enjoy its rustic charms.

It was on such a day, an unusually balmy Saturday toward the end of July, that disaster struck. As usual when anything bad happened, Henry was away. He and Pappy had gone to Lake Village to see about some hogs, so I was alone with the girls. They were making mud pies by the pump and I was sitting under the oak mending one of Henry's shirts. There was a nice breeze and a sweet smell of poison in the air; the crop dusters had flown over that morning. I must have nodded off, because I didn't see Vera Atwood come into the yard. I woke to the sound of her girlish voice, loud and shrill. "Where's your mama at?" she was saying. "Where is she?"

"I'm right here, Vera," I said.

She whirled and looked at me. Her breath was coming in whistling gasps, and her dress was drenched with sweat. She must have run all the way to our house.

"What's the matter?" I said.

"You got to take me to town," she said. "I'm gonna kill Carl."

It was then that I saw the butcher knife in her hand. I felt a surge of raw fear. The girls were standing just a few feet away from her. I stood and said, "Come here, Vera. Come and tell me what's happened."

She came, staggering a little. The girls started to follow, but I made a shooing motion with my fingers. Amanda Leigh took her sister's hand and held her back.

"He's started in on Alma," said Vera.

"What do you mean?"

"He's started in on her just like he done with Renie. I got to stop him. You got to take me."

"He beat her?"

"No."

When I took her meaning my body went cold despite the heat. Renie was the eldest Atwood girl, the one whose baby Florence had delivered in February, just two months before Vera's own. Both children had died within a few days of being born—crib death, Florence had told me.

"He ain't gonna have Alma too, not if I can help it," Vera said.

"Where is he now?"

"He went to town to get some shotgun shells. Said he's taking her hunting this afternoon."

Just keep her talking, I thought. Henry and Pappy were due back any time now. "Hunting?" I said.

"That's how he started with Renie, taking her out to the woods with him."

"How can you be sure? That he . . . ?"

"Renie wouldn't eat nothing they brought back. Deer, rabbit, squirrel—didn't matter what it was, she wouldn't touch it. Said she wasn't hungry. But Carl sure was. Set there gobbling that food like he hadn't et in a week, gnawing on the bones and talking about how nothing tastes better than meat you hunted and brought down yourself. 'Ain't that right, Renie,' he says to her. And her setting there skinny as a rail, staring at that food like it was full of maggots."

Vera was rocking back and forth on the balls of her bare feet, the knife swinging at her side. Her head was tilted, and her eyes were wide and unfocused. She looked like a woman I'd seen once at a hypnotist's show at the state fair.

Just keep her talking. "Did you say anything to him about it?" I asked.

"No. He would have just denied it. When Renie started to show I asked her who done it but she wouldn't say, not even when I got after her with the switch. Just stood there real quiet and took it like she deserved a whupping. I knew right then but I didn't want to know. I told myself if it was a boy then it wasn't but if it was a girl then it was, that would be the proof cause Carl ain't got nothing in him but girls. And when that baby came out and I seen its parts, I knew it for his seed."

I stole a glance at Amanda Leigh and Isabelle. Their gingham dresses were spattered with mud. A streak of it ran across Isabelle's forehead where she'd brushed her bangs out of her eyes, and she was sucking on her thumb, watching us.

"Look at me," Vera demanded.

I obeyed instantly.

"You look at me," she said.

"I'm looking, Vera. I see you."

"A few days after it was born I came in the bedroom and found Carl holding it. He had his finger in its mouth and the baby was sucking on it, and Renie was laying there watching em. Right then I decided to do it."

"What?" I asked. But I knew.

"I waited till they was all asleep that night. And then I took a pillow and I sent that baby out of his reach, like I hadn't done for Renie."

"And your own baby?"

Her face contorted, and then she was standing right beside me and the knife was touching the side of my neck. I could hear my heart thundering in my ears. "You got to drive me to town *now*," she said.

Her breath smelled of rotting teeth. Fighting back nausea, I said, "Vera, listen to me. My husband will be back soon. When he gets here, we'll talk to him. Henry will know what to do."

"No," said Vera, "I can't wait. We got to go now. Come on."

She jerked me by the arm, pulling me toward the truck, but the key wasn't in it; it was hanging on a nail by the front door. Amanda Leigh and Isabelle were watching us with big frightened eyes. What would I do with them? I couldn't leave them alone on the farm—they were too little, anything might happen to them. But how could I take them with us? I didn't think Vera would harm them, but in the wild state she was in I couldn't be sure. I pictured Carl's red lips pressed to Alma's. Pictured Vera sitting next to my children in the truck with the butcher knife in her hand.

"I can't, Vera," I said.

"Why not?"

"Henry doesn't let me drive the truck. I'm not even sure where he keeps the key."

"You're lying."

"I swear it's true. The one time I tried to drive it I almost wrecked it. See that big dent there, on the front fender? I did that. Henry was so mad he took the key away."

Vera grabbed my shoulder hard. Her eyes bulged, the pupils dilated despite the brightness of the day. "I got to stop him!" she said, giving me a shake. "You got to help me stop him!"

I felt another swell of nausea. I sagged in her grip. "Vera, I can't. I don't have the key. For all I know Henry took it with him."

She let go of me, and I sank to the ground. She threw her head back and gave a keening cry. It was a sound of such desolation that I had to stop myself from running into the house and getting the key.

"Mama?" Amanda Leigh's voice, thin with fear. I glanced over at them, then back at Vera. I saw the madness drain from her face.

"Don't be scared," she said to the girls. "I ain't gonna hurt you or your mama." She turned to me. Her eyes were serene and terrible. "I'm going now," she said.

"I'll speak to Henry as soon as he gets home. He'll help you, I promise."

"It'll be too late then."

"Vera—"

"You look after them girls of yourn," she said.

She set off down the road toward town, moving at a steady lope, the knife glinting in the sun. As the girls ran over to me, I felt the first cramp hit—a mocking imitation of labor pains. I sank to my knees and pressed my hands to my stomach.

"What's the matter, Mama?" asked Amanda Leigh.

"I need you to be a big girl, and go and fetch Florence from her house. Do you know how to get there?"

She nodded solemnly.

"Hurry now," I said. "Run as fast as you can."

She went. I felt another cramp, like a fist grabbing my insides and squeezing hard, then wetness between my legs. Isabelle clung to me, sobbing. I lay in the dirt and curled my body around hers, letting her cry for both of us, and for the child who would never be her brother.

THEY FOUND CARL'S body lying in the road halfway between the farm and town. Vera had stabbed him seventeen times, then gone on to Marietta and turned herself in to Sheriff Tacker. Rose and Bill saw her walking down Main Street. They said she was covered in blood, like she'd bathed in it.

I learned these details later. At the time, I was too lost in my own agony to care about anyone else's. I lay in the bed, sleeping as many hours a day as my body would permit, waking reluctantly to lie with my face turned to the wall. I got up only to use the outhouse. Florence nursed me, cajoling me to eat and pushing clean nightgowns over my head. The children brought me gifts: wildflowers, drawings they'd made, a molted rattlesnake skin that I feigned delight with, though it repelled me. Rose paid me a couple of visits, offering news from town between awkward throat-clearings. Henry tried to comfort me when he came to bed at night, but I lay stiff against him, and after a few days he kept to his side.

A week passed in this way, then two. The children grew fretful, and Henry's compassion turned to impatience. "What's the matter with her?" I overheard him say to Florence. "Why doesn't she get up?"

"You got to give her time, Mist McAllan. That baby left a hollow place that ain't been filled back up yet."

But Florence was wrong about that. It had been filled up, and to the bursting, with rage—toward Vera and Carl, toward Henry and God, and most of all, myself. It blazed inside of me, and I fed it just like I'd fed the baby, keeping it alive with what-ifs and recriminations. If it hadn't been Florence's day off. If Henry hadn't left me alone with the girls. If he hadn't brought me to this brutal place to begin with. If I'd just listened to him when he told me there was no room for pity on a farm. I played that phrase over and over in my head like a fugue, cudgeling myself with it. Thinking of Henry's face when he walked in and found me lying in the bed, empty of our child; of the way he'd schooled his features, packing away his sorrow so I wouldn't see it and be hurt by it, letting only his tenderness show. Tenderness for me, the woman who had just lost his baby through her own stubborn foolishness. Yes, I knew miscarriages were common, especially in women my age, but I still couldn't shake the idea that the stress of Vera's assault had caused mine; that if I'd let Henry put the Atwoods off like he'd wanted to, I wouldn't have lost the baby. It had been a boy, just as we'd hoped. Florence didn't tell me and she wouldn't let me look at it, but I saw it in her face, and in Henry's.

I resumed my life some three weeks after the miscarriage, on a Monday. There was no fanfare, no scene between me and Henry, or me and Florence, in which I was lectured on my responsibilities and dragged, flailing and cursing, from my sickbed. I simply got up and went on. I bathed my sour body, combed my hair, put on a clean dress and took up my roles of wife and mother again, though without really inhabiting them. After a time I realized that inhabiting them wasn't required. As long as I did what was expected of me—cooked the meals, kissed the cuts and scrapes and made them better, accepted Henry's renewed nocturnal attentions—my family was content. I hated them for that, a little. Sometimes, in the small hours of the night, I would wake in the stifling airless heat with Henry's skin hot as a brand against mine and imagine myself getting up, dressing swiftly, going into the girls' room and brushing my lips softly against their foreheads, then taking the car key from the nail by the door, walking across the muddy yard, getting in the DeSoto and driving off—down the dirt road, across the bridge, to the gravel road, to the highway, and then straight east until the road ran into the sand. It had been so long since I'd smelled the ocean and immersed myself in that cool bluegreen.

I didn't act on this impulse, of course. But I sometimes wonder if I might have, in another week or another month, if Jamie hadn't come to live with us.

WE WEREN'T EXPECTING him; the last we'd heard he was in Rome. We'd gotten a postcard back in May with a picture of the Colosseum on the front and a hastily scrawled message on the back about how the Italian girls were almost as beautiful as Southern girls. It had made me smile, but not Henry.

"It's not right," he said, "Jamie wandering all over and not coming home."

"I know you find this hard to believe, but not everybody longs to be in rural Mississippi," I said. "Besides, he's a young man, with no responsibilities. Why shouldn't he travel if he wants to?"

"I'm telling you, it's not right," Henry repeated. "I know my brother. Something's the matter with him."

I didn't want to believe it, and so I didn't. Nothing could ever be the matter with Jamie.

He came to us in late August, in the hot, slow days before the harvest. I was the first to see him: an indistinct form, shimmering slightly in the heat, striding up the dusty road with a suitcase in each hand. He wore a hat, so I couldn't see his red hair, but I knew it was Jamie by the way he walked—back straight, shoulders steady, hips absorbing all the motion. A movie star's walk.

"Who's that?" asked Pappy, squinting through the haze of smoke that surrounded him. The two of us were sitting on the porch, me churning butter and the old man back to doing his usual nothing. The girls were playing in the yard. Henry was out in the barn, feeding the livestock.

I shook my head in answer to Pappy's question, pretending ignorance for reasons I couldn't have explained, even to myself. As Jamie got closer I began to make out details: aviator sunglasses, oval patches darkening the armpits of his white shirt, baggy trousers sagging around his narrow hips. He spotted us and lifted one suitcase in greeting.

"It's Jamie!" said Pappy, waving his cane at his son. There was nothing wrong with the old man's legs; he was spry as a fox. The cane was purely for effect, a prop he used whenever he wanted to appear patriarchal or get out of working.

"Yes, I think you're right."

"Well don't just sit there, gal! Go and greet him!"

I stood, swallowing a tart response—for once, I wanted to obey him—and walked down the steps and across the yard. I was painfully conscious of the sweat staining my own dress, of my sun-browned skin and unwashed hair. I ran my hands through it, feeling it catch on the calluses on my palms. Farmwife's hands, that's what I had now.

I was about a hundred feet away from him when Pappy hollered, "Henry! Your brother's home! Henry!"

Henry emerged from the barn holding a feed bucket. "What?" he yelled. Then he saw Jamie. He whooped, dropped the bucket and broke into a run, and so did Jamie. Henry's bad leg made him awkward, but he seemed not to notice it. He pelted forward with the joyous abandon of a schoolboy. I realized I'd never seen my husband run before. It was like glimpsing another side of him, secret and unsuspected.

They came together ten feet in front of me. Clapped each other on the back, pulled apart, searched each other's faces: ritual. I stood outside of it and waited.

"You look good, brother," Jamie said. "You always did love farming."

"You look like hell," Henry replied.

"Don't sugarcoat it, now."

"You need to put some meat on those bones of yours, get some good Mississippi sun on your face."

"That's why I'm here."

"How'd you get out here?"

"I hitched my way from Greenville. I met one of your neighbors at the general store in town. He dropped me off at the bridge."

"Why didn't Eboline drive you?"

"One of the girls wasn't feeling well. Sick headache or some such thing. Eboline said they'd be down this weekend."

"I'm glad you didn't wait," Henry said.

Jamie turned to me then, looking at me in that way he had—as if he were really seeing me and taking me in whole. He held his hands out. "Laura," he said.

I went to him and gave him a hug. He felt light against me, insubstantial. His ribs protruded like the black keys of a piano. *I could pick him up,* I thought, and had a sudden irrational urge to do so. I stepped back hastily, flustered. Aware of his eyes on me.

"Welcome home, Jamie," I said. "It's good to see you."

"You too, sweet sister-in-law. How are you liking it here in Henry's version of paradise?"

I was spared from lying by the old man. "You'd think a son would see fit to greet his father," he bellowed from the porch.

"Ah, the dear, sweet voice of our pappy," said Jamie. "I'd forgotten how much I missed hearing it."

Henry picked up one of Jamie's suitcases and we headed

toward the house. "I think he's lonely here," Henry said. "He misses Mama, and Greenville."

"Oh, is that the excuse he's using these days?"

"No. He doesn't make excuses, you know that," Henry said. "He's missed you too, Jamie."

"I just bet he has. I bet he's quit smoking and joined the NAACP, too."

I laughed at that, but Henry's reply was serious. "I'm telling you, he's missed you. He'd never admit it, but it's true."

"If you say so, brother," Jamie said, throwing an arm around Henry's shoulder. "I'm not gonna argue with you today. But I have to say, it's mighty good of you to have taken him in and put up with him all these months."

Henry shrugged. "He's our father," he said.

I felt a ripple of envy, which I saw echoed on Jamie's face. How simple things were for Henry! How I wished sometimes that I could join him in his stark, right-angled world, where everything was either right or wrong and there was no doubt which was which. What unimaginable luxury, never to wrestle with whether or why, never to lie awake nights wondering what if.

AT SUPPER THAT NIGHT, Jamie regaled us with stories about his travels overseas. He'd been as far north as Norway and as far south as Portugal, mostly by train but sometimes by bicycle or on foot. He told us about snow-skiing in the Swiss Alps: how the mountains were so tall the tops of them pierced the clouds, and the snow so thick and soft that when you fell it was like sinking into a feather bed. He took us to the sidewalk cafés of Paris, where waiters in crisp white shirts and black aprons served pastries made of a hundred layers, each thinner than a fingernail; to the bullfights in Barcelona, where the matadors were hailed as gods by roaring crowds of thousands; to the casino in Monaco, where he'd won a hundred dollars on a single hand of baccarat and sent Rita Hayworth a bottle of champagne with the winnings. He made it all sound grand and marvelous, but I couldn't help noticing how drawn he looked, and how his hands shook each time he lit one of his Lucky Strikes. He ate little, preferring to smoke one cigarette after another until the room was so hazy the children's eyes were red and watery. They didn't complain, though. They were completely under their uncle's spell, especially Isabelle, who made eyes at him all through dinner and demanded to sit in his lap afterward. I'd never seen her so smitten with anyone.

Henry was the only one of us who seemed impatient with Jamie's stories. I could tell by the crease between his eyebrows, which got deeper and deeper as the evening wore on. Finally he blurted out, "And that's what you've been doing all these months, instead of coming home?"

"I needed some time," said Jamie.

"To play in the snow and eat fancy foreign bread."

"We all heal in our own ways, brother."

Henry made a gesture that took in Jamie's appearance. "Well, if this is what you call healing, I'd hate to see what hurting is."

Jamie sighed and passed a hand across his face. The veins on the back of his hand stood out like blue cords.

"Are you hurt, Uncle Jamie?" asked Isabelle worriedly.

"Everybody was hurt some in the war, little Bella. But I'll be all right. Do you know what *bella* means?" She shook her head. "It's Italian for 'beautiful one.' I think that's what I'll call you from now on. Would you like that, Bella?"

"Yes, Uncle Jamie!"

I would heal him, I thought. I would cook food to strengthen him, play music to soothe him, tell stories to make him smile. Not the weary smile he wore tonight, but the radiant, reckless grin he'd given me on the dance floor of the Peabody Hotel so many years before.

The war had dimmed him, but I would bring him back to himself.

HENRY

THE WAR BROKE my brother—in his head, where no one could see it. Never mind all his clever banter, his flirting with Laura and the girls. I could tell he wasn't right the second I saw him. He was thin and jittery, and his eyes had a haunted look I recognized from my own time in the Army. I knew too well what kind of sights they were seeing when he shut them at night.

Jamie was thin-skinned to begin with, had been all his life. He was always looking for praise, then getting his feelings hurt when he didn't get it, or enough of it. And he never knew his own worth, not in his guts where a man needs to know it. Our father was to blame for that. He was always whittling away at Jamie, trying to make him smaller. Pappy thought he had everybody fooled, but I knew why he did it. He did it because he loved my brother like he never loved anybody else in his whole life, not even Mama, and he wanted Jamie to be just like him. And when Jamie couldn't be or wouldn't be, which was most of the time, Pappy punished him. It was a hard thing to watch, but I learned not to get in the middle of it. We all did, even Mama. Defending Jamie just made Pappy whittle harder.

Once when I was home for Christmas, Jamie must have been six or seven, we were hauling wood and we flushed a copperhead out from under the woodpile. I grabbed the axe and chopped its head off, and Jamie screamed.

"Stop acting like a goddamn sissy," Pappy said, cuffing him on the head. "You'd think I had three daughters instead of two."

Jamie squared his shoulders and pretended he didn't care—even that young, he was good at acting—but I could tell how hurt he was.

"Why do you do that?" I asked Pappy when we were alone.

"Do what?"

"Cut him down like that."

"It's for his own good," Pappy said. "You and your mother and sisters have near to ruined him with your mollycoddling. Somebody needs to toughen him up."

"He's going to hate you if you're not careful," I said.

Pappy gave me a scornful look. "When he's a man, he'll understand. And he'll thank me, you wait and see."

My father died waiting for that thanks. It gives me no satisfaction to say so.

JAMIE DIDN'T TALK to me about the war. Most men don't, who've seen real combat. It's the ones who spent their tours well behind the lines who want to tell you all about it, and the ones who never served who want to know. Our father didn't waste any time before he started in with the questions. Jamie's first night home, as soon as Laura and the girls had gone to bed, Pappy said, "So what's it like, being a big hero?"

"I wouldn't know," Jamie said.

Pappy snorted. "Don't give me that. They wrote me about your fancy medals."

Jamie's "fancy medals" included the Silver Star and the Distinguished Flying Cross, two of the highest honors an airman can receive. He never mentioned them in his letters. If the Army hadn't notified Pappy, we wouldn't have known about them.

"I was lucky," Jamie said. "A lot of guys weren't."

"Bet you got plenty of tail out of it too."

My brother just shrugged.

"Jamie never needed medals to get girls," I said.

"Damn right, he don't," Pappy said. "Takes after me that way. I didn't have two cents to rub together when your mama married me. Prettiest girl in Greenville, could've had any fellow in town, but it was me she wanted."

That was true, as far as I knew. At least, Mama had never contradicted his version of their courtship. I believe they married each other almost entirely for their looks.

"She wasn't the only one either," Pappy went on. "I had em all sniffing after me, just like you do, son."

Jamie shifted in his chair. He hated being compared to our father.

"Well one thing's for sure," Pappy said. "You must've killed a whole lot of Krauts to get all them medals."

Jamie ignored him and looked at me. "You got anything to drink around here?"

"I think I've got some whiskey somewhere."

"That'll do just fine."

I found the bottle and poured two fingers all around. Jamie downed his and refilled his glass again, twice as full as before. That surprised me. I'd never known my brother to be a drinker.

"Well?" Pappy asked. "How many'd you take out?"

"I don't know."

"Take a guess."

"I don't know," Jamie repeated. "What does it matter?"

"A man ought to know how many men he's killed."

Jamie took a hefty swig of his whiskey, then smiled unpleasantly. "I can tell you this," he said. "It was more than one."

Pappy's eyes narrowed, and I swore under my breath. Back in '34, when he was still working for the railroad, Pappy had killed a man, an escaped convict from Parchman who'd tried to rob some passengers at gunpoint. Pappy pulled his own pistol and shot him right in the eyeball. A single shot, delivered with deadeye accuracy—at least, that was how he always told it. Over the years the elements of the story had hardened into myth. The terrified women and children, and the cool-headed conductor who never felt a moment's fear. The onlookers who cheered as he carried the body off the train and dumped it at the feet of the grateful sheriff. Killing that convict was the proudest moment of our father's life. Jamie knew better than to belittle it.

"Well," Pappy said with a smirk, "at least I looked my *one* in the eye before I shot him. Not like dropping bombs from a mile up in the air."

Jamie stared tight-jawed into his glass.

"Well," I said, "time to hit the hay. We've got an early day tomorrow."

"I'll just finish my drink," Jamie said.

Pappy got up with a grunt and took one of the lanterns. "Don't wake me up when you come in," he said to Jamie.

I sat with my brother while he finished his whiskey. It didn't take him long, and when he was done his eyes flickered to the bottle like he wanted more. I took it and put it back in the cupboard. "What you need is a good night's sleep," I said. "Come on, Laura made up your bed for you."

I took the other lantern and walked him out to the lean-to. At the door I gave him a quick hug. "Welcome home, little brother."

"Thanks, Henry. I'm grateful to you and Laura for having me."

"Don't talk nonsense. We're your family, and this is your home for as long as you want, hear?"

"I can't stay long," he said.

"Why not? Where else have you got to go?"

He shook his head again and looked up at the sky. It was a cloudless night, which I was glad to see. I wanted the cotton to stay nice and dry till after the harvest. Then it could rain all it wanted to.

"Actually," Jamie said, "it was more like four miles up in the air."

"What was?"

"The altitude we dropped the bombs from."

"How can you even see anything from that high up?"

"You can see more than you'd think," he said. "Roads, cities, factories. Just not the people. From twenty thousand feet, they're not even ants." He let out a harsh laugh. It sounded exactly like our father. "How many did you kill, Henry? In the Great War?"

"I don't know exactly. Fifty, maybe sixty men."

"That's all?"

"I was only in France for six weeks before I got wounded. I was lucky, I guess."

For a long time Jamie was silent. "Pappy's right," he said finally. "A man ought to know."

After he'd gone in I shuttered the lantern and sat on the porch awhile, listening to the cotton plants rustle in the night wind. Jamie needed more than a good night's sleep, I thought. He needed a home of his own, and a sweet Southern gal to give him children and coax his roots back down into his native soil. All of that would come in good time, I had no doubt of it. But right now he needed hard work to draw the poison from his wounds. Hard work and quiet nights at home with a loving family. Laura and the girls and I would give him that. We'd help him get better.

When I went in to bed I thought she was asleep, but as soon as I was settled under the covers, her voice came soft in the dark. "How long is he planning to stay?" she asked.

"Not for long, is what he says. But I aim to change his mind."

Laura sighed, a warm gust on the back of my neck.

• • •

THE HARVEST STARTED two weeks later. The cotton plants were so heavy with bolls they could barely stand up. There must have been a hundred bolls per plant, fat and bursting with lint. The air prickled with the smell of it. Looking out over the fields, breathing that dusty cotton smell, I felt a sense of rightness I hadn't known in years, and maybe not ever. This was my land, my crop, that I'd drawn forth from the earth with my wits and labor. There's no knowledge in the world as satisfying to a man as that.

I hired eight colored families to pick for me, which was as many as I could find. Orris Stokes had been right—field labor was hard to come by, though why anybody, colored or white, would prefer the infernal stink of a factory and the squalor of a city slum to a life lived under the sun, I will never understand. The talk at Tricklebank's was all about these new picking machines they were using on some of the big plantations, but even if I could have afforded one I wouldn't have wanted it. Give me a colored picker every time. There's nothing and no one can harvest a cotton crop better. Cotton picking's been bred into the Southern Negro, bred right into his bones. You just have to watch the colored children in the fields to see that. Before they're even knee-high their fingers know what to do. Of course, picking's like any other task you give one of them, you've got to keep a close eye on them, make sure they're not snapping on you, taking the boll along with the lint to increase the weight of their haul. You take that trash to the gin, you'll get your crop downgraded right quick. Any picker we caught snapping got his pay docked by half. You better believe we had them all picking clean cotton before long.

Jamie was a big help to me. He threw himself into every task I gave him, never once complaining about the work or the heat. He pushed himself hard, too hard sometimes, but I didn't try to stop him. Moodwise, he was up and down. He'd go along fine for three or four days, then he'd have one of his nightmares and wake us all with his shouting. I'd go out there and calm him down while our father grumbled about being kept awake. Pappy thought it was a weakness of character, something Jamie could fix if he just put his mind to it. I tried to explain to Pappy what it was like, reminding him how I'd once had those same kind of nightmares myself, and I was in combat for a lot less time than Jamie.

"Your brother needs to toughen up," Pappy said. "You wouldn't see me quaking and screaming like a girl."

On the weekends Jamie would take the car and disappear for a night, sometimes two. I was pretty sure he was going to Greenville to drink and mess around with cheap women. I didn't try to stop that either. I figured he was old enough to make his own decisions. He didn't need his big brother telling him what to do anymore.

But I figured wrong. One Monday in October I was on the tractor in the south field harvesting the last of the soybeans when I saw Bill Tricklebank's truck coming up the road in a hurry. Jamie had been gone since Saturday, and I was starting to worry. When I saw Bill's truck I knew something must have happened. We didn't have a phone, so when somebody needed to reach us they called Tricklebank's.

I got down off the tractor and ran across the field to the

road. I was out of breath by the time I reached Bill. "What is it?" I said. "What's the matter?"

"The Greenville sheriff's office called," Bill said. "Your brother's been arrested. They got him in the county jail."

"What for?"

He looked away from me and mumbled something.

"Speak up, Bill!"

"Driving drunk. He hit a cow."

"A *cow*?"

"That's what they said."

"Is he hurt?"

"Just a bump on the head and some bruises, is what the deputy told me."

Relief flooded me. I gripped Bill by the shoulder and saw him wince a little. The man was thin as a dandelion stalk and about as sturdy. "Thank you, Bill. Thank you for coming out and telling me."

"That ain't all," he said. "There was a . . . young lady in the car with him."

"Was she hurt?"

"Concussion and a broke arm. Deputy said she'd be all right though."

"I'd be obliged if you and Rose would keep this to yourselves," I said.

"Sure thing, Henry. But you ought to know, Mercy's the one who placed the call."

"Damn." Mercy Ivers was the nosiest of the town's operators, with the biggest mouth. If everybody in Marietta didn't already know Jamie was in jail, I had no doubt they would by nightfall.

Bill dropped me at the house and went on his way. Laura and Pappy were waiting on the porch. I filled them in, leaving out the part about the young lady. I was sorry my wife had to know about any of it, but with the Tricklebanks and Mercy Ivers involved there was no help for it. I figured Laura would be angry, and she was—just not in the way I expected.

"After all he's done for his country," she said, "to throw him in jail like a common criminal! They ought to be ashamed."

"Well, honey, he was blind drunk."

"We don't know that," she said. "And even if he was, I'm sure he had reason to be, after all he's been through."

"What if he'd hit another car instead of a cow? Somebody could have been badly hurt."

"But nobody was," she said.

Her defending him like that nettled me. My wife was a sensible woman, but where Jamie was concerned she was as blind as every other female who ever breathed. If it had been me out driving drunk and killing livestock, you can bet she wouldn't have been nearly so forgiving.

"Henry? Was someone else hurt?"

It was on the tip of my tongue to tell her and knock him off the pedestal she'd built for him—I was that mad at both of them. Lucky for Jamie I'm no rat. "No, just him," I said.

"Well then," Laura said, "let me get some supper for you to take to him. I'm sure they haven't fed him properly." She went inside.

"You want me to come with you?" Pappy asked.

"No," I said. "I'll take care of it."

"You'll need money for bail."

"I've got enough in the strongbox."

Pappy pulled his wallet out of his pants pocket, took out a worn hundred-dollar bill and held it out to me. I gaped at it, then at him. My father was a Scot to the marrow. Parting him from money was like trying to get milk out of a mule.

"Go on, take it," he said gruffly. "But don't you tell him I gave it to you."

"Why not?"

"I don't want him expecting more."

"Whatever you say, Pappy."

AT THE GREENVILLE jail I asked to see Sheriff Partain. I knew him slightly. He and my sister Thalia had been high school sweethearts. He'd wanted to marry her, but she had her sights set higher. Caught herself a rich tobacco planter from Virginia and moved up north with him. Told everybody she'd broken Charlie Partain's heart beyond repair. For Jamie's sake, I hoped she'd been wrong. Thalia always did have an exaggerated idea of her own importance.

When the deputy led me into Charlie's office he came out from behind his desk and shook my hand, a little too hard. "Henry McAllan. How long's it been?"

"About fifteen years, give or take."

Charlie hadn't changed much in that time. He had a little

belly on him, but he was still a good-looking fellow, big and affable, with an aw-shucks smile that couldn't quite hide the ambition underneath it. A born politician.

"How you been?" he asked.

"Just fine. I'm living over to Marietta now. Got me a cotton farm there."

"So I heard."

"You've done well for yourself," I said, gesturing at the badge on his shirt. "Congratulations on winning sheriff."

"Thanks. I was an MP in the war, guess I just got a taste for the law."

"About my brother," I said.

He shook his head gravely. "Yeah, it's a bad business."

"How is he?"

"He's all right, but he's got one helluva headache. Course, drinking a whole fifth of bourbon'll do that to you."

"Can you tell me what happened, Charlie? I got the story secondhand."

He walked back behind his desk, taking his time about it, and sat down. "You know," he said, "I like to be called sheriff when I'm working. Helps me keep the job separate. You understand." His face stayed friendly, but I didn't miss the sharp glint in his eye.

"Of course. Sheriff."

"Have a seat."

I sat in the chair he gestured to, facing the desk.

"Seems your brother and a female companion were parked out east of town on Saturday night. Watching the moon is what she said." Charlie's tone indicated how much he believed that.

"Who is this gal?"

"Her name's Dottie Tipton. She's a waitress over at the Levee Hotel. Her husband Joe was a friend of mine. He died at Bastogne."

"Sorry to hear it. Jamie fought in the Battle of the Bulge too. It's where he won his Silver Star. He was a bomber pilot, you know."

"You don't say," Charlie said, crossing his arms over his chest.

So much for my efforts to impress him. I decided I'd better stick to the business at hand. "So the two of them were parked, and then what happened?"

"Well, that's where it gets kinda fuzzy. Your brother don't remember a thing, or so he claims."

"And the woman?"

"Dottie says he ran into that cow by accident when they were driving back to town. Which I might believe if we'd found it laying in the road instead of smack-dab in the middle of Tom Easterly's pasture."

"You said yourself Jamie was drunk. He probably just lost track of the road."

Charlie leaned back in his chair, putting his feet up on the desk. Enjoying himself. "Uh-huh. There's just two problems with that."

"What?"

"One, he busted through a split-rail fence. And two, he hit

that cow dead on, like he was aiming for it. Had to been going fast too. That was some mighty tenderized beef."

I shook my head, unable to imagine why Jamie would deliberately run into a cow. It made no sense at all.

"Your brother got something against livestock?" Charlie asked, with a lift of his eyebrow.

I decided to level with him. "Jamie isn't well. He hasn't been himself since he got home from the war."

"That may be," Charlie said. "But it don't give him the right to do whatever the hell he wants. To just *take* whatever he wants. He ain't in the almighty Air Corps anymore." He ground out his cigarette. "All those flyboys, thought they were such hot stuff. Strutting around in their leather jackets like they owned the world and everything in it. The way the girls chased after em, you'd have thought they were the only ones putting their necks on the line. But if you ask me, it was the men on the ground who were the real heroes. Men like Joe Tipton. Course they didn't give Joe a Silver Star. He was just an ordinary soldier."

"There's honor in that too," I said.

Charlie's lip curled. "Mighty big of you to say so, McAllan."

I wanted to punch the sneer right off his face. What stopped me was the thought of Jamie in that cell on the other side of the wall. I locked eyes with Charlie Partain. "My brother flew sixty missions into German territory," I said. "Risked his life sixty times so more of our boys could come home in one piece. Maybe not your friend Joe, but Jamie saved a whole lot of others. And now—now he's messed up in the head and he needs some time to get himself straightened out. I think he deserves that, don't you?"

"I think Joe Tipton's widow deserves better than to be treated like a whore."

Then she shouldn't act like one, I thought. "I'm sure my brother never meant her any disrespect," I said. "Like I told you, he isn't himself. But I give you my word, sheriff, if you'll drop the charges and send him home with me, you won't have any more trouble from him."

"What about Dottie's hospital bills and Tom's cow?"

"I'll take care of it. I'll do it today."

Charlie shook out a cigarette from the pack on his desk and lit it. He took three leisurely drags without saying a word. Finally he got up and walked to the door. "Dobbs!" he yelled. "Go fetch Jamie McAllan. We're releasing him."

I got up and held my hand out to him. "Thank you, sheriff. I'm much obliged."

He ignored my hand and my thanks both. "Tell your brother to stay away from Dottie, and from Greenville," he said. "If I catch him making trouble here again, he'll be the one who needs saving."

WHEN THEY BROUGHT him out to me he wouldn't meet my eyes, just stammered an apology while Charlie Partain and his deputy watched. He reeked of whiskey and vomit. He looked like hell too. There was a bad gash on his forehead and one eye was swollen nearly shut.

Still, he was in better shape than the DeSoto, which they'd taken to the municipal pound. We went there first, intending to pick it up, but I didn't need a mechanic to tell me it was undrivable. The front end was collapsed like an overripe pumpkin, and the engine was a mangled mess. Jamie's face went white when he saw it.

"Jesus, did I do that?"

"Yeah, you did," I said. "What the hell happened?"

"I don't know. The last thing I remember is Dolly telling me to slow down."

"Her name's Dottie. And you put her in the hospital."

"I know, they told me," he said in a low voice. "But I'm gonna make it up to her, and to you. I swear it."

"You can make it up to me all you want, but you're never to see her again."

"Says who?"

"Charlie Partain. Her husband was a friend of his."

"I wondered why he was so pissed off. He gave me this shiner, you know."

"He hit you? That son of a bitch."

"I reckon I deserved it."

He looked so hunched and miserable. "Next time, do me a favor," I said.

"What?"

"Go after a rabbit, will you?"

It took him a few seconds but then he started laughing, and so did I. The two of us laughed till tears ran down our faces, like we hadn't done in years. And if Jamie's face stayed wet for a time after we were done, I pretended not to notice.

I dropped him at the Levee Hotel, where he'd been staying. While he was getting cleaned up I drove over to the hospital and paid Dottie Tipton's bill. They were sending her home that afternoon, which I was glad to hear. I didn't visit her—what in the world would I have said?—but I asked one of the nurses to tell her Jamie was sorry and hoped she'd get better soon.

When I picked him up he looked and smelled a little better. We stopped at Tom Easterly's place on the way out of town. Bastard wanted two hundred dollars for his cow, which was a good fifty dollars more than it or any other cow was worth, but I thought of Charlie Partain and paid it. The whole thing ended up costing me close to three hundred dollars, not counting the car. Figured I was looking at another four hundred minimum to fix it, and double that if I had to replace it. I'd planned on spending that money on a rent house for Laura and the girls, but now that wouldn't be possible.

All the way home I dreaded telling her, dreaded seeing that disappointed look on her face.

"We're tapped out," I said, when we were alone in bed. "Even with a good harvest, there won't be enough for a house in town this year. I'm sorry, honey."

She didn't say a word, and I couldn't see her expression in the dark.

"The good news is, Jamie's promised to stay another six months to make it up to us. With his help, I should be able to put enough by that we can get a house next year."

She sighed and got out of bed. I heard her bare feet scuffing on the floor, down to the foot of the bed and around to my side. Then I heard a familiar scraping sound and saw a match flare. She lit the candle, parted the mosquito netting and got in, squeezing in next to me. Her arm went around me.

"It's all right, Henry," she whispered. "I don't mind it so much."

I felt her lips on my neck, and her hand slip down into my pajamas.

JAMIE

BECAUSE OF HENRY. Somehow it always comes back to that.

There I was again, indebted to him for pulling my ass out of the sling I'd custom-made to hold it. He wouldn't tell me how much he was out on my account, but I figured it was close to a thousand bucks.

Henry wasn't the only one I owed. Thanks to me, Laura didn't get her house in town, her indoor toilet and grass lawn. Instead she got another year of stink and muck. She never reproached me for it, though, never even raised an eyebrow at me. She welcomed me home as sweetly as if I were returning from church and not the county jail. A lot of women act sweet, but with most of them that's all it is, an act they learn young and hone to perfection by the time they're twenty-one. My sisters were both masters of the craft, but Laura was something else altogether. She was sweet to the core.

Then there was Dottie Tipton. I snuck into Greenville to see her a week after the accident. (That's how everybody except my father referred to it—"the accident." Pappy referred to it as "your drunken rampage" and took to calling me "the cow-slayer.") Dottie was tickled pink to see me. Nothing was too good for the man who'd given her a concussion and put her arm in a cast. She changed her dress and put on lipstick, one-handedly fixed me a drink in a crystal highball, fussed over my bruises. Was I sure I wasn't hungry? She'd be happy to whip up a little something, it would be no trouble at all. I pictured us sitting at her dining room table eating supper off her wedding china, no doubt with dessert afterward in her bedroom. The urge to leap up and run out the door was as powerful as anything I'd ever felt before battle. It was Dottie's dead husband who stopped me. Joe Tipton stared out at me from his silver frame on the mantel, his expression stern under the cap of his uniform. *Don't you do it, you craven son of a bitch,* that expression said. So I stayed awhile and had a few drinks and laughs with her. The drinks made the laughs come easier, and the lies too. When it was time to say goodbye, I was tender and rueful—Antony to her Cleopatra. *Bravo,* said Joe. *Now get the fuck out.* Dottie clung to me a little when I told her I could never see her again, but she didn't cry. Another thing I owed her for.

All those people whose lives I'd careened into—just like that, they let me off the hook. All that was left was for me to do the same, and that wasn't hard. Booze helped, and remembering: Flaming planes trailing black smoke, falling from the sky. Men falling from the planes, falling with their chutes on fire, falling with no chutes at all, throwing themselves out of the planes rather than be burned alive. The *wuff wuff wuff* of enemy flak, ripping them all to pieces, the falling planes and falling men and pieces of men.

They say you have to hate to be in the infantry, but that wasn't true in the Air Corps. We never saw the faces of our enemies. When I thought of them at all, I pictured blank white ovals framed by blond crew cuts—never bangs or curls or pigtails, though I knew our bombs fell on plenty of women and kids too. Sometimes we just picked a big city and blasted the hell out of it. Other times, if we couldn't get to our primary target, usually a military installation or factory, we went after a "target of opportunity" instead. We called them AWMs, short for "Auf Wiedersehen, Motherfuckers." There was an unspoken rule never to bring the bombs back home. My last run, thunderstorms kept us from reaching the munitions depot we were supposed to hit, so we ended up dumping our full load on a big park full of refugees. We knew from our intelligence briefing that there were SS soldiers there, seeking cover among the civilians. Still, we killed thousands of innocent people along with them. When we got back to base and made our strike report to the CO, he congratulated us on a job well done.

A few seconds before I hit that cow it turned its head and looked straight at me. It could have moved, but it didn't. It just stood there watching me as I bore down on it.

I GUESS I COULD have talked to Henry about the war, but whenever I started to bring it up I found myself cracking a joke or making up a story instead. He wouldn't have understood what I felt. The horror, yes, but not the guilt, and certainly not the urge I'd sometimes had to drive my plane into an enemy fighter and turn us both into a small sun. Henry, longing for oblivion—the very idea of it was laughable. What my brother longed for was right under his feet. He scraped it from his boots every night with tender care. The farm was his element, just as the sky had once been mine. That was the other reason I didn't confide in him: I didn't want to muddy his happiness.

Whiskey was the only thing that kept the nightmares at bay. After the accident I knew Henry, Laura and Pappy were all keeping a close eye on me, so I was careful never to have more than a couple of beers in front of them. I did my real drinking in secret. I had bottles stashed everywhere—on top of the outhouse, out in the barn, under a floorboard on the front porch—and I always carried a tin of lemon drops to hide the smell on my breath. I never got falling-down drunk, just maintained a nice steady infusion throughout the day. A lot of it I sweated out. The rest I put to use. I was the designated charmer of the household, the one responsible for keeping everybody else's spirits up. To play my part I needed booze.

I played it brilliantly, if I do say so myself. None of them guessed my secret, except for Florence Jackson. Her sharp eyes didn't miss much. One time I discovered a half-full bottle of Jack Daniel's tucked underneath my pillow, like a gift from the Bourbon Fairy. I knew it was Florence who'd put it there because it was washing day and the sheets had been changed. I must have left it somewhere, and she'd found it and returned it to me. This one act of kindness aside, she didn't much like me.

I tried to win her over, but she was immune to my charm—one of the only women I'd ever met who was. I think she must have sensed the part I would play in the events to come. Henry would scoff at me for saying so, but I believe Negroes have an innate ability that us white people lack to sense things, a kind of bone-sense. It's different from head-sense, which we have more of than they do, and it comes from an older, darker place.

Florence may have sensed something, but I had no idea of what I was setting in motion the day I gave Ronsel Jackson a lift from town. It was just after the new year. I'd been back in Mississippi for four months, but it felt more like four years. I drove into Marietta to get my hair cut and pick up some groceries for Laura, and some bourbon for me. Usually I bought my liquor in Tchula or Belzoni, but that day I didn't have time. I was coming out of Tricklebank's with my purchases when I heard a loud explosion off to my left. I hit the ground, covering my head with my hands and dropping the box of groceries, which spilled out into the street.

"It's all right," said a deep voice behind me. "It was just a car." A tall Negro in overalls stepped out from behind a parked truck. He pointed at an old Ford Model A moving away from us down the street. "It backfired, is all," he said. "Must've had a stuck intake valve." Belatedly I recognized Ronsel Jackson. I'd only spoken to him a couple of times and only about farm business, but I knew from Henry that he'd fought in one of the colored battalions.

Somebody chuckled, and I looked up to see a dozen pairs of

eyes staring at us from under hat brims. All the Saturday afternoon regulars were on the porch at Tricklebank's, exchanging opinions on whatever passed for news in Marietta—at the moment, no doubt, that crazy brother of Henry McAllan's, the one who killed that cow over to Greenville. Hot-faced, I bent down and started putting the groceries back in the box. Ronsel helped me, handing me some oranges that had rolled his way. The flour sack had come untied, spilling half its contents onto the dirt, but the whiskey was mercifully intact. When I picked it up, my hands were shaking so hard I dropped it again.

If Ronsel had said anything, if he'd even made a sound that was meant to be sympathetic or soothing, I might have hauled off and hit him—God knows I wanted to hit somebody. He didn't give me the excuse, though. He just held his own hand out, palm down, so I could see it was shaking every bit as bad as mine. I saw the same frustration in his face that I was feeling, and the same rage, maybe more.

"Reckon it'll ever stop?" he asked, looking down at his hand.

"They say it does eventually," I said. "Did you walk here?"

"Yessuh. Daddy's using the mule to break the fields."

"Come on, I'll give you a lift."

He headed for the bed of the truck. I was about to tell him he could ride up front with me—it was cold out and starting to drizzle—but then I saw the men on the porch watching us, and I remembered Henry mentioning that Ronsel had gotten into some trouble here awhile back. I waited till we were out of town, then I pulled over, stuck my head out the window and called out, "Why don't you come on up front?"

"I'm doing just fine back here," he called back.

The drizzle had turned into a steady rain. I couldn't see him, but he had to be cold and wet, and getting more so by the minute. "Get in, soldier!" I yelled. "That's an order!"

I felt the truck rock as he jumped off, then the passenger door opened and he got in, smelling of wet wool and sweat. I expected him to thank me. What he said was, "How do you know you outranked me?"

I laughed. "You obeyed my order, didn't you? Besides, I was a captain."

His chin came up. "There were Negro captains," he said. "I served under plenty of em."

"Let me guess. You were a sergeant."

"That's right," he said.

I reached into the box sitting between us, uncorked the whiskey and took a good long swallow. "Well, sergeant, how do you like being back here in the Delta?"

He didn't answer, just turned his head and stared out the side window. At first I thought I'd ruffled his feathers, but then I realized he was giving me privacy in which to drink. *A fine fellow, this Ronsel Jackson,* I thought, taking another swig. Then I had a second, more accurate realization: He wasn't looking at me because he figured I wasn't going to offer him any. He was protecting his dignity and giving me the leeway to be a son of a bitch at the same time. Annoyed, I thrust the bottle at him. "Here, have a snort."

"No thanks," he said.

"Are you always this stubborn, or is it just around white people who are trying to be nice to you?"

He accepted the bottle and took a quick sip, his eyes never leaving my face. The truth was, not that long ago I wouldn't have offered him any, not unless it was the last swig in the bottle. I wasn't sure whether it was a good or a bad thing that I didn't care anymore.

"What kind of an NCO are you?" I said, when he tried to hand the bottle back to me after that one little sip. This time he took a big snort, so big he choked and spilled some on his overalls. "Don't waste it, now," I said. "That's my medicine, I need every drop."

When I took the bottle back from him, I saw him notice my missing finger. "You get that in the war?" he asked.

"Yeah. Frostbite."

"How does a pilot manage to get frostbite?"

"You got any idea how cold it is at twenty thousand feet, with the wind blowing through like fury? I'm talking twenty, thirty below zero."

"Why'd you leave the window open?"

"Had to. There were no wipers. When it rained, you had to stick your head out the window to see."

He shook his head. "And I thought I had it bad, being stuck inside a rolling tin can."

"You were a tanker?"

"Sure was. Spearheaded for Patton."

"You ever piss in your helmet?"

"Yeah, plenty of times."

"We had relief tubes in the cockpit but sometimes it was easier just to use our flak helmets. And at twenty thousand

feet that piss freezes solid in less than a minute. One time I
went in my helmet and forgot all about it. It was a long haul.
When we got close to the target I put the helmet back on. We
did the bombing run and were dodging enemy flak when I felt
something wet running down my face. And then I smelled it
and realized what it was."

Ronsel gave a big booming laugh. "You must a caught hell
back at the Officers' Club."

"My buddies never let me hear the end of it. The ones who
survived, that is."

"Yeah. I hear you."

It was nearing dark and cold enough that I could see his
breath and mine, mingling in the air. I put the truck in gear
and we drove the rest of the way to the farm in silence, letting the bourbon be our conversation, back and forth. When
we pulled up to the Jackson place, Hap was outside filling a
bucket at the pump. The look of alarm on his face when he
saw his son in the cab of the truck was so exaggerated it was
comical.

I rolled down my window. "Evening, Hap."

"Everything all right, Mist Jamie?"

"Everything's fine. I just gave Ronsel here a lift from town."

Ronsel opened the door and got out, a bit unsteadily.
"Thanks for the ride," he said.

"You're welcome." As he was about to shut the door, I said,
"I expect I'll be heading into town again next Saturday afternoon. If you like I'll stop by here, see if you want a ride."

Ronsel glanced at his father, then back at me. He nodded

his head once, as solemnly as a judge. And in that moment, sealed his fate.

Maybe that's cowardly of me, making Ronsel's the trigger finger. There are other ways to look at it, other turning points I could pick, eeny, meeny, miny, moe: When that car backfired. When he got in the cab of the truck. When I handed him the whiskey. But I think it was right then, when he stood half-drunk in the rain and nodded his head. And I believe Ronsel would tell you the same thing, if you could ask him, and he could answer.

III.

LAURA

I FELL IN LOVE with my brother-in-law the way you fall asleep in the car when someone you trust is driving—gradually, by imperceptible degrees, letting the motion lull your eyes closed. *Letting,* that's the key word. I could have stopped myself. I could have shoved those feelings into some dark corner of my mind and locked them away, as I'd done with so many other feelings I'd found troubling. I tried to, for a time, but it was a halfhearted effort at best, doomed to failure.

Jamie set about making me love him from the first day he arrived. Complimenting me on my cooking and doing little things for me around the house. Things that said, *I see you. I think about what might please you.* I was starved for that kind of attention, and I soaked it up like a biscuit soaks up gravy. Henry was never a thoughtful man, not in the small, everyday ways that mean so much to a woman. In Memphis, surrounded by dozens of doting Chappells and Fairbairns, I hadn't minded so much, but at Mudbound I'd felt the lack of attention keenly. Henry was wholly preoccupied with the farm. I would have gotten more notice from him if I'd grown a tail and started to bray.

I want to make one thing clear: When I say that Jamie set about making me love him, I don't mean that he seduced me. Oh, he flirted with me plenty, but he flirted with everybody, even the men. He liked to win people. That makes it sound like a game, and perhaps to a certain type of man it is, but Jamie was no rake. He *needed* to win them. I didn't see that then. I saw only the way he leaned forward whenever I spoke, his head cocked slightly to one side as if to better catch my words. I saw the wildflowers he left for me in a milk bottle on the kitchen table, and the happy smiles of my children when he teased them.

Isabelle was his pet, and I was glad of it. I could never love her enough or give her enough attention. Jamie saw her need and met it with extravagant affection, which she returned in full measure. When he was in the room, none of the rest of us existed for her. He'd come in dirty and worn out from the fields, and she'd hold her chubby arms up to him like a Baptist preacher calling on the Almighty. Jamie would shake his head and say, "I'm too tired to hold you tonight, little Bella." She'd stamp her foot imperiously and reach for him, knowing better, and he'd swoop down and gather her into his arms, twirling her around and around while she squealed with delight. It wasn't just that he loved her; it was that he loved *her*, in particular. That was everything to her. Before long, she was insisting we all call her Bella. She refused to answer to Isabelle, even after Henry spanked her bottom for it. But she's his child as well as mine, at least in stubbornness, and eventually she got her way.

Even dimmed as he was, Jamie charmed and leavened us all. Pappy carped less, and Henry laughed more often and slept more soundly. I came alive again, like I hadn't been since before the miscarriage. I was less resentful of Henry and less mindful of the privations of the farm. He must have known Jamie was the cause of my improved spirits, but if it bothered him he didn't let on. He seemed to accept that Jamie "made the girls sparkle," as he'd told me all those years ago. It would have been unthinkable to Henry that his wife would have sexual feelings for his little brother.

And that's exactly what I was having: sexual feelings, of an intensity I'd never experienced in my life. Anything could bring them on: slicing a tomato, pulling weeds in the garden, running a comb through my hair. My senses were acute. Food was more succulent and smells more pungent. I was hungrier than usual and perspired more often. Not even pregnancy had made my body so strange to me.

Even so, it all might have come to nothing if Jamie hadn't built the shower for me. That shower became the crucible of my feelings for him. To understand why, you have to imagine life without running water or bathrooms. It was an all-day undertaking to get the whole family clean, so we bathed only on Saturdays. During the summer months I filled the tub and let the morning sun warm the water. I bathed the girls first, then myself, praying nobody would come calling while I was naked. For privacy we hung sheets from two clotheslines, placing the tub between them—an arrangement that left the bather exposed on two sides and gave the whole country an eyeful on

windy days. After my bath I refilled the tub for Pappy. When
he was done, I emptied and refilled it again—sometimes with
the old man's grudging help, but more often by myself—for
when Henry and Jamie came in from the fields. In the winter, the tub had to be dragged into the kitchen and the water
hauled in and heated on the stove. Still, for all the work involved, Saturday was my favorite day of the week. It was the
only day I felt truly clean.

The rest of the time, we stank. You can say all you want
about honest sweat, but it smells just as bad as any other kind.
Henry didn't seem to mind, but I never got used to it. I remembered my little bathroom on Evergreen Street with swooning
nostalgia. I'd taken it completely for granted, even grumbled
occasionally about the poor water pressure and the chips in
the porcelain tub. Now, as I took my hasty spit baths from a
pail of cold water in the kitchen, that little bathroom seemed
a place of impossible luxury.

The worst time for me was during my menses. The musky-
sweet reek of my blood on the cloths I wore seemed to fill
the house until I could hardly breathe. I'd wait each night for
the others to fall asleep, then tiptoe to the kitchen to wash the
cloths and myself. One night, as I squatted over the basin with
my nightgown bunched around my waist and my hand moving awkwardly between my legs, Henry walked in on me. He
turned quickly and left, but oh, how ashamed I was!

Jamie must have guessed how I felt. One day in March, I
returned from an overnight shopping trip to Greenville to dis-

cover a narrow wooden stall in back of the house, with a large
bucket attached to a pulley contraption mounted on top. Jamie
was just finishing it when the girls and I pulled up in the car.

"What is it, Uncle Jamie?" asked Amanda Leigh.

"It's a shower, little petunia."

"I don't like showers, I like baths!" cried Bella.

"I didn't build it for you, honey. I built it for your mama."

Bella frowned at that. Jamie tousled her hair, but his eyes
were on me. "Well," he said, "what do you think?"

"I think it's the most marvelous thing I've ever seen."

And it was. Of course, like everything at Mudbound, the
shower required some effort. You still had to heat water on the
stove and haul it outside—two or three bucketfuls, depending
on whether or not you were washing your hair. You lowered
the big shower bucket, poured the hot water in, then raised
it again by pulling on a rope attached to the pulley. Then you
went in the stall and got undressed, draping your clothes over
the walls. When you were ready, you tugged gently on a second
rope attached to the bucket's lip, tilting it and releasing just
enough water so you could soap yourself. Finally, you pulled on
the rope again and rinsed until all the water was gone.

I had my first shower that very evening. It was one of those
warm soft nights in early spring when the air itself seems like
a living being, surrounding and gently supporting you. As soon
as I stepped into the stall and closed the door, I was in a private universe. On the other side of the walls, I could hear the
deep thrumming of insects and frogs, the constant music of the

Delta, and more distantly, the men's voices interwoven with the sound of Amanda Leigh practicing her piano scales. I took off my clothes and just stood there for several minutes in that warm, embracing air. Overhead floated large clouds, stained fantastic hues of pink and gold by the setting sun. I pulled the rope and felt the water stream down my body and thought of my brother-in-law, of his hands sawing the planks, fitting them together, nailing them down. He'd even made me a soap dish, I saw. It was slatted at the bottom and held a small bar of embossed purple soap, the kind they had in fancy stores in Memphis. When I brought it to my nose I smelled the dusky, pungent sweetness of lavender. It was my favorite scent; I'd mentioned it to Jamie once, years ago. And he had remembered.

I ran the soap across my body and wondered: as he was building the shower, had he imagined me in it like this, naked and free under the darkening sky? I don't know what shocked me more, the thought itself, or the heavy ripple of pleasure it sent through me.

HENRY WAS THE beneficiary of all this newfound ardor. He'd almost always been the one to initiate our lovemaking, but now I found myself seeking him out in our bed, to his surprise and my own. Sometimes he would refuse me. He never gave an explanation, just took my exploring hand and returned it to my own side of the bed, patting it dismissively before he turned away. The anger that filled me on those nights was so hot and raw I was surprised it didn't set the bed ablaze. I'd never refused him, not once in all the years of our marriage. How dared he push me aside like an unwanted pet?

I tried to keep my feelings for Jamie secret, but I've never been good at subterfuge; my father used to call me his little trumpeter for the way my face proclaimed my every emotion. One day Florence and I were working in the house together, me cooking and her sorting laundry, and she said, "Mist Jamie doing some better."

"Yes," I said, "I think he is."

Seven months on the farm had done him good. I had no illusions that he was completely healed, but he was having fewer nightmares, and physically he seemed stronger. My cooking had put some meat on him; I was especially proud of that.

"He got hisself a woman, that's why," Florence said, with a sly smile.

I felt a constriction in my throat, like a stone was lodged there. "What are you talking about?"

"See here?" She held up one of his shirts. There was a smudge of red on the collar.

"That's blood," I said. "He probably cut himself shaving." But I knew better. Dried blood would have been brown.

"Well, it sure is some mighty sweet-smelling blood then," said Florence.

The stone in my throat seemed to swell until I could hardly swallow.

"Ain't good for a man to be without a woman," she went on

conversationally. "Now a woman, she likes a man, but she can get along just fine without him. The Almighty seen to that. But a man ain't never gone thrive without a woman by his side. He be looking high and low till he find one. Course Mist Jamie, he the kind come by em easy. They be lined up like daisies on the side of the road, just waiting for him to pluck em. He just got to reach out his hand and—"

"Shut your mouth," I said. "I won't listen to another word of such low talk."

We stared at each other for a moment, then Florence dropped her gaze, but not before I saw the knowing look in her dark eyes. "Now go and fetch some water," I said. "I want to make some coffee."

She obeyed, moving with an unhurriedness that bordered on insolent. When the front door closed behind her, I went to the table and picked up the shirt. I raised it to my nose and smelled the cloying scent of lily-of-the-valley perfume. I tried to imagine the type of woman who would wear that scent. Her dresses would be low-cut and her fingernails would be painted the same shade of carmine as her lipstick. She'd have a throaty laugh and smoke cigarettes from a long holder and let her slip show on purpose when she crossed her legs. She'd be nothing but a cheap little tramp, I thought.

"Smell something you like, gal?" I turned and saw Pappy framed in the front window. I felt my cheeks flame. How long had he been standing there, and how much had he overheard? Long enough and plenty, judging by the smirk on his face.

Nonchalantly, or so I hoped, I dropped the shirt into the

basket. "Just sweat," I said. "You know, the odor that comes from a person's body when they do work of some kind? Perhaps you've heard of it."

I left the room before he could reply.

THE TROUBLE STARTED the first Saturday in April. I was driving the old man to town when we encountered Jamie coming the other way in the truck. As we drew closer I could see Ronsel Jackson in the passenger seat. He'd wisely kept his head down in the year since he'd been home. We rarely saw him, except as a distant figure in the fields, hunched over his plow. That view of him seemed to have appeased Pappy; at least, he'd stopped ranting about "that smart-mouthed nigger" on a daily basis.

"Who's that with Jamie?" Pappy said, squinting at them.

The old man was too vain to wear glasses in public, so he often depended on us to be his eyes. For once, I was glad. "I don't know," I said. "I can't make him out."

The road was too narrow for two vehicles to pass. Jamie pulled the truck over to let us by, and I was forced to slow to a crawl. As we passed them, Jamie raised his hand in greeting. Ronsel sat beside him, looking straight ahead.

"Stop the car!" Pappy ordered. I braked, but Jamie drove on. Pappy's head whipped around to follow the truck through the rear window. "Did you see that? I think he had that nigger with him."

"Who do you mean?"

"The Jackson boy, the one with the big mouth. You didn't see him?"

"No. The sun was in my eyes."

Pappy turned to me, fixing me with his basilisk stare. "You lying to me, gal?"

"Of course not, Pappy," I replied, with all the innocence I could muster.

He grunted and faced forward, crossing his arms over his chest. "I'll tell you one thing, it better not have been that nigger."

We ran our errands and returned to the farm several hours later. I was hoping for a word alone with Jamie before Pappy could speak to him, but as luck would have it, he and Henry were out front working on the truck when we pulled up. The children ran to meet us, clamoring for the candy I'd promised them.

"I'll give it to you inside," I said. "Jamie, would you help me carry these groceries in the house?"

"Wait just a goddamn minute," Pappy said to Jamie. "Who was that you had with you in the truck?"

Jamie's eyes flickered to me. I shook my head slightly, hoping he'd catch on and make something up.

"Well? Are you gonna answer me or not?" Pappy said.

"Girls, go inside," I said. "I'll be right there."

Reluctantly, they went. Jamie waited until they were out of earshot before answering Pappy. "As a matter of fact, it was Ronsel Jackson. What's it to you?" His voice was steady, but his cheeks had a hectic look. I wondered if he'd been drinking again.

"What's this?" asked Henry.

"I gave Ronsel a lift from town. Evidently our pappy doesn't approve."

"Not when he's sitting in the cab with you, I don't, and I bet your brother don't either," Pappy said.

Henry's expression was incredulous. "You let him sit inside the truck all the way from town?"

"What if I did?" Jamie said. "What does it matter?"

"Did anybody see you?"

"No, but I wouldn't care if they had."

They glared at each other, Jamie defiantly, Henry with a familiar mixture of anger, hurt and bewilderment that I'd last seen directed at me. Henry shook his head. "I don't know who you are anymore," he said. "I wonder if you do." He turned and walked toward the house. Jamie looked after him like he wanted to stop him, but he didn't move.

"Don't ever let me catch you giving that jigaboo a ride again," Pappy said.

"Or what?" Jamie said. "You gonna come after me with your cane?"

The old man grinned, revealing his long yellow teeth. He rarely smiled; when he did, the effect was both bizarre and repellent. "Oh, it ain't what I'll do to *you*."

Pappy followed Henry inside, leaving me alone with Jamie. His body looked tensed, poised for violence or flight. I was torn between wanting to soothe and chide him.

"I can't stay here," he said. "I'm going to town."

To his woman, I thought. "I wish you'd change your mind," I said. "I'm making rabbit stew for supper."

He reached out and lightly brushed my cheek with one finger. I swear I felt that touch in every nerve of my body. "Sweet Laura," he said.

I watched him go. As the truck and its wake of dust got smaller and smaller and finally disappeared, I thought, *Rabbit stew. That's what I'd been able to offer him.* It was all I would ever be able to offer him. The knowledge was as bitter as bile.

FLORENCE

I RAN THE BROOM over his foot three times. Said, "Sorry, Mist Jamie, ain't I clumsy today." The third time Miz McAllan gave me a scolding and sent me out of the house, finished the sweeping her own self. I didn't care what she thought, or him either. I just wanted him gone. But he didn't go, not even after I threw salt in his tracks and put a mojo of jimsonweed and gumelastin under his bed. He kept right on coming back, turning up like the bad penny he was.

He was a shiny penny though, with his handsome face and his littleboy smile. Folks just took to him natural, they couldn't help themselves, like the way a child hankers for a holly berry. He don't know it's poison, he just sees something pretty and red and he wants it in his mouth. And when you take it away from him he cries like you taking away his own heart. There's a whole lot of evil in the world looks pretty on the outside.

Jamie McAllan wasn't evil, not like his pappy was, but he did the Dark Man's business just the same. He was a weak vessel. Whiskey on his breath at noon and womansmell all over his clothes every Monday. Now a man can like his nature activity and even his drink and still be the Lord's, but Jamie McAllan had a hole in his soul, the kind the devil loves to find. It's like a open doorway for him, lets him enter in and do his wicked work. I thought maybe he got it in the war and it would close on up in time but it just kept on getting bigger and bigger. None of em seen it but me. Jamie McAllan geehawsed em all, specially Miz McAllan. The way she looked at him you would a thought he was her husband and not his brother. But Henry McAllan didn't seem to mind, that's if he even noticed. Tell you one thing, if my sister ever stretched her eyes at Hap like that, I'd claw em right out.

Even my son was took in by him. I knowed about their Saturday afternoon drives and them other times too when Ronsel went out walking after dark. Only place colored folks round here go walking after dark is to and from the outhouse, if they know what's good for em anyway. No, I knowed exactly where he was. He was out in that ole falling-down sawmill by the river, getting drunk with Jamie McAllan. I seen Ronsel heading off that way plenty of times and heard him stumbling in late at night. I tried to tell him to keep away from that man but he wouldn't listen.

"What you doing, hanging around with that white man?" I asked him.

"Nothing. Just talking."

"You asking for trouble is what you doing."

Ronsel shook his head. "He ain't like the rest of em."

"You right about that," I said. "Jamie McAllan's got a snake in his pocket and he carries it along with him wherever he goes. But when that snake gets ready to bite, it ain't gone bite him, oh no. It's gone sink them fangs into whoever else is with him. You just better make sure it ain't you."

"You don't know him," Ronsel said.

"I know he's drinking whiskey every day and hiding it from his family."

Ronsel looked away. "He's just chasing off his ghosts," he said.

My son had plenty of em too, I knowed that, but he wouldn't talk to me bout em. He was like a boarded-up house since he come back from that war, nothing going into him or coming out of him—at least, nothing from or to us. Jamie McAllan had more of Ronsel than we did.

I didn't tell Hap about the two of em drinking together. I don't like to keep things from my husband but him and Ronsel was already butting heads all the time. That was Hap's doing, he was pushing Ronsel to talk to Henry McAllan bout taking over the Atwoods' old acres. There was a new cropper family in there but Mist McAllan wasn't happy with em, he'd said so to Hap. Ronsel told his daddy he'd think it over, but he wanted them acres like a cat wants a pond to swim in. And Hap just kept on pushing him and pushing him, that was the landsickness talking is what that was.

"You don't stop, you gone push him right out the door," I told him.

"He's a man grown," Hap said. "He needs to get his own place, start his own family. Might as well be here. One of the twins can help him. With the four of us working fifty acres, and if cotton prices stay above thirty cents a pound, in three four years we'll have enough to buy our own land."

Ronsel couldn't a cared less about having his own land, but there wasn't no point in telling that to my husband. Might as well to been singing songs to a dead hog. Once Hap gets a notion a something, he's deaf and blind to everything that don't mesh with it. It's what makes him a good preacher, his faith never wobbles. Folks see that in him and it bucks em up. But what works in the pulpit ain't always good at your own kitchen table. All Ronsel seen was his daddy not caring bout what he wanted. And what he wanted was to leave. I hated the thought of him going but I knowed he had to do it soon, just like I had to set back and let him.

By SPRINGTIME HE was getting drunk with Jamie McAllan every couple days. So when ole Mist McAllan seen the two of em together in the truck, I was glad. I thought it would put a stop to the whole business.

Ronsel didn't mention it to us. Just like the last time, we had to find out what happened from Henry McAllan. He come by one afternoon, all het up, wanting a word with Hap and Ronsel. And just like the last time, I listened in. Reckoned I had a right to know what was being said on my own front porch, whether the men thought so or not.

"I expect you know why I'm here, Ronsel," Mist McAllan said.

"No suh, I don't."

"My brother tells me he gave you a lift from town today."

"Yessuh."

"I reckon it wasn't the first time."

"No, not the first."

"Exactly how long has this been going on?"

"I can't rightly say."

"Hap, do you know what I'm talking about?"

"No, Mist McAllan."

"Well, let me tell you then," Henry McAllan said. "Apparently your son here and my brother have been riding around the countryside in my truck for God knows how long, sitting in the cab together like two peas in a pod. My father saw them today, coming back from town. You telling me you knew nothing about this?"

"No suh," Hap said. "Well, I knew Mist Jamie given Ronsel a ride every once in awhile, but I didn't know he was setting up in front with him."

But Hap did know, cause he'd seen em together that first time. You better believe he gave Ronsel a talking-to that day, told him never to sit in the front seat of a white man's car again unless he was the driver and wearing a black cap to prove it.

"And now that you do know," Mist McAllan said, "what have you got to say about it?"

A silence come down amongst em. I could feel Hap struggling, trying to decide how to answer. It wasn't right, Henry McAllan asking him to take sides against his own son like that. If Mist McAllan wanted Ronsel humbled down he should a done it his own self, instead of expecting Hap to do it for him. *Don't you do it, Hap,* I thought.

But before he could answer, Ronsel spoke up. "I don't reckon my father's got anything to say about it, seeing as how he didn't know nothing about it. It's me you should be asking."

"Well then?" Henry McAllan said. "What in the world were you thinking?"

"White man tells me to get in his truck, I get in." Ronsel's voice was pretend-humble though, even I could hear it.

"You mocking me, boy?" Henry McAllan said.

"No suh, course not," Hap said. "He just trying to explicate hisself."

"Well let me explicate something to you, Ronsel. If I catch you riding in the car with my brother again, you're going to be in a heap of trouble, and I don't mean a nice little talk like we're having right now. My pappy isn't much of a talker when he gets riled up, if you take my meaning. So the next time Jamie offers you a ride, you tell him you need the exercise, hear?"

"Yessuh," Ronsel said.

"You know, Hap," Henry McAllan said, "I expected better sense from a son of yours." In a louder voice he said, "And that goes for you too, Florence."

After he was gone I went to the front door and looked out. Ronsel was standing on the edge of the porch staring after Henry McAllan's truck, and Hap was setting in his rocking chair staring at Ronsel's back.

"Well, Daddy," Ronsel said, "ain't you gone say I told you so?"

"Got no need to say it."

"Come on, I know you're itching to. So say it."

"Got no need."

For a long while the only sound was the crickets and the tree frogs and the squeak of Hap's rocker. Then Ronsel cleared his throat. *Here it comes,* I thought.

"I'll stay till the cotton's laid by," he said. "Then I'm leaving."

"Where you gone go, son?" Hap said. "Some big city up north, where you got no home and no people? That ain't no way to live."

"Wherever I go and however I live," Ronsel said, "I reckon it'll be better than here."

HENRY

By planting time I was about ready to kill my brother, messed up in the head or not. It wasn't just that he was drinking again and lying about it after he swore to me he'd stop. It was his selfishness that really got my goat. Jamie did whatever he damn well pleased without a thought for how it might affect anybody else. There I was, working hard to make a place for myself and my family in Marietta, and having a drunk brother who consorted with whores and niggers sure wasn't helping me. And on top of everything I had to listen to Laura make excuses for him while my father sat there smirking. Pappy thought I was blind to it but he was wrong. Even if I hadn't had two perfectly good eyes in my head, my ears would have told me.

Whenever Jamie was around she sang. And when it was just me, she hummed.

Still, I didn't mean to say what I said, not like that. But Jamie pushed me too far and the words just spilled out, and once they were out I couldn't take them back.

The two of us were in the barn. Jamie had just milked the cow and was taking the pail to the house when he tripped and fell, spilling the milk all over the floor and himself. He started laughing, acted like it was nothing. And I guess in the scheme of things it wasn't but right at that moment it rankled me.

"You think it's funny, spilling good milk," I said.

"Well, you know what they say, no use crying over it."

By the way he ran the words together and lurched to his feet I could tell he'd been drinking. That rankled me even more. I said, "No, especially when it's somebody else's."

That wiped the grin off his face. "I see," he said, in a sarcastic tone. "What do I owe you, Henry?" He reached in his pocket and pulled out a handful of change. "Let's see, there must have been three gallons there, that'd run what, about two dollars? Let's say two and a quarter to be on the safe side. I wouldn't want to gyp you." He started to count out the money.

"Don't be an ass," I said.

"Oh no, brother, I insist." He held out the money. When I wouldn't take it, he reached over and tried to shove it in my shirt pocket. I batted his hand away, and the coins fell to the floor.

"For Christ's sake," I said. "This isn't about money and you know it."

"What's it about then? What would you have me do, Henry?"

"Sober up, for one thing," I said. "Take some responsibility for yourself and start acting like a grown man."

"One pail of spilled milk and I'm not a man?" he said.

"You're sure not acting like one lately."

His eyes got small and mean, just like our father's did when anybody crossed him. "And how should I act, brother—like you?" Jamie said. "Walking around here like God Almighty in his creation, laying down the law, so wrapped up in myself I can't see my wife is miserable? Is that the kind of man I should be? Huh?"

I'd never hit my brother before but right then I was mighty close to it. "Be whatever kind of man you want," I said. "Just do it someplace else."

"Fine. I'll go to town." He started to walk out.

"I don't mean for the night," I said.

I saw it in his face then, that look like he used to get as a boy when one of Pappy's gibes cut deep. Then it was gone, pasted over with indifference. He shrugged. "Yeah, well," he said. "I was getting tired of this place anyway."

He's got nothing, I thought. *No wife or kids, no home to call his own. No idea of himself he can shape his life around.* "Look," I said, "that didn't come out like I meant it to."

"Didn't it?" Jamie said. "Seemed to me it came out pretty easy, like you've been thinking it for a good long while."

"I just think you need a fresh start somewhere," I said. "We both know you're no farmer."

"I'll leave tomorrow, if that's soon enough for you."

I didn't want him going off mad and half-cocked. "There's no need for that," I said. "Besides, I'm counting on your help with the planting."

He acted like he hadn't heard me. "I'll catch the first bus out of here in the morning," he said.

"I'm asking you to stay a little longer," I said. "Just till we get the seed in."

He considered me for a long moment, then gave me a bitter smile. "Anything for my big brother," he said. He walked out then, back straight and rigid as a soldier's. Jamie would deny it but he's just like our pappy in one respect. He never forgets a slight, or forgives one.

LAURA

IF HENRY HADN'T been so stubborn.

If there hadn't been a ball game on.

If Eboline had taken better care of her trees.

It was the twelfth of April, a week after the incident with Ronsel. Henry, Jamie, Pappy and I were having dinner at Dex's. The girls were at Rose's, celebrating Ruth Ann's seventh birthday with a much-anticipated tea and slumber party.

Halfway through the meal, Bill Tricklebank came in looking for us. Eboline had called the store, frantic. A dead limb had cracked off her elm tree that morning and caved in her roof. No one was hurt, but the living room was exposed and there was a big storm headed our way. It was expected to hit Greenville sometime Monday.

"Damn," said Henry after Bill had left. "Wouldn't you know it'd be right in the middle of planting season."

"I'll go," Jamie offered.

"No," said Henry. "That's not a good idea."

Jamie's mouth tightened. "Why not?" he said.

Things were still tense between him and Henry. I was staying out of it; the two times I'd tried to talk to Henry about it he'd practically taken my head off.

"You know why," Henry said.

"Come on, it's been six months. Charlie Partain's not gonna do anything even if he does happen to see me. Which he won't."

"That's right," said Henry, "because you're not going."

"Who's Charlie Partain?" I asked.

"The sheriff of Greenville," said Pappy. "He ain't too fond of our family."

"After the accident, he told me to keep Jamie out of town," said Henry, "and that's exactly what I aim to do."

"This isn't about Charlie Partain," said Jamie. "You don't trust me to go. Do you, brother?"

Henry stood, took a ten-dollar bill out of his wallet and set it on the table. To me he said, "Telephone Eboline and let her know I'm on my way. Then get somebody at Tricklebank's to take you all home. I'll be back in a few days."

He bent and gave me a swift kiss. When he turned to leave, Jamie grabbed his arm. "Do you?" he asked again.

Henry looked down at the hand on his arm, then at Jamie. "Let the tenants know there's a storm coming," he said. "Get the tractor inside the barn and fix that loose shutter in the girls' bedroom. And you better check the roof of the house, nail down any loose edges."

Jamie gave him a curt nod, and Henry left. We finished eating and walked over to Tricklebank's. Jamie and Pappy stayed on the porch while I went inside and called Eboline. Afterward

I bought a few groceries from Bill. When I came out with them, Pappy was at one end of the porch, listening to a ball game on the radio with some other men. Jamie was sitting alone at the opposite end, smoking and staring moodily out at the street. I went over to him and asked if he'd found us a ride.

He nodded. "Tom Rossi's going to take us. He went to the feed store, said to meet him over there."

Tom owned the farm to the west of ours. He was also the part-time deputy sheriff of Marietta. I found it oddly dispiriting, living in a place whose citizens only misbehaved enough to warrant a police force of one and a half.

"You about ready to leave?" I called to Pappy.

"Do I look like I'm ready, gal? The game just started."

"I'll bring him," said one of the other men.

"Supper's at six," I said.

Pappy waved us off, and Jamie and I left to go find Tom.

I sat between them on the ride to the farm, making awkward small talk with Tom while Jamie brooded beside me. As soon as Tom dropped us off, Jamie took the truck and drove off to warn the tenants about the storm. When I heard him return, I went outside. He was striding angrily toward the barn, his hair ablaze in the sun. I called out to him.

He kept going, calling back, "I need to fetch the ladder and see to the roof."

"That can wait a little while," I said. "I want to talk to you."

He stopped but didn't turn around. His body was rigid, his hands balled into fists. I went and stood directly in front of him.

"You're wrong about Henry not trusting you," I said.

"You think so, huh?"

"Don't you see, that's what he was trying to tell you, when he asked you to warn the tenants and all the rest of it. That he trusts you."

"Yeah," Jamie said, with a harsh laugh, "he trusts me so much he wants me gone."

"Don't be silly. He's just sore at you over the Ronsel business. He'll get over it."

Jamie cocked his head. "So, he hasn't told you yet," he said. "I didn't think he had."

"Told me what?"

"He kicked me out."

"What are you talking about?"

"He asked me to leave yesterday. I'm going as soon as we're done planting. Next week, most likely."

I felt a sharp pain somewhere near the center of my body, followed by a draining sensation that made me a little dizzy. It reminded me of how I'd felt when I used to give blood for the war effort. Only now it was all going, all the life and color in me, seeping out into the dirt at my feet. When Jamie left and I was emptied, I would be invisible again, just like I'd been before he came. I couldn't go back to being that dutiful unseen woman, the one who played her roles without really inhabiting them. I wouldn't go back. *No.*

I realized I'd spoken the word out loud when Jamie said, "I have to, Laura. Henry's right about one thing, I need to make a new start. And I sure as hell can't do it here." He waved his hand to take it all in—the shabby house and outbuildings, the ugly brown fields. And me, of course, I was part of that dreary landscape too. Henry's landscape. Fury gathered in my belly, rising up, scalding my throat. I truly hated my husband at that moment.

"I'd better get busy on those chores," Jamie said.

I watched him walk to the barn. At the door, he stopped and looked back at me. "I never thought my brother would turn against me like this," he said. "I never thought he was capable of it."

I could think of nothing to say in answer. Nothing that would comfort him. Nothing that would keep him here.

I LISTENED TO HIM move the tractor, hammer the shutter, climb up on the ladder to check the roof. Mundane sounds, but they filled me with sadness. All I could think of was the silence to come.

When he was finished he popped his head in the front window. "The roof looks fine," he said. "I've taken care of the rest."

"You want some coffee?"

"No, thanks. I think I'll take a nap."

He'd been asleep for maybe twenty minutes when I heard him moaning and shouting. I hurried out to the lean-to, but at the door I found myself hesitating. I looked at my hand on the latch and thought of all the things it had proven capable of since I'd been at Mudbound, things that would have frightened or shocked me once. I looked at the ragged nails, the swollen red knuckles, the slender strip of gold across the fourth finger. I watched my hand lift the latch.

Jamie was sprawled on his back, his arms flung wide. He was still dressed, except for his shoes and socks. His feet were long, pale and slender, with a blue tracery of veins in the arches. I had the urge to press my mouth to them. He cried out and one arm flailed upward, as if he were warding something off. I sat on the edge of the bed and took hold of his arm, pushing it down against the sheet. With my other hand I smoothed his hair back from his damp forehead. "Jamie, wake up," I said.

He tore his arm from my grasp and grabbed my shoulders, his fingers digging into my skin. I said his name again and his eyes opened, darting around wildly before settling on my face. I watched sense come into them, then awareness of who I was, and where we were.

"Laura," he said.

I could have looked away then, but I didn't. I held myself very still, knowing he could see everything I felt and letting him see it. It was the most intimate act of my life, more intimate even than the acts that followed. Jamie didn't move, but I felt the change in the way his hands gripped me. His eyes dropped to my mouth and my heart lurched, slamming against the bone. I waited for him to pull me down to him, but he didn't, and I realized finally that he wouldn't; that it was up to me. I remembered the first time Henry had kissed me, how he'd taken my face in his hands as though it were something he had a right to. That was the difference between men and women, I thought: Men take for themselves the things they want, while women wait to be given them. I would not wait any longer. I bent down and touched my lips to Jamie's, tasting whiskey and cigarettes, anger and longing that I knew was not just for me. I didn't care. I took it all, no questions asked, either of him or myself. His hands pulled me on top of him, undid the buttons of my blouse, unsnapped my garters. Urgent, impatient, speeding us past whether and why. I went willingly, following the path of his desire.

And then, suddenly, he stopped. He rolled me to one side and got up out of the bed, and I thought, *He's changed his mind. Of course he has.* He took my hand and drew me up to stand in front of him. Mortified, I looked down and started to button my blouse back up. His hand reached out, raised my chin. "Look at me," he said.

I made myself look. His gaze was steady and fierce. He ran his thumb across my mouth, stroking the bottom lip open, then his hand dropped lower. He brushed the backs of his fingers across my breast, once, and then again in the opposite direction. My nipples stiffened and my legs trembled. My body felt dense and heavy, an unwieldy liquid mass. I would have fallen but his eyes held me up. There was a demand in them, and a gravity I'd never seen before. I understood then: We wouldn't be swept away by passion, as I'd always imagined. Jamie wouldn't let us be. This would be a deliberate act. A choosing.

Without looking away from him, I reached out with my hand, found his belt buckle and pulled the leather from it. When I released the catch he let out a long breath. His arms went around me and his mouth came down on mine.

When he was poised above me I didn't think of Henry or my children, of words like *adultery, sin, consequences.* I thought only of Jamie and myself. And when I drew him into me I thought of nothing at all.

HE FELL ASLEEP on top of me, as Henry sometimes did when he was tired, but I felt none of my usual irritation or restiveness. Jamie's weight on me was sweet. I closed my eyes, wanting to shut out every other sensation, wanting his weight to imprint the shape of him into my flesh.

It was the thought of Pappy that got me to move. By the golden tint of the light coming in the window, it was late afternoon; he'd be home any time now. Carefully, trying not to wake Jamie, I extricated myself from beneath him. He stirred and moaned but his eyes stayed closed. I picked up my clothes from the floor, dusted them off and got dressed. I went to the mirror. My hair was disheveled, but apart from that I looked like myself: Laura McAllan on a normal Saturday afternoon. Everything had changed; nothing had changed. Astonishing.

I heard the cot springs creak slightly behind me and knew that Jamie was awake and watching me. *I should turn around and face him,* I thought, but my body refused to do it. I left the room quickly, without looking at him or speaking. Afraid I would find shame in his eyes, or hear regret in his voice.

About half an hour later I heard the truck start up and pull away.

HAP

THAT MONDAY AFTERNOON I was out by the shed hitching the mule to the guano cart when Ronsel finally come back from town. By that point I was mighty vexed with him. He'd went in to run an errand for his mama but he was gone way too long for that. Mooning around again, I reckoned, thinking bout going off to New York or Chicago or one a them other faraway places he was always talking bout, meantime here I was trying to get the fields fertilized and needing every bit of help I could get.

"Where you been?" I said. "Half the day's gone."

He didn't answer, it was like he didn't hear me or even see me. He was just staring off with this funny look on his face, like he'd had the stuffing knocked out of him.

"Ronsel!" I hollered. "What's the matter with you?"

He jumped and looked at me. "Sorry, Daddy. I guess I was off somewhere else."

"Come help me load this fertilizer."

"I'll be right there," he said.

He went in the house. Bout a minute later he come charging

out onto the porch, looking all around like he'd lost something. "You seen a piece of paper anywhere?" he said.

"What kind of paper?"

"An envelope, with writing on the front."

"No, I ain't seen nothing like that," I said.

He looked all around the yard, getting more and more worked up every second. "It must a fell out of my pocket on the road from town. Goddamnit!"

"Ronsel! What's in this envelope?"

But he didn't answer me. His eyes lit on the road. "I bet it fell out in that ditch," he said. "I got to go fetch it."

"I thought you were gone help me with this fertilizer."

"This can't wait, Daddy," he said. He took off running down the road. That was the last time I ever heard my son's voice.

RONSEL

THE ENVELOPE HAD a German stamp in the corner of it. It was dirty and beat up from traveling so many miles and passing through so many hands. The writing was a woman's, fancy and slanted. Soon as I seen it I knew it had to been from Resl. The censors had opened it and taped it back up again. I hated the thought of them knowing what she'd wrote me before I did.

When I pulled out the letter a photograph fell out, right onto the floor of the post office. I picked it up and looked at it. Amazing, how a little piece of shiny paper can change your whole life forever. My mouth went dry and my heart sped up. I opened the letter, hoping the censors hadn't blacked anything out, but for once it was all there.

> Lieber Ronsel,
>
> This Letter I am writing with the Help of my Friend Berta on who you may remember. I do not know if it is arriving to you but I am hoping that it will. May be you are surprised to hearing from me. At first I am thinking I am not writing to you but then I have decided that I must do it, because it is

not right that a Mann does not know he is having
a Son. That is what I want to say you—you have a
Son. I name him after my Father und his Father,
Franz Ronsel. He is born in the Nacht of the 14
November at 22:00, in the Hospital of Teisendorf.
I ask myself what you is doing at that Moment. I am
trying to imagine you in your flat Missippi but I can
not make such a Picture in my Mind, only of your
Face which I see everyday when I look at the little
Franz. I am sending you a Foto so that you can see
him. He have your Eyes und your Smile.

At your Leaving I did not know that I am carrying your Child in me and when I learned to know it
my Proud did not let me write you. But now I have
this beautiful Son and I am thinking on the Day on
which he know he has no Father and his smiling
will die. Compared to that my Proud is not important. For Franzl I ask you please, will you come
back and stay with us hier, with me und Maria und
your Son. I know it is not being easy but I have this
Haus und I believe that together we are making a
gut Life. Please answer quick and say me that you
are coming back to us.

In Love,

Your Resl

The letter was dated 2 February 1947, more than two
months ago. My heart was sore thinking of her waiting all that
time for an answer and not getting one. I lifted the paper to
my nose but if her scent had ever been on it, it was long gone.
I looked at the photo again. There was Resl, looking as sweet
and pretty as ever, with the baby bundled up in her arms. In

the picture his skin was a medium gray, lighter than mine would've been, so I guessed he was gingercake-colored like my daddy. She was holding up one of his little hands and waving it at the camera.

My Resl. My son.

A SON, I HAVE A SON. That was the only thought in my head, walking back from town with that letter in my pocket. Knowing I was a father made the world sharper edged to my eye. The sky looked bluer and the shacks that squatted underneath it looked shabbier. The newly planted fields on either side of me seemed to stretch on and on like a brown ocean between me and him. But how in the hell could I get to Germany? And what would I do once I got there? I didn't speak the language, had no way to support a family there. But I couldn't just abandon them. Maybe I could bring the three of them back, not to Mississippi but someplace else where they wouldn't care that she was white and I was colored. Had to be a place like that somewhere, maybe in California or up north. I could ask Jimmy, he might know. Too damn many mights and maybes, that was the problem. I needed to think it through and make a plan. In the meantime I'd help them however I could. I didn't have much money left, maybe a few hundred dollars stuffed into the toes of my boots at the bottom of my duffel bag. I'd write to Captain Scott at Camp Hood, he'd know how to get it to Resl. But first I'd write and tell her I still loved her and was working on a plan, so she could whisper it to my son.

I was so busy thinking I didn't even hear the truck till it
was almost on top of me. Turned around and there it was,
coming straight at me. Soldier's instincts is all that saved me.
I dived into the ditch on the side of the road and landed in
mud. The truck passed so close to my head it like to gave me a
crew cut, then it went off into the ditch right in front of me. I
recognized it then, it was the McAllans' truck. For a minute I
thought Old Man McAllan had tried to run me over but when
the door opened Jamie got out. Well, fell out is more like it,
he was drunker than I'd ever seen him, and that was saying
something. He had a bottle in one hand and a cigarette in the
other. He staggered over to where I was.

"That you, Ronshel?"

"Yeah, it's me."

"You all right?"

"I'm as muddy as a pig in a wallow, but other than that I'm
fine."

"Shouldn't be walking in the middle of the road like that,
you're liable to get yourself killed."

"It'll take more than a drunk white flyboy to kill me," I said.

He laughed and plopped down on the edge of the ditch,
and I got up and sat beside him. He looked terrible sickly.
Red-eyed, unshaven, skin all sweaty. He took a swig from the
bottle and offered it to me. It was more than three-quarters
empty already.

"No thanks, I better not," I said. "Maybe you better not either."

Jamie wagged his finger at me. "Do not think, gentlemen, I am
drunk." He raised his left hand and said, "This is my ancient,

this is my right hand." Then he raised the hand holding the bottle. A little whiskey sloshed out onto his pants leg but he didn't seem to notice. "And this is my left. Oh God, that men should put an enemy in their mouths to steal away their brains! That we should with joy, pleasure, revel and . . . revel and . . . what's the fourth thing, damnit?"

He looked at me like I was supposed to know. I just shrugged.

"With joy, pleasure, revel and . . . applause—that's it, applause!—transform ourselves into beasts!" He twirled his left hand in the air and bowed from the waist. He would've fell over into the ditch if I hadn't grabbed his shirt collar and yanked him back up.

"Hey," I said, "is something the matter?"

He shook his head and stared at the bottle, picking at the label with his fingernail. He was quiet a good long while, then he said, "What's the worst thing you ever did?"

"Killing Hollis, I guess." I'd told him about it one night at the sawmill: how I'd shot my buddy Hollis in the head after his legs got blown off by a grenade and he begged me to do it.

"No, I mean something that hurt somebody bad. Something you never forgave yourself for. You ever do anything like that?"

Yeah, I thought, *leaving Resl.* I was that close to telling him about her. I wanted to say the words out loud: *I'm a father, I have a son.* I'd already told him plenty of things, like about shooting Hollis and refusing to let the crackers in our tanks and the time me and Jimmy went to a cabaret in Paris where the dancing girls were all stark naked. But there was a mighty big difference between that and me having a child by a white woman. Jamie McAllan was born and bred in Mississippi. If he got fired up and decided to turn me in, I could get ten years in Parchman—that's if I didn't get lynched on the way there.

"No," I said, "nothing I can think of."

"Well I have. I've belied a lady, the princess of this country."

"What you talking bout? What princess?"

"And she, sweet lady, dotes, devoutly dotes, dotes in idolatry upon this spotted and inconstant man. Idolatry, idultery—ha!"

So that's what was troubling him. Thinking of Josie, I said, "Ain't good to mess with the married gals, you just looking for heartache there. Best thing to do is put it behind you, never see her again."

He nodded. "Yeah. I'm leaving here next week."

"Where you going?"

"I don't know. Maybe California. I always wanted to see it."

"I've got a buddy lives in Los Angeles. According to Jimmy, it never gets too hot or too cold there and it hardly ever rains. Course he could've been pulling my leg."

Jamie looked at me, a hard clear look like you get sometimes from somebody who's drunk, it's like they sober up just long enough to really see you. "You ought to leave here too, Ronsel," he said. "Hap can manage without you now."

"I am leaving, just as soon as the crop's laid by."

"Good. This is no place for you."

He finished the whiskey and tossed the bottle into the ditch.

When he tried to stand up his legs gave out. I got up and helped him to his feet. "Reckon you better let me drive you home," I said.

"Reckon I better."

Somehow we managed to push the truck out of the ditch, then I drove him as far as the bridge and got out. I figured he could make it from there, and I didn't want Henry McAllan or that old man seeing us.

"You drive careful the rest of the way," I told him. "Try not to run any more colored people off the road."

He smiled and held out his hand. We shook. "Doubt I'll see you again before I go," he said. "You take care of yourself, hear?"

"You too."

"You've been a friend. I want you to know that."

He didn't wait for me to say anything back, just waved and drove off. I followed the truck down the road toward home, watching it weave back and forth, thinking of how surprising a place the world could be sometimes.

Must've been half an hour later that I found the letter gone. The first thing I thought was it fell out in that ditch. Ran all the way back there and looked but all I found was Jamie's whiskey bottle. I kept on going all the way to town and still didn't find it. The post office was closed but I was sure I hadn't left it in there. Only two places it could be: in somebody's pocket who'd picked it up or in the McAllans' truck. I made myself keep calm. If I'd left it in the truck Jamie might've found it. He wouldn't show it to nobody, he'd keep it for me. Maybe he was over at my house right now looking to give it back to me. And if not and it was still in the truck, I could sneak over there after dark and get it before anybody saw it.

By the time I headed back home it was coming on to dark and raining hard. I'd left without my hat so I was soaking wet. I was about halfway there when I heard the sound of a vehicle bearing down on me for the second time that day. I turned around and seen two sets of headlights. I jumped down into the ditch but instead of passing me they stopped right beside me. I didn't recognize the car in front but I knew the truck behind it. There were white figures inside, four in the car and maybe another three in the truck. Seemed like they practically glowed in the dark. When they got out I seen why.

LAURA

JAMIE DIDN'T COME back on Saturday, or on Sunday. When Rose brought the girls home Sunday morning I asked if she'd seen him in town, and she said no. It was a long couple of days, waiting. The sweet ache between my legs was a constant reminder of what Jamie and I had done. I had a few pricks of conscience—seeing Henry's pajama bottoms hanging forlornly from a peg in our bedroom, his comb on the dresser, a stray white hair on his pillow—but real shame and regret were absent. In their place was a riotous sense of wonder. I'd never imagined myself capable of either great boldness or great passion, and the discovery that I had reservoirs of both astounded me. I couldn't stop picturing myself with Jamie. I burned the grits, forgot to feed the animals, scalded my arm on the stove.

Pappy was in a fouler mood than usual. He was low on cigarettes and furious at Jamie for leaving us with no transportation. He smoked his last one early Monday morning and spent the entire day punishing me for it. My biscuits were too dry, was I trying to choke him to death? My floors were so dirty they weren't fit for a nigger to walk on. My brats were making too much racket. My coffee was too weak, how many times had he told me he liked it strong?

Short of walking, there was no way to get to town until Henry or Jamie got home.

"Goddamnit, where is he?" Pappy called out for the tenth time.

"Mind your language," I said. "The children are right here."

He was out on the porch watching the road, which was preferable to having him in the house with us. Florence had gone home for the day. I was sewing new dresses for the girls, and they were making paper dolls. We could hear Pappy's boots clomping back and forth outside the window.

"It's just like him," said the old man, "pulling a stunt like this. Thinking only of himself, the hell with everybody else."

The irony of Pappy complaining about Jamie or any other person being selfish was too much, and I laughed out loud. The shutters banged open, revealing Pappy's scowling face at the window. I was reminded of a malevolent cuckoo clock.

"What are you snickering at?" he demanded.

"Something Bella just did."

"You think it's funny, an old man being without his cigarettes. Just you wait and see how you feel when you get old, and you have to do without your comforts because nobody cares enough to look after you."

"You could always ride one of the mules to town," I suggested, deadpan.

Pappy couldn't stand animals, especially large ones. I think he was afraid of them, though he never admitted as much. It was the reason we didn't have any pets on the farm; he wouldn't tolerate them.

"I ain't doing any such thing," he said. "Why don't you go ask that nigger gal if she'll go? Tell her I'll pay her two bits."

"I'm sure Florence has better things to do than fetch your cigarettes for you."

His face retreated as abruptly as it had appeared. "Never mind," he said. "I see the truck coming."

The girls ran out to the porch to wait for their uncle. I took a deep breath and followed them. I would need to be very careful around Jamie to avoid raising Pappy's suspicions.

"Drunk again," Pappy said scornfully.

The car was weaving all over the road. At one point it went off entirely and into the newly planted fields. I was glad Henry wasn't home to see that; he would have been apoplectic. Jamie pulled up in front of the house and got out of the truck. Bella started to run to him but I held her back. He was rumpled and unshaven. One shirt tail hung out of the front of his pants. "Afternoon Laura, Pappy, little petunias," he said, swaying on his feet.

"You got any cigarettes?" said the old man.

"Hello, son," said Jamie, slurring the words together. "I'm so glad to see you, how are you today? Why Pappy, thank you for asking, I'm fine, and how are you?"

"You can talk to yourself all you want, just give me a smoke first."

Jamie reached in his shirt pocket and pulled out a pack of

Lucky Strikes, tossing them to his father. The throw fell short, forcing Pappy to bend down and pick them up off the ground. "There's only one cigarette here," said the old man.

"Guess I smoked the rest."

"You ain't worth a damn, you know that?"

"Well, I'm worth one cigarette. That's something. Unless you don't want it."

"Just give me the truck keys."

Jamie held them up, dangling them. "Ask nice and maybe I will."

Pappy walked toward Jamie, his steps slow and menacing. "You trying to mess with me? Huh, mister big hero?" The old man's cane was in his left hand, but he wasn't leaning on it; he was gripping it like a club. "Just keep talking, and we'll find out which one of us is a man and which one ain't. See, I know the answer already, but I don't think you do. I think you're confused on the subject. That's why you keep giving me lip, is because you want to be straightened out. Ain't that right, boy?"

When he reached Jamie he stopped and leaned forward until their faces were inches apart. How strongly they resembled each other! I'd never seen it before—I'd always thought of Pappy as ugly—but their features were essentially the same: the arched sardonic brows, the slanting cheekbones, the full, slightly petulant mouth.

"Ain't that right?" said the old man again.

My muscles tensed; the urge to step between them was almost overwhelming. Suddenly Pappy raised his cane, thrusting it toward Jamie's face—a feint, but Jamie flinched and took a step back.

"That's what I thought," Pappy said. "Now give me the god-damn keys."

Jamie dropped them into his outstretched hand. The old man shook the cigarette out of the pack, lit it and blew the smoke in Jamie's face. Jamie crumpled to his knees and retched. Liquid gushed out, not a solid thing in it. I wondered when he'd last eaten. I went and knelt beside him, helpless to do anything but pat him gingerly on the back as his body convulsed. His shirt was soaked through with sweat.

I heard a bark of laughter and looked up. The old man was watching us from the cab of the truck. "Well, ain't you a pretty pair," he said.

"Just go," I said.

"Can't wait to have him all to yourself, eh gal? Too bad he's too liquored up to be any good to you."

"What are you talking about?"

"You know exactly what I mean."

"No, I don't."

"Then why's your face so red, huh?" Pappy started the truck. "Don't let him fall asleep on his back," he said. "If he throws up again he could choke to death."

He drove off. I looked down at Jamie. He'd stopped retching and was lying limp on his side in the dirt. "When he is best, he is a little worse than a man," Jamie said in a hoarse voice, "and when he is worst he is little better than a beast."

"What's the matter with Uncle Jamie?" Amanda Leigh called out.

I turned and saw the girls watching. I'd forgotten all about them. "He just has an upset tummy is all," I said. "Do me a favor, darling, fetch me a clean washrag. Dip it in the bucket, wring it out, then bring it here. And a glass of water too."

"Yes, Mama."

Somehow I got him to his bed in the lean-to. He fell onto it and lay on his back without moving. I took off his shoes. His socks were missing. A vivid and unwelcome picture of them lying abandoned under some woman's bed flashed into my mind. With some difficulty, I rolled him onto his side. When I'd gotten him settled I looked down to find him watching me with an unreadable expression.

"Sweet Laura," he said. "My angel of mercy." His hand lifted and cupped my breast, possessively, familiarly. I felt a stab of desire. His eyes fluttered closed and his hand fell to the bed. I heard a familiar tapping sound on the roof; gentle at first, then sharper and more insistent. It had begun to rain.

IT MUST HAVE been about two hours later that the front door flew open and Florence came bursting in. The girls and I had just sat down to a late supper. Pappy still hadn't come home, and I wasn't going to wait on him any longer. The children were hungry and so was I.

"Where's Mist Jamie?" Florence said, without preamble. She was soaked to the skin and breathing harshly, like she'd been running.

"Taking a nap in the lean-to. What's the matter?"

"Where's the truck then?"

"Pappy took it to town. Now what in the world's gotten into you?"

"Ronsel went to town earlier and he ain't come back. What time did Mist Jamie get home?"

Her high-handed attitude was beginning to annoy me. "Shortly after you left," I said. "Not that it's any of your business."

"Something's happened to my son," Florence said, "and Mist Jamie's caught up in it somehow, I know it."

"You're talking nonsense. How long has Ronsel been gone?"

"Since bout five o'clock. He should a been home by now."

"Well, it's nothing to do with Jamie. Like I said, he's been here since around three-thirty. Ronsel probably ran into a friend in town and lost track of the time. You know how young men are."

Florence shook her head, just once, but I felt the weight of that negation as strongly as if she'd shoved me. "No. He ain't got no friends here, cept for Mist Jamie."

"What do you mean, they're friends?"

"You got to wake him up and ask him."

I stood up. "I'll do no such thing. Jamie's worn out, and he needs his rest."

Her nostrils flared, and her eyes flickered to the front door. *She means to force her way past me and go wake him,* I thought. I wouldn't be able to stop her; she was a foot taller than me and outweighed me by a good forty pounds. For the first time since I'd known her, I felt afraid of her.

"Best if you go on home," I said. "I bet Ronsel's there right now, wondering where you are."

There was real animosity in Florence's eyes, and it woke an answering flare in me. How dared she threaten me, and under my own roof? I remembered Pappy telling the girls one time that Lilly May wasn't their friend and never would be; that if it came down to a war between the niggers and the whites, she'd be on the side of the niggers and wouldn't hesitate to kill them both. It had angered me at the time, but now I wondered if there wasn't a brutal kernel of truth in what he'd said.

Bella started coughing; she'd swallowed her milk the wrong way. I went and whacked her on the back, then looked at Florence. I thought back to the first time we'd met; how crazy with worry I'd been for my children. The memory was like a clean blast of air, clearing my head of foolishness. This wasn't a murderous Negro in front of me, but an anxious mother.

"Watch the girls," I said. "I'll go and ask him."

I knocked on the door of the lean-to, but there was no answer, and when I opened it the lantern light revealed two empty beds. Jamie's pillowcase was cool to my hand. I checked the outhouse, but he wasn't there either, and there was no light in the barn. Where could he have gone, on foot and in such pitiful condition? He couldn't possibly have sobered up; it had been less than three hours since he got home. And where was Pappy? Tricklebank's was long closed, and it wasn't like the old man to miss supper and a chance to complain about my cooking.

It was with a growing feeling of dread that I went back to the house. "Jamie's not here," I told Florence. "He must have gone for a walk to clear his head. He sometimes does that in the evenings. I'm sure it's nothing to do with Ronsel."

Florence headed swiftly out the door. I followed her to the edge of the porch. "I'll send Jamie to your house as soon as he gets back," I called, "just to set your mind at ease. I'm sure you're worrying for nothing."

But I was talking to the air. The darkness had swallowed her up.

JAMIE

THE RAIN STARTLED me awake. The din of a Delta thunderstorm hitting a tin roof is about as close as you can get to the sound of battle without actually being in it. For a heart-pounding minute I was back in the skies over Germany, surrounded by enemy Messerschmitts. Then I realized where I was, and why.

I lay in the dark of the lean-to and took stock of my condition. My head hurt and my mouth was full of cotton. I was still a little tipsy, but not nearly lit enough to face Pappy and Laura. There'd been a bad scene earlier, that much I remembered, but the details were vague and that was just fine by me. Amnesia is one of the great gifts of alcohol, and I'm not one to refuse it. I groped under the bed for the bottle I kept stashed there, but when I picked it up it felt light in my hand. There were only a couple of swigs left and I took them both, then I shut my eyes and waited for the whiskey to kindle me. My stomach was empty so it didn't take long. I might have gone back to sleep, but I had to piss too bad. I fumbled for the lantern on the bedside table and lit it. Pappy's bed was empty. There was a pitcher of water sitting on the table, along with a basin, a neatly folded towel and some cornbread wrapped in a napkin. Laura must have left them there for me.

Laura. It came back to me then, in a rush of images: Her hair falling down around my face. Her breasts filling my hands. The dusky sweet scent of her. My brother's wife.

I went outside. It was full dark, but the lights were on in the house. I stood at the edge of the porch and added my own stream to the downpour, wondering what time it was. A flash of lightning lit up the yard, and I saw that both the truck and the car were gone. We didn't expect Henry till tomorrow, but why wasn't Pappy back? Maybe the old goat had gotten stuck in the rain. Maybe he was sitting in the truck in a ditch at this very moment, cussing the weather and me both. The thought cheered me.

As I was zipping up my pants I saw a light moving near the old sawmill. At first I thought it was Pappy coming home, but no headlights approached the house. The light bobbed along the river, winking in and out like somebody was walking through the trees with a lantern, then it went out. Whoever it was must have gone inside the sawmill. Ronsel, probably, or a drifter seeking shelter from the storm. They were welcome to it. I wasn't about to go investigate, not in that downpour.

I went back inside and got myself cleaned up. I didn't want to face Laura and the girls stinking of sweat and vomit and whiskey. I was half-dressed when I remembered the fifth I had stashed out in the sawmill. As soon as I pictured it, I wanted it. Without that bottle, I'd be on my own with Laura, and then with my father and Henry whenever they showed up. I knew Ronsel wouldn't drink my whiskey without invitation, but a drifter sure would, if he found it. The thought of some bum sucking down my Jack overcame my aversion to getting wet. I stuffed some cornbread in my mouth and put on my jacket and my hat. At the last second I grabbed my .38 and stuck it in my pocket.

I was wet through within seconds of leaving the porch. The wind tore my hat from my head, and the mud tried to pull my boots off with every step. It was so dark that if it hadn't been for the occasional bursts of lightning, I wouldn't have been able to see a thing. As it was I almost ran straight into a vehicle parked off to one side of the sawmill. The hood was warm. When the lightning came again I recognized Henry's truck. And there was another car parked beside it. *What the hell?*

I went around back of the building. Strips of light showed between the planks, and I put my eye up to one of the gaps. At first all I saw was white. Then it moved and I realized I was looking at the back of somebody's head, and that he was wearing a white hood. He wasn't the only one. There were maybe eight of them standing in a loose circle.

"How many times did you fuck her?" I heard a voice say.

One of the figures shifted, and I saw Ronsel kneeling in the center of them. His hands and feet were tied behind his back, and there was a noose around his neck. The rope was slung over a beam in the ceiling. The man holding the other end gave it a vicious yank. Ronsel gagged, and his head came up.

"Answer him, nigger!" said my father.

RONSEL

I STARTED TO RUN but then I heard the sound of a shot-gun round being chambered. I froze and held my hands up. A high tight voice said, "If I was you, boy, I'd stay right where I was." It sounded like Doc Turpin, the sonofabitch who'd messed up my daddy's leg. He'd talked through his nose like that, that day at Tricklebank's. And Daddy had told me he used to be in the Klan.

"Get him in the car." That voice I recognized straight-away—it was Old Man McAllan. I wondered if Henry McAllan was there too underneath one of them hoods. Somebody came up behind me and threw a burlap sack over my head. I flailed out and he punched me in the kidneys, then somebody else grabbed my arms and tied them behind my back. They drug me to the car and threw me in. One of them got in on either side of me, then we started moving.

The wet sack on my head smelled like coffee, I reckoned they got it at Tricklebank's. They must've met up there be-fore they set out to find me. That gave me a little hope. If Mrs. Tricklebank had been there and heard them talking she would've called Sheriff Tacker as soon as they left. He wasn't no great friend to Negroes but surely he wouldn't stand by and let one of us be lynched. Surely he wouldn't.

"Listen," I said, "I'll leave town."

"Shut up, nigger," said the man I thought was Turpin.

"I'll leave tonight, and I won't ever—"

"He said, shut up," snarled the man on my other side.

Something hard slammed into my ribs and all the breath went out of me. The pain was fierce, felt like some of my ribs were cracked. I kept quiet after that and so did they. Somebody lit a cigarette. I'd never been much of a smoker but when my nose caught the smell of it I wanted one bad. Funny how the body keeps right on wanting what it wants even when it thinks it's about to die.

The car made a turn and the ride got rough, I figured we'd gone off the road. A couple minutes later we stopped. They jerked me out of the car and marched me a ways into a building. The rain on the roof sounded like a thousand people clapping, cheering them on. I was shoved to my knees and I felt a rope go around my neck. They tightened it, not quite enough to choke me but one more hard tug and it would. It was hot under the sack and hard to breathe. Sweat and coffee stung my eyes and the burlap was itching my face. How long did it take to choke to death? If I was lucky my neck would break and I'd go quick, but if it didn't . . . I felt panic take ahold of me and I fought it down, slowing my breathing like they'd taught us in survival training. I would keep calm and wait for a chance to escape. And if I couldn't, if they meant to kill me, I'd show these fuckers how a man died. I was an NCO of the 761st Tank Battalion, a Black Panther. I wouldn't let them turn me into a scared nigger.

One of them jerked the sack off my head. At first all I seen was legs but then they stepped back some and I realized where I was: the old sawmill, where I'd spent so many nights drinking whiskey with Jamie McAllan. Seven or eight men stood in a circle around me. Most of them were just wearing white pillowcases but two of them had on real Klan robes with pointed hoods and round badges on the chest. The badges had square black crosses on them with red dots in the middle like drops of blood. I looked up to where the rope was slung over a beam, then followed it down to the hands of one of the men in robes. He was tall, maybe six foot five, and built like a bear. Had to be Orris Stokes, he was the biggest fellow in town. I'd helped his pregnant wife carry her groceries home from Tricklebank's one time.

"Do you know why you're here, nigger?" he said.

"No sir, Mr. Stokes."

He handed the rope to one of the others, then reached out with one of his huge arms and backhanded me. My head snapped back and I felt one of my teeth come loose.

"You say that name again or any other name and we'll make you even sorrier than you're already gonna be, hear?"

"Yes, sir."

The other man in Klan robes stepped forward. It was Doc Turpin, I was sure of it now. I could see his paunch pushing his robe out and his little beer-colored eyes glinting through the holes in his hood. It was plain he and Stokes were in charge.

"Bring forth the evidence," Turpin said.

One of the others held something out to him. Soon as I seen that old yellow hand I knew what had to be in it. Turpin took the letter and the photograph from Old Man McAllan and held them up in front of my face. Resl and Franz smiled out at me. I wished I could climb into that picture with them, into that other world.

"Did you rut with this woman?" Turpin asked.

I didn't answer, even though he had the letter right there in his hand. There were worse things they could do to me than hang me.

"We know you did it, nigger," said McAllan. "We just want to hear you say it."

Another one jerked on the rope and the noose dug into my windpipe. "Go on, say it!" he ordered. His voice was deep and raspy from chain-smoking. No doubt who that was: Dex Deweese, the owner of the town diner.

"Yes," I said.

"Yes, what?" said Turpin.

"Yes, I . . . was with her."

"You defiled a white woman. Say it."

I shook my head. Stokes hit me again, this time with his fist, knocking the tooth he'd loosened earlier out of its socket. I spat it out onto the floor.

"I defiled a white woman."

"How many times did you fuck her?" said Turpin.

I shook my head again. Truth was, I *had* fucked Resl at first. I'd taken what she offered thinking of nothing but my own pleasure, knowing I'd soon be moving on to another post.

When had it gotten to be more than that? I closed my eyes, trying to remember, trying to smell her scent. But all I could smell was my own sweat and their hate. The animal stench of it filled the room.

Deweese gave the rope a hard yank and I gagged.

"Answer him, nigger!" said old man McAllan.

"I don't know," I choked out.

Turpin waved the photo in the air. "Enough times to get her with this—I won't call it a child—this . . . abomination! A foul pollution of the white race!" The men shifted and muttered. Turpin was working them up good. "And what's the penalty for abomination?"

"Death!" shouted Stokes.

"I say we geld him," one of them said.

The fear that took ahold of me then was like nothing I ever felt in my whole life. My guts were churning and it was all I could do not to shit myself.

Turpin said, "And if a woman approach any beast and lie down with it, thou shalt kill the woman and the beast. They shall surely be put to death, and their blood shall be upon them."

"String him up," said Old Man McAllan.

Right then the door banged open and we all turned toward it. Jamie McAllan stood there dripping water all over the floor. He had a pistol in his hand and it was pointed at Deweese.

"Let go of the rope," Jamie said.

JAMIE

"LET IT GO," I said.

One of the others moved, a shotgun in his hands, rising. I pointed the pistol at him. "Drop it!" I said.

He hesitated. For a few seconds everybody froze. Then my father spoke up. "He's bluffing," said Pappy, "and he's half-drunk besides. Point the gun at the nigger. Go on, he won't shoot you. My son don't have the balls to kill a man up close." He stepped in front of the man with the shotgun, blocking my aim. I found myself staring down the sight of the pistol into my father's pale eyes, framed in white cotton. "Do you, son?" he said.

Behind him I could see the barrel of the shotgun, now pointed at Ronsel's head. Pappy took a step toward me, then another. There was a roaring in my ears, and the hand holding the pistol was shaking. I put my other hand under the butt to steady it.

"Stop right there," I said.

He took another step toward me. "You gonna betray your own blood over a nigger?"

"Don't come any closer. I'm warning you."

"Kill me, and the jig still dies."

Hate rose up in me—for him, for myself. I'd lost, and we both knew it. I only had one play left to make. "If you kill him, you better kill me too," I said. "Because if Ronsel dies, I'm going straight to the sheriff. I swear I'll do it."

"What are you gonna tell him, boy?" said the fat one in Klan robes. "You can't identify nary one of us, except for your father."

Without taking my eyes off Pappy, I said, "You know, Doc, white's not your color. Makes you look a little hefty. Now Dex here can wear it because he's so skinny, and Orris, well, he's gonna look big no matter what he has on. But if I were you, Doc, I'd stick to brown and black."

"Shit," said Deweese.

"Shut up," said Stokes. "He can't prove nothing."

"And I don't want to," I said. "I'm leaving here in a few days. Just let Ronsel go, and he'll leave town and I'll leave town and neither one of us will ever say a word about this to anybody. Isn't that right, Ronsel?"

He nodded frantically.

"Let go of the rope, Dex," I said. "Come on now, just let it go."

It might have worked. Ronsel Jackson and I might have walked out of there, if my father hadn't laughed. I'd always hated his laugh. Harsh and pitiless as the cawing of a crow, it broke the spell I'd been trying to weave. Stokes and one of the others rushed me. I could have shot one of them, but I hesitated. They barreled into me and we crashed to the floor. Stokes punched me in the face. My arms were wrenched behind me, and somebody kicked me in the stomach. At some point I lost the gun.

"Nigger lover!" Turpin shouted. "Judas!"

The punches and kicks were coming from all sides now. I could hear Pappy yelling, "Stop it! That's enough!"

Finally a boot connected with the back of my head, and that was all. *Goodnight, Pappy. Goodnight, Ronsel. Goodnight.*

HAP

"Please Jesus," I said, "shepherd Your son Ronsel, keep him from harm and light his way home to us." I was praying loud on account of the storm, hollering at the Lord like He couldn't a heard me elseways. So when we heard that knocking we all just about jumped out of our skins, all of us cept for Florence. It was like she'd been waiting for it to come. She didn't even open her eyes, just kept right on praying. But when I got up to answer the door she grabbed ahold of my leg and held onto it so tight I couldn't move.

"Don't answer it," she said.

I could feel her shivering against me, quaking like a spent mule. I'd never seen my wife brung so low and afraid, not in all the years we'd been married. It hurt my heart to see that. Lilly May let into crying and the twins was hugging themselves, rocking back and forth on their knees.

"Come on now," I said. "Ain't the time for weakness now. We got to be strong."

The knocking come again, harder this time, and Florence let go of me. Ruel and Marlon gave each other a look like twins do when they talking without words, then they helped their mother to her feet and stood on either side of her. Drew themselves up tall, like men, and put their arms around her and Lilly May.

I went and opened the door. There was a fellow standing on the porch, I couldn't tell who it was at first on account of his head was bent, but then he looked up and I seen it was Sheriff Tacker and I thought, *He's dead. My boy is dead.*

"I've got bad news, Hap," the sheriff said. "It's about Ronsel." He looked behind me to where Florence and the children were standing. "You better step outside with me," he said.

"No," Florence said. "Whatever you got to say, you say it to all of us."

The sheriff shifted on his feet and looked down at the hat in his hands. "Seems your son ran afoul of an angry bunch of men tonight. He's alive, but he's hurt bad. They were pretty riled."

"Where is he?" I said.

"How bad?" Florence said.

He answered me and not her. "My deputy's taken him to the doctor in Belzoni. I'll drive you there now if you want."

Florence came over and stood beside me. She took ahold of my hand and gripped it hard. "How bad?" she asked the sheriff again.

He fumbled in his pocket and pulled out a piece of paper. "We found this laying on the ground next to him." Sheriff Tacker handed it to me. It was a letter and it had blood all over it, at first I thought it was just spilled on there but then I turned it sideways and seen the word and the numbers written in it, Ezekiel 7:4, written in blood by somebody's finger.

"What does it say?" Florence asked me.

But I couldn't answer her, fear had closed up my throat like a noose.

"Apparently your son was having relations with a white woman," the sheriff said.

"What? What white woman?" Florence said.

"Some German gal. That letter's from her, telling him he's the father of her son."

"It ain't true," Florence said. "Ronsel wouldn't do that."

I didn't want to believe it either but it was right there on the paper, I could read it through the blood. *You have a son*, it said. *Franz Ronsel.*

"Says there's a photograph with it but we didn't find it," the sheriff said.

"What did they do to him?" Florence said. I couldn't feel my hand, she was squeezing it so hard.

"They could've hanged him," the sheriff said. "He's lucky to be alive."

"You tell me what they done," Florence said.

And mine eye shall not spare thee, neither will I have pity: but I will recompense thy ways upon thee, and thine abominations shall be in the midst of thee: and ye shall know that I am the Lord. Ezekiel 7:4.

"They cut out his tongue," the sheriff said.

FLORENCE

MY SON'S TONGUE.

"Dear God," Hap said. "Dear God, how can this be true?"

They cut out his tongue.

"They could've hanged him," the sheriff said again.

They.

"Who did it?" I said.

"We don't know. They were gone by the time we got there," he said. He was lying though, a five-year-old could a told that.

"Where?" I said.

"The old sawmill."

I knowed right then who was behind this business. "How'd you know to go looking for him there in the first place?" I said.

"We got a tip there might be trouble," the sheriff said.

"Who from?"

"That ain't important. What matters is, your boy's alive and he's on his way to the doctor. If you want to get to him, we need to leave now."

"Why'd you send him all the way to Belzoni? Why not take him to Doc Turpin in town?"

The sheriff's eyes slid away from mine, and I knowed something else too. "He was one of em, wasn't he?" I said. "Who else was there besides him and Ole Man McAllan?"

The sheriff's face hardened up and his eyes got squinty. "Now you listen to me," he said. "I understand you're mighty upset, but you got no call to be pointing fingers at Doc Turpin or anybody else. If I was you, I'd be more careful what I said."

"Or what? You gone cut my tongue out?"

His Adam's apple gave a jerk. I stared him down. He was a scrawny little fellow, no more meat on him than a starving quail. I could a snapped his neck in about two seconds.

"You're lucky we followed up on that tip," he said. "Lucky we found him before he bled to death." His face was like a child's, I could see everything in it. His fear of us. His anger at my son for laying hand to a white woman. His disgust at what they done to Ronsel, and his sympathy for the devils who done it. The little bit of shame he felt for covering up for em. His impatience to be done with nigger business and get home to his wife and his supper.

"Yessuh, sheriff," I said, "we're one lucky family."

He put on his hat. "I'm leaving now. You want me to take you to Belzoni or not?"

Hap nodded and said, "Yessuh. My wife'll come with you."

"No, Hap," I said. "You go. I'll stay here with the children."

"You sure?" he asked, surprised. "Ronsel will be wanting his mother."

"It's better if you go."

My husband gave me a stern sharp look and said, "You keep that door locked, now." Meaning, *You just stay put and don't do nothing foolish.*

And I looked right back at him and said, "Don't you worry bout us, you just take care of Ronsel." Meaning, *And I'll take care of what else needs taking care of.*

I would use Hap's skinning knife. It wasn't the biggest knife we owned but it had the thinnest blade. I reckoned it would go in the easiest.

LAURA

I woke to cursing and pounding: Pappy's voice, punctuated by his fists hitting the front door. "Wake up, goddamnit! Let me in!"

I'd fallen asleep on the couch. The room was pitch dark; the lantern must have burned out. I'd barred the door earlier, something I seldom did anymore, but after Florence left I'd felt unaccountably afraid. The night had seemed full of terrible possibility waiting to coalesce, to shape itself into monstrous form and come for me. As if a flimsy wooden door and an old two-by-four could have kept it out.

"Just a minute, I'm coming," I said.

Either the old man didn't hear me or he was enjoying himself too much to stop, because the racket continued while I got the lantern lit and went to the door.

"About time," he snapped, when I opened it. "I've been standing out here for five minutes." He pushed past me, tracking mud all over the floor, and looked around the room. "Jamie hasn't come home yet?"

"No, unless he's asleep in the lean-to."

"I checked already. He ain't there." Pappy's voice had an edge to it I'd never heard before. He removed his dripping hat, hung it on a peg then went back to the doorway and peered out into the night. "Maybe he missed the place in the dark," he said. "He was on foot, and you didn't leave a light on."

As they were meant to do, his words let loose a storm of guilt in me. Then their meaning penetrated. "How do you know he was on foot? Did you see him?"

"He ain't got a car, that's how I know," said Pappy. "So if he left here, he had to been walking."

The old man's back was to me, but I didn't have to see his yellow teeth to know he was lying through them. "You asked me if he'd come home *yet*," I said. "If you haven't seen him, how'd you know he left in the first place?"

He reached into his shirt pocket and pulled out a pack of cigarettes. He shook one out, then crumpled the pack in his fist and threw it out onto the porch. "Shit!" he said. "They're soaking wet."

I went to him and gripped his shoulder, turning him toward me. It was the first time I'd touched him on purpose since my wedding day, when I'd given him a dutiful, and obviously un-welcome, kiss on the cheek.

"What's wrong? Has something happened to him?"

He jerked his shoulder out of my hand. "Let me alone, woman. I'm sure he's fine." But he didn't sound sure, he sounded guilty and oddly defiant at the same time, like a wicked boy who's done some longed-for forbidden thing: hit his sister, or drowned a cat. A dark suspicion bloomed in me.

"Has this got something to do with Ronsel Jackson being missing?" I said, watching his face.

"Who says he's missing?"

"His mother. She came by here looking for him around seven."

He shrugged. "Niggers go missing all the time."

"If you've harmed that boy, or Jamie—"

The old man's features contorted, and his eyes lit with hate. "You'll what? Tell me what you'll do." His spittle flecked my face. "You think you can threaten me, gal? You better think again. I've seen the way you sniff after Jamie like a sow in rut. Henry may be too thick to notice but I ain't, and I ain't afraid to tell him either."

I could feel my face reddening, but I brazened it out. "My husband would never believe that."

He cocked his head to one side, calculating. "Well maybe he will and maybe he won't, but I bet it sure will stick in his craw. Henry ain't got much of an imagination but with a thing like that you don't need one. A thing like that, a man will always wonder about. There'll always be a little bit of doubt."

"You're despicable."

"I'm wet," he said. "Fetch me a towel."

He sauntered to the kitchen table, planted himself in one of the chairs and waited. For a moment I just stood there, paralyzed by the emotions tearing through me—shame, anger, fear, all battling for dominance. Then my limbs seemed to move of their own accord: walking to the linen cupboard, taking out a clean towel, walking back to him. He snatched it from my hand. "Now fix me something to eat. I'm hungry."

As mechanically as a windup toy, I went to the stove, took

cornbread from the oven and spooned chili onto a plate. Thinking of Henry, and how he would feel if Pappy carried out his threat and said something to him. I set the plate down in front of the old man and started to leave the room.

"If you hear Jamie come in," he said, around a mouth full of cornbread, "you come wake me up. And if Henry or anybody else asks you where I was tonight, you tell em I was right here at home with you, hear?"

I pictured those pale hateful eyes closed, the mouth shut, the skin waxen. Pictured it melting away until there was nothing but smooth white bone, crumbling slowly into dust. "Yes, Pappy," I said.

He gave me a malicious smile, knowing he'd won. Still, I thought, there were plenty of ways for an old man to die on a farm. You never knew when tragedy might strike out of the blue.

I LAY ON MY BED with my eyes open, waiting for Pappy to finish eating and turn in. When I heard the front door open and close, I got up and checked on the children. They were sleeping, with an untroubled abandon I envied. I set about cleaning up the mess the old man had left, grateful for work to keep my hands busy while I waited for Jamie and whatever else would come that night. But imposing order on the house did nothing to ease the turmoil in my mind. *A sow in rut.* Had I really been so transparent? Was that how Jamie thought of me? *A thing like that, a man will always wonder about.* I couldn't bear the thought of causing Henry such pain, even if it meant lying for Pappy. But if he'd harmed Jamie . . .

Suddenly remembering what the old man had said about Jamie being lost in the dark, I took one of the lanterns out to the front porch with the intention of leaving it there as a beacon. It was then that I saw the light in the barn. Jamie—it had to be.

I didn't even stop to change into my boots or put on my coat. I simply walked into the storm, my one thought to reach him. The night was wild: lashing rain, furious gusts of wind that whipped my hair and my clothes. The barn door was shut, and it took all my strength to get it open. Jamie was curled on the dirt floor of the barn, sobbing. The sounds that came from him were so anguished they were nearly inhuman. They mingled with the plaintive lowing of our cow, who was moving restlessly in her stall.

I ran and knelt beside him. He'd been beaten. There was a cut above his eyebrow, and one cheek was red and swollen. I pulled his head into my lap and when I did, felt a large lump on the back of it. Hot rage surged through me. Pappy had done this to him, I had no doubt of it.

"I'll go fetch some water and a clean cloth," I said.

"No," he said, wrapping his arms around my waist. "Don't leave me." He clung to me, shuddering. I murmured soothing nonsense to him and dabbed at the cut on his forehead with my sleeve. When his sobbing quieted I asked him what had happened, but he just shook his head and squeezed his eyes shut. I lay down behind him and curled my body around his, stroking his hair, listening to the droning patter of the rain on the roof. Time passed, ten minutes or twenty. One of the mules whickered, and I felt rather than heard movement, a displacement of air. I opened my eyes. Saw Florence standing in the open doorway of the barn. Her dress was soaked through, and her legs were muddy to the knee. Her face was a blasted ruin. The hairs on my arms rose up and I shivered, knowing something terrible must have happened to Ronsel. Then I saw the knife in her hand. *Ronsel is dead,* I thought, with absolute certainty, *and she means to kill us for it.* I was strangely unafraid. What I felt most keenly was pity—for Florence and her son, and for Henry and the girls, who would find our bodies in the barn and grieve and wonder. There was no way I could stop her; I didn't even think to try. I closed my eyes, pressing myself against Jamie's back, waiting for what would come. I felt a stirring of air, heard a whisper of bare feet on dirt. When I opened my eyes she was gone. The whole incident had taken perhaps fifteen seconds.

For a long while I just lay there, feeling my heart trip and gradually slow down until it kept pace with Jamie's again. A boom of thunder sounded, and I thought of the children. They'd be frightened if they woke and I wasn't there. Then I thought of Pappy, sleeping alone in the lean-to. And I knew where Florence had been headed.

I sat up. Jamie made a whimpering sound and drew his knees up to his chest. Before I left the barn I got a horse blanket and covered him with it. Then I knelt beside him and kissed him on the forehead.

"Sweet Jamie," I whispered.

He slept, oblivious, his breath whistling softly with each exhalation.

I DREAMED OF HONEY, golden and viscous. I floated in it like an embryo. It filled my eyes, nose and ears, shutting out the world. It was so pleasant, to do nothing but float in all that sweetness.

"Mama, wake up!" The voices were piercing, insistent. I tried to ignore them—I didn't want to leave the honeyed place—but they kept tugging at me, pulling me out. "Mama, please! Wake up!"

I opened my eyes to find Amanda Leigh and Bella hovering over me. Their mouths and chins were smeared in honey speckled with cornbread crumbs, and their hands on me were sticky. I looked at the clock on the bedside table; it was after nine. They must have gotten hungry and helped themselves to breakfast.

"Pappy won't wake up," said Amanda Leigh, "and he's not in his eyes anymore."

"What?"

"He's in his bed but he isn't in his eyes."

"We can't find Uncle Jamie," said Bella.

Uncle Jamie. I pictured him above me, mouth open, head thrown back in pleasure. Pictured him as I'd left him last night, curled in a ball on the floor of the barn.

I got up and put on my robe and slippers, then led the girls

out to the lean-to. The rain had stopped, but it was a temporary respite; the clouds were dark gray for as far as I could see.
The door creaked loudly when I pushed it open. I knew what I
would find inside, but even so I wasn't prepared for the feeling
of elation that shot through me when I saw Pappy's body lying
stiff on the cot, vacant of malice and of life.

"Is he dead?" asked Amanda Leigh.

"Yes, darling," I said.

"Then how come his eyes are open?"

Her mouth was pursed, and there was a familiar vertical
furrow between her eyebrows, a miniature version of the one
that creased Henry's face when he was perplexed. I kissed her
there, then said, "They must have been open when he died.
We'll shut them for him."

I pushed down on his eyelids with the very tips of my fingers, trying not to touch the eyeballs, but the lids wouldn't
budge—the old man was contrary even in death. I rubbed my
fingers against my robe, wanting to rid them of the feel of that
cold, hard flesh.

"Does he not want you to shut them?" Bella whispered.

"No, honey. His body is just too stiff right now. It's a natural
part of dying. We'll be able to shut them tomorrow."

There was no blood and no knife wound, but Jamie's pillow was on the floor. She must have decided to suffocate him
instead. I was glad; a wound would have raised unwelcome
questions. I bent down to pick up the pillow and put it back on
the bed. There was a piece of white fabric on the floor beneath
it—a pillowcase, I saw when I picked it up. It wasn't one of

ours; the cotton was dingy and coarsely woven. Then I turned it over and saw the eyeholes cut in the fabric, and bile rose in the back of my throat. I balled the hideous thing up quickly and stuffed it in the pocket of my robe. I would burn it in the stove later.

"What is it, Mama?"

"Just an old dirty pillowcase."

It was impossible not to picture the scene: the taunting men in their white hoods, the sweating and terrified brown face in their midst. I wondered how many others there had been, and where they'd done it; whether they'd hanged him or killed him some other way. Jamie must have found out about it—that was why he'd been so distraught last night. I wondered if he'd seen what happened. If he'd watched his father murder that poor boy.

"Is Pappy in heaven now?" asked Bella.

The old man's face was expressionless, and his untenanted eyes gave away nothing of what he'd felt in his last moments. I hoped he'd seen Florence coming for him and been afraid; that he'd begged and struggled and known the agony of help-lessness, as Ronsel must have. I hoped she'd taken pleasure in killing him, and that it would give her some kind of grim peace to know she'd avenged her son.

"He's in God's hands," I said.

"Should we say a prayer for him?" asked Amanda Leigh.

"Yes, I suppose we should. Come here, both of you. Don't be scared."

They came and knelt on either side of me. Mud from the

dirty floor oozed through the thin cotton of my nightgown. I felt a fat plop of water hit my head, then another; the roof was leaking. The girls waited for me to begin, their small, soft bodies pressing into mine from either side. I closed my eyes, but no words came. I would not pray for Pappy's soul; that would be the worst sort of hypocrisy. I could have prayed for Florence, that God would understand and forgive her a mother's vengeance, but not in front of the children. And so I was silent. I had no words to give them, or Him.

A shadow fell across us, and I turned and saw Jamie in the doorway. The light was behind him so I couldn't see his expression. Bella got up and ran to him, hugging him around the knees. "Pappy's dead, Uncle Jamie!" she cried.

"It's true," I said. "I'm sorry."

He picked Bella up and moved to stand at the foot of the bed. He was still in his dirty clothes from the night before, but he'd combed his hair and washed his battered face. There was bitterness in his eyes as he gazed down at his father's body, and sorrow. I'd expected the one but not the other. It tore at my heart.

"It looks like he went peacefully, in his sleep," I lied.

"That's how I'd like to go," Jamie said in a small voice. "In my sleep."

He looked down at me then, a look of such tender desolation that I could hardly bear to meet it. I saw a brother's guilt in that look, but none of the shame or contempt I'd feared to find. Just love and pain and something else I recognized finally as gratitude, for what I'd given him. Gone was the gallant and fearless aviator, the laughing cocksure hero of my imaginings. But even as I mourned his loss, I knew that that Jamie wouldn't have needed my comfort, or lain with me.

That Jamie had never really existed.

The realization stunned me, though it shouldn't have. He'd given me all the clues I needed to see the weakness at the core of him, and the darkness. I'd ignored them, preferring to believe the fiction. Jamie had created that fiction, acting the part almost to perfection, but I'd been the one who swallowed it whole. I was to blame, for having fallen in love with a figment.

I loved him still, but there was no longing to it, no heat. Already the memory of our lovemaking was beginning to seem distant, as though it had happened to someone else. I felt strangely empty, without all that carnal furor.

I think he saw it in my eyes. His own dropped to the floor. He set Bella down and knelt beside me, bending his head. Waiting for me to begin. For the second time, I was at a loss. What honest prayer could I, an adulteress kneeling with my lover beside the body of my hated, murdered father-in-law, possibly offer Him? And then I knew, and I clasped Jamie's hand in mine and started to sing:

> Praise God, from Whom all blessings flow;
> Praise Him, all creatures here below;
> Praise Him above, ye heavenly host:
> Praise Father, Son, and Holy Ghost. Amen.

My voice was strong and clear as I sang the familiar words of thanksgiving. The girls joined in at once—the Doxology was the first hymn I'd ever taught them—and then Jamie did as well. His voice was raw, and it splintered on the *amen*. I found myself thinking that Henry wouldn't have waited for me to begin. He would have led us in prayer unhesitatingly, and his voice wouldn't have cracked.

JAMIE

THE BIBLE IS FULL of thou-shalt-nots. Thou shalt not kill, that's one. Thou shalt not bear false witness against thy neighbor, that's two. Thou shalt not commit adultery, thou shalt not uncover the nakedness of thy brother's wife—three and four. Notice how none of them have any loopholes. There are no dependent clauses you can hang your sins on, like: Thou shalt not uncover the nakedness of thy brother's wife, *unless* thou art wandering in the blackest hell, lost to yourself and to every memory of light and goodness, and uncovering her nakedness is the only way back to yourself. No, the Bible's absolute when it comes to most things. It's why I don't believe in God.

Sometimes it's necessary to do wrong. Sometimes it's the only way to make things right. Any God who doesn't understand that can go fuck Himself.

Thou shalt not take the name of the Lord thy God in vain—that's five.

THE DAY AFTER the lynching passed with the slow heaviness of a dream. I hurt everywhere, and I had the mother of all hangovers. I couldn't stop thinking of Ronsel, of the knife flashing, the blood spurting, the clotted howling that went on and on.

I took refuge in work. There was plenty of it: the storm had wrecked the chicken coop, peeled half the roof off the cotton house and sent the pigs into a murderous frenzy. Henry hadn't returned from Greenville yet, but we expected him back any time. I'd gone earlier to check the bridge and found it just barely passable. From the ominous look of the clouds, it wouldn't stay that way for long. In weather like this Henry would know to hurry home.

I was in the barn milking when Laura came and found me. Venus hadn't been milked since the previous morning, and her udders were full to bursting. She'd already punished me for it twice by swatting me in the face with her cocklebur-infested tail. Still, it was good to sit with my cheek against her warm hide, listening to the snare-drum sound of milk hitting the pail, letting the rhythm empty my head.

"Jamie," Laura said. I looked up and saw her standing just outside the stall. "Henry will be back soon. We need to talk before he gets here."

With some reluctance I left the shelter of the stall and went to her. She had on lipstick, I noticed, but apart from that she was totally without artifice, probably the only woman I'd ever known who was. That would change now, because of me. I had turned her into a liar.

"How are the girls?" I asked her.

"Fine. They're both asleep. All this has worn them out."

"I expect it has. Death is unsettling. Especially the first time you see it."

"They wanted to know if you and Henry and I would die someday, and I said we would, a long time from now. Then they asked if they would die. I think it was the first time it ever occurred to them."

"What did you tell them?"

"The truth. I don't think Bella believed me, though."

"Good," I said. "Let her have her immortality while she can."

Laura hesitated, then said, "I need to ask you about something." She pulled a crumpled piece of white cloth from her pocket. Even before I saw the eyeholes I knew what it was. "I found this on the floor of the lean-to. I imagine it belonged to Pappy." When I didn't answer, she said, "You've seen it before, haven't you?"

I nodded, the memories exploding like grenades in my head.

"Tell me what happened, Jamie."

I told her. How I'd seen the light near the sawmill and gone over there. How I'd discovered Ronsel with a rope around his neck in a room full of hooded men, my father among them. How I'd broken in on them and tried to get Ronsel out of there. How I'd failed. "I didn't even fire my gun," I said.

"Listen to me," Laura said. "What happened to that boy isn't your fault. You tried to save him, which is more than most people would have done. I'm sure Ronsel knew that. I'm sure he appreciated it."

"Yeah, I bet he's just overflowing with gratitude towards me. He probably can't wait to thank me."

"He's alive?"

"Yes."

"Thank God," she said, her eyes closing in relief.

"At least, he was when I left," I said. And then I told her the first lie: how I'd come to with Sheriff Tacker bending over me, and the others gone, and learned they'd cut out Ronsel's tongue. Laura's hand flew to her own mouth. Mine, I remembered, had done the same.

"Tom Rossi drove him to the doctor," I said. "He'd lost a lot of blood." It had been everywhere: drenching his shirt, pooling on the floor, spattering Turpin's white robes.

"Why?" she asked. "Why did they do it?

I reached in my pocket and pulled out the photo and handed it to her. She looked at it, then back at me. "Who are they?"

"That's Ronsel's German lover, and the child she had by him. There was a letter with it, I don't know what happened to it."

"How did they get hold of this?"

"I don't know," I said. Lie number two. "I guess Ronsel must have dropped it somewhere."

"And one of them found it."

"Yes."

"Who else was there, besides Pappy?"

"I didn't recognize any of the others," I said.

Lie number three, this one for her own safety. I'm sure she saw through it, but she didn't call me on it. She just gazed at me thoughtfully. I had the feeling I was being weighed, and found wanting. It gave me an unfamiliar pang. I'd cheerfully disappointed dozens of women. Why, with Laura, did it feel so bad?

"What will you tell Henry?" she asked.

"I don't know. He's going to be upset enough as it is, without having to know that our father was part of a lynch mob."

"Did Tom or Sheriff Tacker actually see Pappy at the sawmill?"

"I don't think so. But even if they did, this is the Delta. The last thing the sheriff wants to do is identify any of them."

"What about Ronsel?"

"He won't talk. They made sure of that."

"He could write it down."

I shook my head. "What do you suppose would happen to him if he did? What would happen to his family?"

Laura's eyes widened. "Are we in danger?"

"No," I said. "Not as long as I leave here."

She walked to the barn door and looked out at the brown fields and the bleak crouching sky, hugging herself with her arms. "How I hate this place," she said softly.

I remembered the strength of those arms around me, and the surprising sureness with which her hand had gripped me and guided me into her. I wondered if she was that fierce and sure with my brother. If she cried out his name like she'd cried out mine.

"I can't see any reason to tell Henry your father was involved," she said finally. "It would only hurt him needlessly, to know the truth."

"All right. If you think so."

She turned and looked at me, holding my gaze for long seconds. "We won't ever speak of it," she said.

WHEN HENRY GOT home he was already in a welter because of the storm. Laura and I met him at the car, but he barely gave us a glance as he brushed by us to kneel in the fields and examine one of the flattened rows of newly planted cotton. It had started to rain again, and we were all getting soaked.

"If this keeps up all the seed will be washed away, and we'll have to replant," he said. "The almanac predicted light rain in April, damnit. What time did it start here?"

"Around five o'clock yesterday," said Laura. "It poured all night long."

Her voice sounded strained. Henry looked from her to me and frowned. "What happened to your face?"

I'd forgotten all about my face. I tried to think up a story to explain it, but my mind was blank.

"Venus kicked him," Laura blurted out. "Last night, when he was milking. The storm agitated her. All the animals. One of the pigs is dead. The others trampled it."

Henry looked from her back to me. "What in the hell's the matter with the two of you?"

She waited for me to tell him, but I shook my head. I couldn't speak. "Honey," she said, "your father is gone. He died last night in his sleep."

She went and stood next to him but didn't touch him. He wasn't ready to be touched yet. *How well she knows him*, I thought. *How well they suit each other.* He bent his head and stared at his muddy boots. Eldest child, now the head of our family. I saw the weight of that settle on him.

"Is he . . . still in his bed?" Henry was asking me. I nodded. "I guess I'd better go and see him," he said.

Together the three of us walked to the lean-to. Henry went in first. Laura and I followed, coming to stand on either side of him. He pulled the sheet down. Pappy's eyes, vacant and bulging, stared up at us. Henry reached out to close them, but Laura took his hand and gently pulled it back.

"No, honey," she said. "We already tried. He's still too stiff."

Henry let out a long breath. I put an arm around him and so did Laura. When our hands accidentally touched behind his back, she shifted hers away.

I hadn't expected Henry to cry, and he didn't. His face was impassive as he looked down at our father's dead body. He turned to me. "Are you all right?" he asked.

I felt a flare of resentment. Did he never get tired of being the strong one, of being stoic and honorable and dependable? I saw in that moment that I'd always resented him, even as I'd looked up to him, and that I'd bedded his wife in part to punish him for being all the things I wasn't.

"I'm fine," I said.

Henry nodded and squeezed my shoulder, then looked back down at Pappy. "I wonder what he saw, at the end."

"It was a dark night," I told him. "No moon or stars. I doubt he saw much of anything."

Lie number four.

"NIGGER LOVER!" Turpin shouted. "Judas!"

Finally a boot connected with the back of my head, and that

was all—for five minutes or so. When I came to, somebody was none too gently slapping my cheek. I was lying on my side with the other cheek against the dirt. The room was a blur of legs and white robes.

"Wake up," said my father, giving me a hard shake. A half dozen overlapping hooded heads swam over me. I tried to push him away from me. That's when I realized my hands were tied behind my back. He pulled me to a sitting position and propped me against the wall. The sudden motion made the room spin, and I felt myself starting to topple over. Pappy yanked me back up again by my jacket collar. "Sit up and act like a man," he hissed in my ear. "You make one more wrong move, and these boys are liable to kill you."

When the room resettled itself I saw Ronsel, still alive, his head straining upward in an effort to keep the noose from choking him.

"What are we gonna do with him?" said Deweese, waving in my direction.

"No need to do anything," said Pappy. "He won't talk, he told you so already. Ain't that right, son?"

My father was scared, I realized. He was scared as hell, and he was trying to protect me. I think it was right then that I really began to feel afraid myself. My heart started to pound and I felt sweat breaking out all over me, but I made my voice stay calm and confident. For me and Ronsel to walk out of here alive, I would need to give the performance of my life.

"That's right," I said. "Just let him go, and as far as I'm concerned this never happened."

The hulking figure of Orris Stokes loomed over me.

"You ain't in a position to make demands, nigger lover. If I was you, I'd worry less about what happens to him and more about your own skin."

"Jamie won't go to the law," said Pappy. "Not when we tell him what the nigger did."

"What did he do?" I asked.

"He fucked a white woman and got a child on her," Pappy said.

"Bullshit. Ronsel wouldn't do any such thing."

"Is that a fact," said Turpin. "You think you know him, huh? Well, what do you say to this?"

He thrust a photo in front of my eyes, of a thin, pretty blonde holding a mulatto baby. It definitely hadn't been taken in Mississippi. The ground was covered with snow, and there was an alpine-style house in the background.

"Who is she?" I said.

"Some German gal," said Turpin.

"And what makes you think Ronsel's the father?"

He waved a piece of paper in the air. "Says so right here in this letter. She even named it after him."

My feelings must have shown in my face. "See?" Pappy said. "I told you boys he'd be with us on this."

I looked over at Ronsel. He blinked once, slowly, in affirmation. There was no shame in his eyes. If anything, they seemed to challenge me, to say, *What kind of man are you? Guess we're about to find out.* I looked at the photo again, remembering how shocked I'd been when I first saw Negro GIs with white girls in the pubs and dance halls of Europe. Eventually I'd gotten used to it. Soldiers will be soldiers, I'd told myself, and the girls were obviously willing. But I'd never been easy with it, and I still wasn't. And if *I* wasn't, I could only imagine what that photograph stirred up in these white-sheeted men. That, and Ronsel's quiet pride in himself, which must have infuriated them. I knew their kind: locked in the imagined glory of the past, scared of losing what they thought was theirs. They would make an answer. I understood that, and them, all too well. But I couldn't let them kill Ronsel. And if I didn't come up with something quick, they would.

"What do you fellows care about some Kraut whore?" I said.

That earned me a hard kick in the thigh from Orris's boot.

"Just tell em you won't talk," urged Pappy. I could hear the desperation in his voice, and if I could hear it, so could they. That was dangerous. Nothing goads a pack like the scent of fear.

"You're not taking my meaning," I said. "These fräuleins, they're not like our women. They're cold-hearted cunts who'll smile to your face then stab you in the back the first chance they get. They got an awful lot of our boys killed over there. So if Ronsel exacted a little vengeance on one of them and left her with a reminder of it, I call it justice."

There was silence. I began to have a little hope.

"You're good, boy," said Turpin. "Too bad you're full of shit."

"Listen, I'm not saying we should give him a medal for it. I'm just saying it doesn't seem right, killing a decorated soldier over an enemy whore."

Another silence.

"The nigger's still got to be punished," Pappy said.

"And kept from doing it again," said Stokes. "You know how these bucks are once they get a taste for white women. What's to stop him from going after one here?"

"*We're* gonna stop him," said Turpin. "Right here and right now."

He opened a leather case on the floor and pulled out a scalpel. Somebody whistled. Excitement crackled through the room. Ronsel and I started talking at the same time:

"Please, suh. I'm begging you, please don't—"

"You don't need that, he's learned his les—"

Doc Turpin's voice cut across ours like a whip. "If either of them says one more word, shoot the nigger."

I shut up, and so did Ronsel.

"This nigger profaned a white woman," Turpin said. "He fouled her body with his eyes and his hands and his tongue and his seed, and for that he's got to pay. What'll it be, boys?"

They all spoke at once: "Geld him." "Blind him." "Cut it all off!"

I caught a whiff of urine and saw a stain spreading across the front of Ronsel's pants. The smell of piss and sweat and musk was overwhelming. I swallowed hard to keep myself from throwing up.

Then my father said, "I say we let my son decide."

"Why should we do that?" Turpin demanded.

"Yeah," said Stokes, "why should he get to do it?"

"If he decides, he's part of it," said Pappy.

"No," I said. "I won't do it."

My father bent down to me, his eyes narrowed to slits. He put his mouth up to my ear. "You know where I found that letter?" he said. "In the cab of our truck, on the floor of the passenger seat. Only one way it could've got there, and that's if you let him ride with you again. This is *your* doing. You think about that."

I shook my head hard, not wanting to believe it, knowing it had to be true. Pappy pulled away and raised his voice so the others could hear. "You had to stick your nose in. Busting in here like Gary Cooper, waving that gun around and making threats. Threatening me, your own father, over a nigger! Well, you're in it now, son. You don't want him killed, fine. You decide his punishment."

"I said I won't do it."

"You will," said Turpin. "Or I will. And I don't think your boy here will like my choice." He made a crude stabbing gesture toward his crotch. There were hoots and chuckles from the others. Ronsel was shuddering, his muscles straining against the ropes that bound him. His eyes implored me.

"What's it gonna be?" said Turpin. "His eyes, his tongue, his hands or his balls? Choose, nigger lover."

When I didn't answer Deweese swung the shotgun around, pointing it at me. My father stepped away from me, leaving me alone in the shotgun's field. Deweese cocked it. "Choose," he said.

Here it was, the oblivion I'd been chasing for so long. All I had to do was stay silent, and I would have it—an end to pain and fear and emptiness. Here it was, if I just had the guts to reach out and grab hold of it.

"Choose, goddamnit," said my father.

I chose.

LAURA

I WENT TO SEE Florence the day after we found Pappy dead. I wanted to find out how Ronsel was. I also needed to have a private talk with her. I couldn't have her working for me anymore. I didn't think she'd want to in any case, but I had to be sure of it, and of her silence.

I told Jamie where I was going and asked him to watch the children for me. As I was about to walk out the door, he pulled something from his pocket and handed it to me: the photograph of Ronsel's German lover and their child. My arms broke out into gooseflesh; I didn't want to touch it. I tried to hand it back to him.

"No," he said. "You give that to Florence, for Ronsel. Ask her to tell him . . ." He shook his head, at a loss. His mouth was tight with self-loathing.

I gave his hand a gentle squeeze. "I'm sure he knows," I said.

I intended to drive, but both the car and the truck were mired too deeply in mud, so I took my umbrella and set out on foot. The rain had slackened a little since yesterday, but it was still coming down steadily. As I walked past the barn, Henry saw me and came to the open door. "Where are you going?" he asked.

"To Florence's. She didn't show up for work yesterday or today."

Henry still didn't know about what had happened to Ronsel. Hap hadn't come and told him, and we'd been cut off from town since last night. Jamie and I had said nothing, of course. We weren't supposed to know about it yet.

Henry frowned. "You shouldn't be out in this mess. I'll go over there later and see about it. You go on back to the house."

I thought quickly. "I need to ask her some questions. About how to prepare the body."

"All right. But take care you don't fall. The road's slippery."

His concern for me brought a lump to my throat. "I'll be careful," I said.

Lilly May answered my knock. Her eyes were red-rimmed and swollen. I asked to speak to her mother.

"I'll see," she said.

She closed the door in my face. I felt a clutch of fear. What if Ronsel hadn't survived his wounds? For his family's sake, and for Jamie's, I prayed that he had. I waited on the porch for perhaps five minutes, though it felt like much longer. Finally the door opened and Florence came out. Her face was drawn, her eyes sunken. I feared the worst, but then there came a long, guttural moan from inside the house. It was a horrible sound, but it meant he was alive. They must have brought him back home yesterday afternoon, I thought, before the river flooded the bridge.

"How is he?" I asked.

Florence didn't answer, just gave me a cold, knowing stare. I stared back at her, adulteress to murderess. Reminding her that I knew things too.

"We leaving here soon as the river goes down," she said curtly. "Hap'll be by later today to tell your husband."

Relief flooded me, overwhelming the small bit of shame that accompanied it. I would not have to see her, even from a distance; would not be reminded daily of how my family had destroyed hers. "Where will you go?" I asked.

She shrugged and looked out over the drowned fields. "Away from here."

There was only one thing I could offer her. "The old man is dead," I said. "He died night before last, in his sleep." I emphasized the last part, but if she was reassured her face didn't show it. If anything, she looked even more bitter. "God will know what to do with him," I said.

She shook her head. "God don't give a damn."

As if to prove her words, Ronsel moaned again. Florence closed her eyes. I don't know what was more terrible: listening to that sound, or watching Florence listen to it. It might as well have been her own tongue being torn from her body. I shuddered, imagining how I would feel if that sound were coming out of Amanda Leigh or Bella. I thought of Vera Atwood. Of my own mother, still grieving after all these years for Teddy's lost twin.

"I have something for him, from Jamie," I said. I took out the photograph and handed it to her. "It was taken in Germany. The child is—"

"I know who he is." She brushed her fingers lightly across the surface of the picture, touching the face of the grandson she would never see. Then she shoved it in her pocket and looked at me. "I need to get back to him," she said.

"I'm sorry," I said. Two words, pitifully inadequate to carry the weight of all that had happened, but I said them anyway.

Ain't your fault. Three words, a gift of absolution I didn't deserve. I would have given anything to hear Florence say them, but she didn't. All she said was goodbye.

JAMIE

THE FIVE OF US staggered through the mud to the grave. It was still raining lightly but the wind had picked up, coming in violent gusts that seemed to blow us in every direction but the one we needed to go. Henry and I carried the coffin and the ropes. Laura walked behind with the children, Bella in her arms and Amanda Leigh hanging onto her skirt.

When we got to the hole we set the coffin down and worked the ropes underneath it, one on each end. Henry moved to the other side of the hole and I threw him the two rope-ends. But when we tried to lift it, the ropes slipped to the center and the coffin teetered, then tumbled to the ground. The wood groaned, and there was a loud crack from inside the box—Pappy's skull, hitting the wood. One of the boards on the side had pried loose. I bent and pushed the nails back in with my thumb.

"This isn't gonna work," I said. "Not with just the two of us."

"It'll have to work," Henry said.

"Maybe if we stood at either end and ran the ropes lengthwise."

"No," he said. "The coffin's too narrow. If it falls again it could break open."

I shrugged—*so what?*

"No," he said again in a low voice, with a glance at the children.

Laura pointed at the road. "Look. Here come the Jacksons."

We watched their wagon approach. Hap and Florence sat up front, and the two younger boys walked behind. The wagon was piled high with furniture. As it got closer I saw they'd strung up a makeshift tarp in back. I knew Ronsel was under there, suffering.

When they came abreast of us Henry waved them down.

"Don't," Laura said. "Just let them go."

He shot her an indignant look. "It's not my fault, what happened to that boy. I warned him. I warned both of them. And now Hap's leaving me in the middle of planting season when he knows damn well it's too late for me to find another tenant. The least he can do is give us a quick hand here."

I opened my mouth to agree with Laura, but she gave a slight shake of her head and I swallowed the words.

"Hap!" Henry shouted over the wind. "Can you help us out here?"

Hap whoa'd the mule, and he, Florence and the two boys turned and looked at us. Even from thirty yards away, I could feel the force of their hate.

"We could use some extra hands!" Henry shouted.

I expected them to refuse—I sure as hell would have. But then Hap handed the reins to Florence and started to get down.

She grabbed hold of his arm and said something to him, and he shook his head and said something back.

"What are they dithering about?" Henry said impatiently.

Hap and Florence were really going at it now. Their voices weren't quite loud enough for me to make out what they were saying, but I could guess well enough.

"*No, Hap. Don't you do it.*"

"*It's the Lord's doing we passed by here just now, and I ain't gone argue with Him. Now come on and let's see it done.*"

"*I ain't helping that devil get nowhere.*"

"*You ain't helping him, he's already burning in hell. You helping God to do His work.*"

I saw Florence spit over the side of the wagon.

"*That's for your God. He ain't getting nothing more from me. He done taken enough already.*"

"*All right then. I won't be long.*"

Hap climbed down. He turned toward the two boys, and Florence spoke again. Her meaning was plain enough: "*And don't you ask the twins to do it neither.*"

Hap trudged to the grave alone, head bent, eyes on the ground. When he reached us, Henry said, "Thank you for stopping, Hap. We were hoping you and one of your boys could help us get the coffin in."

"I'll help you," Hap said, "but they ain't coming."

Henry frowned and his forehead knitted up.

"It's all right," Laura said quickly. "I can do it."

She set Bella down next to Amanda Leigh and took up one of the rope ends. Henry, Hap and I took the other three. Together we maneuvered the coffin over the hole and lowered it down. When it touched bottom we managed to wiggle one of the ropes out from under it, but the other one caught and wouldn't come loose. Henry cursed under his breath and let the ends fall down into the hole. He looked at Laura.

"Did you bring a Bible?" he asked.

"No," she said, "I didn't think of it."

I saw Hap look up at the sky, head cocked like he was listening to something. Then he bowed it and said, "I've got one right here, Mist McAllan." He pulled a small, tattered Bible from his shirt pocket. "I can send him on if you want. Reckon that's why I'm here." I searched his face for irony or spite, but I saw neither.

"No, Hap," Henry said. "Thank you, but no."

"Done this plenty of times for my own people," Hap said.

"He wouldn't want it," Henry said.

"I say we let him do it," I said.

"He wouldn't want it," Henry repeated.

"*I* want it," I said. We glared at each other.

Laura broke the stalemate. "Yes, Henry," she said, "if Hap is willing to do it I think we should let him. He is a man of God."

"All right, Hap," Henry said after a moment. "Go on then."

Hap leafed through the Bible. He opened his mouth to begin, then something flickered in his eyes, and he turned to an earlier page. I was expecting, "The Lord is my shepherd"; I think we all were. What we got was something else entirely.

"Call now, if there be any that will answer thee; and to

which of the saints wilt thou turn?" Hap's voice was strong and ringing. I saw Laura's head lift in surprise. She told me later the passage was from Job—hardly the thing to comfort the bereaved at a burial.

"Man that is born of a woman is of few days, and full of trouble," Hap went on. "He cometh forth like a flower, and is cut down: he fleeth also as a shadow, and continueth not. And dost thou open thine eyes upon such a one, and bringest me into judgment with thee? Who can bring a clean thing out of an unclean? Not one."

Henry was frowning. I think he would have put a stop to the reading if the clouds hadn't erupted just then, loosing their contents and drenching us all. While Hap shouted about death and iniquity, Henry and I grabbed the shovels and began filling the hole back up.

So it was that our father was laid to rest in a slave's grave, in a hurried, graceless ceremony presided over by an accusatory colored preacher, while the woman who meant to kill him looked on, stiff-backed and full of impotent rage that somebody else had beaten her to it.

If Pappy had woken up when I came in with the lantern, Florence might have gotten her chance. But he didn't. He slept on peacefully, his face relaxed, his breathing deep and steady, the way a man sleeps after a long and satisfying day's work. I stood there watching him for some time, dripping water and blood onto the floor, feeling the fury build inside me. I heard his voice saying, *You'd think I had three daughters and not two.* And, *"My son don't have the balls to kill a man up close."*

And, *"The nigger's still got to be punished."* I don't remember picking up the pillow on my bed, just looking down and seeing it in my hands.

"Wake up," I said.

He jerked awake and squinted up at me. "What are you doing there?" he said.

"I wanted to look you in the eye," I said. "I wanted you to know it was by my hand."

His eyes widened and his mouth opened. "You—" he said.

"Shut up," I said, bringing the pillow down over his face and pressing hard. He thrashed and clawed at my hands, his long nails digging into the skin of my wrist. I cursed and let go for a second, long enough for him to turn his head and gasp in a last breathful of air. I pressed the pillow back down, smashing it against his face. His struggles grew weaker. His hands loosened and let go of mine. I waited another couple of minutes before I lifted the pillow off his face. Then I straightened the covers and closed his mouth. I left his eyes open.

I took the lantern and went to the barn. Laura found me there half an hour later, and Florence found us both not long after that. Laura thought I was asleep by then, but I wasn't. I saw Florence come in with the knife, saw her rage and knew what she meant to do. I wished there was some way to tell her it was already done, that he didn't die a peaceful death. I put my guilt in my eyes, hoping she would see it.

What we can't speak, we say in silence.

HENRY

THIS IS THE LOINS of the land. This lush expanse between two rivers, formed fifteen thousand years ago when the glaciers melted, swelling the Mississippi and its tributaries until they overflowed, drowning half the continent. When the waters receded, settling back into their ancient channels, they brought a rich gift of alluvium stolen from the lands they'd covered. Brought it here, to the Delta, and cast it over the river valleys, layer upon sweet black layer.

I buried my father in that soil, the soil he hated to touch. Buried him apart from my mother, who'll lie by herself forever in the Greenville cemetery. She might have forgiven me for that, but I knew better than to think Pappy would. I didn't mourn his death, not like I'd mourned hers. He wouldn't have wanted my grief in any case, but he ought to have had somebody's. That was the thought in my mind as I shoveled the earth on top of his coffin: that not one of us was really grieving for him.

A few days later I lost Jamie too. He was hell-bent on going to California, even though I'd made it plain I could use his help for a few more weeks now that the Jacksons were gone. That was a terrible business at the sawmill, but nobody could say I didn't warn the boy. I wondered what he'd done, to make those men punish him like that. Had to been something pretty bad. I think Jamie knew, but when I asked him about it he just shrugged and said, "It's Mississippi. There doesn't have to be a reason."

In spite of everything that had happened, I would miss him, and I knew Laura would too. I figured she'd take his leaving hard, thought she'd probably end up mad at me over it. But when we finally talked about it—in bed, after the light was out—all she said was, "He needs to leave this place."

"And you?" The question just slipped out, but as soon as I said it I felt my mouth go dry. What if she said she wanted to leave too, to take the children and go back to her people in Memphis? I never thought I'd come to fear such a thing, not with Laura, but she'd changed since we moved to the farm, and not in the ways I'd expected she would.

"What I need," she began.

All of a sudden I didn't want to hear her answer. "We'll get a house in town after the harvest," I blurted out. "And if you can't wait that long I'll borrow the money from the bank. I know it's been hard for you here, and I'm sorry. It'll be better once we're living in town. You'll see."

"Oh, Henry," she said.

What the hell did that mean? It was pitch dark and I couldn't see her face. I reached for her, my heartbeat loud in my ears. If she turned me away—

But she didn't. She rolled toward me, settling her head in the hollow of my shoulder. "What I need, I have right here," she said.

I put my arms around her and held on tight.

LAURA

Jamie left us three days after the burial. He was bound for Los Angeles, though he wasn't sure what he would do when he got there. "Maybe I'll go to Hollywood and get a screen test," he said with a laugh. "Give Errol Flynn a run for his money. What do you think?"

The bruises on his face were starting to fade, but he still looked haggard. I worried about him being all alone out there, with no one to look after him. But then I thought, *He won't be alone for long.* Jamie would find someone to love him, some pretty girl to cook his favorite foods and iron his shirts and wait for him to come home to her each day. He would pluck her like a daisy from the side of the road.

"I think Mr. Flynn's in real trouble," I said.

The front door opened, and Henry joined us on the porch. "We need to head out if you're going to make your train," he said.

"I'm ready," said Jamie.

Henry gestured at the fields in front of us. "You wait and see, brother. You're going to miss all this."

"All this" was a sea of churned earth stretching from the house to the river, bereft of crops and the furrows they'd been planted in. A newly hatched mosquito landed on Henry's outstretched arm, and he swatted at it irritably. I hid a smile, but Jamie's expression was serious as he answered. "I'm sure I will."

He bent and kissed the girls goodbye. Bella cried and clung to him. He gently pried her arms from around his neck and handed her to me. "I left you something," he said to me. "A present."

"What?"

"It's not here yet, but it will be soon. You'll know it when you see it."

"We'd better be off," said Henry.

Jamie gave me a swift, awkward hug. "Goodbye. Thank you for everything."

I nodded, not trusting myself to speak. Hoping he would comprehend all that was contained in that small movement of my head.

"I'll be back by suppertime," said Henry. He kissed me, and then Jamie was gone, down the road to Greenville, and to California.

In the days that followed, the girls and I looked everywhere for Jamie's present. Under the beds, in the cupboards, out in the barn. How could he have left me something if it hadn't yet arrived? And then, a few weeks after he'd gone, I found it. I was weeding the little vegetable patch Jamie had helped me put in when I spied a clump of small tender plants at the edge. There were several dozen of them, too evenly spaced to be weeds. I knew what they were even before I broke off a sprig and smelled it.

All summer long I slept with Henry on sheets scented with lavender.

AND NOW HERE we are at the ending of the story—my ending, anyway. It's early December, and I'm packing for an extended stay in Memphis. Henry and I agreed I should go home for the birth. The baby's due in six weeks, and at my age it's too risky to stay here in Tchula, two hours from the nearest hospital.

We moved here in October, just after the harvest. Our house isn't as nice as the one we lost to the Stokeses in Marietta, and there's no fig tree in the backyard, but we do have electricity, running water, and an indoor toilet, for which I'm profoundly grateful. Our days here have settled into a pleasant routine. We get up at dawn. I make breakfast for us all, and Henry's lunch to take with him to the farm. After he leaves I get the girls dressed and we walk Amanda Leigh the eight blocks to school. By the time Bella and I return home our colored maid Viola is here. She only comes half days; there's not enough work to warrant having her full-time. I spend the morning reading to Bella or running errands. At three we go and fetch Amanda Leigh, and then I cook our supper. We eat half an hour after sunset, when Henry gets home. Then I knit or sew while we listen to the radio.

Our life here is a world away from Mudbound, though it's only ten miles on the map. Sometimes it's hard for me to believe in that other life and that other self—the one capable of rage and lust, of recklessness and selfishness and betrayal. But then I'll feel the baby kicking, and I'll be forcibly reminded of that other Laura's existence. Jamie's baby, I have no doubt of it; I felt the tiny flare of its awakening that night, a few hours after we were together. I won't ever tell him the child's his, though he might wonder. It's a small bit of dignity I can give back to Henry, that he doesn't know I've taken from him. I give him whatever I can these days, and not just out of guilt or duty. That's what it is to love someone: to give whatever you can while taking what you must.

Jamie married in September. We weren't invited to the wedding; he let us know after the fact, in one of his breezy letters. And then, a week later, we got an almost identical letter telling us the news again, as if he hadn't remembered writing us the first time. Henry and I both knew what it had to mean, but we didn't say the words out loud. I pray his new wife will help him stop drinking, but I also know, as she doesn't, how much he has to forget.

I won't be allowed to forget. The baby will see to that. It will be a boy, who will grow into a man, whom I'll love as fiercely as Florence loves Ronsel. And while I'll always regret that I got my son at such terrible cost to hers, I won't regret that I got him. My love for him won't let me.

I'll end with that. With love.

RONSEL

IT'S DAYTIME, OR IT'S NIGHT. I'm in a tank wearing a helmet, in the backseat of a moving car with a burlap sack over my head, in the bed of a wagon with a wet rag on my forehead. I'm surrounded by enemies. The stench of their hate is choking me. I'm choking, I'm begging please sir please, I'm pissing myself, I'm drowning in my own blood. I'm hollering at Sam to fire goddamnit, can't you see they're all around us, but he doesn't hear me. I shove him aside and take his position behind the bow gun but when I press the trigger nothing happens, the gun won't fire. I have a terrible thirst. *Water,* I say, *please give me some water,* but Lilly May can't hear me either, my lips are moving but nothing is coming out, nothing.

Should my story end there, in the back of that mule-drawn wagon? Silenced, delirious with pain and laudanum, defeated? Nobody would like that ending, least of all me. But to make the story come out differently I'd have to overcome so much: birth and education and oppression, fear and deformity and shame, any one of which is enough to defeat a man.

It would take an extraordinary man to beat all that, with

an extraordinary family behind him. First he'd have to wean himself off laudanum and self-pity. His mama would help him with that, but then he'd have to make himself write his buddies and his former COs and tell them what had been done to him. He'd write it down and tear it up, write it down and tear it up until one day he got up enough courage to send it. And when the answers came back he'd have to read them and accept the help that was offered, the letters that would be written on his behalf to Fisk University and the Tuskegee Institute and Morehouse College. And when Morehouse offered him a full scholarship he'd have to swallow his pride and take it, not knowing whether they wanted him or just felt sorry for him. He'd have to leave his family behind in Greenwood and travel the four hundred miles to Atlanta alone, with a little card in his shirt pocket that said MUTE. He'd have to study hard to learn all the things he should have been taught but wasn't before he could even begin to learn the things he wanted to. He'd have to listen to his classmates talk about ideas and politics and women, things you can't fit on a little portable slate. Have to get used to being alone, because he made the others uncomfortable, because he reminded them of what could still happen to any one of them if they said the wrong thing to the wrong white man. After he graduated, he'd have to find a profession where his handicap didn't matter and an employer who would take a chance on him, at a black newspaper maybe, or a black labor organization. He'd have to prove himself and fight off despair, have to give up drinking three or four times before he finally kicked it.

Such a man, if he managed to accomplish all that, might one day find a strong and loving woman to marry him and give him children. Might help his sister and brothers make something of themselves. Might march behind Dr. King down the streets of Atlanta with his head held high. Might even find something like happiness.

That's the ending we want, you and me both. I'll grant you it's unlikely, but it is possible. If he worked and prayed hard enough. If he was stubborn as well as lucky. If he really had a shine.

ACKNOWLEDGMENTS

If James Cañón hadn't been in my very first workshop at Columbia. If we hadn't loved each other's writing, and each other. If he hadn't read and critiqued every draft of this book, plus countless early drafts of individual chapters, during the years it took me to write it. If he hadn't encouraged and goaded me, talked me off the ledge a dozen times, made me laugh at myself, inspired me by his example: *Mudbound* would have been a very different book, and I would be writing these acknowledgments from a nice, padded cell somewhere. Thank you, love, for all that you've given me. I could not have had a wiser counselor or a truer friend.

I am also grateful to the following people, organizations and sources:

Jenn Epstein, my dear friend and designated "bad cop," who was always willing to drop everything and read, and whose tough, incisive critiques were invaluable in shaping the narrative.

Binnie Kirshenbaum and Victoria Redel, whose guidance and enthusiasm got me rolling; Maureen Howard, friend and mentor, who told me I mustn't be afraid of my book; and the many other members of the Columbia Writing Division faculty who encouraged me.

Chris Parris-Lamb, my extraordinary agent and champion, for seeing what others didn't; Sarah Burnes and the whole Gernert Company team, for embracing *Mudbound* so enthusiastically; and Kathy Pories at Algonquin, for believing in the book and being such a thoughtful and sensitive shepherd of it.

Barbara Kingsolver, for her tremendous faith in me and in *Mudbound;* her help in turning the story into a coherent, compelling narrative; her passionate support of literature of social change; and the generous and much-needed award.

The Virginia Center for the Creative Arts, the La Napoule Foundation, Fundación Valparaiso and the Stanwood Foundation for Starving Artists, for the gifts of time to write and exquisitely beautiful settings in which to do so; and the Columbia University Writing Division and the American Association of University Women, for their financial assistance.

Julie Currie, for the price of mules in 1946 and other elusive facts; Petra Spielhagen and Dan Renehan, for their assistance with Resl's broken English; and Sam Hoskins, for lessons in orthopedics.

Theodore Rosengarten's *All God's Dangers: The Life of Nate Shaw;* Stephen Ambrose's *The Wild Blue;* Byron Lane's *Byron's War: I Never Will Be Young Again;* Lou Potter's *Liberators* (and the accompanying PBS series); and Joe Wilson's *The 761st "Black Panther" Tank Battalion in World War II,* for helping me put believable flesh on the bones of my sharecroppers, bomber pilot and tankers.

Denise Benou Stires, Michael Caporusso, Pam Cunningham, Gary di Mauro, Charlotte Dixon, Mark Erwin, Marie Fisher, Doug Irving, Robert Lewis, Leslie McCall, Elizabeth Molsen, Katy Rees and Rick Rudik, for their unwavering friendship and belief in me, which sustained me more than any of them will ever know; and Kathryn Windley, for all that and then some.

And finally, my family: Anita Jordan and Michael Fuller; Jan and Jaque Jordan; my brothers, Jared and Erik; and Gay and John Stanek. No author was ever better loved or supported.

MUDBOUND

An Interview with Hillary Jordan

A Reading and Discussion Guide

AN INTERVIEW
WITH HILLARY JORDAN

What inspired you to write *Mudbound*?

My grandparents had a farm in Lake Village, Arkansas, just after World War II, and I grew up hearing stories about it. It was a primitive place, an unpainted shotgun shack with no electricity, running water, or telephone. They named it Mudbound because whenever it rained, the roads would flood and they'd be stranded for days.

Though they only lived there for a year, my mother, aunt, and grandmother spoke of the farm often, laughing and shaking their heads by turns, depending on whether the story in question was funny or horrifying. Often they were both, as Southern stories tend to be. I loved listening to them, even the ones I'd heard dozens of times before. They were a peephole into a strange and marvelous world, a world full of contradictions, of terrible beauty. The stories revealed things about my family, especially about my grandmother, who was the heroine of most of them for the simple reason that when calamity struck, my grandfather was inevitably elsewhere.

To my mother and aunt, the year they spent at Mudbound was a grand adventure; and indeed, that was how all their stories portrayed it. It was not until much later that I realized what an ordeal that year must have been for my grandmother—a city-bred woman with two young children—and that, in fact, these were stories of survival.

I began the novel (without knowing I was doing any such thing) in grad school. I had an assignment to write a few pages in the voice of a family member, and I decided to write about the farm from my grandmother's point of view. But what came out was not a merry adventure story but something darker and more complex. What came out was, "When I think of the farm, I think of mud."

So, your grandmother's voice was the one that came to you first as you started writing this?

Yes, hers was the first, and only, voice for some while. My teacher liked what I wrote and encouraged me to continue, and I tried to write a short story. My grandmother became Laura, a fictional character much more fiery and rebellious than she ever was, and the story got longer and longer. At 50 pages I realized I was writing a novel, and that's when I decided to introduce the other voices. Jamie came next, then Henry, then Florence, then Hap. Ronsel wasn't even a character until I had about 150 pages! And of course, when he entered the story, he changed its course dramatically.

But you never let Pappy speak.

Nine drafts ago, Pappy actually narrated his own funeral (the two scenes at the beginning and end of the book). And people—namely, my editor and Barbara Kingsolver, who read several drafts of *Mudbound* and gave me invaluable criticism—just hated hearing from him first, or in fact, at all. Eventually I was persuaded to silence him. The more I thought about those two passages, the more fitting it seemed that Jamie should narrate them.

Still, even without having his own section, it's clear that Pappy really struck a chord with readers. Why do you think that is?

Yes, people really do seem to hate him! Which is as it should be—he's pretty detestable. He embodies not just the ugliness of the Jim Crow era but the absolute worst possibilities in ourselves.

What was the hardest part of writing *Mudbound*?

Getting those voices right—the African American dialect especially. I had a number of well-meaning friends say things to me like, "even Faulkner didn't write about black people in the first person." But ultimately I decided I had to let my black characters address the ugliness of that time and place themselves, in their own voices.

Your book takes on racism on many levels—the most obvious forms, but also the more insidious kinds, like the sharecropping system, for example.

In researching this book, I was astounded by what I learned about the perniciousness of the sharecropping system. Owning your own mule meant the difference between share tenancy, in which you got to keep half your crop, and sharecropping, in which you got to keep only a quarter. A quarter of a cotton crop wasn't nearly enough for a family to live on, so people went further and further into debt with their landlords. And they were so incredibly vulnerable—to misfortune, to illness, to bad weather conditions. Being a sharecropper wasn't that far removed from being a slave.

The climactic scene with Ronsel is absolutely wrenching to read. I imagine it was equally wrenching to write.

Yes, it was. I'd been unsure for months what was going to happen in that scene. And when it finally came to me, all the hairs on my arms stood up, and I called my best friend James Cañón (who is also an author and was my primary reader during the seven years it took me to write *Mudbound*), and I said, "I know what's going to happen to Ronsel," and I told him. And there was this long silence and then he said, "Wow."

I dreaded writing the scene, and I put it off for a long time. When I finally made myself do it, I cried a lot. I was reading it out loud as I went—which for me is an essential part of writing dialogue—and having to speak those horrific things made them that much more real and terrible.

What books would you recommend to those who want to know even more about the period?

All God's Dangers: The Life of Nate Shaw, by Theodore Rosengarten. This is a true first-person account of a black Alabama cotton farmer who started out as a sharecropper and ended up owning his own land, with many adventures along the way. Nate was an indelible character, smart (though illiterate) and funny and wise about people. He was eighty years old when he told his life story to Theodore Rosengarten, a journalist from New York. And what a fascinating life it was.

James Cobb's *The Most Southern Place on Earth.*

Pete Daniel's excellent books *Breaking the Land* and *Deep'n as It Come: The 1927 Mississippi River Flood* and *Standing at the Crossroads: Southern Life in the Twentieth Century.*

A PBS series of documentaries about black history from *The American Experience.*

Clifton L. Taulbert's *When We Were Colored.*

And of course, the works of James Baldwin, William Faulkner, Flannery O'Connor, Eudora Welty, and Richard Wright, among others.

Have you begun working on another novel?

Yes, and it's absolutely nothing like *Mudbound*! After seven years of working on it, I was extremely ready to leave the Deep South, the past, and the first person. My second novel, *Red*, is set in a dystopian America roughly thirty years in the future. It begins in Crawford, Texas, and ends—well, who knows?

A READING AND DISCUSSION GUIDE

1. The setting of the Mississippi Delta is intrinsic to *Mudbound*. Discuss the ways in which the land functions as a character in the novel and how each of the other characters relates to it.

2. *Mudbound* is a chorus, told in six different voices. How do the changes in perspective affect your understanding of the story? Are all six voices equally sympathetic? Reliable? Pappy is the only main character who has no narrative voice. Why do you think the author chose not to let him speak?

3. Who gets to speak and who is silent or silenced is a central theme, the silencing of Ronsel being the most literal and brutal example. Discuss the ways in which this theme plays out for the other characters. For instance, how does Laura's silence about her unhappiness on the farm affect her and her marriage? What are the consequences of Jamie's inability to speak to his family about the horrors he experienced in the war? How does speaking or not speaking confer power or take it away?

4. The story is narrated by two farmers, two wives and mothers, and two soldiers. Compare and contrast the ways in which these parallel characters, black and white, view and experience the world.

5. What is the significance of the title? In what ways are each of the characters bound—by the land, by circumstance, by tradition, by the law, by their own limitations? How much of this binding is inescapable and how much is self-imposed? Which characters are most successful in freeing themselves from what binds them?

6. All the characters are products of their time and place, and instances of racism in the book run from Pappy's outright bigotry to Laura's more subtle prejudice. Would Laura have thought of herself as racist, and if not, why not? How do the racial views of Laura, Jamie, Henry, and Pappy affect your sympathy for them?

7. The novel deals with many thorny issues: racism, sexual politics, infidelity, war. The characters weigh in on these issues, but what about the author? Does she have a discernable perspective, and if so, how does she convey it?

8. We know very early in the book that something terrible is going to befall Ronsel. How does this sense of inevitability affect the story? Jamie makes Ronsel responsible for his own

fate, saying, "Maybe that's cowardly of me, making Ronsel's the trigger finger." Is it just cowardice, or is there some truth to what Jamie says? Where would you place the turning point for Ronsel? Who else is complicit in what happens to him, and why?

9. In reflecting on some of the more difficult moral choices made by the characters—Laura's decision to sleep with Jamie, Ronsel's decision to abandon Resl and return to America, Jamie's choice during the lynching scene, Florence's and Jamie's separate decisions to murder Pappy—what would you have done in those same situations? Is it even possible to know? Are there some moral positions that are absolute, or should we take into account things like time and place when making judgments?

10. Why do you think the author chose to have Ronsel address you, the reader, directly at the end of the book? Do you believe he overcomes the formidable obstacles facing him and finds "something like happiness"? If so, why doesn't the author just say so explicitly? Would a less ambiguous ending have been more or less satisfying?

WILLIAM COUPON

Hillary Jordan grew up in Texas and Oklahoma. She received her BA in English and political science from Wellesley College and spent fifteen years working as an advertising copywriter before starting to write fiction. She got her MFA in creative writing from Columbia University. Her first novel, *Mudbound*, won the 2006 *Bellwether Prize for Fiction*, awarded biennially to a debut novel that addresses issues of social justice, and was the New Atlantic Independent Booksellers Association Fiction Book of the Year for 2008. Jordan's short fiction has appeared in numerous literary journals, including *StoryQuarterly* and the *Carolina Quarterly*. She lives in Tivoli, New York.

Other Algonquin Readers Round Table Novels

Water for Elephants, a novel by Sara Gruen

As a young man, Jacob Jankowski is tossed by fate onto a rickety train, home to the Benzini Brothers Most Spectacular Show on Earth. Amid a world of freaks, grifters, and misfits, Jacob becomes involved with Marlena, the beautiful young equestrian star; her husband, a charismatic but twisted animal trainer; and Rosie, an untrainable elephant who is the great gray hope for this third-rate show. Now in his nineties, Jacob at long last reveals the story of their unlikely yet powerful bonds, ones that nearly shatter them all.

"[An] arresting new novel . . . With a showman's expert timing, [Gruen] saves a terrific revelation for the final pages, transforming a glimpse of Americana into an enchanting escapist fairy tale." —*The New York Times Book Review*

"Gritty, sensual and charged with dark secrets involving love, murder and a majestic, mute heroine." —*Parade*

AN ALGONQUIN READERS ROUND TABLE EDITION WITH READING GROUP GUIDE
AND OTHER SPECIAL FEATURES • FICTION • ISBN-13: 978-1-56512-560-5

An Arsonist's Guide to Writers' Homes in New England,
a novel by Brock Clarke

The past catches up to Sam Pulsifer, the hapless hero of this incendiary novel, when after spending ten years in prison for accidentally burning down Emily Dickinson's house, the homes of other famous New England writers go up in smoke. To prove his innocence, he sets out to uncover the identity of this literary-minded arsonist.

"Funny, profound . . . A seductive book with a payoff on every page." —*People*

"Wildly, unpredicatably funny . . . As cheerfully oddball as its title."
—*The New York Times*

AN ALGONQUIN READERS ROUND TABLE EDITION WITH READING GROUP GUIDE
AND OTHER SPECIAL FEATURES • FICTION • ISBN-13: 978-1-56512-614-5

Saving the World, a novel by Julia Alvarez

While Alma Huebner is researching a new novel, she discovers the true story of Isabel Sendales y Gómez, who embarked on a courageous sea voyage to rescue the New World from smallpox. The author of *How the García Girls Lost Their Accents* and *In the Time of the Butterflies,* Alvarez captures the worlds of two women living two centuries apart but with surprisingly parallel fates.

"Fresh and unusual, and thought-provokingly sensitive." —*The Boston Globe*

"Engrossing, expertly paced." —*People*

AN ALGONQUIN READERS ROUND TABLE EDITION WITH READING GROUP GUIDE
AND OTHER SPECIAL FEATURES • FICTION • ISBN-13: 978-1-56512-558-2

Breakfast with Buddha, a novel by Roland Merullo

When his sister tricks him into taking her guru, a crimson-robed monk, on a trip to their childhood home, Otto Ringling, a confirmed skeptic, is not amused. Six days on the road with an enigmatic holy man who answers every question with a riddle is not what he'd planned. But along the way, Otto is given the remarkable opportunity to see his world—and more important, his life—through someone else's eyes.

"Enlightenment meets *On the Road* in this witty, insightful novel."
—*The Boston Sunday Globe*

"A laugh-out-loud novel that's both comical and wise . . . balancing irreverence with insight." —*The Louisville Courier-Journal*

AN ALGONQUIN READERS ROUND TABLE EDITION WITH READING GROUP GUIDE AND OTHER SPECIAL FEATURES • FICTION • ISBN 13: 978-1-56512-616-9

The Ghost at the Table, a novel by Suzanne Berne

When Frances arranges to host Thanksgiving at her idyllic New England farmhouse, she envisions a happy family reunion, one that will include her sister, Cynthia. But tension mounts between them as each struggles with a different version of the mysterious circumstances surrounding their mother's death twenty-five years earlier.

"Wholly engaging, the perfect spark for launching a rich conversation around your own table." —*The Washington Post Book World*

"A crash course in sibling rivalry." —*O: The Oprah Magazine*

AN ALGONQUIN READERS ROUND TABLE EDITION WITH READING GROUP GUIDE AND OTHER SPECIAL FEATURES • FICTION • ISBN-13: 978-1-56512-579-7

Coal Black Horse, a novel by Robert Olmstead

When Robey Childs's mother has a premonition about her husband, who is away fighting in the Civil War, she sends her only son to find him and bring him home. At fourteen, Robey thinks he's off on a great adventure. But it takes the gift of a powerful and noble coal black horse to show him how to undertake the most important journey of his life.

"A remarkable creation." —*Chicago Tribune*

"Exciting . . . A grueling adventure." —*The New York Times Book Review*

AN ALGONQUIN READERS ROUND TABLE EDITION WITH READING GROUP GUIDE AND OTHER SPECIAL FEATURES • FICTION • ISBN-13: 978-1-56512-601-5

I grab Louisa's arm and click off the flashlight she's holding. She's smart; she doesn't make a sound when she sees the look on my face, just before the light disappears. Behind us, Evelyn opens her mouth to ask one of her loud, yappy questions, but Louisa signals for quiet and Maddie claps her hand over Evelyn's mouth.

We stand very, very still.

There it is again.

Quiet, but unmistakable: out there in the dark, somebody hiccups. And it isn't one of us.

We're not alone.

Someone is following us through the forest.

TOMORROW GIRLS

TOMORROW GIRLS

GIRLS

Run for Cover

BY EVA GRAY

SCHOLASTIC INC.

New York   Toronto   London   Auckland
Sydney   Mexico City   New Delhi   Hong Kong

No part of this publication may be reproduced, stored in a retrieval system, or transmitted in any form or by any means, electronic, mechanical, photocopying, recording, or otherwise, without written permission of the publisher. For information regarding permission, write to: Scholastic Inc., Attention: Permissions Department, 557 Broadway, New York, NY 10012.

ISBN 978-0-545-31702-3

12 11 10 9 8 7 6 5 4 3 2 1   11 12 13 14 15 16/0

Printed in the U.S.A.   40
First printing, July 2011

Designed by Yaffa Jaskoll

TOMORROW GIRLS

Run for Cover

Chapter 1

I'm not like the other girls.

Louisa and Maddie and Evelyn — it's like we're from totally different planets.

It's not just the obvious things, like the fact that I grew up with palm trees instead of pine trees, hibiscus instead of hydrangeas in my yard, tamales in place of tuna fish sandwiches for lunch.

It's not that I'm faster and stronger and better at surviving than they are . . . although I am.

It's not even that my home is gone, or that I watched it being swept away, while they have their nice comfortable houses to go back to, and they can't even imagine anything bad ever happening to them.

It's not all the secrets I'm hiding.

I'll tell you the biggest difference between us.

It's that they think they know what it's like to be scared.

But they have no idea.

We've been in the woods for only five minutes when I start thinking this escape might be a little bit doomed.

Not that we had any choice; we had to run away. Our parents sent us to a hidden boarding school because they wanted us to be safe from the dangers of the War. But it turned out we'd walked right into the worst danger of all.

Country Manor School did seem like a weird place from the beginning. They took away all our electronic devices, snipped off the ID bracelets we've been wearing our whole lives, and forced us to do our homework by hand. *By hand!* With *pens*! I should have *known* they were evil just from that!

But I figured they were just old-fashioned. Plus I liked the outdoor survival training and the friends I was making, and the chance to act like a regular girl again. If I'd been rooming with cooler people, I'd have been happier than I have been anytime in the last three years.

Then everything fell apart. First Louisa's "twin," Maddie, got caught. The headmistress, Mrs. Brewster, figured out that they weren't really sisters (something I could have told her on day two). Then Louisa overheard a TV news broadcast saying Canada had surrendered to the Alliance . . . who, in case you haven't guessed, are the bad guys in the War.

Canada's only a few miles from CMS, but that's not the dangerous part. The really bad news — the news that has us fleeing through the forest in the middle of the night — is that CMS is a sleeper cell and all our teachers are Alliance agents. The children of America's wealthiest

families were brought here to be hostages. Louisa overheard their plans, and we decided none of us were going
to hang around and let Mrs. Brewster use us to manipulate our parents.

So here we are: escaping, in the dark, with no idea how
we'll get back to Chicago. And instead of any of my tough,
cool, outdoorsy friends, I'm stuck with my suite mates.

I glance over at pale, blond Louisa. She can be cool
sometimes. But the others, Maddie and Evelyn, are not
exactly the first two people I would have picked to
run away with. In fact, they're pretty much the last
people anyone would want to drag through the woods.
Maddie — skinny, brunette, brown eyes, looks nothing
like Louisa, in case you're wondering — is always
moping and griping; plus she totally hates me for no
apparent reason.

And Evelyn is a world-class conspiracy freak, convinced that everyone is part of a secret Alliance plan.
She's hyperalert all the time and she scribbles notes in
her little notebook every time anyone says anything. Sure,

4

okay, she's right some of the time, it turns out. But she is also annoying *all* of the time. And PS she hates me, too. Just because I made my own friends instead of sitting with my roommates at meals.

See why I'm a little worried about this escape plan? I'm not sure which is more likely: us getting captured by the Alliance, or Maddie and Evelyn throwing me under a bus the first chance they get. Or me losing my mind. That one could definitely happen, like, by the end of the night.

Maddie starts complaining first. "I'm tired," she says. "My feet hurt. Can we stop and rest?" She leans one hand against a tree and rubs her left ankle. There's a chilly breeze rippling through the leaves, which makes me nervous. It's only September, but we're so far north that it could get horribly cold very quickly — long before we reach Chicago, for instance. I'm not a big fan of the cold. Especially when I know I'll be sleeping outside for the foreseeable future.

"We've barely been walking for five minutes!" I say. Although we're surrounded by dark forest, we can still see the glow of lights from the school behind us. That means we're way too close, since the only lights still on are in the teachers' rooms. We need to get much, much farther away before we even think about stopping. I cross my arms and frown at Maddie.

"Yeah, but we hiked all weekend," Maddie points out, "and I'm still exhausted from that."

"Shhhh," Evelyn says. "They might have bugged the trees." Her dark skin blends into the shadows, but in the glimmers of moonlight I can see her eyes darting around in that annoying everybody's-after-us way that drives me crazy.

"Bugged the *trees*?" Louisa says. "That's a little paranoid, even for you."

Evelyn flares up at once. "I might be paranoid, but I'm right, aren't I? I mean, I was right about the school!"

I roll my eyes. "Maybe one or two of your insane theories were right, but when you're shooting a million ideas into the sky, it's not surprising that a couple of them will land."

"I was right that it was a conspiracy!" Evelyn's voice is getting too loud. "The Alliance *was* luring us into a trap! The secret locations, the weird classes, taking away all our electronics — it was all part of their plan!"

"Shhh, all right," Louisa says. "We're not disagreeing with you. You were right all along. You're a conspiracy-detecting genius. Is that what you want to hear?"

"Can we keep moving, please?" I say. Maddie sighs loudly, but she doesn't argue as we start walking again. I would rather try to find our way in the dark, letting our eyes adjust, but not enough moonlight penetrates the thick canopy of branches, so we have to use a flashlight. I let Louisa hold it, since she has a steady hand. Twigs and pine needles crackle and snap under our feet, and we're surrounded by the Christmas smell of the pine forest. If our situation weren't so utterly terrifying, it would be kind of nice and peaceful out here.

"I don't understand their plan, though, Evelyn," Maddie says after a minute. "If they were planning to hold us hostage for our parents' money, why would they teach us survival skills and all that other stuff? Why train us like we're soldiers? We'd never fight for the Alliance, no matter what they did to brainwash us!"

"Too right," I say. "I'd break Mrs. Brewster's face before I ever helped the Alliance."

"Wow, Rosie," Louisa says. "Tell us how you really feel. No, I'm kidding. I agree with you." A low-hanging branch snags her blond hair and she stops to disentangle herself.

"Maybe —" Evelyn says, and then pauses. Her shoulders are hunched and her hands are shoved in her jeans pockets.

"Maybe what?" I say.

"Never mind," she mumbles. "You'll just think it's stupid."

"I won't," Maddie says, bumping her shoulder. "Go ahead and tell us. I like hearing your theories."

I exchange a glance with Louisa. In the dark I can't see her expression, but I'm sure she's thinking what I am — that it's kind of annoying how Evelyn and Maddie

8

always stick together and encourage each other's worst impulses. I don't say anything, though. As long as we're still walking, leaving CMS behind us, I don't care how much talking everyone else needs to do at the same time. If I were them, I'd be saving my energy, but I can only boss them around so much without someone snapping. I need to pick my battles.

"Well," Evelyn says, "I was just thinking . . . maybe not all the girls there were hostages. Maybe some of them were really on the Alliance's side." She hurries on before we can respond. "I mean, we don't really know anything about them. Maybe a lot of the others were being trained to fight in the War, and they knew it was secretly an Alliance training camp the whole time."

"I did hear something like that," Louisa says slowly. "The teachers were talking about getting certain girls to the cafeteria for a debriefing or something. The kids of Alliance parents."

We all fall silent. I think about my friends at CMS — Mary Jensen and Chui-lian Lee especially. I miss them. They would be a lot more useful out here than Evelyn and Maddie — that's for sure. I'd also take Anne or Erica or Rae or Carole over them any day. But were they all lying to me? Were they secretly working for the Alliance? Would they have turned on me and helped to hold me hostage if — when — everything came out in the open?

"I don't believe it," I say, but my voice catches, and I don't sound as confident as I want to.

Of course, part of me can't help wondering . . . if it's true, is the secret I'm keeping any better than theirs?

An hour later, I let everyone stop for a break. I'm a little worried about how deep in the forest we are. Evelyn is doing a great job with the compass, but I hope we can find a road to follow soon, at least from a distance. At the speed Maddie's going, I'm not sure staying in the woods will get us all the way back to Chicago anytime before January.

I crouch in a dim circle of moonlight under a break in the trees, stretching my aching muscles. I'd never admit this to the others, but I'm pretty sore after our long weekend of hiking, too. Part of me wishes we could have stayed at CMS for one more night, just to get a real night's sleep in a bed. But by tomorrow it would have been too late. Tonight was our only chance of escape.

"I wish we had our ID bracelets," Louisa says, rubbing her left wrist. "Maybe we should have tried to find them and steal them back. How are we going to get anywhere without them? How will we convince anyone we are who we say we are?"

"It's like they took my whole identity, not just a band of metal," Evelyn says. She's perched on top of a boulder. I'm sure she remembers my advice about not sitting down in case her muscles cramp, but if she doesn't care, I'm not going to keep bugging her about it.

"I know," Maddie agrees, climbing up next to her. "I feel naked without mine, especially now that we're away from the school."

I concentrate on my shoelaces. They don't know this, but their ID bracelets will be a lot easier to replace than

11

mine. I tried to act like I totally didn't care when Devi cut it off on the first day, but inside I felt like she might as well be cutting off my hands. Mom and Dad are going to be so unhappy with me when they find out it's gone. I wonder how much a new one will cost us this time, and whether we can use the same guy as before.

"I still don't understand why they took them," Maddie says with a sigh.

"To demoralize us," Evelyn says firmly. "It's classic psychological warfare. Take away our very identities, so we lose our senses of self and become easier to manipulate."

I can't help snorting. They all look over at me.

"You have a better theory?" Evelyn asks.

I hesitate. How much will I give away if I answer truthfully? Will they suspect anything?

Or will it be more suspicious if I don't answer at all?

"They're selling them," I say, rubbing my hamstrings and trying to sound casual. "A recoded ID bracelet is more valuable than a fake passport these days. The

Alliance uses them to get their agents in and out of the country without being caught."

Louisa gapes at me. "They can do that? Change all the information on the tag?"

"You know that," I say, nodding at Madeleine. "Didn't your family get someone to change her tag, so it said you were sisters?"

I hear Maddie's little intake of breath in the dark. "You told her we're not sisters?" she whispers.

"She figured it out," Louisa says. "And yeah, we did get a guy to do that, but all he had to change was her last name and her birthday. And I guess he didn't even do that right, since a ghost of her real info showed up on the tag when Mrs. Brewster scanned it."

I shake my head. "That probably only surfaced because they were trying to reformat and change the whole ID. Most hackers are better at it than your guy. Sorry." I shrug. "But they can construct entire new identities for people using an old bracelet bought on the black market."

I should know.

"Crazy," Evelyn says. "I bet they can raise a lot of money for the Alliance by selling them, too."

Louisa shivers. "I really hate the idea that some bad guy is out there wearing my ID bracelet, using it to sneak around and do horrible things."

I want to tell them that it's not only bad guys who need the black-market ID bracelets, but that would definitely give too much away. Safer just to change the subject.

"Sorry, everyone, but we should keep walking," I say. "Get as far as we can while it's still dark. Okay, Maddie? I know you can do it. You were totally tough on the camping trip." This is not entirely true; mostly she whined and grumbled a lot. But I'm sure she can be tougher with the right encouragement.

She sighs again, but she slides off the boulder and we all start walking through the trees in the direction Evelyn points, which I guess is still south. I try to stop worrying about how soon the Alliance will come after us, or how far we can get before morning, or what we're going to eat

14

when we're hungry. I try not to think about how familiar this feels, the prickling sensation between my shoulder blades like someone is following us . . . someone who might suddenly shove a knife in my back at any moment.

I should feel calmer, out here where no one can see me. At least I'm not going to mess up and get caught by a teacher. No one's going to turn me in to the authorities. I don't have to freak out about following the rules anymore. I'm already so far outside the rules that now I just have to keep running until I get somewhere safe again.

But I won't feel comfortable until CMS is far, far behind us. If we get caught now, I could be in worse trouble than anyone else, even Maddie.

Night noises are all around us as we step cautiously through the trees, using only one flashlight to save batteries. I can hear crickets chirping and leaves rustling and a chorus of weird animal sounds, like snuffling and chittering and hiccupping and croaking . . .

Wait. Hiccupping?

I grab Louisa's arm and click off the flashlight she's holding. She's smart; she doesn't make a sound when she sees the look on my face, just before the light disappears. Behind us, Evelyn opens her mouth to ask one of her loud, yappy questions, but Louisa signals for quiet and Maddie claps her hand over Evelyn's mouth.

We stand very, very still.

There it is again.

Quiet, but unmistakable: out there in the dark, somebody hiccups. And it isn't one of us.

We're not alone.

Someone is following us through the forest.

Chapter 2

"Turn on your flashlight and keep walking," I whisper to Maddie. "Pretend you're still talking to me." Louder, I say, "Sorry, guys. I thought I heard something, but I guess I was wrong."

I tug Louisa behind a tree with me. Maddie switches on her flashlight and walks away with Evelyn close beside her. To her credit, she does a great job of pretending I'm still with them.

"Honestly, Rosie," she says, "you're starting to sound crazy like Evelyn."

"Hey!" Evelyn protests.

"I mean, you're making me totally nervous," Maddie goes on. "I'm sure nobody's even noticed we're gone yet, so we probably don't have to worry for a while. . . ." Her voice trails off into the woods as the little circle of light bobs away. I can feel Louisa tense; she doesn't love the dark settling around us, or watching her friends disappear up ahead. I fumble for her hand and squeeze it reassuringly. My heart is pounding, and I seriously wish we still had the rifles we used on the camping trip.

With the flashlight gone, my eyes start to adjust to the dark and the dim light from the moon, high above the trees. My ears feel like they're going to pop off my head, I'm listening so hard. Is that crack a branch being stepped on? Am I hearing someone's breathing, getting closer and closer?

Louisa sees it first, and she clutches my hand in a death grip.

A dark shadow moves out of the trees behind us and slowly edges past. Whoever it is, they're definitely following the sound of Maddie's voice, stepping lightly where our feet just were.

I crouch quietly and feel for a stick that's just the right size. My eyes scan the darkness, looking for more shadows. I spot another one a few feet away, flanking the one that's just gone by. I don't know if there are more of them out here in the woods. I have to decide whether to risk confronting them, or try sneaking away.

For a moment I think about how far Louisa and I could get on our own — how quickly we'd get back to Chicago, where we could warn our parents about what's happening. They could send help for Maddie and Evelyn. Nothing really bad will happen to them; I'm sure of it. The Alliance people at CMS would want Evelyn safe so they could get as much money as possible out of her parents.

But Maddie is nobody special; she wouldn't be valuable to them. Would they even keep her alive, now that she knows their secrets?

As much as I would like to, leaving the other two girls is not an option. I heft a stick in my hands and touch the end of it — perfect. I place Louisa's hand against the tree and pat it once: *stay here.* Then I creep out, one foot gently before the other, until I'm right behind the first shadow. His friend is ahead and to the left of us, so I can keep an eye on him, too.

I shove the end of the stick into the guy's back. "Stop right there."

He jumps a mile and tries to whirl around, but I've grabbed his arm to hold him in place, facing away from me. "Don't turn around," I say. "I don't know how much damage this rifle will do at such close range, but I bet you don't want to find out. Tell your friends to drop their weapons."

"W-w-we don't have any weapons!" he yelps. "I swear!"

I frown. His voice sounds familiar. And now that we're up close, I'm pretty sure he's only fourteen or fifteen, not much older than I am.

Louisa clicks on her flashlight, illuminating a head of short reddish-blond hair and a sage-green CMS T-shirt over stocky shoulders. The guy has his hands up in the air and keeps twisting his head around to try to see us.

"Ryan?" Louisa says from behind me.

"Louisa?" he says, nearly collapsing with relief.

I lower my fake rifle and let him go. Of course. Just my luck. It's those dingbat boys that Louisa dragged back to our campsite during our survival mission over the weekend — the ones from the boys' school across the lake. The boys who made the other girls so silly that they nearly ruined everything, just for the sake of a couple sandwiches and some flirting.

Nobody cared about what would happen to us if we got in trouble — how we might be sent home, or how the teachers might take a closer look at some of us who'd rather not attract any attention.

The other one comes crashing through the trees toward us. I catch a glimpse of his dark eyes and hair before he raises his hand to block the light. He's Hispanic, like me, and I wonder, not for the first time, where he's from.

21

I put my hands on my hips. "Good grief," I say, "are you guys *still* lost?"

"No!" says the light-haired one — Ryan. "We made it back to school, but then we were sent out again. This time we're supposed to survive out here for a week."

"A week!" Louisa says. "Why didn't they make us do that? That is totally sexist. Girls can survive in the wild just as well as boys."

"Yeah, especially if they happen to run into any boys carrying sandwiches," I point out.

I think she's about to yell at me, but then her face goes thoughtful and she turns back to Ryan. "*Do* you guys have any sandwiches?" she asks. "I mean, I assume you wouldn't say no to them this time, Queen Rosie? Now that we're *actually* trying to survive?"

The boys give her quizzical looks. Before I can answer her, we hear more branches snapping from up ahead of us, and then we see Maddie and Evelyn marching back through the trees. They're pushing a third boy along in front of them.

"Look what we found!" Evelyn says.

"He practically tripped over us," Maddie says. "Not very stealth." Her eyes widen as she spots the guys with us. "Wait — we know you! Ryan! Alonso!"

"Hey," says Alonso, giving Evelyn a friendly nod.

"This guy's with us," Ryan says, punching the new one in the shoulder. "His name is Drew. Drew, meet Louisa, Maddie, Evelyn, and Rosie." I have to admit I'm a little impressed he remembers our names, especially mine, since we didn't exactly meet in the friendliest way.

Drew is taller than the others, Asian American, good-looking, and wiry, with short, straight black hair. He's wearing a pair of sturdy silver-framed glasses and I spot a Swiss Army knife hanging from his belt. There's something about the way he stands and the way he looks at me that reminds me of Ivan — that same aura of secrets Ivan always had, like he knows more than I do.

Maybe it's unfair of me, but immediately I don't trust Drew. Even if he's just a regular guy, even if he would never do what Ivan did to my family, I don't want him around me. Or any of them, actually. Boys are an unwelcome — and dangerous — distraction.

"Are there any more of you?" I ask, scanning the trees. The wind seems to be picking up, and the branches are swaying over our heads so the shadows jump around in all directions. It's a little spooky.

Ryan shakes his head. He seems to be the unspoken leader of the guys, or at least the chattiest one. "It's a three-person mission," he says.

"With sandwiches?" Louisa asks longingly. He grins and nods at her.

"Why were you sneaking after us?" I demand.

"We were curious." Drew speaks for the first time. "We saw your light and wanted to know who else was out here." His voice is quiet and deep.

"Actually, we thought it might be Alliance spies," Alonso says. "Sneaking across the border from Canada and up to no good." He glances at Evelyn again; they both have the same bright-eyed, conspiracy-finding expression.

"We figured we'd get a medal or something if we caught you," Ryan adds with a grin.

I know he's joking, but his words send a bolt of alarm through me. What if they do decide to turn us in, or tell their teachers they saw us in the woods? I shiver, and it's not just from the cold breeze that's starting to whip our hair around.

"What about you?" Drew asks. "Why are you out here?"

"Just hiking," I say quickly, but, of course, at the same time Evelyn opens her big mouth and cries: "We're escaping!"

The boys all look startled. Ryan raises his eyebrows at Louisa, and Alonso's face lights up, but Drew looks straight at me, as if he can tell I'm hiding something.

"Escaping from our camping group," I say, jabbing Evelyn in the ribs. "They're so boring, yakking away

25

about, uh —" I can't even think of anything believable. "Girl stuff. We needed a break, so we're taking a walk. That's all."

"Oh, come on, Rosie," Evelyn starts.

"But we should get back to them!" I say fast. I seize Evelyn's elbow in a way that I hope says, *Shut up shut up shut up now.* "Good luck with your survival mission. See you around." I try to pull Evelyn away, but she wrestles free of my grip.

"We should tell them the truth!" she insists.

"I think so, too," Louisa agrees. Some loyalty! I thought she trusted me to make decisions for the group. But I guess when it comes to boys, she can't even think straight. I should have learned that on our weekend trip when she sided with them over me. I glare at her.

"What do you mean?" Ryan says, looking from Louisa to me and back again. "What truth? What's going on?"

Louisa hesitates, glancing at me. To my surprise, it's Maddie who answers him. "It's not safe to stay at CMS," she says. "We heard something tonight. Well, Louisa did.

The school is an Alliance sleeper cell. They were going to use us as hostages to control our parents. Now that Canada has surrendered to the Alliance, we'd all be in danger if we didn't escape."

I notice that she doesn't mention what happened with her ID bracelet, or that Mrs. Brewster figured out she wasn't a Ballinger and put her in isolation. Even if Maddie trusts the boys more than I do, she still knows not to tell them all her secrets.

"Canada's fallen to the Alliance?" Ryan echoes. "Wow. That is — that is really not good." He crouches and runs his hands through his short hair, taking a couple of deep breaths.

"I knew it!" Alonso says. "I knew there was something weird about CMS! I told you!" He punches Drew in the arm and Drew rubs the spot, looking pained. For a moment I catch a glimmer on his face of the same frustration I feel whenever Evelyn is acting like a nut. Then it's gone, and he looks thoughtful again.

"Are you sure?" he asks us.

27

"I thought you liked CMS," Ryan says, standing up and turning to Louisa.

"I do! I mean, I did," she says. "That's why you have to believe me. I wouldn't say this if it wasn't true. I'm not —" She pauses, and I think she nearly said "crazy like Evelyn." "I'm not happy about it," she says instead. "I wanted CMS to be as great as I thought it was. But I know what I heard. If you're smart, you'll run away with us, too, for your parents' sakes."

"What?" My voice bursts out of my mouth before I can think. "Louisa! You can't just invite them along! We don't know these guys, we can't trust them, and we don't need them! We'd be better off on our own."

"I *do* know them," Louisa says hotly. "I know at least they wouldn't leave their roommates behind in the woods with no compass, like some people!"

"No, all you really know about them is that they'll give you sandwiches," I say. "But if that's all it takes to make you trust them more than you trust me, then maybe you should go with them and I'll find my own way back to Chicago. I bet I'd be safer that way anyhow!"

"Uh-oh," Evelyn interrupts, holding out her hands. A fat raindrop splatters on her palm. We all look up and realize that while we were arguing, the moonlight has been eaten by dark clouds, which have rolled in out of nowhere.

"Oh *no*!" Maddie yelps, and the skies open up.

Chapter 3

There's no way to keep arguing; the thunder drowns out our voices and the wind blows them away. It's one of those terrible storms that have gotten so much worse in the last twenty years, so every bit of rain is practically a hurricane. In moments, the storm is so strong that we can barely even stand under the deluge. I'm soaked to the skin and my backpack is a sodden weight on my back. I can hardly see the others in the dark and through the downpour.

I'm flipping through survival skills in my mind, trying to remember anything about what to do when a busload of rain is suddenly dumped on your head.

Lightning crackles above the trees and I think of flash floods and mudslides and worse. Suddenly I have the clearest memory of Wren's face, the way it changed when she saw the tidal wave coming. I hear her screaming at me to run all over again.

Panicking, I reach out blindly and grab the nearest person, thinking it's Louisa.

"Shelter!" I yell. "We have to find shelter!"

The person leans closer, touching my other arm, and I realize it's not Louisa, but Drew. I start to recoil, but he's pointing and waving something in his hand. I aim my flashlight at it and squint, realizing it's a compass. He pokes it with a finger and points again, off into the trees.

Someone blunders into us and clutches me with thin hands. Before I turn my flashlight on her, I can tell it's Maddie.

"We have to stay together!" I shout in her ear. I can't tell if she's heard me, but when I tug the gold cord out of my hair and twine it around my wrist and hers, she nods vigorously. A light flickers behind her and I see

31

Louisa and Alonso huddling close to us. I lift our linked hands and wave to Louisa to do the same.

Rain batters us relentlessly. It seems to take Louisa forever to work the elastic band out of her hair and loop it around her wrist and Maddie's. Alonso puts the flashlight between his teeth and reaches to help her.

I squint into the dark, searching for Evelyn and Ryan. Drew is still standing too close to me, holding the compass, waiting. I spot another weak circle of light and see Evelyn crouching beside a large boulder with her flashlight, trying to shield her backpack with her body. I point to her and Drew goes over to bring her back to us.

When I look around, blinking in the driving rain, Alonso has tied himself to Louisa's free hand and is working on wrapping something around his wrist and Ryan's. I guess we're stuck with the boys, at least for now.

Drew's hand slips into mine just as a peal of thunder rolls overhead, and I jump. He waves the compass and points again. I nod. I have no choice. If he knows where

32

we can find shelter, we have to follow him, although every cell in my body is screaming not to trust him.

Evelyn joins the end of the line, holding Ryan's hand, although she's still clutching her backpack to her chest with her other hand. I want to tell her that whatever's in there isn't worth it — I guess she's worried about her maps — but there's no way she'll hear me through the screaming wind.

Mud sloshes over our shoes as we slog forward, heads down. The world shrinks down to Drew's warm hand on one side and Maddie's cold, thin hand on the other. The rest of me is wet through and through, freezing and soaked and heavy, so moving is difficult. We slip on waterlogged leaves, stumble through giant puddles. My feet have never been this cold before.

The most annoying part is my hair. Without the cord tying it back, the long dark strands whip mercilessly around my head, stick to my face, and nearly blind me. But I can't reach up to shove it back because both of my hands are occupied. I keep shaking my head, but all that does is plaster more long tendrils to my face.

Suddenly Maddie lets out a shriek and I feel her hand jerk away. There's a wrenching pain in my wrist as the gold cord tightens and my shoulder is nearly yanked out of its socket. I try to let go of Drew, but his grip on my hand is too strong.

"Maddie!" Louisa screams. We both lean over, grabbing for her hands. The ground below Maddie has turned into a river of mud, dropping out from under her so that she nearly slid away down a hill that wasn't there a moment ago. If we hadn't been tied together, she'd have vanished into the dark.

Without letting go of me, Drew helps us and Alonso drag Maddie back onto solid ground. She leans on Louisa's shoulder, and I'm pretty sure she's crying, although it's hard to tell in the rain. I pat her arm awkwardly, her hand hanging limply from the cord tying us together.

"Not much farther," Drew shouts in my ear. I don't

know where he could be taking us. Surely the only shelter nearby is back at CMS — our school or theirs. Is he going to turn us in? I can't help thinking of Evelyn's last theory, that maybe some of the students were really working for the Alliance all along. What if she's right, and what if Drew is one of them?

But there's not much I can do now except follow him.

The rain pours down on us, harder and harder, each droplet like an exploding ice bomb on my bare neck and hands, slithering down into my sleeves. I can't even figure out which direction we're going. Back toward CMS? South, like we were before? I'm totally discombobulated, and I hate it.

Drew stops suddenly and I crash into him. He reaches over with his free hand and pushes my hair out of my eyes, then gestures at a clearing up ahead of us. In a flash of lightning, I spot a dark shape that could be a small cabin.

Everyone moves faster as we cover the last stretch of muddy ground, energized by the sight of shelter. All at once there's a blue door right in front of us: wooden, solid, real. I notice that Drew doesn't knock. He tries the handle, and my heart sinks when I see that it's locked.

But then he crouches and starts picking up large rocks next to the door. I watch him, confused, until he finds a small cavity on the underside of one of them and pulls out a key.

How did he know that would be there?

He unlocks the door, and we all pile inside so fast you'd think it was tigers chasing us instead of a storm. I suck in a breath of dry air and lean against the nearest wall. A wave of exhaustion hits me hard.

The door clicks shut behind us. The howling noise of the storm is instantly muffled. Finally we can hear ourselves think again.

Unfortunately, that also means we can hear one another talk.

"I thought we were going to die," Maddie gasps. She doesn't help as Louisa and I untie the cords around our wrists. As soon as I'm done, she slides down the wall

36

and rests her head on her knees, making little sniffly noises.

Part of me is irritated — she wasn't the only one out there, after all — but part of me realizes that she's never been outside in a storm like that before. I'm probably the only one here who's ever lived through a superhurricane. I glance at Alonso, wondering again if he might have a secret like mine.

A light flickers on overhead and we all turn to Drew, who's found a switch on the wall. We're standing in a kind of vestibule, a small space with an open archway ahead of us into a bigger room. We're all dripping onto a red terra-cotta tile floor. There are neat brass shoe racks on either side of us and a coatrack in the corner. I'm relieved to see that they're empty, although I could probably guess that we're the only people here by the dark rooms beyond the vestibule.

Where is *here, anyway?*

"What is this place?" I ask Drew.

He shrugs. "I'm not sure. I found it on one of my first

solo survival missions, a couple of weeks ago. There wasn't anyone here then, either."

I squint at him. "So how'd you know where the key was?"

His smile is a little condescending, like he thinks it's cute how suspicious I am. I wonder if he'd also find it cute if I punched that smile off his face.

"Lucky guess," he says. "My parents have a rock like that."

Liar, I think. Outside of CMS I don't know anyone who uses real keys anymore.

"I don't care what it is," Louisa says. She's already dumped her backpack on the floor and she's taking her shoes and socks off. "There must be towels here. That's all I want in the world. A dry towel. And some dry clothes. And maybe a hair dryer. And some food. Hot chocolate. And a bed with lots of pillows."

I can't help laughing. "But that's all, right?"

She smiles at me, and I remember why I like her. Nothing ever seems so bad to Louisa. I know that's just because nothing bad has actually ever happened to her, but it's still kind of nice to be around someone who thinks everything will be okay, no matter what. She's like the opposite of my parents, who worry that something terrible is coming around every corner, and they're usually right.

"Whoa," Ryan says, peering into the next room. "Guys, check this out."

The others crowd around him, but I take a minute to put down my backpack, take off my shoes, and wring out my socks and my hooded sweatshirt. I wish I could take off more of my dripping-wet clothes, especially my jeans, but of course I can't, because of the stupid boys. If it were just me, Louisa, Maddie, and Evelyn, we wouldn't have to worry and I'd be able to get dry a lot faster.

By the time I join the others in the main central room of the cabin, which is up two small steps from the vestibule, Ryan has found another light switch and turned on the low-hanging lamp in the center of the room.

I guess I expected couches and a coffee table and a fireplace and maybe a moose head on the wall, like a regular cabin in the woods where people went to fish or whatever in the old days, before the War. Instead there's an enormous oval conference table taking up almost the entire room. The polished mahogany surface gleams in the lamplight. Dark blue swivel chairs are arranged neatly around the oval, with a sort of uncanny precision that gives me goose bumps. The light barely reaches the edges of the table, but under my feet I can feel a textured carpet like the one in my dad's office at home, solid and businesslike.

Creepiest of all, up on the large blank wall opposite us is the seal of the Alliance.

This is definitely not a fishing cabin.

And we are definitely, definitely not supposed to be here.

Evelyn's eyes are huge. "It's their secret Alliance meeting place," she whispers. "This must be where they come to plan their invasion — to meet up with the teachers from your side!" she says to Alonso.

"I bet you're right!" he says. "I bet after they send us all into the woods on our made-up missions, they come here and plan real ones."

My instinct is to scoff at them or crack a joke of some kind, but there's something about the freaky, quiet intensity of this room that makes it too easy to believe what they're saying. I can absolutely picture Mrs. Brewster sitting at one end of the table, calmly passing around file folders full of notes on all the CMS students . . . and discussing how much money they can probably get for each of us.

I wonder what their notes on me would say, and how much they know. Do they realize that my parents will pay anything to get me back, because they're so afraid to lose the only daughter they have left? Is there anything in the CMS files about my missing sister, or is Wren a secret from them, too?

"Well, it's not an ordinary cabin — that's for sure," Ryan says. "I mean, who can afford electricity for a random cabin in the woods these days? It must have its own generator and everything."

We all glance up at the light, and I shiver again.

Louisa's voice breaks the tension. "There's a bathroom back here," she says from a doorway in the far corner. "Not a lot of towels, though. Whatever they use this place for, I don't think sleeping or bathing is a big part of it." She comes out with an armful of lilac-colored hand towels. We each take one and I run mine along my arms, then rub my hair with it. It's not the most useful thing ever, but it's better than nothing.

I notice that Louisa gives Maddie two hand towels and then helps her dry her hair with one of them. I can see why most people would believe that they're sisters. That's something Wren would have done for me. It's only because I think about Wren all the time that I noticed the little ways Louisa and Maddie don't act like sisters.

42

Thinking about my family sends me on a search for a telephone, but of course there isn't one anywhere in the cabin, nor a computer or anything useful like that. The other door off the room leads to a tiny kitchen, although the fridge turns out to be woefully under-stocked. Everything in the cupboards has that NutriCorp logo on it, like the food in the CMS cafeteria. I pull out a box of oatmeal cookies and peek inside. Only half of them are gone.

"Hey, Louisa, guess what?" Ryan says. "I can make one of your dreams come true, at least." He waggles a packet of cocoa at her. She clasps her hands rapturously, looking like a cartoon-character version of happy.

"Wait," Evelyn says, closing the refrigerator door in Drew's face. "Stop! You guys, we shouldn't take anything. Or else they'll know we were here! We can't leave any traces!"

"Ohhh," Maddie says anxiously. "You're totally right. She's totally right! Guys, put everything back exactly

43

where you found it! We should wipe down everything we touched!"

I roll my eyes. "They're not going to dust for fingerprints, Maddie."

"How do you know?" she demands.

"They don't even *have* our fingerprints to compare them to," I point out.

"Oh," she says. "Okay. True. But —"

"But I'm hungry!" Louisa says. "And the Alliance deserves to be stolen from!"

"Maybe they won't notice *one* cocoa packet," Ryan suggests. "Or two? Maybe a couple of cookies?"

"It doesn't matter," Drew says. "We should take whatever we want. They'll know we were here, anyway."

"How?" I ask. *Because you're going to tell them?*

He points down at the floor, then back at the rug behind us. "Even with our shoes off, we've really messed up the carpet. It won't take an enormous brain trust to figure out that someone sheltered in here from the storm."

He's right. There are wet patches and bits of grass and mud all across the pale blue carpet. The hem of my jeans is busily creating its own little mud puddle right here in the kitchen.

"They won't know for sure it was us," I say to Evelyn and Maddie. "They might think it was some of the boys on their survival mission."

"Hey, that's true," Ryan says. "Since they're not expecting me and Drew and Alonso back for a week, they won't even start looking for us until we don't show up."

There's an awkward pause. It takes Ryan a minute to figure out that's because I still haven't agreed to let them come with us, and he gives me an apologetic look.

"Listen, we can't go back to CMS after what you guys told us," he says. "We don't want to be used as weapons against our parents any more than you do. If you won't let us come with you, we'll have to run away on our own."

This sounds like a fine plan to me, but Louisa immediately jumps in. "Don't be silly," she says. "We want you with us. We'll be safer if we stick together."

45

That is blatantly false, but I'm guessing she doesn't want to hear about how a large group will make more noise crashing through the woods, or how much easier it'll be to spot all of us from their helicopters, or how much harder it'll be to find somewhere for us all to sleep safely, never mind finding food for seven instead of four. Safer! We might as well turn ourselves in right now.

"Right, Rosie?" Louisa says. "I mean, look at these poor, helpless guys. They obviously need us."

Ryan tries to make puppy-dog eyes. Alonso's friendly, harmless expression is more successful. Drew, on the other hand, still has that I-know-things face, and he raises his eyebrows at me as if he's curious to see what I'll do, not that it actually matters to him one way or another.

It occurs to me that if he is working for the Alliance, maybe I *should* keep him with us, so I can keep an eye on him.

"Fine," I say, pulling my hair back into a ponytail and wringing it out. "You're right. If we didn't let them come with us, they'd probably end up wandering in circles around the school until they got caught."

"We would," Ryan agrees affably. "We'd be lost without you."

"I'm not as bad as these two," Drew offers. "*I* can actually start a fire, for instance."

"So can I!" Alonso protests. He leans over to the stove and flicks one of the knobs. Blue light flares around one of the burners. "See? I rock at this."

Louisa and Maddie both giggle. Oh, brother. I bet there's going to be a lot of that — laughing at stupid boy jokes that aren't even that funny. I reach over and turn the knob off. We have our own generator at home, too, but I still hate wasting energy.

"So, hot cocoa for everyone?" Louisa says hopefully.

I go back out into the vestibule while the others search the kitchen for mugs. There's a small window by the front door that's covered with a close-fitting dark shade, I guess so no one will see the cabin's lights from the woods. I peek out just in time to see a huge flash of lightning. This storm isn't stopping any-time soon.

"We'll have to sleep here tonight," Drew says from right behind me, peering over my shoulder at the rain.

I whirl around and shove him back. "*Don't* sneak up on me."

"I didn't mean to," he says, raising his hands, palms out. "I came to get the sleeping bags, to see if they'd dry out if I unroll them."

"Me, too," I say. There's only one thing I like about Drew so far, and it's that he seems to have a sensible head on his shoulders. He keeps doing the same things I would do to survive. The problem is, I don't trust his reasons. Maybe he was going to use the sleeping bag idea as an excuse to go through our packs. Or maybe he has a hid-den Alliance communicator in his.

I watch him carefully as we both unpack the sleeping bags and shake them out, but I don't catch him sneak-ing anything out of his pack, or any of the others. We spread the sleeping bags around the giant conference table, head to toe, although there's not quite enough room and one of them has to go under the table, between the chairs.

Despite the drenching downpour, the sleeping bags were pretty well protected in their waterproof bags, and are mostly dry. I wish I could say the same for the clothes in our packs, but they're a little drier than the ones I'm wearing, so I slip into the bathroom and change into new jeans and a warm, long-sleeved black shirt.

When I come back out, Louisa has just emerged from the kitchen with two mugs of cocoa. She sets them down on the table with a flourish. "Maybe they'll stain the wood," she says. "It would serve them right."

"Yeah," I say. "Take that, Alliance! That'll teach them for defeating Canada and kidnapping us!"

Louisa giggles again. To her disappointment, though, the mugs don't leave any marks on the table. They're a plain, institutional white porcelain with the NutriCorp logo emblazoned on the side. I have to look at it twice before I realize it's not the Alliance seal, though. From a distance, and when I'm this tired, the logo and the seal look eerily similar, except that the logo has a maple leaf where the Alliance seal has a giant star.

I barely have the energy to drink my cocoa, although it does warm me up and make me feel a bit better. I have no idea how far we've come from CMS, although I'm very sure it's not far enough. But at least we're safe from the storm, and we can get some sleep before moving on. Hopefully it'll have stopped raining by morning. We're getting out of here as soon as it's light, storm or no storm.

I crawl into the sleeping bag under the table. Louisa, Ryan, Maddie, Alonso, and Evelyn stay up for a while longer, talking. I can hear them giggling as I drift off to sleep. It makes me feel a little left out and a lot grumpy, even though I don't want to join them. Only Drew is sensible enough to also get the rest we all need.

But I'm not going to go out there and yell at them. The girls know perfectly well how I feel about getting distracted by boys, I think. It won't be my fault when they're tired tomorrow.

Something is digging into my back, but I'm too tired to wriggle away from it. I close my eyes and dream, as I always do, of hurricanes and tidal waves, of Wren smiling up at Ivan, of swimming and running and hiding and helicopters, of the look on my mom's face as a new ID bracelet is snapped around my wrist. Only this time, Ivan has Drew's face, and when I look up from my ID bracelet, the person putting it on me, smiling evilly, is Mrs. Brewster.

I can even hear her loud, brassy voice. It's so real. . . .

I jolt awake, all the hairs on my skin standing on end.

It *is* real.

Mrs. Brewster is *here.*

Chapter 4

Runaways," Mrs. Brewster snaps. I'm so befuddled and sleepy and out of it that it takes me another twenty seconds to realize her voice is coming from outside the cabin, not right above me like I first thought. I sit up fast and bang my shoulder on one of the rolling chairs, just barely missing the table with my skull.

"Louisa!" I hiss quietly. I duck my head to look under the chairs and I see Louisa's wide, frightened blue eyes peeking out of her sleeping bag. She hears our headmistress, too.

"Four of them!" Mrs. Brewster goes on. The storm has passed, or else we wouldn't be able to hear her so clearly. If it had still been raining, she would have walked in and found us asleep. "Just when things were going so perfectly! Where could those idiot girls have gone?"

I wince. She's talking about us! Of course, those "idiot girls" are nanoseconds away from being back in her clutches. There's nowhere for us to hide, no way to run before she walks through the door. My heart is pounding and I can barely breathe. What will happen to my family now?

"What is taking so long?" Mrs. Brewster barks.

"I can't find the key," says Devi's voice. "It's like someone moved all the rocks around."

"Connolly," Mrs. Brewster snorts. "He has no discipline."

I scramble out from under the table and nearly crash into Drew's legs. He meets my eyes and holds up the cabin door key, but his face is pale, and for the first time he looks really worried. He never put it back last night, so we're safe for another minute, but not much more.

53

"Is there another way out of here?" I whisper.

On the other side of the table, Louisa shakes Maddie awake and then Evelyn, covering Evelyn's mouth as she opens her eyes to make sure Evelyn doesn't start yakking and give us away. Alonso climbs blearily out of his sleeping bag and pokes Ryan with his toe.

"I don't know," Drew whispers back. "Not that I know of, but I've never, like, hung out here."

"Get our stuff from the vestibule," I say to Louisa and Evelyn. "All of it! Don't leave anything behind. Put your shoes on and roll up the sleeping bags." I don't have time to act like we're all a happy decision-making team right now. I can't believe we're such morons! Of course the teachers would show up here first thing in the morning, ready to discuss their new plans now that Canada has fallen. We could not have picked a worse place to hide.

This turns out to be truer than I first thought as I search for another exit. The bathroom window is way too small for any of us to fit through, except maybe Maddie.

Outside I can see the grayish-blue-pink light of early dawn; it's maybe five in the morning or something horrible like that.

The kitchen doesn't even have any windows, and neither does the conference room. There's no back door. There's only the front door, where Mrs. Brewster is standing, clearly getting more and more impatient. I tug on my socks and shoes as quietly as I can, listening through the wood.

"I'm sorry, Mrs. B.," Devi says. "I found the rock, but the key isn't in there. Someone must have taken it with them last time."

"Idiots," Mrs. Brewster growls. My hopes rise a tiny bit. Maybe they'll have to go away and get a new one, and we can escape while they're gone.

"Connolly and Grifone will be here soon," Devi says. "One of them probably has it."

"I'm not standing here waiting for them like an abandoned dog," Mrs. Brewster says. "Run back to the truck and get our extra key."

"Yes, boss," says Devi.

I dash back into the main room. The others are huddled around the table, looking terrified. "We have maybe a minute," I whisper. "Then it's all over." I press my hands to my forehead, trying to think. There must be something we can do. We can't have failed so quickly, so spectacularly. This has to be the worst escape in the history of the world.

And it's Drew's fault, I think, suspicion bubbling up inside me. But the truth is, if I had known about this place, I probably would have brought us here in the storm, too.

"There are seven of us," Ryan points out. "I hate to say it, but I bet we could overpower her if we try to make a run for it right now."

"Have you seen her?" Maddie asks with a shudder. "She could take all of us down easily."

"Plus she probably has a weapon," Evelyn whispers. "Most likely secret, advanced Alliance technology."

This is such an Evelyn thing to say that Louisa can't help rolling her eyes at me, despite how tense the situation is.

"And even if a few of us get away, she's bound to catch someone," says Alonso, keeping his voice low like the rest of us. "And she'll know exactly how far the rest of us have gone, so we'll all be in cells by the end of the day."

I have no idea what to suggest. My sleeping bag is poking out from under the table, so I crouch down to drag it out while the others argue. I'm a little annoyed no one has packed it up for me while I was searching for an escape route.

The zipper catches on something, and I have to lean in to unhook it. When I see what it's hooked on, I nearly yell with excitement, but I manage to keep my voice down.

"Guys!" I hiss, poking my head out. "There's a trap-door under the table!"

Drew and Louisa shove chairs aside and duck under with me. Together we turn the silver metal handle in the floor until there's a click and we can heave the trap-door up.

I shine my flashlight down the dark hole and we see a dirt floor about eight feet below us.

"This doesn't seem like a good idea," Maddie says.

"All we've got left are bad ideas," I say. I scoot my feet over the edge, drop my backpack and sleeping bag down ahead of me, and jump after them. Quickly I spin with the flashlight, thinking it's a cellar of some kind, and maybe we can hide in it until the Alliance meeting is over.

I catch my breath. Even better. "There's a tunnel down here! We can get out this way!"

"But where does it go?" Maddie frets.

"Away from Mrs. Brewster," Louisa says. "That's all I need to know." She drops her backpack down next to me and swings herself through the hole as well. "Come on, Maddie!"

"Hurry!" I add.

"Maybe Ryan, Alonso, and I should stay here," Drew suggests, to my surprise, as Maddie reluctantly lowers herself through the hole. His face peers down at us, hidden by the shadow of the table above him. "That way if they figure out someone was here, we can pretend we just got lost during the storm. It'll draw attention away from you girls."

Louisa reaches out and catches Maddie as she stumbles away from the hole. Evelyn drops down right behind her. I see the expression on Louisa's face: she knows Drew has made a good suggestion, but she's still reluctant to leave the boys.

It's the perfect chance for me to get rid of them ... but I can't. I know what's likely to happen to them if they stay. Even if Mrs. Brewster believes their story — which she won't — they'll never have a chance to run away after this. And what if Alonso does have a secret like mine? Then he really can't afford to get caught, either.

59

"That won't work," I call up to Drew. "There are seven used mugs of cocoa. They'll know you were with us. Quick, rearrange the room like it was as much as you can, then get down here."

Beside me in the dim light, Evelyn smacks her forehead. "I guess my mom was right about doing the dishes as soon as you've used them."

"We're so dumb," Louisa mutters anxiously.

"We can still get out of this," I say. "If they don't figure out we've used the trapdoor, hopefully they'll think we're in the woods nearby and they'll go out looking for us."

There's a thump as Ryan lands behind us, followed by Alonso. Drew jumps down last, and then Ryan lifts him on his shoulders so that Drew can reach the trapdoor and close it. Just as he turns the knob to lock it, we hear footsteps marching across the floor above us.

We all freeze, holding our breath.

"Of course Connolly is late, as always," Mrs. Brewster grumbles over our heads. "Devi, did you bring the folders on those four girls?"

60

"Of course," Devi answers. "And their ID bracelets. The data history might tell us something about where they're going, if we can retrieve it."

"I wonder if any of the boys are missing, too," says the headmistress.

"I'm sure not. None of the hostages know about what's happened in Canada," Devi says reassuringly. "It's bad timing — that's all. The Ballinger girl was worried about her fake sister. That's why they ran away, so they wouldn't get in trouble. They don't know about us."

"I hope you're right," Mrs. Brewster muses. "But it's a strange coincidence, on the very day we're able to reveal our true purpose. And why would Posner and Chavez go with them? Blast it all. I knew those girls were trouble from the beginning. I should have locked all four of them up on day one."

I wave my hand to get everyone's attention. Fascinating as this is, it can't be long before Mrs. Brewster notices something — the mud on the carpet, or the mugs in the sink, or the extra hand towels draped around the bathroom. We've done a terrible job of covering our tracks. And we need to run. Now.

We don't risk talking or even whispering. Ryan sets Drew down carefully and I head for the tunnel. My flashlight reveals nothing but packed dirt walls all around us. There's no way to know what's up ahead.

But whatever it is, it's got to be better than being dragged back to CMS by Mrs. Brewster so our parents can spend all of their money trying to get us home.

I take a deep breath. And then I lead the way into the darkness.

Chapter 5

It is surprisingly cold in the tunnel, especially since my clothes aren't completely dry yet. My feet squish in my sneakers and my jeans feel clammy against my thighs. I wish I could stop and at least put on a pair of dry socks, but as long as we're moving, I'm not going to be the one to slow us down. Our close call back at the cabin seems to have lit a fire under Maddie and Evelyn, and neither of them so much as peeps a complaint even after two hours of walking.

A drumbeat of worry keeps going around and around in my head. Where is the tunnel taking us? What if they figured out we went this way and are waiting for us at the other end? Drew was the last one through the trapdoor — what if he left a message for them to come get us? I don't see any branches off this tunnel. It goes one way, and one way only. If anyone comes along the tunnel, from either direction, we're as trapped as we were in the cabin.

Not to mention how unexcited I am about finding out where an Alliance tunnel could possibly lead. I'm guessing it won't be Chicago.

After a while, Evelyn pulls out her compass. She flicks on her flashlight — again, we're using only one, to save batteries — checks the needle, and grimaces.

"What?" Alonso asks.

"That's what I was afraid of," she says. "So much for heading south to Chicago."

"Why? What direction are we going in?" asks Louisa.

Evelyn holds out the compass to her. "Due north."

Louisa looks down at it, biting her lip. I know she's thinking the same thing I am. Due north means

Canada. Only a few short miles away. Which has just fallen to the Alliance. We've been walking for such a long time, we might even have crossed the border already.

"What are we going to do if we end up in Canada?" Maddie says, wide-eyed. "Without our ID bracelets, we'll be in such huge trouble."

"Even *with* them we'd be in trouble," Evelyn says.

"That's true," I say. "Now that Canada's on the other side of this war, it's going to be ten thousand times as hard to cross the border and get home again." I know way, way too much about that. I doubt any of my six companions could survive a clandestine border-crossing run.

"Maybe we should go back to the cabin," Ryan says, slowing down and looking back over his shoulder. "Maybe they'll be gone by now."

"That'd be better than getting stuck in Canada," Alonso says. "Most likely in a war zone."

"Unless we run into our teachers coming this way,"

Drew says grimly. "We can't go back. We have to go forward."

I hate agreeing with him, but I do. In this case, the unknown is a much preferable alternative to what we know is back there. At worst, surely we can find a phone somewhere in Canada and call our parents. I want them to know that we're out of Mrs. Brewster's clutches. And once they know where we are, maybe they can come get us.

But as I think about that for the next half hour of walking, I begin to wonder if it's true. Maybe Ryan's plan would be better. My parents certainly wouldn't have an easy time coming to get me from Canada. What if we step out right into a war zone, as Alonso said? What if the Alliance catches us right away? Or what if we get to the border, but there's no way to get across and get home?

I'm about to suggest turning back when, all of a sudden, the tunnel ends.

Maddie's flashlight beam hits a packed dirt wall ahead of us. Dirt walls on either side. We've reached the end, wherever this is.

Maddie just stands there for a moment, staring at the wall in confusion, so I take the flashlight from her and point it up at the ceiling.

A couple of metal rungs are driven into the side of the wall, leading up to another trapdoor, with the same kind of silver metal lock as the one in the cabin. We all gaze up at the new trapdoor, and I'm pretty sure it's safe to say we're all terrified.

"They could be waiting for us," Evelyn points out. "There could be motion detectors in this tunnel that let them know we were coming. Or security cameras!"

Trust Evelyn to make a spooky situation even worse.

"We haven't seen anything like that," I say, trying to sound reassuring.

"The Alliance wouldn't need to put special defenses on their top secret tunnel," Louisa agrees. She combs her blond hair back with her fingers and twists it into a braid like she's getting ready to run.

"Not at this end, anyway," Alonso offers.

Louisa and Maddie both nod like he's said something terribly smart, but the only one he's looking at is Evelyn. She bites her fingernails, blinking at the trapdoor.

"Well, it's forward or back," says Ryan. "I say let's see where we are."

He takes a step toward the rungs, and although I appreciate his boldness, I can't stand letting a guy be the bravest one in our group.

"I'll do it," I say, jumping in front of him. I drop my backpack, grab the handholds, and clamber up the couple of feet to reach the trapdoor. The lock sticks for a moment, and it's especially hard with just one hand, but I throw all my weight at it and finally it slides aside with a *clunk*.

Cautiously, I lift the trapdoor half an inch and peek out.

The morning light is bright enough that my eyes, used to the dimness of the tunnel, take a minute to adjust.

So the first thing I know is that we're outdoors, not coming up into another cabin.

As soon as I can see, my eyes land on a stack of white boxes, all of them with the NutriCorp label on the side. They look like they've been piled up on the grass, waiting to be taken somewhere. Maybe into the tunnel? So they can be smuggled to CMS? But it seems like a lot of boxes. I wonder if there are that many people planning to carry them all the way back down the long tunnel we just came through.

I try craning around, squinting through the small gap between the trapdoor and the ground. Now I can see small wooden buildings and canvas tents, kind of like a summer camp from old movies, back when kids had fun in the summertime, swimming and doing talent shows or whatever. But instead of kids in swimsuits, the people striding around here are all adults . . . and they're all wearing military uniforms and boots.

Alliance military uniforms.

And fluttering above the camp is a giant flag with the Alliance seal on it. They wouldn't dare fly that so openly in the United States.

So I can be pretty sure our worst fear is true: we've crossed the border into Canada, and landed smack in the middle of an Alliance military camp.

Chapter 6

I whisper the bad news down to the others. Maddie lets out a little moan and sits down on the dirt floor, leaning against Louisa's leg. But Evelyn and Alonso actually look excited.

"Maybe we can find something to help the Resistance," Evelyn says.

"The what?" Ryan asks.

She rolls her eyes at him. "Don't you pay attention to the news? The Resistance is fighting the Alliance wherever the military can't. They're exactly the people we need to take down the sleeper cells and training camps. If we could get a message to them, they'd rescue all the girls at CMS."

"Are you serious?" Drew says, pushing his glasses up on his nose. "I thought the Resistance was an urban legend. Where do you get your 'news'?"

Evelyn flushes. "The Internet. And maybe some message boards."

"Oh, message boards," Drew says. "I see. Very reliable."

"Hey, I've heard of the Resistance, too," Alonso says, touching Evelyn's elbow. "I think they're real. *Somebody* put out that fire in Baltimore. They disabled those bombs in Cleveland. They saved that evacuation train full of people when it ran out of fuel in the middle of Missouri. They've been ferrying supplies to the people who are still trying to live in California with no electricity. And I've heard they help refugees get into the country when their own homes get too dangerous." I flinch, remembering kind green eyes behind a makeshift mask and their sad expression when I asked about Wren. "If it's not the Resistance, who's doing all that?"

"Okay, *stop*," I hiss as loudly as I dare, before Drew can snap back at Alonso. There's one way I can end their argument, but it involves offering up way too much personal information. So I decide to go with the other option: grumpiness. "I *don't care* if this stupid Resistance exists. My arms are getting tired, and we have to decide if we're sneaking out of this tunnel right now or not."

"We could wait until nightfall," Louisa suggests. "So we'd be less likely to be spotted?" I could tell she was mystified and bored by the Resistance conversation. Following politics is not Louisa's strong suit. Yet another thing I like about her. She wouldn't understand some of the details of my life story, but she'd be my friend regardless. And she'd understand the really important things, like about Wren. Not that I can tell her any of it, of course.

"That's a good idea," Ryan says. He gives Louisa a

big smile, but she doesn't notice because she's crouching to check on Maddie again.

"No, sorry — I mean, it is a good idea, Louisa," I say, "but we can't wait that long. The Alliance might use the tunnel before then." I peek back out at the boxes. Nobody is near them, but I can't imagine why else they'd just be sitting there. I'm afraid that any minute a crew of soldiers will show up and start carrying them into the tunnel.

"Can you see anywhere for us to hide?" Drew asks me.

I scan the area again, watching the soldiers for longer this time. Most of the activity seems focused around two distant buildings: a big one, which I'm guessing is the mess hall, because people keep coming in and out with plates of food or tin mugs, and a smaller one, which over-looks a field on the far side of the camp. Soldiers are jogging around the field or doing push-ups and jumping jacks in the middle of it.

"I think we've arrived during breakfast," I say. "And morning calisthenics for the other half of camp. There are a couple of small buildings and tents near us that might be empty." I lower the trapdoor again and shake my arm out, thinking.

They're all looking up at me, six worried faces. I don't love what I'm about to suggest, but I don't think I have much choice. If I want them all to follow me, I have to lead. I always figure that's better than following someone else.

"Here's what we'll do," I say. "I'll make a run for the nearest building by myself and peek in the windows. If the coast is clear, I'll signal for you guys to follow me. Okay?"

"What if it's not clear?" Louisa asks.

"I'll find another building where it is," I say, trying to sound confident. "Just watch for me."

"What if you get caught?" Maddie asks, twisting a lock of brown hair around her finger.

Now, there's something I really don't want to think about. "Then come get me," I say with a smile. Then I glance outside again, make sure no one is watching the trapdoor, and shove it open just far enough to wriggle out.

Drew climbs up the rungs right below me, his arm behind my shoulders, holding the trapdoor ajar as I squeeze through the gap. I wish it were anyone but him keeping an eye on me, but there's not much I can do about it. At least he's strong. I crawl free and he lowers the trapdoor quietly behind me.

Immediately I roll into a crouch and run to the boxes, which provide the nearest place to take cover. On one side they face a tall wire fence, not far from a large double gate, with woods pressing up against it that look exactly like the ones we were just walking through last night. I crouch on that side for a moment, peeking out at the rest of the camp.

That's when I see the guards off to my left. More important, I see the building they're guarding, and I see the bars on its windows, and I see the thin figures in black walking in slow circles in a small yard behind another barbed wire fence.

That's a prison.

The Alliance is keeping some of its prisoners in this camp.

Which means . . . which means that at this exact moment, I could be heartbeats away from my sister, Wren.

Chapter 7

Every atom in my body wants to leap out from behind those boxes and run right over to the prison. I want to grab one of those rifles from the guards, bash down the doors, and scream Wren's name over and over until she comes running out and I can throw my arms around her and she can be the one in charge again. How many times have I promised the universe that I would never fight with her ever again if I could just have her back? How many gifts have I offered to give up in exchange for seeing her once more?

I wouldn't care if we got caught; I wouldn't care who

had us or what they did with us, as long as we could be together.

But it's not just me here. I wouldn't call most of them friends, but there are still six other people underground right now who just want to get to safety. They're counting on me not to, you know, freak out and attack some prison guards.

I wonder if they would mind waiting there while I ran over and spied on the prison. I so desperately want a closer look at the people on the other side of that fence. If I could talk to one of them, even, maybe someone inside would have seen a nineteen-year-old girl who looks like me but prettier, with a smile that would have made her a movie star back when they still made movies.

But I can't leave Louisa and the others in the tunnel. Someone could come along and open that trapdoor any minute. We need to find a safer hiding place, and then we need to find a way out of here.

Perhaps if I can stash the others somewhere, then I can go check out the prison.

Or if we find a way out, maybe I can let them go on without me, while I stay and look for Wren.

I force myself to scan the nearest buildings. There's a small guard shack next to the gate, about ten long strides away from me to my left, but through the tall open window I can see that it's empty at the moment.

Beyond that, between the gate and the prison, there's a large camouflage canvas tent, which is probably a dormitory. It faces the prison, away from the boxes and the gate, so the occasional soldier going in and out of it won't see me as long as I stay in the shadows and don't move.

Along the side of the tent, close to the fence, is a scraggly pen with several black-and-white goats, a bunch of scrawny chickens, and one tall, grumpy-looking bird with giant feathers. It takes me a minute to recognize it from the pictures I've seen in books: an ostrich. The Alliance must have taken it from one of the last remaining Canadian zoos. Ostrich eggs are probably huge; I bet one egg could feed ten soldiers.

Okay, I'm totally making that up, but why else would they have an ostrich?

Ahead and to the right of me, between the boxes and the big central field of the camp, are a few low buildings, most of which have steps and doors on the sides. The closest one is only a short dash across a sunny stretch of grass, so I take a deep breath and run, throwing myself down into the shadows below it and slamming my eyes shut, hoping nobody saw me.

There are no shouts of alarm, no rifles poking me in the gut, so after a minute I let myself breathe and open my eyes again. Back at the trapdoor, I can just see Drew's eyes peeking out at me. I think he looks amused, although I really can't tell from this distance, so it's possible I'm just looking for reasons to get mad at him. Then again, he's the type to find my heroism amusing, so I frown at him, anyway.

The window on the back wall of this building is a

little too high for me to see into, so I have to roll a large rock over and stand on it on tiptoes. I grab the windowsill with my fingertips and poke my nose over the edge.

It's only one room, and it must be some kind of filing storage space, because there are piles of papers all over the two desks and the wooden floor. What is with the Alliance and paper? Why can't they use digital storage like normal people? I guess this way they don't have to worry about accessing everything when they don't have electricity. And piles of papers can't be hacked. Or wiped out by electromagnetic pulse attacks, like the ones that wrecked all the electronic equipment in Seattle, Cardiff, and Mumbai a few years ago.

Still, come on, Alliance, join the twenty-first century already. Making kids learn to write with pens and pencils again is just cruel. I swear my right arm is still sore from two weeks of relearning to use a pen at CMS.

A movement in the room makes my heart leap up and bang into my throat. Before I lose my grip from the fright, I see that it's a guy, probably in his early twenties, sorting through some papers with a fierce expression. Then my fingers slip and I tumble back, staggering off the stone and landing on my knees on the dirt beside it. I hold my breath for another minute, waiting to see if anyone heard the thud or saw my graceful crash. But apart from Drew's eyes at the trapdoor, no one seems to be looking my way.

I stick out my tongue at Drew and then slide my hand across my throat, shaking my head. *Not this building. Not safe.* I wave for him to stay put, peek around the side of the building, and sprint to the next one over.

Here we're a bit luckier. There's a drainpipe I can stand on to hoist myself up to the window, and immediately I see that there's no one inside. I'm guessing this is where the boxes were stored until they were moved outside. The room is mostly empty, but the floor is free of dust, as if there were something on it not too long ago. A few stray cans and smaller boxes are scattered across the shelves that line the walls. The only sign of life I see is a gray mouse sauntering boldly around, scavenging for crumbs.

There's nothing in the room that the soldiers will come looking for. It looks like a perfect place to hide, at least until we figure out what to do next.

I beckon to Drew, then slip around the side, up the steps, and in through the door as quickly as I can. The mouse sits up and stares at me, as if it's rather offended I've come to disturb its stolen meal. It looks even more displeased when Ryan thumps through the door behind me, followed by Evelyn, Alonso, Louisa and Maddie together, and finally Drew with my backpack. If I'd been back in the tunnel, I would have made them wait longer between people, but we swing the door shut and wait and there's no reaction from outside. So I guess we're safe for the moment.

"This is perfect," Louisa says, exhaling. She sets down her backpack and pats the faded red wall. Flakes of paint drift to the floor. "See, Maddie? We're going to be okay."

She sounds like she's reassuring herself as much as anyone else.

Maddie rubs her arms and looks around the small, dark space as if she's not convinced.

"What else did you see out there, Rosie?" Evelyn demands, her dark eyes shining with excitement. She peeks out the back window, but there's not much to see in that direction besides the gate and the pile of boxes. There's a dirty front window out onto the rest of the camp, but none of us want to get too close to that in case we're spotted.

I tell them about the guard shack, the tent dormitory, the prison, and the filing storage in the building next door. Evelyn and Alonso both light up at this last bit of information.

"There could be important documents in there!" Alonso says.

"We should steal some!" Evelyn says, and he nods. "To take back to the Resistance!"

"And how do you plan to get these hypothetical papers to this imaginary band of merry rogue heroes?" Drew says snidely.

"I don't know. Maybe we'll post them on the Internet," Evelyn responds in the same spiteful tone.

"Well, it's not safe to go in, anyway," I point out, trying to stop them from arguing again. "There's a guy in there right now."

"I'll watch for him to leave," Alonso immediately volunteers. He hurries over to the door and holds it slightly ajar so he can watch the building across from us.

"All right, well, while you do that very important thing," Drew says, "the rest of us can figure out how to get out of here. Any ideas? Rosie, do you think that fence goes all the way around the camp?"

"I'm pretty sure it does," I say. "Especially since they have prisoners to keep in, besides protecting the soldiers from outside attack."

This makes the others look, if possible, even gloomier.

"Maybe we should wait until dark and go back into the tunnel," Ryan suggests. "If they can use it to get across the border, we can, too. And what are the chances they'll use it at night?"

"Why wouldn't they?" Louisa says. "I don't know. . . . I don't want to go back down there if we can help it. I felt like a rat trapped in a maze. And we'd have nowhere to hide if Alliance agents came from either direction."

"We can't stay here," Maddie says. "They'll catch us any minute."

We're clearly about to have a serious morale problem. What everyone needs is some strong leadership. Even if I don't have any brilliant ideas, I can at least give them that.

"All right," I say, "Louisa, you and Maddie take turns keeping an eye on those boxes out the back window. I bet they'll be going into that tunnel soon, so watch for who takes them and when, and maybe then we can figure out how often they use the tunnel." I turn to Evelyn. She's going to be obsessed with her dopey document-stealing plan, anyway, so I know it's pointless to give her anything else to do. "You and Alonso can keep watching the file storage place next door. But don't do anything risky or stupid. Remember that getting us out of here is more important than stealing anything, no matter how useful you think it might be."

"But we could stop the War!" Evelyn protests. "We could be heroes!"

"Not if we're thrown in an Alliance prison — like, for example, the one right here," I point out. "So let's focus on that first. Ryan, you watch out the front window to make sure no one is coming this way. And Drew, you check these last few boxes to see if there's anything edible in there. I'll go scout around the camp and see what I can find out."

"Um, I don't think we should eat anything in here," Drew says. He points to the floor, and I follow his gaze to the little gray mouse.

"Ew!" Louisa cries.

"The poor thing!" Maddie gasps.

The mouse is lying flat on the floor in the center of the room, and for a horrifying moment I'm sure it's dead. I immediately wonder where a giant stash of poisoned food could possibly be going.

Then I see the mouse's small furry chest rise up and down, and I realize it's sleeping. Drew pokes it gently with the toe of his boot. "Still alive," he says. "But at least some of the food that was in here must be drugged. I don't want to risk it, do you?"

We all shake our heads. I'm even more mystified than before. What is the Alliance planning? Who are they going to put to sleep with that food? I'd sort of figured the boxes might be going to CMS, since the schools are the closest places to the other side of the tunnel. But why knock out a bunch of teenagers? The four of us managed to get out just in time, but I doubt anyone else will even try to escape, especially since the teachers will be on high alert because of us.

I glance at the logo on the boxes again. Does the US government know that NutriCorp is involved with the

Alliance? I've seen their stuff in grocery stores every-where. They could start drugging the whole American population without anyone realizing it.

"So I'll come with you," Drew says, jerking me out of my thoughts.

"No!" I say, too fast, and they all look at me as if I've just bitten Drew's ear off. "I mean — I just mean, I'll be safer on my own. Harder to spot." That is true. It's also true that I don't trust Drew at all. Not only that, but what I really want to do is get close to that prison. I don't want to explain why to anyone else.

But Louisa and Ryan are both shaking their heads. "You'll be safer together," Louisa says. "Please, Rosie. I'll be so nervous if you're out there alone. What if you don't come back? Then what do we do?"

"Drew can watch your back," Ryan says. "He's a great tracker. And he might see something you don't."

Okay, now I'm offended. Remember how I didn't want any boys on this escape with us? Here's one reason why. They always think they can do things better than girls can, and guess what? They're wrong. I guarantee I can shoot straighter, start a fire better, and climb a tree faster than Drew or Ryan or Alonso. And Wren was better than Ivan at everything — except lying, I suppose.

I want to argue with them, but I know it's no good. Drew is going to follow me whether I want him to or not.

"Then you'd better keep up," I say to him, and I'm out the door before he can give me one of his smug expressions.

He catches up to me as I duck inside the guard shack. I was hoping to find something that would open the big gate, but there's no magical ring of keys hanging helpfully from a hook on the wall. There aren't any bolt cutters for the huge links of chain that hold the gate shut. There's no giant button that says: PRESS ME TO ESCAPE! It's just a tiny room with a broken swivel chair in it.

I'm guessing they don't use this gate very much. I wonder if we could climb over it without getting spotted, but we'd have to deal with some wicked coils of barbed wire at the top, which would be the very opposite of fun.

I glance out the window as Drew crowds into the room with me. From this angle I can see clotheslines tied to the back of the dormitory tent, stretching between the tent poles and the fence posts of the animal enclosure. Several Alliance uniforms are hanging up to dry, most of them still pretty wet. I always thought the Alliance had plenty of access to electricity, since they control most of the fuel companies, but I guess even they save electricity by making their soldiers do laundry by hand. My family does that, too, but we pay someone else to do the hard work.

Drew figures out what I'm thinking without me having to say anything. "Let me get them," he whispers. He darts out and runs to the clotheslines, where the flapping shirts and trousers hide him from sight for a moment. At least, from me and the rest of the camp, but I see the ostrich and a couple of the goats whip around and stare beadily at the laundry. Drew's lucky they can't get out, because they look like they're itching to pick a fight with an intruder.

I turn my gaze to the prison. Now would be a good time to try to shake Drew and take off on my own, but I'll be able to get closer if I'm disguised as a fellow soldier. So I wait until he comes scurrying back with two jackets, two pairs of pants, and a hat. We struggle into them, and of course they're too big, although he clearly chose the smallest ones he could find. On the plus side, that means I can put them on right over what I'm wearing. He tosses me the hat.

"In case they make the girl soldiers cut their hair," he explains, pointing to my long dark hair. I twist up my hair and tuck it under the hat. Fine, that was smart thinking. But I'd have come up with it myself; I don't need him.

"Let's split up," I suggest. "I'll go that way." I nod toward the prison. "You see what's going on in the other direction."

He gives me a weird look. "The only thing that way is the prison. Let's follow the fence and see if we can find a front gate to this place."

"Okay, great idea. You do that," I say. "I'll catch up to you in a minute." My gut says to stay with him and keep an eye on him, but I can't fight how much I want to check that prison. I know it's crazy. There's a part of me that knows, logically, that there must be plenty of Alliance prison camps. What are the chances Wren will be in this one, where I happen to show up? But if I can find out anything about her . . . Knowing *something*, anything at all, would be better than the last three awful years of knowing nothing.

Drew studies me, and now he looks like Ivan again, but in the way Ivan's know-it-all look could suddenly turn understanding. Ivan looked at Wren that way whenever she told him about her dreams of saving the planet — the protests she wanted to organize, the petitions and poems and videos, the evidence she wanted to take to the people in charge so they'd actually do something about all the homes that have been destroyed by the superhurricanes and earthquakes and rising oceans.

When Ivan looked like that, it was impossible to imagine he wasn't on our side.

But I know better now. I'm not going to fall for a sympathetic expression again.

"What is it?" Drew asks. "What do you think you're going to find over there?"

"No one," I blurt, and his eyebrows shoot up. "I mean, nothing. Look, just do as I say. We don't have time for arguing."

I pull the hat down so the brim shades my eyes and I march out of the guard hut before he can say anything else. I try to walk past the front of the dormitory tent like I belong here. There are enough uniforms wandering around that I should be able to get by if nobody stares at me too closely.

There's a cold wind whipping through the tents, even though the sun is bright overhead. I'm glad for the thick khaki jacket over my hoodie, and the heavy khaki pants over my still-damp jeans. My sneakers are finally starting to dry, but they're still uncomfortably chilly as I stride across the patchy grass.

Two soldiers stand guard outside the prison door, chatting to each other. There are about fifteen prisoners out in the prison yard, most of them stamping their feet or rubbing their arms to stay warm. None of them are talking to one another. I slow down and study each of them hopefully, but disappointment washes over me as I realize they're all men. Either there aren't any women in this prison, or they exercise at a different time.

Still, they might know something. There's only a tall chain-link fence between me and them. If I can stand next to it without the guards noticing, and if I can get the prisoners' attention, hopefully I can talk to one of them, at least for a minute.

I'm walking past the guards, carefully not looking at

them, heading for the fence, when somebody suddenly takes my elbow in a firm grip and marches me straight past the prison. Fear makes my head spin and my muscles tense.

The Alliance has caught me!

Chapter 8

All I can think is, *What will happen to the others? Can they escape without me?* I hope Evelyn doesn't do anything risky. I hope Maddie can keep it together. I hope Louisa doesn't worry about me. I hope the boys don't wreck everything for them.

Then I'm shoved into another small guard hut, next to another tall gate and just as empty as the first one. I spin around and find myself face-to-face with Drew. He looks mad, but I guarantee he's not as mad as I am.

"Are you crazy?" I nearly yell. I'm so furious I could kick him, but I'm also shaking with relief. I pull off the hat and rub my face, trying not to scream.

"Are *you*?" he asks, closing the door behind us. "What were you going to do? Talk to the prisoners? You really think no one would have noticed?"

"Maybe," I shoot back. "You don't know. You didn't have to barge in and ruin it and give me a heart attack." I sit down in the rickety chair, fold my arms, and glare at him. I don't care that I feel like a teenager arguing with her annoying dad. It's an improvement over the feeling I had a few minutes ago, that everything was over for good.

"I was saving your butt," Drew snaps.

"Who asked you to?" I say. "I can handle this. It'll be worth it."

"What will?" he asks. "What's worth taking a risk like that?"

I press my lips together. If I haven't even told Louisa about Wren, why would I tell stupid Drew?

His face changes, the scowl vanishing like his forehead has swallowed it up. "Come on, Rosie. Tell me. Who are you looking for?"

Then again, if I don't tell him, we're apparently never going to get anywhere.

I sigh and lean my elbows on my knees. "My sister, okay? And don't you dare tell the others."

"I won't." He crouches beside me. "Why do you think she's here?"

"She has to be somewhere." I glance out the window and see the line of prisoners filing back inside. Oh, great. Now I've missed my opportunity, and it's all Drew's fault. Angry, I turn back to him. "This is the closest we've ever gotten to Alliance prisoners. Do you know how much money my family has spent looking for her? And for nothing! No one knows anything! We don't even know for sure if they have her. And maybe I could have found out — maybe someone could have told me — maybe she's even here —" I run out of words and have to shove my hands against my eyes, forcing myself not to cry.

I'm not going to cry until I see her again. That was what I promised myself three years ago. I'm going to be all thorns and no roses, tough and prickly. Wren used to tease me about that whenever I was mad or sulking. "What did you say your name was?" she'd joke. "Thorny?"

But after the tsunami, after we lost everything, or thought we had, she hugged me and said my thorns would keep me strong until we found a home again.

Then she left, and as far as I'm concerned, there's no such thing as home without her.

"How did they get her?" Drew asks, and I'm glad he doesn't pat my shoulder or tell me it'll all be okay.

"She ran away," I say. "With this guy Ivan, her boy-friend." I leave out the part about our town being destroyed. That would invite too many questions, like *What town was this, exactly?* Wren thought she was run-ning away to make a difference in the world, to stop things like that tidal wave from ruining any more lives. But Drew doesn't need to know that.

I shake my hair back and twist it under the hat again. "She left a note that they were going to join the Resistance. She said Ivan was one of them, that he would take her to them. But we think he gave her up to the Alliance instead."

"Because the Resistance isn't real," Drew says.

"No, they are," I say. "Sorry — you lose that argument. I've met some of them." He doesn't need to know how, or where, or, most important, why. "They'd never heard of Ivan. And they said Wren never found them. We have no idea what happened to her after she left us." I point out the window. "But I have a pretty good guess. And I'm going to find a way into that prison, no matter what you do to try to stop me."

He's already shaking his big fat head. "It's too dangerous," he says. Mr. Cliché. I really can't stand this guy. "I get it, okay, Rosie? I get that you want to find her. But if they catch you, they'll catch all of us."

"Not necessarily," I say.

"Remember what you said to Evelyn?" he says. "Nothing risky. This is way too risky. Stay alive first; do crazy brave things later."

All right, I do kind of like that he calls me brave . . .

even if it comes paired with crazy. But I don't care about his clever points or how many of my words he throws back in my face. He's not going to change my mind. I'm about to point this out, when a strange coughing rumble interrupts us.

We both freeze, listening. It sounds like the bus that took us to CMS, but with more of a deep mechanical rattle. It's definitely some kind of vehicle. I scramble up and lean out the window.

"It's a truck!" I whisper back to Drew. "A *huge* truck!"

A gigantic, wheezing monstrosity, half off-white and half rust, is chugging along a dirt road through the woods on the other side of the fence. As I watch it bump and bounce over the path, I realize it's headed for the gate near the trapdoor.

Then I spot the NutriCorp logo on the side.

"The boxes!" Drew and I yelp at the same time.

"They're not going into the tunnel at all!" I say.

"That truck is taking them away," he says, and I can tell his brain is galloping along right next to mine. It is awesome that I don't have to spend an hour explaining my new plan to him.

"Probably back into the States," I say. "Right across the border."

"Think there's room for seven smugglers in there?" he asks with a grin.

I'm tempted to observe that it would have been much easier to stash four people in there instead of seven, but he looks so pleased that I decide now is not the time for a fight. "We have to get back to the others," I say, standing and reaching for the door.

"What about the prison?"

I stop, one hand on the handle. *Stay alive*, says one side of my brain. *Find Wren*, says the other.

This could be our only chance to escape.

This could be my one chance to find my sister.

The others will never make it to Chicago without me.

But maybe they will. . . . Louisa is a lot more capable than she realizes.

It's the thought of Louisa that makes up my mind. I

guess maybe I like her more than I knew I did. One thing's for sure: I can't abandon her. I can't leave Maddie or Evelyn, either. I know how I felt when I woke up and Wren was gone. I'm not going to do that to my roommates.

I turn and glare at Drew. "Fine. Forget the prison. We escape, now. Do *not* give me one of your smug faces about this." I fling the door open, and we hurry around the back of the prison and the dormitory tent, following the line of the fence together.

The truck is just backing through the fence as we sneak between the hanging laundry on the clotheslines. Two soldiers have pulled the gate open, and two others are standing by the boxes with their sleeves rolled up, ready to load the cargo. I catch a glimpse of a pale face in the window where we left the others — I'm guessing Maddie — before she ducks out of sight.

A stocky woman in a navy blue jumpsuit gets out of the truck with a clipboard and starts talking to one of the soldiers as the other three roll open the back and begin transferring the boxes inside. We don't have long; it's a job that won't take them more than half an hour. But how can we get them away from the truck long enough for us to sneak into it?

"If I had a rifle," I whisper, "maybe I could shoot something and they'd have to go investigate." I glance at the back of the tent beside us, wondering if there are any rifles in there.

"It has to be something that'll get all of them to leave," Drew whispers back. "Do you think they'd all chase me if I ran past them? I mean, if I take off the uniform?"

I shake my head. "Not all four of them. Definitely not the truck driver. And besides, what would happen to you then?"

"My mom's kind of important," Drew says. "Once they figured that out, they'd probably be pretty welcoming."

I wonder who his mom is. I also wonder if he's volunteering like this because he wouldn't mind getting caught, since he's really on the Alliance's side. Is this his chance to turn us in? Did he stop me from going to the prison because there's something going on he doesn't want me to know?

I have to stop thinking in circles like this. Drew hasn't done anything obviously untrustworthy yet. It's just a gut feeling I have, and I know that's mostly because of how he reminds me of Ivan. But it doesn't mean I'm wrong. He could be trying to win our trust for some larger purpose. Maybe he'll call in the Alliance to get us later, once he gets some useful information out of us. I really shouldn't have told him about Wren.

"Hello?" he says, waving his hand in front of my face. "Anyone in there? We have to do something, and quick."

"I know. I'm thinking," I say. "I vote no on making them chase you." I look around, wishing again for a rifle, or better yet, a grenade. We learned about all kinds of homemade explosives at CMS. But there aren't exactly a ton of ingredients within reach.

"BLEEEEAAAAAGG!"

Drew and I both jump as a loud, peculiar noise sounds right next to us. I lift aside a flapping bedsheet and find myself staring at a furry nose and sharp black eyes. The goat regards me solemnly from inside her pen. Her face practically says, *Seriously? You didn't think of me right away?*

I glance at Drew, who is grinning — an entirely new expression on him, and one that doesn't look half-bad. Not that I care or notice or whatever.

"Perfect," I whisper.

"You get the gate," he says. "Then go for the others. I'll freak out the animals."

He unclips the bedsheet and heads off to the back of the pen with it. I follow the chicken wire around until I find the spot where the handlers must go in and out. There are a few twisty-ties holding the door shut, and that's it. I glance around, but no one is looking my way. Quickly I untwist the ties and peel back the wire until there's an opening big enough for an ostrich to run through.

A couple of the chickens immediately strut over to see whether I have any food, but the goats and the ostrich ignore me. That part's up to Drew.

I hurry away from the pen and stroll around the front of the buildings so the soldiers by the truck won't notice me. They're all too busy loading boxes to see me slip into the cabin where I left my roommates.

"There you are!" Evelyn explodes as I close the door behind me. "We've been totally freaking out!"

"Well, some of us have," Louisa says, rolling her eyes.

"We've got a plan," I say. "But we have to move fast." I cross to where Maddie is looking out the back window. There's still no movement from the animal pen. Where is Drew?

"Where's Drew?" Ryan asks, echoing my thoughts.

"Working on something. Everyone grab your packs and get ready to run. As soon as the coast is clear, we're getting in that truck." I point out the window.

"Whoa," Alonso says. "I get it. Like fugitives hiding from the law in one of those old movies!" He bumps fists with Ryan, and I think to myself that he can't possibly have a secret like mine, or he wouldn't be able to joke about stuff like that.

That's when I notice that Evelyn is clutching a sheaf of papers to her chest. "Uh-oh. Did you actually —"

"I did!" she says, her dark eyes sparkling. "You should have seen me, Rosie! I was so brave! Like you! Alonso saw the guy leave, so I ran in there, grabbed everything that looked important, and ran back out. Check this out. . . . It's a map, and I think it might show where all the secret training camps are! See, that's CMS —"

I hear a shout from outside and have to interrupt her. "That's totally amazing, Evelyn, but we need to go. You can tell me about it later." It *is* kind of amazing that she managed to do that without getting caught, and if she's right, that would be really valuable information to the Resistance.

Then again, as soon as that guy comes back and finds important papers missing, it's going to set off all kinds of alarms. We could be in a lot more trouble than we were before. But it won't do any good to tell her that. Better to make her feel proud of herself. Our team will work better if we can avoid sulking, worrying, or blaming one another.

I check out the window. Seven goats are galloping toward the men with the boxes, bleating furiously. Right behind them is the ostrich, flapping its fluffy wings and squawking. The bedsheet Drew took is tied around one of its feet and whipping around behind it, which seems to be making the giant bird totally crazy. It keeps spinning and stomping on it and nearly falling over and trying to attack its own tail.

The soldiers practically leap out of their skin when they see the animals running toward them. Two of them take off after the ostrich, grabbing for the sheet and ducking away from the bird's angry, stabbing beak. The other two run for the goats, trying to herd them back to the pen. They're shouting for help, but most of the other soldiers in camp are out on the training field or too far away to hear them.

111

The animals scatter with the soldiers in pursuit, and I see Drew sprinting from the animal pen to the truck.

"Time to go!" I say. I do a quick scan out the door, then send Louisa and Maddie out first. Drew reaches the truck at the same time as they do, and he and Louisa throw Maddie inside and then scramble in behind her. The three of them start rearranging boxes at top speed, making a tunnel to the back.

"Okay, Ryan, you next," I say, beckoning to him. He runs to the truck with Drew's backpack slung onto his other shoulder. Alonso gives Evelyn's hand a quick squeeze before he runs after them. She stuffs the papers into her pack and then stands beside me. I wait a moment until it's hard to see the other five behind the rearranged boxes.

"Let's go together," Evelyn says, taking my elbow. I don't know if she's scared, but it gives me kind of a dumb warm, fuzzy feeling that she wants to stick with me.

"You bet," I say. "Since you're an expert at this stealth business now." She grins.

112

We're out the door and down the steps, nearly half-way to the open truck door, when suddenly I spot the truck driver. I'd forgotten about her completely. She's been standing by the driver's side door, laughing and watching the soldiers chase the goats, but as Evelyn and I sprint across the grass, she turns in our direction.

It's like a slow-motion horror film. There's nothing we can do. In another ten seconds, she'll see us, and the whole plan will be ruined.

Chapter 9

I'm frantically tossing aside options in my head, but before I can do anything, Evelyn barks, "Hey, you, there!"

The truck driver sees us and looks as startled as I am. She squints at Evelyn and me. "Who are you?"

"Who am *I*?" Evelyn says with grand indignation. "*Me*? Did you really just ask me that? Who am *I*?" She gives me an outraged look. "Did you hear that? She doesn't know who *I* am!"

I fumble to play along. "Gosh. Uh, wow. Shocking. Bet your dad won't be happy to hear about that."

"I'll say! He'll be just furious! What's your name?" Evelyn demands.

114

The driver is so taken aback by Evelyn's attitude that she seems to forget she's being bossed around by a teen-ager. "Gladys Cato," she answers.

"Write that down," Evelyn says to me, then sails on while I check my pockets, which of course don't have paper or a pen in them. But neither Evelyn nor Gladys notices. "My dad *will* be hearing about this," Evelyn goes on. "Imagine my own driver not having any idea who I am!"

"Oh, no, miss," Gladys says, rubbing her short blond hair anxiously. "There must be some mistake. I'm here for these boxes. Nobody said nothing about no kid."

"Boxes?" Evelyn says, giving them an airy look as if she's just spotted them. "You mean you're not my ride to Madison?"

"No way," says Gladys. "I'm going to New York. Special delivery. No passengers."

None that you know about, anyway, I think. And also: *Chicago's on the way to New York. Perfect.*

115

"*Oh*," Evelyn says. "Well, *that* explains that. My goodness. You'd better go tell the guy in there that you're only here for these boxes, then. He was sure you were driving my whole family to Madison. He'll need to see your papers and everything." She points at the filing storage building.

"But I showed them to the other soldier —" Gladys starts.

"Doesn't matter. That's the hierarchy, you know? I mean, *I* should know, with my dad at the top!" Evelyn says. "You'd better hurry, before that guy leaves for lunch."

"Yes, right, okay," says the truck driver. She grabs her clipboard and trots off, looking flustered.

We wait until she disappears into the low wooden building, and then Evelyn and I leap into the truck and scramble through the tunnel of boxes the others have built. They've made a hole near the back wall, with just enough room for the seven of us to sit huddled together. As soon as Evelyn and I are clear, Ryan and

116

Louisa shove boxes around to fill in the tunnel, until it looks from the outside like a solid wall of boxes.

"That was awesome!" I whisper to Evelyn. "How did you do that?"

"I always thought I should be an actress," she says, beaming. "You know, there used to be a famous improv group in Chicago. My mom told me about it. I think I would have been perfect for it, don't you?"

"Yeah, totally," I say, and I really mean it. For the first time, Evelyn's actually impressed me.

"Maybe if the War ever ends," she says ruefully.

"But what if the guy in the building says he doesn't know anything about a family going to Madison?" Alonso asks. "Won't they get suspicious?"

"There's no one in there," Evelyn says. "Hopefully Gladys will decide she needs to leave before he comes back." She crosses her fingers.

"And now we know something useful," I say. "This truck is going to New York. We just have to make sure we get out when we're anywhere near Chicago."

"How are we going to figure that out?" Maddie asks.

I shrug. "We'll worry about it when we have to." I'm squeezed between Louisa and Drew, with Alonso across from me, so close our toes are all touching. Sunlight from the open back door filters in through the gaps in the stacks around us. Boxes tower over us, but Ryan has stacked them so they're braced and won't fall on us. I hope he knows what he's doing, because getting crushed by a bunch of canned goods is not on my to-do list for this lifetime.

On Louisa's other side, Maddie fiddles with her messy hair bun and yawns. It's warm and getting warmer in the truck, so I wriggle out of the army jacket and tuck it underneath me as a cushion against the hard floor. Now all we can do is wait, and that's just about my least favorite activity.

"I wish we'd had time to find a phone," Louisa says. She clasps her hands around her knees. "I want to call my parents and let them know I'm all right."

Ryan laughs and we all give him a startled look. "Sorry," he says. "I'm just picturing that conversation. 'Hey, Mom, I'm calling to say I'm okay! No, I'm not at school anymore. Well, actually I'm in an Alliance prison camp in Canada. But, you know, hiding in a truck, so everything's great!' I bet your parents would appreciate that."

Louisa and Maddie giggle, and I find myself grinning, too. All right, maybe not all the guys' jokes are stupid and unfunny.

"Shhh," Drew whispers. "I think I hear them coming back."

We all sit there, trying to stay as still and quiet as we can. My right foot starts to fall asleep, and my arms ache from the way I'm leaning on them, but I'm afraid to move in case something scrapes against the metal floor of the truck, or a box shifts and gives us away. The others are frozen the same way. I'm not even sure Maddie is breathing. She looks pale and terrified. Evelyn has her pack half-open and she's holding it like that, motion-less, clutching the canvas in tight fists. Alonso and Drew both have their eyes closed, as if that'll help them listen.

We hear the soldiers banging around the outside of the truck, bantering about the goats and the ostrich. One of them jokes that the ostrich bite on his arm should count as a war wound. Another one teases his friend about how girls are even better at running away from him than those goats were. They're all in a good mood despite the animal escape, which would be cute if they weren't the enemy. Unfortunately, I guess they're so cheerful because the War is going their way, and that's really depressing.

The truck groans and creaks as they toss in the rest of the boxes and stack them all the way to the roof. We're pretty stuck in here now. Of course, that's when I notice how hungry I am.

Nobody moves or says anything until we hear the back door of the truck roll down and slam shut, leaving us in the dark. There's a long pause. Slowly I ease my legs into a more comfortable position and rub my prickling foot. Through the walls we can hear the muffled voices of the soldiers and the truck driver. But we can't hear what they're saying. After a while, the driver's door slams, and we feel the vibration of the engine starting up.

"I think it's safe to talk now," Ryan murmurs. "She won't hear us over that." It is a pretty loud engine, coughing and sputtering and roaring. With a jerk, the truck lunges forward, and we all brace ourselves as best we can on the piles of boxes around us. It's going to be a bumpy, uncomfortable ride.

But I still feel a small glow of triumph. We're on our way. Maybe this escape is finally taking a turn for the better. Maybe we'll even make it to Chicago . . . although at this point I'd settle for getting back into the States!

Evelyn fishes a flashlight out of her pack and sets it in the center of the circle, pointing up. The light reflects off the boxes, casting a reddish glow over all of us. We all look kind of weird in the shadows, as if we're telling ghost stories around a campfire — something I've read about, but nobody I know has actually done.

"I'm *starving*," Louisa says. "I didn't realize it before, but it's been ages since we ate anything."

I nod. The adrenaline of our near misses has kept us going, but now that we have a moment to stop and rest, hunger is roaring in my stomach, too.

"Kind of ironic," Evelyn says ruefully. "We're surrounded by boxes of food, but we don't dare eat any of it in case it puts us to sleep."

"Or worse," Alonso agrees. "Where do you think it's all going?"

"In New York? Good question," Evelyn muses. "I'll have to think of all the possible targets. . . ."

"Does anyone have any food?" Louisa interrupts her. "I mean, while Evelyn's, uh, thinking?"

We all dig into our packs and empty out all the food we have into a pile in the middle of our huddle. The boys are much better stocked than we are, since they were prepared for a week in the woods. I'm glad Louisa manages not to make any snarky remarks about me rejecting their food this time around. They've got packets of granola, dried fruit, soy cheese, boxes of juice, nine rather squashed sandwiches, and several cans made of a weird lightweight metal, which contain vegetables and tofu chili and things like that.

All I have are a few protein bars and a box of cookies I grabbed at the Alliance cabin. Louisa must have done the same thing; she has a bunch of little bags of trail mix, several envelopes of hot cocoa, and a hilariously large jar of applesauce. Evelyn just has the sugar packets from her original escape stash. Maddie has nothing at all.

But it's reassuring. At least we're not going to starve right away. And we all have canteens of water, which everyone but Ryan and Evelyn remembered to refill at the cabin.

Louisa flaps a cocoa envelope between her fingers, shaking her head sadly. "Guess this is no use until we can light a fire."

"Yeah, we're not doing that in here!" Ryan says.

"This isn't going to be superdelicious when it's cold, either," Alonso says, picking up a can of tofu chili.

"And how are we supposed to eat the applesauce? With our fingers?" Maddie wants to know. She tries to lift the jar and pretends it's too heavy. "Jeez, Louisa, is this food or a weapon?" I smother a laugh.

"You'll thank me for it eventually," Louisa says with a smile.

In the end we share the cheese, the juice boxes, and the sandwiches, which have a nutty spread on them that isn't peanut butter. Drew says it's sunflower seed butter, with a blackberry jam the guys on kitchen duty had to make themselves.

"That is so cool," Louisa says. "I never got to make jam on kitchen duty! I just had to get up at four thirty every morning and chop melons for fruit salad."

"At least you didn't have to scrub that fruit salad off the tables later, like some of us," I say. "Right, Maddie?"

"That was the worst," Maddie agrees. Back at CMS, we were both assigned to the cleanup crew together, but she never talked to me while we were working. I could tell she didn't like me, so I didn't bother trying to make friends. I don't waste my energy on people who are that tough to crack, and I had Chui-lian and Rae to talk to instead, which was a lot more fun than painful small talk with Maddie. Usually she just pushed her mop around looking miserable.

From the day we arrived at CMS I got the feeling that Maddie would be a downer — she never looked happy, and all the conversations I overheard between her and Louisa seemed to be about how much she hated the school. That was the main reason I usually avoided her outside our dorm suite, but it wasn't until Louisa admitted the truth about their ID bracelets that I started to guess why Maddie might be like that. Now I wonder if I should have tried a little harder to be nice to her.

As the truck bumps and jolts underneath us, she leans her head on her knees, her half-eaten sandwich in one hand. Her brown eyes gaze into space like she doesn't really see the rest of us.

"How long have you lived with Louisa's family, Maddie?" I ask her.

Maddie sighs, and Louisa answers for her. "Six months," she says, rubbing Maddie's back. "Ever since her mom got called up for duty. Her dad's been gone even longer than that."

"No word from either of them," Maddie says. "I don't even know if they're alive."

"I thought —" Ryan starts to say, and Louisa shakes her head.

"No, we're not sisters. We lied about that so Maddie could come to CMS with me. I'm sure your mom is fine, Maddie. And you've got me, right? And my parents love you." Louisa's fingers trace her own neck, and I know she's thinking of the locket she lost the night we escaped. It has her parents' photos inside, and I think it was her grandmother's. Most likely she'll never see it again.

Maddie gives her a sad smile. It occurs to me that Maddie and I have more in common than she knows. We're both missing family members, with no idea what's happened to them, thanks to this war. Maybe one day I'll tell her that, but not now; I don't want to turn the truck into some kind of touchy-feely healing-sharing-weeping circle.

Ryan hefts the jar of applesauce. "Hmmm. Think we could use this to play Spin the Bottle?"

We all crack up, even Maddie and serious-faced Drew. I'm sure none of us have ever played anything like that, and I can't imagine a weirder place to try.

Instead we spend the next couple of hours playing goofy alphabet games, like the one where I say, "Chicago," and then Drew has to come up with a city that begins with *O*, like "Ottawa," and then the next person in the circle (Evelyn) goes, "Albuquerque," and then Alonso says, "England!" and Louisa goes, "BUZZ! Cheat! That's not a city! Disqualified!" and Maddie goes, "Wait, I'm confused. Explain the rules again?" And it's all surprisingly funny, considering our surroundings.

I catch myself thinking that I wish my last border crossing had been this much fun. Which immediately makes me start to worry that I'm not being vigilant enough — that having fun means that something is about to go terribly wrong.

But it's hard not to smile when Louisa smiles, or laugh at Evelyn's impressions of Mrs. Brewster, or joke with the guys about how terrible they are at camping. And the truck just keeps driving and driving. There's a long stop once, which might be the checkpoint where the truck enters the States, but there's no real way to know. We keep very still while we're stopped, but nobody comes back to check on the boxes, and it seems like there's no way anyone could know we're in here.

So finally I let myself relax a little.

After a while I pull out *Julie of the Wolves* from my pack, but reading in moving cars makes me motion-sick, so Louisa and Evelyn take turns reading it out loud to the rest of us. I really like the book, but we didn't get much sleep the night before, so eventually I rest my head on Louisa's shoulder, and one by one we each fall asleep.

Chapter 10

I guess it's the quiet that wakes me.

I open my eyes slowly, confused about why my legs and back are aching and my clothes feel uncomfortably heavy. The flashlight battery has died, so it takes me a moment to figure out why I'm in the dark with people squashed all around me. It's especially confusing because there's no rumbling or jolting underneath us. The truck has stopped, and everything is quiet outside. I fumble around until I find my own flashlight and click it on.

The others are all asleep. Louisa and Maddie are curled into each other; Ryan and Maddie are both snoring gently. Alonso is definitely going to wake up with a sore neck from the way he's positioned. Evelyn has her head on her pack, which is in her lap, as if she's asleep at her desk in school.

Somehow in my sleep I've shifted around, so my feet are tangled up with Maddie's and I'm leaning against Drew. I shake feeling back into my fingertips and carefully wriggle without jostling the others until I'm sitting upright.

Then I realize that Drew isn't asleep. He smiles and shades his eyes when I swing the flashlight toward him.

"How long have you been awake?" I whisper, turning the light down to the floor.

"Since the truck stopped," he whispers back. "I think that was a couple of hours ago."

"Oh," I say. "Sorry I fell asleep on you."

"That's okay," he says. "It's kind of fascinating to see you look so peaceful. Not your normal expression." He grins and stretches his arms, and I realize he's probably been keeping still so he wouldn't wake me.

"Well, don't get used to it," I say, but I try not to sound unfriendly. "I wish I had my watch. What time do you think it is?" My watch was confiscated on the first day at CMS, along with everyone's electronic devices. I spent the first week checking my wrist fifty times a day. It was really annoying.

"I bet it's nighttime," he says, "although I'm just guessing by how hungry I am."

"Oh, yeah," I say, and my stomach growls in agreement.

"She's probably stopped somewhere to sleep."

"So maybe if she doesn't come back soon, we could try sneaking out to see where we are," I suggest.

"That's what I was thinking. Maybe find some more food, too."

"Definitely." There're about a million things I would like to do if we could get out of this truck. Stretch my legs. Change my clothes. Brush my teeth. Run and jump and yell and breathe deeply. And find a phone to call my parents.

131

If they've gotten a ransom demand from CMS, they must be totally freaking out. It's possible Mrs. Brewster could get something out of them even though I'm not really there, although I hope my parents are smart enough to do that movie thing where they're like, "Prove to me that she's alive! Send me a photo of her with today's newspaper!" Except there aren't newspapers anymore, so maybe it would have to be someone's updated blog instead.

Drew leans over and pokes Ryan's knee. Ryan wakes up with a startled snort. His reddish-blond hair is squashed over to one side from being slept on, kind of like my cat's fur when she first wakes up.

"Let's start moving boxes," Drew whispers to him. "So we can tunnel out."

It's like one of those puzzles where there's an empty space in a bunch of tiles, and you have to slide the tiles around until the picture lines up right. Drew and Ryan and I carefully shift the boxes around us, freezing every time we make a loud noise. We hear nothing at all from outside the truck. I'm hoping Gladys is inside a motel somewhere, snoring away. Worst-case scenario would be she's sleeping in the cab, and then she'll probably catch us any minute . . . but surely she'd rather be in a bed, right?

Anyway, we have to get out, so if she does catch us, we'll just have to run for it.

Soon the movement around them wakes the others, and they get up to help us. Even with all seven of us working, it takes a long time to move all the boxes until there's a tunnel to the back door. By then I'm pretty sure we must be stopped for the night, so I decide it's safe to get out and take a look around.

I have a small heart attack when I first look at the back door and it occurs to me that it might be locked, or bolted, from the outside. What if there's no way out, and we're going to be trapped in here all the way to New York, where they'll open the truck to find us all suffocating, starving, and losing our minds?

But Louisa finds a latch at the bottom of the door almost right away, and when she pulls on it, the door slides right up. It creaks and rattles and rumbles like an

El train roaring over your head in downtown Chicago. I can't believe it doesn't wake everyone in a half-mile radius, especially since the night outside is so quiet.

Moonlight filters down through scattered gray clouds, illuminating a mostly empty parking lot. I jump down to the pavement and stretch my arms and legs like I'm getting ready for a marathon. Everything aches and twinges. I'm not used to sitting all day; normally I make time for soccer or basketball or running or Pilates somewhere in the afternoon. Even on the rare occasions when my parents turned on the TV back home, I liked to stand up and lift weights or jog in place while we watched the news.

As I'm stretching, I scan the area around us. We're in the parking lot of a run-down motel, in a back corner under some trees where the two sputtering fluorescent streetlights overhead don't reach. The truck sits in a pool of shadows by a chain-link fence, across from a long stretch of faded orange doors and windows with curtains tightly drawn across all of them. On the other side of the fence is another empty lot surrounding a warehouse.

I pivot to see the road that runs past the front of the motel. There are a couple of stores and a gas station across the two-lane street, but all the lights are off except for the glow of a lamp inside the gas station's convenience store.

"I think it's safe to come out," I say. "I don't see anyone around. It must be pretty late."

Drew hops down beside me. Louisa and Maddie stop for a moment on the edge of the truck, and I reach up my hands to help them down.

"Ow, ow, ow," Evelyn groans as she hits the ground, hunching her shoulders and twisting her neck to work out the kinks.

"Tell me about it," Alonso agrees.

"We shouldn't all stay out here," Louisa says. "What if Gladys looks out the window? Or a cop comes by and wants to see our ID bracelets?"

"Good point," Ryan says.

135

"I'll go scout around," Drew offers. "See if I can figure out where we are, or find some more food."

I can't stop myself from thinking he's really going to find a phone so he can turn us in. I know — I feel guilty about it. I mean, he scared an ostrich for us. What more does the guy have to do? But at the same time, there's just something about the way he looks at me, or the way he smiles and ducks his head, or something, that makes me feel jittery and anxious.

"I could go with you," Louisa offers.

"No, I'll go," I say, too fast. I know I'll keep an eye on him better than anyone else can. If he *is* planning something, I'll be the most likely to catch him at it.

Louisa raises her eyebrows at me, then smiles in this girl-conspiracy kind of way. "Sure, okay, Rosie," she says. Her eyes are sparkling, and it takes me a minute to figure out what that face means.

Oh *no*. She thinks I *like* him. Like, *like* him in a boy-friendy way. I want to say, *Man, Louisa, don't you know anything about me yet?* I'm not interested in guys like that.

Mostly they just annoy me. I don't have time for hand-holding and guessing games and flirty jokes and waiting around by the phone and moping over how confusing boys are. Plus I've seen how badly it can all turn out, from watching Wren and Ivan. Really, it can't get much worse than having your boyfriend betray you to the Alliance.

I don't know if the guys notice, but Louisa and Maddie are definitely giving each other those silly match-maker smiles I've seen on other girls. Thank goodness it's so dark, so no one can see how much I'm blushing. At least Evelyn seems oblivious — her keen nose for secrets seems uninterested in relationship stuff.

"See if you can find anything else to drink," she says. "And find out what road that is over there. And if we're near any big highways. Here, use this to write down whatever you find." She hands me her small notebook and pencil, then pulls out her map printout and tries to find a patch of moonlight where she can read it.

"Have fun," Maddie says with a grin I just want to mash into her face.

"Yeah, take your time," Louisa agrees. I think she's trying to wink at me. AAARRGH.

"Well, don't take too long," Alonso says. "We should get back into hiding as soon as possible."

"That's true," I say. "You guys stay hidden. Come on, Drew, let's get this over with." I shove Drew ahead of me toward the road and stomp away from the others, trying to ignore Louisa's giggle. I pray to all the spirits of the universe that the others don't gossip about me and Drew while we're gone. That's all I need — five people ooglygoogling over my imaginary romance when they should be focused on hiding and surviving.

We hurry across the lot and head for the main road, staying in the shadow of the motel. Drew keeps looking at my face as if he's trying to figure out whether I'm mad and why.

"Was that weird?" he asks. "Or was it just me?"

"It's really, *really* not important," I say. "Keep an eye

out for signs or even scraps of paper that might give us a clue about where we are."

The big sign in front of the hotel isn't lit up — that would be a waste of electricity — but between the moonlight and the few functioning streetlights we can see that it says CAMELOT MOTEL. VACANCY. A glass door leads into a small lobby at the front. We peek inside, but we don't see anyone at the front desk. Two candles burn quietly on the counter. There are a couple of sad potted plants, a spinning leaflet holder, and a few orange plastic chairs around a coffeemaker and an unplugged vending machine.

"Do you think it's safe to go in?" Drew asks. "What would we say if someone came out to offer us a room?"

I glance around at the deserted street behind us. From the way it's angled, it looks like the view from the desk wouldn't cover the gas station across the road. "We say our parents are across the street getting gas, and they sent us to ask how much a room costs." Not many people drive nowadays, but the ones who do are pretty wealthy, so I'm hoping that'll encourage the clerk to be friendly to us, or, more important, informative.

"Nice," Drew says, nodding approvingly. He doesn't mention how we don't exactly look related, since he's Asian and I'm Hispanic, but I'm betting the motel clerk won't be rude enough to ask. We also have to hope that curfew isn't as strict here as it is in the cities, or else I'll have to come up with a reason why we're traveling so late at night.

It turns out our cover story isn't necessary, though, because nobody appears behind the desk when we walk in. There's a little silver bell on the counter, and we debate ringing it, but I decide it's safer not to talk to people if we can avoid it. I've pulled my sweatshirt sleeves down over my wrists, but I still feel like it's really obvious that I'm not wearing an ID bracelet, which would be just about impossible to explain. Drew keeps his hands in his pockets most of the time, so I bet he's worried about it, too.

A clock on the wall over the coffee machine says it's a little after midnight.

I turn the leaflet holder, flinching at the squeaky noise it makes. I keep my voice quiet. "My mom told me these used to hold brochures about fun places to go, like amusement parks and museums and stuff."

"Amusement parks," Drew says wryly. "I bet those were awesome."

"But a huge waste of fuel," I point out. "Not to mention perfect targets for bombs and stuff like that. It's no wonder they all got shut down when the War started."

"I know, I've heard the propaganda, too," he says. "But I think that stuff's true of most places where lots of people go. My dad says we shouldn't spend our lives being afraid. Like, if we never do anything fun, and if we spend all our time cowering inside our houses, then the Alliance might as well have won already. You know?"

Spoken like someone who's never had to run for his life from angry men with guns. It's easy for guys like him, who don't have to worry that every knock on the door is the end of the world. I'd give up roller coasters any day for the chance to feel safe, just for a few hours. They sound kind of pointless, anyway, from what my mom's told me about them. I've had plenty of real scares and near-death experiences in my life; I don't need to pay for fake ones.

Of course, I don't say any of that to Drew.

I pull out one of the leaflets. Nowadays the government issues these almost every week, and they tell us about new curfews, new restrictions, new things to worry about. This one looks a few weeks old, and it talks about reporting any suspicious activity along the Canadian border and keeping an eye on anyone coming from that direction. It must be from before Canada surrendered, but clearly the government was already worried about Alliance activity over there.

There's nothing on the leaflet to tell us exactly where we are, though. I turn around as Drew leans over the counter to check the desk behind it.

"Mail," he whispers, glancing back at me. He hefts himself up on the counter and grabs a couple of envelopes that were lying in a black plastic in-box. The address on

142

them tells us we're in Wisconsin. I write it down in case Evelyn can find the town on her map.

"Smart thinking," I say, handing the envelopes back to him.

"You would have thought of it in another minute," he says.

I nod. "True." He laughs, but it is. That's the way my brain works, too.

"I like trying to keep up with you," he says. "There aren't many people I'd say that about." In the candlelight his face looks warmer, cuter, all the angles smoothed out and the smugness wiped away. In this moment he doesn't look like Ivan at all, in fact.

"Well, keep trying," I say, patting his shoulder. "You might catch up eventually."

He laughs again, and I feel a weird flutter in my chest. *No, Louisa is NOT right. This is not flirting. This is ordinary conversation with a guy; it's just hard to recognize because I haven't done it in so long.*

I step away from him so he'll stop looking at me like he knows all my secrets. I check the other leaflets, hoping for more recent news about the War, but none of them have been updated recently.

There's nothing else useful in the motel lobby, so we slip out the glass door and run across the street to the gas station. The clouds have slipped down the sky to the horizon, leaving the moon bright above us. It's shockingly cold, but in a clear, bracing way after the claustrophobic stuffiness of the truck.

I check up and down the road as we cross — no cars anywhere, which isn't surprising — and spot an on-ramp to a bigger highway not far away. The sign points to Route 94 East. I stop by the gas pumps and write that down for Evelyn, too.

It takes me only a minute, but when I look up, Drew has vanished.

Chapter 11

I'm not going to panic. I'm not going to panic.

I *am* going to kill him.

So much for my hypervigilance. Was he just waiting for me to get distracted? Where did he sneak off to so fast? And what is he doing while I'm not watching him?

I hurry to the door of the convenience store, but it's locked. So he's not in there, unless he figured out how to lock the door behind him really quickly. I peer in through the glass, but there's no movement in the dark aisles.

"Drew!" I hiss, whirling around. "Drew! Where are you?" The gas pumps are like tall, silent robots, watching me blankly. The little numbers over the nozzles say that gas is sixty dollars a gallon here.

Silence stretches around me. It's so cold even the insects are holed up somewhere. There's a faraway hum like a generator off in the distance. Then I hear a soft *clink* around the back of the gas station.

I pelt around the corner of the store and run right into Drew. He's standing at a pay phone, holding the receiver in one hand as he slides coins into the slot with the other.

A pay phone!

"Hey," he says, giving me the most harmless, innocent grin I've ever seen. "Look what I found! We really are out in the country, huh? It's like a relic from the last century. Who still uses these? Right? But I'm getting a dial tone, so I figured I'd try it."

I glare at him.

"Who are you calling?" I ask. I know I sound accusatory, but too bad; I *am* accusing him. How dare he sneak off like that! He can't have had time to call

Alliance agents in the minute I took my eyes off him . . . can he?

"My parents, of course," he says. He looks puzzled, like my anger has confused him all over again. "But no one's answering. They might be traveling for work — they do that a lot. I can't remember their cell phone numbers, though." He hangs up, shaking his head, and coins shower into the slot at the bottom of the phone.

I eye him suspiciously. He can't remember his parents' phone numbers? Or is he lying to explain why he's not talking to someone right now? Did he just hang up on the Alliance? "Seriously?"

"Well, I always use my cell phone to call them," he says. "Their numbers are in there, so I never bothered to memorize them. You know?"

I guess I do understand that. We are crazy about keeping track of one another in my family, so I know all my parents' numbers, but I need my phone to call any of my friends or find their e-mail addresses. Yet another

147

annoying thing about Mrs. Brewster taking away our electronics.

"All right, let me try," I say. But as I pat my pockets I realize I don't have any change. Why would I? It's been ages since I used cash at all — not since we left home, probably. We just use our ID bracelets to charge everything.

It's actually kind of weird that Drew has change. I'll add that to my list of Suspicious Things About Drew, although I can't come up with an explanation that points to Alliance spy.

"Here, use these," he says, passing me his handful of quarters. I slip them in and dial home. My anger at Drew starts to fade as the phone rings and my hopes rise. I could be moments away from talking to my parents! Just the thought makes my throat feel tight, like I'm about to cry, although of course I won't let myself do that.

Ring. Ring. Ring.

Where are they?

Ring. One more ring and I'll get the voice mail.

148

Should I leave a message? Or save the quarters and try a different number?

Part of me would love to hang on just to hear Dad's voice on the message, but I know I shouldn't. I'm about to hang up when Drew reaches over my shoulder and hangs up for me. The coins clatter down again, and I frown at him.

"Saving the change," he explains.

"I *know*," I say. "I was about to do that. I'm not an idiot."

"Of course you're not! I know!" He raises his hands in a gesture of surrender. "Sorry. Just trying to help."

There's a pause as I scrape the coins out and look at them, heavy in the palm of my hand. Dread is starting to gather like smoke in my stomach, coiling and twisting around my insides. "Why aren't they there?" I say. "It's the middle of the night. Where else would they be?" I hesitate. "Maybe I should try again."

"Sure," Drew says gently, but I stand there for another minute, thinking. What if something terrible has happened? What if they've been found out, and they had to run? They wouldn't have left home — or, worse, the country — without me, surely. But how would they have gotten me a message, out at CMS with no phones or mail?

What would they do about a ransom demand? Would they call the police? Almost definitely not; they wouldn't want the extra questions, and where I come from, calling the police is a guaranteed way to have a kidnapping end with somebody dead.

Maybe they'd call someone else . . . the guys who made our ID bracelets, for instance. Or the Resistance fighters who helped us get to Chicago. That seems more likely . . . but what could any of those people do?

The horrible part is that we all believed I'd be safer at school. Mom and Dad didn't want to send me away, and I didn't want to go. But it was getting so dangerous in Chicago, and they worried about me all the time. I knew they'd be able to focus on searching for Wren if I were tucked away somewhere safe. We thought that sending me to CMS was the right thing to do. Boy, were we wrong.

The pit in my stomach yawns deeper as I imagine my parents turning over the money. We're rich, sure, but not so wealthy that we can spare as much as Mrs. Brewster probably asked for. What if my parents are meeting Alliance agents on some deserted street corner right now, with a suitcase full of cash and no idea that they won't be getting me in exchange? Will the Alliance let them walk away alive from a meeting like that?

Surely it wouldn't have happened that fast. But now the urgency to get home is prickling all across my skin. I feel sick.

"Try another number," Drew says. He reaches out and lightly runs his hand down my arm. Normally I would shove him away, and I still haven't forgiven him for disappearing, but there's something weirdly comforting about his touch.

151

I dial my mom's cell phone. It rings and rings; no answer. I hang up again, collect the coins, and dial my dad's cell phone.

It goes straight to voice mail. I hang up fast, too fast, without thinking, and the machine swallows Drew's change with a self-satisfied *clunk clunk clunk*.

"Oh no!" I cry. I grab the phone, shake the box, press the lever to return the coins over and over again — but nothing works. The quarters are gone. All I'm getting is a dial tone.

"I'm so sorry," I say to Drew. "I didn't think — the voice mail — I should have just left a message." I hang up the phone and lean my head against the wall, pressing my hands into my eyes. "I can't believe I did that."

"It's okay. Don't beat yourself up," Drew says. He leans on the wall beside me, nudging my shoulder with his. "We'll find more change, another phone. Maybe one of the others has quarters. It's not the end of the world."

I take a deep breath and stand up straight. I'm not a pity-party kind of girl. "You're right. Not the end of the world." I turn around and look at the empty road and the empty lots around us. I've never missed my parents as much as I do right now. I breathe in, out, trying to calm down. I look at him sideways. "Nope, I still feel awful."

"Think of it this way," he says. "Maybe it's better you didn't leave a message. Maybe the Alliance has their phones tapped. You could have led them right to us. Eh? See? Really, you were doing the smart thing. Plus we'll probably be in Chicago by tomorrow. So then you'll see your parents and all this will be over."

He's trying so hard, I can't help but smile. "Nice try. You and Louisa could teach optimism classes."

"I think Ryan would prefer that job," he says. Is he implying that Ryan has a crush on Louisa? I give Drew a quick look, but his face doesn't give anything away. That's the feeling I've been getting, too, but I've also noticed that she keeps looking at Alonso, so I'm not sure Ryan has a chance. Unless Alonso and Evelyn . . . Wow, this is a stupid train of thought. We so don't have time for middle school who-likes-who. The other girls might enjoy that, but it's not me at all.

"Let's get back to the others," I say, shaking my head to clear it. "I don't think we're going to find any food here."

"Not without breaking in," he agrees. "And I don't think we should do anything that people might notice. At least not as long as we want to keep hiding in the truck."

We head back across the road. I keep looking back at the gas station, feeling guilty and confused, but also still a bit suspicious. Why did Drew disappear so fast? Was he trying to ditch me? If I hadn't found him quickly enough, would he have called the Alliance to tell them where we were? What if he's only being nice to me to throw me off the scent?

Or . . . what if I do like him, the way Louisa thinks I do?

Right now, it's hard to decide which would be a bigger problem.

Chapter 12

As we pass the motel lobby, I stop, glancing in through the glass doors.

"What?" Drew asks.

"There is one thing I want to take," I say. "Wait here."

I slip inside and pull one of the chairs over to the table with the coffeemaker on it. I climb up on the chair, then the table, balancing carefully so I don't knock anything over. The clock lifts right off the wall. It's as light as a Frisbee, and I feel a flash of gratitude for whoever decided it was worth spending precious batteries on it.

"Sorry, motel people," I whisper to the lobby. But in

the sunless, muffled space in the back of the truck, we need a way to know what time it is.

Drew nods at the clock when he sees it in my hands. "Yes. Totally useful."

"Hopefully they won't notice it's gone until we're far away," I say.

We sprint across the dark parking lot and climb into the back of the truck. Ryan is waiting by the door to roll it shut behind us. He latches it closed again, and we all crawl back through the tunnel to our hidden space.

While Louisa and the guys arrange the boxes to hide us again, I show Evelyn the address we found. She lights up at the sight of the highway number and slides her map toward me.

"I thought we might be somewhere along there," she says eagerly. "Let's see if we can find the town."

We both study the map in the small yellow beam from my flashlight. The lettering on the towns is so tiny it makes my eyes ache. Maddie leans over to help us, her bun of brown hair looking like a flat, messy bird's nest next to Evelyn's tight, neat rows of braids. I don't even want to think about how my hair must look, after two days without a shower.

"There!" Evelyn yelps excitedly, jabbing the map with her finger. "I found it! So let's see. . . ." She takes out a pencil and measures the distance left to Chicago, comparing it to the scale at the bottom of the printout. "Okay, it looks like we're still about three hundred miles from Chicago."

"So we definitely don't want to get out here," Louisa says. "That's too far. We could get closer if we stay put in the truck."

"But what if she doesn't stop near Chicago?" Alonso asks. "What if she keeps driving all the way to New York tomorrow?"

We all sit in a circle, looking at the map and thinking. Louisa unpacks the food and shares it out so we can eat while we decide what to do.

"We don't have many options around here," I say, peeling the wrapper off a protein bar. "Either we walk the rest of the three hundred miles, or we stay in the truck. I wouldn't risk trying to get a lift from anyone else."

"What if we steal the truck?" Ryan suggests.

Everyone stops eating to stare at him.

"I'm serious," he says. "We take it right now and drive the rest of the way to Chicago. Drew and I took Auto Shop at CMS. I bet we could get it going, even without the keys."

Drew is shaking his head. "Probably, but it's way too dangerous. As soon as she reports us, the Alliance will know exactly where we are, where we're going, and what we're driving to get there. They'll catch us long before we reach Chicago."

"Or the cops will," I say. "There aren't too many cars on the roads these days — I think they might notice one driven by a bunch of teenagers. Then we have to explain why we don't have ID bracelets, why we're out after curfew . . ." *Who I am and where I really come from . . .* I shake my head. "I just want to get back to my parents before I have to deal with reporting any of this. You know?"

158

"Really? I wouldn't mind finding a cop," Maddie says. "They could help us. They'd get in touch with our parents and get us home. Maybe we should be *trying* to do that."

My stomach lurches nervously. I can't explain to everyone why I don't want to involve the cops. They don't know how much trouble I could be in.

"Let's vote," Drew suggests. "Raise your hand if you want to get out here and find another way to Chicago."

Maddie is the only one who raises her hand. She smiles and shrugs like she doesn't really care that much.

"Okay, raise your hand if you vote for stealing the truck," Ryan says. He raises his hand, and so do Alonso and Evelyn.

"All in favor of staying put?" I ask. It's me, Drew, and Louisa. Stalemate.

"So you decide," Louisa says to Maddie.

Please don't say steal the truck, I pray quietly. *Please don't send us out to get caught by the police.*

159

"Oh, dear," Maddie says, twisting her hair around her index finger. "I don't know! What if we get stuck in here and go right past Chicago? They might catch us when they open the truck to unload the boxes!"

"Gladys will have to stop sometime between here and there," Drew offers. "For lunch or to stretch her legs or anything. It's too far for one straight drive. There's a good chance we'll be able to hop out sometime during the day tomorrow. I'd bet on it."

"But —" Ryan starts.

"Okay," Maddie says. "That makes sense. I vote we stay hidden."

I exhale with relief and punch Ryan's knee. "Good work thinking outside the box, though, Ryan. I'd never have come up with an idea like that." *Mostly because it's idiotic, but I'm trying to reassure, not gloat.* "It's pretty cool that you'd know how to start the truck, anyway."

Ryan looks grumpy, as if he really wanted to test out his car-stealing skills. He takes a dried apricot and chews on it, grumbling under his breath. I wonder if I need to try harder to cheer him up, to keep team morale going, but he's been a pretty cheerful guy so far. I'm guessing he'll be back to normal if we just leave him alone for ten minutes.

"So let's sleep in shifts," I say. "That way we won't miss it when the truck starts moving again. When it does, whoever's awake, keep an eye on the time." I set the clock in the center of our circle. "What do you think, Evelyn — four hours to Chicago?"

"Probably more like five," she says. Five is what I thought, too, but I guessed wrong so she'd get to feel smart correcting me. That ought to help if she's feeling stung over being on the wrong side of the vote. But judging from the way she squishes herself in next to Maddie and splits a cookie with her, I don't think Evelyn's going to hold a grudge.

"Great, okay," I say. "Well, I'm wide-awake. I'll take first shift."

"Me, too," Drew says, and I dearly hope he misses the *Ooooooooo* face Louisa gives me.

"And, Louisa, you, too," I say quickly. "That way we can all keep each other awake."

Evelyn, Maddie, Ryan, and Alonso wriggle around trying to get comfortable for a while, but they finally fall asleep. I lean my back against the stack of boxes, combing my hair with my fingers. In whispers, I tell Louisa what happened with the pay phone.

"I didn't even think of that," she whispers back. "I don't know a lot of numbers by heart, either. Like my parents at the hospital . . . I totally haven't memorized their work numbers." She fingers the neck of her shirt where her locket would be. "I wish we could call them now," she says, "but I guess we'll be in Chicago tomorrow. That's soon enough. Wow, can you imagine? We'll be sleeping in our own beds tomorrow night!"

We grin at each other. I have a feeling it might not be that easy, but I want to believe her. For a moment I let myself be Louisa, convinced that things will turn out great.

I let myself forget that there's anything dangerous out there, hunting us.

Chapter 13

A few hours later, we wake Alonso and Evelyn for the next shift. But no matter how I shove the army jacket around underneath me, I can't get comfortable, and I can't fall asleep. My mind keeps going around and around, worrying about all the things that could go wrong, feeling bad about losing the quarters, missing my parents, worrying about Wren, hoping we can get out of the truck safely, and puzzling over Drew. He's asleep beside me, his glasses tucked into the neck of his shirt. He doesn't look like a spy. Why don't I trust him?

It's about seven o'clock in the morning when we hear the cab door of the truck slam. After a moment, the

163

engine starts, and the truck backs up, then rumbles forward, speeding up as we reach the highway. The noise wakes everyone, and we split some of the dried fruit and granola for our meager breakfast. With seven people to feed, the food is going fast. But I can't exactly complain, since it was the guys who provided most of it.

We're all tired and sore from sleeping in uncomfortable positions, so it's a much quieter, more boring ride this morning. Evelyn uses a couple pages of her precious notebook to play Hangman with Maddie and Alonso. Drew and Ryan start an argument in low voices about some book they had to read for English. Louisa rests her head on Maddie's lap and falls asleep again.

I stare at the clock. It moves painfully slowly. I want to be home so badly. I want to walk into my own house, hug my parents, pet my cat, sleep in my own bed. I want to stop worrying about the Alliance catching up to us, or what they've told my parents by now.

Five hours later, the others all go quiet, one by one, as they notice the time ticking past noon. If our calculations are right, we should be near Chicago. But Gladys isn't stopping. Evelyn folds and refolds her map between her short, nail-bitten fingers. I wonder if she's telling herself the same things I am: Well, it's an old truck. It's probably going slower than we calculated. We're probably not *that* close to Chicago yet. We still have time. We'll still be closer than we were last night, even if we're on the other side of the city, if she stops anytime in the next couple of hours.

Then, at half past noon, we feel the truck lurch to the right and gradually slow down.

"Pack up," I whisper, pulling the army jacket back on. "If she's just stopping to stretch her legs and grab some food, we might only have a couple of minutes." Evelyn stuffs her map into her pack; Drew finds room for the clock in his. Ryan gets up and carefully slides a couple of boxes aside as the truck jolts and bounces below us. We all brace ourselves as it clatters to a halt and the engine cuts off.

Louisa takes my hand and squeezes it. She has the

flashlight in her other hand, pointed at the boxes between us and the back door. We wait, barely breathing, until we hear the truck door slam again. Gladys's voice goes past, clipped and muffled with occasional pauses, as if she's talking on a cell phone.

As soon as we can't hear her anymore, we all jump up and start moving boxes. It's faster this time, since we built the tunnel last night and only filled it in with a few boxes. In a couple of minutes we're all crouched at the back door.

"I wish we had a periscope," Evelyn whispers. "Like on a submarine? So we could see outside and know what we're jumping into?"

"Totally," Alonso agrees. "There could be a whole crowd of people out there. Or an Alliance guard."

"It doesn't sound like it," Ryan says. He has his ear pressed against the back door. "I don't hear anything. No cars, no voices, nothing."

"The important thing is not to lose each other," I say. "So don't panic. If anyone sees us, we'll run. But stick together — if we have to run, everyone follow me. All right?"

No one argues with me. I hope they'll really do it. I trust myself to assess the situation and figure out how to escape. But it'll be a lot harder if any of the others take off in the wrong direction. I can't lead them to safety and run around them like a border collie herding sheep at the same time.

"Here goes nothing," Louisa whispers. She reaches down, lifts the latch, and rolls the door open.

Bright sunlight dazzles our eyes. The first thing I notice is the mouthwatering smell of food — soy burgers and tofu dogs and things fried in oil. I hop down while my sight is still adjusting and get ready to run. My sneakers hit pavement and I squint around us.

We're in another parking lot, next to a greasy-looking pizza place with a couple of bicycles locked up out front. It's right off what used to be a busy highway, six lanes divided by a concrete barrier, although now it's probably only used by military and supply trucks, and buses like the one that took us to CMS. There are no cars in sight in either direction. Across the highway I can see a large building with walls of broken glass that used to be a supermarket. Some of the big orange letters in the sign swing loose in the wind.

I scan the area, planning our escape.

Big old stores and abandoned strip malls in each direction. A bridge with a tall fence for pedestrians to get over the highway. Patches of grass growing wild, spreading over the old concrete walkways. An old bus stop, covered in graffiti, with cracked plastic walls.

The pizza place looks like the only functioning business in sight. It must get all the truck drivers who go through here.

The others hit the ground beside me. Ryan pulls the truck door shut as soon as we're all out. He's clanking the latch back into place when the door of the pizza place opens.

Gladys steps outside, holding a paper plate with a limp slice of soy-cheese pizza on it in one hand and a can

168

of soda in the other. No matter how much the country falls apart, you can always find soda wherever you go.

She sees us at the same time as we see her. Her whole face falls open: eyes huge, mouth agape. The pizza and the soda can crash to the ground. Even in her shock, she starts fumbling for something at her waist. A phone? A gun?

I'm not waiting around to find out.

"Run!" I yell.

Chapter 14

I bolt toward the highway. My muscles feel weak and useless after sitting in the truck for so long, but fear makes me fast. I don't look back. I hope the others are behind me.

I fly across the first three lanes and sail over the divider. My backpack slams against my ribs as I run. Chilly air whips across my face and I feel like a runaway train, blasting ahead with no way to stop. I'm far too scared to stop.

Out of the corner of my eye I see a figure running beside me. I throw back my hair and glance over; it's

Drew. I wish it were Louisa or Maddie. I want to be sure that they're safe. Neither of them would be all right on their own, or if they got caught.

I burst ahead of Drew, skid into the supermarket parking lot, and risk a look back. The others are only a few steps behind me — I do a quick count — all six of them. Gladys is standing where we left her, shouting after us. Clutched in her hand is a cell phone. Which is better than a gun, but still bad.

"Come on!" I call to my friends. Evelyn's the slowest, but Maddie looks like she's about to faint or collapse in terror or something. I dart back and grab Maddie's hand, dragging her after me. We pound across the lot and I kick aside the broken glass so we can jump through one of the walls of the abandoned supermarket.

Empty shelves loom up around us in the dark. We hurtle past the wide bins where vegetables used to be, past the cold glass doors that used to lead to ice cream and frozen waffles. There are still a few sale stickers and flags sticking out, relics of a time when there was enough food to throw away tons of it every day.

In the back corner, behind the deli counter, I find a door to a dark kitchen and even darker storage closets. The others follow me through and I slow down for the first time, trying to figure out where each of the doors around us might lead.

"Maybe we should hide," Alonso suggests. "There's enough room for all of us in that old walk-in freezer."

"Worst idea ever," Drew says, and I'm so glad I don't have to say it myself that I want to hug him. "The one thing Gladys knows for sure is that we went in here. The Alliance will check this whole place first."

"So we go out the back," I say, nodding at the employee exit door, "and keep running."

I swing open the door and peek out into the parking lot behind the supermarket. The bulk of the building shields us from view of the pizza place. Gladys won't know which way we've gone.

Still, we stay low as we dash across the sunny pavement. Soon we're running behind one of the strip malls. Nondescript doors and rusty fire escapes flash by. The next large building has a sign on the side that says it used to be a bookstore. For a moment I wonder why they needed all that space for e-readers and flash drives, until I realize it must have sold actual books — old-fashioned ones made of paper, like my copy of *Julie of the Wolves* and the others at CMS.

Then there's a stretch of trees, and I risk a look back across the highway. The pizza place is out of sight. No sign of a truck chasing us down, so that's lucky. But I'm sure Alliance agents are going to come swarming into the area within minutes to find us.

"Back across the highway," I order the others. "Hopefully they'll concentrate their search on this side first." We dash across the wide lanes again, vaulting over the concrete barrier. We pelt through several more parking lots and then hit another patch of trees, where Maddie calls for us to stop. She leans over with her hands on her knees, gasping for air.

"I can't run much farther," she says.

I take out my canteen and pass it around; everyone takes a quick gulp of water. Evelyn collapses beside a tall pine tree, rubbing her legs and grimacing. "We need to figure out where we are," she says. "Are we running in the right direction?"

"Or maybe we shouldn't," Ryan says. "Run in the right direction, I mean. Maybe that's what they'll expect us to do."

"I can't believe she saw us," Louisa pants, holding her hair off her neck. "That was the scariest thing that's ever happened to me."

See what I mean? She has no idea what it's like to really be scared — to think your sister might be dead, to worry that you're going to get caught and lose everything at any moment, to watch your whole life get swept away in an instant. I *wish* Gladys were the scariest thing that had ever happened to me.

Although I'll admit that doesn't make me any less scared right now.

"There are signs along the highway," Drew says. "Let's find one that tells us how far the nearest big city is — and hope it's Chicago."

We find one after another ten minutes of running: a rectangular green sign with sunlight reflecting brightly off its silver back. We duck around to the front of it and discover that Chicago is twenty-eight miles away — and we've been running in the wrong direction.

Maddie sighs heavily.

"It's a good thing," Ryan says encouragingly. "They won't expect us to be going this way."

"Unless they count on us being idiots," Louisa says, looking glum.

"We should get away from the highway, anyway," I say. "Now that we know which way Chicago is, you can use your compass to get us there, right, Evelyn?"

She perks up, nodding as she digs the compass out of her pocket.

"So let's head away from the road and try to circle around." I lead the way down an off-ramp and soon we find ourselves in a suburban-looking neighborhood with lots of trees in between the cute little houses. Louisa visibly relaxes, as if it reminds her of home, but all I can think of is the faces that might be behind any of those sweet lacy curtains, watching us and wondering why seven teenagers are roaming the streets together unsupervised. Who will find us first, the Alliance or the cops? Which would be worse for me and my parents?

We don't see any people out and about — maybe nobody lives here anymore — but I'm still relieved when the houses get more spread out and the trees take over. It's easier in the woods to travel in a wide arc, swinging back around to the far side of the pizza place, aiming for Chicago. Evelyn forgets to grumble about her aching legs as she reads the compass intently.

We've been moving as fast as we can for about forty-five minutes when we hear the distant growling above us.

I stop and look up. Cloudless blue sky, warm sunshine, air as clear as you can find these days when everything's so polluted.

Exactly the worst conditions for hiding from a helicopter.

Chapter 15

Okay, *now* we have to hide," I say, picking up the pace. "Somewhere indoors. These trees are too scattered to give us enough cover." Especially since there are freaking *seven* of us — though I manage not to say that part out loud.

"Inside someone's house?" Louisa asks. She hurries to keep up with me. "Do you think anyone will help us?"

"Not safe," I say. "There must be somewhere else —"

"There!" Maddie points through the trees. A large concrete structure squats beside the road, several yards away. It's our only option. The thunder of the helicopter blades is getting closer.

We race through the trees and across a small stretch of bare pavement. As we get closer, I realize it's a multi-story parking garage. I dart into the shadows of the entrance and turn around to yank Louisa and Ryan in after me. The others just manage to make it inside before the helicopter bursts into view, churning ferociously in our direction.

They can't have spotted us yet. They're just searching, hoping to catch a glimpse of us from the air. We hurry farther into the garage, past thick concrete columns, over painted yellow lines. Space after space, level upon level. It's hard to believe there used to be so many cars on the road that they had to be stacked and packed into garages like this.

"This garage must be attached to something," Louisa points out. "All these parking spaces must be here so people could go somewhere."

Faded arrows on the wall point us toward broken glass doors and dead elevators. We step gingerly through the doorframes and climb the dingy stairs, following the dim yellow circle of Drew's flashlight.

"Oh," Maddie says in a hushed voice as we step out into an enormous open space, crisscrossed with beams of sunshine. A ceiling full of dusty skylights sparkles far above us. Petrified escalators lead up to a balcony lined with glass storefronts. Triangular planters lined with black and silver tiles, crawling with dead vines, are arranged artistically around the walls. All around us, covered in layers of dust, are closed-up carts and door grates and signs in bold, eye-catching fonts.

For a brief moment, looking up at the faraway ceiling and feeling the hushed stillness around us, I think we're in a church. But then I recognize it from stories I've heard my parents' friends tell.

"It's a mall," Louisa whispers, awestruck. I remember the first night I clicked with her, when we joked around about going to a mall like this.

"Oh my gosh, *yay*," I say, grinning at her. "I so totally need a dress for prom!"

She grins wickedly back. "And new *shoes*," she squeals. "I mean, I only have, like, forty pairs. My closet is practically empty!"

"I know!" I say. "I was like, should I wear the purple shoes or the pink shoes with this outfit, and then I was all, if only I had shoes that were purple *and* pink!"

Maddie jumps in, her eyes sparkling. "Oh my gosh, you guys, we totally have to find our dresses before we stop for lunch. After all the fro-yo I'm going to eat at the food court, I'm not gonna want to see myself in the mirror."

"Like, whatever!" I poke her in the ribs. "I bet you can't eat as many burgers as I can!"

"Shyeah, but you'll still be the hottest girl at prom," Maddie says, rolling her eyes. "It's so totes unfair how many guys have asked you."

"OMG, we don't have time for boys!" I say. "We have *shopping* to do!"

"Like, totally!" Louisa says, throwing one arm over my shoulders. "And don't forget we need new sunglasses! You know, like, for our tennis game later!"

The three of us burst out laughing. Maddie and I collapse onto one of the giant planters, holding each other up and giggling. Louisa tries to sit down next to us but misses and ends up on the floor, which makes us all laugh harder.

"Okay," Ryan says, "something weird just happened."

"Maybe it's in the air," Drew says, rubbing his chin. "Something that infects girls as soon as they step into a mall."

"Is it contagious?" Alonso asks. He gives us a worried look that sets off our giggles again.

"Not *all* girls," Evelyn says. "You don't see *me* acting like an airhead from a twentieth-century movie." She shakes her head, trying not to smile.

"Come on," I say, taking Maddie's hand. "This is the perfect place to hide. Let's look around."

"We can pretend we're normal teenagers from before the War," Louisa agrees, taking Maddie's other hand.

"Does that mean *we* have to giggle about prom dresses, too?" Ryan asks as we start walking along the row of closed storefronts.

"Oh, please," Louisa teases. "You know you'd look hot in sparkly green taffeta."

"Sure, but I'd look hot in anything," he jokes back.

"Oooo, freaky," Maddie says, pointing at a window display where a couple of mostly naked mannequins are still poised, like actors waiting for the spotlight to turn back on.

She drops my hand to go over and look at them, and a moment later I feel another warm hand take mine. I look up into Drew's brown eyes.

"So what color dress are you thinking?" he asks. "You know, so I can make sure the corsage matches."

"Why, you forward young man," I say. "You haven't even asked me yet. How do you know I'll say yes?"

"Resist this face?" he says, pointing to his winning grin. "Impossible. Can't be done."

He might be right about that, I think. I can't help smiling back at him.

"Can you imagine what it was like?" Louisa says, jumping up on a planter and pirouetting. "All that time for people like us to just hang out? Walking around and shopping on the weekends?"

"Going to the movies," Evelyn says wistfully. "Enormous vats of popcorn!"

"And video games!" Alonso says. He hooks his hands through one of the grates and peers in at an old display of computer games.

"Plus staying in school until you were eighteen," Drew says. "Or even longer if you went to college. No enforced military service. No hiding from the Alliance. No seven thirty curfew, no food rationing, no tanks in the streets."

We all go quiet for a moment, thinking about what Chicago will be like now that the Alliance is closer and stronger than ever. Everyone goes to work for the war effort at fifteen, which is only a little more than a year away for some of us. I wonder where we'll all be in two years. Or in four years, when we should have been getting ready for a prom for real.

Once we get back to Chicago, will I see my friends again? Will we all survive this war?

I shake my head. I should focus on surviving the next couple of days first. Somehow we have to get home without getting caught. We know where CMS is; the Alliance doesn't want us sharing that information. If they've figured out what else we might know — about the cabin, or the prison camp, or the truck full of doped-up food heading for New York — they could get really hard-core about hunting us down.

Suddenly I'm so tired I actually feel myself wobbling. I didn't sleep all night, and it's finally catching up to me. Drew takes my elbow and guides me onto a beige padded bench.

"You should rest," he says. "We'll travel faster and safer once it's dark, anyway."

Evelyn nods. "I'm going to scout around in here," she says. "Maybe I can find a more detailed map, so I can figure out the best route to Chicago."

"I'll come with you," Alonso says.

Before I let myself sleep, Louisa and Maddie and I find a corner and change into new clothes from our backpacks. It's just a little thing, but because we've been stuck in the truck with the guys for two days, we haven't had a chance. It's not the same as showering, but wearing clean black cargo pants and a fresh blue shirt makes me feel worlds better.

"You sleep first, Rosie," Maddie says. She spreads my sleeping bag out on the bench. "We need you wide-awake to lead us home tonight."

I give her a sharp look to see if she's making fun of me, but she seems perfectly serious, as if she doesn't mind me being in charge anymore. I guess a lot of things about her don't bother me so much now, either. She's been more of a trouper than I expected. Especially now that I know more about her life before CMS. And there's something about the way she fluffs my pack into a pillow that reminds me of Wren.

"Hey," I say, touching her shoulder. "Um. I just want you to know — I know what it's like. I mean — not knowing . . . losing someone and not knowing what . . ." I have to stop, since stupid tears are trying to climb up out of my eyes again.

Maddie tilts her head at me. "Really?" she says softly. "Who?"

"My sister," I say. "Her name is Wren. We don't know where she is or what —" I stop again and shake my head furiously. "Anyway. The Alliance probably has her. But we'll find her one day."

Unexpectedly, Maddie reaches out and hugs me. Her shoulder blades are like bony wings under my hands. "I know you will," she whispers in my ear. "And I'll find my mom. The War *has* to end eventually. That's what I tell myself . . . and sometimes it helps."

She pulls back as the others come over. Louisa looks confused but pleased to see Maddie and me getting along so well. Ryan unrolls his sleeping bag on the next bench over.

"Nobody do anything crazy while I'm asleep," I say.

"Yes, boss," Maddie jokes.

"We'll just stand here and watch you sleep," Louisa says. "That won't be disturbing, will it?" She grins.

"Nothing can distract me from sleeping right now," I say, sticking my tongue out at her. "But wake me if there's any sign of trouble, okay? Or if we need to go. Or —"

"Oh my gosh, sleep already," Drew says, throwing his sweater at my head.

I grab the sweater and add it to my pillow. As I close my eyes, I can hear him chuckling, and the murmur of Maddie and Louisa chatting quietly, and Ryan snoring already. Overhead, Evelyn's and Alonso's footsteps echo as they search the upper level.

We're not safe yet, not by a long shot. But it's the safest place we've been since we escaped CMS. Even with the Alliance chasing us, I feel like we're going to make it home soon after all. I let myself relax, drifting into sleep.

And that is my biggest mistake.

Chapter 16

Something feels wrong the minute I wake up.

It's too quiet. I can still hear a couple of my friends' voices — but not enough of them.

I sit up fast, giving myself a splitting headache.

"Whoa," Louisa says. "Calm down, there's no fire." She's perched on the planter beside me, reading *Julie of the Wolves*. The light has changed — I must have slept for a few hours. The shadows of the escalators angle off in new directions, and there's an orange glow around the skylights, like the sun is close to setting.

I rub my temples and try to shake off my sleepiness. My skin is prickling. I know something's wrong.

"You look a lot friendlier when you're sleeping," Evelyn comments from the floor. She has papers spread out around her — some of them maps, others covered in scribbled notes that I don't think are hers.

"So I've been told," I say. Alonso is crouching beside Evelyn, studying one of the maps. I twist around. Ryan is still snoring on the next bench. And there's no one else in sight.

"Where's Maddie?" I demand, throwing off my sleeping bag. "And Drew?"

"They went to look for food," Louisa says. She puts down the book and frowns at the expression on my face. "What? They'll be right back."

"Don't worry; Maddie's not going to steal your boyfriend," Evelyn teases. I want to grab her papers and rip them into tiny shreds. Does she really think that's what I'm worried about?

"It's okay, Rosie," Louisa says. "I mean, we were all hungry. We're down to, like, three raisins and that jar of applesauce. And of course there's no food in here." She

191

waggles her finger around at the empty stores. "So they're just finding us something to eat."

"They left the mall?" I cry. I grab my shoes and yank them on. "When did they leave? How long have they been gone?"

"Um." Louisa glances at the clock I stole, which is propped up on Maddie's pack beside her. "Like an hour, maybe?"

"An *hour*?" I'm already moving as I tie my hair back. "Which way did they go?"

"What's the big deal?" Louisa hops off the planter and chases after me. "They went out the door down that hall-way." She points, and I see more broken glass doors facing out onto an open-air parking lot. "Rosie, I'm sure they're being careful. They'll be back any minute."

I can't explain why it's a big deal. I can't explain why my heart is pounding or why panic is clawing around in my chest. For one thing, I don't have time. I have to find Drew and Maddie. I just know that it's not safe out there, and I wouldn't have let them go. They could have been spotted — they could have been captured — it should have been me out there, if it was anyone.

"Hey, Maddie was just trying to help," Louisa says, hurrying to keep up with me. "She said she wanted to be more brave, you know? I figure she can take care of herself."

"But she can't!" I say. "She's never been chased like this before! She doesn't know anything about escaping — how to hide, where to run when someone's after you —"

"But you do?" Louisa asks, giving me a hard look. "Why is that?" She grabs my arm and pulls me up short. "Rosie, what aren't you telling me?"

This is the closest I've come to spilling my secret, but I'm too scared for Maddie to feel any extra fear for myself. "Not now," I say, jerking my arm away. "I have to go find them."

I sprint to the door. No sign of helicopters in the pink-and-orange sunset sky. No cars out on the road that runs along the other side of the parking lot. But there's so much empty space out there. Only a few stunted trees cast lonely, thin shadows here and there across the lot. There's nowhere Drew and Maddie could have hidden if a helicopter suddenly showed up.

Louisa's footsteps crunch in the glass behind me as I step through the doorframe. I want to send her back, but I don't want to argue with her, and I know she won't go. I scan the row of buildings across the road. It's a smaller highway than the one Gladys was on. I don't know where Drew and Maddie would have expected to find food out here. They should have waited until dark, when we were all traveling together. *I* would have found them food. I would have done it safely.

"There!" Louisa says, pointing. Two figures are running along the road toward us, still several yards away. I can see Maddie's long brown hair flying out from the slower runner.

"Doesn't look like they found any food," Evelyn says from behind us, and I jump. I was too focused on the outside to hear her coming.

194

"That's fine, as long as they make it back safely," I say, biting my nails. It's a huge relief to see them, unharmed and, as far as I can tell, not being chased. But they're so exposed. I lean forward, wishing for them to run faster.

The two figures turn into the parking lot and jog in our direction. Maddie spots us in the doorway and waves with a big smile. Drew looks pretty cheerful, too. That's not going to last long once I get him inside and give him a piece of my mind. From now on, the rule is: no crazy missions without me.

I'm not just being bossy and controlling, although everyone might see it that way. I know I can handle the risks better than anyone else. What I can't handle is the idea of something happening to one of them — something like what happened to Wren — not when I could prevent it.

Louisa waves back. Suddenly her hand freezes in the air. I hear it at the same time: the roar of an engine starting up.

Maddie and Drew look back over their shoulders. We all see the headlights suddenly blaze brightly in an alley across the road. A truck shoots out from its hiding spot and barrels toward us, driving straight over the curb and the patches of unkempt grass.

This isn't the rusty old supply truck Gladys was driving. This is a sleek military machine, and the men hanging out the window are all brandishing guns.

My sneakers are pounding across the pavement before I can think. I don't know what my plan is, but I'm hoping I can distract the soldiers in the truck long enough for the others to escape.

Maybe Drew has the same thought, because he shoves Maddie toward the mall and runs at the truck, waving his arms.

Everything happens so fast.

The truck swerves around Drew. The soldiers barely even glance at him.

I'm too far away.

I'm running as fast as I can, but I'm too far away.

Two men leap out of the back of the truck. Black masks hide their faces. Maddie shrieks as they grab her around her waist. She kicks and fights and struggles, but they pin her arms and legs.

"Maddie!" Louisa screams, and I think I do, too.

I'm too far away!

They fling Maddie into the back of the truck and jump in after her.

I hear the door slam. I can still hear her screaming.

I'm almost there, but I'm too late. The truck's tires squeal as it U-turns, close enough to blast a wave of exhaust into my face. I see cold blue eyes over one of the masks in the front seat, looking straight at me as the truck wheels away.

But they don't stop for me. They don't stop for Louisa or Evelyn, running out of the mall behind me. They don't stop for Drew as he tries to jump in front of them again.

They swerve right around him and peel out of the parking lot, roaring off down the road.

I fall to my knees on the asphalt, pressing my hands to my face.

I've broken my promise to myself. I'm crying.

And Maddie is gone.

Chapter 17

"Rosie? Rosie, it's okay." Drew drops to his knees beside me and puts his arms around me.

"It is *not* okay!" I shove him away and he flails for balance. "This is your fault! They caught Maddie and it's all your fault!" All my fears about him come flooding back. Maybe he betrayed us after all. Maybe Maddie didn't watch him like I did, and he managed to sneak off to call the Alliance down on us. They clearly didn't want him — the truck went right around him twice.

"I know," Drew says. His voice sounds shaky and his glasses are crooked. "I tried — I'm sorry —"

"You should have tried harder!" I yell. "You should have saved her! You shouldn't have taken her out here in the first place! What were you thinking?" I shove his chest again and he falls backward, scraping his hands on the pavement.

But even as I'm blaming him, running through all my suspicions again, I realize I don't believe it's true. Not after everything we've been through. He screwed up, taking her with him, but I can't believe he meant for her to get caught. I wipe my eyes with my sleeves, trying to shove three years' worth of tears back into my face.

Louisa and Evelyn are standing above us now, looking shell-shocked. I turn away from them, rubbing my face, and see Alonso and Ryan running out of the mall toward us.

"Who took her? Were they Alliance?" Evelyn blurts. "Why didn't they take us? What's going to happen to her? Where will they —"

"Evelyn, SHUT UP!" Louisa yells. Evelyn's eyes go wide and her mouth snaps shut.

200

Louisa buries her face in her hands. I want to get up and hug her, but I'm too mad at them all for letting Maddie go, and I'm so furious at myself for falling asleep and not watching them, and I'm so frustrated that no matter what I do, I can't control everything and make it all work out.

It's crazy how upset I am. Three days ago, I didn't even like Maddie. I would have left her behind in the woods if I'd had a choice.

But now . . . now it feels like losing Wren all over again.

"Maybe they weren't Alliance," Ryan says. "Maybe they were on our side, and once they figure out who she is, they'll take her home."

"Not without an ID bracelet," I say. "Who'll believe her? They'll think she's — she's —"

"Like you," Drew says quietly. He pushes himself up to sit cross-legged a few feet away from me. I nod. Somehow it doesn't surprise me that he's figured it out.

"What?" Evelyn says. "What do you mean?"

201

I breathe in and out, shaky, ragged breaths. "There's something I haven't told you guys." I wrap my fingers around my wrist where my bracelet used to be. It's a stupid time for a confession, but it's as if the words are spilling out of me like the tears, pent up for so long that I can't stop them when they finally all burst out. "I'm here illegally. We — my family — we snuck into the US three years ago, after a tsunami wiped out our town in Mexico and my sister ran away."

"But —" Louisa looks even more shocked. "But that's a war crime!"

"I know," I say. "If anyone caught us, we could be deported — and that's the best-case scenario. The War means every illegal immigrant could be a spy for the Alliance. We're not," I say hurriedly. "But the government could treat us that way. It would be awful."

"That could happen to Maddie," Louisa whispers. "Without ID — they might just throw her in a prison camp and leave her there. We wouldn't even know how to find her."

"Why'd your parents risk it?" Drew asks me.

"We were looking for Wren," I say. "The Resistance helped us get into the country, and they said they'd try to find her." I shift my shoulders and push my hair out of my face. "We couldn't stay in Mexico, anyway. Our home was completely destroyed."

Memories wash over me: Wren's face as the ocean was suddenly sucked away, running away from the beach hand in hand, watching from the hills as the wave swamped over our home. Bodies floating out to sea. Water reaching from horizon to horizon. One of my orange sandals, carried away by the fierce grasp of the flood. The sodden mess of wood and brick that was left behind where my house used to be.

Wren was always talking about climate change and going out to save the world. That was how she met Ivan: he'd come down to Mexico with Greenpeace to help clean up our beaches after the latest oil spill. Or at least, that was what he told us. He must have told her something else — that he was with the Resistance, and together they could make a difference, if she'd run away to the States with him. And then they disappeared.

My parents' money got us into the country, with the help of the Resistance, but no matter how rich we were, it didn't help us find Wren, and it never made us feel safe.

"I've been terrified every minute for the last three years," I say. "It's kind of a relief to tell someone. I'm sorry I had to lie to you for so long."

I guess I expect them all to hate me now, so I don't know what to think when Louisa kneels and hugs me. But that's nothing compared to my surprise when Evelyn does the same.

"We don't care where you were born," Louisa says firmly. "You're our friend."

Alonso and Ryan crouch beside us. I glance up at Alonso's face, so much like the boys I grew up with. "I wondered if you were — I mean, if you might also —"

Alonso shakes his head. "Born here, although we moved around a lot. But it hasn't been easy since the War started — I get stopped and searched all the time. It's scary enough when you don't have anything to hide. . . . I can't imagine what it's been like for you."

"That's how you knew about the ID bracelets," Evelyn says, snapping her fingers.

"And that's what you meant about knowing how to escape," Louisa adds.

"We nearly got caught a couple of times while we were crossing the border," I say. I ball my hands into fists, rubbing them against my cargo pants. "I remember how scared I was. That must be how Maddie feels now. We have to *do* something!"

"I am really sorry," Drew says again. He sounds even more devastated than the rest of us. I lean forward and take one of his hands.

"We'll fix this," I say. "I know you tried to save her. I saw you trying to draw them away." He's not like Ivan. I can trust him. I squeeze his hand, hoping he can feel that.

"They really wanted Maddie," Evelyn pipes up. "Did you guys notice that? They ignored the rest of us and just went after her." She fingers her braids, frowning thoughtfully. "I wonder why. There must be something special about her that we don't know."

"No way," Louisa says. "I know everything about Maddie. We've been best friends since we were five. Trust me, if there were anything about her that would interest the Alliance, I'd know."

"Yeah, they probably just grabbed her because she was the easiest to take," Ryan says.

Evelyn sets her jaw stubbornly. I know her theories are usually a little far-fetched, but part of me thinks she might be on to something, for once. It was weird how the truck went straight for Maddie. But why her? Her parents aren't rich. She doesn't even know where they are. What could the Alliance possibly want her for?

"So what do we do now?" Alonso asks.

"I guess we keep going — get back to Chicago, find our parents, and tell them what happened," Ryan says. "Right?" He sounds like he's not really thrilled about that plan.

"We can't just abandon her," Louisa says.

"I agree," I say. "I don't know about you guys, but I won't be able to handle it when they pat us on the head and make us stay inside after dark while they do nothing. I think we have to be the ones to help her. I think we're the only ones who can. We have to."

"We'll find her ourselves," Drew agrees. I get to my feet and pull him up beside me. As the others stand up and brush themselves off, I straighten his glasses and he traces his fingers across my cheek. His face doesn't look smug to me anymore. He might know all my secrets, but now I don't mind. I'm actually kind of glad.

I look up at the sky, where the orange and pink is fading into dark purple, and heavy gray clouds are starting to roll in, smothering the early stars.

Maddie is one of us. We're not going to leave her out there on her own.

Our flight toward home will have to wait.

It's time for a rescue.

What will happen tomorrow?
Read on for a preview of
Tomorrow Girls #3: With the Enemy.

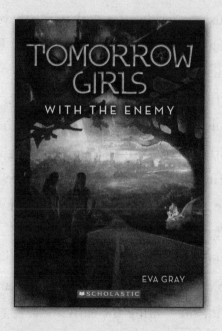

We divide up the food evenly and start eating. I put a berry in my mouth and bite down and it explodes with a burst of tart juice on my tongue. I eat another as I peel off the green skin of one of the nuts and edge the tip of my CMS–issued knife in the crack to pry it open. It takes work but the nut inside is crunchy with a taste somewhere between an almond and a peanut.

Maybe it's because I'm starving but I think these are probably the best nuts and berries I have ever eaten in my life, possibly the best ones in the world. For five minutes the only noise in the snack bar is the sound of shells cracking open.

Until Louisa says, "I wish they'd taken me, too." She puts down her knife and pushes away the rest of her nuts. I'm sitting next to her so I can hear the trembling in her voice.

"Who?" I ask, setting down my knife and turning toward her.

"The people in the — what did Helen and Troy call it — Rover. The people who took Maddie." She looks around at all of us and there are tears in the corners of her eyes. I slide off my stool and give her a hug.

"I hate thinking of her there alone," she says into my shoulder. "Why did they only take *her*?"

My throat feels like it's closing up.

Louisa pulls away from me but keeps hold of my wrist as she repeats, "Why?"

I can't move. I can't breathe. I can't tell them.

"Maybe because she's the smallest," Ryan says after a moment.

"That would make her the easiest to control," Alonso confirms. "That makes sense."

"And to feed," Rosie points out. She brushes the shells from her hands and touches Louisa lightly on the arm.

"Seriously, what if they'd taken Ryan?" Alonso puts in then. "They'd waste all their ransom money on food."

Louisa relaxes the hold on my wrist and gives a little smile and says, "I guess."

Drew sits up straighter. "The truth is, we might not know why. But at least now we have some idea of who took her, and where. Right, Evelyn?"

I discover I've been holding my breath. "Right," I say. "We have something to go from."

Disaster is averted. Eating recommences. Boys are strange but at this moment I am really glad they're here.

We are filling Alonso and Ryan in on what Helen and Troy told us when there's a tapping on the boards over one of the windows.

Followed by a low moaning.

Instinctively, we all turn off our flashlights. What you can't see you can't shoot.

"That's just wind," Rosie says, but next to me I feel her tense. My heart starts to beat faster and my palms get clammy.

Something thuds on the roof of the building, and there's a sound like feet skittering over it.

"What's that?" I whisper to Rosie in the dark, my heart racing.

"Tree branches?" she whispers back, not sounding completely sure.

That's when a voice outside demands, "Who?"

I jump to my feet, panting. "That is not the wind, that is someone —"

"*Who who*," the voice calls again. An owl. It's an owl.

Everyone else starts to laugh but it takes some time

for the "All clear, just nature" message to get from my brain to my heart, which continues running a race in my chest. Our flashlights click back on.

Drew pulls himself to his feet. "Look, I'm feeling much better. This place is creepy and I think we should keep moving."

The speed with which everyone else leaps up and starts shoving things in their packs shows how much they agree.

We skirt the edge of the pavement toward a driveway Ryan and Alonso saw before which we're pretty sure must lead to the highway. It's long past 7:30 — which means long past curfew — but since it's night we decide to risk walking on the road, where we'll make better time. The chance of there being anyone driving on it, with the current price of gas, is remote, and even if there were someone, we'd hear their engine or see their lights long before they could see us in the dark.

Drew and Louisa lead the way, with Ryan and Alonso behind them. Rosie hangs back to walk next to me.

"Do you really think Maddie is in that place that Helen and Troy came from?" she asks.

"It sounds like she was picked up by the same people, and the tire tracks headed to Chicago," I say. The temperature has dropped and our breath is making little clouds in the air. "Why?"

"I don't know." Rosie kicks a stone from the road. "I thought Helen was mostly talking to stall until Alonso and Ryan came back with the food once you pointed out we didn't have any."

My fingers tighten around the straps of my backpack. "I shouldn't have done that. I was just worried they were going to hurt you."

Rosie pats me on the arm. "Believe me, I'm not complaining. You handled that great."

"Really?" I say. I instantly feel a thousand times better.

"Yeah." But then she purses her lips. "Although I do think it's funny that you can talk down two crazy hostage takers and save my life, but you're afraid of an owl."

"I didn't know it was an owl!" I object. "Besides, you were scared, too."

"Nuh-uh," Rosie says.

"Uh-huh," I reply.

"Do I need to separate you two?" Alonso turns around to ask. "I thought I heard my name and I wanted to let you know it's okay if you want to tell me how handsome and brave and quietly brilliant I am to my face — you don't have to do it behind my back."

"Same goes for me," Ryan says. "Although my brilliance isn't quiet."

"Duly noted," Rosie says, gesturing for them to return to their own conversation. She rolls her eyes at their backs, then says to me, "Assuming the school is real, how do we find it?"

"Even though Helen was lying, I have the sense that they told us more than they meant to." I try to think of how to explain what I mean. "When Troy talked about the Phoenix, that all seemed completely real."

"Helen said he made it all up," Rosie points out.

"Which practically guarantees that it's true," I say. I am starting to get excited. "Do you know that feeling where you're close to uncovering an answer or solving a problem but you can't quite touch it?"

Rosie nods slowly. "I do. Remember when we were in that prison camp, the one we broke into?"

I give her my most innocence-filled look. "No, I'm afraid I have totally forgotten about the time when we broke into a prison camp. What was it, two days ago?"

She makes a face at me. "I'm serious. When we were there I — I felt like I was close to finding my sister, Wren. Like maybe if I stayed I could figure out what happened to her after Ivan betrayed her, where she ended up. Is that the same?"

"No," I say. "That's much worse." And then it hits me just how bad. I turn toward her. "You gave up that chance to save the rest of us."

She shrugs, not meeting my eyes. "What choice did I have? You would never have gotten anywhere without me." Her tone is light but I can tell it hurts. "Of course, maybe you would have been better off. Maybe then Maddie would still be here."

I stop walking and pull on her pack until she stops, too, and turns to face me. "You have to cut that out," I tell her. "There was nothing you could have done to keep Maddie from being kidnapped. Whoever took her knew who she was and knew what they were doing. The only thing that could have gone differently was that you could have gotten hurt. Is that what you want?"

She stares at me wide-eyed and I realize everyone else has stopped in the middle of the road and is staring at me, too. Silence falls hard and heavy.

"She's right," Louisa says, coming to stand next to Rosie. "There was nothing you could do."

"Maddie wouldn't want you to beat yourself up," I point out.

Rosie flips her hand in the air, brushing this aside. "People always say that."

That makes me angry — I am not *people* — and

maybe that's why I say, "In this case it happens to be true. Maddie wouldn't want you to be throwing a pity party for yourself because you lost her the same way you lost Wren." I hear Rosie's sharp intake of breath but I don't stop. "She would want you to focus on what needs to happen next, not what happened before. She'd want you, the strongest leader in our group, to help find her. And if we can find Maddie, we can find your sister."

Rosie's jaw is tight and she takes three breaths before she says, "Do you really think so? Do you really think that's true?"

"I do," I say. If I'm not going to mention that I think Maddie might be (as good as) dead, there's no reason to mention I have no idea how to find Wren.

POISON APPLE BOOKS

The Dead End

This Totally Bites!

Miss Fortune

Now You See Me...

Midnight Howl

Her Evil Twin

THRILLING. BONE-CHILLING. THESE BOOKS HAVE BITE!